Akin Minds

ANTHONY MERCIER

Akin Minds
Copyright © 2019 by Anthony Mercier
Cover design credit: Tyler Girard-Meli

All rights reserved. No part of this publication may be reproduced, distributed, or transmitted in any form or by any means, including photocopying, recording, or other electronic or mechanical methods, without the prior written permission of the author, except in the case of brief quotations embodied in critical reviews and certain other non-commercial uses permitted by copyright law.

Tellwell Talent
www.tellwell.ca

ISBN
978-0-2288-1028-5 (Hardcover)
978-0-2288-1029-2 (Paperback)

Sovereign Soul: Akin Minds

<u>Dedications...</u>

To my family and friends who supported this
series from the very beginning.

To those tucked away in these pages, some
of whom may never speak again.

To my characters, for enduring all I've made them endure.

I'll never forget you.

TABLE OF CONTENTS

Part One: Ascension

Act One: Enter Ryoku 3
    Scene One - The Arrival 5
    Scene Two: The Old Forest 17
    Scene Three: Keeper 40
    Scene Four: The Stranger 52
    Scene Five: Last Night in the Old Forest 68
    Scene Six: Unspoken 78

Act Two: Guardianship 97
    Scene One: Becoming True 99
    Scene Two: Magelet 106
    Scene Three: A Daunting Task 116
    Scene Four: Encampment of the Raiders 124
    Scene Five: Rescue? 129
    Scene Six: A Brave New World 138

Act Three: Trickster 151
    Scene One: Tricks and Gods 153
    Scene Two: Werewolf 160
    Scene Three: Hunters 176
    Scene Four: Renegade 185
    Scene Five: The Timeless One 199

Act Four: Blackness 211
    Scene One: Ragnarokkr 213
    Scene Two: Black City 224
    Scene Three: Over Dinner 240

    Scene Four: The Moon Wolf and the Black Demon 261
    Scene Five: Nyctophobia.. 274

Act Five: Bright Manifest **285**
    Scene One: Katiel 287
    Scene Two: The Words 295
    Scene Three: Defenders 304
    Scene Four: Penguin Inn..314
    Scene Five: The Diamond Dragon 326
    Scene Six: Roland Demizen 340

Act Six: Alteration...**363**
    Scene One: He Who Feared 365
    Scene Two: A Shadowed Abode 374
    Scene Three: Violet..388
    Scene Four: Battle in the Capital 400
    Scene Five: Trickster God's Lyric 416
    Scene Six: The Deciding Battle 426
    Scene Seven: Goodbyes 434

Act Seven: Disowned **449**
    Scene One: The Soldier's Father 451
    Scene Two: Brawl in the City 465
    Scene Three: Grasp of Orden 478
    Scene Four: Indecision 489
    Scene Five: Assistance...503
    Scene Six: Fatal 511

<u>Part Two: Descent</u>

Act Eight: Conquer..**525**
    Scene One: Roses 527
    Scene Two: Disarm..545
    Scene Three: Whirling Skies 562
    Scene Four: Ascension to the Sky..574
    Scene Five: Requiem of the Trickster God 586

Act Nine: Separation **601**
    Scene One: Plan of Action..603

- Scene Two: The Keeper of Death 618
- Scene Three: Seeking the Scepter 628
- Scene Four: Tower of the Falling Rain 645
- Scene Five: Choice of Kings 651
- Scene Six: Escape 670

Act Ten: The Serpent's Nest 677
- Scene One: The Serpent Emperor 679
- Scene Two: Bounty Rose 693
- Scene Three: Trickster's Signature 703
- Scene Four: Escape 713
- Scene Five: A Godsend Storm 719

Character Guide 735

PART ONE
ASCENSION

ACT ONE: ENTER RYOKU

Through all-seeing eyes, we are in
Bytold, in the world of Harohto.
It is late evening
On November 3rd, 2017.

SCENE ONE - THE ARRIVAL

The small ringing of a bell barely touched the clamour of the already bustling tavern, a singular noise to fall upon deafened and drunken ears. Brief illumination of the setting sun through the doorway glanced off the frame as a traveler entered, scarcely noted, and quietly grateful for it. A few of the patrons saw his light, golden hair that seemed to flicker in the ethereal evening sunlight, or briefly caught the glance of his forest-green eyes.

"Greetings, traveler," the barkeep called out in greeting. She, a young woman with pumpkin-orange hair, was preoccupied pouring a drink and paid little mind to the boy beyond the notice of a new customer. She hardly caught a glimpse of the unremarkable clothing he wore: a baggy brown shirt, the lace at the chest partially askew and hastily tied, the sleeves pushed up on his slender arms. A brown rucksack sat perched on one shoulder; a brown-handled knife at his hip. His black cargo pants tucked into weathered leather boots. The girl's first thought was that this boy had best not try to buy liquor. His fair face and light eyes couldn't fool anyone; he was legal for it in no lands.

The newcomer caught the girl's glance as she finally looked up, and offered a shy smile. The look caused her to fumble as she went to push a drink across the table to a lad eagerly awaiting it. She recovered in a moment, and slid the drink across the counter without spilling a drop. From then on, however, she had eyes only for the newcomer. The boy glanced behind him for a moment, as though expecting somebody to have joined him, but he was the only silhouette in the doorway.

After a long moment, the boy approached the bar counter to the girl, now eagerly waiting.

"Hello," he finally said. He had a light and fair voice, perhaps dipped with some kind of sophisticated accent. It was certainly more refined than the girl's was, she mused to herself. Perhaps he was a mage. "My name is Ryoku Dragontalen, a... Defender. I've come seeking a room for the night."

If the girl was enthralled before, she might as well have forgotten where she was. What an interesting name! And that title...

"Caryl Cerone," she introduced herself in kind. "The farmer's daughter, if it's titles you're after." She managed a light giggle, and he chuckled, but she quickly went after the meat of his statement. "A Defender? Truly? Don't see much of you lot, especially this far south of the capital."

He appeared genuinely surprised. That was about when Caryl could place the hesitation on his tongue. He was new to these parts. She didn't know much about Defenders, but she knew they must be travelers from abroad. They never seemed to know the area they wound up in.

"That is news to me," he admitted. "Unfortunately, I guess I'll be headed there next. I hope it's half as beautiful as the woods around here."

Caryl smiled lustily, inferring his compliment to her rather than the boring village. She was eyeing up the smooth curve of his neck, the lines of his chest disappearing like a tease beneath his shirt. If she weren't on duty, she'd have a very different goal in mind. "You like these parts?" she mused. "Here's pretty dull. Wait 'til you see the capital city. A special stone they built the walls out of makes it just light up at sunset. That old forest is a bit of a drag, but past that, you'll love it."

Ryoku smiled in a wistful way. By the Creator, was Caryl's poor heart ever beating fast. "I'm sure I'll see," he replied softly. "I had a friend with me who told me some about the surrounding area. I... don't really know where they went. They were right behind me." He glanced back at the doorway, as though the mystery friend might pop up in the doorway now. "I guess I can find my way."

He didn't sound so sure of himself. Caryl wondered if his *friend* was a girl, but she recalled where she was before she asked such an open question. Remembering her duty, Caryl reached back to pick a room key off the shelf behind her. The section she reached for was more favorable, granting a better view of the town for the odd traveler. Normally they cost more, but the owners might never know. That, and she was familiar with that particular bed. Oh, she'd gone up there with travelers more than once in the past. She had to bite back a smile as she turned back to Ryoku and dangled the key teasingly in the air.

"Six gold, friend. Three of 'em get back to you once the room's checked over in the morn."

Ryoku fumbled for the gold satchel at his belt. When he produced it, Caryl saw how noticeably fallow it was. Her heart sank a little. Did he even have enough for the room? The lusty part of her mind reacted like the world was ending. Somehow, she felt like she needed this boy to stay with her. She ignored the fact that the inn was hardly accomplishing just that, but she would entertain the thought.

She was so enraptured by her conversation with the Defender, she didn't notice some chairs nearby scrape back. Their conversation had been overheard.

"Puny gold satchel for a Defender, me thinks."

Ryoku's head inclined toward the voice, but he didn't make eye contact. She saw the bored expression in his eyes, and gave the approaching men a warning look. They didn't have eyes for her – which was odd, to recount. She'd been the apple of this tavern before.

Two burly men sauntered toward the counter. The speaker came to lean heavily on the counter, nodding to Caryl for a drink. She didn't stir. The other rounded Ryoku's other side.

"Think he's got more in that bag, Bruno? A *Defender* has gotta be loaded, I'd say. Legends talk of the different places y'all have been. All the riches ya must have gathered."

His friend guffawed, but Ryoku rolled his eyes. "Not unless dry bread and a sleeping roll go for high stakes in this place."

The speaker cut his laughter short and redacted a little. Apparently, he was surprised to hear Ryoku talk back. Normally, any man Ryoku's size would have balked and handed over their stuff, no matter how meager. Caryl cringed. Defender or no, he was not smart to retort to these guys. As if in response, the man beckoned to his table, where three more men got to their feet.

"Think you're witty, kid?" the man demanded. The man behind him grabbed him by the arm as the first staggered closer. Ryoku didn't stir other than to raise a delicate brow in question. This only made the speaker growl under his breath. Ryoku's nose wrinkled as he closed in. Drunkard wasn't the kindest odor, I knew. "I've half a mind to knock some sense into ye. Who d'ya think yer talkin' back to, kid?"

Ryoku's eyes rolled so hard, they might slip from their sockets. "Half a mind? That cannot be too much, coming from you. You haven't even given me your name."

Caryl could have screamed at him. Why was he talking back to these guys? Did he have a brain between those cute ears of his? Now that he tilted his head, Caryl noted a distinctive point to his ears. Elven, she realized. Not the dagger-like ears that Bytold sometimes saw in summer guests, but with a smaller point.

His retort was all it took. The one gripping Ryoku's shoulder dragged him off his seat, and the speaker lunged at him with a fist the size of a stone. With the speed of a fish, Ryoku sidestepped out of his grip, ducking underneath the incoming attack to reappear on his other side. With a thwack like two stones, the attacker struck his friend soundly in the gut. He moaned, and fell like a rock.

On his other side, Ryoku chuckled. "Sorry about your friend, but I think he was better suited for that hit than me."

Did he realize that hit could practically kill him? Caryl fumed, but she was helpless.

"Ruddy brat!" the attacker swore, reeling around to face Ryoku once more. He swung heavily at Ryoku's head, but the spry Defender easily ducked beneath the blow, causing the drunk to stumble heavily. As Ryoku slid out of the way, Caryl thought she saw something on his arms. A small glint. His weapon?

Ryoku didn't account for the other folk approaching the brawl. One snatched him by the arm. Like a flash, Ryoku lashed out with his knife, but another friend of the original drunk caught him hard by the wrist, causing the knife to clatter to the floor.

Only now did Ryoku's eyes widen in alarm. Did he really think he could outmaneuver them? Granted they were slow as logs, but they still outnumbered and outsized him.

Another man grabbed his free arm. The boy wriggled like a fish out of water, struggling to free himself from captivity. The one who started the brawl sauntered forward, stepping around his unconscious friend on the ground. Caryl's breath caught in her chest. She hated times like this. She was capable for a lass in Bytold, but she stood no better chance at stopping this than the boy did.

"Your lot aren't so big and mighty after all, are ye?" The man spoke in slurred words, closing in on Ryoku like some kind of wild wolf. "Defenders." He spat on the ground, just shy of Ryoku's boot as the Defender struggled to stand tall. The entire inn was fixated on the brawl now, but not a soul rose to stop what was unfolding. This group was a little infamous around here, and interference couldn't go well.

"Ye swoop in from Creator knows where, expectin' the common folk to kiss the ground where ye walk. Well, looky here. I caught me one of the stupid folk. And I'm gonna let the rest of ya know my message."

He raised his fist. Ryoku's head flinched away. Caryl cringed in unison with him. She actually liked him, and here she was, forced to watch as a bunch of angry drunks decided they didn't like the way he looked.

The next sound was a loud, spine-chilling crack, one that seemed to ricochet across every wall in the tavern. It could have easily been Ryoku Dragontalen struck down by this ugly drunk's fist, but something about it made Caryl glance up. The drunk screamed in pain, his full weight thrown off the ground.

A young man had somehow pushed his way through the crowd. Among the crowd, he was the only one who saw something unjust and decided to act. Caryl recognized him – Will Ramun, a crusader from a distant kingdom called Syaoto. He stood taller than many men in the bar did, but he wasn't quite as beefy as the regular drunks were. He was young, too, perhaps about Caryl's age, though his sapphire eyes gleamed with acquired wisdom. Standing in his dark green tunic, he towered over the man he'd knocked down with a single strike like Dante himself.

He casually lowered his fist as Caryl tried to hide a giddy grin. Ryoku's mouth twitched to hide his own evident surprise and relief. Not a soul in the bar stirred.

"Now, now," Will reasoned, though his eyes narrowed. "This is a public place, a respite where food and drink are served with little complaints about your squalor. If you seek a brawl, may I suggest the

Old Forest? Things lurk there which could use the brawn of such men." He looked down upon the fallen man, who struggled to push himself up. "If you sought to do good, I suppose you would find it elsewhere, not targeting such a young lad in evidently uneven odds. Bytold needs men of valor, not petty bullies."

The men who'd been clutching Ryoku stepped away. Ryoku rubbed his hands, but didn't retrieve his knife just yet. He sized up Will as though trying to decide if he were a friend, or another foe. Nobody noticed the one felled by his own friend's strike snatch up the knife Ryoku failed to retrieve.

Will tilted his head toward Ryoku, who stared at him. "Stay behind me."

Half a second later, all five men lunged at Will, including the one who snatched the knife. Will didn't seem to move for a moment, long enough for Caryl to wonder if he really saw it coming.

Then he dropped to the ground. He threw all his weight onto one arm and swung out with his leg. One unlucky man flew from his feet, landing hard against a table and splitting it asunder. The man next to him took the brunt of Will's elbow to his jaw, sending him spiralling backward and over a chair. Will pivoted, and caught the next man around the midriff hard enough to throw his full weight into a fourth culprit, sending both men crashing into the last unscathed chair.

The once silent bar erupted with wild amusement and fear as the brawl sorted itself out. None dared step in to support the thugs, but none helped, either. Caryl knew Will had it covered.

The one with the knife skirted around his fallen allies without fear. Will's glance fell upon him like the decisive stare of the reaper. One well-placed kick knocked the knife from his hands before the man could so much as adjust his grip. The air rang with the sounds of broken fingers and the resounding scream that followed. The knife, freed from the thug's clutches, sailed through the air to land point-first in a nearby table, scaring the wits out of a few other patrons.

The man clutched his broken fingers, cursing as he scanned the room for a new weapon. One of the thugs got up and ran at Will for seconds, but Will reared on him and struck him soundly in the jaw, sending him straight back into the chair he clambered up over. One of the others had gotten to his feet and now hesitated, looking around at his fallen comrades with bewilderment. Will studied him with a small smirk.

"I believe this is finished," he said sharply. "All of you, dispatched so easily by a single man. Your time spent in a bar reflects your fighting prowess. I have seen better fights when I was a lad." When the man looked up at him, Will fixated him in his gaze. "Apologize. Then perhaps I could allow your leave."

The man growled under his breath. However, seeing the state of his friends, he had no choice but to drop his fists to his sides and let out a gravelly sigh. "Sorry, kid," he muttered, just like a child forced to admit defeat. "It's the drink, y'know. Makes us harsher than we mean."

Will gestured to Ryoku, who managed a wry smile. "S'alright," he said softly, coming over to stand with Will. His hands hung at his sides like he didn't know what to do with them. "No real harm done, I guess."

With a grateful nod aimed somewhere between Will and Ryoku, the man went to rouse his friends, leaving only the one with broken fingers behind. When those four had cleared out, Will strolled toward the table where Ryoku's knife lay embedded. One of the men sitting there yanked it free and held it out to Will, who accepted it with a courteous nod. While he walked back to Ryoku with it, he studied the blade, turning it over in his hands. It was a simple knife, with a fine coppery handle and a blade only a little longer than Will's hand.

"I believe this is yours?" Will asked softly, and flipped the blade over to offer it to Ryoku, handle-first. "Perhaps you should keep a better grip on it in the future."

Ryoku smiled sheepishly. "Right. Thanks." He slipped the knife back in its sheath before returning his gaze to Will. "And... Thank you. For saving me, I guess."

Will grinned. He looked older than Ryoku, but not by too much, and handsome in quite a different way. Caryl had the luxury of having seen that body in its full glory before, but nothing about the way Will looked at her betrayed that fact to Ryoku. In fact, why was she even worried about that?

"Not at all, my friend," Will assured him earnestly. "Their idea of an even match is five huge men against one boy. No offense, but you stood little to no chance against *one* of their ilk." He paused, and watched as the last man conceded defeat and ducked out of the inn.

Will watched him go; waiting for a long moment as though he might decide to return, before he turned back to me. "My apologies about the damages. I have some gold to cover it if you wish."

Caryl shook her head, smirking. "No, we go by 'the last man to touch it is responsible.' If you recall, that'd be those flying men there."

Will hid a smirk behind his hand as he returned his attention to Ryoku. Their eyes locked for a long moment, staring at each other with some sort of quiet acknowledgement. Caryl waited patiently, wondering if this had something to do with her. Yet, something about the atmosphere between them made her wonder if they knew one another.

It only dispelled when Will offered his hand. "My name is Will Ramun," he said, "median-rank soldier from Syaoto. I am here on expedition with a small platoon of soldiers led by Field Commander Lancet Cooper."

Ryoku accepted his hand. "Ryoku Dragontalen," he replied, looking a little abashed now. "Um, Defender. Of Brooks, I suppose."

"Brooks?" Will studied him. "Oh. Not Brooklyn, I assume. You do not look the type." Ryoku only looked confused, so he went on. "A Defender, though. That is interesting. Your kind is more likely to appear in places such as my home, not the backwater villages in Harohto. You... must be headed to the Capital. You are a new Defender?"

Ryoku didn't seem to understand much more of Will's words than I did. "Yeah, I'm new," he agreed. "I ran into someone when I arrived, who guided me this far with the knowledge to head to the Capital, seeking the Registry."

"Ah, to officially register as a Defender. A smart move." Will acted quite curious of the boy, and the boy didn't seem to know what he was talking about. Will's brow arched. "Someone met you? As in... When you arrived here? Was it a Guardian?"

Now Ryoku looked confused again. "A Guardian? What's that?"

Will shook his head, chuckling to himself. "How different you are from the normal Defenders I have met." He murmured this mostly to himself, and Ryoku looked offended. Did Will mean to say they were often more impressive and well put together? Ryoku knew he didn't know much about his coming duties, but he liked to think he could figure it out on his own. Will looked back to Ryoku, and smiled. "I see. You have really been hurtled into this life, have you not?"

Ryoku nodded. "It was a hasty decision."

"A hasty decision? To come to a whole new..."

Will trailed off with a glance at Caryl. What was he about to say? He changed his train of thought, then, and looked back at Ryoku. "Well, alright. You say you head to the Capital? A journey of at least three days through the woods for one who knows the trails, and... I presume you do not know the trails." Ryoku shook his head. "The option also exists to scale the cliffs to the far west of the forest. An option for a more fit man with better supplies, and it would be a quicker journey, but it is also highly dangerous. More so than the Old Forest, I dare say. And... You truly do not have your own Guardian yet?"

Ryoku was starting to look quite abashed with his lack of knowledge, and a little frustrated. "No—I don't know what that is, honestly. Don't tell me that I can't go on without one, because I can and will prove you wrong. As long as the forest isn't swarming with angry drunks, I think I'll be fine."

Will couldn't help but chuckle. "No, I would say the forest has anything *but* angry drunks. Perhaps lost ones." He adopted a serious expression quickly. "A Guardian is someone sworn to protect a Defender. Since your lot are from... so far away, they tend to pick out some strong locals to accompany them on their journeys. They swear official vows, and the ritual grants them some rights above the average person. Over all, they ensure the Defender can go about their work without getting their butt handed to them at every corner. It sounds awfully showy, but it is a tedious task."

Ryoku's brow flicked up. "Do you pay them, like mercenaries? Because I honestly don't think I can even afford a room at this inn, let alone some burly bodyguard. Perhaps I should go after those drunks."

Will chuckled, and Caryl's heart sank in her chest. The poor kid didn't have much going for him, did he? He was giving Will a somewhat defiant look. No matter what the experienced soldier would tell him, he might still forge on through the Old Forest. Caryl hadn't been far into the woods at all, and only with her father and an armed escort. It was a dangerous place – more so than her bar, if that was believable these days.

"Hold on a moment," Will told Ryoku, and he went to a table in the corner of the inn. A day bag was resting on the chair. Caryl honestly couldn't recall if he'd been here before the brawl broke out, or whether he snuck in during the conflict. Regardless, he returned after fishing out a gold satchel from the side pocket. It was far deeper than Ryoku's, and the Defender was already giving him a protesting look as Will fished through it on his way to the table. A few of the poorer denizens of the tavern eyed his satchel, but they must know they could never wrest it from Will's hands.

Rather than pool any gold into Ryoku's hands, he slid some across the counter. "Two rooms for the night, please," he told me. To Ryoku's questioning look, he smiled. "I am certain of little in life, my friend, but I can tell you might face a mighty trial in those woods. As of late, they may be even more dangerous than normal. In the morning, we will speak with my team in the village and see about guiding you through those woods. If you must face those ordeals in the woods, then you should not do so alone. If anything, I will accompany you myself."

Ryoku looked completely taken aback. Whatever he thought to happen, it wasn't this. "I-I don't have enough gold to hire some expert mercenary team!" he protested. "I don't... I don't know how this works..."

"You do not," Will replied with certainly, but he was smiling. "It does not matter. There must be a reason for our meeting today. Perhaps my time of ambling around this village comes to an end. I will guide you myself, one way or the other. We will make a few stops tomorrow."

Ryoku's head tilted. "What sort of stops?"

The tone of his voice made Caryl turn to him again. Curiosity and eagerness were knocking aside his hesitation over Will's choices. A spark was forming within him. The promise of a journey. The look of brightness in his eyes made Caryl's heart do somersaults. The look of a boy anticipating adventure was an appealing one.

Will scratched his chin airily. "I will have to speak with my team," he murmured, "and we will stop by the blacksmith. The owner is a friend of ours, and I am sure I can strike a deal for some better tools for you." He looked Ryoku over with an appraising eye. "Hmm. Perhaps a bow or staff."

Ryoku's brow flicked back up. "Do I have the money for—"

Will silenced him with a hand on his shoulder and an easy smile. "Do not think of the money, friend. After all, Defenders do tend to come across money in alarming abundance. For now, we ought to rest. Night falls, and a fit sleep will make for easier travel."

Ryoku only nodded, bouncing on his heels. He didn't look like he needed the sleep at all, despite having narrowly avoided a full-on brawl with several drunks, and it sounded like his whole day was a little odd. The adventure ahead of him would be an even greater trial, Caryl knew. Monsters prowled the Old Forest, along with the raiders and brigands who were rumoured to hold tramping grounds in the northern forest. She knew, too, that more dangerous things haunted the woods. The bounty board at the inn near the edge of town always had some manner of terrifying creature with a price on its head. Caryl shuddered at the very thought.

She caught herself in her thoughts. Caryl still clutched the key she fetched for Ryoku, leaving a red imprint in her palms where she'd been squeezing it. She let go, and quickly swept up another key from behind her. She had no doubts, now, about grabbing two high-quality room keys for the pair. She held them out to the pair. Ryoku reached for his, but Will held up his hand – Caryl tossed him his key, and he caught it expertly.

Ryoku's hand touched hers as he lightly swept up the key, and she met his gaze. His eyes were breathtaking, especially when he was close enough to touch. Now, with nothing else between them, it was like seeing the sun break through the clouds, and she saw everything. He must be scared of the journey ahead, of the impossible tasks laid out for him – of which, the terrifying woods was only the first hurdle. His tavern brawl would hardly hold a candle to the horrors beyond. Caryl heard stories of the outside world all the time. Stories of the horrors of the southern war, of the horrific monsters in the woods across the mountains, and especially those from the soldiers of Syaoto. Even Will had told some dark stories about monstrosities beyond her little village. At least the brave soldier was going with him. That gave the boy some determination to piggyback on his fear. It went unsaid, but there must be something unworldly ahead of him. A reason that Ryoku Dragontalen braved new worlds, dodged drunks, and plotted ways through wayward woods. He had something to fight for – and Caryl felt he might actually be strong enough for it, deep down.

"Thank you so much," Ryoku told Caryl politely, clasping his hands together in some strange, unfamiliar bow. When he brought his head back up from it, Caryl couldn't see past the shields in his eyes now.

She managed a shaky smile. "Of course," she replied, as though helping intriguing and attractive Defenders was part of her job description. "If you need—"

He cut her off in the most unexpected way. In a light, natural movement, Ryoku eased over the counter and lightly kissed Caryl upon the cheek. She flushed red, blind to the looks of anyone else in the tavern.

"I'll be fine," he assured her with a dreamy sort of smile, the corners of his eyes like intricate fans. "Thank you."

"Y-Yes," she stammered, quickly losing grip of her emotions. Ryoku Dragontalen was a rare boy, she knew, and he was slipping from her grasp as if she tried to sweep up the river against her chest. She couldn't explain why, but it felt like her meeting with him was important. He would stay in her mind for a long time, even as he walked away with Will up the stairs. The kind soldier already had his arm around the boy's shoulders, immersed in some kind of topic that made Ryoku chuckle and glance back. She watched them go, wishing she could be the one taking him up to his room.

It was with a heavy sigh that she returned to her duties. The life of adventure, of romance, of promised danger and, most importantly, a spot next to that boy – it wasn't for her. Her father needed her, and she needed to stay here where it was safe.

SCENE TWO: THE OLD FOREST

...Of Act One: Enter Ryoku

In the eyes of Ryoku Dragontalen, we are in the Old Forest, in the world of Harohto. It is early afternoon On November 4th, 2017.

The sun was well into the sky when we set out from the Fallen Unicorn. I hadn't anticipated sleeping in, but the antics of the past day must have taken a greater toll on me than I thought.

Will met me in the morning, now outfitted in armor. Syaoto custom seemed to dictate that they only wore the shoulder pauldron, half of the breastplate, and the piece that flayed out across his hip. It looked impractical to me, but Will wore it with pride. I had to admit, Will would cut an intimidating figure even if his armor were hot pink. I caught a glimpse of myself in the bedside mirror. My blond hair stuck up on all sides, and my clothes looked ill fitting. Obviously one of us was the more intimidating one.

"Good afternoon," he greeted me with a knowing smile. "Come. We will head to Kimball's blacksmith nearby. My squad should be meeting up with us shortly."

I got the impression that he'd been up for quite some time when I agreed. We left the tavern. I hoped to catch a glimpse of the cute bartender from the night before, but a burly man stood in her place, polishing glasses and glancing down his nose at us.

Will remarked on it as we left the tavern. "You liked the bartender from the night before?"

"Caryl? Yeah, I suppose. She was pretty cute."

"Ah, you know her by name?"

"She did introduce herself, yeah. What?" I gave Will a dirty look as he chuckled.

"Oh, nothing." He shifted his bag upon his shoulders. "Just that she is a good girl. Besides being quite good in bed, she takes care of her father. Works at the inn at night, the fields during the day. My troops have helped her before."

"She seemed like a good... Wait, you slept with her?"

Will chuckled. "She could teach you a thing or two, I imagine." When I gave him a scathing look, he put up his hands in an innocent gesture. "What? I was clearly speaking of farming tricks!"

I shook my head, but couldn't hide my smile. Will noticed, and added, "She couldn't take her eyes off you, y'know. If you wanted to stop by her farm before we set out..."

The idea made me blush scathingly, but I kept my eyes locked ahead. "No. I mean, even if I wanted to... I have something I need to do."

Will didn't press the point, which surprised me a little – but was gratifying. I wasn't ready to explain. "Good on you. I can tell you are eager to set out, huh?" He smiled at me. "I agree. Beyond tramping about the village, spending nights at the tavern, stuffing our faces... my field commander has not left much room for actually helping people. We do what we can, but we must follow orders. A friend and I have taken to helping Caryl and her father on the fields. We buy rounds for the veterans of the southern war. I can tell we met for a reason, my friend. If nothing else, I am driven to press against the forces that oppress us."

"Oppress you?" I asked, curious. I didn't guess that Will might be unhappy with his troop.

"Right. Here we are," he said abruptly, only a short jaunt down the road from the inn. "This is the best blacksmith in town – Kimball Cragg runs it, and he has been kind to us. Not many can maintain Syaoto armor and weapons."

I noted the weapons Will carried on his person. A wood-handled lance kept propped over his shoulder by a thick baldric, the steel head covered with a snapped cloth. If that wasn't enough, a rounded blade sheathed at the back of his belt, only a little longer than his waist. If I recalled my vague studies of history in my world, it might be a gladius from the thickness of it.

I shielded my tired eyes to look at the shop ahead of us beyond the gleaming sun. It was a simple one, stuck on the side of the road next to residential homes and a bakery. It looked like a home turned into a shop, and I could feel the heat resonating from the forge within. Despite being late autumn, the air didn't have much of a chill to it, or I might welcome the heat. Barrels loaded with halberds crowded around the open door like the smithy didn't have room inside to hold them, and some of the pikes sat topped with full steel helmets. I took in the sight with surprise. Did Bytold really need so many weapons and armor forged, or was this why the forge was so well stocked?

I wiped sweat from my brow already as Will led the way inside. Inside was just as cluttered as the doorway. Half-made weapons and armor mixed with finished ones among the barrels and finite shelves. The odors of sweat and metal lingered in the air as if they were a part of it. A heavy-looking anvil sat askew on a tilted log, where a hammer and a large pair of steel tongs lay abandoned next to the giant hearth. Though it wasn't currently in use, the hot surface emitted such a steaming aura that I couldn't look at it, and the cooling water next to it emitted steam.

A man stepped out from behind the great bellows, rubbing his neck with a towel. He wore only slacks and an undershirt, his muscular arms stained with burns and scars. Even his short, dark hair looked burnt in places. He was younger than I imagined, too. Perhaps in his thirties.

"Will, is that you?" the man asked, grinning. "What a surprise! Did your armor get mashed up or something?" Then his eyes fell on me, and one bushy brow rose in surprise. A smirk hid behind his trimmed beard. "Ye brought me a customer? In this sleepy lil place?"

"You bet, Kimball," Will started, but I was surprised he could get the words out. Kimball hurriedly strapped a huge mask over his head and started stretching thick gloves onto his hands.

"What'll it be, friend?" he demanded, having to raise his voice as he leaned on the bellows, which made the quieted flames in the hearth scream to life. "You'll have me forge a sword? Some armor? Or maybe – gods, maybe a mallet?"

"Kimball, wait—"

The flames whooshed up again, and we had to step away from the burning hearth. "What's that, Will? Y'know my shop's loud as the fires of Chaos when it gets fired up!"

Will managed to stop the excitable blacksmith with a hand on his shoulder. "Wait, friend," he insisted. "I was not sure a sword or hammer would suit my young friend here. You see..."

He leaned in closer, and I couldn't make out his words over another roar from the flames. When they settled, Kimball was giving me an incredulous look. "Why, a Defender? And one who won't take some glorious new sword, or armor forged from the scales of a dragon—"

"You forge from dragon scales?" I asked, bewildered.

Kimball guffawed. "If ye've the gall to go hunt one in the Border Range, or the Atmos Woods beyond! Only places I think a dragon might hide out. But ye go fetch the scales, and I'll make yer armor!"

I frowned. "I'd have to kill a dragon to make armor from it? No thanks. Don't they just... drop scales once in a while?"

Kimball descended into quite a fit of laughter, leading us away from the forge itself as he managed to stumble amid his piles of weapons and armor. "I like 'im, Will. Better sort than that snide captain of yours. He'd fall for a tall tale like that and be chargin' out into the woods by now."

Will's smirk was a little distant, I thought. "I apologize, Kimball, but the day is getting away from us—"

Kimball raised his hands in surrender. "Say no more, boy," he said, and stumbled through his wares until he reached a much more organized part of the store. A tangible desk emerged from the piles of weapons. Behind it was an assortment of wooden staves and bows of all different sizes. "I don't just forge, y'know, though it takes a mean smith to make a working bow. I'm also a carver. No, I don't do those runes meself. Lindsor Cerone's studied up on those in his old days."

"Lindsor Cerone?" I echoed, curious. "Like Caryl's—"

Kimball swore as he knocked over a barrel of pikes in an attempt to get to the desk. "Gods! Wish one of these villagers would just up and join the army like the good ol' days. Sell me out, for the Creator's sake! Can't just stop makin' arms and armor now, can I?"

"You could always—"

Will couldn't finish as Kimball ducked out of sight, and then reappeared just as quickly, clutching a wooden stick in his hands. It looked like a gnarled tree branch – oak, I recognized, and about three feet long. A red gem crested the knotted end of the staff. In the more open part of the shop, he approached and stuffed the branch in my hands.

"Oak staff," he said. "Yer basic stave. Particularly good fer fire, which's what most new kids like to practice. Ya see—"

Now Will cut Kimball off. "How much?"

Kimball gave Will a surprised look, but the tall soldier wasn't looking at us. He craned his neck to look through a little dusty window near the entrance. I couldn't see what he saw from where I was, but I could guess. His squad was here.

"Right. Six gold, I'd say. Normally this runs over ten gold, but… Just clearin' stock, ya know?"

Will was already rifling through his gold satchel. "Right. I appreciate it, as always," he assured Kimball, stuffing coins in his hand. I could clearly count more than a mere six gold in his palms. "Would you do me a favor?"

"Name it," Kimball said, without hesitation. He wasn't even looking at the gold.

"Could you explain to my friend how to use that? I… must meet with my team."

Kimball's eyes gleamed. "Gonna stick it to the man then, are ye? Very well. I'll take care of it."

Will nodded his thanks before taking off toward the door. Kimball and I watched him go while I clutched the oaken stick. I thought there was something awfully foreboding about the hunch in Will's shoulders. He almost knocked down a display of halberds as he went, shouting back a hasty apology before ducking through the doorway – tall as he was, he had to bend to exit the store. Kimball only chuckled, bemused, stroking his kept beard with a smirk.

"Why does he look like he's going to face death itself?" I murmured, half to myself.

Kimball gave me a quiet look. "Ye must be new here, then. His captain's a character with much to be desired. Every one o' his men's got a heart o' gold, 'cept for him. If nothin' else, it looks like ye inspired him to finally stand up to the dodger." He sighed, gazing down at the staff now. "Right. Then listen good, y'hear?"

I nodded as he gestured to the staff in my hands. I could make out two smoothed-out spots spaced out among the knobby wood. On the other side etched letters of an unfamiliar dialect in dark blue letterings that didn't seem to be made of the staff at all.

"This is yer standard oak staff. Normal ones are charged with a single magical element. Not to say ye can't use it fer other types of magic, but—"

I stopped him there. "This is magic? Like... magic is real. And it's in this staff."

The look Kimball gave me was as though I asked what color the sky was. "Ye're a Defender, and ye're gonna ask me that sort of ruddy question? I wouldn't dare guess how it works, but I know ye must've used some air of magic to get here in the first place."

I had to concede to that. "I suppose magic isn't the weirdest thing I've seen in the last few days."

"Aye, if that ain't the truth," Kimball muttered, but went on. "I suppose ye want the whole ruddy explanation on magic, then, but I'm not the one to ask. I can tell ye it works in elements and whatnot. Your typical staff comes with an affinity o' sorts for one o' 'em. Oak, that's good fer fire. Pine, she's good for earth-type magicks, and birch fer wind. That's not to say ye can't use any ol' type of magic with them, but fire runs through this one like rings of a tree."

"Right," I agreed, as though I knew exactly what I was talking about, "but how do I use it? Will it just... listen to me?"

Kimball sighed. He took the staff from my hands and held it aloft, screwing up his face. I backed away several steps, sure he might just set the store ablaze right before me, but he opened one eye and chuckled. "Not everyone's good fer magic, kid. But if you didn't believe I was about to shoot flames all over my shop just now, then that's hardly a skeptic eye ye have."

I tried to hide my grin. "Point taken."

He handed the staff back to me. "Yer a Defender. Magic must run through yer veins, or else nobody'd run scared of your lot in the bigger cities. I can't tell ye how to use it, but it'll come to ye." He chuckled under his breath. "If I'm wrong, then ye can still club some baddies with this stick, anyway."

I smiled. Yeah, sounded good. Six gold – or more, as I was sure even while Kimball hastily stuffed away Will's coins – for a stick I could've found in the woods.

"Far as I understand," he went on, and tapped the red gem embedded in the head of the staff. "This here's what makes it a staff. Ye could run around tryin' to set people ablaze with the stick, but without this little guy, it's useless. From what I get, the gem tries to take the energies ye need to use it. There's all sorts o' names for that. Mana. Energy. Chakra. Whatever have ye, but it comes down to the same means: it's a cost o' use. Means ye can't just run around settin' people ablaze or whatnot – not as long as you don't have the energy to supply it. I've heard o' mages droppin' dead from the tax of their own spells in the past. Not unheard o'. Ol' Lindsor's brother, he—"

His gaze caught something behind me. I turned, and realized I could see outside through one murky window near the forge. Will was outside, standing with at least half a dozen men all dressed in similar styles to him. It looked like Will was arguing with one of them, a man with a steel helmet and a red cape over his shoulders.

"Right," Kimball said softly. "Don't ye go rushin' out there now. Impractical as their armor is, I don't think they'll like ye very much if ye try clubbin' their knees with this."

I was too worried to chuckle. I'd seen Will easily take down five other huge men, but this group of people might have the same skills he had. If they didn't like me, I might as well just stay in this shop forever.

"Last thing," Kimball said, evening his voice out. "Those letters on the side there are what's known as Charge Runes. If ye plan on gettin' in some big brawl, just sap up some extra magic into the gem and it stores up in these big ol' letters. Doesn't store up for too long, so ye can't just fill 'em up now and expect to have any left when ye reach the Capital. On the flip side, nobody but the guy who put 'em in can use your Charge Runes. That way, nobody else can steal yer fire." He chuckled, bemused by his own joke. "Best not to try 'n' figure all that out in one sittin'. Other magickal folks can explain it better than this ol' smithy, I'm sure. Capital city has a magic school if yer serious about the art – and ye got the time and money to spare."

I nodded, studying the weapon in my hand. I wondered if I'd actually be able to master such a complex weapon. I certainly wouldn't have the chance to study. "Thank you very much," I told him earnestly, and bowed. "I must catch up with Will."

"Hold yer horses," he told me just as I was about to turn away. Kimball shuffled across the store back to his desk. "Will mentioned ye were lookin' fer a bow 'n' arrows, too."

I glanced at him, distracted as I caught a glimpse of Will arguing outside with his captain. "I guess he decided on the staff," I reasoned. "I don't know how to use a bow, either. Nor do I have the gold for it."

Kimball only chuckled, and pulled an item out from below the counter. It was a short bow, almost half the size of the staff and curved taut by a thin wire. He pulled out a small, squared-off quiver chock full of arrows, strapped to a baldric.

"Recurve shortbow," he elaborated, as though that might explain it all. "In terms of archery, a beginner's tool. Far simpler than yer longbow or crossbow." He set the quiver on the counter and demonstrated the movement of the bow. "Ye just loosen up your legs and shoulders, keepin' yer body like a turret. Draw the wire back just to about this length, notch an arrow here…"

He notched an arrow to the bow, moving much more quickly than I was fully following, and then swivelled the bow around and freed an arrow just over my shoulder. I jumped a mile, but the arrow sailed just past me and twanged loudly into something behind me. I spun, alarmed, to find the arrow embedded in a target haphazardly hung on one of the shelves. It had struck dead center.

He took a moment to calm himself from laughter upon my reaction. "Fairly simple when ye get the hang of it. I dabbled with the bow and arrow back in my day." He handed me the bow. "Go on, lad. Give it a shot. Don't worry – only breakable thing to an arrow in here is us."

I ignored his laughter at the idea, since I felt I was more likely to shoot an arrow into my foot than any sort of target. However, with his encouragement, I drew the bow taut. It didn't have nearly as much give to it as it looked when he used it, but I was able to draw the wire back far enough to take the arrow Kimball offered me. As I kept his poise and prepared to shoot, I accidentally let go of the arrow far too soon – it sailed into a straw display covered in armor.

"Huh," Kimball murmured. "Well, ye got it between the plates. Were that a real man standing there, you'd have struck right between the plates! On any man, that's a decisive arrow, mark my words. Forget that yer off a mile from the actual target."

I smiled sheepishly and went to hand the bow back to him. "Thank you. I'm sure I might be able to kill someone with my next bow – intentional or not."

Kimball only chuckled, crossing his arms. "Keep it. Will's been my best customer in a long time. Find me any of these damned sleepy villagers who'll talk about arms and armor with me for hours, or to offer me pointers on how the Syaoto smithies do their work, and I'll sell ye my arm and leg." His smile turned a little wistful, I thought. "Will's a good lad, and I feel I won't see 'im for quite some time. Or ye, for that matter. And any friend o' his is a friend o' mine. See to it that ye take down a few of them raiders with this, at least, y'hear?"

I stared at Kimball incredulously, surprised by his generosity. "Thank you!" I exclaimed, and bowed again. Kimball's brow rose, but he chuckled. I had the feeling the bow I learned yesterday was foreign here. Did that mean the man who took me to Bytold wasn't from here at all?

"Don't sweat it," he waved me off, "but stop by if ye ever return to this sleepy town, and I'll make whatever ye want. Even if ye come across some dragon scales."

I laughed, but it was time to go. Kimball already headed toward the back room, so I forged a path through the strewn contents of the shop, passing by the suffocating heat of the hearth on my way out. The strap of my bag nearly knocked over another display, but I managed to duck away. I was fiddling with the strap of the quiver's baldric as I left when I crashed into someone outside the door. The surprising force threw me back into the door. Stunned and windless, I glanced after a tall figure who rushed past me and down the road.

"Sorry!" a female voice called back. She seemed awfully tall for a woman, I thought, and had a black kite shield bobbing over her shoulder. Before I could say anything, she wheeled around a corner and I lost sight of her. Shrugging, I turned my attention to the situation before me.

My new comrade had his back to me, standing, arms crossed, among a counted eight other soldiers. Three of them wore silver tunics, gold pieces of armor, and helms that shrouded their faces. The one Will stared down wore armor of a higher calibre, polished and shiny, with a red cape slung over one shoulder. He had his visor down, and the sides of the helm spanned out like small wings. The helm didn't end in some tapered feather like old illustrations I'd seen, but had a peak like someone could impale themselves upon it. If I had to guess, that must be Lancet Cooper.

Two more of them dressed like Will in green tunics, steel armor, and with rounded steel caps placed upon their heads. Three more – all of whom looked younger than Will – wore blue tunics and bronze armor. Their attire had to be a sort of ranking in Syaoto terms. The blue-tunics lacked the lances everyone else had as well, but the silver-tunics also had gleaming hatchets at their belts.

"This is the kid?" Lancet asked in a snide tone. I could feel his eyes on me through the visor on his helm when I stepped up next to Will, but I couldn't see his face. "I see what you mean. However, you seem to be making a hasty assumption on the part of the Crown – one which, I remind you, is not in your jurisdiction in any sense of the word."

"I will be escorting him free of charge," Will replied. The icy quality to his tone surprised me. Even to a bunch of angry, drunken men, Will hadn't sounded this... dangerous. "He has very little gold. Next to no supplies. He is armed now, but the Old Forest is dangerous. You know that as well as I – you have seen the bounties. Not that we have acted upon any of them in weeks."

Lancet walked away a pace, a hand on his hips and one upon the crown of his helm, and cursed under his breath. He stayed away for a moment. When he returned, he levelled himself before Will. My new friend was a head taller than his commander was, but nothing about the man suggested he cared about that.

"Will. You seem to be making a rather hasty assumption of what it is we're here for. Do you honestly think we traveled all the way *here*, to this backwater little village all the way from our grand, royal kingdom – to protect the sheep? To escort a boy through the woods so, what, he may not form calluses upon his heels as he walks? To see to it that yet another high-born Defender – useless, in the grand scheme of things – may see himself safely to the Capital of this backwater little world?" He chuckled, but in such a way that I was almost worried. "Please. We have urgent matters to attend to, more urgent than this poor sod of a child. While you and my other men have been frequenting the tavern, sneaking off in the dead of night, and making house calls to wenches—"

"I would go with Will."

A younger soldier piped up, stepping up on Will's other side. By the look both Will and Lancet gave him, he was speaking badly out of line. The boy was almost as tall as Will, with sandy hair and light, clear eyes. While most of the other soldiers looked built and stocky, this particular novice was more gangly and thin. Regardless, he crossed his narrow arms next to Will, setting his freckly face in a scowl.

"You dare—"

"Brom sent us here, to Harohto, to gain experience in our knighthood and do good by the people!" the boy interrupted, no shortage of emotion in his voice. "If I may, sire – we have done neither by your lead. You would have us act as paid swords, offering steep prices to take people through the woods safely. No matter how you word it, we are robbing them. That is not in our code – I have read it all, sire. Have you?"

Will nudged him in the elbow, and the boy retracted painfully. "Alex, stop. Do you realize what you are saying?"

"I do, Will," Alex replied sternly, "and I would be folly not to speak up. Lancet claims we waste our money on booze? I see veterans at the tavern, hardly able to pay for little more than a scarce meal and with none to hear their legends. Did you meet the man with one arm, who lost his wife and daughter in the southern war? We fed him, Lancet! We saw to his medical bills so that the stump of his arm would not rot to disease!"

Lancet took a step toward Alex, a hand on the hilt of his sword. "You insolent little—"

"Alex is right." This time, one of Will's rank stepped in next to him, arms crossed. Lancet stayed his hand, but he fixated the other soldier in his glare now. "You would label us as criminals, sire? Sneaking off in the dead of night? Perhaps you mean how Will, Leif, and I went into the woods to find a child who had run off, scared of getting a needle to cure her of her illness? Is that not true, Leif?"

"The medicine that we went off to get two weeks ago," the other soldier of Will's rank piped up, apparently Leif. "Sneaking off in the dead of night? I did, and would again. The forest is even deadlier at night, and the raiders up north are not sleeping in the night, either." He rolled up the sleeve of his tunic to show bandages wrapped around his upper shoulder, outlining what looked like a deep wound. "By your leave, we would be awaiting a messenger from Lord General Brom on whether or not we could embark on such a task." He turned to me, and offered me a brave smile. "I see little difference here."

"What of all the work we did on the farms?"

Now one of the silver-tunic men strolled around – and came to stand next to Will and Alex. "Helping to plough the fields of one Lindsor Cerone, an esteemed man in the village whose wife passed years ago, and who only has a daughter to work the bar and the fields?" He looked Lancet in the visor and removed his own helm, shaking free a head of shaggy brown hair. "That is right. Helping the man was not of your command. It was by word of Will."

"And his daughter, what a catch she is! H-Hey!"

Will elbowed Alex hard in the ribs. Lancet growled in irritation and spun to his fellow silver-tunic. "What about you, Oliver? Tell me you have more sense than this!"

His fellow man turned to face him. "By your lead, Lancet, we have acted as little more than glorified field guides in this village. No matter what mission Lord General Brom may have assigned you, it does not justify acting this way toward the populace. They do not need bullies and tyrants to tax them – they need gentle guidance, protection – someone to fight for them. If Will proposes a new task for us, then I am all for it. He has not misled us so far despite his inexperience – it outweighs what good we have done under your lead, sire. Respectfully. And I would write home to Lord General Brom and explain just as I have said unto you."

By the time Oliver finished speaking, not one soldier stood by Lancet. All seven of them gathered around Will, hands on the hilts of their weapons – not as a threat, but in a resting gesture to show they were earnest. Will held Lancet's glare evenly.

"Very well, then," Lancet drawled, removing his helm. A mane of silver hair cascaded down from his helm, falling to frame a sharp, angular face with cutting blue eyes. I thought he looked a little different from the others right away. They all had earthy-colored hair and tanned skin, but Lancet was paler with silver hair. Was he from the same place? My heart leapt as his hand went to his sword. "I challenge you, Will. Duel me. If you win, I'll allow your foolish endeavour while I single-handedly complete Brom's mission. Lose, and you shall leave this Defender to stumble through the woods alone."

"That is not fair!" Alex cried. A green-garbed soldier held him back. "We outclass you, ranking or no! Brom will listen to us!"

"Lord General Brom," Will hastily corrected him. My tall friend had already freed the wooden lance from over his shoulder. "Lancet, I accept your challenge."

The other soldiers dragged an argumentative Alex away from Will and Lancet. I followed suit with haste, sure that I didn't want to be caught in this skirmish. I was learning a great deal about my new traveling companion from witnessing this encounter, as scarring as it may be. Could Will win against his commanding officer? I clearly recalled how easily he dispatched five men in the bar, and I felt confident.

Will and Lancet cleared the distance between them with a lunge. Their weapons met with a brilliant spark that seemed to crack through the air like a collapsing iceberg. They locked arms, pressing against each other with all their might. Just when I thought their hold might break, they jumped apart, skidding until they perched on one knee several feet apart, lances drawn back over their shoulders like scorpion tails. Will's hand twitched near the rounded blade at the back of his belt.

The next moment was tense. The soldiers faced one another, their bodies taut and waiting for the opportune moment to strike. There was no sort of telltale movement or signal that I caught when they leapt again, their lances cutting through the air like massive tiger claws. Lancet swept down in a deep thrust aimed for Will's ribs. With remarkable agility, Will pivoted around the lance and swung around to Lancet's other side, his lance curved up in a deadly wild spin.

The next moment was difficult to follow with the naked eye. Both fighters moved with expert agility. In a single move, they landed in entirely different positions. Lancet was on one knee, his lance against Will's upper calf, his raised elbow just above Will's sternum. Will's lance lay against Lancet's collarbone. They stayed, unmoving, for a long and tense moment. My heart stuck in my chest. By the look of it, a move on either side spelled the end of the fight. Will's chest was heaving, but Lancet didn't appear fatigued. Finally, Lancet drew a heavy sigh.

"You win this round," Lancet conceded. Will's weapon drew back slowly, almost with hesitation. Lancet got to his feet, sheathing his weapon over his shoulder. Will straightened, putting away his lance, and their eyes locked. For a moment, I could see nothing but a bitter hatred between them. "You may embark on this foolish quest. Report straightaway to me once this boy reaches the capital. If you receive some sort of payment, distribute it as usual. I will remain here."

Will's eyes did not soften. He bowed appropriately and thanked the elite soldier. He exchanged glances with the seven soldiers who had sided with us, and led the way down the street. People parted for us – we'd drawn a crowd. Bytold probably didn't see much like that, and I could relate. I stumbled to follow them, still clutching my staff and bow as though my life depended on it.

A short ways down the road, Oliver and the others stopped. He and the other silver-tunic looked older than Will and, oddly, Lancet as well. Both had chestnut-brown hair, but Oliver looked a little older and wizened, while being one of the shorter soldiers. "We will go back our things from the Brazen Boar," Oliver told Will. "You look to have all your things. Meet at the edge of town?"

Will only nodded, his expression tight after his confrontation with Lancet. I sensed a great deal of turmoil between the two. Oliver went with the other silver-tunic, Leif, and the other green-tunic, leaving Will and I with the blue-tunics.

I waited for Will to speak up, but he didn't for a long time as we walked through the small village of Bytold. By their expressions, they thought nothing special of the place and had been here for some time. I felt like I was slowing them down as I took in the place with wonder. Honestly, I'd never seen anything like it – from the little brook that babbled through the town, to every meagerly crafted home, most of stones, wood, and even mud. Anglers' rods bobbed in the river, seeking the silvery fish I saw occasionally spring out from the surface, flailing in the air before returning home. Other folk bustled around on their daily business, carting barrels and baskets of all sorts of commodities to and fro. All gave us curious looks as we passed. It was only after I saw Will flash me a quick smile that I realized the truth of it: Will and his troops had been here for some time. I was the odd one out.

The edge of town sprang out at us. Perhaps I'd been too busy looking around the village to see the great wall of earthy-green that stretched out just past the village. Anyone could step between the village and the thick of the woods in a single bound, since nothing separated them.

I began to see why locals dubbed it the Old Forest as we slowed to a halt near the birthing of a dirt path leading into the thick of it. Each tree looked too thick to wrap our arms around, and towered far above our heads, layering part of the road with pine needles, cones, and all sorts of little dried leaves among them. I wondered how old each tree was, truly. Did their lives here work the same as in my world, or were they the ghosts of mine? Ancient trees that went to live on past the life in my world?

Will came to stand at my side, staring up at the intimidating canopy of trees ahead of us. While the village had been little to him, he could still stare up at these boughs with appreciation. He'd even been here before, if my assumptions on the earlier conversations were correct, and probably seen thousands of forests in his time of all sorts, but he still smiled up at those trees like it was the first forest he'd ever seen.

"We are in for an arduous journey, Ryoku," he said, but his voice didn't lack faith. Alex and the others were rifling through their day bags, sorting out their supplies. I could already see Oliver and the others down the way, each of the three men holstering more than one backpack. "Rain will fall before we make camp."

I followed Will's gaze. His vision was surprisingly good. I could only spot the edges of some dark clouds far beyond the west reaches of the woods. "Is that going to deter our hike?"

The look Will gave me was approving. "Not if you are unfazed, my friend. It looks like you appreciate what rises before you. In rain, forests thrive just like a flower in sunshine. The trees seem to stretch even further out, seeking to trap every last drop between their highest branches and their deepest roots. Everything comes to life."

He spoke with unmistakable fondness. "You've seen lots of forests, then."

Will gave me a look. "Have you not?"

I didn't reply. Besides the murky Bytold Woods to the south, this was, technically, my first forest, and certainly the first of its kind. In my world, such a thing was long since gone. I couldn't imagine how to explain such a thing to Will. Did he know what this place really was?

Rather than try to breach that topic, I chose a less worrisome one. "What would have happened if you lost against Lancet?"

His expression clouded over so quickly, I regretted asking. "It would not have," he replied. "Lancet Cooper allowed me to win. Even a man like him knew the others already outmatched him. If he won, he would have to deal with eight men who already expressed their wishes about doing better work. It was just a show to put on for his crew."

"To remind us that he remains our captain, and that he is the superior soldier," Oliver chimed in as he returned, setting down two big rucksacks next to us. He hardly looked fatigued, which was odd considering the impact those bags made on the ground as he dropped them. "Not that Will is short of a prodigy himself." He smiled at me, and offered a hand. "I apologize we were not able to introduce ourselves properly back there. I am Oliver Rouge, a high-rank soldier from Syaoto."

I shook his hand. "Ryoku Dragontalen, Defender. Though I guess you already know that."

"We sure do," Alex agreed heartily, setting down his bag to join us. "A Defender, in the flesh – that is amazing! My name is Alex Retton. Novice rank in the Syaoto army."

Despite his gangly looks and kind, green appearance, he had a startlingly firm grip. "You were brave to stand up to Lancet like that."

Alex smiled sheepishly, but I didn't miss the stern looks Will, Oliver, and the others were giving him. "I have been known to speak out of line in the past. Especially when it comes to our fearless leader." He spoke with a great amount of contempt.

"That does not eliminate the need for respect," Oliver chastised him. "You must be careful. Even I was foolish to speak against our leader, but it was necessary. In the future, you must recall your ranking when speaking toward your superiors. Lancet could demote you for your comment about Lord General Brom alone."

Alex snorted. "Brom cares not for those silly titles," he said. "Will, you are close friends with him. Our kingdom is about so much more than titles and nobility! Even King Lionel—"

"Close friendship does not eliminate the need for respect," Will reasoned, "as you would do well to study. Our kingdom is close, yes. A king may be friends with a servant, but the servant could still face execution or exile for not properly addressing his liege. That works in the army as well, and in life." He glanced at me, a small smile playing across his lips. "Take Ryoku for example. A Defender is a title. He does not offer that as some chess piece to move the room to his pleasure, but it is a powerful title and a relevant note of info. A Defender can be treated differently by different people. In many cultures, including our own, even kings can pay tribute to them. How would it look if even King Lionel paid his respects to Ryoku, but in the same room, you did not?"

Alex cringed at the comparison, glancing at me. "It makes sense when you say it like that," he admitted. "But that is weird. Some worlds do not pay Defenders respect?"

"Not all do," Will said. "It strongly depends on the world."

I looked at Will questioningly. "So you do know where we are? And where I came from?"

Will smiled at me. "We do, but not all denizens of this place know the truth of it all. It is... a complicated setting."

"Soldiers are usually trained to know," Oliver agreed. "Usually, armies in different worlds can be sent to assist other worlds and, in some cases, conquer. I assure you we are here for the former."

Alex was giving me a lasting look. "What is it like?" he asked softly. "The land of the living, I mean. Since we are a part of the spirit realm."

"This might not be the best place to ask that," Leif intervened, approaching with his own pair of rucksacks. He set them down between us and glanced between Alex and I. "For future note, and as a reminder to my forgetful friend – the regular denizen is often unaware of the greater picture. Everyone in this little town – the cute barmaid, her stern father, that energetic blacksmith – none of them realize they are a part of this place. Not in the way you might imagine, anyway."

I already knew not to ask common folk about the spirit realm, thanks to the friend who guided me to Bytold, but he never dived into the specifics. I'd have to ask Will down the road.

"Yes, we will refrain from such topics in the village," Will agreed. He turned to me and seemed to note something. "Ryoku, where did you set down your bag? We can fill it with supplies."

"I didn't..." I hesitated. I was still clutching my bow and staff, but my back felt strangely empty. I hadn't thought to stow my new weapons with my bag in all the ruckus since I left the shop.

"Did you leave it at the armoury?" Alex asked.

I scrunched up my nose. "No," I recalled. My bag had caught on a display on the way out, but I certainly left with it. Then...

With a start, I recalled the woman I bumped into as I left the shop, who sprinted off with something clutched against her chest. Did she...?

I confessed my idea to Will. Alex and Oliver looked alarmed, but Will only waved it off. "It does not matter, really. You had, what, a couple coins and some dried bread? A sleeping roll?"

He gestured for Alex's day bag, who was already handing it off to Will. They rifled through it, counting things off. "Well, here is a new sleeping roll. Some bandages and gauze, in case of emergencies. Fresh bread, trail mix, dried fruit... Oh, and this cloak will fit you."

"We have a *lot* of backup supplies, Ryoku," Oliver assured me. "Take whatever you may need. In the worst case, we may have to top up our stock at the Capital."

"I have only packed some necessities for light travel," Will told me, handing me the bag. "I promise I will see to getting you proper supplies in the city. That, and you would not want a heavy bag on your first traipse through these woods."

"All uphill, too," Leif commented with a smirk. "Not easy on us, either, but easier than it would be for a boy in your shape. Have you done much hiking?"

I shrugged the new bag on. It was ill fitting on my shoulders. "There isn't really the option," I replied, unsure how to really explain. If they knew the truth about my world and the land of the living, then they didn't know it in full detail. This could be a headache. Still, I gave him a friendly smile. "Can't wait, though. It looks beautiful in there."

They looked confused by my wording, but the four of them all turned with me to stare into the woods. "Damned right," Oliver agreed heartily. "She is a beautiful forest. Syaoto has the Royal Forest and all, but this is a gem."

Will smiled at me. "Enjoy the last smells of the village – from here on, there is but pine and mold. Even the most seasoned outdoorsmen tire of the scents."

I sighed wearily, doubting I might tire of it. My ex always told me that I was something of an old soul, aspiring so heartily to be in the woods in a world where it just didn't exist anymore.

It only took a few more minutes for the soldiers to finish sorting their bags. Then, with one last look at the village, we piled down the beginning of the forest trail.

Once we entered the cover of trees, the air got noticeably thicker quickly, and a shadowy darkness settled in around our heads. Dust glinted in the air like falling stars in stray streams of sunlight through the forest canopy, offering the place an even more mystical aura than I personally gave it. We trod along a well-traversed path, littered with fallen logs, tangled brush, and weeds that poked through even the trodden soil.

The soldiers marched along quietly, the shadows of the forest canopy dancing across their steel armor, so I had plenty of time to absorb all the various sights and sounds. Most of the trees were pine, but some grand oaks stuck out now and then, much of their leaves gone in the late autumn season. Not far off the path, the trees clumped closely together, strewn thick with a musky fog that gave me the chills. I stared out into it anyway, wondering if I might see some wildlife if I stared long enough. With the constant clatter of the soldiers' armor above our footsteps, I doubted it. Large boulders sat just off the path, somehow nestled among the trees with no sign of how they'd gotten there. Upon question, Will suggested they came from the Border Range, the surrounding mountain range to the east that presumably split Harohto's main continent in half, a long time ago.

A few hours down the path, Will signalled for the group to stop. It was little more than a clever palm movement, but every one of the soldiers caught it and stopped in the path, turning to Will. I couldn't help but be impressed. Will wasn't their captain, but they sure listened to him.

"Please scout the perimeter for any sign of danger," Will told them. "Alex, Leif, find some berries and provisions from the woods. The less we damper our stock, the better."

"Not that we cannot easily feed the Fallen Unicorn at dinner," Leif remarked idly, but he did not disobey. The seven soldiers broke off the path. Some of them embarked down the path, but Oliver and his fellow silver-tunic ducked down a deer trail to the side.

When all the others were gone, Will guided me to a nearby lichen-coated boulder. "Sit," he instructed. "You are not used to this type of excursion, are you?"

He helped me climb the boulder, assisted by what was practically a naturally formed set of steps along the side. I took a moment to reply, catching my breath atop it. "Sorry, no. Like I said, this kind of thing—"

"Does not exist in your world," Will finished. He sat across from me on the boulder, staring out into the woods. "So I have heard. Despite that, your being here is quite strange."

I gave him a look. "How so?"

I was quickly realizing he'd stopped just for me. When he crested the boulder, his chest rose in easy, even breaths – he wasn't fatigued at all. He sat across from me on the rock, facing the woods we had yet to cross. "Make no mistake. Many corners have heard of Defenders. In worlds where the most exciting things are the gossip at the bar, they hold out for legends. They know that Defenders are more uncommon than a spirit like myself. They come from far away. They speak odd dialects. Sometimes they seem unfamiliar with the most basic aspects of our culture. Common instruction is to refer them to the nearest Registry, located in our capital cities. That is all they know about you.

"Soldiers are made familiar with your kind for a reason. Because your kind seeks war. They require armies and the best weapons possible. You arrive with some kind of purpose. Yet," he went on, peering at me," something about you is different. You have a clear goal, but it must be a noble one. I cannot quite place it. So, if I may be so bold as to ask... what *is* your goal here, Ryoku Dragontalen?"

"What do you mean?" I asked, a little guarded.

He smiled plaintively. "Beyond reaching the Capital to register yourself. You may be armed with a new bow and staff, but the world beyond is much harsher than this place. Do you intend to go on ahead alone, to other worlds? Are there others like you?"

I glanced away, unsure how to answer his questions. "I don't know much," I replied. "I guess you could say I'm... looking for somebody. Yeah."

Will's look was nothing if not curious. "Who, then? A lover? A friend?"

"Not a lover," I replied hastily. "No, nothing like that."

Will sighed. "Ah, I suppose so. Else, that scene at the bar might have been a little distressful." His eyes gouged at mine with pressing questions. "Unless there is another woman in your life as it is? Another Defender? I may be only a guide to you, but you may find my ears quite receptive! Who is she?"

I turned scarlet and glanced away haughtily. "M-Maybe we can talk about this another time. It's not quite so simple."

I thought he would press the question further, but he seemed to sense something about my tone and cut himself short. I kept my eyes away, staring at nothing while my mind worked. Up until the matter arose, the events of the last few days kept my thoughts from the odd matter of my love life – of the unexplained change of heart that I succumbed to about a month ago.

Up until recently, I knew I'd been distraught with the departure of my ex-girlfriend, Annalia Rikalla. Last winter, she'd had to up and move across the country with her family, ending our yearlong relationship. It happened to coincide with a difficult point in my life. I felt the sting of that for a long time. Only during the summer did I start to realize I was holding onto something much more than Anna's abrupt move.

However, timed with the appearance of the strange boy I was seeking out, I developed feelings for a different girl. Someone who I'd dated a long time ago. I couldn't explain why, but it felt like it formed around a new beginning. Something stirred greatly in my life, causing old feelings to vacate and new ones to spring forth. It was a new chapter, spurred on by the appearance of the strange boy who led me to the spirit realm in search of a great many of things – far too vast to explain to this stranger before me without sounding like a lunatic.

It took me a moment to realize Will was giving me quite a concerned look. "I'm alright," I told him flatly, brushing him off with a smile. "Just thinking, that's all."

Will said nothing, only watched my expression as I tried to keep my thoughts from my face. "I understand," he replied simply, still looking at me. "Love has cut you deeply, my friend. Old scars can still inflict pain when the weather is right."

I gave him a quizzical look. "What's that supposed to mean?" I asked. I got the strange impression that Will was able to see something about me that even I couldn't, as though I'd casually mentioned the truth of my heart and forgotten what it even was.

He laughed. "I promise to not raise the subject further," Will assured me, his grin returning as well. We rose to our feet, stretching the ache from our limbs. His glance wandered behind me, and a wry smile lapsed over his face. "Say, Ryoku. That bow you got from Kimball. Mind if I take a look?"

I obeyed. He turned the bow over in his hands, examining it. "Ah, a recurve bow. This is not bad for a beginner such as yourself." He plucked an arrow from my quiver and knotted it to the bow with dextrous fingers. Just as quickly as Kimball, he whirled around and loosed an arrow. I turned, expecting to find some target hidden in the trees, but the arrow had lodged itself in a tree at a haphazard angle. Will smirked sheepishly. "My bad. I believe I wrecked the arrow. I am not too fortuitous in the world of archery, I fear, despite the best efforts of Brom and my father. Show me what you can do."

Hesitant, I mimicked the posture I'd done with Kimball. Will tutted under his breath, appraising my stance. "No, my friend, you must relax. Remove the tension from your shoulders – no, not like that. More like this." He demonstrated a pose, emphasizing how he could freely turn his shoulders. "There you go. Now, notch an arrow. Draw it until the tail is adjacent to your lip. The tail, which would be the feather end of the arrow! Not quite so close to your lips, you might never be able to kiss a pretty barmaid again. Do not look at me like that! There is some force to that whiplash. Okay, now…"

He coaxed me into it until my stance was perfect, and made me keep dropping and reassuming the posture until I could resume it with ease. It wasn't until then that he finally had me make a shot. It was with a great feeling of accomplishment that I watched the arrow sail through the air, past the rock – and directly below the arrow Will shot. Glee and pride shone in his face as he bounded off to retrieve the arrow. "See? It is like breathing once you get used to it. And you even kept the arrow safe." He returned, handing me the arrow with a grin. "Do me a favor, Ryoku Dragontalen – do not forget this. You will surely need it before long."

As I replaced the arrow in my quiver, Will sharply glanced up. I realized, by how quickly he acted, that he had been alert this whole time. I could not say the same. I tried to mimic his agility, but only caught the flash of a shadow flutter over the break in the canopy of the Old Forest. I blinked, but it was gone. It could easily have been a bird, but... I doubted Will would jump for such a thing. Moreover, by the size, it would have been a *big* bird.

As if not spooked enough now, a sudden scream pierced the wind, making my heart flutter in my chest. Will's head snapped toward the sound. It sounded male. Could it have been... one of the squad? The faces of Oliver, Alex, Leif, and the others clouded my mind quickly.

Will cupped his hands to his mouth and let out a strange, loud call. If I had to guess, it might be some sort of owl. The sound echoed so clearly that I was sure they must have heard it, no matter how far they got.

The only response was silence.

"What was that?" I asked urgently.

"We must go," Will said urgently, starting off at a brisk pace. "I cannot imagine how, but it seems we may have angered..." He trailed off, looking me over quickly. "I saw how you did in the bar before I stepped in. Against a smaller or more reasonable foe, you may have been able to hold your own. Should the worst come to worst, however, I strongly suggest you avoid such action in these woods. Stay close to me."

I stumbled after him and gave him a worried look. He only returned a half-smile. "What's going on?" I asked. "Are your friends okay?"

Will gave me a tight-lipped smile, and beckoned me to draw my weapon. I hesitated before drawing my knife, the only weapon I thought I might be able to use easily. "We will find out," Will said. "Be that as it may, I will not let your journey end here. Come."

I drew a sharp breath as Will led me back onto the trail, hoping that I might be able to survive whatever was coming.

SCENE THREE: KEEPER

...Of Act One: Enter Ryoku

*In the eyes of Ryoku Dragontalen, we are in
The Old Forest, in the world of Harohto.
It is late afternoon
On November 4th, 2017.*

The rain we'd seen forecasted in the clouds was quick to follow our departure. A gentle pitter-patter at first, but it slowly hastened until even the shelter of thick trees could hardly keep us dry.

Another scream pierced the humid, wet air. Will's face paled a shade. He quickened his pace, only slowing when the mud caused me to slide back several feet on the path, and he started showing me how to find my footing even along the trudging uphill hike.

Atop the hill from where we'd stopped to rest, a small creature darted out onto the path. It was so quick, I could note little about it. It was red as copper, about the size of a small dog, and, perhaps the strangest, had the stature of a human. Will scared it off with a strange whistling sound. I saw the flash of red eyes, but it vanished into the woods without a trace. When I tried to ask Will about the encounter, he didn't hear me.

Will kept repeating his call every time we entered a new little area, but there was no response from his soldiers. The ground slowly evened out, but the rain only worsened. I kept a solid pace for Will's sake, but my lungs and chest burned with each stride. I feared that if we ran into whatever he was scared of, I might just keel over at its knees. Presuming it had knees. I didn't know what to imagine in this strange new world.

Will finally slowed at the bank of a steady river, capped with the excess runoff of the storm, which only seemed to meet us at this corner before veering off again. Further in the trees, I saw that the extra water crested the river at the corners and forged little streams of runoff through the woods. As we approached it, I studied the water with scrutiny, but my heart soared when I saw how clean it looked.

Will found a spot where the water skipped over a small ledge and lowered his canteen to it. "We will stock up on river water here. While traveling, it is always a good idea to collect fresh water – we all keep extra canteens in our bags for just that. You should have one in your ba—what are you giving me that look for?"

I hesitated. I watched the water fill his canteen and run across his hands, but he still stared at me. "Is that drinkable?" I asked.

Will laughed, shaking his head. "Of course. Natural spring water flows through the woods. Even said, I still find a spot where the river is flowing strong. Points like this, where the water breaks contact with the main body, are especially ideal for taking drinkable water. The only precautions in these woods are during the dry season when the river lowers exceptionally. Why...?"

He stopped himself, staring up at me, his jaw slightly agape. "Hold on. The rumors about your world... Are they true? That it begins to die?"

I didn't respond right away. I stared at the water blearily. In my own world, such a spring would never be safe to consume. They said that what we drank now was less than ten percent of actual water, and less than five percent of what ran through our oceans and rivers. It was heavily chemically modified in order to give us the same sustenance that it had since the beginning of time. But this... I had never seen water so clear, especially running through nature without any sort of filtration system.

"I have heard little but folklore about it," Will went on when I didn't reply. By his tone, he was treading very carefully. "Defenders will speak of it callously. Maybe some spirit-born believe it is just their distant kingdom, but we know the truth. Their world is starting to fall."

"It isn't dying," I cut him off sharply. Will flinched back, surprised by my outburst. I was, too. "The state of things in my world... they're temporary, I know it. The physical realm cannot just... die, can it?"

"Your eyes just now..." Will tilted his head. I gave him a quizzical look, but he lowered his gaze. Wordlessly, he capped his canteen and gestured for me to hand mine to him. I obeyed, and he gently showed me how I would hold the canteen under the runoff to minimize any possible risk. He left out the idea that the tactic was useless in my home.

"I do not know," Will answered finally, watching the canteen fill. "Those that know of your world are clueless as well, I imagine. It is a topic which should not be breached with just anyone."

I watched him in silence for a moment. Maybe I was in the wrong place hoping for answers. "You said spirit-born earlier," I commented. "What does that mean?"

"Ah, right," Will said apologetically. "The people of this realm can be divided into two: spirits, and spirit-born. Excluding you Defenders, of course. Spirits are just as you would expect – those who died in your world, and have come here. I am one myself. Spirit-borns are children that spirits have sired in these realms. Unlike us, who do not age with the passage of time, spirit-borns will live and die just as you do in your home. Those are the people who do not understand your world, and they outnumber us greatly."

I frowned. "How do they know you're spirits, then, without knowing about my home?"

Will shrugged. "We are normal to them – spirits, their forefathers, but not quite as esteemed. Some time ago, it was agreed upon to let the spirit-born believe theirs is the only realm. In fact, such is the law in many different worlds." When he saw my look, he shrugged. "To hear the whole story, one might believe a spirit-born only gets their one life here as a result. Would there be truly be a whole slew of afterlives for those born in different dimensions? Should your kind be the only one who gets to go someplace afterward?"

I considered his words heavily. It gave me a headache to imagine that there was another spirit realm for the spirits of this realm, and then maybe even more after that. "I see," I murmured softly. "That is an elaborate tri ck for the spirit realm to collectively follow."

"In a perfect world, all would obey it."

I nodded, watching Will as he stood. "It's wonderful, though. Imagining a whole other cycle of life taking place here – apart from my own twisted, corrupted world."

Will's eyes sparked dangerously. "This world is still wrought with danger in itself," he said sharply. "Living here does not mean one is safe. Depending on the world, they might be without medicine or proper medical care. Many spirits abandon their children, so as to not explain why they will age as regular folk while their parents stay the same. Many are shadowed with darkness of a completely different sort. Many of these individual worlds will not last for long, condemning millions of spirits and spirit-born alike to their deaths."

I quickly realized I'd offended him. "I'm sorry – I didn't mean to make it sound like that." I studied him for a moment, thinking of what he said. "So there are multiple worlds here. If I understand, we're just in one of them."

"Correct," Will said, his voice still a little brusque. "We currently stomp through the world of Harohto. This is a rather peaceful world, considering. They can vary greatly in design, but all seem to have a general moot point. You might be surprised to see the extent of some other worlds outside Harohto, including my own. Each has norms that do not exist in other realms, or lack things commonplace in most other lands. Each world, too, is somewhat of a different size. Harohto is moderate. Both the main continent and the southern continent are simply labelled 'Harohto,' but that is all to this world."

I regarded him with surprise as he handed me my canteen. "That is all? But... do they not question why their world is so small? Or where you come from? Where *I* come from?"

Will shrugged. "It is commonplace. Your world is made of seven continents, is it not? Why is that all? Must there not be more?"

"Well, yeah, but..."

"As for the other realms, compare it to another aspect of your world." He gave me a small grin. "Aliens. Just imagine if aliens came to your world, mingling with the other folk. They would surely have come from other galaxies far away, but that technology is beyond your knowledge. In the case of Harohto, this world has barely grasped building ships to survive the southern voyage. Some worlds, to my knowledge, do not even carry such vast bodies of water. A surprising amount, to be frank. A denizen of Bonnin or Brooklyn may be alarmed by such oceans, filled with water not immediately drinkable."

I took this in with surprise. "They seriously don't know about that?"

Will shrugged. "Forgive me if my knowledge of your realm is outdated, but are there not small villages within the Amazon Rainforest that have not seen anything more than the great river?"

His knowledge wasn't misplaced, and surprisingly recent. I wondered how long ago Will had been a part of my world. I tried to picture him in my classes, politely listening to the teacher as they explained algebra to the intelligent woodsman, hunched over in his chair because the kids behind him couldn't see the chalkboard.

"And yes," Will went on, oblivious to my train of thought, "these worlds seem to have a finite lifespan. I do not know the details. Perhaps new ones are born from new stars somewhere out in the void."

"So they can die," I derived. My wording caught Will's glance, and I swallowed back my hesitation. "The individual realms, part of this spirit realm, can die. The world seems to go on without them, but can the same be said for my world? Could the land of the living just... cease? Could we go on with half of the world gone?"

"Bold of you to assume your world is half," Will commended sharply. "You have seen but the very tip of the corner of the realms. Hah – not even, to be frank. A small niche in the page. Your indifference can be written off only as such. I will ask again, when you have become a more seasoned Defender. Once you have come with me to my world, and you have seen what exists beside us – a fallen world, one that we cower in the shadow of. The common folk do not know. They cannot see it like we may see the moon in the sky, but I, as a seasoned traveler, have seen it. Worlds can fall, Ryoku Dragontalen, no matter how large they may seem. Take care that it does not happen to your own."

He took a swig of his water and capped it, turning his gaze to the path ahead. I held an open flask in front of me, untouched. Unwittingly, I'd offended Will. His expression was pallid and grey with worry, his eyes bleary. Still, his words rang in my ears. *Once you have come with me to my world.*

He had come so far to protect me. He'd stood up against the likes of Lancet Cooper. Now, his friends and fellow soldiers were lost in the woods, perhaps fallen to whatever beast may be pursuing us, and he still stood at my side. Still, he was my only source of information in this world right now.

"I don't intend to stick around," I told him. "I have a mission I have to accomplish. A few, to be exact. I have questions that need answering. However I may wish for lush forests and drinkable water, this isn't my home."

I was speaking with envy and rage. I didn't need Will's sorrowful look to tell me that. I was watching my conversation with this likeable soldier falling apart, but I couldn't hold back my comments. Why? Was I so full of unspoken words that I needed to tear into Will?

"Try that water," he instructed softly. "I see the way you look at it. I drank it, and I am fine."

I looked closely at Will as though to challenge that opinion, but there was nothing I could find. Gingerly, I lifted the canteen to my face and smelled it, just in case, but was pleasantly surprised. Was water supposed to smell so appealing? I expected to wrinkle my nose in disgust, but my throat twisted instead. I drank from it quickly, as though that might change. It passed through my parched lips and wetted my anxious tongue. The sensation was alarming. I'd never tasted something so refreshing!

"Those who enter these realms will never forget it."

I looked at Will, but he was staring pointedly up the path, his sapphire eyes gleaming like the sky.

"You will never hear the wind without the whispers of our people, or the fire dance in the hearth without whispering the ancient tongue of magic. You will never stare at the failing foliage of your world without longing for our earthy, healthy trees in their stead. You will never watch the tepid tide roll across the beach without picturing this gallant river."

He plucked an apple from the corner of his bag as easily as ever. I realized it was probably convenient to have our food readily available, and thought of mine tucked into my sleeping roll. He held the apple in front of him in a loose fist.

"Up until now, you have likely believed your world is the entire apple, even as it has soured and ripened in age, riddled with worms, bruised... Now you learn that there is another half. While yours is contaminated, ours remains largely untouched, as though fresh from the tree. Perhaps something within the good part of the apple can explain why the other half ended up this way. Why the worms only riddled throughout half of it. Maybe there is even a cure. Maybe one day, both will eventually rot. But one thing remains true."

With a fluid, one-handed motion, he snapped the apple clean in half between his fingers, and held them both side-by-side in his palm. "Now that you know your apple was never the whole picture, it will never be the whole picture." He gave me a wistful look and passed me half of the apple. "You can enjoy your side of the apple, rotten as it may be, but you would never forget the other half."

I didn't reply, regarding the half of an apple as though it might very well be rotten. Moments washed past us with the rushing water in the background. I stared at the wet soil at our feet, ignoring the relentless pattering of rain upon the earth, dampening my body and spirit. Will stared at me, searching my expression. He looked weary and tired. We had merely stopped for a drink of water, but something had caught us into this dangerous conversation. I felt ashamed, and clasped my canteen shut with only a sip taken from it. I felt his eyes on me as I returned to the path, and he followed suit shortly after.

We trudged along the path for well over an hour. The tension eventually subsided between us and I ate the half of an apple he gave me, along with more from my bag. Still, we saw no sign of his squad, nor any signs of struggle nearby. No discarded armor, no blood, nor any baggage spilt across the path. I dared to think they might still be alive, but I was wondering if we went the wrong way. Had they turned down a side trail somewhere? Will assured me that wasn't the case. They knew these woods like the back of their hand. Splitting up only ensured they would meet up later down the path.

Later on, we came to another bend in the river that jutted out into the path like a scar through the woods. Will zeroed in, and I caught up to him as he examined a set of rushed tracks in the mud.

I counted the footsteps long after he stood. It must have been about five of them.

"They were split up," Will murmured, "and they came this way."

It was hard to hear him over the falls. A short waterfall, only about Will's height off the ground, coursed near us like unchained horses made of aqua. Mist sprayed all around, and the ground nearby was beginning to develop a late day fog. Will approached and dipped his hand in. "The rain must be heavier on ahead. The normal flow of the water is escalated. Much of it is warmer rainwater, and not glacial runoff as it should be this high up. I pray the bridge ahead is still intact."

"W-We have to cross a bridge?" I asked, uncertain. Considering the poisonous quality of water in my world, I wasn't particularly fond of crossing or swimming in the stuff, either. I didn't feel that concern ebb away in a new world. Something about looking down and not being able to see the bottom of the river made me shaky at the thought of tumbling into its depths from above.

"It will be easy. One little bridge and we will be on the other side." He stared up the length of the river ahead. "I only hope they are still alive."

He led the way alongside the river and past the falls. We were showered with even colder water than the rain as we passed, and I wrapped myself in my cloak for warmth. The slope was muddy and tough to climb, but Will helped me after deftly making short work of it himself. It was becoming harder to see as, true to Will's word, the rain already began to pick up.

When he led me to a rickety bridge ahead, I halted in my tracks. It crossed the river and was only as wide as we were. A faint creaking noise I dully became aware of seemed to belong to the ropes of this bridge. Churning waters tickled the bottom of the bridge. When it tossed in the wind, I could see the boards making the bridge spread quite far apart. All too easy to slip through.

"It is our only option," Will said firmly. "This bridge has survived worse, I can assure you. If we can cross it and sever the ropes behind us, then perhaps we can shake the entity following us."

I hesitated, surprised to hear such a suggestion from him. "What of your squad? There were five sets of tracks. We don't know if everyone got across, or is even headed the same way." I gripped my knife, more of a reassurance to myself than anything. "Will, if you think we can, I'll stand with you against it."

"I do not believe the option exists," he replied. He sounded as though he'd spent the whole walk reaffirming that thought in his mind. "Besides, there are other ways to cross the river even to those not as resourceful as my group. Perhaps we will find them once we cross, or they are further ahead. There are many crossroads in these woods, and I am sure the truth awaits." He cast a haunted look behind me, as though seeing our apparent pursuer. I glanced, but saw nothing among the ancient trees of the Old Forest. I thought I could hear a faint noise in the distance, but it might have just been my own ears. When I turned back, Will looked grave. "Besides, I assure you that we cannot fight this entity. The only option is escape."

"Are you sure?" I asked. "You mentioned something about bounties in the forest earlier, and I think Kimball said something, too…"

He was searching my eyes. "Ryoku. You have a goal, do you not? A lofty one, I imagine, from that look you get in your eyes. I do not know what, but I wager it must be truly valuable." He smiled at me – it was a grave smile. "I believe in you. I believe that your mission might be something that you alone are capable of. So, can you accomplish your goal if you prowl these woods aimlessly for days? Seeking out friends that may already be waiting at the inn with a cup of hot cocoa?"

"I…"

I hesitated. Will's words touched me. Still, what if we were pressing forward while his friends remained lost behind us? I couldn't voice that opinion, not while he looked like he was trying his hardest to think about anything but that. I had to swallow my hesitation. Here was Will, but one of his squad, able to guide me seamlessly through the woods. Surely his other seven comrades were capable of similar feats, especially all in one pack.

"Come," he told me, and he cleared the mound leading up to the bridge in a single stride. "It is sturdier than it looks."

That was the first time I didn't fully trust the words from Will's mouth. Still, I had little choice in the matter. I tried to ascend the mound in a single stoic step as Will had, but stumbled and turned it into more like six staggered ones. Will caught me before I could fall back, chuckling.

"Do not let yourself get frazzled. I already taught you how to walk up muddy paths! Now come. Think of stairs – they must creak with age, but they will not collapse. We still have nights to spend in these woods."

It took his last comment for me to turn toward him as he started out onto the bridge, strolling as easily as though he headed to the bar. I thought back to our banter about drunks in the woods and almost chuckled at the idea. If only an inn and a warm fire waited at the other side. I'd even take on those drunks again if Oliver, Leif, Alex, and the others were waiting inside.

I didn't consider our combined weight on the bridge until I stepped on and the bridge swayed vicariously. Cool air and mist throttled me as I flailed, sure that I was about to plummet – but a strong hand grabbed my arm. "Steady yourself! This is not a tightrope, Ryoku – just a bridge! Here, let me take your bag and things. There – unburdened. Come on!"

Will let go after stealing my bag, bow, and quiver from my back, and he easily strolled ahead of me with all of it. I still stumbled as soon as he let go, but I steadied myself this time. I dared not look down at the waves that sloshed over my boots, or the waves that reached up on either side like giant hands trying to take me to their lair.

I tried to step in a rhythm, keeping my feet slower than my racing chest, but it was hard to keep my footing on the slippery bridge. I gripped the rope rails until my hands bled, dragging myself forward. If I could snap my fingers to get off this bridge, but land in a circle of angry drunks unarmed, I'd snap my fingers again and again.

Something alerted me to raise my head. Will, standing near the end of the bridge, froze. His neck craned, and he turned to face upstream with an expression I couldn't see.

I began to hear a faint noise. It rang between the sloshing waves and the torrential downpour in oddly clairvoyant tones. It almost sounded like a flute, though there was an odd atmosphere to the sound that made my hair stand on end.

It wasn't until I saw Will break into a dead run ahead of me that I clued in.

The noise somehow elevated above the rain and waves – and it was getting closer, fast.

Run.

The ice shattered. I forced myself into a run, which could easily break my legs at least if I couldn't time my pounding steps with the gaps in the bridge. I half-dragged myself by the rope railing as the sound gained volume. There was a beautiful, haunting tone to it, but it slowly began to sound more like a shriek.

If I thought I was overreacting, my mind resolved when I saw Will clearing the last steps of the bridge, and he freed his lance from over his back like an unleashed scorpion tail.

Then I saw something else. A shape, some sort of entity that caught my eye from up the river. For a moment, it looked like a dark green cloak thrown from somewhere in the trees. It flew at us with horrific speed.

The shrieking noise was now so loud that I couldn't hear the water. I wanted to cover my ears, but I couldn't let go of the bridge. In fact, I couldn't move – not once I saw the hooded red eyes amidst the green cloak-like entity, or the twin sets of ivory claws that it lashed out with.

A noise rose out now above even the shrieking. The splitting of rope, the snapping of wood. Before I could fully comprehend what happened, I hit the water like ice. The force of my fall sucked me down, and water filled my lungs at an alarming rate.

I struggled to free myself of the icy clutches of the river, but I only sank further. I knew the current got me, latching onto me as if the river was its own dangerous entity that hunted us. Every frenzied attempt only served to drag me deeper. Pressure built up on my chest, only letting more water into my lungs.

Unwittingly, I thought of what Will said moments before clambering onto the forsaken bridge. Will said my goal was lofty, but he believed in it. I hadn't told him much – hardly anything at all, really. Nevertheless, he believed in me.

Here I was. Was I to die here? Thrown from the bridge into the relentless river by some mysterious cloaked creature, worlds away from anything *close* to my goal?

Faces flashed across my vision. The strawberry-blond, her blue irises like clear summer skies, her freckles like sunspots in my eyes. I could almost feel her smile. Would I never see her again?

It was no use. Despite my best efforts to rouse myself and free myself from this watery prison, my arms were pinned by the current.

Not even a giant could free themselves from this vicious undertow, and I certainly wasn't even a giant.

My arms felt like lava ran through them, and my lungs much the same. My chest seemed to sink with me. The waves would swallow me here and end my journey, quickly as I had ever entered this place. The clear water I'd tasted for the first time today would now be my grave as it became black as night, swallowing me into its ancient darkness.

The last thing my mind imagined was the slightest, most infinitesimal touch of human skin – and the water turned to fire.

SCENE FOUR: THE STRANGER

...Of Act One: Enter Ryoku

In the eyes of Ryoku Dragontalen, we are in
The Old Forest, in the world of Harohto.
It is morning
On November 6th, 2017.

"Hey, this kid's been out for days. You think he's dead or something?"

An unfamiliar voice was speaking. A girl. Somewhere in the darkness, I could hear her. A warm hand touched my chest. "It has only been two days, Sira. He has a heartbeat. A pulse. He will wake, and hopefully soon. With all the water he swallowed, this is yet the luckiest outcome."

"Whatever, I didn't ask for specifics, Will. Do I look like a doctor to you?"

"Not at all." The sarcasm in Will's voice brought a smile to my face as I inched back into awareness.

"Good news, you're not blind. Don't need to be a doctor to tell you that." She made an irritated noise. "Hey, I think he's waking up. Or dreaming. Do Defenders dream?"

I groaned, and my eyelids finally fluttered open. It was dark, but I could almost taste the coming dawn in the air. There was a chill to the air, but I was wrapped up in a sleeping roll that kept most of it at bay. Branches of trees high above rustled in a gentle breeze, bringing down the scent of pine that I'd grown quite familiar with. I couldn't detect a hint of the rain from last I was awake.

"Does he always look this dumb, or did too much water get in his brain?"

I averted my attention to the two figures kneeling before me. Will looked in disarray, his wavy brown hair tangled with twigs and grass. Little scratches lined his face, and he was unshaven. He looked to have ploughed through a jungle.

The second figure was new. Sira, Will called her. A girl, balancing on the balls of her boots with her arms, bare but for a pair of thick black bracers, crossed over her knees. The look of her made me quickly try to sort myself out; trying to improve my impression on this girl, if that was at all possible. Locks of scarlet hair fell across her face, mostly parted at the brow and kept shoulder-length, and a pair of matching blood-red eyes looked at me in a bored way. For such a sharp, angular face and stubborn chin, she had a cute nose and a dip to her pursed lips that drew my eye. Already I was noticing her figure, dressed in a black sleeveless shirt with a high neck and pants that fit a daunting figure nicely. I spotted the handle of a rather large sword over her back.

"No, he always has," Will joked, drawing an immediately look of ire from me. Still, his smile was worried. "How do you feel, friend?"

"I don't know, that's a pretty vacant expression if you ask me," Sira said bluntly. "I've seen addled cats and dogs with the same look about them. Can you speak, kid?"

"Urk," I replied, and found pleasure in the small grin appearing on her face. "Looks like I can."

"Show-off," she murmured. "Not everyone can string two words together, let alone four."

Now she drew a smile from me. So she was funny. Around then, though, I started to recall the events leading up to my unconsciousness. "What happened back there? With the river, and that... that thing?"

I tried to prop myself up onto my elbows, but the act proved quite difficult. My muscles felt horribly strained, and I nearly fell back hard. Will caught me and lowered me gently. "Careful, friend. Your body will be in quite bad shape. You came close to drowning in that river."

"Seems like you boys got on the wrong end of that thing," Sira remarked, sitting down properly. "Talk in the village calls it the Keeper of the Old Forest, though I think it's a little inflated. Just some monster of the woods that's gotten all riled up. That's how you came upon me." She pumped a lazy fist in the air. "Army of one, versus one pissed-off Keeper."

"You were hunting it by yourself?" I asked. "Why was it after us? We didn't do anything to harm the woods!"

I noticed Will's glance, and an image flashed across my mind. The arrows embedded in the tree.

Sira shrugged. "Probably the raiders set up in the north end of the woods, though that's pretty far from where you guys ran awry of it. Either way, it scattered after I pulled you outta the river. You're lucky as all hell. One more gulp, and you'd be fish food. Still, that's preferable to if that thing decided to finish the job."

I regarded her with shock. "Wait, you saved me?"

Sira smirked – it was an attractive look. "Well, I was around. Saw you go down. You were close enough to the severing point that you went straight in – a nosedive. Willy-boy got to shore safely, but you were halfway downstream before he could even turn around. Lucky for you, I've seen my fair share of storms. Cutting down that river was no easy feat, but I got you before you hit the falls."

I was stunned. She did look cut out for it. I noted a definitive curve to her shoulders, developed muscles on her forearms and thighs. On top of that, she was pretty. There was definitely some dark accent to her lashes and the corners of her eyes, making her scarlet glare that much more attractive.

"Uh, thank you," I stammered – it was annoyingly tough to form a coherent thought around this girl. "I think I remember. I was being pulled down by the current, everything going black, and then... Then I think I felt your hand."

For the briefest moment, I thought I saw her molten look soften, but her sharp brows quickly furrowed. "Don't be stupid," she muttered, and turned to Will. "Hey, Willy-boy. Weren't you gonna heal up this kid so we can get going? I'm not carrying him."

Will was working something with his hands, but a wry smirk painted across his lips. "You mean carry him any further? We did travel almost a day worth in the time—"

Sira cut him off with a sharp look. "Well, you weren't offering," she snarled. Her glance flitted to me in almost annoyance. "Couldn't well make camp right next to that river, could we? I mean, we could have gotten further, but the fact that you weren't moving..." She scowled. "What do you eat, anyway? Grass? I'm sure I've carried cats heavier than you."

I felt my face going red. What was I to say to this girl? How had my world turned so quickly upside-down? I mentally shook myself. Sira had a sharp tongue, but she actually saved me. There was kindness to her. She may be reluctant to show it, but it was there.

Will lifted up a small black mortar and pestle from his lap. I could see a thick bluish paste crushed up inside. "Moonwelt paste," he explained at my look. "Just a few Moonwelt herbs and water. Unfortunately, the plant is best harvested at night, which meant it took some time to find the proper dosage for the amount of water you ingested. Moonwelt is a strong natural painkiller native to Harohto. Alone, it is almost toxic. Dilution by water is necessary for the painkiller to activate." He turned to Sira. "Would you mind lifting his shirt? I must apply it over his lungs, where much of the damage took place."

She rolled her eyes. "Can't do it himself, I guess," she complained, but she knelt forward. She removed a sleeping roll from over my chest and slid my shirt up to just past my ribs. Her fingers briefly brushed against my bare skin, eliciting a response I didn't anticipate. On top of that, I could now see the dark purple bruising across my abdomen. Sira raised a brow at me, but she said nothing else as Will knelt forward, stuck two fingers in the bluish paste, and started applying it over my skin. It felt warm, and dissolved quickly into my skin after he applied it.

When he was finished, Will scraped the rest into a small jar that he stuffed into his bag. "Journeying with you, my friend, I feel the rest will be useful before long." He smirked. "All done. Allow me to go rinse my mortar and pestle, and then we can see how you are doing."

He shuffled into the woods and out of view. By the faint sound of trickling water, we remained near a source of water. I assumed it wasn't the same river.

"Think you can try standing?" Sira asked me dully, offering her hand. At my expression, she smirked. "Stuff works fast, trust me. Haven't you ever used spiritual medicine before?"

"No," I told her seriously, but I took her hand. She eased me into a grip around her forearm and supported me as I pushed myself free of the sleeping roll and steadily upward. Her other hand found my waist with unanticipated gentleness until I found myself standing, and she held onto me for a moment before gently letting go. I teetered, but I remained standing. As she stepped away, I noticed how tall Sira actually was. She might even be taller than Will!

"T-Thank you," I murmured, managing a small smile.

"Don't mention it," she replied. Her arms hung at her sides like she didn't know what to do with them. "Like, seriously. I have a rep. Imagine if all the people I bullied find out I actually *help* people sometimes. A fucking disaster."

She startled a laugh out of me. She was actually funny, and attractive to a startling degree. How had we come across her again? I tried to look anywhere but those challenging, fiery eyes of hers, or that definitive and teasing curve to her hips – and my gaze landed upon the small rucksack by her feet. My old bag that had gone missing after I left Kimball's shop. I pieced the last bit of the puzzle together when I saw the black kite-shaped shield slung over Sira's back across her broadsword.

"You stole my bag!" I cried out, dropping a hand to my waist – only to find my knife was absent. "What the hell?"

She looked ultimately confused until I practically pointed at the bag on the ground. "Oh, that was you?" she asked mildly. "Funny part about when I left my home. I didn't bring shit with me. Not a single gold coin. Just my sword and shield. Normally that gets me by, but I didn't anticipate coming here with all these *woods* and stuff." She spoke of the woods like it was a cemetery.

"That doesn't explain why you stole my bag," I muttered, lowering my hand. "Not that I had much in it, but if I wasn't with Will..."

She chuckled. "Yeah, Mister Bags there. Sixty percent more backpack than human, I hear. Well, you're luckier than me. Your bag didn't have shit in it! A sleeping roll, some dried fruit, and not even enough gold for the inn!" She scoffed, like it was my fault she had to rough it. "But yeah, Mister Bags has us set. I think he could support the village if they moved into the woods for the night."

It was hard to be mad at her, and I quickly realized I didn't have much reason to. She'd saved my life, after all. A petty theft shouldn't change my opinion of her so quickly – should it?

"You sound like you left your home in a hurry," I said. "Why?"

The look in Sira's eyes immediately made me rescind my question. "Save one kid in the woods, and you gotta give your life story out?" She scoffed, annoyed. "Whatever. All you gotta know is, if you ever get the chance to go visit my homeland – *don't*." Then her glare alleviated, and she cast her gaze around. "The hell did Will go? Fall in the river?"

"Where is your homeland?" I asked, but my question fell to deaf ears as Will stumbled through the brush from another direction, smiling apologetically.

"Sorry about that. I did some quick scouting." He knelt down to his bag and stuffed his mortar and pestle away before shouldering the huge bag. "Pack your things. I estimate about a two-day journey from here to the Capital. If we cut through a small deer trail I located to the southwest, then we may be able to shave off that last night in the woods." Then he glanced up at me, as though noticing me for the first time. "You can stand."

I nodded. "Thanks. My mom taught me when I was little."

Sira snorted, and even Will chuckled. "Did she teach you how to navigate the woods, too?"

I smiled as I knelt to roll up my sleeping bag, and found my knife, staff, and bow set next to my bag. "No. Unfortunately, she..." I quickly realized the topic I was about to venture down with two people I'd only just met, and I quickly shut up. When I got to my feet, shouldering my bag, I didn't miss Will's lasting look. With his memory, that topic wasn't going to just die out.

When I stood, however, I noticed Sira had her bag holstered and was waiting for me. "You're coming with us?"

She shrugged. "Eh, I signed on while you were passed out." At my expression, she smirked. "Willy-boy told me about your mission as I told you mine – to hunt that damned Keeper. I don't know what happened to your squad, but one thing seems crystal: I can't do this one alone, and we can get some serious backup at the Capital."

I gave Will a look, who nodded shortly. "Forgive me. I thought that you might consider joining me on this little escapade. You would be useful with what prowess you displayed back at the inn. A little practice would not hurt, either. We can go to the Registry, get you set up as an official Defender, and maybe suit you up with some new gear. It may prove to be a valuable experience for you."

"That, and people listen when a Defender pipes up," Sira said seriously. "Maybe the Capital has some more info about this bastard. Either way, if you come up asking for an army with your Defender writ or whatever in hand, people will listen to you. Not... not an actual army, of course. Just a few hands."

"You want *my* help?" I asked. It was abstract, but this may be my chance to repay both of them. It could be my first job as a Defender. I had a duty I needed to carry out, but this could help me get stronger. I had no idea how strong I needed to be, but I had time.

"This became quite a personal endeavour for me," Will added, almost apologetically. His fists clenched at his side. "I do not know what became of my squad. I only hope they got to the Capital ahead of us, but we are a few days behind. The fact that none of them came across our camp..."

That sealed it for me. I pictured the faces of his squad. Oliver, who stood up for Will and I against Lancet; Leif, grinning at me in support of helping us; and Alex, who offered me his bag and related to me with his outspoken demeanour. Unfortunately, I hadn't exchanged names with the other four, but they had all been nothing if not kind to me.

"Absolutely," I told him, meeting his glance squarely. "If there's anything at all that I can do, I'd be happy to."

Will looked positively moved by my choice. "You have already exceeded my expectations," he admitted sheepishly. "I apologize that my simple guiding mission has gone so horribly awry. I know your mission must be dire, so..."

I stopped him short with a look. "I need the experience. Anyway, I was dumb to think it'd just be a journey from point A to B. More like from point A, through point S, past point W..." They didn't seem to understand my reference, so I smiled. "It's the journey. Anyway, I think I need to get stronger to do what I need to do."

"You could stand to gain some muscle," Sira teased, squeezing my arm. "Will says you did pretty okay in a bar fight in Bytold. I'd laugh, but coming from someone like this guy..." She jabbed her thumb at Will like a private joke. "I look forward to seeing just what you can do.

"Anyway," she cut herself off like avoiding any sort of compliment, and stuck out her hand. "The name's Sira Jessura. I'm an ex-knight from Orden."

I accepted her hand, and was hardly surprised when her grip practically crushed mine, but she eased it a little after a second. "I'm Ryoku Dragontalen. Defender, but I guess you know that." When she withdrew, I kept her gaze. "So Orden is your home? What does that mean?"

She looked annoyed by my question, but Will piped up. "Orden is a neighbouring world to my own. Both are medieval in nature. Orden... well, it has always had more of a penchant for darkness. Their royal line is formed of established dark knights. Men who learn how to swing a sword before they learn table manners. If nothing else, it serves to profess Sira is an excellent fighter."

She looked upset while Will explained her home, but beamed at the compliment. "You bet your ass," she boasted, and tapped the handle of the sword on her back. She turned so I could see the full blade. It hung naked on her back with her black kite shield, and the entire sword was a deep shade of blood red. Altogether, the weapon was easily almost as tall as her. "Meet Sinistra. She's been my blade since I can remember. Most men would wield this with both hands, and they'd be so slow I could cleave them in two before their sword picked up momentum." She lifted it partway from the belt holding it at her shoulder to demonstrate. "Me? I can use this baby one-handed, thrice as effective as anyone with two hands."

I gazed at her incredulously. "You can swing that thing?"

"You named your weapon?" Will asked, intrigued.

"She named herself," Sira replied easily, as though it should have been obvious. "That lance looks like it means something to you. Haven't you named it?"

Will's expression soured a little. "Some weapons are too important to be named." He turned to be without batting an eye.

"Shall we move on? Do recall I mentioned our timing. I would like to leave these parts by nightfall."

"And sleep in bandit territory," Sira remarked dryly. She adjusted her bag on her shoulder with her weapon and smirked at me. "You good to walk? I could stuff you in this bag if you're unsure."

I gave her what I hoped was a fiery look, and tested my legs. I couldn't help but be surprised at their mobility myself. Through our conversation, even the sharp pain in my chest had largely abated. I could hardly feel the sticky residue of the Moonwelt paste on my skin beneath my clothes.

We started out on the path. Everything seemed to work out fine. The path was easier, too. We turned out to be just off the main path, but Will quickly worked us onto a tight side trail before the sun had even fully poked out over the mountain range to the east, now cutting deeper into nature than we had yet. The path wasn't wide enough to travel abreast of each other, so Will led the way, occasionally cutting the thickest of brush aside with his gladius.

I tried to pay attention to every detail as we traveled. Keeping behind Will, he occasionally stopped to inform me of things about our surroundings. Much of the foliage was largely pine or oak, things that stood quite differently in my world. Only in the highest altitudes of our hike did the trees crowd in smaller heights, otherwise they towered over us like castles. He kept an eye on our path, and he showed me the different markings of wildlife – deer droppings and prints, rabbit prints, spots where male deer sharpened their antlers against the trees, and even pointed out a badger den from afar. Even the stalwart woodsman didn't seem eager to tangle with a badger.

Sira wasn't entirely alien to the woods, either. She only explained the odd thing now and then. She pointed out how clouds gathered around the furthest mountains, how they would eventually bring a cloud cover to us, which would cause a drop in temperature. She pointed out how the darker clouds were full of rain, but wasn't sure if we would encounter it.

Our hike brought us on a winding trip up a plateau, and the deer trail we hiked started to snake up a slope along the higher altitudes of the forest. The huge canopy of the woods made it difficult to see the full extent of it, and sometimes it blocked out the sun. We viewed a ravine in the eastern half of the woods that dipped down below sea level. Will scoped out the cliff with me, pointing out how the river – despite being invisible to us from our height – caused a slight decline in the trees along its path, and how it showed a set of falls that brought mist through the valley. While we studied it, there was a great, booming crash from below, and a few trees toppled, spraying a dust cloud that we could see from our sky view. I wanted to see what caused it, but Will whisked me away without explanation.

Atop the plateau, the trees spaced further apart, and a moss-laden rocky outcropping along the edge became our first rest stop of the day at early noon. My legs felt like jelly, and I plopped down easily on the rocks to consume a meager lunch. We shared some food between us, including some fresh berries Will had ciphered along the trail. Even Sira produced a few small, red apples she had plucked from the trees that I hadn't noticed.

Our break didn't last too long. Will explained that if we relaxed our muscles too much, the rest of the hike could be our undoing. He even had us partake in some easy stretches to keep limber over the remaining hike.

At the end of the plateau, Will pointed out something far to the north of us – the edge of the woods. It was hardly visible from where we were, but I could make out a bold stone wall far ahead, laden with fog from our current altitude.

"The Capital," Will said proudly. "I know you can hardly see it, but maybe you needed the motivation. One more night out here, and we should make it by nightfall tomorrow. Wait until you see it at sunset."

I remembered something Caryl mentioned at the inn. "Sunset stones?" I asked.

Will nodded eagerly. "It lights up like a festival at night. Some say it is a beacon for bandits to know their next destination, but others say it keeps wild animals from finding new food in the city. I have heard the stones use some warding magic, too. Nothing quite like the ones in my home, but…" He trailed off, staring at the city from afar. I wondered if he was missing his home.

Sira nudged me with a wry smile. "You might see deer droppings more exciting than this stuffy old place," she informed me. Will gave her a glare, but she only beamed more.

Our hike continued through the heat of the day. True to Sira's idea, a chilling cold began to settle in during the early evening. I enjoyed it at first from the heat of the day's hike, but quickly found my cloak from my bag as we descended from the plateau.

Darkness fell early in the autumn season, and Will began searching for a camping site even as the cold settled in. It took a few hours, and darkness was already getting comfortable in the world of Harohto when Will found his destination. He ushered us under the boughs of a large pine tree, one that had branches touching the ground in a sort of dome shape around us. It was tall enough for both Will and Sira to stand easily after ducking into the entrance, which certainly said something. Underneath was laden with pine needles and the occasional cone. The three of us brushed out a circular area, where Will set to creating a fire pit. Curious, I requested to learn, and it quickly became a group activity.

The first thing Will did was remove a shovel, a cloth sort of tarp, and a black bag from his backpack. "The most important thing is to keep nature as we found it," he instructed me. "We will dig two holes, and everything we dig out goes onto this tarp. In the morning, we put it all back."

I observed carefully and helped him out as he dug one larger hole in the ground, about ten inches around, and then one narrower hole upwind from the first. In our case, it pointed to the entrance to our little den. We scooped out the first part in a sort of plug-shape and placed it on our cloth tarp. The rest was loose, but Will explained we wouldn't have to worry about putting that all back in order.

"This sort of campfire is preferable for many reasons," he told me. "It keeps relatively smokeless thanks to the ventilation hole – the narrow one – which is important for stealth and for our den. We do not wish to be smoked out of here, do we? Additionally, since we carved everything out, we can make ourselves undetectable. I cannot say whether the Keeper is intelligent or not, but by morn, none will be able to tell we made camp here. Were we more worried about raiders in this part, this sort of fire would make even more sense.

"And due to it being in the ground, we require much less tinder." At this point, he reached for his black bag and pulled out a fistful of dry reeds. They were fresh enough that I realized he'd plucked them throughout the day for this very reason. "You want your tinder to be mostly lifeless. This outer layer will be what our fire burns into, so it can be a little fresher. The inside, though, will catch instantly."

He folded the tinder up into a sort of diamond-shape. The innermost part was a dried sort of fluff, like cotton, while the outer layers looked like the reeds that grew alongside the path on the plateau. With this, he pulled out a small black box from the corner of his bag, producing a piece of flat steel and a small, earth-colored stone – flint. In a swift motion, he struck the two together, and a spark immediately ignited the pile of tinder. He quickly put this into the small hole, and there we had our fire. Will was right – it produced very little smoke.

Sira had been watching Will's process with interest, but she left at this point and returned shortly after with a pair of dead rabbits – struck dead by arrows she borrowed from me, without asking. Will kept the fire fed only by handfuls of kindling he kept in another bag, still whittling some away with a knife from the tree we camped under. He found a longer stick, sharpened it, and used it as a spit to cook the rabbit. I kept purposefully away from the smell. Sira regarded me like I was an alien for it. Will, on the other hand, roasted a few apples on a stick and offered it to me. I tasted it, and liked the crisp difference in taste when they were cooked.

As we ate our dinner by a gently lit fire, we talked about our homes. Will's stories of Syaoto were fascinating. He talked about his liege, King Lionel Pendragon, who ruled Syaoto with a kind but firm hand. By the sound of it, he was quite close to his king. I recalled Alex saying something similar before.

It sounded much like any medieval story I'd ever encountered. Will was a member of the army, though somewhat esteemed among the soldiers because of his father – he conveniently left out the details of that part. The army normally divided soldiers not only by their ranking, as I'd established, but by their work. Will and his squad were field soldiers, which meant they usually worked outside the city and served as supplementary forces to other worlds. Other soldiers either served in the castle or as auxiliary forces in the army. The different ranking of each one that he listed was dizzying at best. Above it all was Lord General Brom, the leading commander of the King's Own, the *entire army*, and second only to the king himself.

In contrast, Sira spoke little about her home. She only elaborated on what Will said about her dark empire, and she gave no names. Only the emperor through royal bloodline, who kept little to no advisors, council, or other assuagements to the royal duty, ruled the empire. The emperor kept only the general of the army and a set of vassals, usually powerful figures sent from other worlds as a form of allegiance. Again, she listed none of them, and they seemed like sensitive subjects to her.

I couldn't get far in describing my own world, but I realized they each had a little knowledge of it. Sira hadn't explained, and she offered no elaboration, but I figured she must be a spirit as well. Will knew of steam technology, of war and guns, and early vehicles, but fell short when I started on paved roads, industrialized cities, and of the lengths of science and medicine. Sira knew little of it, and she regarded the idea of industrialized technology with a fair distaste. While Will listened with fascination, Sira remained sure that she was better off. I couldn't help but agree, knowing the state my world was currently in. I avoided mentioning it now, and Will respected it this time.

We cleared spots for our sleeping rolls and retired for the night. Will kept the fire going with a few carefully chosen logs to offer us warmth without creating a smokier fire. I fell asleep easily and dreamt of strange things, imagining noble knights of Syaoto and the tyrannical empire of Orden. In my dreams, Syaoto knights kept handsome and clean-shaven, with shiny armor and were all as tall as Will, while Brom stood like a skyscraper above them all. Sira's dark emperor was different, a shadow cast over the world, and I saw the face of the boy I was seeking in his wake. Behind him, her clothes worn and torn, was my sister.

I awoke in a cold sweat, only to find Will and Sira both awake and packing up our campsite in a hurry. The holes of our fire were already covered. Sira cast a glance my way and signalled to her ear. Confused, I listened – and stiffened when I heard the distant, haunting call. The Keeper.

I got to my feet quickly, all but forgetting my troubling dreams, and kept my weapons close. This time, I wasn't going to back down.

I expected the monster to bear down upon us when we left our comfortable tree abode, but we set off on a rushed journey down the path into the thick of the woods. Will and Sira kept close, their glances whisking off into the trees with every noise. I could still hear the faint noise of the creature. After a while, I wasn't sure if I was actually hearing it or just imagining it.

I froze up when we reached another bend of the river, all too similar to the one we crossed before. Sira groaned at my reaction and grabbed my wrist, leading me across a much sturdier-looking bridge than before. Will kept quiet as we crossed.

Despite her assurance, Sira's fiery glance kept into the trees, and she withdrew as soon as we reached sweet land on the other side. I wondered if she really hated me that much, but then I saw her reaching for Sinistra.

"Damn it!" she snarled, pushing me behind her. "Will, it's here!"

Will sidled around me with the ease of a branch rustling in the wind, his lance drawn and ready. From the moment Sira's scarlet sword hit the open air, I swore I could feel some sort of presence from it. I couldn't quite explain it, but the weapon seemed to radiate some sort of aura that made my hair stand on end. The face of the weapon looked razor-sharp and looked like fire in the wind. With her kite shield strapped to her other wrist, she made quite the imposing figure. Hearing her boast about the weapon and seeing her wield it were two different things altogether.

Something about the sight made me feel brave, and I tugged out my staff from its holster on my back. All I had to go on was Kimball's brief lecture on magic. I had yet to try it out myself.

"What the hell good's that gonna do?" Sira muttered darkly in my ear. Her closeness to me surprised me, and I felt an unwilling chill taper down my spine. "We can't do anything here but scare it off, if we're lucky. Do you even know what you're doing?"

My own automatic response felt foreign on my tongue. "I won't let you fight it alone."

Sira cursed. "We can't do much like this." She urged me forward with her, scanning the trees with her fiery eyes. I couldn't see a thing in the sea of trees, but both Sira and Will were on high alert. The whistling noise had come to an altogether halt. "You better know some decent magic if you'll choose that piece of wood over solid steel."

I had the impression that Sira wasn't overly fond of magic. I swallowed, running over the brief words Kimball had explained about magic. He assured me that I would know what to do when push came to shove, but could I trust that? It seemed like a better idea than trying to shoot the thing with an arrow or stick it with my knife. For an alien creature of the spirit realm, an alien art of magic might just be the trick.

My comrades stopped abruptly. Something alerted them, and I missed it. I was turning out to be quite the hero.

Sira whipped around with lethal speed, her sword screaming through the air like a wind of flames. Will yanked me back as Sira's blade scathed the air, leaving a bright scar in the air where it cut. I almost missed the dark green figure that seemed to float just astray of the weapon. As soon as I saw it, the entity lurched forward with revolting speed.

The sound of shattered steel pierced the air. I thought Sira landed a hit, but then I saw her black shield crumple like ash, leaving only the handles dangling from her wrist. She fell back with a cry.

My heart leapt in my chest, but Will shoved me away with so much strength that I stumbled down the path away from the creature, scraping my knees on disturbed brush on the path. I cursed, forcing myself upright, and spun on my heel.

When I turned, I froze.

It was floating before me. I couldn't tell if it was but an instant or a full minute, standing there with the full height of the monster before me. It must be taller than Will or Sira, covered head-to-toe in a ratty green cloak that smelled of the deepest corners of the woods. Only darkness stared at me from under the wide-rimmed hood. Dust streamed off the creature like it had just risen from the earth itself.

It floated there in complete, gut-wrenching silence. Even the dirt tumbling from its cloak didn't make a sound. In the moment, I couldn't place just where Sira or Will had gotten to, and I hardly registered that I clutched my staff tightly enough to drive splinters into my palms.

As silently as the night, the creature lifted an arm. At least, it might be an arm. The appendage looked twisted and black, ending in a row of razor-sharp blades that seemed to cut the very air with the simple movement. I kept eerily reminded of an executioner's axe, hanging in the air like the very sentence that spelt certain death.

An emotion welled up in my chest, so strongly and powerfully that it paralyzed me. I was no stranger to it, but now it coursed through me like a physical being, drawing from every last breath in my chest to feed it like a fire.

Everything went black.

SCENE FIVE: LAST NIGHT IN THE OLD FOREST

...Of Act One: Enter Ryoku

In the eyes of Ryoku Dragontalen, we are in The Old Forest, in the world of Harohto. It is mid afternoon On November 6th, 2017.

The breath slammed from my lungs as I hit the ground. Sira fell beside me, and I saw Will on my other side. Behind me, a piercing shriek cut through the woods like lightning. I spun around, scrambling for my weapon – but there was nothing.

Sira got to her feet, dusting her tight pants off with a grin. Will offered me a hand up, smiling too. Confused, I accepted, and he lifted me with unnerving ease.

"What... what just happened?" I asked, dazed.

"What the hell do you mean?" Sira demanded, but she was smirking. "Quick thinking on your behalf for once. Guess that has its costs, but don't waste my momentary gratitude. Literally never thought of using fire against that thing. Besides my sword, but... *fire*. Actual damn fire. I didn't know you could do it."

I tilted my head at her. "How did you...?" I trailed off, noticing the straps of her shield dangling uselessly off her arm. The broken metal shards of her shield splashed in a wide arc across the path, showing the monstrous velocity of the Keeper's strike. "Your shield."

She only grunted, ripping the straps from her arms and tossed them into the woods. "Whatever. Thing only reminded me of my home, anyway. Sinistra? She's a part of me, not Orden. And you," she added, "only apologize if it's damned necessary. Did you smash my shield with your puny fists? No? Didn't think so." She tossed her hair as she turned away, smirking at me in a somewhat teasing way. "If you apologize for everything, it makes your real apologies worthless."

"Sorr—"

I cut myself off, shaking my head. "Ugh. Okay, well what happened?"

"You summoned fire and surprised the Keeper at a precise moment," Will explained, but with the tone of speaking to a moron. His expression changed when I regarded him blankly. "Do you... honestly not recall?"

"It was the most useful thing I've seen you do," Sira remarked with a grin. "It was right there, and could have easily taken any of us down with those claws. Then you were there, and you threw up your staff, and there was this bright flash. You must have used a real burst of magic. I haven't seen anything like it, to be honest, but Orden's pretty unfamiliar with magic. And your eyes—"

I almost missed it, but Will silenced her with a sharp look. I looked at him until he turned his sapphire eyes to me with the innocence of a child. "My eyes what?" I asked accusingly. I looked between the two of them, who both, for the first time, appeared equally hesitant.

Will knelt down and retrieved my staff from the ground, where I hadn't noticed it next to a sizeable scorch mark across the dirt path. Were it not for that, I might not believe their story. It wasn't the first time I had a short gap in my memory, but it still smelt of trouble.

"Your eyes only looked rather red for a moment," Will assured me gently, placing the staff in my hands. His eyes were so earnest that I couldn't help but listen. "I believe it was but a reflection of that brilliant blaze. It was quite a batch! I am no more a magic practitioner than Kimball is an organized baker, but I have heard that staves may borrow your energy in a time of need. You fell almost immediately after. I followed, fearing you might strike your head on a stray rock – that would be an abrupt end to our journey!" He smiled complacently. "It might explain why you do not seem to recall."

I could only nod. Amid a pair who liked to save my life at regular intervals, it was hard to remain suspicious. He wouldn't keep something harmful from me, I felt. Kimball said something about staves borrowing energy when needed. "Will it be back?" I asked instead.

Will shrugged. "It was likely but scared off for now. Such a beast is stronger than a single spell, even a fully charged one. Something angers it, and I fear we might not see the end of this until its rage is quieted. That is why we must press on, and hopefully avoid running into it until we are prepared. We still have time to reach the Capital. We packed up early and have kept a good pace this morning."

"Fear's a good fuel," Sira remarked. "Still, doesn't the Capital close their gates early at this season? Bytold wouldn't shut up about the raiders and bandits."

We started down the trail again. "I don't understand," I piped up after a few minutes of silence. "The shopkeeper told me I'd figure out how to use the staff when I really needed it, but I don't remember at all."

Will shrugged. "I am not well versed in magic, but I believe adrenaline had a large role in that. My presumption is that your body supplied the necessary energy in a time of need, and the rush of the moment nearly knocked you unconscious. Perhaps we should take a moment in the city to gain some proper insight on the fact. Next we run into that creature, I imagine it would serve you well."

"Or practice with a real weapon," Sira suggested dryly. "There's a reason magic's all but extinct in Orden, except in the royal family: it's dangerous, mostly to you. Drawing untold amounts of energy from your body whenever it wants? A real weapon never does that to its host." She stared off into the trees. "Still, guess that fire did come in handy. You control that, and we might have this hunt in the bag."

Since neither could tell me much more about magic, I dropped the subject and focused on our hike. The terrain closer to the Capital was different. The trees spaced out more, and I even saw some signs of clear-cutting. It seemed the Capital taxed the forest far more than the people of Bytold, who largely left the woods alone. Autumn leaves showered the path around us on what turned out to be a mostly levelled-out path.

To my glee, I spotted some more wildlife around here. Will pointed out a small pack of deer mulling over the corner of a creek a ways off the path. Only one buck herded them, one with antlers in an impressive array around its head and laden with moss, and a few fawns with them. I wanted to get a closer look, but Will strongly recommended against it. Apparently, the normally docile creatures could be territorial.

Further down, Will stopped me at a set of tracks. He informed me that they belonged to a type of beast he called a Ragul. It sounded something like a bear from his description, but the huge mammals often had hides of greenish, moss-like tints and known to be quite aggressive. He showed me how the edges of the print betrayed how recently it had been there, which he wagered to be within the last twelve hours. It was with this in mind that he quickly turned us down another deer trail, this one arcing toward the Capital in a straighter line.

We took a brief rest around midday, but our moods kept different from our last break atop the plateau. Will and Sira sparred with each other, an impressive feat I was sure I would never see replicated. Will moved like a stream, his footsteps careful and planned, and his lance like a bend in the river. Sira was like fire. She never stopped moving, and her eyes kept alight with the promise of battle. From afar, they looked to be an even match even as they both practiced wildly different styles. I tried my hand at practicing with them, but nothing I could do matched up to their expertise. Will tried to practice with his gladius against my knife, but I always wound up in situations that would have killed me in a brawl.

For a spell, he tried to teach me how to use his lance. I couldn't muster up enough strength to do much with the weapon, even with his advice on footwork and how to hold my shoulders. He let me swing it around, trying for angles over my head and behind my back, but I dropped the long weapon frequently. Then he offered for me to try his gladius. The blade was just longer than the distance between my longest finger and elbow, plus a hand and a half for the handle.

No matter what, though, I couldn't seem to keep a grip on the weapon. When I went to swing it exactly as Will asked, it lurched from my grip like something snatched it from the air. Will watched with curiosity, switching me back and forth from the gladius to the knife and watching my form as though it might explain something. I never lost grip on my knife, though.

As we forged on, the path ascended again as we made the final climb toward the Capital. The sun remained a glowing red beam upon the mountains for much of our walk through the woods as evening neared. When I asked Will about the length of time it remained for, he said our altitude and the forest canopy affected our perception of daylight. Behind us, darkness already shrouded much of the forest, especially at the dip in the valley between us and the plateau of our last camp.

Before the sun finally dipped behind the mountains, Will stopped me and led me through a gap in the trees. I followed, arms wrapped around myself for warmth even under my cloak in the evening chill.

At the opening in the trees, my eyes fell upon the Capital of Harohto while the sun lowered behind it. Light reflected off the stone walls in shimmering waves like an aurora, but in a slew of warm colors from a set of summery watercolor paints. Brilliant waves of red, orange, gold, and white hung around the walls and into the sky in the most breathtaking sight I'd seen yet. It gave off a sort of mirage that clung to my vision even as we left the sight behind us. Will looked disappointed as Sira dragged us onward. My favorite thing about Will was how he'd likely seen this a thousand times, and similar other beauties, but it never ceased to be beautiful to him.

Will explained the phenomenon as we walked. Sunset stones were mined from deep within the Border Range, the mountains we hiked alongside to the east. He wasn't sure about the possibility that they might ward off unwarranted threats, but he knew they'd been discovered when an avalanche revealed part of the sunset stone mine, which had been largely unremarkable until the sun fell and the valley had been showered with an array of color. In terms of strength, the material was little different from regular iron and coppery ores, which meant it could be refined into standard armor. Apparently, they kept that purpose mostly for ceremonial usage rather than direct combat. I imagined a squad of soldiers caught when they tried to enter the enemy base because their armor started glowing.

A deeper chill set in as we climbed, and Will daydreamed of November snow in Harohto. Sira dismissed it as ridiculous, but I wondered about it. Snow wasn't a good thing in my world, just like water and rain. Here, it could easily be a thing of beauty like so much else.

Our pace quickened as darkness fell, mostly out of fear of being stuck in the woods another night. The moon hadn't appeared to guide our path, so Will led the way with a makeshift torch. Within an hour, his idea dampened as clouds arrived from nowhere to begin a steady stream of rainfall upon us. Will cursed, abandoning his torch, and we were forced to forge ahead in darkness. I fell so many times on the path that my body felt a seemingly permanent ache settling in. Atop the tenderness in my legs from our day of travel, it was almost unbearable.

It seemed like forever until the trees finally came to an abrupt halt around us, and we stumbled out into a clearing. I felt an immediate change in atmosphere when the great walls of Harohto's Capital stuck out before us, lit by a pair of sheltered torches alongside an iron gate. The walls shone no longer and appeared just like simple stone, slick with rain. From this close, it all seemed larger than life, spanning along the edge of the forest with no clear end in sight. The forest curved around the walls until either side of us looked back into the woods.

"Welcome to Harohto," Sira droned, "the capital of boredom."

Will choked at this, but I couldn't spark a smile. Everything about the huge city seemed immediately intimidating. Would they let us in, or were we condemned to another night in the woods? It hadn't been all that bad, but I was soaked to the bone in such a way that I wondered if we could even start a fire.

As we worked our way across the field, a thought occurred to me. "Do they speak a different language in the city?" I asked.

Sira muttered something about me, but Will didn't laugh this time. "That is actually an interesting trait about Defenders, one which I am not surprised you are unfamiliar with. I could not begin to explain why, but Defenders are known to be something of a natural bridge between languages. Sira and I are spirits, so we are professed in several languages and can understand each other regardless. However, if that weren't the case, we might not be able to understand one another if we were apart. Say she spoke the Ordenite tongue, and I spoke Syaotoan.

"Harohto does have its own common tongue," he added, "varied only slightly from that of Syaotoan. Harohtian is a mere stone throw from common English, a little less dignified than Syaotoan."

I raised a brow. It was a much bigger response than I expected, and focusing on the topic was helping alleviate the cold. "So I never have to learn another language while I'm here?"

"Apparently not," Sira replied, but there was a strange sort of accent to her words. When she spoke again, it was gone. "You understood that, right? See? You just picked up on the Ordenite tongue, and that ain't as common as Syaotoan."

"I heard the accent," I replied, perplexed. "That's all, though."

That seemed to surprise both of them, and they exchanged glances. "Orden has an accent?" Sira asked Will.

"Syaotoan certainly does not," Will replied formally, and his own words had a sharp, dignified accent to them almost like the people in Bytold. As he said, it sounded more crisp and refined.

"It does," I informed him with a chuckle. "Nicer than I expected."

"You sound something like this, Will," Sira imitated his accent, but in a drawn-out and exaggerated way. Then she cleared her throat, and spoke, "'Your cow looks like a mate.' How's that for Syaotoan?"

Will's brow rose, and he smirked at her over his shoulder as we walked. "What did you try to say? If that was a greeting, I hope you have never spoken to a Syaotoan farmer."

The expression on Sira's face was well worth the smack on the shoulder I got for laughing. I wished I could hear how their own languages sounded, but being a permanent translator might be interesting on its own.

The rain only picked up as we crossed the plains. Puddles formed quickly in the mood, reflecting the bright glow of a full moon that started to poke out around the western clouds, which burst apart as we trampled through them.

"They could easily refuse us at this hour," Will said as a warning. "This season is wrought with thieves and bandits. Without writs, we could be dismissed, and it would be justified."

"But they won't," Sira reputed. "We have a Defender, and we're both international soldiers. If they've got half a brain between their shoulders, they'll let us in."

Will cleared his throat. "An unregistered Defender, a member of a missing squad, and a soldier from Orden. I am uncertain."

Guilt gripped my chest. In the fun of traveling with this pair, I'd almost forgotten about the missing squad. I didn't dare voice that thought.

Lightning flared across the sky. The resounding boom came from nearby, scaring the wits out of me and rocking the earth like a cradle in rough winds. A bold flash of light shone across the stone walls of the kingdom, shedding light on a pair of soldiers winging the gates and awaiting our arrival.

When we closed in, one raised a gauntleted hand in greeting. "Hail, travelers!" More thunder rolled nearby. The storm was worsening more quickly than it would rescind. "Give us a reason to shelter ye for the night! This eve, we've turned away our fair share o' travelers. Raiders flock around their camp in the eastern woods, strugglin' to steal a dry room from us!"

The pair of guards dressed in what I could only call traditional European, plain steel with full helms and gleaming plates, though it was ill maintained – I noted rust on the sockets of their armor. They saw many a rain, and little a fight.

Sira saluted them. "Sira Jessura, swordstress of Orden. Uh, ex-soldier."

"I am Will Ramun, from the patrol of Field Commander Lancet Cooper. I am a crusader, deviated from my original company in favor of..."

He gestured to me, implying my title might be all that was necessary. I swallowed hard. "Ryoku Dragontalen. Defender."

The guards shifted uncomfortably, like thin bolts of lightning shot through to their armor.

"A Defender, ye say?" one of the guards asked. "Long time since we seen one o' your kind around here. Yer a novice, by the look o' ye. Can ye fight well? Or use some kind of otherworldly magic?"

"He can, and it has been a long journey for us," Will replied. Out of the three of us, he seemed the one who'd talk our way into the city with the most ease. "We come to the city in search of aid. A foul beast plagues the Old Forest. Much of my squad may have been lost, or may have come through here ahead of us. We seek to regroup, acquire help, and get to the bottom of the situation."

"Aye, that'd be the Keeper." One of the guards tipped the visor of his helm, peering at Will with jaded green eyes. "Ye did say you were from Lancet's team, didn't ye?" he asked. "A couple o'em came through here not long ago mutterin' about such things. Must've been… two days past, I'd wager. Rough shape."

Will and I exchanged glances. His eyes were sharp. "How many, exactly? There should have been seven of them."

The guard shrugged. "Beats me," he replied. "Like I said, rough shape, and I don't watch this bloody wall day n' night. Could've been three, could've been more. Though you Syaoto lots sure stand out." He turned to his partner, who nodded once. "Right. You got can go on in. Best o' luck an' all that." He reared his head back toward the gate and shouted, "Open the gates, ye ol' codger!"

A great roll of lightning shook the field as he shouted and battered my eardrums so loudly that I thought I might faint. The next sound was the resounding roll of grating steel, almost as aggravating as the thunder itself. The gate was lifted by great black chains, folding up somewhere within the stone entry. I thought I recalled the medieval word associated with the type: a portcullis.

"One last thing," Will said as we stared into the city gates, where a few citizens and guards poked their heads through, curious of what travelers were allowed entry at this hour. "Where might I find these other members of my squad?"

The other guard guffawed, which caused Will to give him a look I'd only ever seen the friendly soldier conjure up once: against Lancet. He quickly straightened, and replied, "That'll be the Grand Hospital. Southwest from the gates as soon as ye go in. It'll be closed to visitors at this hour, much like anything else but the bars and inns. Best bet is to wait. That is, if the one o' em's still alive."

The foolish soldier had the nerve to guffaw again. By Will's expression, it took all his might not to strike the soldier down where he stood. Thinking of the faces of Oliver and the others, and imagining them injured or dead, made me barely resist the notion myself.

As it was, Will harshly pushed his way past the man without a word of apology, landing the man on his rump in the mud. Sira snorted, but she didn't dare laugh for the sake of either Will or the soldiers.

I gazed up nervously as we passed through the entry into the Capital. Amid the stormy weather, I spotted homes of a decidedly European style, though with peaked roofs and constructed mostly of brick, stone, or hardwood. I kept close to Will and Sira as we entered the largest city I'd ever been in, wondering just what awaited me inside.

SCENE SIX: UNSPOKEN

...Of Act One: Enter Ryoku

*In the eyes of Ryoku Dragontalen, we are in
The Lamenting Lion Inn, in the world of Harohto.
It is late night
On November 6th, 2017.*

"You lot look drenched! Travelers from outside the city, I presume?"

Will nodded, pushing drenched hair from his face as he addressed the polite young innkeeper. "From Bytold. We spent nights in the Old Forest on our way, so this will be a treat."

Sira was eyeing the people of the inn like a guard dog, watching the trio of big men watching us at a nearby table, the girl who twirled her braid between her fingers coyly, and especially the figure who leaned near the door in a brown cloak that shrouded his face. "We should get settled quickly. Do you offer food in-room?"

The innkeeper nodded. "Of course. Will you be taking one room, or multiple? Meal included, they go twelve gold apiece."

Will grimaced, glancing into his satchel uneasily. "That is a steep price," he muttered under his breath. I couldn't speak with experience, but I knew it was twice the price of the Fallen Unicorn in Bytold. He looked questioningly at Sira. "Two rooms?"

She scowled at him. "Why waste money? Just one suits me, so long as there's room and a damned shower." With a lasting glare at the cloaked stranger near the wall, she added, "Makes it easier to keep an eye out for each other."

"Alright, I'll see to it," the innkeeper replied with a short bow. I tried to note the gesture, since what my first friend here taught me seemed foreign in these parts. He plucked a key from the wall, spun it on his ring finger, and went upstairs to check out the room. While he was gone, Will leaned against the counter to face us.

"Seems we will wait out the rain here tonight. The clouds earlier suggested this is a brief storm. Should be gone by tomorrow, and we can go about our business."

"You call this a storm?" Sira retorted. "Go to Orden once, I dare you."

He smirked, but went on. "Tomorrow we can check out the Registry at last," he said with a look at me. "I would like to go to the hospital as soon as time allows. We can check out the smithy and wherever else. I... want to see if you can wield a different sword, since the gladius wouldn't work for you. If all goes well, we may be able to set out against the Keeper before long."

"And once our mission is complete, I'll be headed out," I said. Both Will and Sira turned to me, looking quite surprised, but I glanced away. "I have a mission I have to carry out. We'll work things out here and do what we can against the Keeper. For your squad." I met Will's glance. "But then I must go. I have things I have to do."

The door opened behind us, letting a freezing breeze into the room that made all three of us shudder as a young couple entered, tucking away a drenched umbrella as they came in. The wind blew astray the hood of the cloaked man near the door, which he hurriedly fixed. Still, I caught a glimpse of stark-white hair. Could it be...?

Unconsciously, I took a step toward the figure. He turned his head, and I saw violet eyes that regarded me levelly. It was him. When he realized I saw him, he wrapped his cloak around himself and ducked out the door before it could shut, disappearing into the storm outside.

"What the...?" I murmured to myself, stunned.

"What was that about?" Will asked me. "Did you know him?"

"I traveled with him," I told him quietly. "Kioru was his name. He's the one who helped me reach Bytold. He gave me the bag, my knife. He met me right when I appeared in the woods, like he was waiting for me."

"Stay the hell away from him."

I turned in shock. Sira stood on my other side, but she had an oddly wary look in her eyes. She even looked a little pale. "Why? He helped me—"

"Room's all checked out," the innkeeper's voice made me jump. He tossed the key to Will, who caught it as easily as he did back in the Fallen Unicorn. "First one on the right up the stairs. I can have dinner brought up to you in about a half hour. Enjoy your stay, lady and gents."

"Absolutely," Will assured him with a polite grin, and led the way up the stairs.

We passed a fogged window at the top, where I briefly paused to stare out into the storm outside. Rain raced down the panes of glass in rivulets. It was now pitch-black outside, with only the odd sheltered lantern and lightning to offer any solace to the darkness. Rainwater poured from the rooftops in sheets to the cobblestone street below.

I saw a brown-cloaked figure darting down the road beside the inn where we stayed. He stopped in the middle of the road, raising his hooded head to the sky. I could see the white tinge of his hair from here. A clap of thunder slapped across the sky like the very world fell victim to it, and the resounding flash left me blinking away spots. As quickly as the flash abated, Kioru was gone without a trace.

Will ushered me over as he was already unlocking our room. I followed him, looking at my new friends and wondering if they, too, might run from me in time, flinching at my name and braving storms to avoid speaking to me.

The room was much nicer than what we had in Bytold, which somewhat made up for the steep price. Still, I wasn't sure fitting three people in here was a comfortable idea. Three small rooms made up the interior. The main room was finished with hardwood, where a large, wood-framed bed with a plush-looking mattress sat with its back to the wall. Bookshelves lined the walls, save for the entries to the second room and the bathroom, as well as one part taken up by a fine maple wardrobe for our things. From what I could see, the second room looked to have only a folding bed with a window overlooking the city outside.

Will stretched his arms wearily. "I know not for the two of you, but exhaustion bears down on me. We should prepare for rest. Once our food arrives, that should be the end of my day."

I didn't quite relent, and turned to Sira as Will started unlacing his boots. "What do you have against Kioru, Sira? He helped me when I first got here. So did you, so I'd say you're both good people."

She turned away, glaring out the distant window. "He's from Orden, too. Did he ever tell you that?"

A flash of lightning illuminated the second room, casting brief light on us. A chill crawled down my spine as I recalled my dream in the woods, but I shook it off. "No, but you're from Orden too. I don't see how the home automatically makes you a person of evil nature. Or should I learn differently by you?"

She was quiet for a moment, kneeling to unlace her own boots. I realized I was baiting her to snap at me. Why was I so uneasy?

"Just trust me," she finally muttered. "He was in bad company last time I saw him. Anyway, are you going to soak the whole place or take off your wet stuff? I, for one, would prefer our inn room remains dryer than outside."

I decided to listen, but I wasn't going to let that point fade altogether. I had an easier time with my boots, kicking them off by the door, and I joined the others in putting my weapons and bag in the wardrobe. Will rifled through his bag quickly, and then ducked away into the bathroom. He returned in a dry undershirt and beige pants. Without his tunic and armor, I usually forgot that Will was quite well muscled. He had a faded scar across his shoulder that almost looked like a wide streak of lightning, but far more jagged.

With a lack of dry clothes, I borrowed an extra shirt and pants from Will to change into. Sira changed into black sweatpants and a baggy shirt, which still did nothing to hide the appealing curvature of her figure. While we waited for our dinner to arrive, we crowded together on the couch in the second room. The scent of rain still filled the room, but I was close enough to my two friends that I felt comfort in their increasingly familiar scents. Will always carried an earthy smell to him that reminded me of the forest, and Sira had a sweet fragrance that made me imagine flowers stained with blood.

"So, you plan to leave Harohto after we finish up with the Keeper?" Will asked.

I nodded. "I'm not all too sure where I have to go yet, but I can tell it isn't Harohto."

"What is your goal?" he asked in turn. His abruptness surprised me. He'd asked before in the Old Forest, but now there was a different fire to him. It was a question that, more or less, he wanted a real answer to. At my reaction, he chuckled lightly. "Come now, friend. Surely you do not still doubt me after all we have been through. Perhaps you are not quick to trust, but we have been through a great trial together. If anything, I feel a little more worthy to know your truths."

"What's there to be scared of?" Sira demanded. "If we didn't want you around, there was literally a whole forest to ditch your sorry ass in. You think you could outrun us in that twisted old wood? Or survive a fall off that plateau? Sorry, kid. You lived because we wanted you to."

I wasn't sure whether to take comfort in that, but her look was anything but angry. "Do you even know how to cross worlds yet?" Will asked gently. "Leaving Harohto involves that. If you wish to leave, you would do well to learn how, or find somebody who does."

I glanced down. "My goal is… complicated." I found it difficult to speak for a moment. Why was I so nervous to explain my reasoning to these two? They were not the first I had to explain my motives to. If I told the whole story, it'd be far easier. "I'm looking for someone. Finding this person… is going to help me find somebody else. Somebody who I've almost given up looking for in my own world, and something tells me I can find out more here. That is… if the person I'm looking for was telling the truth."

Sira stared at me. "Okay, weirdo. Now tell it again, but not vague as all hell."

"It does sound complex," Will agreed. "You have been looking for somebody for a long time?" To my relief, he didn't seem to recount what we talked about before. I didn't feel like talking about love in front of Sira, and this had nothing to do with it.

"Okay," I started, and took a deep breath. Telling a story to these two might require more patience than I had. "I'm looking for the person who taught me how to come here. A spirit, presumably, who appeared before me in my own world. He asked me for my help – to save him from something. He didn't quite elaborate, promising I would find out more when I got here."

"Was it Kioru?" Sira asked sharply. "Cause that bastard doesn't need saving."

"N-No, it wasn't him," I told her. "I half-expected him to be here when I arrived, but there was Kioru instead. While I was hoping to find information about my charge, I didn't ask Kioru. I couldn't be certain that he was on my side."

"Understandable," Will said, and Sira nodded furtively. "So you seek to save somebody from... somewhere in the spirit realm. You surely understand just how many realms are out there, right? Seeking one person in them is farfetched, even for you. You seem like a good, kind person who would have done exactly for Sira and I what we have done for you, but..."

"But I have to," I insisted. Something about the tone of my voice made focus on me. "There is some kind of connection between us. It has to be how he found me. And if that connection exists, if I didn't imagine it... then maybe he *can* help me find my sister."

I began to speak mostly to myself, and Sira and Will both regarded me sharply. "Your sister?" Will asked. "So by connection, you mean perhaps a blood relation."

"Is your sister a...?" Even Sira couldn't finish the question.

"To be honest, I don't know," I said quietly. Speaking the words aloud made them somewhat more real, and I felt the double-edge of the words against my tongue. "Last time I heard from her, she was, but I can't contact her. I've tried really hard."

"You're separated from her," Sira realized aloud.

"We are both foster children," I explained. "Our mother and her entire side of the family died in a horrid fire five years ago. My father isn't in the picture. Her father, my stepfather, died in a tragic accident a year later. After that, nobody would take the two of us in. Not our stepmother. Not my father. Nobody on my stepfather's side. We were considered cursed children. After all, who goes through that kind of suffering all at once?"

Sira put a hand on my arm, which almost shocked me out of the darkness I was crawling into. "You're not cursed," she insisted. "I mean, it's pretty shitty luck to have met me, but you did meet Will."

I almost laughed. Not quite. "I have a godfather. Even he can't do anything because, apparently, my blood father is still alive according to government law. Also, he's not a guardian to my sister. Half-sister, if you didn't figure that out." I took a deep breath. "So we both went into the system. I guess we were treated differently. I didn't put up much of a fight. Being a few years older than my sister might've done it, but I think I was just tired. I reacted differently, and so I found a new home easily.

"But Roxanne, she wasn't the same after our mother's death," I went on. "She was listed as a more difficult foster child. Level three, they call it. Complicated kids who act out. They're problematic, and need certain foster parents to take them in. It meant we were separated, and I was left with no way to contact her. Even my social worker can't connect us. Not until she settles down."

My comrades kept silent. I wasn't sure if they could hear the emotion in my voice, the tears written behind my words. "And so I need to find him," I said softly. "The only person left in the world with a connection to me, who might have a connection to her."

"What is his name?" Will asked. He sat on high alert, reminding me of some kind of mastiff with the way his shoulders curled defensively. It almost looked like he would run off at the mention of the name, returning only with the boy caught in his teeth, dropping him at my lap. If only it were that easy.

I drew a breath. I hadn't spoken the name aloud to anyone yet, even my friends involved in the same world. "Chris Olestine."

Sira turned away quickly. I wasn't sure if it was related to the name or not, but she didn't meet my glance. "Okay," Will said, "and do you have any clues to go on? Anything about... his looks? Heritage? Those hailing from a certain word tend to clump in characteristics, even spirits."

"Ordenites have odd colorings to their hair," Sira muttered, still not looking at me. With a stray hand, she parted her hair behind her ear, and I could see a black undertone to her hair. "Even spirits."

"You met many of my squad," Will said. "You might be able to notice kindred qualities to us, even though none of us are related."

"Big and dopey," Sira muttered, "tall as a fucking tree, and about as smart."

She startled a laugh out of me, and Will glared at her. "No, I don't think he looked much like either of you."

"Then again, you did say he was a prisoner somewhere," Will recalled. "He could be in an alien world. If we had some roots to go off of, perhaps we could still find which world he came from and start there."

I shook my head sadly, not fully listening to Will's words. "There's a lot I don't know," I said softly. "I don't know where to begin. Chris taught me how to get to the spirit realm. Kioru got me to Bytold. Will, you got me out of that stupid bar, then through the old forest. Sira, you too. Now, I need to figure things out for myself. I need a plan of action, to figure out where to go. After we deal with the Keeper, I have to press on. If I can—"

"There's a damned lot of *I* in that statement," Sira muttered. "You think we're just gonna fuck off after we get your help, don't you?"

She turned to me, and I looked into her fiery eyes, lit by a startling amount of emotion. "What do you mean? Will has his squad, and you..." I trailed off. Had Sira mentioned what she was going to do?

Sira didn't relent. "I remember thinking you might be smarter than you looked when we first met. You had that dopey look on your face, having slept forever after you nearly drowned. Well, it looks like I was wrong. You're pretty dumb, Ryoku Dragontalen."

"Perhaps you are being a little presumptuous, Sira?" Will asked gently. "We know very little ourselves. We both stumbled upon this idea in the most inopportune ways. Myself, from stepping in on a one-sided bar brawl. For you, simply being in the right place at the right time." He looked at me, and a wistful smile lapsed across his face. "Truth be told, it seems very little like a coincidence."

I frowned. "What are you talking about?"

"It could be simple coincidence, but I have my doubts," Will went on. "Meeting you, that is, in the ways that we did. Finding you as you stumbled your first steps into our realm, seeking something that could be far more important than it seems. For me, it was as simple as stepping in to save you, but finding that our lives might be intertwined in a less apparent way. Choosing to guide you through the woods was hardly even an option for me – it was a necessity. You see, I needed to see where this journey would take you. What sort of passion *drove you* to coming this far, even if it had been on your own."

He gave Sira a sheepish smile. "I sound foolish. I have never been quite so good at placing my thoughts into words."

"Yeah, you sound like you're about to propose," Sira muttered wryly, but she was hiding a smile with her fingertips. "Maybe it makes a little more sense coming from me. I mean, how the hell would I end up here, of all places? Running from Orden, this is damned far, and pretty coincidental, or whatever. I zeroed in on one of the highest-paying missions on that stupid bounty board with no clue what I was gonna do after. Make some cash, then what? Keep running?" She scoffed. "No, I landed right where I needed to, at just the right time. I never really was a believer in fate or whatever, but..."

"Okay, you guys both sound really weird," I murmured. "What are you trying to say? That you ran into me for a reason?"

"Nothing creepy, like where your mind is going," Sira snapped. "To help you. And, in the same breath, to help us. To fix this annoying feeling of unrest I've carried for a long time."

"This could resolve a great deal of issues," Will agreed. "You see, Ryoku, the spirit realm is a great, vast, and ever-changing place. Were you to leave and come back in a year, it might be very different. I spoke to you already about worlds that die, but some can change, too. Many worlds with unstable origins can accelerate time at rapid rates."

"Orden is one," Sira told me. "Orden runs on a different sort of season than the rest of the spirit realm. So I could leave and come back, and it could accelerate ten, fifty, a thousand years. Not much seems to keep it in place."

I frowned. "That sounds insane. How does that make any sense?"

"You walk in the realm of the dead while you still draw breath," Will said flatly. "You wield a staff capable of summoning fire. You *fended off an ancient beast in the woods*. Yet, you might tell us still about impossibilities?"

I cleared my throat. "Good point."

"It just works the same as any law," Sira added with a shrug. "Like Harohto gets four seasons, Vortiger gets two. Summer and winter. They change, very rapidly. You'll probably see one day if you're really unlucky."

"I am very unlucky," I pointed out. "But you guys are getting to something. What is it?"

They exchanged glances. "There was... a rather large change in the spirit realm, about two months ago." Will sucked in a deep breath, and I half-expected him to start singing or something, but he carried on in the same voice. "These worlds I have explained to you. They... have not quite existed in the same form this entire time."

"What do you mean?" I questioned. I touched the couch material gingerly.

"You see, something dire must have happened about two months ago," Will explained. "Sometime in September, something caused the spirit realm to rewrite its core structure. It was once split into realms of a sort, but not quite as myriad as they are now. It was simpler things. Worlds deigned to the elements. The Astral Plains, known as a central ground for spirits."

I started paying attention. Things had gotten weird for me in September, too.

"Things like Chaos and Peace," Sira elaborated. "Uh, your world might call those heaven and hell."

I raised a brow. "Those actually exist?"

"They did," Will explained, "up until a few months ago. Every spirit-born that used to be alive prior to that seems to be... gone. Erased. Now, only us spirits remember what used to be, and not quite... all of us. Or all that there is to remember, even. Matters took quite a serious dive."

Sira made an irritated noise. "You're tellin' me," she muttered. "All these thousands of realms popped up. Orden. Harohto. Syaoto. Thousands, literally thousands, of others. Spirits were split up among them, and..." She struggled to find the words, appearing thoroughly frustrated about it. "It's like something *tried* to make us fit. Gave us lives in these new worlds. It's fucking weird. Like, as much as I remember being alive, I also remember being a soldier of Orden for a long time. Since we need magic to cross the worlds now, too, I couldn't even leave."

Will shrugged. "Same here," he agreed. "I remember a full life in Syaoto. My father. The army. Everyone in it. I do recall being alive in your world.

"The point being," Will went on, turning his attention to me again. "Is that we do not remember our lives before."

"Only that the worlds changed," Sira scowled. "We remember it, but not why."

"Or how." Will sighed deeply. "Our memories appear to be deeply affected by whatever transpired here in September. Many Defenders do not seem to recall it, either, or else they are keeping quiet. Coming to a world that had changed quite massively, I do understand keeping quiet."

"Did you experience anything?" Sira asked me. "Anything at all?"

I frowned. "I'm not sure." I didn't feel right trying to explain my sudden change of heart between my ex, Anna, and a girl I dated when I was younger. I might tell Will later, but my feelings about Sira felt too complex to explain anything of the sort to her right now. But...

"I did meet Chris Olestine in late September."

Sira snapped her fingers. "That makes fucking sense," she agreed readily. "He must have something to do with it! And in association, you..." She looked me dead in the eyes, and there was that fiery passion in them again. "You must have something to do with it. You have to. I can tell."

"Possible answers," Will agreed, looking at me as well. "Our quests may intertwine, Ryoku Dragontalen." There was a knock at the door, which made all three of us turn sharply. Will smiled sheepishly. "Right. Food."

We got up to get the door, where a team of four chefs awaited with platters of food. There was a roast beef with stuffing, corn on the cob, mashed potatoes, a bowl of seasoned fettuccine alfredo, and a full Caesar salad garnished with parmesan. Thanking the chefs profusely, we returned to our couch, where Will pulled out a table from the bedside to put our food. The chefs provided cutlery and paper plates, so we loaded ours up for our first proper meal in days – honestly, my first in my time in the spirit realm.

We kept the conversation lighter while we ate, simply talking about the quality of food, the storm, our travels through the forest, and light gossip about the town. The consumption of food started to make me sleepy.

However, when we all ate our fill, the food was pushed aside. I found Sira and Will facing me once more. I gulped. They'd been waiting until the food was done.

"Ryoku," Will started. "I doubt very much that our meeting was by chance."

"I outright deny that it was," Sira agreed. "Coming to Harohto to run away from Orden? I had to be delusional."

"We do have other things to achieve," Will reasoned. "I must find my squad. Even if they are spirit-born and may have little to do with this ominous, ultimate truth, they are my family."

Sira shuddered. "And I just have to run from Orden."

I regarded them both sleepily. "I have to find Chris and my sister. That's my priority."

"What if they were linked?" Will asked me. "Even the matter of your world and its lifespan. What if the longevity of your world was linked to what happened here in September?"

I hesitated. "But the world has been dying since I was young."

"Who knows if the change was immediate?" Sira asked. "Maybe it was a long time coming. Maybe something dozens of years ago triggered something and we don't even know it."

"That sounds like you're reaching," I pointed out.

Sira threw up her hands. "Maybe I am," she complained, "but there is a reason. And I think the three of us can figure it out."

I felt like I was a mile behind the conversation. "You mean, you guys want to help me? To save Chris, and find my sister?"

Will and Sira exchanged glances. "Is he stupid, or are we not explaining this properly?" Sira asked him dryly.

He shrugged. "How easy is it to explain something we do not fully understand?"

They shared an odd look between them. "What are you...?"

Without a word, Will and Sira got to their feet. I stood as well, hesitant, and they both retreated to the main room. I stood there awkwardly, wondering if I'd just said something wrong. Sira returned with her naked broadsword, and Will with his wood-handled lance. As I was wondering what I'd possibly done to turn these two against me, they dropped to one knee in front of me, weapons crossed over their upraised knees.

"Ryoku Dragontalen," Will began, taking a deep breath. "I no longer have reason to be in Harohto. Above all, it may be that my reason for being here was you. I must check with my squad, and we will deal with the Keeper, but this is the immediate future. Beyond that, I long to see my homeland of Syaoto again. My brave and noble homeland could offer you the truths you seek if we went abreast of one another. I can protect you. I know my way around medicine and herbology. Wherever our path may lead, I can guide you."

"Ryoku Dragontalen," Sira started without a breath's pause after Will. "I'm more than done with Harohto, too, once we get our money's worth of this place. You're still weak, and you could use a badass like me to look out for you. Really, there's nobody better for the role than me – forget about Will for a second. Together, we can unravel this shit-storm and figure out the truth. We can save Chris Olestine. We can find your sister. Whatever's going on in this world, we can solve it. I don't really care where we go, just as long as I avoid my home."

I stared at them both in stunned silence. They kept their eyes downward, staring at their weapons. "This is where you say something," Sira stage-whispered, keeping her eyes down.

"Uh," I started, pursing my lips. "Um. Well, this could be... a really dangerous road." I started to draw strength from my own voice. My whole life, especially with the loss of my family, that had been the source of my strength. "I feel like a great truth awaits me. Maybe it's the same one you guys are looking for, but it might not be. I don't know what to tell you. I don't know fully where to go, or what I'm supposed to do. I'll need to get stronger. I'll need experience, supplies, and gold. And..." I hesitated over the last thought, the one that had been on the tip of my tongue since the dream I had in the forest. "What if I have to go to Orden?"

Sira paled at the prospect, and I feared that whatever she was proposing, I was about to lose her. It was a hardly developed idea, and more of a gut feeling that clutched me like a dark hand. The shadowy figure in my dream, the dark emperor of Orden... what more did I have to go on?

Just as I feared she would up and leave, Sira lifted her chin and met my gaze head-on. "Then I'll go with you," she replied firmly. "I don't care. If it's with you, then I'll feel safe. I'll go wherever you go. I just... I sense that I can't just sit out on this. No matter what."

"I agree," Will cut in, his voice terse. If there was a playful smirk on his lips from Sira's words, then he hid it well. "So I, William Jesse Ramun, median-rank soldier of Syaoto..."

"...And I, Sira Midati Jessura, ex-knight of Orden..."

Their words came with an odd clairvoyance, an understanding between them that they must have rehearsed. Sira appeared both more emotional and more serious than I had ever seen her, and Will's professionalism was with the same heart he used when talking about his home.

In unison they concluded, bowing their heads over their weapons until their brows almost touched the floor.

"We pledge our services to you, Ryoku Dragontalen, the Defender, as your official Guardians!"

Somehow, in spite of the little I had learned about my role in these realms, I failed to see this coming. Will had briefly explained the role of a Guardian before, back in the Fallen Unicorn Inn. They were chosen spirits who served as guides and protectors to a Defender as they sought to complete their task and aid the people of the spirit realm. Seeing as I was a Defender – almost officially, as of tomorrow – that person seemed to be me. I clearly recalled the things Will said about Defenders, both who they were and how they should be. People expected better of them, but they hardly received it.

There was more to it. Looking at Will, I remembered how he led me down the path after our short rest at the rock, forgetting his friends to keep me safe. The moment in the tavern where he leapt in to save the day, hardly hesitating in order to protect me. The determined look in his eyes as he tried to protect me from the Keeper. The focused hunch in his shoulders as he worked his Moonwelt solution for my injuries. Every laugh, every smile, every private joke and the glint in his sapphire eyes through almost every moment as he guided me here through the Old Forest.

Sira. I remembered her eyes when I first looked at her. How she led me across the bridge, my hand in hers, and how she leapt into the raging river to save me. The feeling of her arm around my shoulder as she led me on. The fire in her eyes when she stood up for me, losing her shield in the process. The emotion just now in her eyes as she said she'd go anywhere with me – even the place that terrified her the most. There was a lot of emotion between us that made precious little sense for having met so recently, but I wondered if I could do this without her now.

The last thing I considered was my goals. To save Chris Olestine, to discover the roots that bound us and connected us to my sister. To fill the strange gaps in my memory and solve the mystery of the spirit realm. Along the way, I needed to learn the ways of this world and how to defend myself – I could hardly call myself a Defender without it. I needed to become self-reliant and strong somehow. For that, my two newfound friends would be invaluable.

"I accept your vows," I replied quietly. "As your Defender, I will do everything in my power to protect you."

Sira leered up at me. "Idiot," she muttered, but a smile danced across her lips. "We're the ones protecting you. Just let us do what we have to."

Will grinned as well. "If we are to journey together, I suggest making due course for my home, Syaoto. If your idea is correct about Orden, then Syaoto may be able to help. King Lionel is wise and bold in equal measure. If he cannot tell us with surety about the location of your charge, then he will help us with supplies and the means to find him."

After all Will said about his kingdom, I almost shared his longing to visit the place. "Okay," I agreed. "We'll make course for Syaoto after we're done here."

"One more thing," Sira said. "World travel isn't simple. In my case, I had to find a relic capable of world-crossing magic to cart just *one* person here. You could learn how to cast magic, but learning how to get *exactly* where you want to go, with passengers, is harder than you'd think."

"She is right," Will agreed. "If you learn magic, your best shot would be a random travel spell. Beginners learn it quite quickly, but, as the name implies, it does not always lead you exactly where you want to go. Our path to Syaoto may not be so linear, unless you wished to spend a very long time studying magic."

That didn't appeal to me at all. "No, we don't have time for any of that," I murmured. "Maybe we can find somebody capable of crossing worlds. If not, I'll learn the random spell, though I can't guarantee I can actually pull it off. As backwards as it sounds, heading to random worlds might be smarter than going directly there."

I thought they'd protest, but both nodded. "You need to get stronger," Sira agreed. "Syaoto would coddle the life out of you. No, you need random travel, so we can cross worlds, gain some intel, and work on getting you stronger. It might not be easy, but it'll be faster – and way more exciting – than learning how to cart your ass straight to Point B."

I smirked at her. "Done. I guess we'll figure that out as we go, then." Although I didn't voice it, I wasn't sure how much time I had to find Chris Olestine, let alone my sister.

Will smiled wearily. "If all is decided, then we should retire for the night. It has been a doggedly long day for us, and tomorrow may yet be as long."

I nodded my agreement. "Yeah, let's sleep." As Sira rose to put away her sword, I realized Will had set his things up in this room – on the one-person couch. Sira had set hers by the bed. Unconsciously, I'd set my own things down in the main room. "Uh, where am I sleeping?"

The cordial smile Will gave me was all I needed to see. "How could we make a Defender sleep on the couch?" he asked teasingly. "You will share the bed with Sira. She has the closest-range weapon so she may watch over you as you sleep. I am here, of course, to watch the window. Should anyone attempt to clamber through and make an attempt on your life, then I shall put them down swiftly. And, should somebody bust through the front door, then Sira and her giant sword would make quick work of them."

"Don't be ridiculous," I growled, dragging Will down to my level by the collar of his shirt. "Nobody's hunting me! You're just trying to—"

"Is there a problem?"

I halted, turning slowly to face Sira. Her hands were on her hips, a pillow tucked under one arm, and a sly grin on her face. "You wouldn't make a girl sleep on the couch, would you?"

"What? No!" I exclaimed, and shot Will a dark glare. "Will, why don't you...?"

Will tutted under his breath. "Your hesitation would not have to do with your previous scandals, would it? Perhaps out of chastity for the innkeeper in Bytold?"

Sira took a step closer. "What did you just say to him?"

I blanched. "N-Nothing, just..." I reserved a very dark look for Will, who choked. He quickly made it out to look like he was merely choking on a fistful of corn he'd snatched up, but I doubted Sira was fooled. I straightened. "Very well. Let's get off to bed."

"Good," Sira muttered. "I didn't want to give up that comfy-ass bed for your sake." She grabbed my hand and pulled me from the room. "Don't worry, kiddo. Nothing's gonna happen. I'll keep an eye open all night."

She shut the door to Will's room behind her, and I wasn't sure I liked the idea of any of this. Sira managed to be equal parts sexy and horrifying in a combination I might never be ready for. That, and Will swindled me into this, I knew it.

"Right side is mine," she announced as she moved to the respective side. I timidly moved to the other side. I contemplated sleeping without a shirt, but didn't quite feel safe enough, so I slipped under the covers. When I glanced back, Sira had shamelessly removed her shirt and pants, and was stretching luxuriously by the bed. I tried not to stare, and I knew she'd kill me if she turned around at that moment, but her well-cut figure drew my gaze. Her fitness was anything but unattractive, and her lack of clothing only served to embolden her features in a way I might never witness again as long as I lived.

As I watched her, I noticed the long, snake-like scar that ran from the nape of her neck to below the hem of her underclothes at the small of her back. It didn't look like an old scar, either. The high-necked shirt she wore before concealed it perfectly. It couldn't be a coincidence. My first thought was of her fear of Orden and the emperor. Had they done this to her?

"What are you staring at?"

I practically jumped out of my skin when Sira snapped at me. I wondered whether she had a third eye hidden somewhere on her back until I noticed the mirror wedged among the books on the shelf, where her crimson eyes beset into a glare.

"Haven't you seen a girl before, kid?"

I didn't know how to respond, so I retreated under the blankets where I might avoid the intimidating girl's wrath. I wasn't sure what scared me more about her: how easily she could kill me, or how easily I found myself falling for her.

My avoidance tactic didn't seem to work as she pounced on me above the covers. I let out a surprised noise of anguish and managed to wriggle my head free of the blankets, where I came face-to-face with her. Her expression wasn't murderous, really. Her delicate brows were furrowed, but she had a playful smirk written all over her face. Her sickly-sweet scent invaded my senses quickly.

"Gotcha," she murmured, and pinched me under the blanket. I nearly cried out, but caught myself as I remembered Will in the next room. "Next time you wanna check me out, why don't you check for mirrors first?"

I hesitated, staring into her mesmerizing, fire-like eyes. "Sira, that scar..."

Every bit of playfulness evaporated from her face. "Oh. That." She rolled off me in a fluid motion, settling in on her own side of the bed. "And here I thought you were lookin' at my ass."

I didn't want to admit that I, in fact, had spent a good minute looking at the details of her body as she'd moved. The fluidity of her movements, the way her muscles stretched as she bent over and, most certainly, her backside. I wanted to press her about the scar, too, but I could already tell that was a sensitive topic. We'd breached so many of those today, I wasn't sure if she could handle another.

"Get some sleep, kid," she murmured sleepily. "Like Willy-boy said, could be a long-ass day for us." She added a sleepy chuckle. "And not like it's the last chance you'll ever get to check me out, either, if that's what you want."

I felt myself blushing furiously. She fell asleep quickly, so I didn't have to worry about her reaction to that. After a time, I got to my feet and checked out the bookshelves. There was a vast medley of books, anything from Harohtian history to beginning magical theory. I plucked out a few and sat awake for a long time, reading well into the night.

...End of Act One.

ACT TWO: GUARDIANSHIP...

*In the eyes of Ryoku Dragontalen, we are in
Harohto Capital City, in the world of Harohto.
It is early afternoon
On November 7th, 2017.*

SCENE ONE: BECOMING TRUE

I glanced at Will, seeking his confirming nod before I slipped through the open wood door. He and Sira followed, my silent shadows.

The Registry was hardly what I expected. A maple wood counter sat at the other end of the room, where a friendly-looking young woman behind it gave us a practiced smile. Behind her stood several steel filing cabinets, haphazardly piled in tilting towers that practically swayed with the outdoor wind. I wondered if each file in those regarded another Defender like me. A few people sat at benches surrounding a table piled with reading material. With linoleum-looking floors and walls of maple, the Registry looked more like a dentistry office than anything. In fact, it almost looked like it was straight out of my world.

Will led me straight to the desk, Sira in tow. To my dismay, I still found my gaze lingering over Sira as she moved. Everything from the way she walked to the glint in her crimson eyes kept bringing my eyes back to her. I pictured that long scar snaking down her back. Since last night, I couldn't bring myself to ask about it.

The woman behind the counter smiled again as we approached. "Hello there," she greeted us. "How may I help you?"

"We are registering a new official Defender," Will spoke for me, "and his two Guardians."

I still found the titles unnerving. I'd been taught to speak my title whenever I was asked my name, but it still felt like I was introducing someone else, or merely playing a role assigned to me.

Then there was the part about Will and Sira becoming my Guardians. I tried not to pay much mind to the title. Guardians were supposed to be the designated protectors of a Defender. Seeing as we were both accustomed to a different world, Guardians were meant to guide and protect Defenders as we set out to protect the spirit realm. The large assumption was that, by protecting this world, we protected our own as well.

Of course, I had my own reasons for entering this life that seemed to differ from many other Defenders, causing me to set out in search of Chris Olestine and develop these strong bonds with my newfound friends. As a Defender, though, registering meant I was obligated to stop and help any in need. It also gave me certain rights above the average spirit or spirit-born, which extended to include my Guardians. That included being able to have them, of course, and for them to act in my stead or on my behalf. It also included the benefit of requesting aid from any, be they spirits, spirit-born, kings and queens, or soldiers.

"Alright," the receptionist's face turned from mock delightful to businesslike in an instant as she rummaged through her desk. She pulled out a couple documents and laid them on the table. "Who's the Defender?"

"Me," I replied. It took me a moment to realize she was asking for something a little more specific. "Uh, Ryoku Dragontalen."

The woman nodded, scribbling madly on the paper. Considering I'd only given my name, I felt she was writing a *lot* more than that. "Any other Defenders in your family?"

I vaguely realized she didn't have the usual Harohto accent, but her question threw me off. "Not that I know of." It didn't matter much, I thought. None of them was around anymore.

She only nodded. After another minute of scribbling, she pushed my document aside and stamped it once. I saw the page briefly. Somehow, she'd produced a rather lifelike sketch of my face, and stamped it with black ink labelled 'Defender'. The rest was practically illegible. "First Guardian, please."

"I suppose that would be me," Will mused, polite as ever. "William Jesse Ramun."

She kept on scribbling. I watched with fascination, wondering if she'd be able to read this later. "Alright. What is your home world, Will?"

For a split second, I wondered why she hadn't asked me. Obviously, I could only be from one place. Any specifics, like my country, province, or even city, seemed irrelevant.

"Capital of Syaoto," Will replied. The woman went on scribbling. As soon as she pushed that page aside and stamped it with 'Guardian,' Sira started.

"Second Guardian, Sira Midati Jessura." She smirked, letting the woman's frenzy grow as she struggled to finish the paper. "Orden. The Capital."

For a brief moment, I thought I saw a reaction in the receptionist's eyes. Fear, and possibly alarm. Before I could be sure, her head lowered again, and she finished Sira's document just as quickly. She stapled all three files together and bound them with a string of red tape. Then, she held the stack over an empty stack of papers, and she ran her hand over them in a fluid motion. Her fingers glowed, then she removed the first stack and handed us the other stack. I stared at it in surprise. It was an exact copy, possibly produced better than a machine might do.

"You may need these documents to prove who you are. If they're lost, you may get another copy at any Registry located in any Capital city, or any city that acts as a Capital might. Your information will be readily available in the system for all of time until you depart from these lands altogether. Perhaps even beyond then."

I handed the documents to Will, who safely stowed them away in his bag. I probably lost my belongings too often to try to keep them safe. While he put them away, the receptionist handed me a small red stone, shaped similarly to the circular band around our documents. "This device is for registering new Guardians. Merely have them hold their hand over the stone and state their name, title, and home. Next time you go to a Registry, you can claim the official documents if you so wish."

I took the item in reverence. There was an item for this? "Thank you," I told her, surprised.

"You're welcome," she told me with a smile. "That's all you'll need. You're free to go."

I smiled in reply, having assumed this would take longer. However, as Will and Sira made to turn away, I stopped and turned back to her. "Are you... able to find people?"

She looked bewildered. "Locate? That's distinctly possible, as long as their world has a Registry. It also may not be perfect, depending on the world and their technology, but we do keep some records in many worlds. What is the name?"

I pictured his face in my mind, as clearly as I'd seen him when he first appeared in my world like a ghost. Jet-black hair, with olive skin and a delicate nose. The boy who asked me to save him, but deigned to tell me later. Maybe, I hoped, he could help me find my sister.

"Chris Olestine."

"Okay," she replied cheerfully, and turned to a niche in the wall where I was surprised to see a computer. I wasn't sure whether it was a quirk of this world, or whether the Registry was some sort of hole in the world that ignored the regular cultures of it all.

"You think she can actually find anything?" Will asked quietly. I nodded hopefully. Sira seemed a little distracted, staring off at nothing away from me. She reacted oddly to the name the day before, I recalled. Did she know something?

The receptionist returned after a short moment. "I'm sorry; I cannot locate Chris Olestine at this time. Is there anything else I can help you with?"

I felt stunned. She couldn't find Chris through an apparently detailed system? It had been five days since I last saw him, but I knew I still had some time before things went south. Did they catch him reaching out to me? Did they already carry out his sentence?

"Is there anything in the system about him?" Will asked on my behalf. "A homeland? Anything about him whatsoever?"

The receptionist frowned studiously. "If the man does exist, then it's not within our systems at all. Are you sure you have the correct name?"

I nodded numbly. Will cast me a glance. "That will be all, then," he told her. "Have a good day, madam!"

The woman simply nodded in response, lowering her attention to other documents on her counter. Will gently coaxed me to turn away. There was nothing else we could do here.

When the three of us turned away, though, something else caught my attention.

A large brown board hung on the wall, labelled at the top with black letters declaring 'Hunts.' A mix of portraits and writs scattered all over the face of it, some overlapping, and in no particular order. Each portrait declared a hefty price in gold.

What stood out about it, however, was a poster right in the middle of it all: a rather lifelike sketch of my face next to one of Kioru. Next to the pictures was written '12 million gold coins.'

"What is that?" I asked hollowly.

The receptionist answered my question, though I wasn't sure she saw why I asked. "That is a bounty board, extended for use by Defenders and other world-traveling folk. Normally bounty boards are used exclusively within a world. This one spans all worlds and is accessible to any who cross regularly. People all over the worlds report identities of people or monsters needing to be hunted, captured, or killed. Defenders, hunters, or simply travelers can tackle the challenges for rewards directly from the commissioner, and sometimes from the government of a world.

"If you wish to take on a hunt, you must report to the commissioner directly to gain first seat on the respective hunt. Return with proof of the deed, and the bounty is yours."

Sira and Will stood like statues on either side of me. Will's expression was unreadable, but Sira looked absolutely pissed. While they didn't move, I approached the board to examine the poster. Text under the illustrations of Kioru and I read:

Ryoku Dragontalen: Defender, no greater than twenty years of age. Green eyes. May be armed and dangerous. May have Guardians. This boy is a threat to the entire spirit realm and must be brought to justice.

Kioru Rasale: Rebellion leader of Orden. Armed and dangerous. White hair, violet eyes. Possibly travels alone. This man is a threat to the Royal Crown of Orden, and to the entire spiritual realm. Seen in collaboration with Ryoku Dragontalen.

Report to the Royal Crown of Orden to act upon this bounty. Ryoku Dragontalen must be brought alive. Kioru Rasale and any Guardians may be killed for additional bounty with proof of the deed.

-By the righteous decree of the Crown of Orden.

"Why are they hunting me?"

Will seemed oddly calm next to me. "I may have heard of this before," he said softly. "I apologize. Bounties decreed by royal kingdoms are made aware to any and all field soldiers. I'm glad Lancet did not realize who you were, for I did not connect the dots."

Sira strolled up and ripped the poster free of the wall. If the receptionist thought this was odd or unacceptable, she said nothing. "No need to worry about this crap," she muttered, waving the paper at me before she ripped it asunder. She threw the remnants in the trash, and came back shaking her head. "Damn it. If I knew what they were doing... if I was still connected to the army..."

"That's okay," I murmured, though my own voice sounded empty and strangely hollow. It was like the warning of my coming death made my soul retreat within myself. More importantly, though, I noted the part about Kioru. Were his words as false as the ones about me? If not, Kioru might turn out to be an extremely valuable ally – if I could only track him down without him running away.

"Twelve million," Will murmured, and whistled lowly. "It has sure risen since I last heard." He turned to see Sira's glare, and raised his palms in a friendly gesture. "Worry not – I do not heed the work of Chaos, no matter the bounty. Besides, Ryoku, we are your Guardians now. They would duly earn that bounty if they could get past us."

"Does this mean I'm being pursued?" I asked. "Hunters and soldiers actually know about this? What did I do? I just got here!"

"Do not worry, friend," Will replied. "Soldiers respond to the immediate threats." He gestured to another posting in the corner of the board. I looked upon a harrowing illustration of the Keeper, accurate even to the dust streaming from its cloak. "Bounties like this are their immediate concern. Monsters. Raider captains. Those with reason to attack their fine city. And for what they cannot do, they will post bounties here for possible Defenders and hunters, like us, to take up."

"Who's seriously gonna be threatened by that picture of you, anyway?" Sira said scathingly. "There's more fun things to hunt, and hunters are all about the fun. Check these out!" She scanned through a bunch of posters along the left side. Most detailed images of horrific monsters. On one, I saw a sketch of a spiny dragon with eyes that seemed to bore through the picture. Another showed a strange creature with antlers like a buck. "Figures none of these are in Harohto, either. Told you this is the Capital of boredom."

I looked at the poster of the Keeper. "Do we have to register to take up this bounty?"

"Not so traditionally, anyway," Will replied, looking over the poster quickly. "This one is abstract. People theorize that the Keeper has actually been in the Old Forest for a very long time, and is only riled up due to the raider activity and other happenings in the woods. It may be possible to defeat it, but perhaps not necessary. I was thinking on it while we traveled through the woods." He turned to me with an odd look in his eyes. "But we will get to that. For now, I would like to go visit the squad at the hospital and see about undertaking our mission. Do not let this bounty get the best of you, Ryoku."

"Yeah, you got us to look out for you," Sira agreed, grinning. "If any hunters are dumb enough to try you, they won't make it out alive. Trust me." Her grin fell, then, as easily as though it had never been there. "This does clear something up though, big time. I think we know where we're headed."

The smile I'd found at her confidence faded, too, for I knew what she meant. If Orden had reason to place such a bounty on me, it was unmistakable. At long last, I knew where to look.

SCENE TWO: MAGELET

...Of Act Two: Guardianship

In the eyes of Ryoku Dragontalen, we are in Harohto Capital City, in the world of Harohto. It is early afternoon On November 7th, 2017.

"Well look here, a girl all alone in the streets!" The voice made me turn my head.

"How unfortunate fer 'er!"

A set of sinister cackling followed. "How fortunate fer us."

Just around the corner from the Registry, a circle of seven or more huge guys surrounded a lone girl. The sight immediately made a chill crawl down my spine. The girl was probably close to my age, with what looked like silvery hair glinting in the bright morning sun, and dressed in light colors. A staff hung at her side, but she looked far too afraid to raise it. Against these sizes of men, would it even do anything?

Sira tried to keep walking, ignoring the events unfolding right there, but Will and I weren't so complacent. He quickly drew his lance with a warm-up spin, catching their attention wordlessly. My chivalry threatened to fade under their huge figures and dark glares, but I held my ground. Muttering under her breath, Sira drew Sinistra from over her back, the blade seeming to ignite like the sun in the air. I chose to draw my bow and kept an arrow under my finger, praying Will and Kimball's lessons remained fresh in my memory.

"What're you two lookin' at?" one of the bigger ones demanded. I dutifully noted either a crack at my height, or that they didn't even consider me an obstacle. He took a threatening step toward us. Will didn't react. I flinched. Nobody noticed.

"These ugly-ass guys on the road," Sira replied, pointing her sword right at the man. "Freakin' hilarious. Wish you could see 'em."

One of them chuckled. Most of them just cracked their knuckles, and I wondered if they got the joke at all. "Girl has a mouth on her," one of them said. "Wonder if that mouth does more."

A few more of them guffawed. The way their intentions played out across their faces lit an angry spark in my chest, and I took a stride forward, levelling an arrow to point directly at the speaker's throat. He only chuckled throatily, holding my gaze. I wondered if he would really see the arrow coming.

Will slid out in front of me, perhaps saving me from a movement I could regret. "You would do better to focus on level opponents. Picking out the youngest fighter among us speaks volumes of your skill." He gestured easily toward them with two fingers, the other hand gripping his lance rigidly. "Come now. Which of you is foolish enough to try me first?"

The man chuckled eerily, jabbing his thumb at the girl behind them, frozen stiff. "You think we give a rat's ass about some fight? Could whallop a boy like you in my sleep, but these kids are money. A boy for horse keeping sells well. And a pretty girl?" His laughter turned sharp. "Similar to horses, but for the quiet of a man's bedroom."

Will's voice came out terse and stretched. "Stay behind me, Ryoku," he murmured. I didn't think he would strike first. He proved me wrong, and sprang forward with his lance as easily as walking. The men hollered and fanned out, all drawing weapons of their own. One of them lunged at Will with a hand-axe clutched in his meaty fist, and their weapons clashed in the midst of the street.

The side street of Harohto held little action, but I noticed anyone who kept about started to quickly evacuating as the fight began. Sira, who started to laugh with the promise of a good fight, rushed to help as a second man went after Will. Their swords clashed, and Sira's weapon forced the enemy sword to the ground like lightning.

The girl behind the thugs looked terrified. She might have been able to escape now that a brawl started, but she looked too afraid to move. If one of them started after her, we might not be able to stop them. Her snowy-colored eyes darted between them frantically. I started to wonder if she was worried for herself, or for us.

Will's opponent nearly forced him down, but Sira, forcing her own target to the ground, lunged and cleaved Will's opponent from shoulder to hip with an enraged scream. He cried out, eyes bugged, and his weapon clashed to the ground. The released force sent Will's lance straight through him. I cringed back, but still saw the splash of blood.

At the fall of their leader, all the remaining thugs swarmed forward with a clamor. They split up – three after Will, and three after Sira. My heart hammered in my chest. How could they handle three? Shouldn't they have abandoned ship when their leader went down?

Will rushed to defend himself. He thrust a sword astray with a bold lunge, then danced back and knocked the second assailant back with the butt of his lance. He spun it in a quick arc and came about to cross weapons with the third. At his side, Sira slammed the full weight of her weapon against an oncoming sword, knocking the vibrating weapon into the air. The powerful strike forced her into an awkward back step to dodge the second attacker, but she recovered enough to ram the pommel of her sword into the third.

I had to do something. If I didn't act, my two Guardians might be overwhelmed here. All it took was one half-second too late to block, and one could go down. I put aside my mediocre amounts of skill and refocused on my arrow, taking aim on one of the thugs running at Will. When I took aim, though, the thug saw me and turned my way, grinning in an ugly way. I lost the element of surprise, which was really about the only element I had.

As he advanced on me, I panicked, and shut my eyes as I released the arrow. In retrospect, that moment of panic wasn't the best of ideas. The arrow missed its mark and struck the leg of one thug battling Sira, inciting a scream of pain. I cursed, stuffing away my bow and yanked out my knife.

I blocked his club as it came at me. Sparks flew from nails embedded in the wood weapon. Whatever force I'd anticipated from this huge man's swing, it wasn't like this. My knife became my lifeline.

I caught a warning glance from Will, but he couldn't untangle himself from combat to help me. Sira fought like a dog, Sinistra screaming through the air like a monster and knocking every blow aside with all her strength. One of them was the one I'd struck with an arrow, but he somehow kept on fighting. I started to wonder how I thought we could handle this.

I had to move. Summoning every last drop of willpower I had, I forced myself to the ground. Dropping my weight against his club sent the weapon sailing over my head, where it struck and destroyed a patch of cobblestone road. I used my moment of momentum to swing myself around in a way I'd gleaned from Will's fight in the bar, slamming my legs into his with all my might. If I hadn't caught him by surprise, it'd be like hitting a tree with an arrow, but I lucked out. He crashed down like a rock.

Living off adrenaline, I lurched toward Sira and jumped in the way of one of her attackers, blocking his sword with my upraised knife. This time I was ready for the force, and I kept his weapon at bay with both hands on my knife. Even the odds, I thought. If Sira and Will each only had to fight two, then we could clear this out way faster. Unfortunately, it meant I had to deal with two as well, and I wasn't sure I could.

Sira continued her battle against the remaining two like a storm of fire, her blade screaming through the air as easily as I swung my knife. I caught a glance from Will. If he realized what I'd done to even the odds, he didn't appear fully approving of it.

I tried to lash out with a kick at my enemy, but he stepped out of the way easily. I didn't anticipate when he took a hand off his sword and grabbed my arm. My stomach lurched. The thug's ugly mug spread into a grin. The one I'd knocked down was off the ground now, and he approached, whacking his club against his open palm with a menacing glare.

A blue flash lit the air, burning lights into my eyes. It came with a strange, sweeping sort of noise, and a crackling noise like ice giving way underfoot.

Before my very eyes, a blue beam shot from afar and struck my assailant in the shoulder. He let go of my arm in a panic, trying to shake something off. I caught a glimpse of it. Ice was thatching its way across his shoulder, increasing to envelop most of his arm and back through his meager, torn clothes. I stared incredulously. Was that… magic?

I saw the culprit. In the midst of all the panic, the young girl had stepped forward, and now she held up her staff in both hands before her. A blue gem similar to the one in my oak staff gleamed upon the head of hers.

Luckily for me, I wasn't the only one to freeze up, and I gathered myself in time to lash out at my second opponent, who'd been staring at his friend incredulously while ice latched onto him. My knife struck true and bit into his side. He stumbled away, dropping his club as he grabbed his side.

I turned away victoriously, but the thugs had other ideas for me. A sword came swinging out of nowhere. I rolled away and it struck the road, spraying rocks and sparks everywhere. The thug that was quickly becoming an icicle swung at me in full rage. I stepped away again, this time just out of range of his weapon. I felt the wind of his slash, and I thought I could almost smell blood upon his weapon from how closely it cut.

Another blue flash illuminated the area. I saw the blue beam, and it spun out like a web as it fell upon my other opponent – the man I'd cut had been clambering to his feet, his club retrieved and ready to strike again. Now he fell, and ice spread across him with haste. Now I owed the girl, and I was supposed to be saving her.

My enraged opponent dropped his assault on me, turning his gaze to the girl with her staff held up. He, too, realized she was doing more damage than I was. She dropped her staff under the man's glare, clearly terrified.

The thug flexed, and the ice encasing most of his shoulders shattered, crumbling to the ground like broken glass. Freed of its effects, he advanced on the girl.

I had to act fast, and the girl's magic gave me an idea. Stowing away my knife, I pulled out my oak staff from my belt. I hadn't brought out the weapon since I unconsciously used it against the Keeper, if Will and Sira told the truth about that. Truth be told, I was a little nervous about the item. Kimball and Will both warned me that it could sap my energy to use it. If I wasn't careful, it could kill me.

It had to serve its money's worth, right? Will had bought this weapon specifically for me. If anything, that meant my stalwart friend believed I could use it. I'd thought him foolish with his money at first, but he was careful and wise about his spending later. No, Will believed it would do well in my hands. So it had to, right?

This time, as I raised the staff, I felt a strange spark in my hands. It was almost like numbness, a course of strange, warm energy rushing up my arms, but it made my fingers twitch. The energy seemed to flow in a pattern along my skin. Symbols, I thought. Images of the sun, of fire. They seemed to crawl from the staff, along my arms and into my mind as I suddenly envisioned them quite clearly. I hung onto those images and clutched my staff tightly. Was this it? Magic?

The sensation arrived with clarity through all my senses. It came with a dusty sort of smell, like an ancient library untouched for decades, its pages inviting eager hands and minds. A sound hung in the air that felt like it was only for my ears, like a thousand ancient voices whispering encouragement for the elements. My tongue felt thick with ash and heat.

The final sense came with a savage *whoosh.* From the red stone upon my staff, flames leapt up as easily as the campfire in the woods, but with unprecedented velocity, like we'd thrown our clothes into it. Heat lapsed through my entire body, leaving me oddly winded and cold after the flames shot forward, soaring to a height well above my head – and crashed straight into my target.

The regret came instantly, washing away every bit of glee and wonder I felt at the magic. The thug let out a banal, unhinged scream as flames enveloped him, bringing him straight to the ground. Regret washed through me like the girl cast her icy magic on me, settling like a pit in my stomach, knowing that I just sentenced this man to death.

I rushed past the fallen man and hurried to the girl as she fumbled for her staff, running justifications repeatedly in my head. If we hadn't intervened, they would have done much worse to this girl. If I hadn't fought with my all, then they would likely send me to Orden in exchange for that sizeable bounty. I wouldn't be able to save Chris *or* Roxanne that way, not like this. As a Defender, this was my responsibility. As much as the thought repulsed me, I might have to do this repeatedly, but it would be to save others. To keep such a soul alive and in good health. I had to.

"Are you okay?" I asked when I reached her, just as her trembling hands found her staff. "I hope we arrived just in time."

Then she levelled her staff at me. I stepped back, stunned, but she cried out, "Ryoku, watch out!"

Wow, was I ever a legendary hero at this point. I clued in at the last second what she actually meant, and spun around. The girl unleashed another blast of cold energy past me as the second thug I'd been facing ran at me, club raised. I strayed awfully close to her magic, and it felt like opening a door into the dead of winter before it shot through the air toward the incoming enemy.

However, the same trick might not work all the time. He threw up a piece of a leather doublet, possibly either torn from him or his fallen friend, and the magic struck it in his stead. I heard the girl gasp behind me.

Alright, I thought, and stowed my staff away in favor of my knife again. This fight was getting old.

My last opponent fell upon me. I ducked under his oncoming assault and rammed my elbow into his chest, inciting a pained growl. His hand caught me by the shoulder and sent me to the ground. My back scraped the cobblestone. Frantically, I lashed out with my knife, but the thug danced out of the way. I jumped to my feet, readjusting my grip on my knife.

We circled around one another. I was careful not to let him past me. All it might take was one hand on the girl behind me, and this fight would be for naught. I needed to settle this.

"Hey!"

A voice came from afar. I partially turned toward the noise, but dared not look away from my opponent. An object sailed into my vision. As the thug rushed at me, my other hand unconsciously grabbed the object. Was it the lid to a trash can?

Haphazardly, I used the item to block the club, causing a resonating smack that jolted my arm. Still, it was better than taking the club straight to my arm. He struck again, once, twice. Each blow rammed the lid in my hand, and I almost lost my grip on it. Using the added defense of the lid, I lashed out with my other hand. The knife bit into skin. The thug let out a savage growl and lashed our again. I blocked with more purpose this time, using enough force that it made my enemy stagger backwards.

Getting bolder, I pushed out again with the garbage can lid. I managed to use enough force to send the man to the ground. My heart leapt up in my chest, and I lunged, forgetting my temporary shield – and stopped short.

An arm came around the thug's throat from behind, trapping him. Another arm grabbed his and broke his grip, knocking his club away. A second later, and the thug was on the ground – Will loomed over him like a hero, pinning the last enemy to the ground with the butt of his lance. His chest was rising and falling steadily, his skin flushed, his hair tousled, and a wild light in his sapphire eyes. Sira was right behind him, Sinistra steadily dripping blood from its face as she fought to catch her breath.

"It is done," Will said vehemently. "Your friends are all dead. Would you press us to have you join them?"

Instantly the thug started screaming profanities at Will, who appeared unfazed. Rather than follow through, Will stepped aside, and a pair of Harohto guards stepped in to apprehend the thug, dragging him away.

That was around when I noticed the crowd. The streets were empty last time I'd looked, but now people flocked. Women, children, and men lined every nook of the street around us. Many of them were cheering, applauding, whistling. In my focus, I'd been entirely deaf to it. Will and Sira finished off their own opponents just in time to step in. If nothing else, I could be glad I didn't have to take another life as the guards led the last thug away. He screamed bitterly, enraged, and I saw his glare long after the guards dragged him past the crowd.

"You did well, kid," Will told me, clasping my shoulder firmly. "A fair step from your bar brawl. I wonder, if I let you assist me back then, if you could have done as well as you did here."

I gave him a sheepish smile. I didn't think I did well. I just survived, barely. "I couldn't have done it without you," I told him squarely. "If the bar would have ended badly, then this would have been a horror story."

Will chuckled. "Perhaps. But it is only my job as your Guardian, my friend."

"Are you a Defender?"

The girl spoke from behind me, drawing my attention to her. She looked uneasy around all the attention, her staff still held tightly in her grip. This close, I realized she was probably around my age, dressed in a white skirt that reached her knees and a low-cut pink shirt that ruffled around her neckline. A thin pink hair band tucked most of her silvery hair from her face. Was that normal in Harohto? I'd never seen anyone *close* to my age with silver or white hair, except Kioru. Kioru was so strange that I'd come to accept that more readily.

"Yep, that's him," Sira replied as she approached us, looking the girl over. "We're his Guardians. He's new, but not all bad, surprisingly. What's your name?"

Coming from Sira, that was like praising my name in the streets. The young girl gave me an odd look, as though waiting for my reassurance that my friends were okay. I gave her the slightest nod. Then she said, quite softly, "M-My name is Lusari Atella. I'm... I am a mage from the Harohto Capital Magical Academy. I'm afraid I've been absent for a few weeks, though, and I'm a little rusty. I'm just glad I was able to help."

Sira nodded to her. "A mage, huh? Well you did alright out there. I'm Sira Jessura." She jabbed her thumb to Will, who was letting Sira do all the talking for some reason, his gaze somewhere else. "The guy with the spear's Willy-boy. Likes to be called Will Ramun, though, for some reason."

Will sighed, and Lusari giggled. The sound was like wind chimes. "Willy-boy it is, then."

"Please do not," Will said sheepishly, scratching his head.

"And this is our Defender, Ryoku Dragontalen," Sira introduced me by way of poking me with her thumb. "I'll let you know if I find a better name for him."

Lusari smiled at me, and curtsied. "I would eagerly await that."

The four of us turned toward the great-amassed crowd. People still cheered at us. Men whooped and sang our names in praise. I wasn't sure how knew them in the first place. I thought I saw a young girl swooning over Sira, but she retreated behind her mother's skirts. Women were fawning over Will, who absently sheathed his lance over his back and stared out over the crowd.

"Would you?" Sira asked shrewdly. "Maybe we can talk. We've been sorta lookin' for a mage, if that's something you're interested in. You handled yourself pretty well back there, and probably saved our little Defender."

Lusari blushed heavily. "A-Are you serious?"

"Only if you are," Sira replied. "But we got stuff to do. Tag along, if you want, and we'll talk. Maybe Willy-boy's the one you'll like better."

I thought Lusari looked a little timid before Will, but he was easily the friendliest among us. Moreover, had it not been for him, I might not have won in the last part of my fight.

A thought occurred to me, and I scanned the crowd. I wasn't focused, but clearly, somebody from the crowd had tossed me my makeshift shield. Without that, I wouldn't have survived a minute. I looked for signs among the sea of faces, and saw something near the back of the street. A man in a brown cloak, his white hair like snow beneath his hood. There was no mistaking it. He gave me a curt smile, and vanished into the thick of the crowd with a wave of his cloak.

We had to track him down, I realized. He was the only other one stated by name on my wanted poster. If he would just let me catch up, we could help each other!

I tried to grab Sira's attention, but she didn't follow. Instead, she grabbed my arm and thrust it into the air with hers. The crowd erupted into a rancorous cheer, jumping into the air and shouting our names.

Will came around to my other side and took my hand, mimicking Sira's motion.

"This is it, friend! The beginning of our journey – a heroic Defender and his Guardians!"

"I think you have it backwards," I murmured, but he didn't seem to hear me.

"Now we're talkin'!" Sira declared excitedly. "This is what it's gonna be like from now on! The heat of battle, the roar of a cheering crowd, prevailing over evil!"

She gave me the most gleeful, almost child-like grin I could have imagined from her. With her tone, it was almost euphoric to her. I gulped, adopting a shaky smile. What Sira found exciting only made my heart tremble. I still saw the burnt corpse of my first kill, even as guards carted off the extinguished body, and those of the men Will and Sira had killed.

If it were all to be like this, how would I ever survive?

SCENE THREE: A DAUNTING TASK

...Of Act Two: Guardianship

In the eyes of Ryoku Dragontalen, we are in Harohto Capital City, in the world of Harohto. It is mid afternoon On November 7th, 2017

"You made it."

Will nodded, looking upon his friends with worry. Of course, it wasn't his entire squad. Out of the missing seven members, only three remained: Oliver, Leif, and Alex. Oliver lay on the infirmary bed, his chest and head heavily wrapped in bloody bandages, but his dark eyes looked up at us weakly. Leif and Alex sat with him, both in much better condition. Alex only had a few scrapes and bandages across his face that I could see, while Leif's arm hung in a brace.

Will took a seat next to his friend in the bed. I sat with him, while the others stood around the room.

"What happened to you? I only thought you went off to scout, but then we heard screams..."

Oliver stared out the window upon the bright city outside. "The Keeper," he murmured. "It fell upon us like a storm. Alex and Leif came running from down the path, having heard a strange noise. Julian and Ray were the first. They..." He dropped his gaze. "I let them down. I am the most senior of our squad next to Lancet, and I failed them."

Will, Leif, and Alex all put hands on his shoulder. "You could not have done anything more than us," Alex insisted. "Will, we think someone else angered it. I talked to the guards at the city gates. They say the raiders have cut down a massive section of the woods and made camp there! If I were that beast, I would be enraged!"

Will nodded. "We thought the same. Other than that, the forest is quiet. We traveled up to the central plateau and saw everything." He turned his attention to Oliver, watching his senior squad member for a long moment. "If there is blame to be had, it is with me. I only thought to let Ryoku rest, and you could scout out a path ahead."

"Nay, the blame is not with you, either," Leif replied, to my relief. He gave me a small smile. "He is here with you. A lesser man would not dare to come here and face something he may find guilt in. We chose our charge wisely."

"I agree." Oliver grimaced at me. "In a forest where four of us lost our lives, you kept our boy Will safe. For that, I would owe you an eternal gratitude."

I gave Will a look. "I think it's the other way around."

He raised a brow in return. "You do recall falling in the river and everything after, right? I was worried your memory would be soured. That is a long tale, Alex. The important thing is that we intend to settle things with the Keeper. For that, I would ask your assistance once more."

"You mean... you want to go after that thing?" Leif questioned.

"That might not be necessary." Will took a seat in the chair next to Oliver. After a moment where he looked like he was going to dive into an explanation, he caught Sira's glance. "R-Right, of course. Fellows, I have yet to introduce my new comrades. This is Sira Jessura, and Lusari Atella. Speaking of... Lusari, you can come in."

Our newest friend hung in the doorway, apparently quite nervous of the room. Sira had offered her a place among us, and so she came. Along the way, she explained that she had nowhere to go. Her mother and father were victims of the latest raids upon the Capital, her reasoning for her tardy attendance at the magic school – only a week prior to our arrival. Eventually the rent for her family home would pile up, and she, with no current employment and none who might hire the girl with the silver hair, would wind up homeless before long.

Before arriving here, a few of the city guard escorted us to the town hall, where a man by the name of Governor Thorne offered us a tidy bounty as thanks for defeating those thugs. According to him, the city sat upon its head with the recent raids. Thugs and brigands thought they could get away with anything with the guard force stretched thin.

"A-Are these your friends?" Lusari asked Will, still quite hesitant to enter the room.

Alex beamed at her and strode forth gallantly. "Milady! Alex Retton is my name, a man of the Syaoto Army, at your beck and call!"

Lusari flinched back. Leif pulled Alex away, cringing. "Alex Retton is but a novice in the army, Miss, before you decide to file a harassment file on us. I am Leif Cartos, a median, and akin in ranking to your friend Will."

"And I am Oliver Rouge," Oliver waved from the bed. "High-ranking soldier. I apologize that I cannot rise to greet you properly. You... are local to Harohto?"

"I'm not," Sira replied, raising a hand. "Ordenite."

The gazes of all three soldiers turned sharp. Leif even reached for the gladius at his hip, but Will stopped him with a firm look. "Still yourself. She is an ex-soldier of their army, and she is a friend. She saved both of our lives on the way here."

Alex relaxed easily. "Oh, you are a friend, then. Sorry, Sira. We have had nothing if not ill encounters with Orden soldiers."

"Noted," Sira replied, appearing hardly affected by their reactions. "Consider me Ordenite in name only. And besides, you're gonna need my help with Willy-boy's plans."

Now all eyes turned to Will. Leif chuckled, nudging his friend. "Hear what she calls you? Have you picked up a girlfriend in your travels?"

Before Will could even reply, Sira stood behind Leif's chair, cracking her knuckles. "The hell did you just say?"

"N-Nothing!" Leif proclaimed, dodging away from her in his chair. "Nothing at all! Say, Will, what is this plan you speak of?"

"Coward," Sira muttered, but she stepped back.

Will slammed his palm with his fist, startling the already on-edge Leif. "We attack the raider camp!" he declared. "If they are the problem which riles up the Keeper, then we may strike down two birds with one stone."

"By ourselves?" Alex asked. Despite the idea, he didn't sound nervous at all – the idea clearly invigorated him. "The camp is massive – we caught a glimpse of it on our travels. Perhaps you saw it as well. Could we truly hope to cause any damage?"

"They are also raiders," Leif argued. "Starved men, mostly peasants turned bandit. I doubt many of them could stand against our expertise."

"It could be wise to reach out to Captain Lancet, as well," Oliver added gravely. His words made Will, Leif, and Alex forget their vigor and their shoulders dropped. "He will not be happy with what happened to us. Saving face now could prove better for us in the long run."

I saw Will's reaction. His mouth opened to reply, and I knew the heaviness of the words that would come out – but Alex cut in, punching the air in his bravado. "Lancet can wait! We have an important job to do – we must avenge our people! Even a snide, berating dog like him can—"

Oliver gave him a sharp look. "Only because he is not here can you possibly get away with such words, Alex. Mind your place."

"This could end up paying off if we take down the raider camp." Leif crossed his arms, staring at the ground in thought. "Say what you will about Lancet. We bring him back a tidy sum, and he would hardly bat an eye at our reduced numbers."

Oliver laughed dryly. "I could not disagree. Still, with that in mind, how are we to proceed?"

Will looked to me, so I stepped forward. "I can talk to the city guard. With their help, we might be able to actually do something."

Oliver frowned. "Could we, though? Surely you have seen Harohto's forces. They tire, and stretch like paper used to make a bridge. Harohto does not believe in honor like Syaoto. They do not have the manpower, or the initiative for others to train their entire lives and join the army. In truth, much of their militia is roughly-trained men."

"Perhaps I could be of some assistance."

All heads turned toward the door. A man stood there in Harohto armor, a medium helm tucked under one arm. Shaggy brown hair fell across his shoulders. He had brown eyes outlined with dark circles. His face, albeit young, kept lines of stress and scars that pockmarked his skin.

"Mosten Clienne, captain of the city guard, at your service." He bowed shortly toward Oliver. "My condolences for the shape you're in, but I can tell from your wounds what you faced."

Oliver nodded back. "Not at all. I apologize for my words about your people."

"Don't," Mosten replied curtly. "They're not a far cry from the truth." He turned his gaze, then, toward me. "I saw your lot in the Governor's office. I apologize for following you. In normal circumstances, I might have acted more honorably. I'm afraid times are tough."

"No need to apologize," I told him. "What brings you here?"

He straightened, folding his arms behind his back. "Word has spread of your arrival. A new Defender does not see Harohto's walls very often these days. Of the few that do, they hardly make such an impact as you have. Word says you seek to hunt the Keeper. In turn, you're seeking to attack the raider fort."

"Could you offer us any assistance?" Will asked.

Mosten's jaw tightened. "Aye, but your friend is right. Our forces stretch nearly to breaking. The raiders attack our walls day and night. Some break through into the city and raze buildings to the ground. They beat our people, slay our livestock, and rifle through our resources like we grew it all for them. The more they attack our city, the more join them. Many don't have a choice. Many are orphaned by them, and we cannot support that many mouths with no source of income."

The words were clearly getting to him, and he clenched his fists into his helm. "We have little option left, and even littler men for it. I can spare you a small group. Perhaps fifteen or so men, including myself."

Leif frowned disapprovingly. "Fifteen men? What are we to do with that?"

Sira shrugged wryly. "Walk up to their gates and nicely ask them to stop?"

Oliver, however, scratched his chin airily. "We *could* cause quite a ruckus with a smaller group. If you and your men have some knowledge of the area, perhaps we could use the Old Forest to our advantage. Under the cover of night, we could burn their food supply. Perhaps even torch their tents and cause damage to their camp. If they are truly active at night, we might be able to hit them where it counts without putting ourselves in danger."

"Is that not a little... cowardly?" Alex sounded disappointed.

Oliver raised a brow. "Cowardly? Well, Alex, if you think you could waltz into the front gates and do battle with a force of thousands, then go ahead, but you would not risk any more of my men."

Alex's head fell. Reading the room, I felt like all the Syaoto soldiers wanted nothing more than just that. With their expertise, it almost seemed possible, but I knew that was a foolish notion.

"This might sate our old friend, the Keeper," Sira agreed softly. "This'll take a lot longer than just beating the crap outta the monster, but this might be the only way." She turned to me. "What do you think, Ryoku? This plan sound good to you?"

I mulled over it for a moment. Part of me wanted what Alex and the others desired: to fight the raider force head-on like a proper battalion. Still, I knew it would cost lives. I didn't want more lives on my hands if I could help it. Like Sira said, this might be the best way to avenge the others against the Keeper. Defeating a timeless beast like that could prove impossible in the end.

I caught Lusari's glance. She stood with her hands folded by the door, still ultimately nervous of everyone in the room. Despite that, she had a determination in her eyes that she made plain to me. Lusari had lost her family to the raids recently. If I wanted the mage-girl to accompany us, to help us get to the next world, then I would do right by her. This might not bring her parents back, but it would strike a blow against the wretches who did it.

"What happens when we attack the camp?" I asked. "What if we torched their food, so they just attacked here and gained it all back?"

"I will double the city's defenses during our mission," Mosten told me. "If we hold out the walls for long enough, they'll hand themselves over. We imprison the worst of them, set them to work on the fields of the lives they robbed, and we start replenishing our stores before winter sets in on us. Even then, we have our ways to acquire resources. Winter in the Capital lasts until mid-spring, and we are more than accustomed to providing in the harsh circumstances."

"You have thought this out," Oliver commended.

Mosten nodded. "It has been a plan with no action for some time. With your help, it can come to fruition."

"Then we'll do it," I agreed. "If we act wisely, we can avoid an all-out brawl and end this."

I was surprised, looking around at the others, to see how much weight my words carried. The Defender supported them. Alex and Leif exchanged eager looks. Sira grinned cordially at me. Lusari flashed me a private smile. Will squeezed my shoulder.

"I owe you already, for even considering my task," Mosten regarded me gravely. "I assure you that I would not request something impossible of you. We've considered the angles. I can send out a few men right away to find the best entry point, but I already have a good idea of where to start."

Will turned to face him. "Let us know. Even if the specifics change, we would have an idea of where to begin."

"Very well," Mosten agreed. He finally entered the room and leaned against the window, arms crossed over his chest. "To the eastern end of the plains. Right along the edge of the Border Range, there's a trailhead leading into the Old Forest. Path cuts right down to the plateau. More importantly, circles right around where they've made camp along the higher plains. Somewhere along there has to be the breaking line. If we take out maybe one guard team, it could be a free run to the heart of the camp."

Sira nodded approvingly. "So we just bust in, take some down, burn their supplies, and whatever else we can do, huh? Fine by me."

Will turned to Leif. "Can you join us? How fares your arm?"

Leif rotated his shoulder in its socket, pulling at the sling he kept his arm in."You bet. I only had a bit of a sprain going, so they made me wear this. Not the arm I injured back in the woods a few weeks ago, either, so... Count me in."

Will looked to Oliver then, sadly, who smiled up at him. "I have to sit this one out," Oliver said. "You would be the next in charge. Given your stance in Bytold and all you have done since, I believe I have little to say. You could be better suited for the role than I ever was. Certainly far more than our commanding officer."

Will smiled tightly, clasping Oliver's shoulder. "I will lead us to victory in your stead. Hold tight until we return, alright?"

Oliver nodded sombrely. There was a moment of silence between the two of them. I wondered if Will was going to tell him, then, that he planned not to return to Lancet. Would his friends still treat him the same way? Would Oliver, who treated Will like an equal, still do so if he knew he had decided to become my Guardian? Would Alex and Leif still look up to him like an older brother?

Mosten nodded to us. "Right, then. I will go and set some things up. At nightfall, meet me at the northern trailhead I mentioned. Come prepared."

He shook the hands of the Syaoto soldiers and I. He gently touched Lusari's hand in a respectful gesture. He hesitated before Sira, and the swordstress stuck out an irritable hand to shake. Smiling, Mosten took it – and returned with a reddened hand. Grimacing, the soldier took his leave, and our company followed suit for the last of our preparations.

SCENE FOUR: ENCAMPMENT OF THE RAIDERS

...Of Act Two: Guardianship

In the eyes of Ryoku Dragontalen, we are in Harohto Sunset Plain, in the world of Harohto. It is early evening On November 7th, 2017.

"Well, here we are."

Will reaffirmed himself with a quick glance at the map, using a small light shimmering in Lusari's palm. He nodded again, whether to confirm to himself or the rest of us that we were in the right place. A red circle on our map marked the spot. Next to it, a larger blue circle embodied our target: the raider camp.

I could already see it through the trees. Logging and clear-cutting marred the hills like old scars, where dark tents sat in their stead. Some clumped quite close together, some even pitched onto one another in a form of chaos only raiders could allow. Even though Mosten confirmed a large part of their forces leaving before sundown, it still looked like hundreds of men swarmed the camp, squatting around campfires with weapons in their lap, or else strutting around like they owned the place. Pikes stuck out of the ground every few feet, bearing black flags that hung listlessly in the windless night. Even as we watched, one flag caught fire, and a few raiders rushed to put out the flame, clambering over one another in their effort.

"Stupid bastards," Sira muttered angrily, but she chuckled nonetheless. "If we left them, they might cook each other alive."

Mosten laughed quietly. "If only."

I shuddered a little, wrapping my cloak tighter around me. A wintery chill started to settle in; I longed for the warmth of the little campfire Will, Sira, and I made back under the protective boughs of the Old Forest the other night. We were here now, though, squatting in the trees and waiting for our signal to attack. Only Sira seemed warm, like the promise of a fight radiated heat from her.

A crow cawed loudly near us, and I jumped a mile. My hand found the hilt of my knife in wariness. Of course, our attempt to try my hand at a sword seemed to end in failure again. I couldn't keep a grip on a weapon much longer than my knife, and so I kept it. Sometimes, the weapon on my hip seemed to offer me some solace. It was one of the first things I learned in the spirit realm, and it sometimes reminded me that this wasn't my place. It made me think of my own world, where I currently sat in bed poring over a book I'd read a hundred times, my mind wholly on my task here. If anyone else thought it odd that I could be present in both worlds at once, they didn't remark. I never let my attention lapse on my task here, though I might space out a little more in my world.

Sira was staring at me, her eyes on my knife I gripped tightly. A Guardian's instinct, maybe. The two of them had seemed much more in-tuned to me since they placed their vows. Sira wordlessly gestured to look ahead.

A ways down the hill, at least two dozen men began to make their way upon the hill, seated upon half-starved ponies, some of them on foot. This was the main scouting force. Mosten suggested we take it out before we enter the camp to ensure we wouldn't have our escape route blocked. Still, we had to do it quickly and efficiently. A stray yell could capture the attention of the camp. We'd wind up cooked for sure in that case.

Will hand-signalled in the air. I thought nobody else would see it, but the resulting sound of quieted footsteps followed. The soldiers around us shifted, crouching in the trees on either side of the path. Will drew his lance as noiselessly as a natural part of the night, and

Sira followed suit. I tried to mimic them with my bow, but the bow clipped against its holster, the arrow twanged quietly against my bow. Even those telltale sounds fell dead to the night. Lusari knelt next to me, her staff in hand. There was a determination to her eyes I hadn't predicted.

The sound of hooves drew ever closer, until it finally crested, and the sounds turned flat as they traveled along the path. One of them jeered about some woman he'd had his way with that day, and the rest laughed like owls.

I didn't imagine the reactions of that statement until I felt something ice-cold pass me. A bluish bolt, as silent as wind through the trees, shot past me and struck the speaking raider in the chest. The raider let out a shocked cry, tumbling off his horse in an attempt to knock away the ice forming across his chest.

I turned to Lusari in surprise, but the girl's chin kept stubborn even as a tear or two stained her cheeks.

The raider didn't make another sound. Forced from hiding, Leif leapt from the trees and buried his sword hilt-deep into the raider. He was the first into the clearing, and he straightened, looking the dozen or more raiders in the face, and smirked.

One of them raised his hand and was about to shout, but Sira's mighty Sinistra broke through the man from his shoulder, cleaving him in two seamlessly. Mosten was upon the next man, snapping his neck in his arms. Will vaulted past him with the aid of his lance, and buried the same weapon in the throat of another man about to let out a telltale scream. Alex sprang out of the shadows next to him and grunted with effort as he ran through another man with his longsword. For a moment, Alex looked proud – but then he looked down at his crumpled enemy on the ground, and ghosts appeared on his face. Had Will's young friend ever actually killed before?

Then, in rhythm with our forces, Lusari and I braved the open.

My first arrow kept truer than my last attempt at archery. When the raider fell to the ground, though, I felt my chest whither. The target rolled over on the ground – a dirty, rugged young man hardly older than me, with worn, sparse clothing. Even given his youth, his pockmarked face sported a spotted beard. His lifeless eyes stared up at me with accusations.

I tried to force myself into mental armor. We'd known already that the raiders were a ragged lot, forced to fight and steal for their living. It didn't excuse the lives they took. This man had laughed about a man forcing a woman to his will. They all had. This young man could have attacked Harohto himself already, killing dozens, or could have even held the sword that killed Lusari's father. Either way, he'd taken more lives that he was worth. That number remained the same for all: one. Now I had taken two lives.

The sounds of battle around me sounded like they were upon pillows. Not one raider uttered another noise as the soldiers pursued them, eager to exact judgement upon those who'd killed fellow soldiers, brothers, wives, neighbours and all.

As I saw Leif impale another man on his blade, I wondered about the prospect of death. Though we were in the spirit realm, as I knew it, these spirit-born were able to die. Where did these raiders go beyond? Was there a whole other realm for spirits from here, or were they reborn elsewhere in a form of reincarnation? Would these raiders live a better life, or continue to bloody their weapons? Maybe the cycle would reverse, and the raider Leif just killed might be reborn a toddler in my world. If that was true, I felt it was a fate worse than ultimate death.

I tried to notch another arrow to my bow, but my next target fell victim to Sinistra crashing through the shadows. Will struck a raider on horseback. I thought he was still alive, watching him with my bow until the horse galloped, and the man toppled off like an abandoned puppet. Searching for my next target, I wondered if this was how they thought. A methodical rhythm between kills.

My next target fell victim to Lusari's ice. The older, bearded raider toppled from his horse, ice catching the moonlight like crystals, but he found his way to his feet. As he stood there, icicles thatching across his chest like spider silk being strung before me, I saw how dreadfully thin he was. These weren't thugs like we fought earlier. They weren't men who lived at the bar and ate richly to strengthen their muscles and drink until their bellies swelled. These were poor, starved men, forced to kill to stay alive.

Before I had fully comprehended this new thought, steel burst through his chest from behind. Mosten rolled out of the shadows, yanking his rigid blade from the man's chest with a forceful tug. Blood sprayed from the raider's frozen chest as he succumbed into a block of blood-splattered, jagged ice.

My self-proclaimed armor trickled away as the battle sped by. I loosed an arrow with no target, trying to fight the sick feeling in my chest. By some ill luck, a raider running at Will stepped in the path of the arrow, and it sliced a jagged line down the length of his bare arm. He uttered a gasp of pain, and Leif dove from the cover of darkness, finishing the man with a single strike.

Before I could set after another target, Sira's crimson sword shot through the night like a stray flame, swallowing the next raider. The most experienced fighters like Sira, Will, and Mosten needed no second strike to finish off their target. Their blades were sudden death: instantaneous and hopefully less painful.

I found it within me to shoot a last arrow, landing in the throat of an unsuspecting raider. Lusari finished him off with a burst of icy magic, and that was the last man. The brawl was over, and I was at least partially responsible for three of their demises. Sira, Will, and Mosten had likely taken out most of them. Some of the horses stampeded down the trail, now without a master. My stomach lurched as the trained soldiers took off after even them, and soon they laid down the path with their fallen riders.

"All in a day's work," Sira muttered, dusting off her hands. "What was that, a few dozen? A good chunk of their force. What next?"

"I'd think that's time to drop your weapons."

For a moment, I thought the second voice belonged to one of our soldiers. Then I saw the steel glinting against Sira's throat. She cleared her throat, annoyed, as a man appeared from the shadows behind her, guiding her by a weapon to the throat. I felt cold steel appear at my own neck, and I straightened.

They surrounded us.

SCENE FIVE: RESCUE?

...Of Act Two: Guardianship

In the eyes of Ryoku Dragontalen, we are in The Raider's Camp, in the world of Harohto. It is early evening On November 7th, 2017.

"What do you hope to accomplish?"

The captain struck Will for his question. He grunted in pain, clutching his chest, but a glare at the man in question showed he wasn't about to let up. Mosten spat at the raider captain's feet. Sira instinctively reached for her sword. Not only was it absent, but trying to move only made the rope binding us even tighter. She grumbled something about not being able to believe someone snuck up on her. I could relate.

Through our controlled attack, the raiders hardly uttered a noise. We put effort into ensuring they had no time to scream out for assistance. Except for...

I caught Lusari's glance across the room. She had her back to Will's, next to Sira and me. Even if her attack earlier alerted them, I found it hard to blame her. Hearing the raiders talk about their victims would have been triggering for her. Still, here we were – trapped in their camp. They had Mosten, Leif, and Alex bound up in the other corner, and I wasn't sure where they'd taken the others.

The captain gave Will a snide look. He looked much better fed than the rest of the army. He kept his beard neatly trimmed, his armor finely polished, and his dark eyes glimmered with contempt. It was clear how their systems worked.

"Oh, and don't think I didn't notice yer mug." The raider captain was looking at me with a sinister gaze. "There's a good bounty on yer head, so the men say. That sort of coin'll feed us for years! We can build a whole new Capital. Give and take as we please – no need to fight over scraps, then. Some of ye could join us. As the help, o'course."

I grimaced. Word must have spread about my bounty. The petitioner, Orden, might be what held Chris captive. I wanted to get there of my own accord, not strapped up and shipped for a bounty. How would I get out of this?

Sira struggled behind me. "You'll sell him over my dead body." Her words kept sharp as a dagger, but I couldn't miss a moving devotion for me behind them. "Orden would kill every last one of you. You don't seriously think they care about anyone but themselves? If you saw a coin of that bounty, then I must be an ogre."

The captain struck her across the face. Her head snapped to the side, but she kept her shoulders firm. "Shut yer trap, wench. Ye just don't want us to get rich, don't ye?" I saw him studying her up close. "Come t'think of it, yer a pretty wench. What say ye shack up with us? Get a fair shagging on the day, and ye can even fight with us. Ye'd get a tidy sum, that's fer certain."

His words made something like Sira's fire rumble within my chest. Before she could retort, as I knew she would, I found myself speaking. "Keep your hands off of her, you filthy bastard."

The captain turned his attention to me, looking thoroughly bored. "Now the pup's utterin' threats, too? Curse Orden. The bounty says to keep yer mug alive. Didn't mention ye'd have a mouth bigger than yer damned bounty poster."

He stepped toward me and lowered his head down to my level. He may be better groomed than the others, but he still stank like them. He grinned in an ugly way, boasting missing and damaged teeth. "Did say alive, didn't it? But not entirely undamaged."

"Don't you fucking dare," Sira growled from behind me. "You touch him, I swear to the Creator—"

Akin Minds

The captain growled in annoyance, and whistled with two fingers. A few more raiders entered the tent, similarly groomed to the captain. Must be his top men.

"Start with the wench there, men. Leave a lot of 'er for me."

My jaw dropped – more out of rage than surprise. Sira growled behind me as the men approached her. "Try it. When I'm out of these ropes, you'll wish you starved to death."

I looked the captain in the eyes. "Lay another hand on her, and you will face the true wrath of my world."

The captain chuckled. Behind me, one of the men stuffed a gag in Sira's mouth. She tried to scream through it, but her angry words came out muffled. "Is that so? Cause, we're gonna lay a few hands on her."

"It is so." I was surprised to hear Will backing me up, though his words came to my ears like he spoke from behind a wall. "I have seen it with my own eyes. The force that drives the forest into unrest. You have felt it, seen it, and experienced it. Have you not? The force which my Defender awoke."

I heard the men behind me stop. The raider captain glared at Will. "What're you gabbing on about? No way this little runt is responsible."

"You would guess so?" Will asked gently. "Tell me; have you met a Defender? Yet, have you ever *fought* one? Even heard of somebody fighting one?"

One of the other raiders cleared his throat. "Boss, that fight we heard about in the Capital earlier..."

The other one gulped. "And boss, the Keeper! The monster that gots Reed and Lonfrey last night! Ya don't think..."

The captain snarled in frustration. "Don't tell me yer scared of a lad! Pups like these just need breakin' in. I'll show ye!"

He got up and approached Sira. *No*, I thought angrily. I couldn't let them touch her!

I felt hands behind me. One of them was untying us. I got my hopes up, but they didn't let my hands out. They brought Sira to her feet. One pushed her, causing her to stumble, and the other caught her, groping her bottom obviously. She let out an angry noise through the rag shoved in her mouth.

As the three men closed in on Sira, I thought I heard a strange noise. It rang slightly above the energy building up in my chest, as though the force abated so I could hear the sound. Something about it was horribly familiar. The darkness within me spoke.

"I warned you."

It was only loud enough for the three men to hear me. One of them paused, still clutching Sira's backside. In their momentary lapse, a scream lit the night from outside the tent. Everyone whipped around to face the noise – except me. Something about the entity rising within me made me know it was already coming.

"What the—?" the captain growled. He reared around to me, standing in front of me with an incredulous look. "Joff, go check it out. One of the men probably lit themselves on fire again. If this kid thinks he's gonna scare us, he's never met me. Joff, if ye give me that scared look for a second more, I swear I'll—"

The sound of ripping cloth cut him off. The tent around us burst asunder as a bundle of green cloth split through the tent, tearing through one of the raiders as it dove upon the raider captain. Blood splashed everywhere. The raider captain let out a shrill, horrific scream. A set of ivory claws shot through his chest. They stopped short, blood-soaked, an inch from the rise and fall of my chest.

Whatever it was, the darkness flooding through me already had it all figured out. We remained in the Old Forest, even ransacked as it was to make room for this raider camp. Even in ruin, these grounds belonged to the forest, and the Keeper was bound to protect it. I only prayed it would prioritize the raiders as its enemy.

"Holy shit." Sira's voice was the first noise I heard past the scream. Before my eyes, the raider captain fell through the Keeper's claws, cutting their way through to break free of his skull without the Keeper moving at all. Now it hovered before me. I stared into the darkness under its hood. Even as this was the second time I stood before the beast, I couldn't tell if there was anything underneath.

The other raider in the room finally gave, and let out a horrified scream. The Keeper spun around. Leaving only its shrill, flute-like noise in its wake, it carved back through the tent, dragging the top half of the raider with it. The disembodied legs kicked, seizing up, and fell.

I shortly thought it left altogether, but then I heard screams outside. Blood splashed up in our view through the wrecked tent.

Will was the first to speak. "Get the weapons. Now!"

The ice that gripped everyone broke with the urgency in Will's voice. Sira stepped away from the two mangled corpses. She was the only one unbound, so she made for her sword.

While I waited for her to free us, I stared out into the wreckage outside. I couldn't spot a single live raider, only blood splashed across the ground in thick puddles. I was strangely impressed, but mortified in a deep, rooting way. I could imagine the faces of the three men I'd helped kill out in the woods. Hundreds of men like that, all slaughtered by this beast without a fighting chance.

A warm presence appeared in my hand, trying to drag me away. For a moment, in my stupor, I imagined it was somebody else. The girl with blond hair, shaking me to my senses as I stood over a body in my school classroom. I could almost see her freckled face, her blond hair falling across her shoulders in loose curls, the urgency in her blue eyes.

It faded away abruptly, and I stood before Sira, giving me a puzzled look. It faded quickly, and she let go of me. As she went to free the others, I went for my weapons. I let her free them with Sinistra as I replaced my knife, bow and arrow, and staff on my person. Already, the odd feelings of the darkness and that horrifying memory started to fade into the recesses of my mind.

"That thing's still out there and it's angry as all hell," Sira muttered to us. "Can we even get out?"

Mosten looked her in the eye. "We must. My men are somewhere in this camp. If we don't get out, that thing can't differentiate us from the raiders."

"We need to be ready to fight back," Will agreed. He turned to Lusari and I – the mage-girl was hanging onto his arm, her other hand clutching her staff. "You two, be ready to use all the magic you can muster. Lusari, can you use fire?"

"I might be able to," she agreed. It sounded like she was trying to tell herself more than anything.

"Good," Sira told her. She brushed her hand over the face of Sinistra. "Maybe my old girl can be useful, too. Hopefully it doesn't come to it."

With one last, unanimous look between us, we burst out of the tent. As soon as I got outside, though, I almost turned right back around in disgust.

The entire clearing was painted in gore. Slashes cleaved every tent in sight asunder. Bodies of raiders hung everywhere like listless flags. Some lived, screaming at the top of their lungs and crying in agony. Great gashes split their chests apart. Some held their insides together with their hands, screaming to us for help. Fires raged rampant through the field, and some raiders had caught flame. For the survivors, it was a game to see what took them first: their grievous injuries, or the unsafe flames of their own camp.

I wasn't the only one scarred by the sighting. Will's face turned into a mask. Leif, Alex, and Lusari all looked like they might be sick. Even Sira was shaking her head out of sorrow. We all knew they were enemies only by what life gave them.

Shouts from behind us caused us to turn around. The other soldiers from our group emerged from a nearby tent in a similar fashion, some still strapping on their armor. I wasn't sure, but I thought there might be less of them than when we'd arrived. Mosten turned to greet them. I lingered with Alex and Leif, unsure I liked the look on Mosten's face.

Mosten met them and urged each man forward with a pat on the back, stopping only to revel in the fact that they were still alive. I watched, stunned, even as Alex and Leif tried to urge me along. We stood in the middle of slaughter grounds, true, but I couldn't help but watch. At the last man, Mosten stopped him and asked a question close to his ear. The man's chin sank and he shook his head. Mosten's fists clenched and he glared off into the night behind us, staring into the flames as though the men he lost might return from them. I couldn't believe it. It may have only been two or three men, but the loss clearly touched Mosten deeply. If I was ever to be a soldier and chose my commanding officer, it might be Mosten.

After a short moment, Mosten returned at a full pace. Sira grabbed me by the shoulder. "Don't lose sight of us, idiot," she muttered, and dragged me ahead. Leif and Alex followed me, and I wondered if they felt the same way I did after watching Mosten.

Ahead of Will, the flames caught some sort of fuel and soared up into a tower of flames, blasting all of us with its sheer heat as it seemed to touch the sky. Our footing suffered as we danced around bodies on the ground, dodging the living who grabbed at our ankles. Sira and Will tried to put down each living raider that fought to bring us down, but there was little we could do. Too many suffered in this field. I fell deafened to it all, a wild montage of prolonged screams and the quiet roar of fire. Mosten's soldiers caught up to us and formed a ring around us, with Mosten holding up the rear.

I saw the occasional unharmed raider. Men scattered around in the relentless smoke and fire, their weapons in hand and smeared with blood, their eyes popping with fright. Sometimes our soldiers tried to reach them, but the smoke would billow up, then away to reveal just another body. Once or twice, that cost us another of our men, and Mosten cursed the horrific night.

Among it all, we were certain the Keeper still prowled. We saw it only as the occasional shadow, the haunting whistling in the distance, but we knew it wasn't far.

The raider camp wasn't all too big, but the setting made our trek across it feel like an eternity of walking through hell. We finally reached the edge of the camp looking out into the plains before the city. The fire hadn't reached this far, but black smoke billowed up from the camp like a living monster. The majority of the raiders must have flocked to the camp when the Keeper attacked.

"We're almost free!" Mosten called out. "Once we leave these woods, we will be safe from the monster!"

"Just a little further," Will added encouragingly, waving everyone forward. Leif stumbled behind him, and Mosten offered the soldier a hand up. Behind us, a small band of raiders shot out from cover of some trees. Our soldiers took up the defensive, Alex leading them. Lusari and I assisted with magic and arrow, picking the survivors off until not even one remained. I waited while Mosten rushed to check up on his soldiers, ensuring not one more loss.

Sira was at the head of the group to cross the boundary, free of the ancient grasp of the woods. She stabbed Sinistra into the earth and bent over in exhaustion, hands on her knees while she struggled to catch her breath. Will caught up to her ahead of much of the pack. I caught his glance, and he stopped dead in his tracks. Sira straightened next to him, and I saw her reach for Sinistra again.

"It returns! Hurry!" Alex rushed me along. Soldiers around us drew their weapons. Will, Sira, and the soldiers who'd made it out readied to charge. I found Lusari's arm grabbing mine. Mosten hesitated, torn between flocking his soldiers and challenging the ancient beast that drew closer. I could hear its haunting cry increasing rapidly in volume.

My legs felt heavier than ever as I tried to keep pace with Alex and Lusari rushing me along. Something caught my ankle suddenly – a felled raider, using the last bit of his life force to try to drag me down. I dropped like a stone, knocking the wind from my lungs. Lusari and Alex came down with me, but Alex rolled, drawing his sword with an enraged shout. Lusari pulled out her staff in a fluid motion and thrust it out behind me. Knowing I had precious seconds left, I kicked the hand holding me down and spun around with my own staff.

The Keeper of the Old Forest seemed right at home. Ashes and heat waves fluttered around it like a part of it. The dim flames of the raider camp gave it a terrifying sort of aura as it loomed before me for a third, and final, time. Beneath that frayed hood, for the first time, I thought I could see a pair of golden eyes.

I flung my staff forward in unison with Lusari. I expected flames to hurl from our staves, but something different happened. White light shot out from our weapons, splitting out into several smaller rays of violet. Rather than strike the monster before us, the light shot around to all sides – and returned with the fire from the camp, creating a personal inferno with new vigor.

The flames rose with more aggression and intensity than I'd ever conjured before, and worse than as we tried to leave the camp. They burned so brilliantly that they left angry bright patches in my vision, spinning and whirling in the air, given strength from the flames all over the camp.

The Keeper shrieked in a way that would likely hammer my eardrums for days. It seemed to stretch to every corner of the forest. Somehow, the sound seemed to resonate within me like it caught within my lungs. I felt every animal in those woods turning its head as the sacred Keeper took a serious blow – both animals I expected, and strange monsters that hid in the deepest recesses of the woods. A strange, antlered figure dressed in clothing like leaves. A large bear colored moss green with large, rabbit-like ears. The last one I saw was a tall, lion-like creature who stood on two legs with moss-green fur and a determined gaze, clutching a spear that oddly resembled the Keeper's ivory claws. For a strange, eerie, moment, I saw everything.

Then, as suddenly as it occurred, the flames vanished; flickering away like a fell wind was enough to extinguish them. With them, the Keeper was gone – defeated or otherwise – and I felt a considerable weight lift from my shoulders.

Hands appeared to help me to my feet. Alex yanked his blade from the raider that had dragged me down. Even with the Keeper and all the fire gone, Sira's hands on my arms felt just as intense. She pulled me along until we all stood safely outside the raider camp, and then she spun around.

I seemed to watch her fiery hair in slow motion, her scarlet eyes leaving afterimages in the air – and a tear. Then I was in her arms. I thought to pull away quickly, but she held me tightly against her chest, her palms pressed tightly against the back of my shoulders in an oddly relaxing way, her chin resting against my head. Sinistra lay on the ground, the blade still seeming to reflect the brilliant blaze from moments before.

"That was brilliant," Will whispered from beside me. I could hear the swelling pride in his voice. "Good job, Ryoku. If this is what a Defender can really do…"

"Lusari, you did excellently!" Alex proclaimed, touching her shoulder in a gentle but enthusiastic gesture. "What you did with the fire…!"

Lusari was shaking her head. "That magic wasn't me. I've never done something like that before."

I glanced at her over Sira's shoulder, as she still didn't let me go. "I never have, either. Maybe it was both of us?"

She smiled timidly. "Maybe."

A thought remained in my mind as we stood, ashen and breathless, in the fields outside the Old Forest. If we could pull something like this off, what sort of trials could possibly wait ahead?

SCENE SIX: A BRAVE NEW WORLD

...Of Act Two: Guardianship

In the eyes of Ryoku Dragontalen, we are in Harohto Capital City, in the world of Harohto.
It is dawn
On November 7th, 2017.

"Thank you all for what you have done for us."

I smiled to the small crowd around us. The governor of Harohto's Capital, Thorne, stood before us at Mosten's side, who remained in his soot-stricken armor, helm tucked under his arm. Some of the other soldiers remained, but many had gone home to their families. Some, I knew, went to where they buried their families, bringing their departed souls the good news of the raider defeat. Alex, Leif, and Oliver joined us as well, the latter seated on the steps to the garden in city hall. It was an enclosed space, well away from prying eyes, and would be our departure point.

The battle continued long after ours was finished. We joined the effort in defending the walls against what remained of the raider force. Given the state of the camp, they had nothing to return home to. At the sight of their camp up in flames, many had fled off into the woods to fight another day. The army apprehended or killed the rest. Mosten told me that the prisoners wouldn't be treated harshly. After all, we knew many of the raiders were simply starved or orphaned citizens. They would be given jail time depending on their behaviour, provided with commodities and food until they were ready for release. In the meantime, Mosten planned for them to help with the fields and gathering food until winter truly set in.

"We could not have done it without your help." Will stepped forward to shake hands with Mosten, and their eyes met solidly for a moment. I felt they were quite alike in all I'd seen of Mosten during our mission – and I was coming to know Will quite well.

"The same can be said for you, friends," Mosten told us earnestly. "We assimilated the raider effort last night. Thanks to your efforts, we torched their camp. Of our reports, a scamp few hundred may have escaped into the woods, and they'll return to us before long. Our people can live in peace."

"For a time, at least," Thorne agreed gravely. "We yet must deal with the prisoners. I imagine many will cooperate, but the rest will expend our dwindling resources. We have but a few weeks left to bring in our harvest before the snow. Still," he added, and a bit of a smile overcame him, "it has been a long time since our kingdom has seen something so kind and true from a Defender. I would be ignorant to not commend your valiant gift to our city: her freedom."

It took me a moment to realize he was referring to the city as a woman. Was that a real medieval notion? Cities were the last thing that should be applied a gender, I thought. It was an entity: a strong, bold, and humble one held together by great people. Still, I smiled all the same, because a Defender might sound insane to comment on their ways.

"I hope your reward money serves you well on your journey," Thorne went on. "Gold is of unending service to a new Defender, but recognition and fame may be even more so. Harohto will remember your services for an era, at least. Once our fine city catches up, should you ever return, we would gladly offer you a hand – nay, a thousand hands! – should you require it."

"Um, thank you," I said hesitantly. "Are you sure this money would not better serve your city? You said how hard the winter will be…"

Sira nudged me. "Don't you dare give up our gold!"

Thorne chuckled. "No, my young friend. This is not just government money. It has been pooled together by the soldiers who can finally let their families rest in peace, and some from the families who lost their fathers, sons, husbands, and all else in the war. We have allotted a large chunk, too, for those children without fathers; for the wives without husbands; for the damages to our fine city. I assure you, this money is yours to take."

"Do not look a gift horse in the mouth, friend," Alex warned, nudging me. "You have a huge goal ahead of you, no doubt. And... This will, no doubt, assist in the well-being of my dear friend."

Alex, Leif, and Oliver all turned toward Will, who stood at my side. Will went to speak, but Oliver raised a hand. "You need not explain. For all you have done for us, I could never let you leave in ill spirits. You have found your calling, my friend, and I would only ever wish you the best."

Will frowned. "What about Lancet?"

"Let us deal with him," Alex declared, putting his hands on his hips gallantly. "We have a tidy sum as payment, so he cannot say we simply came here to smell the flowers. And if he says anything about you, or *you*—" he pointed at me "—I swear I'll stick his lance where the sun don't shine!"

Oliver, Leif, and Will all turned on Alex. Sira doubled over in laughter, and Lusari hid her giggling behind her hand.

"Mind your tongue," Oliver warned, "and your language! Have you been rolling with the pigs while your friends fought for this city? I should return you to Lancet as a new leather coat! I could explain that you are the only one of us whose body I came across, stuffed in the backside of a bear in the woods!"

"He has a point, though," Leif agreed, throwing his arm over the taller Alex's shoulder to bring him down to his level. "Lancet has his reasons to stay in the village, and that might be all he cares about. The only thing he cares about more is showing you up, Will. He might even be happy you have left us. It means less challenge to his position!"

"More importantly," Alex spoke from the crook of Leif's shoulder, "we support your cause, brother." Leif let him go, and he rose to his full height, smiling at me. "You found a rare person among a rare sort of people. I have no doubt that you are about to do great things!"

Will grinned at me, clasping my arm. "I agree. We have a long way to go." He looked his friends down earnestly, meeting their eyes.

"Thank you all. Oliver. Leif. Alex. You all have done more for me than I could ever ask for from fellow soldiers."

Leif scowled at him. "Hey, you helped me out back in the village the whole time! I could not have fetched the medicine for that poor girl or tracked her down in the woods without your expertise! Your wisdom is certainly far beyond your years – even as a spirit."

"And ploughing Lindsor's fields?" Alex chimed in. "Helping out old Kimball? Can you imagine what a stuffy experience Bytold would have been without you?"

"It would not be the same upon return," Oliver added, sighing. "I do hope Commander Lancet meets whatever goal it is that Lord General Brom assigned him, and soon. Without your bravado, Will, we might actually get caught helping the people. Can you believe those words just came out of my mouth?"

Mosten and Thorne exchanged furtive glances. "Perhaps we could chip in," Thorne suggested. "A small platoon of soldiers could escort you to Bytold. Sniff out any trouble, and perhaps set this Lancet back in line."

Alex and Leif turned to Mosten hopefully. "Could you...?"

Mosten sighed. "Unfortunately, the city needs me right now. If you remain for a while, I'd happily visit in the spring. My wife and I could use a good voyage once the coming snow would abate."

Leif scowled. "I hope we are not here over winter!"

Alex nodded heavily. "I would sooner take up Oliver's offer about a bear rump, or whatever that business was."

Will chuckled heartily. "I will miss the lot of you. Syaoto is one of our destinations, so perhaps our paths will cross again soon."

"I hope so," Alex agreed. "Ryoku, when we meet up, you must tell me of all the wonderful places you see! As a Defender, you must get to see many of them! I have been to some on missions like this, but..."

"We could wind up anywhere," Will said. "It is a disquieting unknown, considering how many prospective worlds out there we may face."

Those words fell upon us like a wave, and I felt certain trepidation behind them. Even Harohto had turned into a winding mess. What else could possibly await?

Thorne nodded sadly. "He is strong-willed, as are all of you. You have displayed that to me in full. I'm sure you will all grow strong and, in time, face the darkness that presents your bounty."

My brow narrowed. The dark kingdom that issued my bounty, and the likely captor of my charge, Chris Olestine. Orden.

"Have you heard anything about them?" Will asked. "Perhaps some word has reached Harohto of them? Anything we might not know?"

Thorne shrugged cordially. "Not as far as I have heard. Orden is quite far from here. There appears to be some minor unrest in the royalty of Jerule, and Brooklyn is as chaotic as ever. That is about the height of news I have. All we know of Orden is the common knowledge of their swordplay. They say their emperors and soldiers alike are trained to wield a sword before learning how to eat with manners." He shuddered, as though the thought repulsed him. "They are savages who live for battle. No offense, milady."

Sira grunted. "None taken."

Alex was looking at Lusari, who tried to hide her face away from him. "Lusari, are you going with them?"

Shyly, the girl nodded. "They need me as a method of travel, and I have no other place to go. Besides..." she smiled up at Will and I. "I think I might like traveling with them."

"Have you sworn a Guardianship vow?" Mosten asked curiously.

"N-No," she replied, her glance turning nervous. "I, um, well..."

Mosten laughed, waving her off. "That isn't a prerequisite, don't worry," he assured her. "You don't have anywhere else to go in the city. No legal guardians or parental figures?"

Lusari shook her head. "No family left. It was just me, my mother and father."

"Hmm," Thorne murmured. "Normally I would not suggest such a thing, but these circumstances are a little unusual. I feel that your friends have taken better care of you than any foster parent might. Still, if it is your wish to return at any time, I hope your newfound friends would escort you. In that event, you could come to me, and I would see to your comfortable return to the city."

He looked to Will as he spoke, who nodded solemnly. "If you decided to return, I would guide you myself. Ryoku, you would likely do the same."

"Of course," I agreed vigorously. Lusari beamed at me, and I returned the smile. "I hope you feel welcome with us. I mean, you're not just a method of travel, either. You saved me back there."

She wiggled her brow. "I think you did all the saving, Ryoku Dragontalen."

"You have to stick around long enough to see my world!" Alex butted in, grinning at Lusari. "You think this old place is beautiful? We can stroll through the Royal Forest together, picking daisies from the ferns and chasing foxes! Why, I know a perfect viewpoint of the sunset from atop Clamber's Plateau…"

Leif twisted Alex's ear, causing him to cry out. "Come on, Alex! You said the same stuff about Caryl back in Bytold! You want me to tell her who you lust after now?"

Alex pulled away, stumbling over his own feet, and Oliver steadied him. "Leif! You are the worst! Heed not his toxic words, Lusari!"

She only giggled in response. Alex took off after Leif, chasing him in circles around the garden. Lusari watched, amused, next to Leif. In the lapse of conversation, I turned to Will. A thought had occurred to me.

"Will, you said you're a spirit, right? So you used to be in my world?"

His expression, just bemused by Alex, faded a little. "Yes. I thought you might ask about that sooner than later." He turned his attention to me. "About a hundred years ago, I would say. I died in your world when I was fourteen. A fire took my family home, killing myself, my mother, and brother. "

Hearing about his death made a strange chill run down my spine. "You died at fourteen? But…"

Will smiled easily. "Yes, I look older. Spirits are able to fluctuate their appearance in age by a certain degree, which helps when we associate with spirit-born who are unsure of our origins. It includes the ability to appear older than you were before passing. Spirits will often appear at the age they died, or else an age they attribute a strong emotion with. An old man might appear as a young child, for instance, because that was when they felt happiest. In other cases, a child grows older. Many children want to grow up, right?"

I nodded slowly, trying to make sense of that. "So you appeared older? You seemed to know a lot about the world at the time you were alive."

"Yes," Will agreed. "I fought in the first World War of your world. At the time, doing so at my age was somewhat expected, although I did lie on a few extra years. I learned many valuable things in that war, but I lived through it." He trailed off for a moment, watching Alex as he ran around after Leif. The young soldier had donned a cloak over his head, and I felt he might be impersonating the Keeper. "Of course, the army was not my first life. It is only the freshest memory that prevails. As, I am sure, your current life is not your first. It is only what prevails in your mind."

I put up my hands. "Wait," I stopped him. "Reincarnation, you mean? So you've lived other lives?"

Will nodded. "It is not the case for all spirits, and this world was not always the same. Many spirits eventually reappear in your world as newborns. I suppose it happens after death as well. My memory is… a little foggy on the specifics. I imagine that is for a reason."

I took this new information in. Could this relate to what Will and Sira were saying back at the inn, just before swearing their Guardianship vows? Did this involve a past life of mine somehow?

"Give it time," Will commented, putting a hand on my shoulder. "Surely we will all understand where you came from before long."

I looked up at him, about to ask what he meant by that, but Sira approached, her hands shoved in her pockets. "You were gonna ask me, too, weren't you?" she asked. "I died a few years older than I am now. I haven't come into your world since the middle ages, I guess. And you probably haven't heard of my home." She grinned. "Not yet."

I looked at her, surprised. She dismissed all of her spiritual past as a mere fact, though with little detail. Those details likely hid the pain behind her wretched smile, the ghosts burning away in her eyes. One day, I thought, I would find out just what it was.

"I do not believe we have met other spirits yet, either," Will said, though he was giving Sira a lasting look about her own history. "Lusari is spirit-born. Alex. Leif. Oliver. They would age in our company. Our forms may change a little, but Sira and I will never age. You would only age in your world, unaffected by any odd flow of time in ours. Still, time can affect you in certain ways. Your hair may grow out. Your features may sharpen. They could grow quite different from what you entertain in your homeland."

"You could put on some muscle!" Sira squeezed my arm painfully, and I winced away.

The thought, however, was interesting. "So I could look older here than at home?"

Will nodded, watching Alex and Leif chasing each other still. Lusari watched, giggling, and drew her hair back across her shoulder. At that moment, despite her silvery hair, fair skin, and snow-colored eyes, she looked remarkably... human. Contrary to my first ideas about a spiritual realm, she lived here, growing up by the day and living just as anyone else in my world. The same went for Alex, rushing around with his cloak drawn over his head, and Leif, who fought back laughter as he vaulted over a vat in the garden. Oliver and Thorne looked on, ready to intervene if they broke something. Oliver was older than the others, but he still looked like a youth next to the portly Thorne, who leaned on the stairway and twirled his black moustache.

In an odd, startling contrast, I turned back to Will and Sira. Will stood with one hand resting on the hilt of his gladius, the other relaxed at his side, and a relaxed smile on his lips. His tousled brown hair shimmered in the wintry sunlight; his sapphire eyes shone with life. Sira stood next to me, arms crossed, a faint scowl on her face as she watched the others running around. Her scarlet hair reflected the light like the center of an open flame, and her eyes shone no less. There was something perfect about the two of them, like they passed the test of time and now challenged the world as its equals. As spirits, they accentuated the world in such a way that they naturally seemed to draw my gaze. It was odd, and wondrous. I never imagined finding anything like this.

Alex and Leif grew tired. Leif sat down on the stairs, and Alex strolled over to us, hands in his pockets. Lusari sat down with Leif, and the two engaged in some kind of conversation.

"Bytold will be so boring," Alex moaned. "No raiders. No ancient Keeper of the woods. What is a Syaoto soldier to do?"

Will chuckled. "Indeed. A Syaoto soldier should be very happy that their place of residence is safe."

"You make a villain of me!" Alex proclaimed, raising his hands in an open gesture. "The news of the raider defeat is splendid for the people!" His shoulders sagged, and he sighed. "For me, however, it means returning to sleepy old Bytold, where I must tell Lancet that the son of the hero is gone. He shall have my head, whether for that or for the pike—"

Oliver cut him off with a warning noise. Will only laughed. I didn't miss that title Alex gave him – an odd one, for a spirit. Will approached Alex, standing before him for a moment. Despite having the same home, the two looked quite different. Alex's hair was sandy and unorthodox, his arms ganglier, a bit more of a bend to his posture. With one hand, Will removed the steel cap upon his head. Quite gently, like a crown, he placed it on Alex's head.

"I should have my doubts about less action where you are concerned," Will told him. "In that case, you may find my cap to serve you better than the standard issue."

Oliver gave Will an awestruck look, while Alex touched the hat with a single finger like it was made of gold. I couldn't imagine the importance behind this gesture, but it seemed great. Did it have to do with Alex calling him a hero's son?

With that, Will turned to me, smiling. "Should we be on our way?"

Sira stretched and yawned next to me. The antics of the last day left us sleepless, eager to meet the next world. Either that or the social interaction bored Sira to tears. "Might be best. You know how easy I get bored of this place, and we've been here *way* too long. Where do you think is next?"

Will shrugged broadly. "There are many worlds nearby." Lusari approached us, pulling out her staff. "What is there? Brooklyn, Lysvid, Jerule... any of them would be a fair chance."

"Be wary in Jerule," Thorne told us. "As I mentioned, matters seem to be turning sour there."

Oliver input with a sour expression. "And I do not need to lecture you on Lysvid. That is a dangerous and hostile place."

"Where does that leave us? Brooklyn?" Sira curled her lip. "Never liked that place. They put more money into acting and theatres than their army."

Thorne smiled, and looked around him to the other soldiers. "Lusari is preparing her spell. We should hurry along, lest we get dragged into their spell."

Leif balked at that idea. Alex, who had been slowly turning red as a beet with his new cap upon his head, shot his hand to his head in a bold, emotional salute. He held it for several seconds before Oliver and Leif fell in alongside him and mimicked the salute. Will planted his feet firmly and returned the gesture. I tried to follow suit.

"It was good to meet you, Ryoku. Sira. Lusari." Oliver flicked out the salute in a finishing gesture. "Until we meet again."

"Thank you for all your help," Leif told us. "Will, I am on my way to becoming an elite soldier. Guess I would have you beat soon, huh?"

Oliver chuckled. "Maybe in rank."

"And I will be a median soon," Alex told Will firmly, still holding the salute. "With your cap, I will go on. Maybe I will command my own squad one day."

Mosten came to stand with them and saluted in kind. "You will always be welcome here. Ryoku, if you ever deign to learn the ways of the sword... I'd be honored to instruct you on its ways."

I smiled, still holding my awkward salute. "If it's possible."

"May it be in as good terms as this," Will agreed.

"And maybe when Harohto gets more exciting," Sira ventured.

The others laughed, but it was time to go. Alex and Leif rushed ahead to the door leading outside the garden, Alex tugging at Leif's sleeve. Oliver followed, arms folded behind his back and staring up at the early rising sun. Mosten walked alongside his governor. Just as easily as they had all arrived, they were gone.

I sighed, a little sadly, and turned back to Lusari. She held her staff before her, and a greenish glow emanated from it. Green energy hung around her like dust in the air. As she put more energy into it, energy began to etch out around her feet and stretched out across the ground in a wide circle, easily enough to fit at least ten people. It easily encompassed the four of us, though we didn't stand closely together. Symbols started to etch up from the ground in green light, things that seemed to tug at my memory in odd ways. One of the symbols near me looked something like a star intersected with a triangle, and I stared at it until it burned into my eyes. Still, it didn't make any sense to me.

"You'd better be ready," Sira told me firmly. "We could easily land in a hostile world."

I gripped my knife apprehensively. I'd only heard what little they said about the worlds today, so I wasn't sure what to expect. Orden seemed too far away to land in. Syaoto must be, as well.

Lusari seemed to finish preparing her spell, her snowy eyes now opened. Green dust still glinted all around her, gently lifting her silver hair as if in a short breeze. "Are we ready?"

For a moment, I hesitated. I'd made friends in Harohto that I could visit if I returned, and ones who would meet us in Syaoto. What if this was the only place like that? What if every other world was full of darkness and enemies? Of thugs trying to get at Lusari, or Keepers chasing us to the ends of the earth?

As I thought that, though, I looked around at my friends. Will smiled at me bravely. Sira's fingers drummed impatiently on the hilt of Sinistra. Lusari only smiled, appearing a little fatigued by her spell.

I knew, as long as I went with these three, I would never be alone.

I managed a brave smile, and nodded to Lusari. She returned it, and shut her eyes again. With the fluttering of her lashes, the green walls of the spell flared to life, rising up around us like some kind of personal aurora. The symbols around us seemed to rise from the earth and join us like holograms.

Beyond the green aura, Harohto seemed to fade into the background. First went the sky, then the tall buildings around us. I watched darkness swallow the adornments of the garden until it stretched to our very feet, and the grass itself vanished. I expected to lose my footing, but something held me still.

Lusari's head twitched. At the edge of the spell, some sort of black energy rippled through the outer layer of the spell. Every glyph in the circle spun madly, aggravated by the disruption. Two of them turned jet-black.

"What the—?"

Sira's voice seemed to echo through the circle. I tried to reach for my knife, but I couldn't move under grip of the spell. Panic welled up in my chest. Had Orden found us?

Then, across from me, something different crossed into the spell, levelling out the turbulence somehow. A flicker of golden energy licked across the edge of the circle. Two of the glyphs turned emerald-green.

"Lusari, what do you sense?" Will asked uneasily.

Lusari frowned, her eyes shut. "I... I cannot say for sure. I have never world-travelled before. But... um, I feel like somebody latched onto our spell. I think we're being followed."

...End of Act Two.

ACT THREE: TRICKSTER...

*In the eyes of Sira Jessura, we are in
The Black Plain, in the world of Lysvid.
It is early afternoon
On November 7th, 2017.*

SCENE ONE: TRICKS AND GODS

When the world opened up around us, I was almost certain that it'd just been some kind of glitch. I mean, nobody was ever conscious during the arduous process of crossing realms. It didn't look like we ended up anywhere. Everything was dark.

I could dully detect the presence of the others around me. Will always carried an earthy scent, though not an entirely unpleasant one. It was as if he grew up among the trees with an added manly spice to his atmosphere. Lusari's aura was one that oddly reminded me of watching the rain from afar, sitting at a warm hearth with a nostalgic feel to the air.

Then, of course, Ryoku was the unmistakable one. He had an oddly light scent to him, something like the sun streaming through the boughs of tall, wise trees, dancing rays across the scattered stones. The whole time, despite all the good Will had to say about the kid, I expected the worst. Men weren't easy to trust. Even Will, with his etiquette, bold voice, and charming personality, seemed like a snake to me. It could be a ruse, meant to pierce the thousand shields that every sane woman put around her. I expected the same of Ryoku.

That all changed when he woke up. Since then, I was annoyed. His forest-green eyes were like a pair of stars shining through the night, already stabbing questions at me from the second he saw me. His voice was light and casual, but I could tell he thought his words over before he ever spoke. He was perceptive, but not enough to see the way I looked at him. All of that was enough to piss me off – I didn't like letting people in, and it was as if his green eyes already rolled out the red carpet for himself, straight into my life. I had yet to decide whether that red carpet was made of velvet or flames.

What a terrible, annoying pain.

It took a moment, but everything slowly came to focus. It was actually just dark as night, but the darkness seemed unsettling even for me. A pale moon hung in the sky like some eerie, singular ornament to try to enlighten the strange place we were in. I felt dry, crisp grass beneath my boots. I started to pick out some eerie-looking trees in the darkness. Given time, my eyes might adjust to a better state.

Then I remembered what Lusari mentioned. The last thing before everything went dark, like falling asleep. Somebody was tailing us.

My hand shot to Sinistra. No matter no dark it may be, I always knew where to find my sword. I heard Ryoku fumble for his knife. Just as quickly, Will and Lusari winged in on either side of me. I could see the green of Ryoku's eyes in the darkness next to the hulking frame of Will. Lusari, though she wore the lightest-colored clothes, seemed to swim in the darkness.

Will broke the silence. "What is this? This darkness..."

"Listen!" Lusari's soft voice brought us to edge, but nothing happened. We looked to her, and she whispered urgently, "The birds!"

Now that she mentioned it, I could hear the rhythmic songs of birds nearby. A small figure took flight from a nearby tree.

"Birds?" I echoed oddly. "That means... it's daytime?"

"How is that possible?" Ryoku asked us. "I mean, we left during the day, but... its pitch black."

Will sighed. "I know where we must be. Lysvid."

I groaned. "Seriously? What a dumb world."

"Do not let them hear you." Will only dissuaded the look I gave him with a chuckle. He must have been able to sense Ryoku's questions boring into his back, because he added, "Lysvid is the world of vampires. As far as is known, it may be their capital world. That is, a place where all vampires gather. And it is cast in eternal night."

"Vampires? Seriously?"

I snorted. Ryoku's humor was sometimes as dry as mine.

"Well, yes," Will said. "I mean, you could consult the magic stick on your back if you suggest I would lie to you about something so simple. Perhaps you could ask another spirit. I mean, here, in the spirit realm."

I grinned. Will was just as amusing.

"I'm okay, thanks," Ryoku groaned. "But... are they going to attack us?"

"They should not. Laws in their Capital normally forbid feeding on travelers. That is, unless we encounter the Ritual. A cult, one which essentially believes humans are just walking snacks for vampire-kind."

Ryoku sighed. "Okay. Great." He fumbled for his bag. "Do we have something for light?"

Will and Lusari went for their bags. I knew I didn't have anything, so I waited, staring up at the pale moon. How did their moon system work? A world like Lysvid might have two moons that swapped out through day and night. Many worlds had their own system. Most only had one sun and moon. Others, like Orden, worked differently. Orden's three moons cycled through the seasons.

I turned around just in time to see Lusari raise her staff. A second later, everyone was cowering before an absurdly bright light emanating from her.

"Ouch! What gives?"

Lusari only giggled timidly. "Sorry. I thought you wanted light."

"That's a handy trick," Ryoku commented, rubbing his eyes, "though a little warning could have been nice."

Only Will looked unperturbed. I suspected he had a soft spot for the mage, but I didn't dare voice that idea. Will was perceptive, and I knew he saw how I looked at Ryoku.

"Well," Will started, looking around. "Seems we appeared on the path. So, which direction...?"

He broke off as he turned to the path behind him, and reached for his lance. I tightened my grip on Sinistra.

"What?" Ryoku asked, turning toward where we stared.

A portal stretched the fabric of the world just ten feet down the path, appearing like a fresh wound splitting skin. Within looked like a starry night sky, out of place on the path ahead. Tendrils of violet mist seeped into our realm.

"Somebody approaches," Will warned. "That is a single-person portal. Some may cross the worlds alone. Whoever it is..."

"They must have been the one who tracked us!" Lusari cried.

My heart felt encased in ice. All I could think of was how vassals of Orden's royal family – and the emperor himself – frequented single-man portals. Had they found us?

A shadow appeared within, becoming clearer as the portal reached human height. Then it dropped abruptly, leaving a well-built man standing in the middle of the path. His skin was almost as dark as the world around him, but his hair and baggy pants stood out as stark white. I caught the steel glistening of thick bracers on his arms, but I couldn't spot another weapon. Honestly, by the size of him, he might as well be the weapon.

He strolled toward us with as purposeful a gait as though he hadn't stopped walking whilst he crossed worlds. As soon as the man dropped into our world, I could sense the power he radiated, like the coming of a storm as electricity crackled in the air, foretelling certain lightning. The ability to sense power was dilute in me, but I bore no doubts about it. This man was dangerous.

We kept close to Ryoku, weapons drawn. The man sauntered forward with the ease of a cougar. As he closed in, I noticed the most unsettling fact about the man: his eyes were jet-black. I thought it was a trick of Lysvid's night at first, but there was no mistaking it. I could see the whites of everyone else's eyes.

Without any indication to us, Ryoku stepped toward the man. Will and I both made to wing him, but the man's hand twitched in a noticeable gesture. My muscles seized up. I couldn't move an inch.

"What the—!"

Will growled under his breath, his expression strained. He, too, couldn't move. "W-What sort of sorcery is this? Who are you? State your business!"

The man laughed. I associated the noise with a lion looming over paralyzed prey. He didn't offer an answer. His eyes remained on Ryoku. Inches from our Defender, the large man had a serious height advantage on him. Ryoku didn't make a noise. I couldn't tell if he was paralyzed like us. His face didn't betray anything.

"You are Ryoku Dragontalen?"

The man's voice was deep and rich, tinged with a bit of accent. I cursed Ryoku's abilities. Now that we were his Guardians, the same translating barrier applied to us, meaning I couldn't properly guess this man's lineage. Vortigeran? No, his white hair and black eyes weren't common there. The same went for Id, the next desert world I could think of.

Ryoku nodded slowly. "And you are?"

His voice made chills run through the pit of my stomach. There it was again. The darkness. It was that voice he used the other day when he spoke to the raider captain in Harohto. The voice that, I believed, caused him to use magic so fluidly without prior experience. It was equally thrilling and terrifying.

If the stranger thought anything of this voice, he said nothing. A cold, wry grin etched out over his face like it was slowly drawn on. "At last, I've found you. My name is Jesanht Olace. Perhaps you do not recall. I was born into a world without a name because of your deeds. My father was somebody you destroyed not long ago. For your plight, I was born into this world lacking the things you take for granted. A family. A purpose."

I didn't think Ryoku knew what the hell the man was talking about, but he didn't respond. Jesanht raised a hand and pressed it directly over the center of Ryoku's chest. Still, Ryoku didn't move.

"Your oaths of Guardianship are freed – you may go as you wish." Jesanht seemed to be speaking to us, though he didn't remove his eyes from Ryoku. "Once your Defender is exterminated, there is nothing left to bind you. My quarrel does not exist with you." His eyelids fluttered, his head tilted. "This is for my father."

Before anything could happen, something hurled Jesanht Olace to the side. His hand jolted from Ryoku's chest. As he soared, I saw a lance of dark energy burst from his hand in an arc that would have pierced Ryoku's heart instantly. Whatever it was that broke their connection looked emerald-green and left a burning golden spark in the air. Will and I stumbled – the magic holding us snapped. I rushed to Ryoku's side as a new stranger appeared where Jesanht stood.

"Who are you?" Jesanht Olace asked, quietly and vehemently. Despite how far he went, the panther-like man was already on his feet.

The stranger smiled. He was a young man, maybe with about ten years on the rest of us, with spiky golden hair and an angular face. The emerald-green blur seemed to be his tunic, pressing against his wiry figure, arms crossed over his chest. A kingly sword sat at his hip, lined with rubies all along the hilt.

"Leave now, Jesanht Olace. Put this event behind ya, or you shan't live to regret it."

His voice was smooth and quick, but layered with daggers behind each word. Jesanht Olace raised an eyebrow, but didn't move.

"I don't believe you heard me, stranger. I asked for your name."

The green-eyed man chuckled like wind chimes in the breeze. "I suppose I could tell you, but you'd have to run along now before I kill you for it. Oh, and you can get the word out, too." His eyes snapped open – as they did, I suddenly sensed energy bursting from the man. "Loki the Trickster god's lookin' out for this kid."

I stared at the guy incredulously. Was he kidding? Loki the Trickster god? Nevertheless, even as he boasted such a thing, the energy he gave off backed him up. Where Jesanht gave off a powerful, almost primal energy, Loki gave off something like white lightning, clear and focused in its rage.

When I turned to Jesanht to see his reaction, I realized he'd vanished, leaving only a dark afterimage of himself with the hanging noise of world travel behind him.

Loki smirked, and the power around him relaxed. "You're welcome," he told Ryoku, as sincerely as though Ryoku actually thanked him already. "You alright? Pretty sure I got him in time, but one cannot be too careful. That magic would have killed you."

Ryoku stared at him. "Are you really... Loki?" he asked. His voice returned to normal, which made my shoulders sag in relief. "From Norse mythology? *That* Loki?"

"In the flesh, or so to speak," Loki said, putting his hands on his hips. "Gods cannot simply waltz out of Immortalia without a price, so I'm a little weaker than I should be. More than enough to make Jesanht Olace turn tail, though."

"Why was he after me?"

Loki frowned a little, scratching his head. "Uh, beats me. Didn't he say why?"

"Nothing that made any sense," Will spoke. "What brings you to Lysvid anyway, Trickster god? Should we consider you a threat? You claimed to be 'looking out for Ryoku,' but I did not catch you while we, actually, have been doing that job."

I raised a brow in quiet surprise. Was that distaste in Willy-boy's voice? I had to admit I wasn't immediately fond of Loki's demeanour myself, but wasn't he still a god? Gods didn't like disrespect, if mythology had anything to say about the notion.

"Most should consider me a threat, Will Ramun of Syaoto," Loki professed, giving Will a sidelong glance. "I wouldn't dismiss the idea from your head just yet. Still, you're quite wrong in one aspect. I didn't come to harm Ryoku. On the contrary—"

"How do you know our names?" Ryoku asked, cutting him off in a way that made Loki's brow twitch. "And I thought mythology names you a giant."

I had to choke back a laugh. The golden-haired man was only a few inches taller than Ryoku, and scowled at him. "Mythology misunderstands, my friend, I assure you! Besides," he added with a smirk. "Mythology would also tell you a man in the sky made *everything*, and that you should believe him or die for it. Could be wrong, but isn't there a whole spiritual realm here disproving that? Your own two friends have likely been reincarnated more times than you could guess. Or is that just the Creator's way?" Loki shrugged cordially, fixating Ryoku in his emerald-eyed gaze. "Perhaps don't trust everything people tell you. Better to see it with your own eyes before you place your beliefs someplace."

Ryoku nodded slowly. I had to like the man's point. "You didn't answer his first question," I pointed out. "How do you know our names?"

Loki's emerald eyes flashed. "Isn't that odd, Sira Jessura of Orden?" He chuckled in a mischievous way. "The answer is truly simple, and yet as complex as the stars, the moons, and the worlds themselves."

Loki held his hand out to Ryoku. The young Defender stared at it for a moment, contemplating, ruminating over the possible dangers in his mind – but he reached out and accepted Loki's hand. Rather than shake it, Loki put his other hand over Ryoku's, smiling at him like a merchant who'd just sealed the deal.

"Ryoku Dragontalen, I'd like to offer my services on behalf of Immortalia, realm of the gods, as your Guardian."

SCENE TWO: WEREWOLF

...Of Act Three: Trickster

In the eyes of Sira Jessura, we are in Lysvid's Capital, in the world of Lysvid. It is early evening On November 7th, 2017.

"Well, here we are."
Will gazed on ahead of us into the literal monster nest. Not something I would ever call them aloud, but it was true. For things that lived off the blood of other creatures, a monster was a good word.

By first impression, the city was enormous. Streetlights dotted the expanse of the city until they disappeared into a dark fog as far as the eye could see. The buildings, all tall and black, lined the sides of the street like standing coffins, their windows spray-painted black to keep out even the city lights they installed themselves. Even considering Orden, it was one of the dreariest cities I'd ever stepped foot in. Rumor stated that almost every vampire alive lived here – or so to speak, anyway. Alive was a tentative term for these people.

The dreary bastards dressed all in dark clothing. Males clad in heavy coats, robes, and cloaks sauntered down the street, challenging anyone to meet their crimson-eyed gaze. The women wore almost nothing, slipping in and out of the crowds and alleys like slinking shadows.

"We'll make for an inn," Loki told us. "Lysvid keeps their inns central. Meaning, we must traverse much of the city to get there."

I sighed. "Like walking into a damned spider web."

As we started into the city, Loki glanced sidelong back at Ryoku. "Watch out. They like to make eye contact with their food. I'd keep my head low, and my blade high."

Ryoku gulped. The poor kid looked horribly uneasy around the vampires. We'd passed some of them on our way to the Capital from our entry spot, so he wasn't entirely alien to them by this point. Still, I couldn't imagine meeting vampires when you didn't acknowledge their existence before, especially in such bulk.

As we started into the city, it became clear that the vampires had a preference. Females lurked near Will and Ryoku especially, tracing their clawed hands across their arms, their hips, and honestly reaching for anything they thought they might get away with. Ryoku didn't know what to do. At least Will seemed assertive enough to put some distance between them. Lusari waved her lit staff around to dissuade them, while Loki and I only needed to boast our weapons. Against that, the males constantly tried to assert themselves before us. Many bumped chests with Loki or Will. Lusari and I seemed a bit safer.

Hours trickled by as we delved deeper into the lair of desolation. I thought the city might never end, or else we passed the inn already. Our anxiety grew as the populace thinned. Luckily, they seemed more distracted around the city's center, too. Maybe the sounds and smells of the big city helped cover us up.

Somewhere deep within the city, we saw a column of odd-looking vampires dressed in full-black uniforms, their hoods drawn over their heads. They marched down the street in single file, crimson eyes locked ahead, hands on their weapons.

"The Ritual," Loki muttered to our unanswered question. "Vampiric cult, essentially. Believes that the blood in our veins is their Creator-given right. Blood banks and donors are sacrilegious to their ilk. We'd best stay clear of their kind."

Ryoku watched them go for an awfully long time, a wary hunch in his shoulders. Will mentioned this cult earlier. The leader walked like he was the city's gift to us, his shoulders swinging as he walked, the tail of his black coat fanning behind him as he walked. For a brief moment, I was sure he glanced our way. I saw his curls of brown hair beneath his hood, the glint of his crimson eyes. However, as the thought entered my mind, the leader turned, and they went on down the street. We drew breath only once they rounded the next corner.

"As hostile as they are to us, they're like the guardsmen of this city," Loki explained, though he spoke with distaste. "Them and the Night's Watch – those are friendlier to us, FYI – protect the city and its folk from harm."

"What sort of being could harm vampires?" Lusari asked. It almost sounded prejudice, but possibly just her idle curiosity.

Loki fanned his shoulders. "Werewolves. Vamp hunters, too, though I doubt they get much of a foothold in this place."

Will's brow shot up. "The vampiric capital has werewolves? Truly?"

Loki nodded. He still gazed after where the Ritual folk had disappeared as though they might return. "Every world's got its vice. Harohto's supposed to be friendly, but it's wrought with war and strife. Syaoto, she has her demons. Orden has its rebellion, too. Parallel to your world, Ryoku, is our own. A world rife with life."

I saw the look in Ryoku's eyes. His world was a sensitive subject. I interjected, whether to save Ryoku or Loki. "It's always night here. How do werewolves function?"

Loki glanced at me. "They remain in their wolf forms, of course." He gestured toward the sky. Only then did I realize that the original moon we'd been looking up at was gone. In its place looked to be two moons. one blue, one red. "Lysvid runs in a cycle of moons. The one you saw earlier – a moon by any world's standards – passes over during early morning and noon. Later on, the red one rises from the north, the blue from the south. As they meet in the sky, it marks evening. Once they set, nightfall. No moon shows overnight. At dawn, so to speak, the first moon rises." He rambled all of that like it was common knowledge. "You see? No sun. So the wolves can't go back to normal once they're bit."

"You know much about this world, Loki," Will commented aridly. "Have you spent a lot of time here?"

Loki smirked. "You could say that."

He didn't elaborate. Even given the piousness of this Trickster, pressing him for answers couldn't possibly be a good idea.

"Thanks for the history lesson," I muttered. "Now, how about something useful? Maybe the distance to the tavern, or the regular price of good rum."

I heard Ryoku chuckle behind me. When I looked at the Trickster, though, his eyes had turned sharp. His hand shot to the hilt of his sword. I reached for mine, glancing around. Had another vampire gotten too close? Had the Ritual members turned around after all?

No, that wasn't it. Loki's piercing emerald eyes scanned the crowd in search of something. I followed suit. Will's footsteps came up beside me.

Sensing the danger was an acute ability for me, especially compared to something the Trickster could muster. Even Will had better sensing abilities than I did.

I focused, trying to zero in on the disturbance. Ryoku's footsteps behind me sounded like they were miles away.

"...could such a foul creature enter the city? Isn't the Ritual doing their jobs? What of the Night's watch?"

"You think they care about us? All it is for them is blood, blood, and more blood. Even if it comes from our own kind."

There it was – a snarl. Screams erupted in a wide circle around the noise. People near us still cast disgusted looks in the way of the noise. The female vampires clustered behind our company while a few of the males stepped up around us, flexing their venomous muscles and snarling under their breath.

It was difficult to make out. Slowly, I became aware of the cold energy of the vampires. That was always present even while we weren't directly aware. It was why the five of us had our cloaks wrapped tightly around us in this city.

Beyond that, though, came a different sensation. Amid the cold, tantalizing aura of the vampires appeared heavy warmth. A primal, wild energy that slowly rose up until it felt like it might suffocate us. Then came the arid scent of wet dog.

My eyes shot open just as the beast bounded into the street ahead of us. Vampires screamed just like normal humans in any crisis, pushing and falling over one another in their struggle to escape the beast. Its head shot up, and it lunged at one of the vampire women who'd tripped on the cobblestones. Her screams lit the city like a flame, just as her blood spurted out in huge splashes. Did vampires have blood, or was that their toxin?

Full-on panic took the streets by storm. Some vampires in dark-brown uniforms blew on white horns that looked like they came from demons. Some hung around near the monster with airy hesitation.

Loki stepped forward, and the beast reared on us in an instant. Could it smell that we were different? The monster straightened over its victim, towering to a height that must rival my own. Ribs pressed out on its wiry chest like upraised scars, covered in coarse grey fur from head to toe. Its facial structure looked more wolfish than anything, but its eerie gait suggested otherwise. Insanity crawled in the depths of its wide golden eyes. If I were like it, I thought, I'd be just as insane.

"A werewolf? Here?" Will muttered, eyes locked on the beast. "How did it get so deep into the city?"

"City guards' not doing their job," I guessed. "Oh well. Guess we get one fight that *won't* piss off this damned city."

"It's a smidge worse than that," Loki commented. The sharpness of his tone made me turn. "This is not a werewolf – it's a Warg. They're sacrilegious even among other wolves. Wolves infected with the Lycanthropy gene. It turns them feral and beyond any possible reasoning!"

He swung his sword in a practicing way; the wolf mimicked his movement. He lifted his chin toward a nearby vampire in a brown coat. "Go! Get her to safety! The rest of you, to me! With your heads about you!"

He barely finished speaking before the Warg lunged. To my surprise, Loki darted around the incoming strike and brought his silver blade down upon its back. Dark blood rained upon the pavement as the monster howled in agony.

The other vampires seemed inspired that Loki could actually harm it. A few of them scooped up the injured female, who was groaning and crying in a right mess. The others came to wing us against the wolf.

The beast turned on Loki as I stepped into its blind spot, closely followed by Will. One trait I admired about the soldier was his willingness to go up against anything, even monsters he'd likely never faced before.

I swung heavily with Sinistra, but the beast dodged all but the furthest bite of the edge. It let out another horrific noise. It writhed in pain, lashing out at us. We danced around each strike nimbly, keeping a careful distance between us. I blocked a lash of its claws with Sinistra's broad face. Sparks sprayed across the road. It let out a savage growl rumbling deep in its throat.

Ever wary, Will stepped up to wing me as the monster prowled toward me. Its body tensed up so that it could easily close the distance between us before I could draw a breath.

It sprang without warning. Will stepped out in front of me and blocked it with the breadth of his spear, tossing it to the ground unceremoniously. Loki made to strike, but the creature already got to its feet and retaliated at Will aggressively. Will blocked the first strike, but I stepped in before it could lash again and swung headlong at the beast. It ducked underneath and tried to bite at our ankles. Loki dissuaded it by choosing to step in, and it staggered away, retreating to pace almost on all fours.

Prints of blood followed the beast as it lurked, a low growl rumbling in its chest. Lusari and Ryoku remained behind us. I was sure they could do some damage with their magic, but this monster might just rip their heads off before they could muster a single spell. It could easily go after any of the vampires nearby, but it trained its golden orbs on us.

I would've rather fought the beast alone. Loki and Will, along with the few vamps circling around us, would only get in the way of my broadsword. I was better suited to lone combat. Still, I shacked up with this group. It meant I might always have this stalwart soldier and deluded Trickster at my side. Still, as long as I had Ryoku at my back, it might be okay.

As the beast prowled, I thought its fur began to look reddish. Surely we hadn't struck it enough to soak its entire coat.

I thought I saw a change in Loki's expression, and he added a second hand to the grip of his longsword. I gave him a questioning look, but he didn't meet my glance. The Warg's fur was definitely turning red. Were its abilities so different from those of a werewolf?

"Step back," Loki warned us quietly. When neither of us made to move, he shot me a sidelong glare. "Seriously! Get back or I'll—"

"You will what?" Will challenged. "To be a Guardian suggests I must stand between Ryoku and danger at all times."

"Even when it could cost you your life?"

"Especially," I barked. "What about you, Trickster? Would you fight without a crowd?"

A shriek from the monster nearly cut my sentence short. Somehow, with the way its skin turned red as blood, the Warg's capabilities took a turn for the worst. It cleared the space between us in a single bound and bore down on Loki with both claws. Loki, caught off guard, reflected with the edge of his sword. It didn't seem to do much to the Warg, but stone cracked around Loki's feet from the sheer force of it.

Will and I had to help. We seemed synchronized as we lurched toward the monster. Will swung his lance like a baseball bat at the monster while I raised my sword above my head. The Warg's eyes flashed.

In an instant, it was upon us. One strike dissuaded Will's lance, causing him to teeter in an attempt to regain his balance. All I saw of the monster was the golden trails its eyes seemed to leave in the air as it closed in. It struck the face of my weapon with such force that I struggled not to drop the blade, or else break my arms trying to hold on. The beast lowered itself in front of me, and charged.

Whoosh!

The beast lurched to the side, ice beginning to thatch across its fur. I smirked. Lusari's ice magic. The sheer power of it ran a chill down my spine from this close. Still, the beast's radiating flesh was melting away the ice as quickly as it formed.

It gave me enough time to recover, and I switched my grip on Sinistra to swing headlong at the beast. Even with ice forming across its flesh, it proved much faster than me, ducking beneath with ease. Will tried to stick it with his lance, but the creature rolled away, leaving a trail of melting ice behind it as it went.

By the time Loki made to connect his sword with the beast, it had fully recovered and lunged at him without relent. Will rammed it with the blunt end of his lance, but the creature only jolted, latching onto Loki with its claws out. Loki cried out, trying to shake the beast off. I hesitated. Could I cut the monster without cleaving Loki in half, too? Furthermore, did I even care?

One of the vamps sprang behind Loki and struck the beast soundly in the jaw, driving relief through my chest as the creature hit the ground between us with a pained yelp. It quickly got to its feet, however, and swung at Will. As the soldier stepped away, I swung heavily and with as much haste as I could muster.

A consequent set of sharp twangs shot through the air. Before my eyes, three arrows pounded directly into the throat of the Warg. Each one landed atop the other in fluid motion, busting all but the last arrow and driving all of them deeply into the creature's neck. Blood spurted out like a cork pulled from shaken wine.

The creature let out a savage noise unlike anything I'd ever heard, reeling on the spot. Its crazed golden eyes turned even more fervent, searching desperately for its attacker.

There he was. Ryoku, his bow drawn with another arrow already strung to it. A cool, confident smirk hung on his face. It only lasted for a second before his eyelids fluttered, and something changed about his pose. He suddenly looked confused – and the Warg, now fully enraged, locked onto him.

It took little more than that for us to launch into action. Lusari unleashed a wide burst of ice magic, smashing into the Warg like a window that shattered before his chest. The impact must have slowed him enough for Loki to dart forward and bury his sword in the beast's shoulder. It let out a fervid wail, lurching on its hind legs as it struggled to free itself from us. Its frantic movements dodged my swing, though my sword cleaved the surviving arrow in its throat asunder and sprayed reed shrapnel everywhere.

As it spun, however, the head of Will's lance burst through its chest. Blood and guts sprayed a sizeable distance, luckily clear of the lot of us. Now, finally, I saw the life fade from the monster's deluded eyes, and it went limp. Will pulled away just in time as the beast collapsed unceremoniously in the middle of the cobblestone road – alone, and quite dead.

We stood there, chests heaving from our battle. Loki stretched out his sore arms, sword still in hand. Will stared at the fallen monster with remorse. Lusari was giving Ryoku quite an incredulous look. No doubt she was trying to piece together how he'd mustered such a fatal blow while the beast was in full movement. She wasn't the only one.

Slowly, hesitantly, the vampires came out of hiding around us. Only the one that struck when Loki was trapped looked at least a little unperturbed. The women were quick to fawn over the men, and Ryoku had an untoward amount of attention coming his way. Hostility from them was at an all-time low.

"How did this get into the city?" Ryoku asked. The fool only had eyes for me, not the hundreds of bloodsuckers on him like some sort of fresh snack.

"Who knows," Loki muttered. He strode toward the Warg's body. Without explaining a word of this, he brought his sword down upon the Warg's neck with a sickening *thud,* arrows and all. Everyone reared back in disgust as the beast's head rolled down the road. Only now, I noticed, a certain light faded from its golden orbs.

"It would have gotten back up," Will seemed to realize aloud, giving Loki an incredulous look. "Wargs could survive such an attack?"

Loki wiped the blood on the Warg's hide with disregard. "Keep their spinal cord intact, and they'll rise from anything. Easiest way is to just lop off the head. Even those arrows missed their mark. Though," he added, giving Ryoku an unreadable look, "I imagine they wouldn't have if the bowman knew exactly what he was shooting at."

Loki looked his blade over and, with a scowl, rammed it back into its scabbard. "Wargs are vicious, unlawful monsters, and they must be killed whenever the opportunity should arise. In most cults, creating a Warg is an unforgivable sin. It violates the laws of nature, and werewolves are supposed to be a tree-huggy sort of monster. "

I couldn't help but see why. Though wolves were harmful to humans, they often kept to themselves. A violent guise such as Lycanthropy didn't suit them.

"But something is creating them up here," Lusari said.

Loki shrugged. "To be expected. Lysvid's in a state of war. The wolves, I bet, are losing. Some might turn to this."

Ryoku looked like he must be bursting with questions. "Why did its fur turn so red?" he asked. "It got... stronger, didn't it? Somehow."

Ryoku's inquisitiveness must have been perfect for Loki, who beamed like a teacher asked to profess his knowledge. "It's what we call their 'last hunt,'" he explained. "Like how a predator draws on all their adrenaline when their life is endangered. Only, when a Warg does it, their strength and abilities increase at least tenfold. That's why we had to fight so seriously back there – and, speaking of which, why I'm so impressed with you!"

His expression changed like the weather. His eyes brightened with enthusiasm. "Three arrows in a moving target in rapid succession! Not to mention the target was a Warg in its last hunt! I haven't met many capable of such a feat except…" He hesitated, mulling over his words, but smiled again."Truly, I chose the right Defender."

Ryoku just smiled. I could tell he was eager to ask Loki more questions like an arrow notched to a bow.

"You're pretty knowledgeable in the field of Lycanthropy, old man."

The female voice, honeyed to the nines, belonged to a small, ivory-skinned girl who entered our midst. She was unmistakably a vampire for her crimson eyes, and almost looked about Lusari's age, though that didn't say much for their kind. She could have been my great grandmother for all we knew.

She kept her midnight-black hair strung up in pigtails. That was about where her childishness ended, for she wore a decidedly adult expression with her luminous eyes on Ryoku. She also dressed in a style no kid should ever wear. Her white dress-shirt was tied off at the base of her ribs with more than half the buttons undone, baring a lacy black bra that *had* to be a push-up. She even had her black thong hiked up by her hips above her tiny skirt, cutting off far above the fishnets she wore with it. The more I studied this newcomer, the more I could tell she was older than she looked. She was diminutive and slender, but the black make-up around her eyes hid some years from her. She could be as old as Loki looked.

When she appeared, the battle-wizened men of our group quickly became boys again. Will only glanced at her for a moment before his eyes trailed off, then he shamefully averted them altogether, staring away to find Lusari giving him a hilariously stern look. I had to clear my throat sharply for Ryoku to draw his gaze from her waist, and he only gave me a sheepish smile, his face flushed. Loki, however, didn't seem to avert his eyes at all.

"Perhaps I am," Loki replied. His tone was dreamy and distracted, baring his silvery tongue. "And who might be inquiring? Such a pretty lilac amid the city of the undying."

Gross. Even first impressions must put years between the two. The girl didn't shy away. Seducing vulnerable men was an asset of female vampires. She gave a formal curtsy that very obviously flashed anyone standing behind her. Oddly, though, all of the vampires behind her pointedly averted their eyes. Not one must have caught a glimpse of her rear. What did she mean to these people?

"My name is Cleria Nightfang," she replied in her silky voice. She sounded just like a prostitute, I realized. Sharing company with the emperor of Orden unfortunately made me quite familiar with their ilk. However, the presentation of her last name suggested I was right. "Your ample knowledge of Lycanthropy makes me suspicious of you, old man. Just who are you, exactly? Are you a werewolf of some sort?"

Loki seemed to clue in for the first time what she was calling him. Maybe he even detected that sickly-sweet tone she used on him. "O-O-Old man!?" he demanded. I tried to catch his look and warn him, but he was too enraged. "I'm Loki! That's Loki the Trickster god to *you*, little girl! And if you knew much about Lycanthropy at all, then you'd know I couldn't walk out as a human in a place like this!"

It was only after he crossed his arms defiantly and snuck a glance at Cleria's expression that he noticed mine, and he froze. The fool had just openly declared his name while the rest of us were trying to blend in. A hefty bounty sat upon Ryoku's head. Considering that and the wealth of information on him, it wouldn't surprise me if Orden already knew that Loki was with us.

He did manage to create a shocked look on Cleria's face. "Really?" she asked shrewdly, much of her honeyed voice absent now. "The Trickster god? You?"

Cleria's expression was fully condescending. Regardless of his handsome visage, expensive attire, and the way he held himself at all times, Loki didn't quite fit the image of god. However, she lost interest in him before he could spit out a reply, and turned to the object of her initial interest – Ryoku.

"Who are the rest of you? World travelers, clearly. Are you looking for work?"

I chose to step in. I wasn't sure I trusted Ryoku to muster up a lie. Even then, I wanted as little contact between him and this vampire as possible.

"The name's Roxy Cleon. Swordstress, from the world of Id."

Cleria scrutinized me carefully. I'd been mistaken as a resident of Id before in other worlds aware of the outer spirit realm. Of course, thousands of vampires couldn't hang out in one world without being minutely aware of the outside. Id was known for its desert lands, where the people had darker skin, strangely colored eyes, and hair kissed by the sun. Only the undertones of black in my hair hinted my true heritage, but I usually styled my hair to hide it. Even among good company, I didn't boast about my homeland.

I noticed Ryoku giving me an odd look, too. No, he knew we had to lie. What was the emotion in his eyes?

"How is Id this time of world-year?" Cleria asked in a mocking-polite tone.

I scoffed. "Hot. What else?"

Now Ryoku sidled around me, offering Cleria a hand. "Ronyx Curtis," he introduced himself, surprisingly smoothly. "Nice to meet you."

He didn't try to lie about a world. Nothing he'd ever heard of might explain away his golden hair, his easy smile, his fair skin...

Still, I felt he could have called himself Rumpelstiltskin and the girl would have accepted it. If I ever found myself looking at Ryoku or anyone in the same way she did, I'd sell my own bounty.

"A pleasure," she told him sensually, practically devouring him with her eyes. She took his hand and lightly ran her nails across his knuckles. At least, if Ryoku felt anything from that, he had a solid poker face. "Soft hands. Bitten, but dirty. You work for a living, or you did somewhere else. Maybe a... cook, of some sort?"

He smiled sheepishly. "Yeah, I guess you could say that."

I wouldn't let them see how mad I was that she could guess things about Ryoku that *I* didn't know. "Were I the one in charge of Ellithea, I'd make a pretty boy like you a prince. Still, I suppose the pure line of elves is a snobbish one."

She'd handed him his own alibi and the name of one of the biggest elven worlds in the spirit realm. I could see the twinkle in his eye from here. He hadn't heard a word of her flattery. All he heard was the world of elves. I hadn't decided if his curiosity was cute or annoying yet.

Lusari approached next, perhaps to stop Ryoku from asking questions about his apparent homeland. Her snowy eyes concealed a depth of intelligence behind her timid, cutesy act. As she curtsied before Cleria in a practiced, refined manner, I knew she had a lie painted on her lips like a canvas.

"Hello, Cleria. I'm Belle Collier, a fledgling mage from a small academy in Fayzr. It's a pleasure to make your acquaintance."

I gave Lusari a surprised look. I could easily believe she was actually telling Cleria the truth and had lied to us. Even her regular stutter was gone! Cleria only looked bored. Lusari seemed the least interesting to her, probably because of the alarming difference in their personalities. Cleria could be horribly wrong, though. For a girl we'd met surrounded by thugs in a compromising situation, Lusari carried herself well.

"A pleasure," Cleria agreed half-heartedly. "So that makes a god, a warrior from the hottest of worlds, a mage from the coldest, and a pretty elf boy. That brings us to..."

Will jumped when his eyes fell upon her. The tall, good-natured warrior had been staring out into the sea of faces with a dreamy, spacey smile on his placid face. I'd seen him trekking through the Old Forest's dizzying hills with expertise, but he looked bored in the painted city of Lysvid. He was certainly a country boy, unimpressed by illustrious buildings or ornate lamps, but by the mighty trees in the woods that skyscrapers only tried to impersonate, clutching for the sky with hands of leaves and branches. Here, standing before Cleria, he looked like he was in the wrong painting.

"Me?" he asked, shocked, as though he should be the last one giving his name. The poor lug was a mile behind the conversation. He had the most time to conjure up a fake name, but the look on his face showed he hadn't used it at all. Loki, who missed his own cues earlier, started gesturing frantically to Will from behind Cleria – waving to the lamppost, his sword, and even a moustachioed vampire who stared at Loki like the Warg returned through him.

"Uh, right!" Will said after a horribly long pause. "Silly me! How could I forget? Why, my name is Jeffrey! Uh. *Sir...* Jeffrey... uh, Lampsword. I hail from Bonnin!"

The gallant pose he struck afterward was too much. I choked trying to hold my tongue. Ryoku and Lusari giggled in fits behind Cleria, who was staring at Will, clearly thinking he was touched in the head. Loki buried his face in his hands.

"Right," Cleria said in a tone as dry as the desert I claimed my home. "Of course. That would make a god, a warrior from the desert, a mage from a wintry world, a pretty elf, and... You... what was it?"

He raised a polite hand in greeting. "Sir Jeffrey Lampsword, miss. From Bonnin."

"Right," Cleria said again, either deaf or ignorant to the chuckling behind her. "Sir Jeffrey Lampsword, an apparent knight from Bonnin." She gave Will a lasting look before turning back to Ryoku, who quickly shut his mouth. "I'd love to get the story of how your little group came to be, but I came here for a reason. Tell me, are you lot looking for work?"

"For work?" Ryoku echoed softly.

"Why, of course we are!" Loki agreed, the only one who kept his natural identity. To be fair, I thought he'd burst at the seams if he tried to act normal for five minutes. "Our stay in Lysvid will surely not be for long, but we're seeking an inn and hoping to stock up on supplies and funds before we depart once more."

For the first time, Cleria brightened up after hearing Loki speak. "Perfect! I can refer you to an inn just down the way." She stopped to point in the direction we'd been heading before the Warg appeared, though a little more to the west if the moon's angle was to be trusted. "The Resolute Mire's a great inn and pub. Tell them I sent you, and they'll cut your cost by at least forty percent." Her smile returned, and her fangs peeked out from her dark lips. "So, are you lot interested in becoming werewolf hunters?"

Ryoku's brow rose, and I could almost read the plaintive thoughts on his face at a glance. I shared some of his sentiments – it had taken all of us to defeat the one Warg. If we fought more, would we survive? On the other hand, Ryoku seemed to feel sorry for the likes of them. A race of humans and wolves turned into monsters, unable to revert to their human forms.

"There's no real catch," Cleria reasoned. "One, it's no real commitment. You get the night at the Resolute Mire, and then come to the Defender Registry in the morning. What?" she added at Ryoku's expression. "The Registry's good for more than just Defenders, y'know." She said the world *Defender* with a little spite, I noticed. Probably a good thing we hid Ryoku.

"Register there with us, and the clerk will give you registry papers. You bring those to the gear shop down the way; they'll outfit you in our own special weapons and armor. They'll augment anything you insist on using, too. See, we've got all sorts of tonics and herbs suitable for taking down the wolves with ease.

"Either way," she went on, watching Ryoku's face like she might find answers there. "Back to my point: there's no commitment. You keep those papers, and you can sign up anytime you come back to Lysvid. It's no contract, per say, but gives you permission to engage in our territorial war. If you didn't have them, then the wolves could just kill you in the middle of the streets, and nobody could lift a finger. That, and we don't hold any real responsibility if you die on the job."

Loki already looked sold. "Discount at the inn, and free gear?" he echoed, as though that had been all she uttered. "Sign us up! We'd love to clean the streets of their ilk, wouldn't we, Jeff?"

He elbowed Will mockingly, who glowered at him. I shared a smirk with the Trickster. No way Will was ever going to live this down.

Will was the first one to look to Ryoku. "What do you think?" he asked. "Werewolf hunting? Hardly clean work by the sounds of it, but we can earn extra money. Until we get to Syaoto, funds cannot be underestimated."

He deliberately avoided using Ryoku's fake name, since he probably didn't catch it. His tone gave Cleria surprise, though; by her expression, she hadn't realized Ryoku was the leading voice among us, and regarded him in a new light.

"It'll work," Ryoku agreed. He didn't seem to give it much thought. What else would we do to earn money here?

"Excellent," Cleria replied with a smile. "Then I'll see the lot of you in the morning. And," she added, with a wink to Ryoku, "the woman who was injured is being treated, if you were wondering. Considering the *usual* impact of a Warg attack, the city owes you a great debt. Consider my job offer as something of my own personal amends for the fact, if you will. But if that isn't enough…"

She whispered something close to Ryoku's ear, and before a blushing Ryoku could stammer out a reply, she slipped away in the crowd. I glared after her, wondering if the vampire girl was worth trusting. Finding us in the middle of the city to offer us a job seemed too convenient. Maybe, as much as I would never say it aloud, I didn't like how she looked at Ryoku.

The crowd started to disperse around us and some guards came to remove the body of the Warg I caught Will's eye and raised a brow at him. "Really? Jeffrey Lampsword, of fucking Bonnin?"

Our group started laughing anew. Watching Ryoku's face light up again, I realized I didn't really care where we ended up or what we did – as long as I was with him.

SCENE THREE: HUNTERS

...Of Act Three: Trickster

In the eyes of Ryoku Dragontalen, we are in Werewolf Camp Gaevrel, in the world of Lysvid. It is early afternoon On November 7th, 2017.

"You ready, kid?"

I nodded confidently. On the inside, though, I wasn't sure. Killing one Warg in the city was a daunting task. Loki assured us that werewolves weren't quite as tough, but still... we were about to attack a village full of them.

Sira grinned in response, stuffing away the cloth she used to polish Sinistra. She wore new clothes apparently more suitable for werewolf hunting. Whenever she wasn't looking, I admired her in them. Any pants less baggy than the kind she preferred would help emphasize her shapely hips and bottom. These ones flared out around the ankles in an Asian flair. Oddly, she also donned a hair band similar to Lusari's style, and it helped emphasize the attractive curve to her cheekbones. If she ever saw me staring, she didn't remark on it. She seemed a little less surly than usual.

Lusari charged her staff up nearby, speaking in some archaic tongue that made a blue light climb through the runes on her staff. The normally shy girl had donned a sexy style of skirt cut shorter at the front and long at the back, paired with calf-high boots of dark leather. She swapped out her bright, low-cut shirt for a black dress-shirt with wide, lacy cuffs on the sleeves. I couldn't tell if she was trying to act more as a fake alias in Lysvid, or if this was just an augment to her style. Either way, it took work to avert my gaze.

The girls weren't the only ones outfitted in new styles. It was the first time I'd seen Will willingly put away his Syaoto armor, something that must have been tipping others off to his origins. Instead, he found a similar style of armor decorated in ivory, complete with a long-sleeved black shirt and black pants beneath. He looked as though he'd been reborn as a vampiric soldier.

Sira stayed with Lusari and me. I guessed she didn't care much for their plans. If I knew Sira at all, she preferred to rush in with Sinistra and cut down anything that moved. Two other groups of similar sizes crouched elsewhere in the brush, each about ten strong.

Our group consisted of us, Cleria, and four other vampires – two males, two females. The males appeared annoyed by our company, but the females just stayed near Cleria, who dressed the same way as she did back in the city. The men carried weapons, but the girls seemed deadlier with their claws. I thought the long claws could be brittle, but Loki professed otherwise. Apparently, they were as sturdy and sharp as bones.

Loki described vampires as 'the perfect predator.' Both males and females were sturdy as rocks, though females appeared softer to the touch. The lack of blood flowing through their system left their bodies cold and desolate. In its place flowed vampiric venom, a toxic, poisonous life force. Loki claimed the venom came from an ancient magic long ago. It fed off the blood that vampires so lustily pursued, but, in turn, reinforced their entire bodies in a way human blood could never achieve. Their muscles and veins swelled doubly, offering them immense strength and affected every muscle's abilities. Their legs grew faster, their hearts more durable, their lungs capable of their extreme feats. Even their brains took on effects from the venom, making them smarter and able to think on their feet. The combination made them incredibly fearsome predators.

Of course, they weren't completely immortal, but not in the ways my world believed. Garlic was useless against them; a stake to the heart would simply shatter; they didn't particularly like sunlight, but it didn't cause them to melt or set aflame. No. According to Loki, there were three ways to kill a vampire: to poison blood they took in, to prevent them from taking blood, or the bite of a werewolf, their natural predator.

Werewolves were much simpler to understand. The Lycanthrope virus wasn't quite like vampiric venom. In fact, it seemed to have more earnest roots. Vampires descended from elves long ago that chose to dabble in blood magic. In tandem, werewolves were their natural predator. Men who became werewolves initially accepted the role of an animal spirit. It took their bodies during moonlight, offering them animalistic strength and senses to rival the vampire. They might live around two hundred years or more, depending on how they lived their lives, and were killable in combat. In truth, I was glad circumstances chose us the easier foe.

A hand caused me to jump. "Quit zoning out." Sira's words cut through my thoughts like a hot knife, and I reflexively winced. If she noticed, she didn't comment. "We're your Guardians, but our abilities are limited if you space the hell out all the time. Focus."

I gave her a sheepish smile. For a moment, I thought her stern scowl might ebb away into a smile, too.

"I'm ready," Lusari whispered, loud enough for Will to hear at the edge of the main group nearby. The soldier nodded and stood with the others. The four vampires looked us over curiously, though with measured distaste. No doubt, they were unhappy to be around us.

"Got it. Everyone else?" Will asked quietly.

We all stood in silent reply, and everyone merged together at the edge of the brush overlooking the camp. Loki returned through the edge of the field. His guise was in a completely different field than the others, and he might never have gotten away with it if he hadn't spilled the beans on who he was. I was sure he'd somehow seen the old Dracula movies from my world, or else he was terribly racist. He'd gone off with the quartermaster and returned in a white ruffled dress-shirt – the collar popped, of course – and tight-fitting black pants. If that getup wasn't already concerning, he later added a short red and black cape to pin to his shoulders. Pretty sure he was wearing fake fangs, too. He might pretend it was some kind of illusion to fool the wolves, but I wouldn't take the bait.

He greeted me with an unnecessary friendly shove. "Ready, Ronyx?" he asked, his silvery tongue making easy work of my alias. Something about my expression made his smirk slip. "Worry not – I won't let them harm you. You have ample protection here, my fair-haired friend."

I gave him a tepid stare, but he smiled like I told him he was my hero.

"What did you see out there?" one of the vampires asked Loki.

The Trickster smiled. "Fear not – there's little of them from what I can tell. Perhaps thirty or less. All holed up in muddy shacks along the swamp-front. I'd guess at more, but somehow I doubt they comprehend living underground or in tree lofts – mitts cannot be useful for such things. Their ruddy shacks, bridges, and whatnot should fall to but a single sword strike. If you ask me, our work's cut out for us."

"They've surprised us before, old man," Cleria warned. "Were the torches lit?"

"What?" Loki frowned, puzzled. He temporarily lost his composure at Cleria's nickname for him, but he composed himself before eyes turned to him. "Perhaps. Well, yes. Most of them."

One of the males growled. "Then they know we're coming. Damn it. I'd bet my fangs the elf let slip our little plan."

"Then you would lose your fangs," Loki replied like a gunshot, turning on the vampire with an emerald-eyed glare. "He's with us – do you want our help or not?"

Before the vampire could advance on Loki, Cleria let out a low, inconspicuous call resembling something like an owl. It stopped the vampire. Around us, I heard the other companies coming in to surround us.

"Of course they're wary, you nitwit. We're at war with their kind, remember?" She growled under her voice and rose to her full height, addressing the entirety of our hunting group in a low voice. "We're ready. Split up – we'll tackle them on all sides. Vallous, you take the north. Greil, east. We'll handle the west. We surround them and press them against the southern marshland. Greil, your group will take out the bridges spanning the bank, trapping them on our side."

The confirmation was merely both parties taking off into the woods. We rounded up our group and readied ourselves. Will appeared at my shoulder with a brave smile.

"Fear not, my friend. You have the lot of us here to protect you. You remain quite the amateur. None expect you to fight alone. If we are to gamble against luck, we may yet outnumber this pack of wolves."

"So we'll surely be outnumbered ten to one." I rolled my eyes. Our luck was not quite something I'd place bets on.

"I would not toss us to the wind just yet," Will told me with some confidence. "These are not the seasoned warrior Wargs we faced in the city – these are starved wolves, forced to live in unwholesome conditions in a world alien to their race. Victory will surely find us."

I felt a sudden and strong empathy for the wolves. They really didn't belong here, did they?

Will saw the look in my eyes. "I do not disagree."

We didn't need to speak. It was one thing to defeat a group of thugs intent on raping a young girl. Even the raiders in the Old Forest weren't entirely evil or set against violence on purpose. Even though these wolves couldn't walk as humans here, there remained that aspect to them. They were just humans stuck in the bodies of wolves, forced back into swamps and woods while vampires prospered. Neither had exactly been friendly to us so far – we'd fought a few stray wolves along the way – but I found myself sympathizing with the wolves. Still, we might never find other work here among their kind, and it had jumped out at us. Our stores from Harohto would only last so long.

We rose to a crouch and went to follow the others, Loki in the lead. The golden-haired Trickster caught my gaze and gave me a bold grin. We only locked eyes for a moment before something leapt upon him from behind, throwing him straight into me.

I tried to catch him, but my position and weight just brought both of us crashing to the ground and knocked the wind out of me. I caught the glimpse of a dark shape leaping over his shoulders. They found us first.

I heard the unmistakable swing of Sira's mighty weapon. The whisper of chilling ice crackled through the air. Will cried out, and I heard his gladius freed into the air.

Loki got to his feet in seconds, using me as a sort of landing board to push himself up. He landed easily on both feet behind the wolf, his silver blade already in hand. Cursing, I got to my feet and scrambled for my weapons.

Something slammed into me. Luckily, it hit my knife before it struck me, and a canine whimper nearly brought me to the ground with it. A rumbling, cold sense of dread thundered inside me. I'd just taken a life. I couldn't yank my knife free without twisting my arm beneath the wolf, so I lost my grip and stumbled back, bumping into something else. I spun around, scrambling for my bow or staff, but it was just Will.

"I do not take kindly to being trampled!" he declared jokingly. Even immersed in battle, his sense of humor never evaded him. Will already had a fine scrape down the edge of his cheek that made my stomach lurch. His lip hung in a pained grimace because of it. More than ever, I wish I could call myself professed in magic enough to heal my friend. It almost made me feel worse than taking lives.

The fight dissolved into a full-on brawl around me, the shouting of my friends and allies mixed with the pained, savage howling of wolves. I couldn't spot them in the dark, but I could hear them. Large forms streaked through the bushes so quickly that to blink might cost me my head. Sira led the charge, swinging her mighty Sinistra like an axe. Loki backed Lusari as she unleashed chilly bursts of ice over any opponent in sight. More than one frozen wolf hung in her tracks, crouched as if ready to break free and lunge. Loki buried his sword in one, and it fell in an avalanche of ice shards and blood.

A tough hand grabbed me, and suddenly I was bowling into Will again. My meager weight would never faze him. With alarming speed, he hurled me behind him and buried his lance through the skull of an incoming wolf – one that pounced where I'd just been standing. I flinched away from the gory sight. Was battle really a place for me?

"Draw your weapon!" Will ordered, shaking me around the shoulders. "What happened to your knife?"

"I—"

I didn't have time to explain. A wolf lunged from the shadows. Will met it mid-air and broke through it with his gladius, cleaving the beast from head to tail in a gory mess. Without meeting my glance, Will shoved an object into my hands. A dagger made of surprisingly heavy metal. The sheath was a clip, so I quickly attached it to my belt.

"I expect that back!" Will said, and turned on his heel to follow the others. I stole a quick glance around as I yanked the dagger out. Just as I turned, I spotted a smaller wolf, its fur jutting up from the brush like a coat of steel feathers. I barely held an advantage – it lunged, clearing the distance between us with a mighty leap.

Before my dagger could meet it, a silver sword shot out from the side, severing the beast with enough force to hurl it aside. Loki dragged his silver blade free with a heavy tug, and flashed me a grin like he was having the time of his life.

"A Guardian lives and dies for their Defender. Should you have to use that blade before you're ready, I'll have failed you."

"Loki, I already killed—"

He was gone, rushing ahead, leaving me to follow with my petty dagger. Luckily, nobody seemed to be around to hear him slip up from my alias.

Will and Sira battled a massive wolf ahead of me, one that made the others look shrimpy. This one had mangy, thick fur that hung off its skin in huge tufts. On its hind legs, the monster towered well over even Sira's head, but the two didn't cower.

Will ducked under a swipe of its giant claws, and Sira lunged, her blade streaking through the air like a bloody quarter moon. One of the nearby vampires buried its sword in the monster's thigh. It emitted a pained howl – awfully human sounding. At the same time, Will's lance and Sira's mighty sword swung for blood, and I flinched away in disgust.

Only my timely flinch found me face-to-face with another wolf. A mass of brown fur and golden eyes. It snarled like tearing cloth and flew into the open air between us, a mix of claws and fangs. I shoved my blade forward, but I already knew I was in harm's way. The full weight of the monster crashed into me, buckling my knees and forcing me to the ground with the monster atop me. Searing pain shot across my chest, followed by the smothering heat of the wolf's body.

Blood was everywhere. My blade found the wolf's heart, luckily, but it brought the limp beast down on me. In the moment, I couldn't imagine that this wolf used to be a human, or that it might shed its fur if the sun ever rose in Lysvid. To me, deep in the throes of pain, they were monsters once more.

I couldn't make a sound. Pain shook my entire body. My legs and chest ached horribly. Had my legs broken underneath me? Was the open wound in my chest the reason my vision swam like heat waves upon summer pavement?

"Damn it! Damn it damn it damn it!"

Sira's string of curses was unmistakable, even as my ears felt like someone put them in a box far from my body. I heard her enraged growl of effort. Sira dragged the beast away with one arm, and hurled it like careless litter before stooping down next to me. I couldn't say what made her eyes so livid and beautiful at the same time, or whether it was a trick of the horrid feeling coursing through me. Her eyes landed on my chest, and I watched the color drain from her skin.

Then she was gone, and then dragging a distraught-looking Lusari into view. Lusari clambered atop me, and then my vision flickered. She had one hand on her staff, the other on my chest. The tips of her eyelashes glinted. Were those tears?

Her hand started to glow. The runes on her staff responded. I thought to question it, but I couldn't possibly. Were people able to channel magic through their hands normally? I focused so intently on that matter that I almost didn't feel the pain ebb away, or note how my vision straightened.

Lusari grabbed me by the collar and pressed herself against me. It was such an abrupt movement that I almost didn't catch her whisper through her strawberry-scented hair or the dusty odour I associated with magic.

"That's only battle healing. It's supposed to last until I can get a good look at you. So for the time being, try not to do anything dumb, okay?"

I could only nod. Even Lusari, the timid little mage from Harohto, seemed taken by a lust for battle. A husky undertone clung to her voice like blood in the grass. Such emotion wasn't something I expected from her, and it made the blood rush to my face.

She remained atop me, her face next to my ear and her measured breath dancing against the lobe. It took me a moment to realize she probably hadn't noticed my nod, so I murmured, "Yeah. I'll try."

Whether I was right or she'd just gotten distracted, Lusari drew away from me. The ice-elemental girl had a blush rising up in her cheeks when she rose, and she ducked away into the shadows. Sira reappeared where Lusari vanished, and stuck out a hand to me without looking.

As my thoughts started to culminate again, I was having about enough of looking like the weak link in the group. I pushed myself to my feet. In Sira's eyes, that was the right move. She looked a little stunned, but she flashed me a smile.

"Come on, moron. Or do you wanna get hurt again before we get into the stupid village?"

I rolled my eyes. We followed the others into the brush, and into the thick of battle.

SCENE FOUR: RENEGADE

...Of Act Three: Trickster

*In the eyes of Ryoku Dragontalen, we are in Gaevrel, in the world of Lysvid.
It is late afternoon
On November 7th, 2017.*

Sira and Will were the first ones I saw. The bright color of Sira's fiery hair burnt my eyes. Will's kind eyes loomed closer, and I felt the back of his rough hand on my forehead.

"You waken," Will stated, and quickly withdrew his hand. "And are evidently feverous. How do you feel?"

Sira turned away when she saw my eyes. Loki's head popped into view, his golden hair in disarray like the werewolves electrocuted him. "Check his pulse," he told Will as though I weren't there. "And his hands. I'll..."

He stuck a finger in my mouth, curling up my lip. I tried to pull away, but I suddenly felt the state of my body. I felt wholly numb save for a fiery feeling behind my face. My fingers twitched, but I couldn't muster the strength for a fist.

"No fangs," he confirmed, as though that were some great surprise.

A different voice I didn't recognize cut in. "Lycanthropy won't just pop up in a matter of hours." It belonged to a young male, I thought. A deep, thoughtful voice. "Surely you know that."

"You never know," Loki replied. "Better to be safe than sorry." He paused, and then gestured to Will. "Jeffrey?"

The fake names. Will's always made me laugh. Not this time. "His pulse is regular," Will said. I only then felt his hand on my wrist. "No claws, if that is what you expected."

"Lycanthropy?" I asked, in the first opening I could seize.

"A mere precaution." Loki waved me off.

I didn't like the sound of that. As I listened to their voices, the events started coming back to me. The wolf that struck a grievous blow on my chest. The quick attempt at healing Lusari had made. What had happened after? I only remembered rushing after the others.

Will stuck a cool, damp cloth under my head when I tried to move, which helped me get a better view of the room. It was a run-down sort of shack made of mostly greying old wood, dried mud shoved between the cracks to connect it all. Will and Loki remained close, but Sira kept a few paces back, her face turned away from me. Lusari lay against the wall, her eyes closed and a cloak thrown over her. Next to her was a stranger, a tall vampire with black hair and gleaming red eyes who dressed in somewhat refined clothing. He only offered me a small smile when I saw him.

"What happened?" I asked, fixating Loki with a bleary glare.

My voice came out weaker than I felt. I tried to lift my head, but a stab of pain cut my vision short. A heavy feeling started to well up in my chest, and I felt short of breath. Being so vulnerable reminded me only too well of a day earlier this year where I landed in the hospital. It took weeks to recover. I couldn't let the same thing happen again.

"We won the battle!" Loki declared triumphantly, pumping a fist in the air. "A wolf tackled you as we entered the village, and you struck your head on a stone. Luckily, we caught on right away and fought our way into the village, where we fortified this shack to protect your prone body!"

"Your wounds reopened in the process of carting you here," Will told me apologetically. "We have done what we could, but you are not yet in peak condition. A... little far from it, I'm afraid."

Slain wolves filled the doorway to sell their point. A mass of greys and browns, all splashed with pungent red blood. The stack of bodies was high enough that we'd have trouble leaving that way without moving them. Slash and claw marks pockmarked the doorframe. Ice clung to parts of it, too, evidently from Lusari's potent ice.

Even at the macabre sight, I managed a small smile. My friends were strong, that was certain. I could have never helped them fortify such a beaten shack.

"Cleria led the other vampires off to the square," Will added, as though plucking the question from my mind before it surfaced. "She did not like how they were acting near you." When he saw my puzzled glance, he added, "Blood."

Right, of course. Vampires wouldn't have made for the best company with an open bag of food in front of them. Still, I caught the glance of the sole remaining vampire, the tall one in a long brown coat. He kept his left arm out of its sleeve, drawn against his chest and hidden from view. Despite the bloody color of his eyes, there was a gentle calm to them, like the sweet red of apples.

When he saw my glance, the tall vampire nodded curtly. He had a young voice for the seriousness of his face. "Rex Dougo," he introduced himself a little awkwardly, a reluctant smile on his face. "I've been around."

I tried to stick out my hand, but the motion only shot pain through my chest. I gave the tall boy a small, friendly smile instead. "Ronyx Curtis," I introduced myself. Again, were it not for Loki, I'd have forgotten to give my fake name. As friendly as Rex's eyes looked, I couldn't base trust off my instinct just yet. It had failed me before.

"Rex showed up among the hunters in another group," Will told me. "He is the only one who could remain around the blood. He offered to help us get you to an old healer near the town of Xactyr. Cleria vouched for them."

I saw the lack of trust in Loki's eyes. I couldn't imagine why. If Cleria and Rex both thought some healer would help us, then I didn't see why we should doubt them. Cleria had been good to us so far.

It didn't take long for everyone to be on their feet. Sira and Rex cleared a path through the piles of wolves. Will gently coaxed Lusari to stand. I could tell she used a lot of magic. Her footsteps were sluggish and almost seemed drunk.

Loki packed up my belongings next to me. He flashed something to me - my knife, the one that I misplaced in the gut of a wolf. "We looted this off the wolves outside the village," he told me with a playful smirk. "Better you lose your knife than your head, but you should learn to hold a grip on your weapon. Remind me - I'll show you a trick when you're better."

I hoped I would remember. At present, my chest felt so tight that I wondered if I wouldn't just die during the trip. My comrades seemed worried, too - not that that was entirely unusual from them.

When everyone was ready, Will helped me onto Sira's back. I felt small and frail, carted around like expensive goods, and it only reminded me further of my hospital time. I'd only known this girl for a precious few days, and she liked saving my ass as much as she liked insulting me. What was I to make of her?

Outside the hut, the werewolf village was in shambles. Most of the other shacks burnt down or still blazed. Every semblance of the others was marred, thick with blood, assuaged with weapons, or else vandalized by the vampires. Werewolf bodies took up the majority of the marshy ground, given an ethereal appearance by the glint of flames and the pale shine of the moon. Blood shone on every spot of ground like rust. Where there wasn't either, the odd vampire body stuck out like a stone amid the dark, earthy colors of the area.

I felt more empathy for the wolves than ever before, and I hoped my allies wouldn't drag me into another brawl with them now. Who were we to dictate their fate because of the world they lived in? In another world, I could have befriended these wolves, who were still people even as the moonlight hid their faces.

Vampire hunting parties scattered around the remains of the village – some putting out fires, looting bodies and homes, or else just standing and conversing amongst themselves. A few groups turned toward us when we surfaced from the ruined cottage, but I didn't see Cleria among them. Some of the vampires who'd fought alongside us remained, though, and they didn't spare us any kind looks.

Our group didn't break pace, and we departed to the edge of the village where a collapsed stockade acted as a gate out to the path through the Black Woods. A group of vampires lurked there, whispering amongst themselves and sparing cold glances our way. I didn't sense any kindness from the folk we'd fought alongside. More than ever, I wondered if we were on the right side.

Nearby, one of the tall male vamps called Loki over. The Trickster hesitated – he, too, didn't seem too fond of the company we were with, or else he just wanted to hurry to our destination. "Go on," Will told him urgently. "See if we cannot glean some last helpfulness from them."

Loki only nodded, sparing me a parting glance before jogging over to the vampire. The rest of us continued to the gate, where the pack of shady vampires watched our approach with unreadable eyes.

It took me a moment to realize the prime source of their distaste – it appeared to be Rex. One of the males drew back his lips and hissed at Rex, who didn't meet his gaze. Was it judgemental of me to think those of the same race should get along? Humans certainly didn't all like one another, but I wondered why they were all giving Rex such hateful looks. Had he done something against his own kind? Cleria didn't seem to be here to keep her hunters in line, either.

One of the bigger males appeared before our company in the blink of an eye, making me jump. Their movements were eerily fast and hard to detect, especially in hostility. Rex was at the head of our group, but Will surreptitiously stepped up next to him, a tight grip on his lance.

"You're in strange terrain, Dougo," the vampire growled, crossing his arms. The way he stood, he clearly didn't want Rex to leave. "What are you doing here? Your kind is all dead."

I saw Will and Sira exchange curious glances. Rex couldn't be a werewolf, could he? They should always remain in their wolf form during the moon.

"Only passing through, Azrael," Rex replied, a little meekly. My stomach lurched. Was he going to let the vampires talk to him like that? Suddenly, I had very little doubt about the matter – we'd arrived on the wrong side, and I didn't want much to do with being a werewolf hunter anymore.

The vampire shoved him. Sira winced as my fingers dug into her skin, and I quickly released my grip when I noticed. Rex was unperturbed, really. He stood still, his feet dug into the mud a little. The hunch in his shoulders and the look on the other vampire's face was making my blood start to boil.

In another instant, the vampire grabbed Rex by the coat, lifting him a few inches from the ground. I felt Sira stiffen in anger. None of the vampires made to move. Will's hand was on his lance, ready to draw at a moment's notice. I saw Loki with the group of vampires, but he'd noticed what was happening and started jabbing his finger toward us, shouting words I couldn't hear at the vampires.

"You aren't supposed to be here," the vampire said coldly, each word enunciated like the tip of a dagger. "Among humans, too? Werewolf hunters, no less. Do they know who you are?"

"Do not label us as hunters," Will spoke. His voice sounded hard and cold, and eerily reminded me of his tone when he spoke to Lancet, his field commander. "We are travelers, passing through, and Rex is with us. Pardon me, but did you lift a finger to help us when our friend fell?"

The vampire hissed at Will, refusing to back down. "You are an outsider. We have no obligation to you and your people. You may have helped us, human, but tell me: would you have if not for the gold?"

By now, I had slid off Sira's back without a word. Sira was too angry to notice, and nobody gave me a second look as I approached. The injuries upon my body didn't seem to hinder me – no, even better, it was as though I was in better shape than ever.

Images ran through my head so vividly that I was losing track of the real scenario: the glint of a knife, the crack of fist against bone, grunts of pain, and a white-hot flash through my eye. It peaked with the smug voice of a boy I used to know.

Everything turned red.

(Meanwhile, in the eyes of Sira Jessura...)

I didn't notice Ryoku slide off my back. He was so light; it was like carrying a little backpack in addition to my own. However, I caught sight of him all too quickly – he appeared beside Will and the vampire. Even the flickering flames of torchlight didn't seem to throw any light on him.

A loud *crack* shot through the village. Any heads that didn't already see the confrontation turned. I saw it happen, but it seemed like a broken image. Entire scenes of the moment seemed to vanish. Ryoku stood where the vampire was, who was staggering back, clutching his shoulder with his fangs fully drawn. Ryoku's bare fist hung in the air. It stayed for a moment before falling back to his side.

"I hate people like you."

The statement was so calm, yet so livid. The voice came from Ryoku, but it bore the patience of a god who was only slightly irritated with his people. His hand seemed to vanish into the darkness altogether.

Nothing happened for a moment. The vampire must've been shocked. How had Ryoku even done damage barehanded? He was still as a statue. Will hung close, ready to intervene when the vampire struck.

"Who the hell do you think you are?" the vampire demanded. His words were slow, angry. "Striking a vampire in war territory? Bah. You humans aren't safe with the label of hunters, I assure you."

The rest of his squad stood at the ready. The females had their claws out, the males with taut fists at the ready. Rex stepped up next to Ryoku and Will. Lusari stood behind Will, though I doubted she could muster up a spell in her current state.

Among it all stood Ryoku. Despite the grievous injuries he bore, he stood with the regality of a king. Blood dripped from the bandages around his waist and head, but he didn't regard it. I couldn't see his eyes from where I was.

I'd had about enough of these vampires, and strolled forward, hand on Sinistra. As I moved, Ryoku's head lifted.

"I am –"

His voice cut off abruptly. Without warning, his kingly posture fell apart like a glass window. He crumpled to the ground. Whatever ferocity took him, it seemed spent in his current condition.

In a flash, Rex slid out before Ryoku. Will and I went to our Defender – he was out cold already, and blood soaked well through his bandages.

"You will not lay a hand upon my company!" Loki's voice cut through the village like thunder. I had never heard him yell before, especially with such power. It made me recall that he was a god. A fairly important one.

As he charged into our midst, I swore I saw currents of electricity running through his golden hair. For a moment, I thought he might strike down every vampire before us. Even the angry vampire in the coat relented before Loki, dropping his gaze and adopting a hunch in his shoulders.

He stood before us, chest heaving, eyes locked on the circle of vampires. It took a long moment for him to speak through his thunderous rage. When he did, it sounded like a full current charged his words.

"We'll take our leave. Next time you think to hire humans as hunters, think again. As long as we remain in Lysvid, you will keep your distance unless you wish to take trial by fire."

He snapped his fingers, and a ball of flame shot from his fingertips to land amid the circle of vampires. I'd forgotten mythology considered Loki a god of fire, among other things. They were outmatched, and they knew it. All recoiled at the sight of the flames. Will quickly helped Ryoku onto my back once more, and we rushed to catch up with an enraged Loki as he stormed past the gate into the woods.

Near the gate, a vampire ambiguously sniggered behind us. A bolt of lightning escaped from Loki and slammed into the ground at the vampires' feet. Hair on end, they fled, retreating into the village and allowing us to leave without another word. We followed Loki in silence, a little more aware of his presence now than before. I had to admit, I was glad he was on our side.

(Meanwhile, in the eyes of Ryoku Dragontalen...)

I woke up in the thick of the dark woods. The steady rise and fall of Sira's stroll was the only thing I felt beneath me. Brush and branches crackled beneath the feet of my comrades in a silent trudge. I could hear noises out around us - the odd hoot of an owl, unfamiliar chirping, and, in the distance, howling.

My head throbbed, so I kept my head against Sira's shoulder while we moved. I could occasionally catch the golden glint of Loki's hair ahead of us, or the odd time a streak of moonlight caught the barb of Will's lance on his back. By the timid crunching of leaves alongside me, I wagered that Lusari was on her feet as well. I drew comfort knowing they were near.

Little conversation occurred. I could hear Loki and Rex whispering to each other, but I couldn't make out their words. Will and

Lusari eventually fell in beside one another and spoke quietly, too. Sira walked alone with me. Will was generally the only one other than me who conversed with the tall warrior. Did she intimidate the others? I wondered if she was ever lonely. She'd been nothing but sweet to me since we met. In her own way, of course.

I faded in and out of consciousness as we walked. The dark woods never seemed to cease, and my comrades never picked up a full conversation. The forest felt cold, but I had no way to keep myself warm other than to stay as close to Sira as possible. Nobody lit a torch as we walked. Maybe it was to keep ourselves concealed should some threat arise. If we still walked in the Black Woods, Cleria told us they were common stomping ground for the werewolves. In that event, sympathy to their plight wouldn't be enough to help us.

At some point, I finally fell into a solid slumber against Sira's back.

(Meanwhile, in the eyes of Sira Jessura...)

"He's out again," I announced dully, keeping my voice low. I could feel Ryoku's chest lift and rise steadily against my back. His bandages had soaked through again. The second time since we left Gaevrel. I kept my steps as light as possible, but it never seemed to be enough. His injuries were too severe.

"Good," Loki remarked icily. The anger he'd displayed in Gaevrel hadn't settled. It probably wouldn't until Ryoku was safe. As Rex walked ahead with Lusari, Loki fell back to speak with Will and I. "These... occurrences of his. They seem to take a lot out of him."

I nodded shortly, careful not to disturb Ryoku. "A demon. But even he can't control Ryoku when he can barely stand."

"He managed to for a wink," Will added. "It was enough."

Loki rose a brow at us. The way the moonlight caught his emerald eyes seemed to give his gaze a tricky shine. Were he not such an impetuous, lordly brat, he might be attractive. "You two are familiar with this. Once in the capital with the Warg, and again back in Gaevrel. He's displayed this before?"

Will and I exchanged brief glances. In the end, only because Ryoku seemed to trust Loki, we explained the scenarios we both saw. The time Ryoku summoned fire after I lost my shield, driving away the Keeper of the Old Forest for the first time. Then, of course, in the raider camp. Sometimes the entity seemed to step in alongside Ryoku, helping him act stronger than he was. Ryoku, however, never seemed to notice.

"Hmm," Loki said when we finished. "And you think it's a demon?"

"It has to be," I replied. Will didn't argue, either. As soldiers, we'd likely both seen our fair share of demons. Seeing them in human habitation, however, was a little different. It wasn't unheard of in a place like Orden. Highly rare, though. Syaoto would have to be familiar with such things.

"What does it matter to you?" Will asked. Clearly, he was still a little apprehensive of the Trickster. I couldn't blame him. Why had he come to save Ryoku when Jesanht attacked? How had he known?

Loki stared ahead into the darkness for a long moment. "Well, maybe this demon will introduce himself before long. It seems he needs Ryoku alive in order to be here, so we share mutual interests."

I wanted to argue, but he had a point. The darkness only stepped in to protect Ryoku. Why was it there?

Our conversation broke apart when Rex turned to us.

"Xactyr is just beyond those hills," he told us, gesturing with his good arm. Ahead of him was the crest of a hill, and the dark, twisted trees of this forest broke off below. I could see some dim torchlight ahead – the city of Xactyr. "Our destination lies beyond the city, not far past the east exit and into the woods. Cutting through the city would be faster, but…"

Loki's back straightened. "No buts. We must take the fastest route, or we risk his life. Come, everyone! Let us travel with due haste."

It didn't take long for us to descend the hill. Even taking care not to jostle Ryoku on my back, it scarcely took a quarter of an hour before we stepped onto the pavement of Xactyr.

It was a different sort of city from the capital, surely. Caravans and wagons flocked the busier parts of the street, stemming from a road that skirted around the forest we came from, while the sidewalks looked more trafficked by foot. The buildings seemed richer and more elaborate. If I had to guess, I'd say Xactyr was some sort of trade or merchant city. From our viewpoint, the slums hid behind the elaborate buildings, as was common with trade cities. They kept their ilk to the alleys and beneath the big buildings, like nobles hid their chamber pots as though they could hide their disgusting human habits. Vampires clearly took to the more vain side of humanity.

As soon as we started into the city, we fell into the thick traffic of vampires on the sidewalk. It was annoying and tedious. There didn't seem to be a polite way to pass, so we walked along the fastest routes we could. I noticed Rex getting the same sort of dirty looks as before. The way he held himself as he walked, it was like he pretended to be walking alone, immune to the judgmental looks of the populace. I could relate.

Will strolled up next to Rex, flashing his lance when a vampire seemed ready to step in Rex's path. "Thanks," Rex murmured, not meeting Will's gaze.

"What is it that makes them spit in your wake, friend?" Will asked gently. "The ones at Gaevrel said something about the wolves, but you look like a vampire to me."

Rex still didn't meet Will's gaze. When he didn't reply, Will went on. "You have been naught but an excellent guide to us, and a friend. You helped us protect our friend, and were the only one not to curl your fangs at the sight of his injuries. You helped us change his bandages without bloody lust in your eyes. You have brought us this far – I plead you; share your plight with us. I dare say you have naught but a set of ready ears from us, and sound, sympathetic minds."

It took Rex a long time to respond. When he did, deeper into the noble city of Xactyr, we hardly heard him. "I am a half-breed."

Will looked at him, studying him. "A half-breed? Of... vampire and werewolf?"

It made sense, in a way. Rex had all the appearance of a vampire, but the usual look of bloodlust didn't seem to take him like it did the others. He retained a human form and just as much strength as the other vampires. With the constant racial war in Lysvid, it made sense why people regarded Rex like filth. To them, his werewolf features stood out on his face like ink.

"Surely you must judge me now as well." Rex was quiet, but his open hand balled into a fist. "I have been cursed with this half-form as a result of my deeds in life. I am a spirit assigned this curse, not born of it. In Lysvid, however, it wouldn't make a difference. They hate werewolves. Their toxins don't match up, and each can kill the other. Even the Ritual labels me as a heathen, a being who shouldn't exist."

"That's insanity," Loki muttered spitefully. "Werewolves and vampires. Let it be recalled that vampires were born of the darkest blood magic – the result of elves tainted by corruption. Werewolves, as legend says, were created to destroy them. That was thousands of years ago, and the races are no different than elves and dwarves, of half-demons and the Aroz. This world's petty rivalries are archaic."

"Mixed breeds are not that alien, even in Sy-- uh, Bonnin," Will said, suddenly sounding ridiculous. We were getting comfortable around Rex, forgetting the need for aliases. He cleared his throat. "Uh, my cousins in Syaoto have told me stories. They are host to many demi-human races. And, well, Ronyx is a demi-elf, of course. Such things are not unheard of. Love is not a thing that merely exists between a human and a human, or an elf and an elf. In a world where werewolves are not confined to their animal form, it is not unthinkable."

"Lysvid is rigid in its ways," Rex said. "A half-breed shouldn't exist here."

"But you do," Loki told him. "And that is a boon to us. Some folk aren't meant to please everyone they meet. They might even rile up crowds with just their appearance. But," he went on, waggling a finger like he was speaking to a child, "those people tend to be less valuable to the populace, and more so to a select few. Phenomenally, in fact."

His words served to stun us all. I didn't think the Trickster was able to be nice to anyone but Ryoku. Rex managed a weak smile toward the Trickster.

"His words apply to us all," Will told him boldly. "That, and our unconscious friend is the most accepting person I know. If he thought twice about you for your blood, then it would make no sense to travel with any of us."

"Especially Loki," I muttered with a sly grin. The Trickster didn't miss that, and spared a fiery glare toward me. I only grinned.

Rex's smile said it all. Beyond the frightening red shade of his eyes that was normal for vampires, there was a certain kindness. During the initial conflict at Gaevrel, I swore I'd seen Rex hesitate, as though trying to pick a side. He claimed to be from one of the other groups, but I had my doubts. He seemed like he arrived during the conflict somehow. Maybe he'd been a part of Gaevrel after all. When

Ryoku fell, and all of us surrounded him to protect him, Rex hesitated no longer and rushed to our aid. In the diplomacy of a war between races, friendship was easier to understand.

Ryoku stirred on my shoulders. Surprised, I smiled. When he was awake, Loki said, he must have been feeling better. I flinched when he coughed, and his body shook on my back. I didn't even realize what the problem was until Loki and Will both reeled around, drawing their weapons in a flash.

Here, in a vampire-infested city, we carried a bleeding elf.

I cursed myself a thousand times for not considering the idea. His wounds opened again, and I could already feel his blood soaking through my shirt. Normally that would upset me enough, but this was different. He was in danger.

Vampires appeared on all sides of us. No matter how dressed-up they were, vampires were monsters. Like sharks, they turned on us at the smell of Ryoku's blood.

When I hesitated between my sword and Ryoku, Rex stepped out in front of me. "Take him to the castle!" he said urgently. "Just outside the eastern exit! I'll hold them off!"

I hesitated. Many of the vampires around us donned the blacks of the Ritual cult. We weren't safe here. Could I even outrun them?

"You can't hold them off alone," Loki insisted, stepping forward as well. "There's too many of them!"

"Forget that," Lusari murmured – the first time she'd spoken in some time from her fatigue, and now she sounded scared. "We're surrounded. We'll never make it out of here without a fight – all of us."

Will had an idea. He appeared between Rex and I. Before I knew it, Will carried Ryoku off my back and pushed him toward Rex. The Defender lost consciousness once more, and Will handled him easily.

"You have to take him! You are the fastest of us! Cut through the crowd and get him to the castle. We will open a path!"

As much as I didn't want to let Ryoku out of my sight, it seemed like the only option. Maybe only Loki could get out of here in one piece, but losing the Trickster might spell our demises in this fight. The rest of us wouldn't make it off the sidewalk.

Cursing under my breath, I drew Sinistra with a violent ring that cut through all sound in the city. Feeling the huge blade in my hands filled me with vigor once more, and I knew I was making the only viable choice.

"Go, Rex!" I snapped. "Do as he says! I swear to the Creator, if you let any harm come upon him…"

The vampires were closing in. With no choice left, Will and I lashed out at the vampires with steel. Loki was quick to step up, both with his blade and bursts of fire that sparked up from his angry hands. Even Lusari, still worn from her efforts at healing Ryoku, summoned bursts of icy energy to match her fully charged staff. When there was a split second, the slightest window of opportunity, Rex darted between the oncoming vampires. I watched him go like it was in slow motion, Ryoku's golden-haired head bobbing against the shoulder of his coat – and then they were gone.

SCENE FIVE: THE TIMELESS ONE

...Of Act Three: Trickster

*In the eyes of Ryoku Dragontalen, we are in Gaevrel, in the world of Lysvid.
It is late afternoon
On November 7th, 2017.*

I dreamt of waking several times. Often it was blurry and confused, or waking before some kingly man who served to heal my wounds. Each time, my friends weren't there. I would look around at all the unfamiliar faces, seeking out the fire of Sira's red hair or Will's easy smile. I saw people I recognized, but never them. The people around me still loved me, and promised that I would never be hurt if I stayed with them. There was no Will, Sira, Lusari, or Loki though. Not even Katiel, Anna, or Dawn – so I couldn't agree.

When I finally woke to Will's worried, sky-colored eyes, I meant to sigh in relief. Instead, I shot up in a bout of pain when the draw of breath pierced my lungs.

"Easy, Ryoku," Will told me calmly, easing me back to the ground. I felt a soft blanket beneath me, but the ground below was hard and cold. "Your injuries are not entirely gone. The Timeless One has seen to you, but your injuries require further healing now that you are awake. You... are awake, yes?"

I didn't register his words for a moment, occupied by realizing my surroundings. We sat in a cellar with the iron gate ajar. A shade-covered bucket sat in the corner. I only wore my pants and the bandages spanning my chest, where I could feel the lingering pain of my wounds. However, blood hadn't soaked through them yet.

Will was dressed oddly, too. He wore an all-black outfit of a tunic with pants and long sleeves. His lance and gladius were gone, his bag elsewhere. A jagged cut on his cheek was beginning to heal. Just how long had I been out?

Will nudged me, so I replied. "Yeah, I'm here," I replied weakly. "Where are we? What is this cellar? What happened after...?"

"Perhaps one question at a time, my friend?" He offered me a small smile. "I apologize for your lodgings, as likely the master of the castle will as well. Your injuries nearly resulted in your progression into Lycanthropy. The chamber was a precaution in case you did manage to turn. Luckily, that particular toxin seems to be out of your system."

A chill ran down my spine. As much as I felt for the werewolves of Lysvid, I didn't particularly plan to join them. "And I suppose werewolves don't get waterbeds," I said sourly.

Will tilted his head, and I realized he might not even know what a waterbed was. He handed me a change of clothes. I changed behind Will as I asked him questions about the place. "Who is the Timeless One?" I asked. "How did we get here? Is everyone else safe?"

He wouldn't answer. "You will meet him momentarily," he assured me. "And everyone is fine. You will surely hear the tale soon."

I grunted my annoyance, but I finished changing and Will helped me stand. For a moment, looking at Will with his hand outstretched, I recalled the more cheerful Will I'd met in Harohto. Here in the vampire world, Will seemed to react badly to the dark atmosphere and lack of sun. His skin almost looked sickly, and I wondered if he was all too well. I wondered how well the soldier could handle hostility from each passerby, as seemed the norm for a human in Lysvid.

The moment passed once I got to my feet, for my stomach lurched dangerously and I retreated to the pail in the corner to vomit bile. Will waited patiently until I felt better enough to walk, and he closed the cellar door behind us

"You look like shit."

Her voice was unmistakable. Sure enough, Sira was leaning against the wall just out of sight. If we'd spoken a word about her, she would have heard it. I grimaced at her, stumbling along behind Will, and her eyes softened a little. She'd changed a little since we met, I realized. She was kind, even though she liked to hide it – from helping a stranger get through two days of forest, to waiting outside the cellar door of the same boy. Was I growing on her, like she was for me?

"Thanks," I replied with a healthy dose of sarcasm. She responded well to sarcasm.

Sira also wore the same style of tunic as Will, and it fit her curves nicely. As she unfurled her crossed arms, I caught her wince. She had difficulty moving her right shoulder. Almost forgetting my own injuries, I stepped toward her. She flinched for a second, like a dog hit in the same fashion before. The movement from her surprised me, and I stopped in my tracks, swaying in place.

"My arm?" she asked dully, though her eyes kept shields over them. "Minor skirmish involved in getting you here. No big deal, really, but we sorta got our asses handed to us. Nothing compared to you, though." She brightened a little when she saw my expression. "Don't worry about it. We're all fine, and you will be before long. So stop giving me that dumb look."

I screwed up my face. When I stumbled again, Sira put her arm around my shoulder. She was taller than me, and such a notion seemed odd from her. "Come on, now," she murmured. "The old bat who lives here says you need to be awake for the last step. If you fall down and crack your skull open, then you might end up a brain-damaged werewolf. A regular werewolf, I could handle."

I thought I caught the hint of flirting behind her tone. Looking up at her, she didn't give it away at all. So far, she kept flirting to a bare minimum with me.

"Our disguises fell through, by the way," Will commented as we started walking. He kept close, too, in case Sira got mad at me and decided to drop me. "As soon as Rex got you here, the Timeless One knew your name. Not only that, but all of ours, too. Loki probably served no help in that category."

"That includes Cleria, too," Sira added, with a definite note of distaste. "She's here. She claims our disguises never fooled her for a second."

I laughed, easily picturing how Cleria might react to such a thing, but the act of laughing made me almost double over in pain. Sira's arm tightened around my shoulders, and I practically fell into her. "Be careful," she muttered, and, to my shock, I felt a quick brush of her lips against my temple. It must have taken her considerable effort to stoop down, so I didn't immediately think it was an accident. I tried to meet her gaze, but she returned her fiery eyes ahead like death itself awaited us. Will, on the other hand, flashed me a grin like he just found his Christmas presents early.

We ascended a flight of stairs. Both Will and Sira had to help me climb them due to my chest. At a second flight, Sira lifted me up onto her back and ascended the steps two at a time, muttering about how slow an injured person could be. I only smiled.

At the end of the steps awaited a set of large oaken doors, big enough that Sira and Will could stand on each other's shoulders and still enter the room without stooping. Looking at us, Will jogged ahead to push on the great doors. A pair of vampires in black tunics appeared to help Will open the great doors, revealing a rectangular room ahead of us.

Torches lined nearly every crook in the wall of this chamber. I thought there was no ceiling above us, but I dimly noted the reflection of torchlight on what seemed to be a large glass dome sheltering us. The sky beyond showed the red and blue moons beginning to set on either side of the horizon. Nightfall.

A large, rectangular table split the room in half. Many vampires sat here, their pale skins and black clothes like a scene from an old movie. I spotted Loki's golden hair near the head of the table easily. He, too, dressed in the traditional black tunic of the castle. He was with Lusari, Rex, and Cleria, and chatted with an unfamiliar vampire with spectacles. The bespectacled one was the only vampire in the room who wore anything but the standard tunic – he wore a white coat over it. Of all the vampires in the room I hadn't met, he was the only one who flashed a friendly smile, adjusting his glasses meekly. I noticed that the spot at the end of the table was absent. Was he the Timeless One?

Loki, Lusari, Rex, and Cleria all stood at my arrival. I didn't miss that Lusari still had difficulty rising.

"The old vampire was right," Loki breathed, sounding surprised. "You've woken. At last, my friend. It is good to see you alive and well."

"I'm not so sure about well," Sira remarked icily. "Where the hell is—"

"Welcome, Ryoku Dragontalen!"

A booming voice came from the empty head of the table. I wasn't the only one to jump, which I took some minor satisfaction in. Sira swore, almost letting me fall in her surprise, but Will steadied me.

"Welcome to the Timeless Castle!" the disembodied voice continued. The bespectacled vampire near the head of the table gave me an amused look, but his lips weren't moving. He wasn't the speaker. Some of the booming quality faded, and a voice continued that was much... squeakier. "Here, I am in your care, my friend."

As I stared at the empty spot at the head of the table, confused, a head popped into view. The figure looked old, but with skin papery-white and as smooth looking as velvet. The collar of his own black tunic popped to frame his thin neck, and a wide-rimmed top hat accented the peak of his head, where wispy white hair curled out in short cascades. His eyes appeared white as fog, which left me blinking, stunned, for a long moment.

The bespectacled vampire cleared his throat into the silence. "I believe he meant to say, 'You are in my care here,'" he suggested, adjusting his glasses. The bespectacled one was much younger than the old vampire, his smile brighter. His wavy brown hair was only a little longer than average and well groomed. He smiled politely when he spotted my searching gaze. "Forgive my master, his brain seems a little scattered these days. Such is my main role as his assistant – to correct him where his faulty tongue may get him in trouble. My name is Relus Ashbane. It's a pleasure to finally meet the wakened Ryoku Dragontalen."

"Um, you as well," I replied, a little stunned. "Forgive me, but..."

"How do we know your name?" the Timeless One guessed my question. "How could we not? You are the very visage of Ryoku Dragontalen. The color of your hair is a little odd, but your eyes are unmistakable – you are he, the hero of whom the spirit realm has patiently waited for – nay, the entirety of our realms! But..." his expression fell, and I thought it looked like an extra layer of fog passed over his eyes. "Now is not the time for such bantering. You are injured, and finally conscious. I must see to your wounds properly. Come here, child."

I gave Sira a wary look. She only shook her head in a slight way, and she and Will led me forward. I felt horribly uneasy. Nothing about the little vampire was remotely *unfriendly* – on the contrary, he seemed quite friendly – but the scenario made my stomach lurch. What was he talking about?

"There are plenty of matters to discuss with you at length once you are healed," the vampire told me placidly. "Simply put, this must come first. Um, you, with the hair like fire. Would you kindly remove his bandages?"

Sira glowered at him. "Why me?" she muttered, but she obeyed nonetheless.

"Now, I hear you are searching for a young man," he told me as Sira finished unravelling the bandages around my chest. I tried not to stare at the wound I could feel there, raw from the removal of bandages being stuck to it, but it didn't seem to bleed. He studied the wound intently – at least, due to his apparent lack of pupils, I felt like he was. "Chris Olestine is his name, correct?"

Surprised, I nodded. I supposed that any of my friends could've mentioned the name.

"I'm afraid I don't know his location, to be exact," the Timeless One said gravely. When my expression fell, he gave me a small smile. "However, I'm sure you know where to start looking."

"Orden," I replied, maybe a little too quickly. Why was I so able to trust this little old vampire? Despite his short stature and comically squeaky voice, there was a certain look to his eyes that kept me rapt with attention – a timeless quality. Perhaps his title was more than a simple moniker.

"Correct," he announced. He leapt from his tall chair and directly onto the table, where he could better place his hand on my wounded chest. Only Relus Ashbane didn't appear surprised by this move, but rather politely tolerant. Even standing upon the table, he was hardly taller than any of those currently seated. With the hand not placed on my chest, he relied on the support of a thick black wood staff, about the size of an average shortsword. "Orden is quite a dangerous place, and renowned for that fact. They're hardly quiet about their distaste for you, my dear boy. Bounties spread far and wide, their name proudly plastered over it all... I have been to this place many times in my long life. Were I wiser and braver in my youth, I suppose I could have prevented some of their current corruption. As they say, life's tragedy is that we get old too late, and wise too soon."

Like clockwork, Relus cleared his throat. "I believe you meant, 'we get old too soon, and wise too late,' sir," Relus said without a note of exhaustion in his voice. To my friends, under his breath, he added, "I do despise when we have rare guests. My master gets so frazzled at dealing with newcomers."

Rather than anything else, the Timeless One raised a single, gnarled finger from the grip of his staff. "Don't listen to him," he said directly to me. "I am no master, as they are not my slaves. Rex, Cleria, Relus. Every vampire in this room is under my study, and another you may soon meet. They are lost souls, ones who needed a firm hand. They are my apprentices, no more." He smiled in a certain way that felt familiar. "Either way, enough about me. Yes, Orden is a dark and terrible place – it's no small wonder they placed a bounty on your head! But why, that is the true question."

An abrupt movement occurred beside me. Without so much as a glance, Sira tore her arm from my grip and marched off, headed to one of the doors behind where the Timeless One's chair was. The door nearly broke off the hinges with the force she slammed it with, leaving the rest of us in a silent room.

"Oh my," the Timeless One murmured. "I must have offended her. My apologies."

I stared after the door she disappeared through, and the Timeless One's hand pulsated in an odd way. He glanced down, his papery brows raised in alarm. "Oh dear – what a significant response! I do hope you understand, I felt that through your chest. Why, it's enough to interrupt my magic! Surely a deep and powerful caring for the young woman!"

I barely heard him. Somehow, I felt I understood Sira in a way that I couldn't relay to the others. She came from a place twisted and defiled by corruption. Perhaps hearing about her home pushed her off the edge. Even if it was a dark place, she must have family and friends there nonchalantly clumped with the terrible things we said. Kioru was from there, of course, and Chris Olestine might be. Could a whole world be called evil?

"You must go speak with her, my boy," the Timeless One reassured me, removing his hand from my chest. "I sense you understand the darkness within your friend." His eyes got a distant, cloudy look in them. "Perhaps in another life, the two of you could have made dutiful apprentices of mine…"

"Yes, do go speak with her," Loki agreed, though his words weren't as kind. If I didn't know better, he may have been speaking with distaste. He rose and put a hand on the Timeless One's small shoulder. "Perhaps we could have a word as well? Something may have just arisen which we should discuss, as colleagues."

I watched him with suspicion. First he didn't trust the Timeless One, and now he called him a colleague?

"Your wound won't open until I see to it again," the Timeless One assured me, "unless you land yourself in some impressive fight in the next room."

I smirked. "That's not entirely unlikely," I murmured. I rose to my feet without help now and slid away from Will – the soldier gave me an approving nod, like I went with his blessing. I supposed I was the best choice to talk to her even if I didn't fully understand why she stormed off. Will and Sira had an odd friendship, but I wondered just how much of her the friendly soldier understood. Loki didn't seem to like her, and Lusari gazed on with impassive eyes. Sighing to nobody in particular, I excused myself and headed for the door Sira left through.

I found myself entering what looked like an abandoned kitchen. Everything seemed caked in dust, cleared only in a certain radius around the door. Ancient-looking kitchen equipment, even by spiritual standards, littered the kitchen. I spotted an old range with elements that looked unperturbed for decades. A large cleaver and a row of sharp knives caught the dim torchlight reflected from the room behind me, until I closed the door.

I saw her. Sira stood at the far end of the room, facing the wall, her hands balled into tight fists. Was I really going to try to talk to her now?

I summoned any ounces of courage left in my chest, and approached. She didn't seem to hear me until I stood close to her.

"Sira?" I asked softly.

She didn't move for a moment. Then, "I thought you'd follow me." Her voice sounded hollow.

I considered my words carefully before I spoke. After all, with all the gleaming knives around the room, it would be awfully easy to make Ryoku stir-fry in here.

"I was worried about you."

She scoffed, making me flinch. "Why the hell should you be worried about be?" Before I could reply, she laughed softly to herself. "Although I guess that would be a turn of events. You worrying about me for once. Not me worrying about your dumb ass."

I scowled at her even though she wasn't looking. "I worry about you plenty," I insisted. "When we fought the raiders, those stupid thugs in the capital, the Warg, all those wolves... Sira, you charge in without thinking. It'd be so easy to get hurt. I've seen it happen. That's why I have to get stronger."

Sira chuckled again – I thought she sounded less cynical than usual, but that might be the tone leading up to Ryoku stir-fry. "You know you've gotten hurt like every single one of those times, right?" she remarked dryly. Then she hesitated, her fingers twitching. "Hey, you've lost somebody that way, haven't you? Just to something simple."

I could only manage a nod. I didn't even think about that she faced the other way, but my silence seemed to speak for me. "I'm made of stronger stuff than most people. Either way, I think you've got the wrong idea."

I took her words out of context for a moment, and felt oddly stung. "What, uh, what do you mean?"

She snorted. "I'm your Guardian, dumbass. I'm supposed to be protecting you."

I laughed softly, which she seemed to notice as her head rose slightly. "That's not how I see it," I murmured. "Besides, I don't even really know why you decided to protect me. You or Will. Or Loki." I frowned. "Anyone, really. I just came here to save my sister through Chris Olestine. Why do you think I'll actually accomplish anything else? Me – Ryoku Dragontalen, the boy knocked out before we even got into the wolf settlement. Who can't use a sword."

She stiffened. I froze, hoping I hadn't struck some kind of nerve.

"You don't think you're anything special, do you?" she asked softly. Finally, slowly, she turned around. I had to prevent my jaw from dropping – tears streaked down her cheeks, cutting paths through her light makeup, dripping silently from her smouldering eyes.

"You think I left because of that remark about Orden? You think I actually care about that place? Not a chance. I *hate* Orden. I hate it more than anything in this world. Yet, I said I'd go there. I'll go there for your stupid ass, Ryoku Dragontalen. I spent the last three days literally carting your ass from Gaevrel all the way to this stupid castle. I didn't even realize it took that long, honestly. Your wounds kept reopening. You remember what your dumb ass did in Gaevrel? You probably don't remember, cause your stupid wounds reopened and you almost got yourself killed!

"Then I had to fucking give you up." Her voice broke as she spoke. I almost empathized with her, except she was talking about *me* and I couldn't remember it. "Your wounds reopened in Xactyr. A city chock-full of these creepy bloodsuckers that turned on us like a fucking gourmet unveiled in the streets! I had to hand you off to Rex to get you out of there. Luckily, Cleria, that glasses guy, and some of the old bat's assistants came to help us out, or we'd be bloodbags by now.

"And then, you know what?" She didn't pause long enough for me to guess. "I didn't get to fucking see you. After fighting our way to this castle, we couldn't even get to you. That old bat practically quarantined you as soon as you set foot in here! Locked you up in the dungeons. Only stupid Will got to see you after two full days. I sat outside that little dungeon. I slept there! Nobody told me a damned thing, not even Will. For all I knew, you were dead."

When she could find no more words to speak, she lunged forward and into my arms. I felt ridiculous, and stupid, and blown away, and horribly guilty. It was just her and I, alone in this dusty old kitchen. Her fingers clutched my back so tightly that I feared she'd tear through my clothes, but even that seemed like a minor affair in the back of my mind.

Slowly, gently, I returned her embrace. I felt like she might act like a rabid dog and bite my hands off if I touched her, but she let me. She felt horribly warm, like the fire I always associated her with. She smelled awfully sweet, like some spicy mix of flowers and heat. I realized it was familiar, as I'd always been around her and just put the facts in the back of my mind. Her hands felt like warmth from open flames grasping at me through a wintry breeze, seeking to cast its warmth upon me.

When her lips met mine in the darkness, they tasted just as rosy and familiar as though I revisited an old memory. In another time, I might have laughed at how soft her lips were for such a fiery girl. In another light, it didn't surprise me. I already guessed at how soft her lips were. I had imagined them once or twice against mine, and against my skin.

Our hands traced down the length of our bodies until they met at our fingertips. Then she took my hands, her nails biting into the backs of my hands, and I didn't notice as I fell to the kiss like foliage before the flame.

It felt as purposeful and divine as each lick of a flame's tongue, but she was the tongue of the flame. Her hands caressed my skin, exploring like fire consuming me from head to toe. Her hands found my belt, and mine slid her shirt over her head, my fingers brushing along her skin. We found the counter in the darkness and I somehow pushed her down onto it, sliding her underwear down her long, slender legs.

She let me move her, caress her, kiss her, and touch her in every possible way, pushing aside kitchen supplies and whatnot to clear the way. Even then, her skilled hands pulled away my clothing until I was atop her. Our lips only parted from one another to kiss each other in different places. Her tongue slid across my neck, inciting a surprised moan from me, and I ran my tongue between her legs. She whispered sweet nothings to me, things I never thought I'd hear her say. She wanted me in all the ways I wanted her. We became the only essences in the room – the forest and the fire, meeting in a way that shouldn't have been possible. I found my way inside of her as she let me into her warmth, her crimson eyes glowing like the hearth of a fire.

A sharp rap broke the moment. Sira and I sat bolt upright, our combined gazes turning to the door.

"You're taking an awfully long time in there," Loki's voice wavered through the previous passionate silence. "Do you need help?"

Sira muttered a curse nothing like the sweet things she'd been saying. "One step closer and I'll kill you!" she shouted back. The following silence suggested her method was effective. Then we were clambering to our feet, rummaging around in the darkness for our tossed clothing.

We had only assembled our underclothes when Sira drew me back to her with a gentle hand below the belt. "You tell anyone what happened here, and I'll kill you, too," she muttered, but she spoke playfully. "That damned Syaoto boy-scout is going to have a field day, and by the Creator, if Loki founds out—"

I stole the moment to slide in and kiss her on the lips. The movement surprised her and caused a flirtatious smile. "Screw you," she murmured, and drew me back in for another kiss before we found the rest of our clothes. It was a process, since it seemed we found a lot of difficulty keeping our hands to ourselves.

My mind felt foggy and distant, like I was watching someone else's life unfold. My hands felt drawn to Sira, and my lips kept seeking that intoxicating warmth of her kiss. I felt happy – but I wasn't going to let her know that just yet.

...End of Act Three.

Act Four: Blackness...

In the eyes of Ryoku Dragontalen, we are in
The Timeless Castle, in the world of Lysvid.
It is late evening
On November 7th, 2017.

SCENE ONE: RAGNAROKKR

"Welcome back, kids."

I felt my face ultimately betraying me as I stepped back into the room. The Timeless One beamed at me like I was his son. Sira didn't let go of my arm and kept at my side. Will had taken a seat, but looked thoroughly amused at the sight of us. Loki's hand cleverly covered a wide smirk. Even Rex was chuckling to himself. Was my hair messed up? Was Sira's tunic inside out?

Despite the interruption, I felt better than I had before. I stood next to Sira as strong as ever, even with the injuries bared on my chest that started to ache deeply. Something about the fire that Sira breathed into me gave me a brave, shaky adrenaline that left me standing before the Timeless One in all seriousness. It felt like I had war stripes where her tongue crossed my skin.

The Timeless One's minute size didn't hinder the eerie silence in his eyes, a look that added to the effect of his ominous name.

"Well, Ryoku Dragontalen," the Timeless One boomed. I flinched at the sound of his full voice – I'd forgotten just how loud he could make himself. "It seems your wound will let me heal it now! As well, I think I'll be able to help you with some other matters. But let us deal with that first."

The Timeless One beckoned me over. When I stood before him, he put a papery hand on my chest. Even with whatever magic had ebbed away much of the pain, I could feel it sting at the contact. Sira's arm clutched mine a little tighter.

Once the vampire shut his milky eyes, I could already begin to feel the magic pouring out into the world. The air felt oddly thick around magic, as though the act was simply air condensing into a thicker, more potent form. A light, dusty smell wafted through the air like an ancient library, its texts recently leafed through to scatter dust in the air. I felt the tips of my ears perk, as though there were some key lament whispered through his fingertips and into my skin. The dusty scent of libraries mixed with an unfamiliar spice settled on my tongue.

The last sense magic could trigger was sight. Slowly, as though it existed all along, a thin gray mist began to seep from the Timeless One's clawed hands. Almost all magic that I'd seen was visible in some way. I wasn't sure if this was standard, but it obeyed similar laws to what I'd already seen. I could recall similar reactions in the world every time I'd seen magic so far – at least, when I paid it due mind.

I could feel the wound beginning to stretch. I hadn't found my gall to look at it yet. It felt like a set of slashes across my chest, but perhaps there was a certain gouge in the middle of it. I could feel the scar tissue mending – an awful and grotesque feeling, to be concise. It was like the Timeless One's misty magic wove needle and thread through the skin, drawing it back together as though it had never been apart.

The sensation became one of increasing discomfort. My stomach churned and tossed. My head spun like my eyes followed the threads of his magic. My legs felt like jelly beneath me, and each breath like I was breathing through sandpaper. Sira's grip on me grew stronger, and I couldn't tell her how it made my stomach lurch even worse.

It felt like eons before the old vampire drew his hand away. "Sorry about that, my boy," he told me in a chipper tone. "The worst of it is over. Why don't you take a look now?"

It took a moment for the nausea to ebb away, but I glanced down. Where I'd felt the horrid discomfort remained only a dark scar etched against my pale skin. It looked like a mass of scar tissue with the edges of a rake of claws framing it.

"That will remain for some time," the Timeless One told me. "A commendation of what you went through – and, dare I say, a reminder of what you must never do again."

I sensed satire behind his voice, but his milky eyes betrayed nothing. Sira and Will both chuckled at this, while Loki only furrowed his brow.

"Obviously, that scar will only affect you in this world, Defender," the Timeless One told me. "That must be a truly disorienting sensation for you, as will many things be in this realm. Exercise caution, for you can still die here. A death in our realms would render your body comatose unless another spirit took it over in your stead, which is not an untoward idea. Many have done it in the past!

"Now," the Timeless One said as he gestured for Sira and I to take a seat. We obliged, taking seats close to the little vampire and across from the others. "I hear you have some trouble properly using weapons. Will tells me you cannot seem to properly wield a blade any longer than your knife, which is hardly satisfactory against most opponents you might come to face." There was a certain twinkle in his eyes, I thought, like a private joke. "Your archery is potent, but it must face proper trial before you can do any real damage with your arrows. Your magic, of course, requires work. All mages are a constant study, as I'm sure you will discover. I have something to offer you."

"Like what?" I asked. The Timeless One didn't immediately answer, and snapped his fingers instead. The sound came like a bullet in the silence of the room. A door near where Will and Sira brought me from opened slowly, as though a figure had been waiting just beyond it. A shadow stepped into the room out of the torchlight, masked by the shadows.

"To your ill-trained skills," the Timeless One said with a smile, "I offer you, a teacher."

(Meanwhile, in the eyes of Will Ramun...)

Nothing about the figure was readily apparent until he stepped into our midst, for the lighting in the Timeless Castle left much to be desired. There stood a tall man with a young, angular face, perhaps aged in about his early thirties. Something kept his dark hair a little spiked up, which served to bolster the youthful handsomeness of the man. He dressed in the same style of black tunic as the Timeless One's castle called for, his hands lightly pushed into his pockets. He didn't carry the atmosphere of a fighter or wizard, I thought, nor any sort of rogue. I couldn't place what he was.

His almond eyes fell upon Ryoku right away, and I saw ghosts in them for a moment before they masked over again. When I saw Ryoku's expression, I knew the truth. This was a man from his own world – at that, a spirit. Somebody he lost.

"M-Mr. Guildford?" he asked, his voice tentative and weak, as though he thought speaking them might serve to make the truth unapparent before him. Loki, Sira, and I wildly glanced between Ryoku and the man. Was this some kind of teacher of his?

The man calmly raised a nonchalant hand in greeting, but a somewhat giddy grin gave him away. "Long time no see," he said, his voice as calm and friendly as he appeared. "I never thought I might see you again – especially while you still lived. At least, so says the Timeless One. I think I had a few assignments left for you to turn in. And… it's just Guildford, if you would. I don't see a classroom demanding etiquette here."

Ryoku didn't reply, staring at Guildford like he was seeing a ghost – as, I realized, he quite literally was. Guildford strolled around the table, keeping a steady pace until he came to stand behind Ryoku and put a hand on his shoulder. "This will be a lot different than teaching you history or grammar. I'm afraid they didn't offer magic or fighting lessons at my particular university. But, all the same, I hope I won't let you down."

It took Ryoku a long moment to smile. I wondered what the boy was thinking about. What would I feel if somebody I thought I lost forever appeared in front of me? Plenty of soldiers I fought alongside in the past, I would delight to see again. Of course, I thought, this seemed like a big one for Ryoku.

Involuntarily, I found myself picturing a girl: she had curly brown hair, and a face fraught with freckles accented by sunlight. Her brown eyes looked like glistening stones. Just as quickly as ever, the memory faded into the back of my mind. Sara, I thought, but I could never quite get further than that in my memories. I only knew that I had lost her somehow.

To stop my eyes from watering, I glanced around the room and noticed the Timeless One's expression. He didn't look surprised in the least to see that Guildford and Ryoku knew each other. Had he planned it this way? I wasn't sure whether to call it a blessing or a cruel curse to reunite with those you lost...

"H-How did you get here?" Ryoku asked. He sounded like a thousand questions formed in his mind and he picked the simplest, hoping for a rounded answer.

Guildford appeared hesitant, but a nod from the Timeless One encouraged him. "I've been here for some time," he said. "After... well, after everything, this seems to be the first place I came. The Timeless One took me in quickly, and has taken care of me and taught me ever since. I can use a sword now," he added, and gestured to a modest longsword clipped to the belt of his tunic. "Surprising, right? I've done a great deal of studying in this world. I can teach you about that, too, if you'd like. The Timeless One tells me you haven't been here for very long."

Ryoku was flinching at everything his teacher said. I watched him with trepidation. How would he react to this?

"It's only been a few days." Sira spoke up for Ryoku, seeing him tongue-tied. She turned and offered her hand out to Guildford. "Sira Jessura, one of Ryoku's Guardians. I guess you... were close to him?"

She almost spoke bitterly. Was that jealousy in her voice? Seriously?

Guildford smiled nervously after shaking Sira's hand – if anything, her tight grip probably scared him. Sira was all bark *and* bite. "You could say that," Guildford replied. "I'm not sure what you know of the physical world, but I was Ryoku's history and English teacher two years in a row. On top of that, I owe the eventual success of one of my toughest students to him, and that of... well, many of his friends." He gave Ryoku a private sort of smile, which the Defender shakily returned.

I almost didn't want to step forward and introduce myself. Getting anything out of Ryoku about his past had proven very difficult, and I longed to know exactly who we were dealing with. Still, I brought myself to stand and bowed to the teacher, which drew a politely alarmed look from him.

"William Jesse Ramun, at your service," I told him plaintively. "I am a Guardian of Ryoku as well. If you are to instruct him, then I shall do my utmost to protect you likewise."

Guildford appraised me for a moment with a warm smile. "You might not find him so helpless," Relus Ashbane inferred from his chair, adjusting his glasses. "Guildford has trained with me, and his sword skill is excellent for a recent arrival to our realms."

Guildford smiled modestly, scratching his head. "Well, I suppose," he said, "though Relus is quite remarkable himself." He offered his hand, and I shook it. He had a firm grip, but not weathered like many soldiers I knew. A golden ring glinted on his finger – a wedding band, or I was a fisherman. "Well met, William Jesse Ramun. Will for short? I seek comrades, not a guard team."

I grinned. Like student, like teacher. "Of course," I told him, "though I have sworn to guide Ryoku through thick and thin already."

Ryoku gave me a telltale smile. "That was only through the Old Forest!"

I shrugged nonchalantly. "It turns out I was meant to guide you further."

Loki thrusting his hand in Guildford's face interrupted any further argument on Ryoku's behalf. "I bet you've been dying to meet me," he said with the tone of a hero. "The name's Loki, the god of tricks and fire. A pleasure to make your acquaintance!"

Guildford took his hand, scowling for the first time I'd seen. "Loki?" he asked thoughtfully. "Doesn't mythology call you a giant?"

Loki immediately frowned. "Perhaps they only spoke of his ego," Sira suggested, to a quiet chuckle around the table.

"Mythology in your world has been wrong on many accounts!" Loki insisted, though he didn't look happy. "Thor and Odin are my brothers. Does your mythology detail that? Or, perhaps, that our family births from the Ancients?"

Guildford only frowned. "Interesting," he murmured, "though I have read about the Ancients in my studies as of late. Those are something like the inner circle of gods, correct?"

"That is correct," the Timeless One exclaimed, beaming at his pupil. "The most powerful of gods from each sect is said to descend from them. Odin, Thor, and Loki would count as 'the big three' of the Norse gods, and all hold positions in other sects, so that would make them indubitably descend from the Ancients. Zeus, Poseidon, and Hades would be those under Greek mythology, and… well, I'm sure those serve as example enough."

"The Ancients are not quite gods, so to speak," Relus added – he appeared to be waiting to correct his master, and looked surprised when he didn't have to. "While gods serve and watch over the world of the living, the Ancients are in charge of the deeper aspects of Creation – they'll rarely meddle in earthly affairs."

The conversation dwindled away, and I noticed Ryoku hadn't moved an inch. Guildford saw, too, but he looked around the table at us. "I wager I have the three of you to thank for keeping Ryoku safe. For that, I will always be grateful. But..." he trailed off, catching the eye of Lusari next to me. "You as well?"

Lusari smiled shyly. "I've not sworn a Guardianship vow," she said. "I'm Lusari Atella, a mage from Harohto. Ryoku has certainly saved me more than I could ever do for him. Perhaps he is my Guardian."

Ryoku blushed furiously, a notion that Sira didn't miss. "Not true," he murmured. "You saved me when the werewolves injured me. Without you, we couldn't have gotten away from the Keeper of the Old Forest!"

"And, if I recall, you served to help just as much against the Keeper," I told him. "Not just the once, mind you. How would we have escaped the first time without your fire?"

"What of the Warg in the capital?" I was surprised to see Cleria pipe up, watching Ryoku across the table with a playful smile. "You're skilled, even if you're a bit of a liar, *Ronyx Curtis*..." Inevitably, her crimson gaze slid to me, bemused. "Speaking of, Sir Jeffrey Lampsword..."

I grinned sheepishly, scratching my head. "My apologies. You see..."

The Timeless One cut me off with a booming chuckle. "Fret not, my little sheep," he told us. "I understand the need for disguises. You certainly must continue with them, of course. Such may even serve to give you an advantage when you finally land in the serpents' lair. The less they know about you, the better."

Sira gave me a pointed glare. "Maybe some of us should think on ours a little more next time."

However, even that fell to silence again. I couldn't fully laugh, seeing the look Ryoku was still giving his old teacher. It took a long time for him to voice his thoughts.

"You died." He spoke simply, his voice hollow. Guildford flinched, and Ryoku's stubborn chin softened. His forest eyes fell past Guildford, past the vampires, past everything else that was here before him. "We fought for you, you know. Katiel. Dagger. Joey. Me. We got our vengeance, and we won. Well, sort of. Varis left the country."

Silence hit the room like a tangible creature. It occurred to me now that, when I asked Ryoku if he'd ever fought before, his answer belonged to this deep and terrible thing he'd done, an inky stain on his past. It was why he knew a little of what he was doing. Why even the big lugs in the bar hadn't really scared him, and he still managed to stand with us against Lusari's would-be rapists in Harohto. He might have seen worse.

"You shouldn't have," Guildford chastised. "You know that could have ended badly for you. Varis and his cronies have sent senior students to the hospital. Adults, even. His family is so renowned in Brooklyn that nobody could win against him. So, how…?"

Guildford and Ryoku locked eyes for a long moment. I remained silent, sensing that there was much more behind their words and expressions than I could imagine. Sira was staring at Ryoku just as intently. Something must have happened between them earlier for the expectant look in Sira's eyes. That wasn't there before.

"Are you intending to meet up with your friends?" Guildford finally asked.

Ryoku nodded. "Soon. Katiel, at least. I'm not so sure about the others yet."

Guildford smirked. "I doubt you'll be able to hide from Dawn," he said knowingly. "As soon as she catches wind of where you are. So long as it suits her, I suppose."

Loki shot to his feet. "Hold on!" he half-shouted, turning on Ryoku. "You don't mean to say… you have other Defender friends?"

Ryoku and Guildford exchanged glances. How could the teacher know such a thing? I could even see the confusion on Ryoku's face, though he didn't speak them just then.

"There's a few, yes," Ryoku explained hesitantly. "Katiel is my best friend. I'm planning to meet with him soon. And… then there's Dawn and Anna. And Virgo."

"Your world has some strangely diverse names," Loki commented, scratching his chin. "Well, go on. Are we to meet them soon?"

Ryoku only smiled. "Katiel won't keep me waiting. That's all I know right now."

Loki didn't press the question, which led me to believe he'd only pester Ryoku further in a different setting. Perhaps without his teacher's adamant backing. Instead, he turned to the Timeless One, who took something that Relus pulled out from under the table. A thick parcel, about the length of a particular longsword.

"If we are done with the questions for the time being," the Timeless One commented, "then I have something for you."

With a push of vampiric strength, the Timeless One slid the item across the table. Ryoku missed it by a mile, but Sira stopped it just after him. She went to hand it to Ryoku, but the item didn't budge. Confused, Sira glared at it like that alone should make it melt out of shame. Ryoku, paying that no mind, plucked it off the table and took it in his hands. Sira stared at him with her jaw agape. The item was wrapped in brown cloth, and a small bronze medallion clasped it shut, masking the true item from view. Every vampire clothed in black and white around the table glared at the weapon unforgivingly.

"That sword was heavy as all hell," Sira muttered, giving Ryoku quite a bewildered look. "I went to push it, but it wouldn't budge."

"But you did stop its momentum," Relus pointed out. "Such an immobile item should have broken your hand, no?"

Ryoku didn't seem to hear them. "You acknowledged that I can't use swords, right?" Ryoku asked. He kept his tone polite, but there was certain skepticism in it. "You did mention that?"

"I did," the Timeless One said, and for a moment, his voice sounded just as old and heavy as his name. "You may find this particular weapon to act differently than most. You see, Ryoku Dragontalen, this is your sword."

"What do you mean by that?" Ryoku asked. I could hear a strain of impatience in his voice by now. I didn't disagree. The Timeless One was leaving something out, some key detail that he should have explained the moment we entered this room with Ryoku.

"I might not be the one to explain everything to you, Ryoku." The Timeless One's milky eyes glistened like light. "You may find your name is older than the presence you have in these realms. Such a name. Ryoku Dragontalen. Have you never wondered why you carry such a title? Surely it stands out in your own world."

Ryoku shook his head, but he contemplated the words before he spoke. "No, not at all. I mean... should it?" He fell silent again, staring at the cloth-wrapped weapon as though he stared through it, through everything below it, and into something that may offer him untold answers.

The Timeless One frowned thoughtfully. "Well, yes, I would say. That is a little odd. But go on! Open it. Perhaps looking upon it will enlighten you to something you have been missing."

That seemed to push Ryoku a little more. Guildford unclasped the item from the cloth, and it fell away in Ryoku's hands to unveil a smooth, black blade, about three or four feet long and with a rather wide blade. The hilt was diamond-shaped and wrapped in thick, black chains that dangled free and connected to the sword's squared pommel. I knelt closer to study the blade. It looked like pale runes danced across the flat of the blade. I couldn't recognize them, even given the automatic translator I now had as a Guardian.

There was something hauntingly familiar about the weapon, and of Ryoku's slowly dawning expression as he examined it. It seemed like a painting of reunited family where neither recognized the other, or perhaps coming across the charred remains of one's childhood home.

"It looks fairly light," Lusari commented. "Sira, you said it was heavy?"

Guildford reached for the handle of the blade. Ryoku stirred, but he didn't stop his teacher as he grabbed the handle. He gave it a tug. The item didn't budge. Ryoku glanced up at his teacher in confusion as he easily lifted and dropped the weapon in his outstretched hands.

"I apologize that the weapon doesn't come with a sheath," Relus told Ryoku. "Of all things, we could not seem to recover that. That cloth is made of a material that even your sword won't cut through. I took the liberty of installing the means to clip it to your baldric."

"You recovered it?" I asked. "From where?"

Relus only gave me a knowing smile and didn't reply.

"Give it a try, young one," the Timeless One suggested. "It may prove the same experience you have had with swords until now, or it may not. One mustn't judge his eggs before they hatch!"

Relus cringed. "Or that you might never know if you never try." He adjusted his glasses studiously. "Perhaps, I might suggest, not in this room. Will tells us the weapon is unable to stay in your grasp, and there are many in this room."

"Why not try it in battle?" Sira suggested. There was a fire in her eyes once more. Whatever she felt for Ryoku, it magnified when she imagined the lust of a fight. "Why don't we have a bout, you and I?"

"In the world of darkness?" I asked dryly. "That sounds an excellent way to kill one another."

Sira gave me a livid look. "Shut up, Jeffy. I forgot, okay?"

Everyone else hung around Ryoku and the sword. Sira gave it a curious look like one might stare at a deadly snake at a distance. Guildford and I both seemed to appreciate the masterful craft of the weapon, though I still kept my distance. Something about looking at the weapon seemed cloudy, like looking at an old friend who appeared after a long time and appeared ultimately unfamiliar. Lusari couldn't take her eyes off it any more than Ryoku could, who'd scarcely looked up since he unveiled the black weapon.

Of all of us, though, Loki fervently kept his distance, lurking at least two chairs down behind a vampire who kept giving the Trickster nervous looks. Loki only had eyes for the sword, and he stared at it like the end of all things good, and a sure slayer of whatever dreams he entertained. What personal vendetta could Loki have against it? One day, I'd get the truth out of him on why he was here, and this was a page in that mystery.

"Its name is Ragnarokkr," the Timeless One's voice boomed, "and it has clearly chosen you, my friend."

SCENE TWO: BLACK CITY

...Of Act Four: Blackness

*In the eyes of Ryoku Dragontalen, we are in Leudis, in the world of Lysvid.
It is late night
On November 7th, 2017.*

"Check the map again, Loki."

The Trickster obeyed with frustration, unfurling our map of Lysvid for what seemed like the billionth time. Guildford peeked over his shoulder at the map while the rest of us stopped, looking at the city ahead of us.

We had reached what the Timeless One referred to as the Black City – Leudis, a major town a few miles from Xactyr. People knew it as a war-like town, the secondary capital to Lysvid as a leading force against the werewolves and other invaders. Black gates at the city entrance loomed to the sky like a pair of coffins on either side of the road. The vampires at the gate dressed finely and heavily armed, which seemed like a commodity thanks to their granite skin. They barely glanced at us when we passed them into the city.

"Town square," Guildford said for Loki, pointing at a spot on the map – a close-up of the city of Leudis, marked with a square near the middle. "Home of the Bloody Mare."

My teacher had changed out of the Timeless Castle garb, and now wore a simple white shirt with an open collar and black breeches under a thick brown cloak. A modest longsword hung at his belt. I felt like my teacher was in some Shakespeare play or something rather than neck-deep in a world of vampires alongside me. Of course, Loki returned to his attire as a mock-Dracula, which looked even more ridiculous next to Guildford. The two appeared close in age.

"Doesn't look far, at least," Sira muttered, peering easily over the shoulders of both men to see the map for herself. "A mile through vamp-infested city streets? Can't be too bad. I think we've seen the worst of this place."

"I hope so," I murmured in agreement, and Sira clutched my hand a little tighter. That was a new thing, a side effect from what transpired between us at the Timeless Castle. All had been fast-paced ever since, and that left no time for us to finish what we started. We only held hands, a mere spark compared to the inferno of that dusty old kitchen.

After acquiring my new sword, Ragnarokkr, from the Timeless One, we spoke a little more before the Timeless One suggested our next course of action – bounty boards. Using the very thing that threatened to condemn me as a method of gaining funds wasn't my most favored notion, but it made sense. Nobody wanted to hunt werewolves anymore after what transpired at Gaevrel. Even Sira seemed to swallow back the idea. That and the attack in Xactyr pushed us out pretty quickly. The next best place to go was here: Leudis, the black city. It was the nearest place, and known for its availability of bounties.

True to its name, everything seemed even darker than in Lysvid's capital. Buildings sat along the streets like rows of shadow-cloaked tombstones, and their denizens like pale, well-dressed ghosts among them. Traffic was high during Lysvid's nights, though I saw little difference save for the lack of a moon in the sky once more.

Walking with the new sword bobbing against my back felt strange. All that the Timeless One told me about it was that it belonged to my name somehow. Ryoku Dragontalen. I had to admit, I thought little of my name. It turned some heads even in the spirit realm, especially to those who knew me as a Defender. The name itself felt strangely distant from me. A moniker, I thought, more than my true name. Could I even say that with confidence, given how much transpired in the last month?

The odd quirk about it was that the blade felt light and normal in my hands. Nobody else could lift it from the ground, let alone hold it aloft. I didn't dare try to wield it yet, and the prospect of wielding a sword bubbled in my chest like a faint promise.

Loki hesitated at the entrance to a particularly dark alley. "This would shorten our journey a great deal," he mentioned. "I don't know about you, friends, but my stomach dearly longs for some true grub. The Bloody Mare is next to the city square. We could squeeze in for a proper dinner if we allow this minor shortcut."

"Is there a time Lysvid stops serving food?" Will asked curiously.

"After dawn," Guildford explained, with a quick glance at me. "The least trafficked time for vampires. We do have time. If you feel this shortcut would be wise..."

Loki shrugged. "Of course," he replied quickly. "What worse danger could we face in this accursed place?"

Sira was shaking her head as Loki veered off toward the alley. "That's a damned challenge if I ever heard one," she muttered, and Will chuckled.

The alley turned out to be busier than the streets, and with even less light. Vampires in long, dark coats walked briskly down the alleys and past shopkeepers who operated from behind shoddily stacked crates. In the darkness, I could only discern living from inanimate by the glint of red eyes.

Nobody spoke as we sidled through the alleyways, carefully avoiding contact with the vampires. Lusari kept the light on her staff low enough to only cover us and view anything just outside our tight circle. Will and Sira kept close to either side of me, their eyes dancing madly over the passing vampires like any might attack out of the blue. If I had the story straight from before the Timeless Castle, it wasn't entirely impossible.

After a few minutes, the traffic in the alleys seemed to dwindle until we could walk apart in the narrow alleyways. Loki breathed a sigh of relief, walking backwards to face us with his arms crossed casually behind his head. "This place consumes my anxiety to no end," he said airily, smirking. "To find a vamp-less spot here is like a vacation, don't you think?"

Guildford glanced at the god sharply. "That might not be the wisest idea," he said, but not before Loki bumped into a vampire while strutting backwards. The vampire, a tall male with a black coat, hissed widely at him. Loki turned calmly, glaring at the vampire.

"What's the big idea?" Loki snapped. "Sorry for walking backwards, but, no offense, you lot are like mice with the way you show up outta nowhere."

"Loki, step away!" Will said urgently. "He is of the Ritual."

"That is right," another voice approached from the darkness into the light given off by Lusari's staff. A tall vampire with curly brown hair strolled into our midst, arms crossed. He held himself with a gait that reminded me eerily of Jesanht Olace, and I had to note his eerie crimson eyes to assure myself it wasn't him. "My name is Gale Destrow, and we are of the Ritual. Your people are causing a lot of trouble in paradise."

I realized I recognized him. When we entered the Capital, he was one of the vampires walking with the Ritual. Locking eyes with him filled me with a strange trepidation that left me staring, certain he was going to rear his head. Of course, here he was. His strange accent seemed ill suited for a vampire. It was almost... modern.

A hand grabbed onto my arm. I thought it was Sira, but stiffened when a second hand went around my throat, sharp black claws against my skin. Sounds of struggle around me suggested that the same was happening to my friends.

"Are you serious?" Loki drawled, pure annoyance emanating from him. "Step down. You're messing with the wrong folk if you think—"

Gale lunged. I didn't see him even move, but the force threw Loki back into the vampire he'd run into, who grabbed him by the arms and pinned him. Loki fought back, but the vampires' strength seemed too much for even him to break free.

"That's enough," Gale snapped. Several vampires emerged from the shadows to back him up. I quickly realized that everyone was pinned like I was. He stood in the center, his arms dormant at his sides while he examined us. "First, the Warg that breached the capital, then what happened at Gaevrel. Your alliance with the half-breed, Rex

Dougo. And, of course, your little fight in Xactyr. You lot have stirred up far too much trouble."

Sira growled, struggling to break free. "What the hell does that matter to you? Like the Ritual is actually doing anything for this place! So we got rid of your Warg and your kind like to attack us?"

"Our actions had nothing to do with your people," Will agreed angrily. I could see him and Lusari as outlines in the dark. He wasn't fighting his captor, but the muscles in his arms were taut and ready to press back. "Are you suggesting we let the Warg into the city?"

Sira glanced at Will. "No way. Is this guy that dumb? How the hell're we supposed to smuggle one of those into the city?"

"Lest you forget, we *defeated* that Warg," Loki snarled. "Where were your people then?"

The woman vampire embracing me started to kiss my neck, which drew unelected feelings within my chest as I struggled to pull away. Loki caught my glance, and his eyes spoke untold words: *I will not let them hurt you.*

Gale only glared at Will and Sira before returning his stare to Loki. "Whoever you lot are, you've caused enough mayhem in my world. That, and the elf..." His crimson eyes flickered over me in mere annoyance before flitting back to Loki. "Enough is enough. You and your company are guilty, and your sentences will be carried out here – repaid to my people with your blood."

He struck Loki again. Loki could only stand and take it, pinned taut by the vampire binding him. I watched the moment flicker by like a slideshow: Gale lurching forward, the impact, Loki's rebellious glare as the vampire struck him.

The next thing I knew, I broke out of the vampire's grip, and the sound of naked steel rang through the air. It was a glorious, reverberant sound that felt... right. Ragnarokkr. It came to my hand as instinctually as scratching an itch. I barely registered tugging the blade from my back. It seemed to pulse in my grip like a living thing. I connected to it in a way that I didn't seem to with any of my weapons. I could feel it longing to strike. I knew it could cut these vampires.

"Oh, look," Gale muttered dryly, only glancing at me from the corner of his eye. "The elf brings a black sword to the black city... how oddly fitting." A slow, menacing grin spread across his lips, and he drew two of his slender, clawed fingers into the air over his neck. He didn't need to state the order.

My company sprang into action. I heard Sira's shout as she slammed into her captor. It jarred him for a moment, but he caught her and struggled to restrain her. Lusari cried out, trying to reach her fallen staff. Will threw all his might into pulling himself free, but it was useless. I could hear Guildford struggling in the shadows, dragged behind me and out of view.

Three vampires advanced. I stood alone, holding only a sword I wasn't sure I could use, and suddenly felt quite naked. What was I doing?

A shadow shot between the others. A loud *crack* shot through the air – stone to stone. The closest vampire dropped, and the shadow swung at the next vampire, forcing him back. It darted away and sprang at the leader, and I caught a glimpse of the figure as he passed the light of Lusari's fallen staff. My heart soared.

"Rex!" I exclaimed, surprised. Another shadow appeared into our midst, and then Loki fell forward. The Trickster was nothing if not smooth, however, and had his regal blade freed and sprang to right himself before he could hit the ground. In the same movement, he spun and brought it down upon the back of the leader's neck. In his wake slid Cleria, a set scowl on her face.

"Ugh!" Gale growled, rising to his feet – apparently Loki's sword could only serve as blunt impact to the vampire. "The halfbreed dares show up here? And you – Cleria Nightfang. You're with them?"

"Screw you, Gale," Cleria retorted, and she extended her claws out like unleashed knives. "You joined the Ritual, and I told you what that means! You're dead to me."

Gale growled under his breath. Rex shot for him again, but another vampire threw himself upon him and the two grappled in the shadows.

"You're making a mistake, Cler. Siding with these folk? You probably still visit that rotten old vampire in the woods, too, don't you? Enough is enough. You've hit my last nerve!"

More vampires appeared in the darkness around us. I hesitated, wondering if my sword I so bravely drew would be any use here. Rex sprang from his opponent in the shadows and struck Will's captor, freeing my friend from their clutches. Will didn't hesitate, and spun around, drawing his lance in a full arc to slam the blunt end into the same vampire's chest. The force hurled the vampire into the shadows with a resounding crash, but two more appeared in his place. Will was already moving, headed for Sira.

Before he could get to her, Sira drove her elbow into her captor. In the moment, she spun around and yanked Sinistra free without hesitation. The blade screamed through the air, and I swore it gave off light as it arched through the air. To my surprise, Sinistra cleaved her foe asunder.

Guildford appeared from the dark behind me just as Lusari reached her staff. As soon as she made contact with it, the small light on it grew to several times its size. I threw my hand over my eyes as light flashed through the alley, illuminating every corner of the fight – and unveiling at least twenty vampires surrounding us, only slowed down by the blinding light.

The first thing I saw when I could see was Guildford throwing his hand forward, and a burst of flames shot from it against the nearest vampire. Lusari already followed up with batches of cold energy lancing through the air like frozen waves of water. Gale picked up a sword somewhere and dueled Loki in the center of it all, with Rex backing Loki up using his singular fist.

A grotesque shriek stole my attention. From the darkness lurched the strangest vampire I'd ever seen. It was taller than the others, its claws so long that they dragged along the pavement behind it as it swaggered eerily toward me. Greasy black hair fell in clumps around its stone-grey face, with oddly unfocused crimson eyes. Every button of its Ritual trenchcoat was done up, but the creature's long neck still stuck out above the tall collar.

Perturbed, I stumbled away, but the vampire creature was fast. It toppled into me like a swinging coat rack, wildly swinging its claws without reason. One claw bit into my arm as I frantically tried to put distance between us. Ragnarokkr slipped from my grasp. Panicking, I snatched at it, my best possible defense against this insane monster. Instead of grasping it by the handle, I caught it by the chains jangling from its hilt, and dragged it toward me.

Suddenly, the blade felt heavier than before. A flash of cold fear gripped my chest. Was I not worthy of the weapon after all? When the eerie vampire lurched again, my only thought became to put the sword between us.

Before I realized what I was doing, I swung the weapon with all my might, my grip still on the chains. The momentum behind my slash ran through the monster like a knife through warm butter, spun, and stuck into the ground on its other side.

I stood there for a moment, my chest heaving, clutching the chains of Ragnarokkr. The monster loomed over me, its eyes wide and buggy as though it lived through the mighty attack. Then, I watched as the top half of it slowly slid to the side, and then fell toward me with a grotesque spray of purplish blood. I cried out, falling back, and lost my grip on Ragnarokkr.

A pair of hands grabbed me by the waist. I thought it was Sira until I felt the claws pinch my skin. Before I realized my mistake, the vampire dragged me back, slapping one hand over my mouth.

Nobody could help me. Each of my friends was in their own fight. Sira and Will fought back-to-back in their opposite styles that somehow worked. Loki and Rex skirmished with Gale in the middle, while Cleria, Guildford, and Lusari backed them up against the outer circle of vampires that didn't seem to end.

Nobody looked back as the vampire dragged me off. As she dragged me around the corner, everyone was already out of sight.

She spun me around and slammed me into the wall, one hand still over my mouth. The other pinned both my behind my back. I found myself face-to-face with the vampire. Her dark orange hair framed her face in a cute, stylish bob that curled over her shoulder. Her opal eyes bored into mine with intensity, accentuated by dark makeup around her eyes. She was, admittedly, quite beautiful.

"Where is he?" she demanded. Fangs slid behind her lips while she spoke. She gave me a look. The implication was obvious: don't make a scene. I nodded, and she pulled her hand away like removing tape. "Bring him out!"

The situation ceased to make sense and, I realized, she was not a vampire.

Orange markings lined her cheekbones in a strange, almost tribal fashion. Her dark skin was far unlike the regular pale skin of vampires. Even the touch of her hands was softer than a vampiric touch. Her eyes weren't even crimson.

"What?" I asked, confused. I tried to free my hands, but she had me pinned.

"You know who. The prince. He who walks in the darkest corridors of your mind. I know he slumbers there even now. Call him out!"

Her words sounded alien to me. Even then, though, they made sense. Images flashed through my mind. When I blacked out in the woods, and woke to the retreat of the Keeper. The dark confidence that ran through me when I needed it most. It propelled me to act sometimes without thinking, resulting in surplus amounts of skill I didn't normally have. Burying three arrows into the throat of the Warg, or summoning magic for the first time.

The worst part was that the occurrences weren't limited to my arrival in the spirit realm. Time and time again, the darkness swelled through me to carry me through tough situations. However, prior to meeting Chris, even those events seemed oddly foggy. The time after Guildford's death had felt like a nightmare. Was it even real?

"Speak!" she demanded. To my alarm, she reached between my legs and grabbed me. "You know who I refer to! Bring him out, or I'll—"

"I don't know what you're talking about!" I said urgently.

"Nonsense! You are Ryoku Dragontalen, and he lives in you – I can almost smell him!"

Her face was very close to mine. A sickly-sweet scent wafted from her, like dewy roses glimmering in a morning sun. She stared into my eyes like a challenge. "Perhaps I must draw him out. Surely you are too weak to hold him back, but if I can appease him..."

Her grip between my legs turned startlingly gentle, and she started moving her hands in a way that made me jerk upright. "W-What are you doing?" I demanded. "Who are you? What do you want with—"

Her hands slowed to a stop, even as a wry little smirk pulled at her lips. Still, she didn't remove her hand. "Hmm. Maybe he is weakened. There is no way he died in the blast, but... Doing such a thing should surely please him..."

She abruptly pulled away, and I nearly fell back against the wall in my relief. She retreated to stand just a few feet away, scratching her chin in thought. She was intensely pretty, I realized. She looked the type of girl considered popular by default in my home world. She dressed nicely, too, in a silky white shirt with tapered sleeves and a medium-length black skirt that hugged her shapely thighs. Every part of her skin that showed was marked with the same strange stripes on her face. Was she even human?

"That might explain the different hair color," she murmured to herself, "but not the eyes. And the sword – there's no way that isn't Ragnarok, but it looks so different." Her black eyes flitted back to me, and I flinched. "Still, you do know what I'm talking about. It's no good to lie to a demon, you know. Especially not one like me. I could make you regret that. Should I?"

"N-No!" I said frantically, pushing myself against the wall. "I mean, I didn't lie! Not really. I don't know what you're talking about, but it does make a little sense."

"So you have experienced him?" she asked sharply. "He does live?"

"Who?" I asked. "You say the darkness, but you act like there's somebody else in me. A demon?"

She stared at me for a long moment. I felt like my face was giving away my emotions. She was alarmingly beautiful in a way that I didn't like letting myself think.

"You truly don't know," she muttered, and the hope in her opal eyes seemed to dwindle. I almost felt bad. "Well, I suppose you should be grateful. I saved your life just now. A kid like you should have been ripped apart in a fight like that. You don't look much like you used to. With my Prince at his prime, they would not dare to meet your glance. At least you managed to kill that odd vampire. Surely the Prince would have stepped in were your life truly endangered. He… has before, hasn't he?"

I didn't respond – her words were hitting quite close to home. I harbored almost no doubt what she was speaking of. The nameless darkness inside me. Smiling, she sauntered toward me once more, pressing me back against the wall. "You don't even know what I am, do you? Who you are?"

I felt like I stood at the edge of a cliff. What was she talking about?

"Ryoku, I'm a demon," she said, smiling all the while. She turned around, pressing her shapely backside against me. I tried to avert my eyes, but then something touched my face. Stunned, I glanced down. The first thing I saw was the lacy black band of her underwear rising over her skirt, but then I saw the object – a long, furry tail, the same color as the stripes on her skin. The tail touched my nose in a way that suggested she had full control over it. As distracted by her as I was, I wished *I* had a tail.

"You've never met a demon before, have you?" she asked demurely, smirking up at me over her shoulder. "Especially a demon like me. I'm rather unique. Those like me and the Prince stand above the common ilk that run amok in the realms. Of course, we have better powers and other *talents* too."

As she spoke, she rose in a catlike fashion, pressing her back against me until her neck was at my lips, her hands running across her thighs. She glanced sidelong at me with a sultry look in her eyes. "I suppose my Prince must not be at his full strength just yet. He is there, though, I am certain. Perhaps he needs... something to return to?"

"What do you want?" I asked, but my voice came out weaker than I'd hoped.

She giggled huskily, rolling her tongue across her fangs in a suggestive manner. "I thought that was obvious, boy."

She tilted her head around until her lips were inches from mine. There was a look in her eyes I couldn't break away from, like she had all the time in the world to play and wait for her supposed 'Prince' to return. Maybe she did, if being a demon was anything like I imagined.

As I felt lost in her gaze, her hand slipped between my legs and gripped me again. I gasped sharply, but I couldn't pull away from her glance. "My Prince rests in that pretty head of yours, boy. This body is his as much as it is yours. That includes this." She stroked between my legs boldly. "That's his, too. And it's been everywhere you can imagine on me. I'll certainly come back for him, and you can feel *everything that I make him feel.*"

She drew closer with every whispered word until her lips pressed against mine. Her grip on me became sensational, turning my breathing quick and heavy. Stunned and confused, as well as horrendously turned on, I found myself kissing her back.

It only lasted seconds. Before I knew it, her lips drew away. She removed her hand. My eyes fluttered back open, and she was gone without a trace.

"What the hell?" I murmured, dazed and a little annoyed. I fell back against the wall, trying to catch my breath and relax. What was she even talking about? It was like that entity in me was a completely different person. A different life, one that had somebody waiting for it to return. What did that mean? How, in all I'd come to know, was that even possible?

"Ryoku!"

Loki's shout alerted me from down the alley, causing my breath to catch in my lungs again. Oh, crap. What was I going to say? It sounded like the fighting was over. Honestly, he would only draw in more vampires if he kept shouting. I stole a glance around me, but the corner the girl dragged me around seemed vacant of any vampires. That was definitely a good thing.

Cursing, I steadied myself and rounded the corner.

The alley was a mess. Lusari's light radiated over the area, completely free of vampires now. Ritual members littered the ground. Blood, both human and the purplish of vampires, stained the walkway. I couldn't spot Gale, but all my friends appeared present and accounted for. Loki was gazing the other way, sword in hand. Everyone else was rifling through the bodies, apparently searching for me among them. Guildford had his hand on the hilt of Ragnarokkr, still stuck in the ground next to the severed, crazed vampire I killed, and scanned all around in search of me.

Lusari was the first one to notice me, and she uttered a squeak of glee. Her noise alerted everyone else. Guildford sighed in relief, nearly dropping to his knees. Will gave me a brave smile. Sira's feet looked like they rooted to the ground. Loki sheathed his sword and jogged toward me.

"What happened to you?" he asked urgently, grabbing me around the shoulders. "Are you hurt? Did they do anything to you?"

"One of them tried to drag me off," I lied. "I dropped my sword and I couldn't do much against them. Another vampire scared them off down the alley." I looked over the scene around us with what I hoped looked like an approving smile. "You guys did great. They had us outnumbered badly."

Loki nodded gravely. I expected a vain smirk to appear on his face and for him to gallantly profess his feats in combat, but he seemed oddly serious. "Three Guardians. One teacher. One mage. Two vampires. And none of us could help you."

I realized the route he was going down. "It's okay," I told him firmly. "I can take care of myself."

Loki said nothing. He seemed to take this to heart. Why was he even with us, anyway? Why did I need such Guardians? I subtly shook my head in disbelief and went to draw Ragnarokkr from the ground near where Guildford stood.

"Did the sword work?" my teacher asked.

I managed to yank it free with a single pull. I expected to find the dark blade stained with vampiric venom, but it was flawless. In the near-pitch of night, it seemed to glint warningly. "I don't know," I admitted. "I almost dropped it, but I swung it by the chains. It felt heavier that way, but clearly it worked."

Will approached, scratching his chin in thought. "Perhaps that is a work-around to this curse. That is the best word for it, is it not?" he asked when I looked at him. "A curse? Any normal man can wield a sword. You can wield a knife just fine. I tested it with the dagger I lent you in Gaevrel."

At my expression and a curious sound from Guildford, he sighed and took out the fine dagger from his backpack. He motioned for me to hold my knife out. Putting them side-by-side, the dagger was about two inches longer than my knife. Then, handing me back my knife, he brought out his gladius. I blinked hard. The dagger was only two inches shorter than his gladius.

"The absolute limit to your curse," he told me. "And, I profess, proof that it exists."

"How could he possibly be cursed, though?" Lusari asked gently. "He only just arrived, didn't he?"

"But there was Jesanht, and then this bloke," Will said, jabbing his thumb at Loki. The Trickster still appeared disturbed, but he listened to our conversation. "So, yes. Stranger things have happened to us."

"Well, who would curse you with a sword?" Guildford asked. "Do you have any enemies? Other than—?"

I shook my head quickly. "No. I mean, I haven't even been here long." I turned to Will. "You really think this is a curse of some kind?

I don't get it. Who cares if I can hold this thing properly or not? I just showed I can still use it if I have to."

"Against a deluded vampire?" Loki asked. "Sure. But what about, say, the dark emperor of Orden? Could you trust such a skill against a fully trained knight?"

"I..." I hesitated. The thought of actually fighting an emperor sounded horribly distant. Was it necessary? Couldn't I just find another way to free Chris and find my sister?

"We should get going," Rex cut in with a hand on my shoulder. "Before more Ritual cultists show up." When I looked to him, he gave me a quick, warm smile. "It was foolish of us to let you go on ahead alone. Cleria and I will help you through the mission you're going to take, whatever it may be, or until you leave Lysvid. Lysvid seems to have a thing for you, doesn't it?"

"Our departure should be soon," Will told me. "One more bounty. Refresh our stocks of money and supplies. If we have the Ritual after us, I cannot stress enough the need to move on."

"To a new world?" Lusari asked, beaming.

"To *any* other world." Sira fell in next to me. Her tone made me glance over at her, but she didn't meet my gaze. "I've seen more vampires now than I ever needed to in my life."

Loki sighed. "Agreed."

We started down the alley, continuing the way we'd been going before the ambush. I subconsciously fell behind; watching the shadows like the demon-girl or any of the cultists might materialize in them. However, it was Guildford who fell in at my side.

"You have not changed much," he remarked, giving me a once-over. "I mean, you look a little stronger. The darkness of this world can't do much to put you down, can it?"

I shook my head, a little gratified by his words. Did I look happy?

"You made it so far without your friends' help," he added with a smirk. "Katiel, Dagoriph... they always helped you out in the past, but you made it this far without them. You still would rather shoulder the burdens of the group than alleviate the weight."

I turned to him questioningly, but he stared into the darkness after my friends. "You continue to swallow back your fear for your friends. I..."

He turned to me with a suddenly quite serious expression, and I felt I was about to be scolded. "I don't know that you realize the gravity of your situation. The danger of your quest. Nothing I have ever taught you might prepare you for what lies ahead. You could wind up seriously injured, or even die. Do you know this?"

His words triggered something in me. Will and Sira spoke the same way to me before they made their vows, and it stank of the strange things that characters like Jesanht and that demon girl spoke of. Things that pulled at my unsung memory like loose threads.

This world felt familiar with me. That, alone, could easily wind up my undoing.

It was bad enough that I entered this strange new world, discovering things like magic and vampires *actually* existed. My goal was solely to find my sister. That involved saving Chris, though, which inordinately stuck the dark empire in my path.

"I know," I replied softly. "I know it all. At least, part of me does."

Guildford gave me a stern look. "Is your knowledge of the matter enough? Acknowledging a fire does not put it out."

"But it is the first step," I whispered.

I expected Guildford to look mad, but he adopted a small smile.

"Yes. I suppose it is the first step."

He sighed sadly, staring off ahead. For another long, drawn-out moment, I recalled the fact that my teacher was dead. His death only came seven months ago. Hundreds, if not thousands, of people in my home were missing this man. They would give anything to see him again. I was sure he'd do the same for many of them, to stand at the head of his classroom before thirty or so students, book in hand and pointing to the chalkboard, about to call on one of them to answer a question.

Now I stood beside him, clad in outlandish garbs with a sword at his belt, talking about dark empires as we strolled through a vampire-infested alleyway, leaving dozens of unconscious or dead cultists in our wake.

Loki eventually beckoned Guildford to the front, as apparently the Trickster needed his help to make it out of the alley. As he left, I caught Sira's glance, who walked a little away from the rest of us. Her scarlet eyes flashed, and she turned away with a scoff.

A nervous feeling birthed in my stomach. Was she mad about our conversation? Of my weakness at not being able to wield a sword?

Or, I thought, had she seen through my lies?

SCENE THREE: OVER DINNER

...Of Act Four: Blackness

In the eyes of Ryoku Dragontalen, we are in Leudis, in the world of Lysvid. It is past midnight On November 10th, 2017.

"By my fellow gods, remind me to never cut through an alley in Lysvid again."

The silence that followed Loki's words only showed how much we all agreed. Getting out to the heavily trafficked streets felt like a close shave to what could have ended up a lot worse. I watched Sira as we walked, but she didn't return my gaze. I wondered if that was some sort of silent ending to what happened between us at the Timeless Castle. Just a brief chapter, a sneak peak, and nothing more.

The Bloody Mare was a huge building, much larger than any place we'd been to yet. Even the government buildings of Harohto threatened to pale in comparison. It stood at least three stories tall and built of dark red brick. Torchlight spilled out through the cracks of boarded windows. From outside, we could already hear the sounds of a busy place. Guildford pointed out how the entrance broke off into two doors. One led to the diner, and the other, presumably, to the hunters' den.

"You will like this place, Ryoku," Rex told me, smiling. Somehow, he was the only vampire who could do that without baring his fangs. "Loki picked it out of the inns we knew in Leudis for good reason. The Bloody Mare is a well-trafficked spot for bounty hunters to post and take on hunts, but it's also one of Leudis' most esteemed bars. My master paid for everything, so you'll have four rooms and a four-course meal at your disposal."

Food sounded good right now, I had to admit. But... *four courses*? Who could swallow up that much food in one sitting?

"I'm glad we have a reservation," Cleria said. At a look from Lusari, she smiled thinly. "We were on our way to meet you, anyways, so we're included. Don't you worry – we won't be sitting out this experience."

We climbed a short flight of stairs up to the main doors. We could see another set down below. Guildford noted a sign on the door decreeing it as the hunters' den. "I'll go check out the bounty boards while you guys get set up."

Loki's nose turned up like a dog smelling meat. "I'll go with you. Surely my expertise will help us find a suitable mission to embark upon!"

Wordlessly, Will joined them in rushing ahead. He didn't say why, but I wondered if he was scouting out the bounties posted about me. That left Sira, Lusari, Rex, Cleria, and I to the other door. Sira still didn't utter a word, so Rex and Lusari walked ahead with me. Rex easily opened the door ahead with one hand, and gestured for Lusari to go first. He mimicked the gesture for Cleria and Sira. Cleria happily obliged, rubbing against Rex's arm as she passed. Sira only gave us a cold stare, though, so Rex gestured for me to go ahead.

I quickly discovered that we were in for a treat. The Bloody Mare looked something like a castle. Brightly lit chandeliers hung from the ceiling, the flames casting pale shadows to dance across the elevated seating area and the bar. The walls and floors were hardwood, despite the exterior made of bricks, and lent the room a surprisingly warm atmosphere. The kitchen was right in the middle of it all, and vampires dressed in white chef coats bustled around, tossing heaping pans of wings on open flames, dicing vegetables at a stupendous rate, and working in flawless tandem. I watched that with more curiosity than anything when a tall, redheaded vampire came to meet us.

"Welcome," she spoke in a silvery-sweet voice, clutching a stack of menus against her chest. "A table for...?"

"Eight," Rex told her kindly, "we have a reservation."

The hostess certainly brightened up at that. "Oh, you're the, um, 'Avenging Eight,' is it?" she asked, unable to keep the hint of humor from her voice. "Reservation for the eight four-course meals and four rooms?"

Rex and I exchanged dry glances. Whether that was the Timeless One or Loki, either made sense. "Sounds like it," I replied. "The rest should be behind us shortly."

As she scribbled something on her notepad, my gaze wandered back to the sight of the kitchen, watching the bustling pace of the team as they fought to complete every bill. The six or seven vampires in tuxedos who ran the bar kept calm, easy paces, making small talk with the folk who drank there. Young-looking vampires ran the food to and from tables. I watched an elderly vampire couple anticipating the arrival of two plates, one of lobster and another of steak, each heaped with sides of mashed potatoes, rice, and vegetables. I never thought I could call a vampiric restaurant *friendly*.

The vampires seated at fine tables were nothing like the disturbing ilk that lurked the streets. The girls wore elegant ball dresses that glittered in the candlelight, emphasizing their ivory skin and offering deluge to their dark hair. The men were strapping, dressed in full tuxedos with their dark hair trimmed short or tied back.

"Alright, I'll take you to your table," the hostess told us with a genuine smile. She led us along past the kitchen. A vampire dicing vegetables flashed us the friendliest smile I thought possible.

"Would you like smoking or non-smoking section?"

"Smoking, if that is fine by you," Rex said, looking to me for direction. He waggled a black pack of cigarettes at me, which I saw had red filters. "Blood cigarettes. They make a meal all the more appetizing, and I'm afraid I'm rather addicted to it. But only if you don't mind."

"That's perfectly fine by me," I told him, though I wondered if I was really the one he should be asking. Sira still looked angry.

Lusari was glancing around wildly, clearly never having entered such a rich place before. I could relate. Cleria, on the other hand, strutted alongside me like a fancy cat, clearly used to places like this. I wondered if she was really from some royal family in the Capital. Did that tie in with how she knew the Ritual leader, Gale?

"Very well," the vampire told us, flashing Rex a rather private smile. She led us to a table near the edge of the elevated area, overlooking much of the finer seating and the kitchen. It was quite distant from the rest of the customers. I settled in next to Lusari – Sira sat across from me, as far as she could get, next to Cleria. The server smiled around at us in a way that didn't bare her fangs. "I'll be right back to take your drink orders."

She bustled off to another table where three vampires in tuxedos waited to give their orders. Loki, Guildford, and Will returned before they took our drink orders. I didn't miss the glares Loki got for his Dracula-esque attire. Guildford, on the other hand, got a lasting look from our hostess as he walked past – he was all too ignorant to it, however, as he watched a few cooks carting out a full turkey to a waiting table. I could almost see his mouth watering from where I sat.

"We found the perfect mission!" Loki declared gallantly as he spun into an empty chair next to Cleria, who looked most displeased by this. "Tomorrow morning, we'll be headed north via train to the village of Peul, where we shall be hunting *the Moonwolf*."

He spoke the name as though it were some delicacy. Everyone looked to him in interest. "Trains run in Lysvid?" Sira asked, a little too surprised to keep her angry face on.

"Lysvid does seem to favor the steam era," Guildford said informatively, slinking into a chair next to Loki to practically bury himself in a menu. Will took a seat next to me, flashing me a quick, knowing grin before he disappeared into a menu, too.

"What is this *Moonwolf*?" Lusari popped the question. Her fingers toyed with the edge of her Lysvid-styled skirt under the table.

Loki adjusted himself in his chair. It seemed that was an attempt to get the lighting to cast mysterious shadows across his face, but it failed, and he cleared his throat. "Nobody knows. Only that the Moonwolf has been causing absolute mayhem in Peul – attacking villagers and their livestock, damaging property, and prowling the woods to effectively trap its people in the village."

Lusari emitted a shocked squeal. "That's terrible!" she exclaimed. "We must deal with it at any cost!"

More than one set of eyes turned to me. "That would be primarily up to our Defender," Loki said. "We did accept the mission, but it would be easy to resign if you wish."

I caught Will's glance next to me, and I felt a thick sense of relief. He was giving me a look that showed he'd have no respect for me if I didn't take on such a mission, no matter the danger. After all, I had him to watch my back. As long as she stuck around, nobody would mess with Sira. Then there was Loki…

"We'll do it," I said, as simply as ordering a drink. "If people are in danger, there's no question."

Will wasn't the only one who gave me an approving smile. Only Guildford looked quite worried, still. "Despite being a highly rewarding bounty, it has its due dangers. The people know little to nothing about the beast. Few have even seen it and lived to tell the tale. Mostly the tracks and the sounds tell us it is a wolf."

"We need the money," Will said pointedly. "Honestly, it was the only mission I saw that does not stink of werewolves."

Cleria looked at him from under her lashes. "But it is a wolf. How do we know it isn't a werewolf?"

Loki was the one with a telltale smirk. "Because the Ritual doesn't fund the bounty. Bastards'll back any anti-werewolf propaganda they can smell. If they're not touching it, it's because evidence says it isn't a werewolf."

"But then," Rex added softly, "what else could it be?"

Nobody had an answer. After a moment, Lusari chimed in about the menu, and the tension faded as our stomachs took over.

The three new arrivals scooped up menus just as our hostess returned for our drinks. She hung oddly close to Guildford, stooping next to him with her neckline plunging quite low. Guildford paid about as much attention to the fact as he did anyone else at the table.

Loki ordered some kind of exotic dwarven ale, while Guildford chose a delicate red wine. Will ordered some dark rum, and Sira requested something that sounded even worse. Rex and Cleria both ordered a drink that sounded like it had blood in it – it probably did. Meanwhile, Lusari and I both decided to order mango juice, an apparent favorite of the house.

Once drinks were in order, Rex pulled out one of his red cigarettes and lit it. He did so with his one usable arm – he was quite versatile with it, I was starting to see. Guildford watched him with some interest for a moment, and then glanced at me.

"Did you ever stop smoking, Ryoku?" he asked me.

I nodded. "Just after your funeral, I guess." I left out a chunk of that story, not ready to discuss the aftermath of my teacher's funeral just yet. Images flashed through my mind. The kid who brought a gun to school. Guildford confronted him. Then, the darkness.

Guildford only nodded. Whether or not he saw the look in my eyes and decided to drop it, I couldn't tell.

"Sorry," Rex told me, and exhaled away from the table. "It's just a unique way to attain blood without drinking in front of normal people. Relus invented it, I believe. It… works exceptionally well for somebody of my breed."

At my quizzical look, Will explained. In a quiet voice, so little more than the three of us could hear, he told me Rex was a hybrid – vampire and werewolf. That intrigued me. "Both? Really?" I asked curiously. "So you don't need blood as much? But, you also don't take wolf form here like the other ones."

Will gave me a sharp look to speak quietly as another table glanced over. "Don't bother," Rex told him. "Being quiet about it doesn't change it. The vampires always smell it on me. Even though I spend most of my time in vampire cities, they don't like me much. And no, Ryoku, I'm not stuck in wolf form. I can freely change into it at night, but the full moon – in some worlds – is mandatory. It'll happen either way. I have the blood lust, but I need less than most other vampires do. I have less vampiric defenses, but more werewolf strength."

I nodded eagerly, taking it all in. Being a hybrid didn't sound so bad, really, except for how his own people treated him. He should just stick around people like us, who had nothing but respect for him.

"Say, Ryoku," Rex piped up. Some of the others were dissolving into their own conversations, besides Sira, who had already closed her food menu and glared at the empty table next to us. "You used to smoke regular cigarettes? How long were you smoking for?"

I thought about it. "Since ninth grade, I guess. Two months in. So almost two years, it would have been. How about you?"

Rex looked surprised I asked. "Well, I don't think it matters. A long time. Once, tobacco wasn't such a bad thing. At least, we thought as much."

Guildford nodded in support before glancing at me. "You started shortly after you met Dagoriph, I assume. That makes sense. How is he doing?"

I cringed a little at his assumption, but answered nonetheless. He was one of the only teachers who tolerated Dagoriph. "He graduated. Just this last summer, he earned enough credits to finally do so."

Guildford looked surprised. "What a relief! I was sure he'd have at least another semester to finish. You were a great boon to him, then."

"Dagger said the same thing." I could only nod. I swallowed back anxiety. "He moved away this summer, to Abronal. He might actually go to post-secondary."

Guildford's eyes lit up, and I knew he was connecting the dots. "In the summer? Does this have to do with Varis?"

I averted my gaze. I knew he'd figure it out. I didn't want to get into the details with him right now, either.

A different hostess brought us our drinks. Our regular server remained close to Guildford, who was too busy interrogating me to pay her any mind. As I sipped on my mango juice, I noticed Loki trying very hard to look like he wasn't listening. When he saw me noticing, he balked.

"Ryoku!" he exclaimed. "Why don't you tell us about your friends in the real world? I've been so curious, what with your old teacher here now..."

Guildford didn't look surprised by this in the least. "Dagoriph – Dagger for short. Were it not for his family name, I believe the young man would have been holed up in a facility of some kind. The school held him back several years in high school, but his influence kept him in regular classes rather than independent learning. His family is one of drug lords, one of two prevalent families in Brooks."

Loki slammed the table dramatically, mortified. "A drug lord?" he echoed. "So he would sell to the students?"

"It was suspected," Guildford admitted. "However, there was little anyone could do about the matter. His family, the Neseru's, holds power over much of the district. Even caught red-handed with drugs, I imagine they would paint the picture quite differently. Dagger's family was very intent on his learning, even as much as the boy himself was not.

"He came close to expulsion several times for his rivalry with another student from the opposing influential family. Varis El'Salandier. I believe their hatred for the boy was what made Ryoku and Dagger such fast friends."

I could only nod my agreement. Without Dagger, I never would have made it through that day. The Day of Black, we called it now. The day of Guildford's funeral, and of our vengeance.

Loki couldn't glean much more from Guildford, and the topic eventually drifted. I saw Will studying Rex's arm, tucked away in his coat.

"How did you come to lose use of your arm?" he asked.

Rex took a long drag of his blood cigarette, and then drew his other arm out from within his jacket. I didn't realize he could still use it. He put the bare arm out on the table. There was a large, circular hole taken out of his palm. It looked long since healed over, but it must have been a gruesome injury once.

"It's called a thief's mark," he explained gently, and exhaled a drag of his cigarette, surrounding himself with the reddish smoke. "Carried in from when I was alive. Despite that our anatomies change often after we die, our scars will remain."

"What do you mean, our anatomies change?" I asked.

"Often our injuries or debilitations can heal here," Rex told me. "A missing eye. Loss of the ability to walk. When we die, such debilitations usually go away. That, and sometimes we can be different races. It's part of our soul that comes here, and it doesn't always listen to the rules of our body. I wasn't a half-breed while I was alive. I was a human, just like you. Apparently it was punishment for my sins in life."

I absently touched my face, wondering if the same applies for Defenders.

"You were a thief though," Loki remarked. "Weren't you? So becoming a hybrid could be punishment for that."

Rex didn't reply for a moment, staring deep into his dark red glass. "Sort of," he replied distantly. He took another long drag of his cigarette, and exhaled as he spoke. "I stole some things. Many things, I suppose. Life works in the way that you sometimes need to. But this?"

he asked, holding up his useless hand. "What earned me this wasn't my doing. For this, I was framed."

"But you were a thief nonetheless," Loki absolved. "Perhaps that mark is merely your thefts catching up to you."

Loki clearly didn't think highly of thieves. Rex didn't respond, but I felt there was a great story behind that mark. Today, clearly, wasn't the day to share it.

"He's not quite so simple, old man," Cleria warned, sipping delicately from her glass like it was red wine. "We all carry ghosts into this world, cursed to remain unresolved for all our days."

"And what was it with you and that Gallon character?" Loki asked. "Was he a ghost of yours?"

She glanced at him sharply. "Gale Destrow, you mean. Sure. He was an ex of mine. He cut that off himself by joining that silly cult. Not that he was ever a good man. It only took that sort of edge for me to cut him off for good." Loki's expression looked curious, but Cleria stoned over. "Nothing you need concern yourself with, old man. I can take care of myself."

Another server returned to start on our orders. Everyone picked out an appetizer, but, with Lusari and I still trying to examine the full menu, we left it at that for now. I kept it safe with a starter Caesar salad, one of the few appetizers that sounded normal. I'd gauge just how normal everything else was by seeing the fancy appetizers everyone else ordered.

Shortly after that, our red-haired server abandoned trying to grab Guildford's attention and returned to her job. Loki gave Guildford an incredibly incredulous look for some time until he could finally glean the reason behind his ignorance.

"Damn it! You're married, aren't you? *That's* why you're ignoring our scrumptious snack of a waitress!"

Loki jabbed his finger at Guildford's hand, which had been strategically stowed in his pocket at the table until he took a sip of his wine. Guildford stared at him like Loki had just proposed to him. "The waitress? What are you going on about now?"

Loki ignored him. "How fantastic!" he swooned. "Your devotion to your beloved wife holds you to your sacred vows, even after death! Utterly incredible!"

"He has only been with us a few months," Rex pointed out, but Loki feigned deafness.

Before Guildford could find the words to stave Loki off, our 'scrumptious' waitress returned to take our dinner orders before our appetizers arrived. I picked out something that I hoped was mozzarella sticks, and some spicy-sounding pasta. At the demand to pick out a third course, Lusari and I timidly picked out a platter of what I hoped was scalloped potatoes to share between us.

"What is the matter with you?" Loki asked me callously after our server left. "That's scarcely a meal you have there! And not an ounce of meat?"

I blinked. "Loki, you ordered enough to feed that village of werewolves twice over."

Loki gazed at me incredulously. "My boy, you are surely delirious from being famished all the time! I'm on a low-carb diet!"

Once more, the Trickster left me at a loss for words. I caught Will's glance – he was near bursting with laughter. The expression made me chuckle, and then laugh outright. Soon, the laughter spread all across the table. Lusari giggled into her hands. Guildford was clutching his stomach from laughing so hard. Even Rex hid his mouth behind his napkin as he struggled to repress his laughter, and even the Trickster started to chuckle.

Of course, one person at the table didn't laugh, and nobody dared ask why. Sira kept to herself like she was at a table full of misbehaving children.

Our appetizers arrived shortly after, and Guildford studied me with interest. "That's right – you're a vegetarian, aren't you?"

I nodded. Everyone besides Guildford and Lusari shot me incredulous looks. Even Sira glanced over at this, but she quickly averted her eyes.

"You live without meat?" Will asked.

"No wonder you're so slight!" Loki declared. "How will you ever learn to flail that mighty sword with no muscle mass?"

"There are ways to cope without," Guildford remarked, notably giving Loki a dirty look. "The right diet works wonders."

"I'm the same way," Lusari piped up, perhaps to alleviate the dumbfounded expressions from me. "I grew up mostly without it. The raids in Harohto have been bad for years, and sometimes the price of meats and other commodities would climb due to unavailability."

"That is understandable," Guildford said sympathetically. "The Timeless One has told me much about the states of other worlds. Due to world-travelers and spirits, sometimes common luxuries we take for granted can be quite rare in other worlds."

"What about you, Ryoku?" Loki jabbed at me with his fork. "You're a grown lad! How could you survive like this?"

I shrugged, hesitant under the pressure. "Just... the treatment of the animals in my own world. Animals aren't cared for properly in my world. Not much is, really."

"Ryoku is something of an environmentalist," Guildford added. "He joined many of the proactive clubs in the school. Animal cruelty, fighting pollution, all sorts of things."

I didn't miss the understanding in Will's eyes. Loki, however, made a noise over his mouthful of food. "How could such a thing exist? The world's dying, isn't it? What's left to save?"

"It isn't dying!"

I found myself on my feet, and my voice came in unison with Guildford's as he, too, took offense. The two of us stared down Loki, eyes blazing. The Trickster appeared wholly alarmed by our reactions.

A hand on his shoulder from Cleria gently coaxed Guildford back into his chair. Will's hand appeared on my shoulder. "You must forgive him. Loki is a rash god. I do not believe he meant offense."

I looked Will in the eye. For the first time, I noticed empathic specks of gold in his sapphire eyes. If Will was defending Loki, then I had to concede. Not only was he not wholly approving of the Trickster, he was the most understanding out of all of us. Loki seemed to think I could do great things, but he overlooked the steadfast Syaoto soldier.

"You believe me?" I asked. "That it isn't dying?"

Will smiled. "How could I doubt your steadfast belief? If you told me the sky would turn the colors of the rainbow and stay that way for all of time, I would have to agree. Your determination would make it so."

His words made me feel a little better. I met Loki's glance as I sat back down. His eyes were apologetic, but he said nothing. If he was a major god, did he know something about it that I didn't?

Either way, now was not the time to press that. Our waitress returned with our first courses, and everyone dove in like their appetizers were made of paper mache.

Oddly enough, Guildford seemed to note something as Loki dove into his food.

"You were married once," he said, a statement rather than a question. Loki glanced over at him, and the teacher nodded to his finger where a diamond marriage band sat. With the talk of his own marriage, perhaps it was a stab at revenge.

Loki chewed his mouthful slowly. "I was married long ago, yes," he said heavily. "Early in my godhood."

Much of the usual mischief twitching behind his smile was fading. Ghosts traveled across his face like speaking about them brought them back again.

"That must have been an interesting time," Rex commented. His hand twitched near his pack of cigarettes, but he drank deeply from his glass of blood to battle that particular craving. "Godhood. Were you chosen by somebody, or were you always this way?"

"It differs for each god," Loki said. He stole a glance at me, but averted his eyes when he saw me already looking at him. "Some are chosen for their accomplishments in life. Some, by their sins. Others are born into it. As one of the 'big three' of the Norse gods, one could say I was born into it."

"Are all the legends real, then?" Lusari asked.

Loki only smiled. Much of the usual spirit behind his grin was absent. "Some. Not all. To converse about the true origins of mankind over dinner would take a much grander feast than this, my dear."

"Did something happen to your wife?" Guildford asked. "Was she... Is she a god, too?"

I realized his first inference was correct. Loki didn't reply for a moment, taking a deep drink of his ale. "You see," he spoke, and his words sounded like delicate steps on a floor of broken glass. "The trouble with being a god is often the immortality."

I saw the problem quickly, but it didn't seem to be apparent to the others. Rex finally broke and pulled a cigarette from his pack. "That would be why many want to become gods, I imagine."

"Teoe, my wife," Loki said softly, "wasn't a god like I was. I met her early on, It was among... well, most of the things you hear about in Norse legend. Many of those are recorded, but not all. Back in the days, I helped attain some of the most legendary weapons of the gods, and played a role in the building of Asgard's great wall!" He grinned, as though recalling fond memories, but it trickled away. "None of this matters anymore, since the spirit realm has quite drastically changed."

He glanced at me again, cleared his throat, and went on. "Yeah. Long, long ago, I met a girl in an old village in Midgard – the physical world, essentially, but by an old name. The gods are a fickle sort, you know. A cousin of mine slept with a giant, and my future children... well, that is a story for another day.

"The one thing," he went on, and the anger in his voice started to show, "that the Norse gods seem to have no tolerance for, is to bed a mortal. Perhaps due to our difference in lifespan, or maybe for their own good. It didn't matter long, anyway, since my own brother broke those rules later in life." He deliberately avoided my glance, now, and it took a moment for him to continue. "I kept our affair secret for a very long time. We had a daughter together. We didn't name our daughter for some time. It just seemed a difficult task to name such a girl, such an embodiment of beauty and innocence.

"It was around then," he paused, taking a deep breath, "that I decided to tell my brother about her. To seek his blessing, I guess. I thought our love was strong enough to conquer anything. Surely Odin would realize that it was meant to be."

He didn't finish his statement. To my surprise, the Trickster started to tear up, and he slowly buried his face in his arms on the table. Everyone at the table felt the Trickster's pain, if not to the same degree. Guildford and Cleria both put hands on his shoulder. Even Sira paid attention, watching Loki with true pity.

It took some time for Loki to regain his composure. Our second courses arrived just after he lifted his head. I found myself pleased with the pasta I ordered. Apparently, Loki thought the same about the large steak placed before him, plated with a bowl of rice, steamed vegetables, and a slice of garlic toast, for he seemed to brighten up then.

However, before he lifted the food to his mouth, he paused, his eyes seeing something far past the diner.

"After that happened, I finally named my daughter. Teoe – after her mother."

After effectively leaving the room floored, he kept eating. Everyone fell silent for a long time. We chose to clear their plates rather than stir the pot.

Finally, after we were well into our second courses, Will's curiosity got the better of him. "Your daughter," he asked. "Is she a god as well?"

"Yes," Loki replied, without missing a beat. "I am known as the reigning Trickster, but there are other, smaller Trickster gods who carry out my bidding – especially as of late. Teoe is one of them. She, too, is a Guardian."

That surprised me. Loki's daughter was a Guardian as well? But, to who?

Loki waved his fork at me. "Ryoku," he said, still speaking with his mouth full of food. "Tell us about your other Defender friends. Guildford mentioned them, right?"

He took me by surprise again. "Oh, okay," I murmured. "Well, what about them?"

When Loki only gave me a dirty look, Guildford cleared his throat. "That would mostly be the main three, wouldn't it?" he asked. At my expression, he turned to Loki. "Ryoku's been friends with this group for as long as I know. Katiel, Annalia, and Dawn."

I felt mixed feelings stirring up in my heart, my trepidation with the two girls. Annalia, or Anna, was the girl I'd been dating around this time last year. We dated over the winter, but her family moved across the country in the spring – just before Guildford's death. While I recalled recently still having strong feelings for her, they changed abruptly in the recent months. It was like the memories of her slipped into the gaps, replaced with her: Dawn.

Dawn and I started dating in middle school. The details about its beginning, middle, and even the ending still felt foggy to me. I only recalled how strong we had been. As strange as it felt, I knew it was real. I knew we'd been in love, somehow. I remembered standing up to her stepfather in front of her, and defending her from... somebody. Trying to recall all the details made me dizzy. I supposed the fight hadn't ended so well, but we didn't talk about it nowadays.

That, and it felt strange to think of her after whatever Sira and I sparked up. It only added more confusion to the part of my life that was easier not to think about.

"I would bet some top coin that those three are Defenders, too," Loki chimed. "Is that right, Ryoku?"

I nodded, which made everyone give me a look of interest. "Many Defenders seem to be unaffiliated with one another," Will told me. "After all, becoming a Defender is not a common phenomenon in your world, correct?"

"You must be quite close to them as well," Loki ventured. "You've spoken of Katiel before. Who is he?"

I nodded, pausing to finish a mouthful of food before I explained. "My best friend. He's something of a gamer, but he's kind, brave, and likes to keep the mood light. He's usually the peacekeeper out of us, but strong enough to have our backs if anything happens. He basically helped me get through middle school, and he's stuck around no matter what a pain I've been."

"No matter what you've been like?" Lusari asked skeptically. "It must be so hard to put up with a boy who saves girls from thugs on a semi-regular basis, or sets out on quests to save strangers."

A few laughs echoed around the table, but I blushed. "It does get old after a time," Will agreed, but couldn't hold back his chuckling.

Loki, however, remained vigil even as a grin made his lips quiver. "What about the others?" he asked. "Annalia and Dawn?"

Guildford smiled at this. "As I understand, he dated each of them at different points," he said, a little amused. "I did not know Ryoku while he dated Dawn, but that relationship was the talk of the school. He and Anna separated just before I died, when she moved across the country."

Guildford mentioned his death with relative ease, but I had a feeling he was just using the word without thinking about all it entailed. Meanwhile, Will stared at me expectantly. He knew that this was reaching what we'd briefly spoken of in the woods. I remembered his words, too.

"I guess Anna's a strong Defender, too," I told them. "All my friends seem to be. She's supposed to be this amazing archer. Katiel told me my shoddy archery would have nothing on hers. I haven't talked to her in a long time." I took a short sip of my mango juice, and saw Sira turn away abruptly, feigning ignorance. "She's a little unapproachable at times. Reserved, quiet, studious. Occasionally she opens up, and it's like a floodgate opening up. Despite that, I guess, she does care about us, I think. Still, she likes to tackle stuff on her own."

Loki got a certain look in his eyes. Before I could realize what it meant, he took a heavy swig of his ale. He slammed down his empty flagon, and our server quickly replaced it with another full one. He was drinking quite heavily, I realized – perhaps his third or fourth helping, and it was starting to show. "What about Dawn?" he demanded.

My first instinct was to smile wistfully, which made Loki raise an eyebrow. "She's like the healer of our group," I told him. "She's happy and full of life all the time, even though she's had just as fucked up of a past as we have." The last bit slipped out, and I hesitated, but nobody interrupted me. "She's the type to take care of us after a fight, reprimanding us the whole time about it. Despite that, she's sweet and caring about all of us."

"She was a known ace in all her classes," Guildford told them. "Although I believe she spent more time passing notes with Ryoku and the others than actually studying, she somehow makes it through." His smile faded a little. "Of course, much of the student body didn't seem too fond of her."

Will raised a brow. "Why on Gaia not? She sounds like a wonderful girl."

"Her father's work, I believe," Guildford explained. "He was an officer that I worked quite closely with, but he was killed in the line of duty about... perhaps four or five years ago?"

Rex regarded Guildford in a new light. "As in, a police officer? You're a police officer?"

Guildford smiled. "An auxiliary officer, mind you. It means I worked the post part-time."

"And the school didn't like Dawn for this?" Loki asked incredulously. He was starting to get quite into his mead.

Guildford sighed heavily. "Because of the likes of Dagger and Varis, both of whom come from quite illegitimate families," he said. "The two families deal heavily in substances. Even if the kids might be clean, many of their parents weren't. They programmed the bias against policing families into their children's' heads. It was easy enough, I imagine, hating on the authority figures stamping down on the drug abuse. As such, students like Ryoku and Dawn weren't quite popular among them, no more than I was as a teacher."

Will looked at me with newfound respect. "Your family was involved with the police, too?"

I nodded shortly. "My stepfather, Darrold Vornaire. The chief of police."

Will nodded approvingly, but he halted. "Ryoku, you said..."

The table went silent. Guildford picked up the silence. "Yes. An accident at home. He was a good chief, and his death fell on the same year as the death of Dawn's father. It landed the police force quite short on bodies. I took a year off to help the force. I returned just in time for Ryoku to enter my classes. He didn't know me, but I knew his stepfather and reached out to him."

Loki nodded slowly. "No wonder you were his favorite teacher." He took a long, slow dip of his drink. "Say. When, exactly, did you kick the bucket?"

My teacher flinched visibly. Will and Rex both made to step up for him, but Guildford met Loki's glance equally. "April 15th, of this year. Why?"

"Hmm," Loki murmured thoughtfully. "No reason. Merely connecting the dots in this modern little story."

I remained silent. April 15th. The day that he brought a gun to school. The Day of Black followed a week later on a rainy April day. Thinking of that month only ever succeeded in bringing me back to a time of darkness.

It was a while before our next plates of food arrived, and conversation eventually turned to a lighter, less personal, note. They discussed the Ritual, and whether or not we dissuaded their efforts to kill us. Cleria ensured us that they had thousands of numbers on us. The brawl in Xactyr and in the alley scarcely a yard from where we stood only boasted a few of their numbers.

The Ritual put up a guise as a mercenary force serving to protect the people. Behind that curtain, they worked with a darker intent: illegally claiming blood, practicing dark magic and, worst of all, converting new vampires from elves. Cleria casually revealed that the latter might have been a reason to come after me, which disturbed me to the core. Corrupting elves usually earned a priestly status of those among the Ritual. Turning an elf would almost kill them, but the resulting vampire was usually insanely powerful.

Eventually, Loki ascended from his rather sour mood and took on the full effects of his liquor. He sang at the top of his lungs, flirted with the waitresses, and danced openly until his chair toppled over. Guildford winced as Loki grabbed our server's backside. I was sure that, for a moment, the server hoped it was Guildford coming onto her, but then immediately turned sour.

At some point, Loki borrowed a vampire gentleman's top hat and took the stage on top of the table. His scrambled dancing nearly toppled everyone's' plates, who snatched them up like it was all they might ever eat in their lives. I failed to save my drink as it perished on the floor of the diner. I exchanged glances with Lusari, who nodded. We pushed our plates aside and stood.

Guildford glanced up at us. "Done already?"

I nodded, but he already had a mouthful of food. I couldn't stifle my laughter as he tried to chew as quickly as possible. "Give me a moment, and I'll go up with you," he finally blurted once his mouth was freed.

He watched Loki for a moment, amused, but quickly dived back into his meal. Lusari and I leaned against the chairs, watching Loki's antics with some amusement. Most of the diner had emptied out. Our waitress was watching our table discreetly, I noticed.

Will finished his last plate as well, rising like he actually put on a belly from his food – I wouldn't be surprised. Guildford finished right after him, and he flagged down our waitress. "May we be shown to our rooms?" he asked politely, but had to raise his voice a little – Loki just transitioned from dancer to rock star.

"Certainly," she replied with a polite smile, and beckoned us to follow her. She led us up the stairwell behind our table. I glanced behind us at the others just as Loki tried to drag Rex onto the table with him, who looked and acted like a stone. The vampire raised his single hand in defeat, easily breaking free of Loki's grip, and came to join us. Sira didn't look at us, but Cleria waved and winked at me. Loki waved enthusiastically at us as though we must be leaving on a twenty-year journey, never to be seen again. I waved back, bemused.

We took the stairs and went down the first hallway, then around the corner to the next. In that hall, she gestured to four doors in a line down the way, giving us a warm smile. To Guildford, her expression still seemed suggestive, but he paid it no mind. She lingered for a moment, and I almost wondered if she might approach Guildford – but finally, she left, returning to her duties.

"Alright," Guildford said, "room arrangement. We've got four rooms, and eight people."

"Who set that up?" Will asked wondrously. He needed no answer; the Timeless One and Loki made the reservations.

"Cleria and I will share a room," Rex told him. "Forgive me, but I'm not sure either of you would like sharing a room with a vampire. This will be easier."

Guildford cringed, but handed Rex one of the four keys. "Goodnight, Rex. I'll let the others know their rooms afterward."

"Goodnight," Rex said, and gave me a warm smile before taking the farthest room down the hall.

"I will take the room with Sira," Will said quietly. I gave him a look, surprised, but he didn't meet my glance. He gave Lusari a very subtle nod. How strange. I had a feeling they must have planned this after seeing how Sira was acting.

"And I'll pair up with Ryoku," Lusari said, stifling a yawn. When she realized who remained, however, her expression fell.

"Oh no, Guildford..." Will moaned. "I would hate to leave you with the local drunk downstairs! We could switch our arrangements..."

"That's quite alright," Guildford told him, looking past Will with a grin. He gestured behind us, where two burly vampires carried an unconscious Loki toward us. Cleria and Sira tailed behind them, both shaking their heads in pity. "Goodnight, friends."

"Goodnight," Will, Lusari, and I chorused. Will went to the third room down the hall, while Guildford directed the pair of vampires to the second room. Lusari and I made for the first. I fumbled with the key at the door and dropped it. When I picked it up, I caught the glance of Sira as she stood next to Will. For a moment, I thought I could sense the energy behind her eyes, the same feeling as when we got closer than ever before in that old kitchen – the spark, the fire that I craved about her. Then it was gone, and she disappeared into the room, leaving me feeling somehow emptier than before. Just when I thought she couldn't hurt me anymore.

Lusari and I entered our room. The place was just as impressive as the dining area. Two single-person beds faced us that looked like they could comfortably fit two each. The comforter and pillows looked like something out of a heavenly dream. One boarded-up window was above the beds facing the street, covered with a dark curtain, but even that couldn't make this wondrous room look foreboding. A large maple wardrobe took up most of the far wall, and the other side led to a white-tiled bathroom.

"A bathroom," I breathed, surprised. I went to check it out, and found myself impressed. "Running water. A shower. Sink. Toilet, even. Wow." I didn't expect Lysvid to be so accommodating. The inn at the Capital hadn't been as modern. I turned back to Lusari, who was taking in the room with just as much wonder. She didn't seem accustomed to riches or fineries, especially in other worlds. "Lusari, do you mind if I shower quickly?"

"S-Shower? Of course, go ahead," she replied, managing a smile. She sat down on the bed and hugged her legs against herself. Her snowy eyes seemed a little distant. I wondered what she was thinking about, but she smiled up at me when she saw me studying her. "Go on, silly. I'll probably get ready for bed and fall asleep in the meantime. It sounds like tomorrow will be another big day, and I have Mana to recover."

I almost obliged, but her wording caught me. "Mana?"

"That's just a name for magic energy," Lusari explained, sounding tired. Her eyelids fluttered a little, and I realized she wasn't kidding. "My sources aren't unlimited, you know. A good night's sleep will do me just right."

I only nodded. Of course, another spiritual term I didn't know. I took a minute to unpack my things near the wardrobe, and carefully placed Ragnarokkr against the wall with my staff, knife, and bow and arrows. I developed quite the arsenal, I thought, even though I could do little with what I had. I picked out the outfit I started out in the spirit realm with – a lace-up brown shirt and black pants. They seemed suitable for sleeping clothes, especially when I was sharing a room with a girl.

I caught Lusari's glance as I retreated to the shower. Was I imagining the look in her eyes? It seemed almost impatient, even lusty. She hadn't moved since I started unpacking. When I thought about it, she was the one of us I knew the least about. Will and Sira – even through the latter's mysterious behavior – seemed like they'd drilled their ways straight into my heart. After Loki vented to us, it was hard to see him as the distant and cold Trickster anymore. Even Rex and Cleria seemed quite warm with us, but there was a distant quality to Lusari. I felt close to her, still, but I wasn't sure how she felt about us.

I was almost sure I was overthinking it, so I went to shower. The hot water would surely clear my head. It sure felt relaxing once I stepped in. I hadn't realized how sore I became after the day, let alone the constant pace of action we seemed to face ever since I stepped foot in Bytold's inn. I had only been here for a few days, but the flow was starting to feel... natural.

The recently healed scar on my chest tingled oddly in the water. It didn't hurt, really, but felt strange. I could still glance down at it and picture how it looked before it healed. It was the worst of any injuries I'd gotten here so far. I washed the skin tenderly, as though it might break open on me again.

I spent much longer basking in the hot water than I intended, and caught myself before I properly dozed off. I stepped out into the cold world again, wrapping myself tightly in a plush towel to battle off the sudden chill. I caught my own glance in the mirror, and stared at myself for a long moment. Somehow, as impossible as it seemed, I thought I looked more mature than before. Had the fights with vampires, werewolves, thugs, and raiders added that darkness to my eyes? Did my cheekbones always look quite so prominent?

When I finally left the bathroom, Lusari was fast asleep on her bed, only partially wrapped up in blankets. Laying there, her silvery hair spilled around her head like snow, she looked like the innocent girl I'd seen at the mercy of a group of thugs. I smiled sadly, a little angry at myself for my concern about her. I went to adjust her blankets, but quickly realized she was mostly unclothed under them. I steeled myself, mindful of how cold the room was, and fixed them so she was fully covered. It wouldn't do any good for our mage to be sick tomorrow, I told myself.

When I laid down in my own bed, already blurry-eyed from readiness to sleep, I thought I saw Lusari turn over in her bed, facing me. I smiled wearily; I was sure I imagined how dark her eyes looked in the lack of light. I was surely already asleep.

SCENE FOUR: THE MOON WOLF AND THE BLACK DEMON

...Of Act Four: Blackness

In the eyes of Lusari Atella, we are in North Woods of Peul, in the world of Lysvid. It is early morning On November 10th, 2017.

"Remind me, Loki – whose fault is it that you're hung over?"

"You're a teacher," Loki grumbled. "You shouldn't let me drink so much in one sitting."

"Not *your* teacher," Guildford replied, but he smirked.

"You have the worst timing," Sira growled. She trudged ahead as she held Ryoku's hand. As far as I knew, she hadn't elaborated on that. "We don't know how tough this Moonwolf thing is gonna be, and our strongest fighter is useless."

Loki eyed her with a wicked smile. "You think *I'm* the strongest? Truly, coming from the mighty Sira?"

Will was at my side, his cautious eyes scanning the perimeter, but he spared that a side comment. "I think she meant the strangest."

He drew a laugh from a couple of them: Guildford's was that of a young man, rich, powerful, and undeniably charming. Ryoku's, in comparison, was like the brief illumination of an orchestra, tapping into his beautiful, hidden vocals in a way that seemed to send everyone spinning. He turned to face us, walking backwards to briefly and blindly entrust his safety in the fiery and fickle hands of Sira Jessura – and he smiled.

That was it. Ryoku Dragontalen's secret weapon. His golden smile borrowed the warmth from the hottest suns in the spirit realm to blast us with its brightness. Combined with his beautiful green eyes, the delicate curve of his nose, his cheeks, and the soft cascade of his golden hair, Ryoku Dragontalen was a force to be reckoned with. I was startled he hadn't been able to win over an enemy of ours with just that coveted face of his.

I kept silent, though I made sure he saw just how easily his smile summoned mine. I had to. With the fiery Sira attached to his hip, she'd never let me get close. She couldn't decide whether she was in love with him, or only lusted for him. If I had it right, she helped him get through the Old Forest and fought for him before we met. Ryoku had saved my life. Without him, I would surely have been dead... or worse. Sira didn't need him like I did.

That said, I wasn't sure what I could do anyway. Where Ryoku was preoccupied with everything else, Will watched out for me. He made certain to watch over me especially while we traveled through the unknown territory of Lysvid. He was sharp and wary, never quite taking things at face value – except for me. I could tell he still saw the same helpless girl, surrounded by a bunch of thugs. When his eyes darted to the shadows, it was as though he saw the same men approaching again, this time garbed in the dark attire of the Ritual.

That, and Will seemed almost as preoccupied by the Defender as I was. It wasn't in a sexual way, though, I hoped. Ryoku and Will always seemed to have an understanding and close comradery between them, even when I first met them, and it only grew and grew. I was envious of it. No matter how I tried, Ryoku never lowered his guard around me. Not like he did around Will, Sira, Guildford, or even Loki. The vampires weren't exempt, either. Rex seemed to warm right up to Ryoku. The insidious Cleria wanted to as well, I could tell.

No. For the time being, I was the odd one out. The black sheep of the group. Will may love me, but he had duties and honor that would always come first, whereas I thought Ryoku might jump off a cliff for Sira. Probably for anyone, really. Sira loved Ryoku, whether she accepted it or not. Loki loved himself. Guildford loved Ryoku as a student, and he might eventually teach us like the rest of his class, too.

Being the odd one out was okay, though. From the sidelines, I could watch everyone with comfort. I could study how easily Ryoku spaced out, or how Sira stared at him while he did so. How Will would study his landscapes, his hand always on the lance with carved initials in it.

Loki gave Ryoku odd looks, I thought. It was as though he looked at him and expected somebody else to turn his way. When Ryoku Dragontalen smiled absently back at him, Loki gazed away, and I could almost sense the self-loathing behind his silence.

Rex smoked a lot, despite that he battled his cravings when we first brought Ryoku to the Timeless Castle. Cleria skipped along like a moving shadow, usually somewhere between Ryoku and Rex. It seemed like everyone in the group had their favorites. A ragtag bunch for the history books.

The most accepting of the group, besides Ryoku himself, was surely Guildford. Perhaps he raised the bar a little for Ryoku, but he treated *everyone* like equals. It didn't matter whether we hung out in a vampire-infested bar or the castle of an eerie old bat. It didn't matter whether we traveled with the fiery Swordstress or the Trickster. It didn't matter whether we fought bands of the Ritual cult or went after savage wolves in the north – Guildford was with us all the way and never complained. In fact, I thought he enjoyed it.

"We'd best be on guard," the teacher warned as I studied him, stowing his map into his cloak in favor of his longsword. He didn't see me looking. "We're near its territory now."

Everyone slowed down until we all traveled in more of a tight flock. Ryoku nervously kept the lead, his hand on the strange black sword that the Timeless One gave him. Did he notice how easily he swayed toward that new weapon?

Will squeezed my hand. "Are you ready?" he whispered. His eyes shone like lagoons in the dark world of Lysvid. They bore an unrestrained love for life. Despite having just as dark a past as any one of us did, he held it well. Almost nothing could shatter his deep enthusiasm for life, even the dark world of Lysvid.

I took my staff from its holster over my back. It was already glowing with charged runes. I'd taken the time to do so during our train ride to the village of Peul. Will smiled, taking out his lance. As he did so, a raccoon-eyed Loki drifted up next to him like some sort of bog ghost.

"We should buy you a new spear, my friend," he muttered, observing the plain lance with discretion. "That's like the kind soldiers use. You're a Guardian, Will."

Will grimaced quickly. "A soldier would not use a weapon lacking quality," he replied. "Regardless, I am but a guide and Guardian. It is a noble position. I need no new weapon, Trickster."

Loki regarded Will like the soldier had just made an ill comment about his weight. He jabbed his thumb at Ragnarokkr bobbing on Ryoku's back. "You sure you don't want something like that? I'm a god, Will – I'm sure I could get you whatever you please. Perhaps something like Gungnir? Sleipnir? Gods forbid it, but the Gae Bolg... Indulge yourself!"

"I could not be more confident," Will replied. His voice sounded more strained now. He gave his spear an experimental spin. When he laid it to rest on his shoulder, I saw the initials carved just below the blade. 'J.R.'.

"There it is!" Guildford declared, pointing ahead with the blade of his sword. Loki and I flinched, but Will didn't react – even in conversation, the soldier was always alert. He stepped ahead of Ryoku and Sira, as they drew their weapons. Rex and Cleria joined us. I heard the quiet *shink* of Cleria's claws extending. Not quite as deadly as Rex's rock fist, but she was strong, too. She caused a lot of damage when they arrived to save us from the Ritual.

We'd come to an end of the forest where the path staggered off into thicker woods, laden with large boulders and rocky ledges all over. The trees shot out to the sky, gnarled and twisted like claws of the earth reaching for the only lights in Lysvid. If we delved deeper, it'd be hard to tell where we were going in the pitch of Lysvid without the lead of Rex and Cleria, who both seemed to see in Lysvid's darkness eerily well.

Ahead of us, atop a part of the ledge between the trees, the wolf stepped out into the open. Its fur was as dark as the world around it, and resonated with some sort of energy that made the air feel like static. Its black eyes studied us from atop a fang-filled snout, the lip curled up into a silent snarl. It was at least double the size of a normal wolf. The atmosphere it gave off was not unlike that of Jesanht Olace, the interloper who attacked Ryoku when we arrived in Lysvid.

Even before Loki let out a startled cry of realisation, I knew we'd just stepped into something more than we'd intended, like children who wandered into the deep end of the pool by mistake and found nothing beneath their feet. Guildford eased Ryoku back carefully with a touch of his arm, and Will's grip on his lance fastened like a shark's maw.

Loki stepped out before us, a hand on his royal sword. "Geri."

In response, the wolf seemed to be grinning. Its lip curled up in a way that suggested it took humor in Loki's appearance.

"Loki," the wolf growled in a deep male voice. It took me nary a second to realize it was the wolf speaking. It bounded part of the way down the hill, stopping a ways before us to stretch lazily, never taking its eyes off the Trickster. "Fancy meeting the Trickster in a place like this. I thought the gods ventured far from the world of Lysvid, but here I find you. Or you find me, I suppose."

"Not lately," Loki replied. His hangover magically dissipated once an actual threat rose. To Ryoku, he subtly whispered, "This may not be the best place to train, kid." Before he could protest, Loki continued toward Geri, his hand at his sword. "Where's Freki, Geri? Is she with you?"

The wolf let out a rippling snarl, holding its ground. Ryoku attempted to follow Loki, but Will and Guildford held him back, both watching the encounter with hawk eyes.

"Freki has vanished," Geri growled, "as of two months ago. The spark of the new world, and she has disappeared. Do you know anything about that, Trickster?" Before he could get an answer, his nose suddenly perked up. "Interesting."

An intense feeling of dread washed over me as his gaze slid from Loki, to Ryoku.

"How interesting," he repeated, stepping down from the upper ledge further. Loki stepped in his way, but Geri seemed to look right through him. "To find the Trickster god lurking in the shadows of Lysvid. And, with him… a Defender."

I could've sworn I saw Loki's shoulders sag half an inch in relief. Why he would look relieved about that, I couldn't imagine.

"Get back!" Loki shouted, and stepped in the way of Geri just as the huge wolf lunged, clearing the rocky slope like an anthill, and bore down on Loki with his rows of sharp fangs. Loki caught the wolf by his shoulder and jaw, his sword still sheathed at his side. Will and Guildford urgently pushed Ryoku back and stepped forward. Ryoku fell to the ground from their force. Ragnarokkr clattered to the ground behind Guildford. The teacher's glance darted between Ryoku and Loki.

I didn't hesitate, and hurried to Ryoku's side, where I nearly crashed into Sira. "We need to get him the fuck outta here," she told me urgently, as though the thought might never have occurred to me. "Come on, you."

"I can't," Ryoku replied, as simply as if we asked him to go to the markets with us. He ignored my hand and rose to his feet on his own. "That wolf has been hurting the villagers. Somehow, I need to stop it. We took that bounty."

Sira slapped her forehead in exasperation. "That's a fucking god, kid. You realize that? We're looking at the same *massive wolf god*, right? This is no time to be acting like a full-fledged Defender!"

Ryoku seemed to be looking past her and didn't hear a word she said. He only looked at Loki, his heels digging into the earth, struggling to hold Geri back. The wolf bounded around Loki, trying to force him back, but the Trickster held his own. Guildford and Will hung back, waiting for their opportunity to step in.

Without a word, Ryoku lunged for Ragnarokkr behind Guildford. Sira glared after him like fire following a trail of gasoline. Amazingly, Ryoku didn't seem to flinch at this. If there was a side of Ryoku I could claim to love, it was this. The boy who acted brave in the face of danger. We both knew he didn't stand a chance, but he rushed to protect his friend – a god, of course, and Ryoku was only human.

"Hey! Wolf-head!" Ryoku shouted, waving his sword at the wolf. In another context, I would have surely dropped to the ground laughing at Ryoku's small attempt at an insult. "You're after me, aren't you? A Defender?"

Geri relented. Loki fell forward on all fours. He looked pale. Fighting against a fellow god must take a lot out of him. Geri circled around the fallen Trickster, approaching Ryoku with just as much caution as we regarded it with. Will and Guildford hung near

Loki, stuck somewhere between helping Ryoku or Loki. In the end, Guildford stooped to help Loki to his feet, and Will cautiously circled Geri toward Ryoku's side. Sira and I kept right behind Ryoku, though Sira looked just as ready as Geri to sever Ryoku's head.

Geri closed the distance to Ryoku. Sira made to dash in front of Ryoku, but he was too fast. The wolf god flipped into the air and rammed his hind legs into Ryoku's chest like a kangaroo. I felt the wind as Ryoku flew past me, rolling over twice before slamming into a grinding halt on his knees. Impressively, he still had a grip on Ragnarokkr's chains surrounding the hilt.

Shouting obscenities, Sira swung at Geri with all her might, Sinistra screaming through the air. Geri danced around it. The blade struck the ground hard enough to cleave into the earth, spraying dirt everywhere. Will lunged next with his lance, but the wolf caught it in its fangs and used the weight to hurl Will aside, where he landed hard against rocky ledge. Cleria darted out from Will's shadow like a ghost, her claws outstretched for blood. Geri dodged the first swipe, then closed in and rammed into the vampire girl's side. Even the stone-skinned vampire was knocked astray and fell into Rex. He caught her and held back to study the wolf's movements.

Only Guildford and I didn't act. The teacher tried helping Loki to his feet – the only one of us who really stood a chance – and I stepped closer to Ryoku, clutching my staff as a lifeline. My magic would be necessary for healing, I knew, but I needed to be between Ryoku and his enemy.

"What a peculiar scent," Geri growled, resuming a saunter toward Ryoku. "Defender. You smell bright for a human being. And... somehow, quite different."

Everyone struggled to rise. Sira couldn't free her sword buried in the earth, but she looked ready to start swinging at Geri with her bare hands if she needed to. Rex helped Cleria stand and moved toward Geri defensively, but kept distance between them. One false move, and this wolf could easily kill Ryoku.

Ryoku didn't respond, struggling to his feet. The hands clutching Ragnarokkr trembled badly. Just as suddenly as before, Geri sprang into him. His wiry tail struck Ragnarokkr hard enough to create a sound close to steel-on-steel. Ryoku flew back once more, but he used Ragnarokkr to slow his impact and attempt to steady himself. The chains were slickening with blood.

"There is something else in you," Geri decided, sniffing at Ryoku while he lurked ever closer. Ryoku managed to find his footing, but blood was dripping down his face and hands. "I smell it. A sickly-sweet scent. Humans always have it, but I have never smelled such a potent... *darkness.*"

Geri snapped the last word, and Ryoku flinched, stumbling forward against his blade. The blade held, but Ryoku looked fully reliant on it to stand. Loki made to move, but he stumbled. Guildford had to lunge to catch and steady the Trickster. Sira finally dragged her sword free of the ground and turned to rush Geri, only to find Will's hand stopping her. He put a single finger to his lips. What was he thinking? Didn't he see how Geri advanced on Ryoku like a predator?

I couldn't heed his warning. I rushed to Ryoku's side and raised my staff up toward Geri. Energy crackled around my hands, ready to unleash everything I had. Geri briefly sniffed the air at me, but then returned his attention to Ryoku. I was of no consequence.

"Leave him alone, Geri!" Loki demanded, trying to find his footing as he leaned heavily on Guildford. "None of us have anything to do with Freki, I promise you. Why don't you just go to Immortalia and ask the Ancients?"

Geri's laughter came out as an angry bark. "Immortalia is worthless! The gods are weak, imprisoned in a pallid excuse for a godly realm. The Ancients are nowhere to be found, and, more importantly, neither is my sister." His black eyes slid back to Ryoku. "No, Immortalia is not the answer. I have found something worth my while."

Sira struggled against Will, but he surprisingly kept a firm grip on her. Rex and Cleria had slowed to a stop. Only Loki and Guildford approached slowly. Did they feel as useless as I did?

"Do you know what I speak of, boy?" Geri asked. I stole a glance at Ryoku without dropping my staff. He looked like he could collapse at any moment. His hair fell into his face, his head tilted downward. He trembled so violently that I was surprised he could still hold his sword. In fact, after two strikes from a god, I was thoroughly impressed.

"Turn your ears, Ryoku!" Will shouted, still keeping Sira at bay, who looked like she might try to tear Geri limb from limb. "Do not listen to this fallen god!"

Ryoku didn't reply. Geri turned his head to Loki and Guildford, who still attempted to close in despite the rough shape Loki was in – had fighting off Geri really taken that much out of him? "Fallen god? I only speak the truth. Does the mighty Trickster not sense his presence?"

His grip on his regal blade shuddered. "What are you on about, Geri?"

Geri grinned in such a way that a quiet snarl escaped his lips. "You call yourself a god, but you do not notice his energy? The primal darkness that stirs within your precious Defender? Is this not why you chose Lysvid, the darkest world, to hide away in?"

Loki staggered away from Guildford, who only let him go when the Trickster found his footing. Loki didn't pay Guildford any mind. His attention turned fully to Ryoku. Geri slowly turned his head to face the Defender standing behind me.

It was only then, watching the expressions of two gods, that I realized they weren't the only energy here.

I turned as Ryoku raised his head. Wait, was that Ryoku? His skin looked darker. He'd been struggling to stand, but suddenly rose to his full height, rolling his shoulders back in an eerily quick movement. The darkness seemed to cling to his hair, and not a trace of its usual gold shone through – it had turned jet-black.

In the same way that a terrible fright coursed through my body, something else was there, too. Excitement. The way Ryoku could stand up to powerful forces without fear, the dripping threats in his voice when he had nothing to back it up. I remembered seeing the red flash in his eyes when he faced the Keeper in Harohto, or when he shot three arrows in impossible succession into the throat of a Warg. In Gaevrel, when he stood up to the vampires threatening Rex.

It all made sense now.

"What is that?" Will demanded. He lost his grip on Sira, but the fiery warrior stood frozen to the spot.

Ryoku's head snapped up, and I saw the final touch. One eye closed from the blood running down his face, but the other zeroed in on Geri – and it was as red as blood.

He uttered a cold, cruel laugh. It was nothing like Ryoku's. Where his voice sounded musical and happy, this was an enemy.

Ryoku's laughter was like wintry bells; his was like the sound of the Reaper's chains.

"I can breathe," the demon spoke. His words almost sounded like Ryoku's, but there was an odd quality to them. Darkened, tainted. He lifted Ragnarokkr with one hand, holding the blade aloft at an easy weight, examining it. He tilted his head a little to see it. His closed eye didn't open. "What a strange form you have taken, Ragnarok. The darkness that weakened me so greatly seems to have taken its toll on you." He studied it a moment longer, and then flicked the blade. What looked like dark energy tapered off the blade in ribbons, inspiring a satisfied smile from the demon. Then his eye slid, ever so slowly, to lock onto Geri.

I felt Rex's hand pull me back. A loud crack shot through the air. A current of wind threatened to floor me, but Rex held me steady. Will caught Cleria. Loki, a look of horror on his face, fell back into Guildford. Only Sira held her ground, watching what unfolded with wide eyes.

The demon that took Ryoku moved. The crack was the sound of a full swing of Ragnarokkr cleaving through the air, which Geri met with a whip of his wiry tail. I caught a brief glance of the demon's face. It was one that would serve to haunt me, imagining Ryoku with that impassive look on his face, his open crimson eye devoid of emotion.

Ryoku's body moved with effortless speed. Geri narrowly dodged Ragnarokkr as the blade cleaved the stone where he stood – the stone fell to pieces in the blade's wake. Geri lunged at the demon and caught his arm in his snout. I cringed, ready to intervene with anything I could muster. Demon or no, that was Ryoku's body.

"This is what you wanted?" Loki cried, struggling to find his footing. "You wanted to fight instead of finding your accursed sister?"

Geri howled in laughter as the demon flung him back, cut short by a whimper as his back struck stone. "We are gods, Loki!" he screamed. "How often do we find a feasible fight? Something we can actually try for?"

"A fight?" the demon spoke. His voice grated my ears. I hated hearing Ryoku speak such dark utterances. It was nothing like the moments of insidious confidence. This was the full monster. "You invoked me for a *fight*?"

"You would thank me for it, demon," Geri snarled, pacing around the demon. "You were trapped within the mind of this mortal. Were it not for me, surely you would still be sound asleep!"

The demon watched Geri pace for a moment, and chuckled in a way that sent shivers down my spine. "Huh. Mortal body, you think." His laughter turned dry, cynical. "Wolf god, you interfere in matters you do not understand. You believe this is an even fight? You believe you truly stand a chance against me?"

Geri laughed dryly, but did not let down his guard. I noticed Ryoku's arm was bleeding from Geri's fangs. The demon used it like it had no damage whatsoever. "I know you are weakened, demon," Geri replied. "You have been asleep for months. Perhaps longer, and in different time. Like all else in this world, you are weaker than ever."

The demon stopped, regarding Geri with a look devoid of any emotion. Then, ever so slowly, a smile crept along his lips. It was nothing like Ryoku's smile. It was sinister and dark. "What an insolent god. Let me show you just how wrong you are."

If I had chosen that moment to blink, I may have missed the outcome of the fight. Suddenly, the demon was gone, leaving only an upstart of dust in his wake where he stood.

"Let's end this!"

It seemed to come from all around us, like the demon took to the air to invade our lungs. We all looked around, alarmed. He was nowhere in sight.

He reappeared in the air above Geri. By the wolf's expression, he hadn't the slightest inkling of what was happening. The demon's sword – Ryoku's sword – rose above his head, and tangible dark energy spiraled around it.

Three words shot through the air like thunder in a valley. Were they even words? It didn't sound like a language I knew, but I could feel power and darkness in them. The words struck straight through to my very core. My soul stirred, fluctuating, in response to the demon. Somehow, I knew I would never forget those words.

"*Rai Shin Kai!*"

With that dark utterance, the demon brought down his sword, and the darkness came free of it like a living thing, falling upon Geri like a flash storm. The sound was immense, powerful, and deafening. It came like a meteor striking the earth, jarring the ground beneath my feet both with a thunderous impact and the mighty boom of magic. It cleaved through the earth, and Geri, in an instant.

An eternity could have fit in that powerful moment where the demon unleashed something unlike anything I had ever seen. He landed lightly on his feet behind Geri, his blood-colored eyes impassive. With one hand, he easily put the sword away over his back and gazed back over the maimed body of Geri. His powerful attack had left a scar in the earth, a sizeable gash like he'd swung at a mere pile of sand with a shovel. Geri lay within, a ruined wolf at the bottom of a tear in the earth. For the first time, I felt pity for the wolf god.

It dawned on me, then, what I had just witnessed. The complete and total defeat of a god.

When I finally brought myself to look at the demon again, he changed. The reverse of his demonic transformation came much quicker, as though some deity from above simply readjusted Ryoku's color. In one swoop, his hair turned shining gold again, his skin paled, that horribly impassive expression on his face faded into shock – and he collapsed.

"Ryoku!"

Out came several cries of worried Guardians and friends as we rushed to his side. I was the first to reach him. He lifted his head by himself in my arms, but his eyes remained closed. A small smile warmed up his face as though that cold soul had never been here. Sira took him from me and helped him to his feet.

Then he opened his one eye, the one that didn't have blood dripping over it. Previously as green as a beautiful forest, it had changed into a swirling, toxic violet.

Sira dropped him in uncharacteristic panic, scrambling away. He flailed for a moment, unsteady on his legs, and the flimsy Loki managed to steady him on his feet. The Trickster stared into his eye for a long moment, expressionless. Everyone was silent, studying the change in our favorite Defender. He only stared back, mute and confused. I wasn't sure he had the energy to speak.

"We've been in Lysvid long enough, I think," Loki murmured. "We'll report back on our hunt, and then we're gone."

"Okay," Ryoku replied – to my horror, a trace of that darkness in his voice came through when he spoke. However, when he cleared his throat, his normal light seemed to return. "We should stop by the Timeless Castle. I think I have a few questions for him."

I couldn't tell whether the tapping motion he did on Ragnarokkr's hilt was intentional or not. For that matter, did he remember losing control? Had he allowed the demon to step in, or was it an unconscious surrender? Was it benevolent to him, or just as harmful to him as it was our enemies?

The strangest thing, surely, was the look Sira was giving him. Sira, who had watched in shock when the demon took over and didn't back down, didn't flinch away, and who relentlessly tried to save him from Geri – recoiled from Ryoku as though his skin were made of acid. If she was afraid of the demon, why did she rush to his side as soon as he collapsed?

No, I realized, it had nothing to do with the demon. As Ryoku stared back at us with that violet eye, I realized that must be the very thing Sira feared above all else.

SCENE FIVE: NYCTOPHOBIA

...Of Act Four: Blackness

In the eyes of Ryoku Dragontalen, we are in The Timeless Castle, in the world of Lysvid. It is early afternoon On November 10th, 2017.

"So the time to continue your journey has arrived."

The nod of agreement in our company had a strange finality to it, as though we'd all had enough of this dark world. That was easy to assume. I longed for sunlight, for adventure. I wanted to find my friends from my world. I was making new friends fast, but reuniting with Guildford made me long for them, too.

We gathered around the long, rectangular table in the Timeless One's hall once more, dressed in our regular clothes again. I bought a new outfit with my share of Geri's bounty. A simple white long-sleeved shirt and pants not torn to shreds. New bandages wrapped around my right arm where Geri had apparently bitten me quite deeply in battle. The wound didn't hurt as much as I thought, but I was growing tired of getting bandaged up.

I noticed that the Timeless One was giving me an odd look. Just as I opened my mouth to ask what strange emotion was in his cloudy eyes, he turned to Guildford. "You will be traveling with your student now, I presume."

My teacher nodded. "Yes. I was unable to teach him of any value during our last few fights, I'm afraid. I want to travel with him until I can instruct him more fittingly. If not, then I will find him a more suitable instructor."

I silently protested that. If anyone could teach me, it was undeniably Guildford. Even if it was magic and combat.

"Then you want to take these with you," Relus said. He handed Guildford a small bag of books, small enough to fit into his own rucksack. "Magical theory and study; the same ones I taught you with. If nothing else, they'll help you recap anything you need to teach Ryoku."

Guildford accepted the books with a nod. "Thank you, Relus," he acknowledged, giving the vampire a curt bow.

"That's fantastic!" the Timeless One exclaimed. "I'm sure that will serve you both well. As they say, the wisest mind is one with something yet to read!"

Relus pushed his glasses up over his long nose. "I believe you meant to say..."

"'*The wisest mind is one with something yet to learn*,'" I finished, recalling the quote from school. "And I guess I'm the wisest of all, because I have a *lot* to learn."

The Timeless One smiled fondly at me. "Even I do not know all there is to know," he said vastly. "Not a soul in this room knows all there is to know about any given subject. Loki does not know every trick, nor does Sira or Will know every strike they're capable of."

Loki raised a countering finger, but the Timeless One kept going before he could interject. "I have much I could teach you if you were to stay in Lysvid. I wish I had the time. You seem like an excellent student, if Guildford is a reliable source of that information." I caught Guildford's bemused smile. "However, you have a journey you must complete – one which, I dare say, may be more pressing than the knowledge your soul desires. The duty must pass to my pupil, the teacher who must have quite a bit to learn himself."

I smiled at Guildford, who rubbed his head, abashed, in reply. He seemed quite amicable with the Timeless One and his pupils. "I'll do all I can."

"This matter falls under my witness as well," Will said, grinning at me from a few seats down. "I am his sworn guide, after all. It is only proper that I should assist in his education."

"My guide through the Old Forest," I repeated – not for the first time, and surely not the last.

"And I as well," Loki added gallantly. "I fear our recent battles have left little room for our Defender to grow, but I have much I can teach my favorite n—Defender, in the long run!"

Loki laughed at his own words. I studied him, trying to figure out what he was just about to say. Since the fight with Geri, the Trickster seemed off. He dragged his feet as he walked, and walked with a slump in his shoulders that he quickly did away with when he noticed me watching. Had the battle weakened him?

However, he was not the only one. In fact, everyone seemed a little different since that fight. Guildford and Will kept a close eye on me at all times. Rex and Cleria, who often kept to the shadows while everyone else chattered and laughed, seemed to be always watching me as I went.

A long, drawn-out sigh followed from across the table. Yes, of course. The unintelligible habits of Sira Jessura had returned. Just when I thought she had warmed back up to me, there it was again. She sat with her head down, arms crossed, feet up on the table – yes, she was the fiery picture of apathy once more, only it seemed even worse this time. She wouldn't even look at me. Whenever our eyes happened to cross paths, some dark emotion ignited in her scarlet eyes, and she turned away like I might transfer the bubonic plague between us.

I felt like I knew the reason, but I didn't voice it. Perhaps I feared it to be true, and my own deceptive thoughts couldn't confirm those mere shadows. After whatever happened in the last fight, they watched me like a ticking time bomb. They didn't think I could fight on my own.

It made sense. Sira would never respect me if I couldn't defend myself. Will and Guildford were always ready to jump in. Everyone seemed ready to help, but, more than ever, I needed to do this on my own. I needed to save Chris and find my sister. Ever since I had stepped into this world, it felt like I *had* to be here. I needed to step into these shoes, even if they were too large for me right now.

The Timeless One laughed, something between a squirrel's chattering and a choking bird.

"It seems you have no shortage of instructors," he claimed, smiling wide. Rex cleared his throat ambiguously, and the Timeless One's eyes flitted to him. When he turned back to me, the little vampire was all business. "Ryoku. You are aiming to reach Syaoto in your travels, correct?"

Will perked up, and I recalled what he said to me back in Syaoto. *Once you have come with me to my world.* It was an immediate goal for us if we didn't stumble upon Orden first. According to Will, his king would gladly supply us with any help we needed. I wondered if that meant I might lose Will to his kingdom. He had sworn to be my Guardian, but the meaning of such a thing remained unclear to me. How long would he travel at my side?

"We hope so," I replied. "As long as we reach there before Orden."

"It's fully possible," Loki agreed. "Syaoto is a friendly nation, sympathetic to a good Defender's plight. In terms of nearby worlds, it stands directly in the way of the dark empire."

I thought the Timeless One's brow furrowed in distaste. Then he was grinning easily, like that was all he knew how to do. "Rex Dougo wishes to reach the world of Syaoto safely, though he doesn't have world-traveling magic of his own," the Timeless One told us. "Perhaps you would be interested in allowing him to travel with you?"

The dark haired half-breed stood bolt upright. "I wouldn't be a burden to your journey," he addressed his boots stalwartly. "I can fight, and pay for my own food and lodgings. Whatever trouble you may land yourselves in, you have me."

Loki assessed the boy carefully. We'd all seen Rex fight alongside us, and we knew he was more than capable of keeping his word. He was reliable, honest, and had a surprisingly bright outlook to him that I liked. I could tell he had an important reason to go to Syaoto. I could see it in the way he stood, practically begging us to bring him along. He couldn't make the journey alone, or he saw that we needed him just as much as he needed us. His posture, his eyes, the corners of his smile told a story I was starting to read; he had somebody he needed to protect.

"We could use another sword arm," Loki said thoughtfully, scratching his chin. I couldn't tell if he was seriously debating or just pulling Rex's leg. "You would help us protect Ryoku should the worst occur? We have attained some powerful enemies, Rex Dougo."

"Of course," Rex replied quickly. He glanced over at me quickly, his dark hair brushing past his crimson eyes, and he smiled. "He may end up the one protecting us before long."

Loki laughed heartily. "Very well then," he said heavily, as though the decision was truly a difficult one. "Welcome aboard, Rex."

The change in Rex was immediate. He bowed deeply before us, hiding a brave smile behind his dark hair. "Thank you! Thank you so much. I won't let you down, I swear."

"We know you will not, friend," Will told him plaintively. "Loki only seeks to bring unnecessary stress to all living things. Be at ease."

Rex took his seat, but he couldn't erase the grin on his face. Was he that happy to travel with us?

"Now that that's settled," the Timeless One said, "there is something I'd like to discuss with the Trickster. If we may be excused?"

Loki didn't look surprised, and his playful grin wavered. "Agreed. We should speak in the back room." His emerald eyes found me, and winked. "I shan't be too long. Then we can leave this dark and dreary world, my friend."

I smiled in response, unsure how to reply to the Trickster's antics. He addressed me like a child who needed to leave an uncomfortable situation. All the same, he was becoming an unlikely fast friend to most of us. Loki met the small vampire at the head of the table. The Timeless One hopped down from his seat and they walked together. I wasn't the only one trying not to laugh, seeing the Trickster walking next to the pint-sized vampire.

When the door shut calmly behind them, everyone dissolved into separate conversations. Most of my friends either dissolved into their own conversations or appeared entirely unapproachable – Sira, mainly.

"If I may inquire?"

Guildford's sudden voice from behind me made me jump. I turned to face him. His brow furrowed in a playful sort of way.

"Before I decide to join you on a reckless journey through the realm of the afterlife," he started, coming to sit next to me. "I want to know what happened after my death."

I glanced away quickly, unsure if I was ready to impart this information on him. He sighed. "In light of what you told me, I hardly think that you, Dagger and Varis sat down together to sing Kumbaya around the campfire. The police force must have been in an uproar as well Varis El'Salandier, with his family prestige and the police backing him, would not have waltzed out of the city on a red carpet. So... what happened to your eye?"

I jumped outright, nearly falling from my chair in shock. Guildford's hand on my shoulder steadied me. I stared at him in disbelief. How did he know?

"You've kept up the illusion quite well," he spoke softly, aware that I wasn't ready to tell everyone. "You've adapted your hearing extraordinarily to your left side. With your quick reflexes, someone else might not even notice the delay. You're a quick learner, I'll give you that. Nevertheless, don't forget who told you that story in the first place. Also, it was likely Dawn who reminded you of the story, wasn't it?"

I gave him a look, and he smiled. "An officer who lost his eye in a struggle against one particularly violent outlaw. Facing possible expulsion from the force due to his disability, he implemented a glass eye. He worked closely with a particular optometrist in developing this eye, and trained around the clock to perfect his reflexes and make up for the loss. Within months, he was better than ever before."

He fell silent, studying my expression, waiting for the truth to dawn on me. When it did, I took a sharp breath. "No way. That was Dawn's father?"

Guildford nodded. "She was quite adamant about keeping that story anonymous. Even to you, it would seem. It has been some... what, four years since his premature death? As you are with your mother and stepfather, so is she with her late father. That, and I don't believe her remaining family is much to count on."

I nodded silently. I still had trouble speaking of my own family, and Dawn's father was about all she had besides her sister, Alyssa. I still had my foster parents, my friends, and a strong group of support around me. Even though Dawn's situation had somewhat improved recently, there were some things harder to get past.

"The eye had one small weakness that couldn't be hidden or fixed," Guildford went on. "Of course I noticed you acquired the same sort of eye. It connects to your optic nerves and simulates the different directions and expressions quite well. It adapts to most lighting. Even your friends, who seem quite keen on reading each other at a glance, likely couldn't tell that your left eye was anything but real. That optometrist of yours is quite good, still, but the dilation of a pupil due to lighting is extremely difficult to simulate. Your one pupil will always show less dilated than the other in certain lighting. In regular daylight, you might never notice. In the dark of Lysvid, however..."

I stared at my teacher in disbelief. "You saw through all that? That's almost like you were looking for it."

Guildford smirked. "Only once I saw the eye in your hand."

I gave the teacher a grumpy look. Of course. Geri had knocked the glass eye out in the brawl in Peul. I quickly snatched it up until I could slip it back in unnoticed. I thought I could pass it off as just getting blood in my eye, but Guildford was far too perceptive. Of course he'd play it off, too, until I admitted it on my own.

"I can only hope you didn't act too rashly on your own," Guildford went on. "You must have gone after them, didn't you?"

I swallowed. "Yeah." *Please*, I thought, *stop asking about it.*

Guildford shook his head sadly. "Dagger's family is keener on honor and strength than the El'Salandiers," he said. "Varis' family readily relies on their connections and hired muscle to keep them safe. They lack the honor that the Neseru's value. Taking them on in a head-on confrontation was foolish. Tell me that none of your friends suffered such grievous injuries as you did. Perhaps, out of usual teacher context, I hope your enemies came out worse."

I grinned in spite of myself. What a Guildford thing to say. "They're fine," I told him. "I took the worst hit."

"Of course you did." Guildford sighed. "I suppose the eventual outcome was Varis' banishment from the city, so I do commend you for that. I only wish the price wasn't quite so steep." He then tilted his head at Rex subtly. "Rex may be able to help you. He suffers from weak vision along with the inability to use his arm. He's skilled in combat and has honed his senses quite well. He may be a hybrid and have combat skills quite unlike yours, but you can certainly learn a thing or two from him about fighting at a disadvantage. He seems quite fond of you as well."

The door opened. Loki and the Timeless One returned, and the pair both gave me grim looks.

"The time nears for your departure," the Timeless One addressed us, drawing the attention of my group. "Loki has taken a bag of supplies for you on my behalf. Should the next world you land in prove as unfriendly, you will have the supplies to make it for a time."

I stood and bowed before the little vampire as he approached the table. "Thank you for all your help," I told him earnestly. "I don't think we could have survived this world without you."

He chuckled lavishly. "Do not sell yourself short, Ryoku Dragontalen. You have proven yourself a resourceful and promising young lad. I'm sure you would have made it."

I only nodded idly, knowing I never would have made it here otherwise. That, and I'd probably be a rampaging werewolf to boot. A thought occurred to me, and I met the Timeless One's milky gaze.

"Were my actions in this world right? To join the vampires against the werewolves? To battle the Ritual in Leudis? To pursue Geri?"

The Timeless One's gaze turned soft. "Who knows? Affairs could have turned out quite differently if you trusted the wolves instead. Even as they are people, they remain perpetually in the state of their wolf forms. Tell me, Ryoku. If you lived the life of an animal for as long as you knew, wouldn't it simply feel natural to you? Wouldn't you scoff at the humans who acted with civility, abashed of their dignified ways?"

I hesitated. It was easy to think something was normal if we'd done it for so long. One day, I might even think this world was normal.

"Furthermore, the Ritual is an insidious force in Lysvid. They've bought the cities into their pockets. While the general practice of the Ritual is, luckily, not as common, the fact remains that they control the cities and the law. It is all too easy to bribe the city guard with a few coins, especially when it's made of their own men. I'm proud of you for standing up to them. Putting a damper on their plans means this world is a little safer for other races."

"As rare as they are," Loki added bitterly. "I wouldn't recommend this place to travelers."

"And Geri," the Timeless One added quickly, probably to intercept Loki. "Your friends have told me the details of your encounter with that particular god. I don't believe you had a choice. Some gods are quite unreasonable, and events as of late have riled a great many of them up. I'm afraid I cannot explain in full detail, but more than a few gods may find blame upon you for such things. Geri, of course, is a god that serves no master. Should he seek a fight, he will certainly take it without regard for his own life."

Relus interjected with a raised finger. I thought he was going to correct something the Timeless One said, but he turned to me instead. "Did you draw Ragnarokkr during your plights?"

I nodded hesitantly. "Sorta. I didn't really get to use it properly. I used..."

"The chains?" Relus guessed.

"Yes," I replied. "I thought I was going to lose it against... well, a very unsettling vampire that the Ritual summoned against me. I managed to grasp it by the chains and it worked. Against Geri, though, I didn't really get to use it. I just supported myself with it."

I held my hands up, showing them my knuckles torn asunder by the chains, though the bleeding had long since stopped. Grooves in the print of chains sank deeply between my knuckles.

Relus nodded, studying my hands absently. "I'm glad it could serve you well," he said. "Practice with it, and I'm sure it'll prove invaluable. Are you familiar with the blade's namesake?"

I thought about it. The name did sound vaguely familiar, I thought. Had I learned it in one of Guildford's classes?

"Do you mean Ragnarok?" Guildford asked. "If I recall, wasn't that the war of the Norse gods? So claimed, the end of their world?"

"Indeed," Relus confirmed. "Ragnarok was the name given to that particular war, the battle between the gods. It translates to *Twilight of the Gods* – the '*kr*' sound at the end is a suffix apparently granted to the blade at some point in time. It means *dark*, so perhaps *Dark Twilight of the Gods,* or *Twilight of the Dark Gods.*"

"Could it mean *Night of the Gods*?" Lusari asked suddenly.

Relus gave her an appreciative smile. "It could," he agreed. "The sword has undergone a great deal in its time as a weapon. It was once a sword of light, but... as you see before you now, that has changed. One fact about the blade remains true, though. It is a weapon capable of slaying gods."

My eyes widened. I swore that I felt something about the blade behind my back, something tugging at my memory. I fell unconscious during the fight from Geri's intense onslaught, but... was Ragnarokkr instrumental in his defeat? To the massive scar in the earth, where the ruined wolf's body lay?

"There is much to learn about the sword," Relus told me. "There is a man who may be able to properly teach you the history of your weapon. He is quite hard to find."

"Who?" Will asked. As he listened intently, Loki instructed Lusari to begin preparing the world-travelling spell. She stepped away from the table, holding her staff aloft, and light began dancing in a circle around her.

"He is a possibility," the Timeless One agreed, "though a notoriously difficult man to find. None have seen him for a thousand years, at least." He scratched his top hat oddly, as though the hat were a spot that could get itchy. "Perhaps restoring Ragnarokkr to its true form would help. It is hard to say, although such a change may only be reversible in credit to your own strength."

Loki looked puzzled, crossing his arms as he watched Lusari prepare the spell. The way he watched her, it was as though he'd never seen it before. "Who are you speaking of?"

Relus and the Timeless One exchanged glances. "A man who goes by Nocrier," Relus answered. "An acclaimed master of the sword. They say he trained the last true wielder of Ragnarok. However, his whereabouts and the likelihood that he still exists are both quite foggy. The world is in quite a disheveled state as of these last few months."

I tilted my head. "What do you mean?" I asked him.

He didn't immediately respond. Everyone was rising to their feet as Lusari's spell grew. With the size of her spell, it was more than enough to accommodate our three new arrivals. Loki, Guildford, and Rex.

"Perhaps I am not the best man to reveal that certain truth." Relus shifted in his seat. He and the Timeless One exchanged odd looks. Loki also fixated them in a glare that quickly dissipated when

I looked his way. "You may be starting to learn some truths on your own, Ryoku. That sword plays a great role in that journey. In truth, you may have more to accomplish than merely saving Chris Olestine."

"What do you mean?" I asked. "This sword is just a means to an end, right?"

"Come, Ryoku," Loki urged me. "Lusari's spell is ready. We must say our goodbyes and depart from this dreary world."

I gave Relus a desperate look, begging him to share whatever it was he kept hidden from me. He only gazed back, the lights of Lusari's spell reflected in his spectacles.

I sighed heavily and gave in. We made our goodbyes to everyone around the table. Cleria embraced me in a startlingly gentle way. I shook hands with Relus and the Timeless One. Both returned it in kind, secrets hidden behind their eyes.

With all said and done, I stepped into the circle with my friends. Lusari stood in the center with Will, and Sira kept to the corner of the spell. Rex, Guildford, and Loki awaited me with kind smiles.

As the spell was starting to activate, Relus seemed to reaffirm himself. "Ryoku, I have one last thing I must tell you. One last piece of advice for which you must build your resolve on."

He locked his crimson eyes on mine, which seemed to flicker behind the reflected light on his glasses. "Ryoku, you mustn't ignore the darkness inside you. You must not give in to its creed."

I froze. His eyes seemed to demand my attention with a strange ferocity. "W-What do you mean?" I asked, unsure if I wanted the truth or not.

He opened his mouth. As he spoke, the lights of Lusari's travel spell flared up, and I couldn't hear what he said. I tried to shout to him, to ask him to repeat himself, but there was no chance he heard me. When the arc of light fell from before me, Relus vanished.

The darkness inside me... What did he mean?

I could still see the Timeless One, and glanced at him, wondering if something about his milky eyes could tell me whatever Relus was trying to say. Before the magic of world-traveling fully enveloped me, I saw the Timeless One's eyes turn orange.

...End of Act Four.

Act Five: Bright Manifest

*In the eyes of Ryoku Dragontalen, we are in
Bonnin Capital, in the world of Bonnin.
It is early afternoon
On November 10th, 2017.*

SCENE ONE: KATIEL

"Huh. Well, this seems a lot more cheery."

Everyone chuckled at Guildford's introductory comment. I gazed around us in wonder, transfixed by the idea of a happy world after the intense darkness of Lysvid. Everything around us looked almost abnormally bright and cheerful.

It looked like we appeared in some quiet block of town. Brightly colored ceiling tiles stuck out on the buildings, reaching up to an almost cloudless blue sky. I heard the chipper songs of birds, the distant chatter of folk bustling around a marketplace. I found myself studying the powder-blue sky above us, the scattered, rolling drops of clouds across its surface – and then the sun high in the sky, which I could somehow gaze at easily due to a huge pair of shades on it. It seemed to stare back, and grinned.

"It does looks like a cheerful place," Loki agreed. "Certainly a desirable change from the darkness of Lysvid."

"There's something off about it," Rex said. "I can't quite place it."

"Everything is so bright," Lusari said. "How could you mistrust this? The sky is so... oh! What is that?"

A little green bird flew past me. It stopped on the top of a cherry-red roof and chirped amicably, studying us with its round, black eyes.

Loki sighed in apparent understanding. "I think I know where we are. This could only be one place. And still your weapon, Will," he added after the slight sound of jangling steel. "It's not that kind of place."

"Did the sun just grin at me?" Lusari asked quietly.

Will seemed to realize as well, for he chuckled under his breath. "Well, well. I wondered if we might end up here. Welcome to the sunny world of Bonnin."

Sira snorted. "You mean the home of Jeffrey Lampsword?"

A long, drawn-out silence fell over our group. We looked at one another, and I met Will's expression just as he cracked up.

It was inevitable. We all started laughing. Even Sira succumbed, clutching her chest as she laughed openly. Hearing everyone else laugh only made the rest of us laugh harder. Rex struggled to control himself with a hand over his mouth. Lusari doubled over in a fit of giggles. Loki fell on his backside, slamming the ground as he cackled like a hyena.

It took minutes for the laughter to subside. Rex almost got control of himself before he laid eyes upon Loki, a hysterical, cackling god on the floor, and he doubled over again in laughter.

I found myself lying on my back, swallowing back a frog in my throat from laughing so hard. My eyes felt both dry and teary as I stared up at the sky. A feeling of ecstasy wafted over me. This was the kind of adventure I wanted.

"You guys really aren't fooling anybody, you know."

A boy's voice spoke from above me. Nearly forgetting where I was, I sat bolt upright before I recognized the voice – it was my first time hearing it in these realms. Then, I beamed.

"Katiel!"

I heard everyone scramble to their feet with me to face the boy standing behind me, hands on his hips. Katiel had dark red hair that fell to his shoulders and into a long braid from there, his bangs pinned out of his face with a small black comb. His face was sharp, angular, and intelligent. He didn't seem to need glasses for his golden eyes in this world, or else he just didn't have them. Their absence somehow made him look sharper. Combined with the long black and red coat he wore, Katiel looked impressive. An unfamiliar girl with reddish-brown hair clung to his arm.

"You finally made it," Katiel said, exasperated. "I've been in Bonnin for days. I forget what sadness looks like now, and I never thought I'd say it gets old." He grinned at my expression, and then gestured to the girl on his arm. "I guess you haven't met Kaia, either."

The girl on his arm mildly glanced up. She had pretty blue eyes that shimmered like the waves of an ocean. Her outfit was pretty, too.

She wore a white shirt beneath a silky sort of cardigan, and her skirt tapered like the waves of a lake.

"You must be Ryoku," she said softly. "I'm Kaia Oceyen, a water-specialized mage. It's a pleasure."

She held out a hand gingerly, and I took it. "Yeah, that's me. Ryoku Dragontalen," I introduced myself regardless. She had a stunning smile.

"Katiel and Kaia, eh?" Loki chimed in, stepping up next to me. "What an adorable couple! I'm Loki, the Trickster god!"

Everyone turned to Loki sharply, but Katiel laughed. "We're not dating, *or* related," he said simply. He looked like he was about to continue, but to my surprise, Lusari stepped forward.

"My name is Belle Collier," she said softly, and curtsied before him. I blinked in surprise – at least Lusari knew to disguise ourselves and took the initiative, but...

"You don't need to give fake names here," Katiel said, surprising Lusari enough that she took a step back. "Least of all, to me."

I didn't miss how Sira jabbed Will in the ribs. "Hear that, Lampsword?"

"Bonnin is a peaceful place," Katiel explained. "They only share bounties for monsters. Even the freakin' Trickster shouldn't bag you too much negative attention." He waved to Loki after leaving him hanging, and bowed lightly to Lusari. "Greetin's. I'm Katiel Fereyen, Defender and friend of Ryoku."

Loki flicked his index finger to his forehead like some kind of gang sign. Lusari didn't give her proper name, only stepped back in mild alarm. Apparently, Katiel unnerved her somehow.

Everyone else came forward to introduce themselves. Kaia retreated behind Katiel shyly. When Guildford stepped up, though, Katiel noticed him for the first time and stopped dead in his tracks.

"G-G-Guildford? Is that really you?"

Guildford nodded solemnly, but a telltale smile crept onto his face. "I figured we would cross paths soon enough. How are you, Katiel?"

I saw each word from the teacher hitting Katiel like a train – it felt the same to me not long ago. "Sorry," I told him quickly. "Everything's been so hectic since I got here, I forgot to mention..."

"T-That's okay," Katiel murmured, still shocked. "I'm doin' alright, Guildford. It's... good to see you again. School hasn't been the same since."

Guildford's responsive expression was too sad, so Katiel forced on a smile and turned to me. "So Ryoku, you got Guardians. Good work. Most people can't pick them up so quickly."

"Not all of them are my Guardians," I told him. "Lusari, Rex, and Guildford are just traveling with me. These three, though, they've done the whole official thing."

Katiel raised a brow in surprise. "Wow, good on you. A lot of Defenders I've crossed paths with are quick to label everyone they're traveling with. People can travel with you easily without swearing the dumb vow. I mean, look at me. I don't have Guardians."

When Loki stared pointedly at Kaia, hiding behind Katiel's back with her arms around his narrow shoulders, he added, "She's not my Guardian. I travel with a regular set of friends, but I haven't let them swear vows. That way, they won't go and do something stupid to protect me. They can come and go as they please."

"I would protect you anyway," Kaia said quietly from behind him. "Anyone who messes with you has to get through me."

Katiel laughed. "So she says, but she hasn't sworn those vows. I also travel with two others who haven't taken the vow. Artos is around here somewhere. Hopefully you'll get to meet him, but he's pretty shy. Doesn't take to people as easily as Eckhardt. Artos is like a ninja, while Eckhardt's the white knight. Then there's Mayfield, who looks a lot like... well, never mind. She isn't here right now, anyway. I... have told you about them before, haven't I?"

"A bit," I said, trying to take in everything he said. "Maybe not in so much detail. Does that fly at the Registry? Not having Guardians, I mean?"

Katiel shrugged. "Never bothered. I mean, sure, using the Registry is great for you. But it's a new idea, and not one I really could benefit from."

I looked at Will pointedly. "So I didn't even have to do it?"

"It is recommended," Will reasoned. He gestured wildly to try to encompass a point. "Say the Timeless One wanted to check up on us. He could simply go to the Registry and ask about us. As long as we check into a Registry in each new world, our old friends will be able to find us if the need arises."

"That doesn't sound very convenient," Rex muttered, crossing his one arm over the other. "Orden could just look him up then, couldn't they?"

"There are some security checks," Loki explained. "They have a… somewhat up to date repertoire of our journey. It's a Registry thing. No use asking me. Just means the emperor can't waltz into a Registry no matter what he says. They won't let him."

"Even in a worst case scenario, they cannot access your information," Guildford advised. "Do you recall seeing something… modern, in there?"

I had to think a moment. Katiel was giving me a look like I should know. It finally clicked. The computers.

"There's still no point," Sira said. "They have ways to find out what they need to know without some Registry crap. They got those bounties out for you, didn't they? If the Registry's really on our side, then how did that happen? They've got other methods, too. Stuff that's lower on the radar."

My chest plummeted at the thought. Loki put his hand on my shoulder. "I wouldn't worry about that. Orden clearly knows enough already. Why do you think I put my name out there?"

Katiel scratched his head. "If I've heard right about Orden, that might not be enough. Haven't checked it out much myself, but the tales spread across all worlds. A friend of Mayfield's works in the rebellion. It sounds like Orden has mustered up a *lot* of firepower."

Our group fell horribly silent. Nobody liked hearing how strong our enemies were. In turn, what did I have that could stop them? A knife, a bow, a staff, and a sword I could hardly use.

Loki shrugged after a moment. "Oh well. It would do some good for us to hear about *them* for a change. 'Know thy enemy,' am I right? Anyway…" He broke off before anyone could respond, stretching his arms lazily behind his head. "What do you say we check out the local clothes shop? Dress up so we don't stick out like vampires in a rainbow?"

He earned a black glare from Rex for that one. "Didn't you hear him?" Rex asked, using the tone one might adopt when speaking to a child. "They won't post his bounty. We should be safe here."

"Better safe than sorry," Sira agreed with a shrug, to my surprise. "Say they won't post it. Who knows, really? Maybe some little town hangs it up on their wall. People travel, too. Anybody could walk down this street and see Ryoku fucking Dragontalen with the giant bounty on his head. Who doesn't want their shot at a huge cash reward?"

She addressed me, but she didn't even look at me while she spoke. Her mood was somehow becoming even stranger. She still spoke to the others and, occasionally, to me, but she wouldn't look me in the eye. If she did, she immediately whirled away in distaste.

"Perhaps you are right," Will said. "Traveling among people all clearly foreign is just begging their attention. We should try to blend in to some degree."

Katiel shrugged. "Well, I guess. Still think we're safe, but if you'd rather be sure…" He grinned at Will. "They do have armor available. Bonnin is protected by a small militia. Suiting up as one of the Meow-cenaries would probably garner less attention."

Sira choked on air. "Meow-cenaries?" she echoed, blinking rapidly. As we started down the cobblestone road into the heart of the markets, I saw her jab Will in the side. "Hear that, Lampsword? You'll fit in here like a dream."

"At least I can *fit* into something," Will responded dryly. She nudged him again, throwing him off balance and nearly into the wall of a market.

We left the quiet little square of town we arrived in and started into the heart of the markets. Much of the city was made of refined stone and wooden buildings, like some sort of castle town. Pathways spidered over one another as the inner city became one of multiple levels. I saw a group of kids playing across a stone walkway crossing overhead, chasing a cat that walked proudly along the rails.

Katiel fell alongside me as I walked near the back of the group, letting Loki find his own way.

"You have a thing with that girl? The redhead?"

I glanced at Kaia, who still hung on his shoulder like a doll, but she seemed unresponsive. It didn't seem to weigh Katiel down at all, walking at a full stride with a girl swinging like a cape.

"Maybe," I admitted. "Not sure. Not anymore, maybe?"

"Huh," he replied, watching her for a moment. She kept beside Will and avoided the others as much as possible. Will looked around at all the sights and sounds, but Sira just seemed annoyed by it all. "She really your type? I mean there's Annalia and all, but..."

I shrugged. "I don't know. Things just happened, and they fell apart just as quickly."

"Like a one night stand? From you?" He grinned innocently at me, and I glared back. He was technically right, though. He paused, thinking something over in his head. "She said she's from Orden, didn't she?"

"Yeah," I replied. "Sira's from Orden, and Will from Syaoto. They're like polar opposites until something threatens me."

"Huh," Katiel mused. "Maybe... I could be wrong, but give her some time. People from Orden are messed up, especially their soldiers. The whole place fucks them up. They're not that easy to approach and have a hell of a time speaking their mind. Mayfield's friend, he's an interesting type."

"That doesn't make sense to me," I muttered placidly, shoving my hands in my pockets. "I'm easy enough to approach, aren't I? And she became my Guardian. She could take that back any time if she regrets it. Why won't she just talk to me?"

Katiel shrugged, a movement that didn't affect Kaia's grip in the slightest. "Who knows? I mean, you're the kid with the million-gold bounty. Clearly somebody regards you as a threat. Some people might find you hard to approach from that alone." He studied my expression for a second. "How's that glass eye treating you, Ryoku?"

I darted my glance around, but nobody seemed close enough to hear what he said. If Kaia was listening, she did a good job of playing it off like she wasn't. Still, something about Katiel's words flipped a switch in my head.

"Do you have any idea what's going on?" I asked earnestly. "The Timeless One told me this sword was given to *my name*, whatever that means. The Trickster came out of nowhere to swear allegiance to me. Did I tell you about Jesanht Olace, the freaky panther man who attacked me *also* out of nowhere? Or maybe Geri, who had a problem with me *out of nowhere*, and..."

"Whoa, whoa. Slow down!" Katiel insisted, slowing me to a stop. He quickly glanced ahead, but Loki led the rest of the pack at a continual pace as he gallivanted ahead. Kaia gave me a dirty look, like

I was distracting her perch. "Okay, walk with me. Tell me everything that happened since you got here."

I obliged. We kept a good pace behind the others. I told him everything, from when I met Kioru Rasale in the Bytold Woods to leaving Lysvid. With an additional glance to make sure nobody was listening, I told him about the demon girl who appeared in the alley.

"Even Will and Sira are acting off," I continued exasperatedly. "We met by chance in Harohto as we all ran around doing different things. When they swore their vows, they said something about the world being in a different state before. They thought my quest with Chris might link to the state of the worlds somehow. Could that be why everything is just aligning like this?"

By the time I finished explaining, we reached the markets. Sira checked out a stall full of unique swords. Will and Lusari looked over one filled with carvings. Loki vanished into some store, and Guildford and Rex walked together ahead, conversing quietly about something. The array of commodities sold here was alarming for such a cheerful world. If I didn't think Katiel might have some answers for me, I'd be just as enthralled as the others.

"That's all pretty messed up," Katiel admitted. "Nobody explained a thing? Loki just... showed up to protect you? And you think Jesanht had you confused with somebody else?"

I nodded. "It all seems like a string of coincidences."

"Could be," Katiel agreed, "but I think you're smarter than that. If Will and Sira can see ties between your cause and theirs, maybe they're not the only ones. Maybe Loki did, and the Timeless One..."

I glanced away. He had a point, if a point could even be made of all the odd things that happened so far. Katiel snagged my attention again, pointing to a stall filled with a colorful array of candies – lollipops, gumballs, and all sorts of different sweets filled almost every inch of the stall.

"Bonnin's specialty," he told me. "Come on. Why don't we check it out? Use some of my gold; I've got more than enough. Let's see who can eat the most!"

I grinned. "Okay, you're on!"

As we rushed to the candy stall, thoughts still plagued my mind. Was the answer as simple as Katiel suggested? Or, with the darkness welling inside of me, was there a darker truth?

SCENE TWO: THE WORDS

...Of Act Five: Bright Manifest

In the eyes of Will Ramun, we are in Bonnin Capital, in the world of Bonnin. It is mid afternoon On November 10th, 2017.

"You *must* be joking."

Sira didn't want to leave the doorway. I was only able to stifle my laughter because I was in no better state. The style of Bonnin seemed to heavily lean towards cat-like things. She wore a sweater of which had a pair of lifelike cat ears on the hood. Bonnin custom also dictated that women didn't wear pants, and so Sira wore the longest skirt she could find – it still came to just above her knees, so she covered the rest of her legs in black stockings. I even spotted that her belt came with a black tail that she tried to hide.

"Are you sure this is what the locals wear?" Ryoku was asking one of the shop attendants, who shrugged at him and simply held his hand out for money. I thought Ryoku wasn't that bad off, since nobody could be as angry as Sira. They outfitted him in a light blue sweater with a hood of cat ears, combined with dark khakis and a customary blue cat tail at his back.

"T-This is unbelievable," Lusari muttered shyly. They only gave her a shorter skirt, and she wore black tights beneath. Of course, they swapped her headband for one with pink cat-ears, and she carried a matching tail.

Guildford added his grunt of annoyance. To him, nothing could have been worse. When he entered the outfitters alongside me, they exclaimed that he was the look-alike to a famous Bonnin hero and a member of the 'Meow-cenaries' – the Cheshire hunter. As such, they wrapped Guildford up in a ridiculous set of black- and purple-striped gear that fit him somewhat snugly. The others weren't able to keep a straight face around him now.

Katiel and Rex embraced their simple choices. Katiel swapped his coat for a similar one, though this one was sleek-black and came with a giant set of cat ears on the hood, which he wore with pride. The pretty girl around his neck donned a new light blue cardigan with cat-ears and a long tail. Rex, too, swapped out for a sleeker coat with cat ears, but he kept his far from his head. As he walked out, I swore the hand tucked in his coat wore a giant black paw.

If the outfitters treated anyone handsomely, it was Loki. The Trickster somehow strutted out of the shop in a ruffled blue shirt and white pants. No cat ears, no tail, and no other semblance to Bonnin's icon. Everyone looked ready to kill him.

I'd been in a shock when I asked for armor. Like what Katiel claimed, the Meow-cenaries seemed to be the only fighting group in all of Bonnin. I finally understood why everyone gave me such odd looks as Jeffrey Lampsword. They outfitted me in a light orange tunic similar to my original, but adorned with white steel plates similar to what I wore in Syaoto. A set of orange bracers hid a set of steel blades just like cat claws, which I solemnly vowed never to use. I'd come out from the outfitters to a series of stifled laughs.

"We are running low on funds," I told them once Ryoku finished paying the shopkeeper, who hastily shut his door after us. "Almost everything we got from our last bounty just went to this irritable clothing salesman."

Loki sighed heavily. "I fear my choice of clothing store was a little on the costly side."

"We should conserve," Ryoku suggested – his tone carried unnecessary apology. "I don't mind staying at a cheaper inn. Maybe we could camp outside the city?"

He spoke with a great deal of longing. After our journey through the Old Forest, I had an idea of Ryoku's idolization of the outdoors. His world lacked such simple fineries as camping outdoors or trekking through days of overgrown woods. He loved it.

Loki looked at Ryoku like he'd just suggested climbing inside of a bear. "Don't be ridiculous!" he cried. "You may have made due while traveling with the bumpkin soldier, but you travel with me now! I don't stay in shacks and shambles! I won't let you suffer, either."

"Who are you calling a 'bumpkin soldier'?" I asked sourly.

"Who cares about your godly needs?" Sira retorted sharply at Loki. Ryoku started playing with his thumbs anxiously, but Sira didn't look at him. "You're not traveling with some royal family with endless pockets – you're traveling with us, and we have to earn our keep. All of us."

"Why don't we check out the Registry?" Guildford asked, to steer gently from the conflict. "We can take on a mission. I'm sure there's something we can do to pay our way for now. Maybe something for tomorrow as well."

Loki was deaf to his reasoning, glaring at Sira. "You seem to forget that we're traveling with a Defender. We've an important mission to undertake. Ryoku must be in peak physical form. A fine rest in a fine bed, not the frosty soil beneath a tree or a bed filled with lumps. And to properly protect him, we must see to ourselves in the same way."

"Perhaps somebody will take us in for the night," I suggested. "We could see to the Registry. If any are offering cots to a Defender and his entourage, they would post up there."

"There's still the matter of our enormous bounty," Rex pointed out – when I shot him a look, he shrugged. "Best to not get too social with the townsfolk, or we'll give ourselves away. Bonnin may be peaceful, but the lives of a few strangers versus over a million gold aren't much of a contest to the average citizen. If they found out, it would be simple to bag our Defender."

Loki glared at him like he'd just ruined the end of his favorite book. "But Ryoku is a hero! Surely there are people with kindness in their hearts yet, especially in such a cheery little world."

"Mind your chatter about 'worlds,'" Katiel reminded Loki, glancing sidelong at a passerby cloaked in dark colors.

"Who are you calling a hero?" Ryoku asked. Whenever Sira wasn't directly in the argument, Ryoku managed a bit of a voice. "Whose opinion is that?"

"Not everyone's some happy-go-lucky elf or something," Sira protested, ignoring Ryoku. "All those vampires and werewolves that came after us? Just cause the fucking sun's grinning at us doesn't mean anything."

She earned a hostile glare from Rex for her comments. Ryoku appeared crestfallen, clutching the sleeve of his sweater with a white-knuckled grip. "There were good vampires, too," he managed, lifting his head a little. "Rex, Cleria, Relus, and the Timeless One."

Rex gave him a warm smile now. The Defender looked like he needed the encouragement.

"Rare examples," Sira dismissed easily. "The worst thing in all these damned worlds is people. Just people! If someone here shouted about your large bounty, I'd have trouble finding anyone in this marketplace that wouldn't risk my blade just to sell you out and live luxuriously for all their lives. Most of them wouldn't feel an ounce of guilt."

"You're effectively doing just that, Sira," Loki warned, peering into the crowds cautiously.

"There are good people still," Ryoku protested. "The barkeeper back in Harohto was nice. Alex, and Oliver, and Leif, and Mosten, and everyone we met in Harohto. And..."

He trailed off. I could tell he was scrambling for names.

"Really, Ryoku?" Sira asked dryly. "Barkeeps are paid to be nice. What, are you gonna say our hostess in Lysvid was nice, too? That's what she gets *paid* for. Kindness can only get you a certain distance. For the rest, there's money. Gold. You're a Defender, and people think they can cash in favors. What, are you going to suggest we can offer Orden a peace treaty next?"

The look in Ryoku's eyes was breaking my heart. Why would he listen to Sira? Why was she being so scathing? Getting angry, I turned on Sira.

"How can we ever complete our mission if we doubt everyone?" I demanded. "If we arrive at every world expecting horrid treatment wherever we go, then there is little point in our mission. Tell me you have not personally vowed to stamp out the darkness of Orden more than once. Tell me you have not mentioned it in your curses, or toss and turn in the night over what the empire has done to you? You may be scarred, Sira, but even those can heal."

Sira visibly hesitated when I turned on her. It made me feel a little guilty, but Ryoku had to be my priority.

"We don't *need* to go to every world," she finally said. "Just Orden, Syaoto if we make it. Obviously one of the places pressing Ryoku's bounty is keeping Chris captive. If not Orden, we check Raansata, Jerule, wherever else has joined up by then. For that matter, we don't need to round up a freakin' troop of friends. We just need to get his friend out, and we kill the emperor. That's all."

Ryoku looked taken by the idea. Thinking of the boy he was here to save. "We need Ryoku to train," I insisted. "He cannot just take on Orden as is. We need to help him become stronger. You really think they are not waiting for our intrusion? The emperor waits – and we must defeat him."

Sira crossed her arms angrily. "Who cares if Ryoku's strong? He just needs to save Chris, then boom – we're in."

Ryoku flinched away from her. I kept my eyes on Sira. Why was she lashing out against him so strongly? Was it his one violet eye? The namesake of the empire of Orden? Then, if so, why had she been so aggressive to him earlier? It all seemed to start after the Timeless Castle…

Before I could reach any conclusions, Loki stepped in by putting a hand on Sira's shoulder. She flinched, but his grip held. His emerald eyes filled with rage, the likes of which I'd only seen when he stood up for Rex and Ryoku in Gaevrel.

"Ryoku could die against the likes of our enemies," Loki told her flatly. "You know the might of Orden yourself, Sira. You know the minds of our opponents. Even I will struggle against them. If Ryoku fought them as he is now, he would die." He paused, letting his words sink in. "Is that what you want?"

She snarled, wrenching Loki's hand off her shoulder and spinning around to face him. "I don't care!" she screamed, and turned on her heel. I made to go after her, but a hand on my shoulder from Guildford stopped me.

"Let her go," he murmured, and nodded in Ryoku's direction. The poor kid was standing there like he didn't know how to do anything else. Lusari's arm slid around his waist familiarly, and Katiel approached his friend, Kaia still perched around his neck. The girl was looking at Ryoku with soft eyes. "Let her calm down. She'll return."

"Are we sure we want her to?" Loki asked coldly. Ryoku and I turned to him, surprised. "This is not the first time she's acted like this. We need allies with unflinching resolve – allies we can count on."

"But she's one of our strongest," Lusari said. "Nobody can wield that sword like her. What would we do? Leave her in Bonnin, stranded?"

Loki sighed heavily, crossing his arms as though withdrawing from the weight of the world. "I don't know, but we can't let this happen again."

"Let's wait it out. Perhaps she will return. It would be better for things to return to normal." Guildford glanced pointedly at Ryoku, a look that the young Defender was blind to. It was evident what he was referring to.

Loki didn't look like he relished the idea, but he followed us as we headed to the nearby stone fountain in the markets. If Sira went back to the clothing store, we'd see her. Ryoku plopped down at the edge of the fountain with Lusari.

One of Katiel's friends returned – he was a tall man clad all in black, with long brown hair wrapped in dark cloth that fell across a hardened face. I listened vaguely as Katiel and Kaia went to meet him.

"Any idea where the others are?" Katiel asked the young man.

He shook his head. "Mayfield's pouting. Eckhardt went to help a nearby village. Niin, I believe."

Katiel nodded. "Round them up if you can, Artos. I think we won't be here for much longer."

The ninja nodded, looking relieved. "Got it." He glanced past Katiel, at Ryoku. The poor boy sat by the fountain, staring at the water as it sprayed all over. "Is that...?"

"Yeah, that's Ryoku," Katiel told him. "Looks different, huh?"

"A little," Artos agreed. "The same eyes, though."

They kept talking in whispers, and I lost track of their words. It was only a few more minutes before Artos darted into the crowds. Katiel and Kaia returned to us.

Loki paced back and forth like he was in a marathon. Rex returned from the market with a link of sausages to sit with Guildford and I as we aimlessly waited. Lusari, of course, stayed with Ryoku.

"This is ridiculous," Loki was muttering under his breath. "If it weren't for that girl's petty outbursts, we could have been training by now, or found ourselves a hunt. Now we'll be lucky if we make the inn."

"You do understand why, do you not?" I asked quietly.

The Trickster finally slowed, coming to stand before me with an impatient expression. "Why what?"

I lowered my voice. "What upsets her. That eye. It is the color of the Ordenstraum royal family."

This clearly hadn't occurred to Loki. He pondered over it for a moment, considering. "Sira does seem sensitive when it comes to matters of her home world. However, the question remains. What did that event with the demon have to do with Orden? What has it done to poor Ryoku's eye?"

"Have you seen the scar on her back?" Guildford asked. "The tip is visible from the nape of her neck. I could be wrong, but it looks like a sizeable scar."

"It is," I replied. "It goes all the way down her back."

"That came from Orden somehow?" Rex asked.

"I would stake my bachelor's degree on it," Guildford said solemnly. Everyone looked at him, confused. I wasn't quite sure what he meant, either, so he smiled. "A certificate in my world that says I can teach classes. Either way, that scar must be a part of her past."

The thought already occurred to me, and I subconsciously clenched my fists. The emperor clearly committed terrible things upon Sira, and still she marched with us to its gates. Even though she'd just acted terribly toward us, I understood a little of how she felt.

"The important thing," Loki repeated, "is Ryoku. His eye. What was it about that episode that made such a thing occur?"

"It came just after the battle with Geri," Rex said, his voice hushed. "Right after that... whatever it was, let go of him. What could that mean?"

"And why only his right eye?" I asked, somewhat to myself.

"That's simple," a voice inferred – Katiel returned to us with Kaia. The girl on his shoulder didn't seem to weigh him down at all. She looked at us like we were interfering. "His left eye? It's made of glass."

Loki and I both turned to him in shock. *"What?"*

Guildford nodded sadly. "I've not been told the details, but it happened after my death. Yes, that makes sense. His glass eye would remain the same no matter what ailment affected him. He clearly hasn't seen it himself yet."

Rex didn't look ultimately surprised, but he didn't comment, either. He watched Ryoku from afar, who was blind to all our gazes. How could I not have noticed Ryoku's eye? How had some of the others?

"How did he lose his eye?" Loki asked hoarsely. He wouldn't remove his eyes from Ryoku. If I didn't know better, I thought he was showing actual empathy. Guildford also looked to Katiel for answers, who glanced away.

"It was the Day of Black, or so we call it. Ryoku, Dagger, Joey, and me." He fell silent for a moment, searching himself for the words. Kaia touched his face lightly, and it looked like the touch brought him back to us. He found Guildford's searching gaze. "On the day of your funeral, we chased down Varis and his gang once and for all. Ryoku... he wasn't himself. If I heard you right about the fight with this Geri character, that about sums it up."

"That darkness," Rex said. "Hence dubbing it the Day of Black?"

"This wasn't the first awakening of that beast," Loki said. "You've met before."

Katiel nodded once. "Sorta. In the past. We think he's always been with Ryoku one way or another. Like two sides of a coin. He doesn't seem to recall anything about it, though. That, and on the day, we all wore the colors. Having just come from a funeral, obviously." He glanced down briefly, but came back up with a small smile – Kaia was holding his hand. "We started off good and all, but... Varis and his crew, they're rough. If it makes you feel better, the guy who did it? He's dead."

Guildford didn't look relieved. "How?"

"It was one of his cronies that did the dirty work," Katiel explained. "He cut out Ryoku's eye. In return, Ryoku took his head off."

Loki's eyes widened. "Seriously? In... Your world, he did this?"

"How did that not land the lot of you in trouble?" Guildford asked sternly. "Ryoku went into some detail about this, but... it doesn't quite add up. Such a grievous cost, too."

Katiel shrugged. "It all evened out in the end. Dagger took care of it."

Guildford didn't look impressed. "Of course he did. I suppose if it had to happen, then Dagger's presence was necessary."

Loki wasn't listening, glaring glumly at his feet. "To think, Ryoku has been missing his eye all this time," he murmured. "We've been teaching him to fight, dragging him into battle after battle, and he's disabled?"

"Disabled is a heavy word," Guildford said, furrowing his brow. "Ryoku has adjusted very well. His other senses have grown to foster the lost half of his sight, even though it's only been months. Without telltale signs, I might never have figured it out. I mean... I never expected it to happen to my student, least of all him."

"He's sensitive about it," Katiel said. "It is a disability to him. The less people know about it, the better."

While he spoke, Kaia gently slid off his shoulder. It was the first time I saw the girl on her feet – I'd begun to think she couldn't walk on her own. She was quite a bit shorter than Katiel.

I wasn't sure Loki heard Katiel at all. He was watching Ryoku as he sat sadly by the fountain. The whole time, Ryoku hadn't done so much as glance at us. "We'll honor him, then," he decided. "That knowledge stays within this circle." He saw my look of surprise, and smiled gently. "When somebody works so tirelessly for something, they have a right to hold it, do they not?"

I nodded, relieved. "So be it."

SCENE THREE: DEFENDERS

...Of Act Five: Bright Manifest

In the eyes of Ryoku Dragontalen, we are in Bonnin Capital, in the world of Bonnin. It is late afternoon On November 10th, 2017.

The fountain spray caught the sunlight like a stream of diamonds as it gushed. The fountain wasn't deep, and a wealth of small gold coins littered the bottom, catching the sunlight like a bronze finish. I wasn't overly fond of water, but a shallow fountain was something I could still admire. The water created a light mist across my face, my clothes, and my hair. I let it, to remind myself that I was here.

For all my life, I always had questions. Nothing ever seemed to add up. The deaths of my parents. My separation from my sister. My childhood. Everything leading up to this moment. What was the reason behind it all? Why had Chris Olestine brought me here to the spirit realm?

This was now the third world I'd been to. Harohto had been a moderately pleasant, but tough, world that presented its challenges. I met Will, Sira, and Lusari there. I made friends. I experienced loss when the terrifying Keeper picked much of Will's squad off. In the end, I helped save a city. Then it was off to Lysvid, where I learned just how dangerous this world could be. I stood head-to-head with Jesanht Olace, Gale, and Geri, opponents so powerful that I never should have been able to walk away. The Trickster joined me. I met my long-lost teacher.

Now I was here in Bonnin, and I was discovering an even more dangerous thing – love.

It was difficult to call it that. I didn't love Sira. Not in the way that we were supposed to, with butterflies and dating and cute quarrels with one another. I loved her as a person. I saw the girl behind her scars, a girl who could smile and laugh and love like anyone else. Maybe even a little more. She was so scared, so traumatized by her past, that the idea of love scared her. At least, that was what I thought I felt from her.

Sira Jessura was scared of something, I knew, and I had a horrifying gut feeling that it was me. Something I had done. Now she'd run off by herself in the capital city of Bonnin after blatantly insulting me. I didn't take her words personally. If I had Sira figured out, she didn't really mean that. But... why had she run away? Was this the end of us?

My questions threatened to boil over me when somebody plopped down next to me. Kaia threw her legs over the rim of the fountain, removing her sandals with a light kick – they landed on my lap – and stuck her feet in the water. She emitted a light squeak from the temperature. On my other side, Lusari got up to walk over to Will. We'd sat in silence together for a long time, and I wasn't sure if she liked that or not.

"Katiel's being boring." Kaia cupped out her hands over the water. "Talking about things we already know. There's no point."

I leaned in closer, watching her as she held her hands over the water. The slight waves in the aqua surface fluctuated like a living thing. She started wriggling her fingers, and the waves of water sprang up to touch her skin like hands. I nearly fell back in shock. She giggled, and played with the water like one might play with a pet, even stroking the water-hands in a tickling fashion. The whole fountain churned in what might have been a happy reaction.

"What are you doing?" I asked curiously. I turned the same way as her, crossing my legs rather than sticking my feet in the water. "Are you... playing with the water?"

She didn't look at me. "I'm a water mage, silly," she told me, as though that were implied. "Water likes me." She giggled as a purposeful little wave splashed across her hand.

I was sure I misheard her. "It… likes you?"

She glanced at me, and then twitched her pinkie finger. A small burst of water shot from the fountain and into my face. I nearly fell from the fountain, stunned and a little annoyed. Yet, fascinated. Kaia laughed.

"Of course it does! Water's just like you or I, but a lot smarter. Especially than you."

I was tempted to splash her back, but not ready for a playful water fight with a girl who could control it. Instead, I put my hands out above the water. I let my hands hover just above the surface, which seemed to still only around the radius of my hands. Kaia watched me in silence.

"It's not going to listen to you, y'know. You're not such a big shot anymore, are you?" She sighed, wiggling her fingers and making the water dance below her fingertips like a puppet. "Well, you are. You always will be Ryoku Dragontalen, one way or another."

"What are you talking about?" I asked.

"Nothing," she replied easily. "You want to learn how to do this?"

I almost entirely forgot what she'd said before. "You can teach me?"

"Don't expect to be a water whisperer by nightfall," she told me stubbornly. "Or at all, honestly. You're going to have to coax the water like nursing a cut. She doesn't like you much."

I eyed the water warily. "Why?"

"You're afraid of her," Kaia replied simply. "Maybe not of *her* directly, but of her sisters and cousins and aunts and mothers. Other waters. Maybe things scarier and deeper. This one's pretty."

I wasn't sure what to say. "She is."

She tutted under her breath. "Just keep your hands right there. Close your eyes."

I obeyed. Kaia didn't speak for a long moment. I felt her slide close to me and place her hands over mine. She smelled something like the crisp, cold air coming from the fountain, but with a salty sort of spray. I had never been near it, but her scent made me envision the ocean.

"There's a lot of interference," she murmured. "Maybe you need a staff. Or maybe she just won't accept—wait. Wait, wait, wait. Do you feel anything? See anything?"

A sensation appeared in my fingertips. It felt like the tide slowly lapping over my hands. I almost opened my eyes, but I realized something quickly – my hands were dry. The tide-like feeling on my hands felt almost like pins and needles. Images flashed through my vision. I pictured that I sat on a sandy shore, its waves gently lapping over the land. Kaia's scent filled the air around me.

The vision increased until it seemed more real than anything else. I could make out each grain in the sand, and how they trickled away as the waves lapped over them, sometimes leaving crabs and abandoned shells in their wake. I could see a babbling brook cutting through a thick forest; feel the roots of trees as they licked up bits of water in the soil. Then I was in the middle of the ocean, watching the wild, unbarred lapping of waves with no land to interrupt it. Each wave came powerful and rich. Fish and large water creatures lurked beneath the surface, tranquil and uninterrupted.

Kaia's excited squeal made my eyes open. For a moment, I watched the water lapping across my hand, almost like the tongue of a dog. As soon as I was aware, the water fell back to the fountain.

"You did it!" she cried. "I didn't think... Most people in this new world need staves to channel magic, but you..."

She met my glance for a moment, and I noticed how similar her eyes looked to the deepest, most free part of the ocean. There was an excited glint to them, like the sun reflecting off the waves. As much as everything about Sira screamed *fire*, the same about Kaia whispered about *water*.

It was the thought of Sira that eventually turned my gaze away, though I couldn't hide my smile. As little as it was, I could do water magic.

"Hey, Ryoku." Kaia wasn't looking at me now. Her hands were back over the water, which lapped up quickly across her hands. "You know you don't need somebody to be happy, right? Not somebody who'll say such mean things to you, at least. Stay with people who'll build you up like you deserve."

I looked at her for a moment, stunned by her words. "But don't you need Kat? I mean... how you cling to him all the time."

The waves lapping over her hand seemed to falter for a moment, but she didn't blink. "Don't be ridiculous," she murmured. "I don't need him – he needs me. I'm being a good girl by sticking by his side. Poor Katiel wouldn't know what to do without me. Luckily, I don't mind sticking around as much as possible. It's a balance – just like you and your darkness."

Her words threw me for a loop, but I didn't have time to react – she sent another jet of water into my face. I spat out water and glared at her irritably, but she beamed at me like I called her pretty. Which she certainly was, a fact I couldn't ignore. Mist seemed to cling to her auburn hair, glittering like she strung her hair with diamonds. And her bright blue eyes...

"I've decided," she said. "You can be my little brother. I think I need to look after you now, little storm."

I tilted my head in confusion. "Little storm?" I asked hazily.

Just then, a hand appeared on my shoulder – Will's. He stood with Lusari, who smiled down at me even as my face dripped with water. Glancing up at them, I realized it was getting late. The shades-clad sun emitted a great yawn from behind a tall building, lurking close to a set of hills below. As odd as the sun was in Bonnin, it offered a beautiful red shimmer to everything like autumn leaves.

"Perhaps we should look to an inn for the night," Will said apologetically, glancing at Kaia with what looked like genuine concern. "Our characteristic sun looks tired. According to Katiel, the Registry is right near a popular inn just down the way. If Sira does decide to return..."

"She'll find us easily," Lusari finished for him. "We tend to camp near Registries whenever possible. Even Sira should know that."

The mention of Sira made me vividly recall the anger in her eyes when she essentially told me I should go die. It had been well over an hour, surely, and she hadn't returned. Will knew this as well as I did, but he seemed more worried about how it affected me.

Suddenly, I felt angry. Ever since Harohto, I hung onto everything Sira did – every word, every action, trying to find some meaning behind it. When she insulted me, I waited for the little smirk she gave me after. When she looked annoyed, I waited until it passed. Back at the Timeless Castle, she'd drawn me in with little to no effort.

Because I was expecting it. Hoping for it. Hoping that I was reading correctly into Sira's frantic, unhealthy actions. When we kissed, and when we slid each other's clothing out of the way, it felt like the ending of a good book coming to fruition.

However, just as suddenly, it evaporated. Since that kiss, she seemed like she wanted to paint the walls with my blood. It had let up for a bit after our stay at the Bloody Mare in Leudis, but then returned in full fury after the fight with Geri.

Was it... over? Whatever it was? On the other hand, was I a fool for thinking there was anything at all?

"Let's go," I replied shortly, hopping to my feet. Will glanced after me for a moment, surprised. Kaia and Lusari fell in line with me. I avoided the looks of Katiel, Guildford, and Rex when we passed them, but they followed us. Loki had walked away a short distance, turned, and smiled at me – but it seemed to waver when he saw my expression. He, too, fell in at my side as I led the way.

Only... I wasn't quite sure where I was going.

The market was quieter at this late hour. People bustled around on the last of their evening business, perhaps purchasing a late dinner or running home to their families. Busy mothers shepherded their children towards home while lampposts came to life around us, but many kids still prowled the street in search of make-believe treasure. Kaia, temporarily retiring from Katiel's shoulder, frolicked among the children, summoning water from the gutters and from cracks in the walkways, making the droplets dance around excited children.

While I was watching, bemused by the childish Kaia, I bumped into someone. I caught a glimpse of curly brown hair, tanned skin, and a red sweater. I realized, when he backed away and his teal-colored eyes caught mine, that I knew him.

"J-Joey?"

It was my friend from school – another example of somebody I *didn't* expect to meet here.

"Ryoku?" he asked. "What are you doing here?"

"I could ask you the same thing," I cried. "Tell me you're not dead!"

I startled laughter out of him. "No, no," Joey assured me anxiously. "I just... I never thought you might be... another one?" Then he saw Katiel behind me. He actually looked relieved. "Well, okay. You're with Katiel. That actually makes sense."

I frowned. "You don't think I could do this on my own?"

Guildford came around the bend behind me, one hand on the sword at his hip, the other taking a hefty bite out of a cat-shaped candy apple. By Joey's look, I swore he was ready to faint.

"M-Mr. Guildford!?" he asked, a clear mix of delusion and joy.

Guildford saw him, and laughed. "I suppose death fogs up the memories of my dear students. It's just Guildford, as I already had to remind Ryoku."

Joey laughed. "Yeah, guess so," he said, but his voice sounded sad. I felt for him. Our world was strange and alien with Guildford just as much as this one was to him. The feeling of being at school without hearing his voice, or standing in his classroom under a different teacher, was still alien to me.

I jabbed my thumb back at our teacher. "He's traveling with me. Teaching me how to fight, and use magic."

Joey raised a brow. "Really?" he mused. "That's ironic. You should've seen Ryoku on the Day of—"

A stern glance from both Katiel and I silenced him, and he quickly remembered who he was addressing. "You were there as well, right?" Guildford asked.

Joey scratched his chin nervously and didn't reply. My eye itched, and Katiel rubbed his arm. I decided to change the subject before it reached places I didn't want to go again. "I haven't seen much of you this year," I told Joey.

He smirked. "Yeah, too bad we've got no classes together this semester," he said sourly. "Since Dagger's gone, I guess they realized pairing us up is actually a bad idea!"

Katiel laughed. "Funny. When he was around, we were saints tutoring him all the time. Now he's in the big city, and we're like regular dropouts again."

"Definitely!" Joey chuckled. "The drug lord helps us dumb kids focus." He cleared his throat, turning to me. "You got any classes with the old gang this year?"

"Mostly with Katiel," I replied. "One with Virgo, one with Dawn."

"I'm with Alan for three blocks," Katiel said sourly, causing Joey to laugh outright. "You got any classes with that freak?"

The two dissolved into a rant about our friend Alan, which I found myself tuning out. Loki edged closer to me, studying my friends with interest.

"If I could get you to clarify something for me?" he asked gingerly. "Perhaps it's not the best time to ask."

"What is it?" I asked distantly.

"Alright. Well, I noticed he and Kaia can use magic without a staff's aid."

I nodded, leaving out the fact that I'd just done the same, thanks to Kaia. "Katiel's a natural mage. According to him, he was born with the art so he doesn't need to study actual magical theory, but he can recite it like a professor. He knows his stuff."

Loki looked curious. "A gifted mage, eh? That's rare, even among Defenders. It takes a lot to pick up the art with such ease. In your world, that would be like understanding rocket science from birth."

I couldn't even fathom his comparison. "That's insane," I said softly, watching Kaia as she turned a particularly decadent dewdrop into a living butterfly, which fluttered into the air to land on the nose of a dirt-smeared boy.

"Right, Ryoku?"

I jumped at the mention of my name, turning to face the others. Will and Guildford joined in on the conversation between Katiel and Joey, and all four looked at me. Rex watched me with a smirk of interest. I had to ask Will to repeat himself.

"The look on your face when Sira and I gave you our vows," he said easily, grinning. "It was similar to the one you have just given me."

I grinned in spite of myself. His words made me remember Sira, running around somewhere in the capital. However, his words made me think of something else.

"Say, Joey," I turned to the other Defender. "Where are your Guardians?"

I could instantly tell I'd struck a soft spot in my friend, and regretted my sudden question.

"Yes, you do look like a seasoned Defender," Loki supported. He pointed at something I hadn't immediately noticed: a longsword hung over his back with a shiny black handle. "A seasoned Defender would have certainly picked up a few Guardians by now."

Joey smiled wistfully. "Well, I don't have any. Not anymore."

My jaw dropped in shock. "What? What do you mean? What happened?"

Joey glanced at the sky, crossing his arms over his chest. "I had one. He... he met his end honorably."

Will put a sympathetic hand on Joey's shoulder. "I see," he said. "An honorable end for a Guardian." To me, he raised a solemn brow. "To die protecting their Defender."

"That is the most honorable way," Loki agreed sadly. "My condolences, Joey."

Joey only nodded. He looked so distant; I thought he might not be here at all. Then a bell tolled in the distance. Joey glanced up as though awoken, looking around – then he returned his focus to me.

"I've got to get going," he told me. "It was good to see you again, especially here. I wish you and your friends the best. Maybe we'll see each other again soon!"

Before I could work up a reply, he rushed off into the crowd. I tried to follow him with my eyes, but he worked his way through the meager crowd like unoccupied space, and was gone.

"He lost his Guardian...?" I murmured, to nobody in particular.

"It is not highly uncommon," Will reasoned. He came to stand next to me. "You recall the vows Sira and I made – our lives are a shield to your own. To die protecting you would be the greatest conceivable honor. If I passed in your service and Syaoto was told, I would be honored."

I looked at him and Loki, who both gave me measured looks. My expression wore down on them somehow.

"I don't want that," I replied. "That's not what I signed up for. To let you guys practically search for a speeding train to run in front of. No, that doesn't fly. We're in this together."

"Your mission is a dangerous one," Loki said, frantically looking to Will for guidance. "Should the likes of the great emperor come seeking to kill you, our lives are the coat to lie across the puddle."

I shook my head irritably. "That's why I need to get strong, isn't it? So that doesn't happen. So that when the emperor shows his face, I'll be ready." Loki and Will both gave me a look. "What? That's what we're doing, right? That's why I have this dumb sword – because this is my fight. I need to find Chris no matter what, and through him, find my sister."

My group fell silent for a moment. I realized I didn't talk often about finding my sister. Kaia studied me with interest, water from a puddle hovering around her like birds.

Finally, a grin broke out over Will's face.

"Fear not then," he said gallantly, swinging his gladius over his hip as he turned away – the picture of a gallant soldier dressed as a cat. "I am your guide, am I not? As such, no matter what oblivion shall rise up against us, I will guide you to its end. I am no gentleman. I shall *not* be your coat across the puddle if you would simply stomp through the mud next to it. We shall stomp through the mud together."

He started marching angrily, but I remained on the spot. When he finally cast a discreet glance over his shoulder, seeing if we followed, I burst into laughter. Loki followed suit, hysterically clutching his chest to laugh at Will's endeavor. Even Rex hid his face behind the hem of his coat, laughing uncontrollably. Then everyone was laughing, even Will.

"What is so funny?" Will asked with a twitching scowl, holding back his own laughter.

I shook my head, unable to stop smiling. "Should I ever wonder why I keep you around, do something like that again. Despite everything, Will, you're surprisingly easy to laugh at – or with, I mean, of course."

He snorted, grinning obnoxiously, and threw his arm across my shoulder. "I deign to take that in the best possible context. Should I wonder why I still follow you around, do make me make you laugh again. Ryoku Dragontalen, do not think I will die so easily."

I grinned, and let my guide lead the way down the road to the Registry. My journey, however long, arduous, and saddening, couldn't be without laughter and joy for long.

SCENE FOUR: PENGUIN INN

...Of Act Five: Bright Manifest

*In the eyes of Ryoku Dragontalen, we are in Bonnin Capital, in the world of Bonnin.
It is late evening
On November 10th, 2017.*

"We'll book five rooms for the night, if you please."

Loki slid Will's hefty satchel of gold across the table. The innkeeper – who happened to be an enormous seven- or eight-foot penguin – caught the satchel with its curved flipper and started counting out enough gold for the rooms.

"Are we sure this is the right place?" Guildford asked under his breath.

"Of course," Loki replied confidently. "The Penguin Inn. It's a high-end inn located right next to the Registry. We'll book these rooms, run over, accept a mission, and be set for the morning."

The large penguin slid back the satchel of gold along with five room keys – each key carved in the smooth design of a penguin. "Welcome to the grand Penguin inn!" the penguin declared, and spread its large flippers out in a dramatic fashion. "Our qualified staff of penguins will see to your every need during your stay. Half your gold goes back to you in the morning, after checkout, which is at... 11 am!"

"They literally don't have any clocks," Katiel murmured to me, studying the expanse of the Penguin Inn's lobby. The desk was at the heart of the room, stairs extending on either side of it in much the same fashion as a pair of flippers. Everything in sight was black and white.

A team of men in cat-like armor were lugging out a heavy suitcase, aided from behind by a poor, regular-sized penguin that put his all into pushing the luggage. Amused, Rex approached and lifted their suitcase with his one good arm, drawing gazes of amazement from the team of presumed Meow-cenaries. Kaia departed from Katiel's neck to walk the lobby of the Penguin Inn, debating over a couch that looked like a stupidly wide penguin accepting seats on its lap.

"Thank you very much," Loki told the innkeeper, and turned to the rest of us. "Alright. Now if Guildford and I head to the Registry to accept a mission, you lot can get started on divvying up the rooms. We fine gents will take the remaining room." He tossed all but one of the keys to Will, who caught them easily.

"Kaia and I will take one," Katiel told me as Loki and Guildford already started out the door.

"I could pair with the tall, dark one," Rex said, returning from having helped the Meow-cenaries – he was alluding to Katiel's other friend, who'd met us at the door to the inn when we arrived. Artos was his name, a tall boy garbed in dark clothing, with long, brown hair and his head largely wrapped in what looked like a turban. He looked at Rex in such a way that suggested *he* was pairing with the tall, dark one.

Will turned to Lusari and I with a brave smile. "That leaves us," he said, and stopped talking when the door opened to the Penguin Inn once more. Looking particularly annoyed, Sira stepped into the lobby, having to duck to enter the doorway.

"You guys really had to pick this place?" Sira asked dryly. She didn't look at any of us. Nobody offered to give her a reply, but she stepped into our midst, skeptically analyzing the place. "Figures. Look for the biggest, most expensive inn in Bonnin, and Loki will have bought rooms there."

Will and Lusari exchanged glances. "You can share a room with me," Will told Sira, meeting her sardonic gaze. "Everyone else is paired up already."

Sira looked confused, but, admittedly, not nearly as angry as she had earlier. "Sure," she agreed, but her eyes were on me. It took her a long moment to tear her gaze away. "We waiting for something, or...?"

Will shrugged. "Loki and Guildford headed to the Registry," he said. "Nothing stopping us from getting set up."

A small herd of penguins appeared seemingly out of nowhere. One snatched the bag from my shoulders, chirping, in broken English, about how it would shoulder my burdens for me. A particularly brawny penguin managed to wrest control of Will's huge rucksack as well. They waited as we looked around at each other, stunned, before Will distributed the keys and we made our way to the stairs.

"It's me and you for the last room, then," Lusari told me timidly, latching onto my arm. She smiled up at me. I returned the look, though I was uneasy. Will and Sira walked together ahead of us, and they'd somehow already sparked conversation. If I heard right, it was something about Bonnin politics, but he still managed to make Sira laugh. Why could everyone do that but me?

Deciding to leave the fate of our next mission to Loki and Guildford, we found our rooms. Will and Sira's was at the start of the ground floor hall. I watched the bulky penguin nearly crash through the door, turning red in the face, as it struggled with Will's bag. The soldier gently helped alleviate the weight from the penguin, which didn't look at all grateful for it.

"Do we have any context on these penguins at all?" Sira muttered. "Like, how do they talk? Or control an inn, for that matter?"

"None," Katiel said sadly. "Bonnin just kinda has its own laws. At least it's largely non-hostile."

Sira shrugged, and followed Will into the room without as much as a look at us. The rooms for Katiel, Kaia, Rex, and Artos ended up being upstairs. Katiel gave me a wry smirk before taking off up them. Kaia lingered by the foot of the stairs, then winked and meowed at me before charging up the steps after Katiel. Rex and Artos followed, their silent shadows.

"What do you think the rooms will be like?" Lusari asked me as we headed to our own room down the end of the first hallway.

"I can only be so worried," I told her with a sigh. She reached the room first, and waited as I unlocked it with our own penguin key, which seemed fatter than the others somehow.

I couldn't have been ready for this.

The penguins squeezed past us to hurl our baggage on the huge queen-sized bed, adorned with a black and white blanket. The fluffy quilt looked softer than a dream. Next to the bed was a large wardrobe, shaped like a penguin with handles of extended flippers.

The whole room was largely schemed the same way. The floors were a plush white carpet, the walls a display of striped white and black. The curtain looked like glazed ice, matching a wonderful chandelier of sculpted ice with drawn penguins dancing around the bulb of light. Another door, shaped like a penguin, led off to a plush-looking bathroom as well. In the corner, kitchen supplies and the like all appeared to be of the same setting. I saw penguin pots and pans, a penguin coffee maker, and even penguin-shaped teabags next to the pot.

"Wow," Lusari breathed. "I honestly shouldn't be surprised."

"Right?" I agreed. "Where do they find all this stuff?"

I automatically went to the right side of the bed. I hadn't known we were supposed to share a bed in our room. Were all the other rooms like this? Lusari said nothing about it and set to readying herself for bed on the other side. If she was intimidated somehow and told me, I'd have no problem sleeping on the floor. It looked almost as comfortable, anyway.

I took my time setting my belongings beside the wardrobe. Seeing my repertoire of weapons made me feel funny. The knife I got from Kioru, my bow and staff from Bytold, and the black blade of Ragnarokkr. How had I come in possession of such things?

I carefully removed my hoodie as well, leaving me in just a white shirt and black pants. It felt relieving to remove the cat-like gear that was so customary in Bonnin.

"Are you planning to shower?" Lusari asked me, surprising me. "I mean, you never know when our next world might not have the luxury."

I shrugged. "Sounds good. Somehow I don't think Syaoto has the commodities Bonnin does, even if Bonnin's are... oddly frightening."

I looked at her across the bed. She'd sat down, her hands smoothing her skirt around her legs. "You don't want to go first?"

She shook her head, smiling at me without looking directly at me. "No, you go first. I'll take the time after you go to sleep. Besides, we, um, didn't have showers like these in Harohto. The one in Lysvid was the first one I've used."

I nodded, though something felt a little off about her words. I took my leave into the bathroom. The bathtub looked like a penguin, of course, and the showerhead resembled a penguin's head with its beak open wide. Shaking my head, I undressed and went into the shower.

Despite all the penguin paraphernalia, the shower was one of the most relaxing I could ever recall. The water felt the perfect temperature at the ease of turning a knob. The shampoo and soap smelled like exotic fruits, not like penguins as I'd half-feared. Although, the little black eyes on everything did feel a little unnerving.

I stood there for a long time under the water, pondering over all the things that happened to me since I entered the spirit realm. I felt like I was close to unmasking some sort of hidden truth. Something perhaps to do with my sister, or Chris, or how everyone said the realms had changed, or the sword linked to my name. With each passing day, more mysteries seemed to present themselves, and I knew I couldn't figure them out on my own.

The water felt so relaxing; I spent almost an hour just basking in the warmth. The hot water didn't run out as I expected, either, but I hurried nonetheless after realizing I was spacing out. I pondered over a penguin robe for a moment before switching into some of my regular clothes. I tried to fix my hair in the mirror, but the glass hopelessly fogged up. I couldn't even see my face, and it didn't show any signs of defogging soon.

Lusari was still awake, sitting on the bed and twiddling her thumbs. When she saw me return, her face brightened. "You take forever to shower, you know."

I smiled apologetically. "Sorry. It's really nice. I just hope I didn't use all the hot water."

"That's alright," she said softly, and gestured for me to sit with her. "I don't feel like I can sleep. Since I met up with you, so much seems to be happening. I feel as if I've been caught in a storm."

I nodded furtively. "I agree. First the whole deal with the raiders and the Old Forest's Keeper, then Lysvid and everything that came with that."

Lusari nodded, but her expression said she was thinking of something else. "You're becoming less of a mystery, you know," she said teasingly. "Since meeting Guildford, and Katiel, and the other Defender in the square, we're starting to get a better idea of who you are."

"Oh?" I asked, a little coyly. "Well, what do you think of this 'better idea of me?'"

I didn't realize that might come across as flirtatious until the words left my mouth. Lusari giggled, and I swore she edged a little closer. "That I was right when you first stood up against those men in Harohto. You're brave, selfless, and kind – almost to a fault."

I smiled, uneasy at her compliment. "To a fault?"

She giggled again. "Yes. I feel like anyone could apologize to you, no matter how insincerely, and you'd accept them with open arms. Even if they're horrendous to you."

I sighed inwardly. She was talking about Sira. I shut my mouth when she turned at the sound, and she smiled warmly at me. "Just forget I said that, okay? I still think you're amazing."

She was definitely getting closer. I gulped. "I'm not that great," I said defensively. "Have you seen Will? I couldn't ask for a better friend, one more noble and true than he is."

I'd thought to unintentionally push her away with the mention of Will, but it didn't work. She only smiled at me. "He's a good man," she said plaintively. "A vigil crusader and a warrior of the heart. But he isn't you."

Now I was almost sure she was flirting with me. Was I reading too much into it? My mind raced to change the topic. Was it my fault for my initial comment?

"Lusari," I said softly. "Have you... did you have a good life in Harohto? I mean, before we came in."

Lusari gave me a surprised look. "You mean after my parents were killed by raiders?" She spoke without hesitation, and I felt a bit of edge to her tone. Was that insensitive of me?

"I spent a few weeks living between inns," she said, and briefly glanced away. "The deaths of my parents exempt me from my studies at the magic academy. I do wish you could have gone there – you would have liked it. I never really got by there, but I'm sure you would have. People didn't like me for my non-Harohto traits. They would have liked you."

I looked at her with renewed interest. I supposed she didn't look quite like what the average Harohto citizen was. If I'd observed well enough, they traditionally had British-esque accents, with dark or fair hair and somewhat rural atmospheres. I hadn't seen a single person with silver hair during my time there – besides Lancet, who wasn't from Harohto as far as I knew.

"You didn't get on well at the school?" I asked gingerly.

Lusari shook her head. "They were pretty mean to me up until the deaths of my parents. I wasn't quite as fast a learner as most of the class. Sometimes my magic had… adverse effects. They liked to use their magic on me as though it might sink in that way. And not in a very friendly way, either." She scowled in a cute way. "Lifting me in the air with wind magic, or freezing my clothes in the dorm rooms. I don't like to think about it much. Some of the students did apologize to me after my parents passed, but it didn't feel sincere. Then, of course, you swooped in and saved me at my darkest moment. Were you not there…"

She shuddered violently, and somehow ended up pressed against me. I instinctively held her, although I knew she hadn't shuddered because of the cold. Those men had very nearly taken something precious from her. As much as I didn't like how Lusari seemed to idolize me for it, I was glad we'd intervened. Of course, Will and Sira had done far more than I had for her. Why did she still insist on thanking *me* for it?

"What about your family, Ryoku?" Lusari asked softly from against my arm. "You talked about them back in Lysvid, but you didn't explain much. I feel like you hid behind the talk of the police force and your hometown. You must have family at home of some kind, right? Do they know you're here, risking your life in the spirit realm?"

I hesitated, and she lifted her head to look at me. Suddenly, with her so close, I could smell the sweet strawberry scent of her hair.

"No, they don't," I told her solemnly. "My mother died when I was younger. Her whole side of the family, in a tragic inferno. I don't know my father. Clearly he doesn't care for me all that much. My stepfather took me and my sister in after, but he died in a tragic accident, too. Based on our reactions to that, my sister and I were separated. They found her to be... more troublesome, and had to go to an orphanage accommodating that. I found a home much more easily."

Lusari looked at me in silence for a long moment. I wondered if maybe I'd said too much. I didn't tell many people about my sister.

"That's terrible," she murmured, her voice little more than a whisper.

As close as she was, I could hear her easily. Unwarranted images of Sira passed across my vision: her tear-streaked cheeks, her emotional scarlet eyes, the way she kissed me, how her hands traveled across my body like they had wanted it since she laid eyes on me... Was that really all it was?

"I guess," I replied just as softly. "It's the past. There's nothing I can do for it now but find my sister."

She looked at me, and there was softness to her snowy eyes that made me think of the promised snow in Harohto, a beautiful and intoxicating thing. "Is that why you're doing all this?" she asked me. "Parading across the spirit realm? In search of your sister? Is she...?"

"Yes," I replied, and I realized my tone came out like a dagger. I softened my voice. "And, no. I felt... connected to Chris somehow. Maybe that connection has to do with Roxanne. I don't know how I know, but..."

I'd never told a spirit her name before. Even Will and Sira had never gotten that from me. Lusari merely looked at me. There was such tenderness in her eyes. I felt like I could tell her everything, and she would treat me as softly as snow in response. There would be no judgement, no telling me that I should have tried harder or done something differently. No, there was only love.

She was laying against me now, her snowy hair spilling across my lap. "I'm so sorry," she said softly. "I know that doesn't make a difference, but I'm here. And I'll go with you, all the way."

It took me a moment to realize the weight of her words. Suddenly she was sitting upright, and she slid her legs onto my lap. She raised her head until her snow-white eyes were level with mine. A fresh snow, to blanket a thriving forest.

"Would you accept me?" she asked, each word like a snowflake in its gentleness. "As your Guardian? I know I hesitated to do such a thing, and it was stupid. You've given me nothing but kindness. I guess I've been scared that I won't be able to help you, but that doesn't matter anymore. I know I'll lay my life on the line for you, title or no."

I couldn't break away from her gaze even if I tried. After speaking with Katiel and Joey, I wasn't sure I wanted *any* Guardians. I didn't want people to die for me. Was that selfish of me? To strive not to lose anyone else at my age?

"I'm so sorry," she whispered, and her lips drew closer to my ear. Each breath she took caused strange sensations to ripple through me, but she held me still. "I shouldn't pounce such a question on you, should I? But... is there ever a better time? A time where we can actually talk other than now?"

She breathed fully into my ear with the last word, and I was now fully aware she knew what she was doing. My body pulsed with unwitting pleasure, and my hands found the backs of her shoulder blades, pulling her closer. She made a small sound of satisfaction, and then she whirled around. I saw her face, her cute button nose, and the delicate lashes of her snowy eyes – before they fluttered, and she pressed her lips against mine.

A thousand thoughts burst through my head. What about Sira? What were we after she displayed so much aggression and hatred toward me? Was our moment in the Timeless Castle nothing special to her?

Lusari was a great kisser. Her soft lips pressed against mine, searching thirstily for a response while her hands ran the length of my arms. No, she wouldn't be satisfied with just kissing.

What harm was there in reciprocating this? Lusari was cute, a *great* kisser, and she actually seemed to care about me. Sira was sexy, but she seemed to hate my guts half the time. She kept the worst temper and seemed to favor insulting me over everyone else. She'd only come around for a brief time after the Timeless Castle, and since then I'd felt like a glorified pincushion. It had gotten to the point that even Will doubted whether she should be with us.

This wasn't the best time for debate. Lusari's lips pressed into mine like they sought the other half of themselves, her tongue slipping in between my lips. Shivers of inevitable pleasure ran down my spine just as her hands worked around my arms, begging for a response.

Of course, while I tried to debate between the two girls, I couldn't forget my life in the land of the living. My ex-girlfriend, Anna Rikalla, and then the one I recently felt stronger feelings for – Dawn Elethel.

Anna had been a sore spot for me for months. We'd had a strong relationship in mid high school, cut short when she moved across the country. We hadn't spoken in months, and I didn't know how she felt. The emotions tied with Anna were confusing and pieced together. The words of Dagger and Katiel remained inevitably in my mind: if she loved me, then why did she want us to separate when she moved away?

It had been years since Dawn and I dated. I couldn't easily explain how those feelings rekindled. We'd barely seen one another over the summer, I thought. Those months had gone by in a blur, but I could recall Dawn hardly having a role in them.

No, I thought, with more finality than I'd mustered in months. I couldn't do that to her now. To storm back into her life with unrequitable feelings. The answer was as simple as the feelings begging for reciprocation right in front of me.

I met the tug of Lusari's persistent, sweet lips. I finally kissed her back, and I felt her smile against my lips. She pulled at my arms and forced me onto my back on the plush bed. She perched on my lap like an extravagant, snowy bird, her lips and tongue exploring mine with fervent pleasure. She pressed against me so tightly that I could discern every curve of her body.

When she finally pulled back for a moment, her hair disheveled from my hands running through it, her cherry lipstick stained – I hadn't noticed she wore such a thing until now. "I can't believe it," she murmured shakily, smiling. "I've... I've wanted you for so long."

I barely had time to smile before she was kissing me again. Then she was running her lips down my neck, gliding her tongue across my skin, her hands scratching at my back. I kissed her in every opening I found, kissing at whatever skin I could find, inciting slow moans when I kissed the right spots. Her hands began to work at my shirt, and she only pulled away long enough to slide my shirt over my head. Then my hands were at her top, and then working the clasp of her bra. She pressed against my bare chest, moaning quietly as she began to work at my belt, then she began to slide my pants down my legs.

As soon as my pants were down, Lusari pulled away from my lips with a silvery smile. My eyes widened when she went down on me, and I found myself clutching the bed sheets in an attempt to keep quiet. She didn't stay down for long, however, and was quickly tugging her undergarments down from beneath her skirt before she mounted me.

Everything was going so fast and feeling so good, I could hardly breathe. Each movement she made seemed to suck out my air and replace it with pleasure. My skin tingled like it longed to burst into flames at the hot touch of this snowy girl.

It was somewhere after our pleasure finally peaked in a release of tandem. Long after she pulled away, her mouth slightly agape with pure ecstasy, and after she kissed me again like she belonged there. It was long after she fell asleep against my chest, the last of her clothing finally gone in our wild lust.

Then, like a hawk waiting to snatch up its prey, the guilt ensnared me.

I stared at the ceiling, and thoughts pervaded my mind. I saw how Will looked at Lusari when she drifted to my side, his sapphire eyes a little distant and lost. The way Sira turned away from me so hastily, but a part of her hesitated, drawing back to linger over my face a last moment before feigning ignorance.

It began to set in, inevitably, that I'd done something horrible.

I watched Lusari's slight face just below my breast, a soft smile on her face even in slumber. How could I break such a thing?

Easily, I thought, if for the sake of my best friend, but it wouldn't be quite so easy to do. How could I draw away after such an exchange? She would surely be broken, if her words were any indicator of her feelings.

I couldn't sleep after that, wondering just how I could face Will again. Surely I would look at my friends in the morning, and they would see the sins written across my face as though written there by her lips. There would be no escaping it.

Why couldn't I have just pushed her away?

It felt like ages before sleep finally wrested me from my dangerous thoughts. Lusari woke sometime in the night, and she pulled the plush blanket around us where the passion no longer provided our only warmth. My heart felt broken. She was such a sweet girl, but did I feel the same way she did? Or had I simply used her to sweep aside the broken glass? To cover my shoddy tracks in the snow?

SCENE FIVE: THE DIAMOND DRAGON

...Of Act Five: Bright Manifest

In the eyes of Ryoku Dragontalen, we are in Outskirts of Bonnin Capital, in the world of Bonnin. It is early morning On November 11th, 2017.

"And here you have it. Our gallant task during our stay in Bonnin."

The Trickster displayed the bounty like a badge of honor. A hunt for an entity called the Diamond Dragon, apparently a dangerous monster inhabiting the mountains northeast of the capital and harrying the regular trade route. The sketch created for the purpose looked like a ferocious monster that wouldn't hesitate to gobble us up, even in the innocent world of Bonnin.

"Every world has its dangers, I suppose," Will shrugged. "So be it. We will see to the safety of Bonnin."

I exchanged a dry look with Will. Neither of us had a female tag-along today. After the events that transpired last night, it seemed that Lusari and Sira had become friends. I'd left my room early in the morning to avoid talking to Lusari, and found Will outside before the break of dawn, lazily munching on a shank of ham.

Akin Minds

Both of us were the bearers of guilt. Once he saw me, he told me what happened with Sira just as I explained what happened with Lusari, leaving us at a strange bypass. Neither one of us could be truly mad, so we bonded instead. What were the odds that we would both make the same sort of error?

Still, it filled me with a sort of trepidation that I did not voice. Lusari, who Will bore quite strong feelings for, seemed attracted to me. Sira, who already displayed a great deal of affection to me in the Timeless Castle, spent a night with Will. What did it mean for us?

When we'd come inside, we saw Lusari and Sira talking together as though nothing happened. Seeing our confusion, Loki commented that we must have done something wrong in bed. Will and I teamed up to take him down while Kaia assaulted him with waves of bubbly magic. It took time, but the Trickster relented to the bubbles while Will had him in a headlock.

To the events of the morning prior to our departure, I found myself wholly confused between the matters of Sira and Lusari. As Loki reported, though, it did seem I was safe in Bonnin. The Registry didn't post my bounty. Even then, my safety was only temporary. Moving onto the next world would surely resume the need for aliases and secrecy. Danger would surely follow.

By the time we set out, I felt I had learned a lesson. Friends would come before matters of the heart, no matter what. What would I have done if Will never forgave me?

Now we walked outside the city walls, Will and I exchanging guilty glances. It would take some time for that to ebb away. Sira and Lusari weren't entirely cold to us – no colder than usual, anyway, in Sira's case – but they certainly didn't hang alongside us as they normally did, so we kept to ourselves.

Along with our mission, Guildford and Loki graciously accepted the request of a local to escort their cart of supplies through the mountains to the village of Niin. It was on our route, and Katiel highly suggested we meet with his friend Eckhardt there regardless. Artos and Rex handled the wagon well enough on their own atop a pair of cute-looking ponies, suitable to the world of Bonnin.

A short ways out of town, Guildford came to walk with Will and I. "I fear to ask what happened between the lot of you," he said, nodding to a skulking Sira and Lusari behind us. "Regardless, I thought I might take the opportunity to teach you some magic along the way."

I blinked, surprised. In the drama, I'd almost forgotten I was still in the beginnings of a learning curve. I hadn't told the others that Kaia had helped me use some minor degree of water magic. Maybe it would help later.

However, a few paces ahead, Will came to an abrupt halt, nearly causing me to run into him. I turned, curious, and saw a look of dread in his usually cheerful eyes, locked onto the mountains.

"What is it?" I asked him, reaching for the handle of Ragnarokkr.

He was silent for a moment. A few of the others had stopped, too. The ponies nearly trampled Loki as he stopped in the road. Katiel and Kaia both halted, Kaia's arms still swinging around Katiel's neck.

"I sense something," he murmured. "Some source of power within those mountains. Something will stand in our way." He noticed me looking at him with eyes full of questions, and he managed a very small smile. "Sensing is an acute ability for those with some modicum of power in the spirit realm. Become adept with your magic, and I am sure you will develop it soon, too." His smile faded. "Regardless, something powerful and threatening is there. I can sense it."

"Do you think it's the Diamond Dragon?" Guildford asked, looking between those who had stopped with some confusion. I noticed that Sira and Lusari both stopped, too, and hung quite near Will and I.

"Nah, there's something familiar about it," Katiel chimed in, but there was none of his usual humor in his voice. "Can't quite place it, but I've felt this before somewhere."

"I recognize it, too," Kaia said. "It is dangerous, I can tell. We're a big group, we should be fine. Right?"

"Of course," Loki agreed heartily. "You've got me with you! I'm sure it'll turn tail and run as soon as it senses *me*!"

"Maybe when it smells you," Sira muttered, and Lusari had to fight off a case of the giggles. Lusari caught my eye for a moment, but turned away. So much for pretending nothing happened.

It took a moment for everyone to calm down and keep going. Everyone pulled their cloaks from their bags as a deeper autumn chill began to set in with the landscape changes. Nearer to the mountains, even Bonnin began to turn more barren and chilly. Will said he could spot snow up on the peaks, but I was sure he just saw the rim of the clouds peeking through. Will liked to imagine early snow in all places.

After we resumed our pace, Guildford kept his word and fell back in line beside me, pulling out one of the books Relus gave him on magical theory. Will kept close, listening with some interest.

"First off is the elemental circle," he explained. "Your staff controls fire, right? Oak is apparently a strong material for fire magic."

I nodded. "I've used it a bit before, through the staff," I told him. "Only when I needed to, though. It just sorta happened."

"Do you know the relation of fire to the elemental circle?" he asked.

He had his book opened to a page with a series of symbols all connected via arrows. When I shook my head, he showed me the page. Each little symbol seemed to be an element, and all intersected with little arrows. He pointed to one symbol on the chart – a flame. Easy enough.

"There's fire," he said, and started tracing the arrows connecting it to other elements. "Consider it just as simple elements in our own world. Water puts out fire. Fire also melts ice, and can be sparked by certain concentrations of electricity. Soil – earth magic – can stifle a flame."

I started to get what he was showing me by looking at the chart. "So this is just what elements interact with each other, and how," I said, trying to simplify his terms.

"In a way," Guildford agreed. "Think of that, and relate it to the world of magic. Magic calls upon certain energies within your mind and can put them out into the world. However, since magic essentially comes from aspects of your mind, you must cast carefully. Using the wrong magic in the wrong situation can be deadly to your state of mind and to your person."

I raised a brow in surprise. "Okay, nobody told me that. Go ahead. Start from the beginning."

Therefore, Guildford explained the elemental circle. I tried my best to follow, but he presented many twists I didn't anticipate. Fire magic could melt ice, meaning ice was useful against water because it could freeze it. Water, then, could put out fire. Against water, one could utilize electricity, and earthy magic was the best choice against electric magic users. Earth magic could also put out fire, while wind magic could strengthen it. Stalwart earth magic could stand against wind.

There was a lot more implications with those choice elements, each drawn and noted in small arrows, and addressed on other pages in more detail that Guildford explained to me. Each element had some sort of effect on another depending on its usage, and the possibilities were endless. One could incite flames from a lightning strike, and wind could put out flames. Ice could be potent enough to freeze fire or infiltrate earth magic. Ice, too, was synonymous with water magic. All it would take was to freeze the water you cast, or to melt the ice you summoned. It was starting to make my head hurt, trying to remember each one and how they connected.

Then Guildford wanted me to try each element out. The way he tried to explain controlling the elements wasn't quite making sense – it involved visualizing each element with a respondent energy in my mind. When I finally got to the point of holding my staff out before me and trying to visualize fire, I felt a different response. I imagined the hearth of a fireplace, the beating sun above, the waves of heat upon the sidewalks in the dead of summer as I had done when I practiced with Kaia. It elicited a quick response. Guildford and Will leapt in joy when flames lashed out from the head of my staff.

I repeated the process with the elements one by one, as we crossed the fields of Bonnin. The further I went, the more difficult it seemed. I wasn't sure if it was because of the elements themselves, or my distraction due to the world around us. Seeing the animated plains of Bonnin, the ominous mountains, the trees dotting the landscape, and everything that popped up around us might be a once-in-a-lifetime experience.

When Guildford saw me getting distracted, he alleviated my studies a little and walked with the others for a short time. I landed beside Loki, who seemed prone to questioning me at all times. Now he asked about the names of my fellow Defenders.

"Why does your name differ from theirs?" he asked me with a barely perceptible glint in his eye. "The names don't sound like you hail from the same place. Ryoku? Katiel? Then Annalia, Dawn, Joey? Dagger, even? Are they from different places?"

I couldn't answer that. I'd come from a town not far from where I currently lived. I was born in Petalburg, but I often called

Brooks my home now. The difference between the two was only a few hours' drive, both in the same province. Anna and Dawn were both from Brooks, and Katiel was from the big city a few more miles north – Baleton. I wasn't sure about Joey. Obviously, Dagger was born in Brooks, too, as well as Varis. Over all, I tried not to think about the matter too much.

We started nearing the base of the mountains around noon and only because we set out quite early. Trekking through the mountains themselves would take a few hours. We started our way up the mountain, keeping close together for both support and warmth. Guildford and Will stayed with for much of the hike. Rex and Artos had difficulty with the horses at the onset of the path, so Loki, Katiel, and Sira helped push the wagon and alleviate the weight from the horses. Kaia and Lusari walked together, immersed in some kind of topic.

We took our first break after an hour of hiking uphill. Our campsite was a vantage spot at a small plateau a few miles up. Some sparse forest surrounded a pond fed by an icy mountain stream. Cliffs still soared far above our heads, and Loki told us that the territory marked on his map belonging to the dragon was still quite high up. We dared not break for too long; else, darkness might fall before we reached Niin.

I helped Will start a fire for warmth, and ate dried bread and fruits from our bags while we rested our legs. Guildford and Rex fed the horses. Will and I refilled our tankards with icy spring water, using the tips he showed me back in Harohto to ensure the water was safe to drink. Afterward, I kept to myself while we sat, running through everything Guildford taught me in my head. It was the most anybody had taught me yet, and I didn't want to mess it up in action. Especially, of course, since Guildford told me the possible costs of it.

When the others weren't looking, I practiced using the elements without my staff. It took time to muster. Using them earlier, I'd gotten used to the aid of my staff and found the response slow in my fingertips. Fire came out less potent without the aid of the gems, but it worked. By the time I cycled through each of those elements, I felt pins and needles in my hands.

I stayed close to Will when we started up again. He gave me helpful tips in the upward climb, such as how to pace my breathing and how to walk without hurting my legs so badly. It was different than hiking through the Old Forest. These hills were sparser, and I found a certain lack of oxygen in the air at higher altitudes. Despite having a heavier bag, Will never seemed to run short of breath. With or without his instruction, my chest still burned like I'd swallowed my practice flame.

Over an hour later, Loki stopped us at a point where we crested a hill overlooking much of the path we'd taken uphill, cut short by a stream that led down to our break spring.

"Guardians of Ryoku," he declared, his map furled up in his hand, "protect our Defender at all costs. We don't know the strength of the entity we're approaching, but our cost for learning its strength won't be his life. If the odds aren't in our favor, protect him. Surround him. If he gets tired, carry him. If he gets hurt, expend nothing less than your *last breath*, if he should require it, to ensure he survives."

I thought he was being dramatic and ridiculous, but my company didn't seem to think so. Will went rigid as a stone and nodded with the confidence of a hero. Even Sira and Lusari threw aside their abhorrent expressions and nodded like soldiers.

Rex gave me a furtive nod. "I told you that I would help you in any way I can. Whatever I can do for you now, merely say the word. Treat me no different than those who have sworn their lives to you."

"The same goes for me," Guildford agreed. I'd never seen my teacher look so serious, either. "I'll get you through this. I may be a new spirit, but I have grown stronger than I ever was in life. I'll do anything I can to protect you, my old student."

"You got us, too," Katiel chimed in, gesturing to himself, Artos, and Kaia. "We ain't no pushovers, either. When push comes to shove, I'll show you what I can do."

"While I am curious," Loki drawled, "I'm sure your abilities won't be necessary." He jabbed his chest with his thumb. "I'm the Trickster god, and my full power is devoted to protecting my charge. Unless the emperor of Orden himself was to climb out from those bushes, I severely doubt anything stronger will be necessary."

I stared at the Trickster, bemused and unsure if these were mere vows of protections or of marriage. That wasn't all, though – a quiet cough echoed from behind me, and I turned to face Lusari, her hands clasped before her.

"I swore to be your Guardian last night," she said softly. "I'll hold to that vow. I won't break that promise. Whatever you need, I am here."

I felt sore from her words. I wasn't sure if she was speaking with any malevolence at all, but I could imagine daggers behind her sweet voice. Even now, I had to admit I would have loved to repeat the events of last night. My friendship with Will would see to it that such a thing never happened again.

Then, to my other side, I heard a heavy sigh. I didn't even have time to turn before an arm stuck itself around me. Her scent was unmistakable as she pulled me against her side – Sira. She glanced down at me like I was about to say something annoying, but she didn't utter a word. I thought it looked like she stared pointedly into my right eye, but maybe that was some sort of Sira coping method. There was no way to tell with her.

When I turned back, Lusari fell in beside Will, who looked gratified. I felt a weight lifted from my chest. Was everything back to normal?

Loki witnessed the silent play of emotions, and he hid his smirk behind a flamboyant hand and a quick turn away.

"I'm ready," I told him expectantly. "Let's keep going."

My friends kept surprisingly wary. It was true that we'd encountered a few hairy situations up until now, like Jesanht, the Ritual cult, and especially Geri. Still, their worry didn't seem to shake.

It seemed stronger than ever as we resumed our pace up the mountain. Will and Sira kept on either side of me just like the days back in the Old Forest. Guildford and Katiel swapped out to guide the horses and the wagon up the hill, while Artos and Rex pushed from behind. Even Will wouldn't keep a proper conversation with me while we walked.

While Sira still deliberately stared at anything but me, I caught the occasional glance from Kaia as she walked alongside the wagon. The pretty auburn-haired girl smiled at me. When I returned her smile, I caught a glimpse of something behind her. A little red figure stood near a boulder. I wouldn't have noticed it if I didn't look at Kaia, since the figure didn't move a muscle until I looked at it. It looked like a small human, but with horns and bright red skin. Then it grinned, baring rows of fangs, and vanished.

"Watch out!"

Will pushed me practically to the ground as he dove over me. A red flash briefly illuminated my vision, accompanied by the sound of something sizzling. Sira caught me around the shoulders and steadied me. Will struggled to rise to his feet. The back of his armor was warped somehow, the scales blackened. A shrill cackle came from nearby.

I saw the little monster jump into the air. A jettison of icicles from Lusari's staff struck the earth where it had been. When it lunged, Rex swung and grabbed the little thing by the ankle, sending it wailing to the earth with a crash. It was hardly the size of Rex's torso, a gangly and thin little creature with horns and a spiked tail.

Despite how small the creature seemed, Sira pivoted around me and brought the mighty blade Sinistra screaming down upon it. I flinched away at the last second. I heard its pitiful scream ignite the air like a siren. Artos tightened the wrap on his head around his ears, and Loki dutifully covered his own as though the dying noise of the creature were a mere annoyance.

When I looked back, there was nothing remaining of the little creature – just a scar in the earth where Sinistra struck, though it seemed blackened with ash. Sira helped Will up with one hand. Guildford and Katiel fought to steady the horses, and Rex practically lifted the wagon with his one arm to alleviate the pressure. Loki was running to me like I'd just fallen from the mountain.

"Are you alright?" he demanded, and started scanning me for injures.

"I'm fine," I replied, unable to keep a bit of spite out of my tone. "What was that little creature?"

"An imp," Will told me. He was brushing Sira away, but he eyed the marred part of his armor mournfully. "Nasty little creatures. They are skilled wielders of fire, but little else."

"And they should not be in these realms," Loki added with distaste. "I'd thought most demons remained in the old worlds. These new ones shouldn't be able to sustain their ilk. Nobody's seen an imp in months."

"Who cares," Sira muttered. She sheathed Sinistra over her back and dutifully returned to my side. "They're nothing. Mere pests."

I still wondered if it was worth killing such a small creature. It technically hadn't hurt any of us. How long had it sat there until I saw it?

Once the horses were calmed down, we resumed our pace. Nobody was very talkative after the little encounter, keeping their eyes on the sides of the road. Only Kaia seemed light-hearted still. While the soldiers marched up the hill, she would make funny faces at me from down the path, or conjure bubbles from her flask to flutter around the others like butterflies. Even Will and Katiel, who I could normally count on to lighten a situation, hardly flashed a smile at the sight of the bubbles.

She helped the journey seem shorter, and it felt like minutes when we crested the hill we'd been climbing, leading to another semi-flat zone. Mountains still soared around us on all sides, but I could make out the path ahead of us that seemed to dip down after. The stream we mostly followed up here ran through the rocky outcroppings and from a mountain further to the west.

Will nudged me. When I looked at him, he nodded toward something near the river. It looked like another large outcropping, but something about it caught the light of the passing sun.

"You don't think...?" I whispered, suddenly realizing the need to be quiet. Will nodded. That was when I saw part of it flit.

Katiel hopped off his horse, handing the reins off to Artos. Once Guildford realized what he was doing, he vaulted from the other horse in a surprisingly expert maneuver, landing lightly on his heels. Keeping as quiet as possible, the dark-clothed Artos leaned close to the horses, whispering to them as he led them away.

"There it is!" Loki cried, abruptly breaking what I thought was a purposeful silence.

As soon as he shouted, the structure rumbled, and two great wings shot out on either side. The dazzling effect against the sun cast a spray of harsh light over us, stinging my eyes and forcing me to shield them. When I lifted my head, the structure was gone.

"Loki, you..." Guildford started, but he stopped when the sky suddenly darkened. The air quickly rang with the sound of drawn steel as everyone prepared themselves.

The shape that soared overhead was as I imagined dragons to be, just as mythology often described a typical European dragon:

a lizard-like body with two great, bat-like wings, four strong limbs, and a long, spiny tail that dragged behind it in the sky. With a shrill, wailing noise, the dragon came crashing down right in front of us. The impact shook the earth so roughly; I thought our long climb might be for naught as the mountain itself might give.

The dragon was the most beautiful creature I'd ever seen. Its scales seemed to either be made of diamonds or a very similar makeup. It perched on four legs before us like a guard dog, its long, spiny tail flitting behind it. Its mighty wings flapped with such force that everyone fought to stay afoot. Overall, it was probably twice Sira's height, as wide across as two of our wagons, and about as long as four of them. It's great, crystal-laden jaw could swallow up one of our horses in a gulp, let alone any of us.

Its catlike eyes left me transfixed. Situated on either side of a singular ruby embedded above its snout, the dragon's eyes seemed to shine with every color that reflected from its diamond texture. Besides its smooth face, its body was laden with full, jagged diamonds that seemed to stick in one direction like the fur on an animal.

Sira pushed me back to join Will and Loki ahead of me. Katiel didn't draw a weapon, but he pushed his sleeves up like it was a chore.

"What is it?" a female voice broke through the air. The voice struck me in an odd way, like it cut through the texture of Bonnin and spoke to me through both worlds. It sounded exquisite, defined, and full of purpose. I knew it belonged to the dragon.

"We are here to stop you," Loki replied loud and clear. He used his silver tongue in its full splendor, but it somehow sounded pallid with the voice of the dragon. "You've preyed on many a traveler through these mountains. I'd say your time is up."

I couldn't take my eyes off the dragon. She remained silent in the face of Loki's drawn sword, unmoving. "Very well," she spoke softly, a forked tongue flitting from her diamond-studded snout. Her stance evaporated into a new one – ready to pounce. "I must warn you, Trickster. I am not one to lay down and die."

That was all the warning she gave. She lunged. Her claws struck Loki with such force that dirt and stone sprayed in an arc behind him. He managed to keep his footing, throwing all his weight into the counter to dissuade her attack. She backed away, then slithered back to dodge a lunge from Will's lance. Sira followed a breath later, Sinistra arcing through the air. The dragon repented like a snake, then lashed out again in Sinistra's wake at Sira's exposed side. Will stepped in the way, blocking the strike with the length of his lance, and pushed back mightily. The dragon let out a fierce roar, staggering back for only a moment before regaining her balance. Even in the heat of battle, she looked glorious.

"What a mighty foe," Guildford murmured. He had both hands open before him, and I was sure the energy radiating from them was his own magic. Lusari was doing something similar with her staff. "Such an extraordinary beast. To harm her brings me nothing but distress."

"It'll protect the people coming through these mountains, though," Katiel said, but sighed heavily.

Loki, Will, and Sira kept on the front lines against the dragon while Guildford, Lusari, Kaia, and Katiel held back to charge their magic. Rex stayed near, ready to step in if one of them got hurt. I wasn't sure what to do. My eyes darted between everyone anxiously. I felt like I was waiting for something, but I wasn't sure what.

While the three fighters traded blows with the mighty dragon, I found what I was looking for. When the dragon skirted around Sira's blazing sword, her eyes flashed to something behind her.

There. Right behind where she had been resting before Loki blew our cover. It was far away and difficult to make out by the riverside, but I caught the glint of diamonds just behind an outcropping of regular old rock.

I had no doubt left in my mind. The reason the Diamond Dragon attacked passerby in the mountains, not allowing any to pass through to the village of Niin. Her egg.

Everything ran in slow motion. I saw Loki, Will, and Sira rear back their weapons in deadly unison. Rex drew near as he readied to strike. Lusari levelled her fully charged staff forward. Katiel, Kaia, and Guildford raised their hands, and the energy glared around them like lampposts in the day.

Surely even the glory of this mighty dragon would fall before their combined might. Who could stand against my friends and live to tell the tale?

I knew what I had to do.

My feet worked before I understood why. I moved fast, my footfalls hardly kicking up dust on the rocky outcropping of the mountain. Wind rushed past my face like it fought my choices, but I knew it'd be worth it.

I heard magic roar to life behind me. The whoosh of livid fire, the crackling of ice, the rushing of water. Then I was darting past Rex, whose eyes flashed in confusion when he saw me lurch by.

I landed before the diamond dragon, my back to her. Ragnarokkr hung heavy in my hands, the chain wrapped tightly around my fingers. I couldn't recall drawing it, but there it was, humming with tense energy just like that which resonated through my body. I had no way of knowing the dragon wouldn't just strike my exposed back. I was putting myself to the test.

Before I knew it, I was face-to-face with Loki. I saw his eyes flicker in abrupt surprise, but not quickly enough to stay his blade. His brilliant sword struck Ragnarokkr with unforetold might. Golden sparks rained down on me. When I pushed back, I was sure I only thwarted the Trickster's footing by sheer element of surprise. I didn't have time to test my mettle against his sword – I would surely lose in a true contest, and he was only the first.

Time seemed to trickle like water. I saw each movement as a droplet, and I knew what pebbles I could throw in to stay them. Will's lance drove through the air like a train. I caught it with the edge of Ragnarokkr. The force threatened to tear my arm off. The pull on the chains was like an earthquake ripping at my body. Only then did I see the confusion shimmer in his eyes, like he only just realized I was there. I managed to divert his attack.

Then I threw my blade up in time to meet mighty Sinistra in the air. It was like poking a boulder hard enough to break my finger. Every bone in my body rattled. I swore I lost an inch of height just from the impact. It took a tricky maneuver to tilt my blade without losing either the weapon or my life, diverting her attack to tilt away and slam into the earth.

I had only an instant to tilt my blade down and prepare for the next impact. What came was an unworldly force. Without preparation, even Sira's impact would have floored me. Now, I wasn't sure if the blade could hold as a maelstrom of the elements slammed into it.

I couldn't see. A mix of mist and steam throttled the air around me like a smoke bomb. The blade flashed hot and cold like a fever. My arms quaked, and the chains of Ragnarokkr turned hot from Katiel and Guildford's combined flames.

My mind raced frantically. Rex was the only one who didn't strike, but he stood back, transfixed by the elements throttling me. All my other friends were on the ground or unable to help. What could they do, anyway? I was rooted to the spot. I couldn't move if I wanted to.

A force appeared at my back – the dragon's head. I knew that I hadn't made a mistake. Her head kept me grounded, inspiring me to keep defending her. If I stopped, we would both surely die.

A strange sensation began to appear in my hands. When I looked to them, certain they would burn, I saw a shimmering aura appear around them. Before I could comprehend it, a flurry of images ran through my head. A searing desert. A frozen lake. A stream of sunlight in a dusty library. Lightning snaking through the sky. A single sapling bursting through the frosty earth.

More followed, so quickly that I couldn't properly absorb them all, until everything around me seemed to fade and the images came to a sudden halt.

Then, like a train thrown from its tracks, everything culminated before me. Each image burst into a living thing, and all weaved into a glimmering golden wall before me. The weight dropped from the head of Ragnarokkr suddenly, and I nearly fell to the ground with relief. Only the dragon's head on my back stopped me. In the shimmering wall, I saw all the images that flashed through my head, all playing like memories in the mirage.

. Ragnarokkr fell from my hands, clattering to the rocky ground below. The last thing I remembered seeing was the shimmering golden wall of energy. I felt the dragon's teeth clamp onto my shirt, and she gently lowered me down.

"Don't hurt her," I was whispering. "She... her egg... let her go."

More hands appeared to help me. "Her egg?" Loki whispered, dumbfounded. Then, a last, clairvoyant voice took over, filtering the rest of the world out.

Thank you. Your friends are safe. My young one and I will leave this world. I will find you again, and I will repay what you have done for me. My name... is Sapphense.

SCENE SIX: ROLAND DEMIZEN

...Of Act Five: Bright Manifest

In the eyes of Ryoku Dragontalen, we are in Niin, in the world of Bonnin. It is late afternoon On November 11th, 2017.

"He's waking up!"
    I groaned at the first instance of daylight trying to break through. Kaia's voice kept me from trying to let slumber take over. My eyes fluttered open, and everything through my normal eye looked like fog. I saw Kaia's pretty face briefly, before it split apart into several thousand, and my head lolled to the side, shuddering with a severe migraine. My eyes willed themselves shut again. A rougher hand appeared to steady me, and the warmth on the back of my neck made me feel sick. I started to realize the pain coursing through my body, and groaned.
    "Eckhardt, have you finished that tonic?"
    Even in such a state, I could always recognize Katiel's voice – I had gone through this before.
    "Almost," a light male voice with a sophisticated accent replied. "Just a few more touches, and a dash of healing magic." I heard him sigh. "You're lucky I've been stationed here. This particular tonic is rare. Not many know how to heal such a thing."

"I know that," Katiel replied, sounding a little annoyed. When he spoke again, though, the tension lessened. "Thank you, Eckhardt. I... couldn't handle losing another friend."

"He wouldn't die," Kaia insisted. "Well, I don't think so, anyway. He just channelled a *lot* of magic, but he had the energy to provide. Didn't I tell you how easily he used water?"

Katiel sighed in relief. "Of course. He is a Remnant of *him*, after all. A gift in the field of magic makes sense. Although, this might even be a little stronger. And that barrier he used..." He fell silent for a moment, and then tilted my head with his hand. "Oh, you're still awake. That's an improvement in itself."

"What..." I tried to speak, but a soft finger on my lips hushed me.

"I said you wouldn't die, but that can change really fast," Kaia chastised. "Not another peep until you drink Eckhardt's tonic. I told you that you're my little brother now. You're not getting out of that."

Katiel laughed. "Trust me, she's right," he told me. "She'll drag you back from the River Styx if she has to. After all..."

He sounded like he meant to reference something, but he fell silent again. Finally, he said, "Alright, looks finished. Let's add the final touch."

Unable to see, I heard a faint bubbling noise, followed by a sound that made me think of twinkling stars. A moment later, something appeared at my lips. I smelled blueberries. "Drink," the newer voice told me gently. "You'll feel much better."

I had no choice but to obey. The mixture that went down my throat was thick and tasted sweet. As it went down my throat, it carried warmth that spread through my body like wildfire. I thought I would be sick for a moment – but it passed quickly, and my eyelids fluttered open.

The migraine that felt ready to split my head apart moments ago vanished. My skin felt alive and flushed, my limbs quickly regaining feeling. Delighted, I sat upright in bed. I half-expected to fall back immediately, but I didn't. Kaia, Katiel, Artos, and a newcomer all gathered around the bed and smiling at me, relieved.

The newcomer was a brown-haired young man with about the same build as Will, his face dabbled in freckles. He dressed in a simple shirt and pants, but a gallant sword lay across his lap. Behind him was a display of full white armor that looked too large to be practical. We appeared to be in some cottage with a small fire blazing in the furnace behind Katiel.

"Welcome back," Katiel told me with a chuckle. "I have to admit, you scared the hell out of me. Jumping in front of us like that! You could have..."

"Quite easily," Artos added with a wry smile. "Even I wasn't fast enough to get to you in time. In a matter of seconds, you shrugged off everyone's attacks. Never seen anything like it."

"How did you get so fast?" Katiel asked me. "I swear you were hanging pretty far back, but then you got between us without alerting any of us. Did you use magic?"

I shook my head, far too pleased with how good I felt to take the conversation seriously. "No, I just ran," I said simply. "Where's everyone else?"

On immediate cue, the door to the room shot open. "You *idiot!*" was the first thing I heard. Sira made to charge in, but several pairs of arms caught her and held her back.

"Sira, you mustn't hurt our Defender again!" Loki protested angrily. "He's still recovering!"

"Actually, he should be fine," Kaia chirped.

"Oh, well in that case..." Loki let Sira go. I sprang out of bed and she slammed into me like a train. Sira's crimson eyes glared down at me more intensely than the fire I'd just fought off, her hands pinning me against the wall – at least that meant her sword wasn't on hand.

"Do not act irrationally..." Will pleaded, stepping into the room like the floor was made of upright shards of glass.

"*Irrationally?*" Sira screeched. "*Irrationally.* You mean like jumping in front of a full-on assault aimed at a dragon *without telling anyone?*"

She didn't avert her gaze, and I held it. I knew I had done what I needed to.

"Perhaps," Will reasoned, "but our Defender does have need of all his appendages. Surely what you said in the capital was out of anger, Sira. This is your chance to speak truly."

He spoke knowingly. I realized he must have actually talked to her about it.

"*All* his appendages?" Sira asked, glaring down at me. Very deliberately, she lowered her gaze between my legs.

"All of them," Loki said quickly, and winked at me.

The room hung in pained suspense. I didn't break away from Sira. I couldn't even if I wanted to, since she had my shoulders pinned against the wall. Whatever it was that Katiel's friend Eckhardt made for me, it made vigor swim through my veins unlike anything I'd ever felt before. Without it, I wasn't sure I could look Sira in the eye for so long knowing how mad she was.

What happened next took me completely by shock – she slammed me back against the wall and kissed me. She pulled away quickly, but she kept a gentler hold on me than she had before. The room fell silent around us. I briefly saw Lusari, Rex, and Guildford clustered around the doorway, too. Guildford raised a brow at me.

"Don't do something that dumb again," Sira told me in a low voice, and let me go. I felt like my shoulder would hurt in any other situation, but I felt fine, holding her gaze levelly.

"She had to protect her child," I said guardedly. "I saw her egg behind where she'd been when we got there. Afterward, she told me she was going to leave and take her child with her. You guys heard that, right? So you know I did the right thing."

Loki and Will exchanged confused glances. Sira let go of me, but her angry aura still kept me against the wall. "She spoke to you?" Katiel asked.

"It makes sense," Kaia said, rolling her eyes. "He's a Dragontalen, right?"

Will's confusion cleared right up. "You are absolutely right, Kaia. It does make sense."

"What are you talking about?" I asked, irritated. "Of course she spoke to me, Katiel. But... what does that have to do with my name?"

"Quite a lot, I imagine," Loki said. He took a seat on the bed. He looked oddly weary. "She spoke to us before we challenged her, yes. After you defended her, she flew back to her nest and watched us as we picked you up and took you here on the wagon. Lusari said she saw the dragon fly overhead during our hasty retreat. She... did not speak another word to us. Though I suppose she did let us go because of you."

I contemplated his words. They hadn't heard her, clearly. They hadn't known about her egg and that she was fighting us for a reason.

"There was some rumor about that," Katiel's brown-haired friend admitted. "Our last travelers claimed a few different things.

Way back, they said there was a second dragon that roamed through these mountains. Now, as of late, there was rumor she had an egg. Only one person out of a guard team claimed such, though, so it was quite easily dismissed." He looked at me, and smiled apologetically. "My apologies – I never introduced myself. I am Eckhardt Bright, a paladin and close friend to Katiel."

I carefully sidestepped around Sira to shake Eckhardt's hand – she let me, but followed me like a shadow. "So you are Eckhardt. A pleasure," I told him. "I'm Ryoku Dragontalen. Defender." I shook his hand, and found his grip well calloused and rough. Clearly the armor behind him wasn't just for show. Eckhardt was a warrior, and not a lazy one. I was getting the impression of a good man who knew how to work hard.

"The pleasure's all mine," Eckhardt told me, and I thought I saw familiarity in his light eyes. "I'm glad my tonic worked well for you. It's an old and uncommon recipe, but it works."

"It sure does," I agreed heartily. I turned, and noticed I had the attention of the room. The thought occurred to me. "What are we doing next? Have we delivered the supplies? Is it back to the capital now?"

"We brought the supplies to the village square," Guildford told me. "They were well received. The people here have been low on stock for quite some time."

"And we reported our success to the Registry already," Rex added. "The mayor of Niin saw to our reward. The next while should see us a little better suited for our expenses."

"We can depart from Bonnin whenever you wish," Loki said.

"Depart already?" I asked, a little surprised. If I had only been asleep for a night, then that made our stay only two days long. Harohto and Lysvid both turned into elongated stays.

"Niin doesn't have anything worth doing," Sira didn't seem too enthralled as she spoke. "Unless you fancy rounding up pigs or picking apples in the orchard, we're left hanging here."

Eckhardt raised a finger. "You *are* welcome to stay at this cottage I've rented out for however long you please," he said kindly. "However, I'm sure you agree with Sira. For a fledgling Defender looking to become stronger, there is little of value in this town. The capital is a day's trek, but staying at the inns would dry up your funds quickly. You... do travel with a relatively large group."

I sighed. He did have a point. I glanced out the window absently. The bright blue sky took up everything but the mountaintops we'd just descended from, giving the air a wide and open feel despite the strange grinning sun in the corner. Near the base of the mountains, I saw trees that looked rich in bright red apples – the orchards Sira had mentioned. Between us and the orchard, an abstract boulder sat in the middle of the clearing, where a group of neighboring children were at play.

"Let's go out and enjoy the town for the day," I suggested. "We'll depart closer to night. I feel like I have boundless energy. Wherever we may go next, who knows how it will be? We could land back in Lysvid, for all I know."

"I should hope not," Loki said bitterly, "but I admire your energy. It's never a bad thing to explore these many worlds in our realms. There are myriads of them, and this is quite the little nook in Bonnin."

"There are that many worlds out there?" I asked wondrously. I gazed up the bright blue sky, like I might see some in the distance like stars in the daylight.

"Thousands," Loki professed, like he had made them himself. "Millions, even. We cannot keep track of them all."

"They differ in size quite a lot," Katiel said. To explain, he picked up an apple and a small bead. "Bonnin is something closer to the bead, I think. I've been here for a bit. There's the Capital, the mountains, a lake, and only about four or five towns all around. There's no ocean. It just sort of... loops around. If you kept walking past Niin through the rest of the mountains and forest, you would wind back up at the Capital."

That surprised me. "That's possible here?" I asked. "Doesn't anyone wonder why?"

Katiel shrugged. "Doesn't our world just wrap around? Nobody asks about that."

"But it's so small," I murmured, but I had to admit his point. To some, maybe Earth was small.

"Lysvid is quite large, in comparison," Rex said, pointing to the apple. "I haven't seen it all, but the Timeless One and I, with the other assistants, traveled quite a bit. Cleria travels a lot as well."

"Was that before I arrived?" Guildford asked curiously. Rex gave him a look, and I was almost sure I missed something there.

"Well, Lysvid *is* the vampire world," Loki said. He pulled himself off the bed with some difficulty. "There's not many worlds filled all with one race. It's even perpetually night so they can thrive. Many worlds have a... quirk, of sorts, to them. Like Lysvid, clearly."

I listened with interest. In turn, everyone started explaining something about different worlds. Orden and Syaoto were gigantic, apparently, so it took a large Capital to keep the world together as a whole. Each had several cities, big and small, with various landmarks of all sorts. Syaoto was a range of few forests and rolling plains, stretching out in all directions to include things such as jungles, catacombs, enormous temples, and even tundra further north. Their quirk, as Loki called it, was a demonic problem; the entities roamed the outside plains at night in large flocks. Will frantically assured me that it was completely manageable, and that the demons never attacked the cities.

In comparison, Orden was a medieval world filled with gothic structures, enormous cities, and landscapes such as dense rainforests and expanses of desert. According to Sira, the storms that Orden experienced were of an intensity no world could truly rival. They constructed buildings especially to withstand lightning and torrential rains. She almost professed it like it was a competition.

As immersed by the topic as I was, I felt antsy. I paced around the room, tapping my heels, examining the paintings on the wall of the living room, watching the flames in the fireplace. The cottage Eckhardt lived in only had one bedroom and a cot in the living room, but was well decorated. A painting of a long dragon hung on the wall over the mantle. Different suits of armor littered the place, all with a theme of white.

Sira got to her feet eventually and turned straight to me. "You want to check out this boring-ass town? Let's go. Better than sitting here talking about where we might go."

Rex pushed himself from the wall and nodded. "I'll join you, if you don't mind."

Loki, Katiel and Kaia ended up coming, too. The others remained at Eckhardt's with the promise of lunch. I felt hungry, but more anxious than anything. I had enough gold to stop by the markets if I wanted.

Outside Eckhardt's home was pretty. Autumn leaves plucked up from the ground in a light breeze to flutter across our view like dusky rose petals. A well-traveled trail led the way from Eckhardt's cottage in the woods to the actual village, atop a small hill past the trees.

The walk through the woods was quick, but scenic. Small animals scurried across the path, from rabbits to squirrels. A large hare paused in the middle of the path to study us with interest. Some deer sipped from a narrow stream nearby, culminating in a pond riddled with the ambience of frogs.

At the village of Niin, a fruitful market ran along the main street. Vendors hollered out their sales, mostly consisting of apples and other local commodities. One shopkeeper sold stones he claimed to have mined from the diamond dragon herself. One look at those, and I knew it was a lie.

There wasn't much to do here, like the others said. Kaia played with her water magic for the children of the town while the rest of us watched in amusement. Sira checked out a meager armory stall and returned scowling. Loki went to visit a nearby clothing store. I bought a few apples from the orchard. Rex and Katiel stayed with me as I took more interest in the world around us.

"It's a pretty place," I said absently, leaning on a fence overlooking the forest. I could see Eckhardt's cottage from there. The children playing on the rocks were like ants. "Simplistic. Calm. Not much seems to happen here. I'm not sure when we'll see more of this."

"It's not as uncommon as you think," Katiel said lightly. "This *is*, theoretically, the afterlife. After living in our world, some people go on to live peacefully for the rest of their days."

Rex scoffed under his breath. "Or in hell," he muttered. I turned to him, surprised, but he made no indication he was willing to elaborate. Just then, Loki popped up behind him, absolutely beaming.

"Ryoku, you'll never believe what I found!" he exclaimed giddily, holding something behind his back. "It was such a good piece in the market, and, well, I thought it suits you quite well!"

He produced an article of clothing from behind his back: a white sweater with red stripes down the sleeves that pointed inward to the chest. It had a relatively large hood and folded sleeves. He approached and stuffed it in my hands. "You must try it on!" he insisted.

"That's an interesting style," Katiel commented as I slipped into the sleeves. "Not usually of Bonnin craft, is it?"

Loki smirked and winked. "Of course! It's quite a lucky find, right?"

I turned around in the sweater. It was lightweight, but fit me perfectly. Even the arms, though narrowly cut, fit my body somehow. "It's incredible," I admitted, a little surprised. "Thank you, Loki."

The Trickster actually blushed. "Not at all, my boy. It was simply—"

Suddenly, the Trickster turned bolt upright, his hand stopping mid-air. Katiel and Kaia both pivoted in the same direction – facing back toward Eckhardt's home. I exchanged nervous glances with Rex.

"What's going on?" I asked cautiously.

Loki didn't move, but his emerald gaze had fixated on the cottage. "Something approaches. I…"

"The same thing we sensed before." Kaia left her puddle of water and turned questioningly to Katiel. "You don't think…?"

Katiel sighed in a huff. "Of course. This close up, there's no mistaking it. It's—"

A sudden gale roared to life in the marketplace, nearly wrenching the lot of us off our feet. Loki grabbed onto me and held me fast, emerald-colored energy like fire pulsating around his feet. Katiel and Kaia clung to one another. Only Rex seemed to have no trouble standing. Screams erupted around us as chaos enveloped the Niin markets. I saw Sira clutching a child that nearly sailed off into the wind, then hurriedly handing them off to a grateful father before running through the violent winds to us.

"What the hell is this?" she demanded, looking at Loki for the answer. The Trickster had none, focused on keeping me grounded.

"Another of his damned inventions," Katiel muttered spitefully. When we turned to him, he focused elsewhere, staring across the field at the cabin where Eckhardt lived. "This ain't targeting us. Not now. We gotta get back to the cabin before—"

A particularly violent gust drowned him out as it wrought through the markets, tearing signs from the ground and forcing us to group together to stay on the ground.

"Whatever we gotta do, let's do it fast!" Loki cried. "People will get hurt here!"

I heard a set of children's screams. The sound seemed to carry over the wind somehow until it reached my ears, turning my attention to the cabin. I realized quickly what I was hearing: those children sitting upon the boulders near the cliffs. I could see them from where we stood. Three of them struggled to hold on while they clasped the hands of a little girl, her legs flailing in the air as the wind threatened to drag her off. If we didn't get to them soon...

My mind tumbled like clockwork. A jumbled idea came to my mind as I saw Rex, the only one with enough weight to stay standing since he had vampiric and werewolf blood. Perhaps Loki would have been a sound idea, or even Sira could have helped me somehow. Katiel and Kaia might have been able to work with me if I stopped to discuss it, but I needed to act fast. Somehow, by the way Rex's head turned where nobody else's did, I knew he heard the children. Guildford had mentioned his accelerated senses.

"Rex!" I cried, and wrenched myself from Loki's grasp. Immediately my feet lifted from the ground – I was far too light to gamble with the winds like this. Still, I could feel its current, and it would get me where I needed to go. I just needed something to keep me from missing my target. "Grab on!"

I wasn't sure what led the surprised half-breed into obeying, but he did without question, clearing the gap between us and kicking off the ground. Images flashed through my mind at a second's response – the wind, a sail blowing in the gust, picking up waves off the ocean. Before I knew it, he caught my leg, the two of us sailed into the wind with ease, hurtling across the forest between us and the cabin like Rex clutched a kite, not a human being. With the aid of my novice magic, strengthened by my resolve, it somehow worked. He knew where I was going right away.

We sailed over the trees, and it took all my strength not to look down and begin to fear my choices. The roaring winds from the attack worked in our favor, and we zipped across the open air toward our destination – that large boulder where the kids were.

As we closed in, Rex swung his weight around until we pivoted downward sharply. He landed first, landing on both feet, and halted my descent before gravity could crush me. I rolled with my landing and quickly lunged across the stone. My hands found those of the three boys just as the wind ripped them from the boulder and into the air. They all screamed in panic. I kept their hands and dug my feet into stone-made footholds. Luckily, all three still had a grip on the girl, who hung in the air like a flag.

"Hold on!" I cried. The combined weight of all of them dragged me against the rocks, scraping my skin as I struggled to hold them. Rex stumbled behind me, having more trouble finding pair footing. Without his help for the moment, an idea caught in my mind as I saw the glint of Ragnarokkr on my back. I couldn't possibly reach the blade with the kids holding onto my arms, but I had a different idea.

Using the same visions of wind as my aid, I channelled them to drag the chain of the blade out from around Ragnarokkr's hilt. The images burnt into my head like tattoos. It took more precision than I thought to direct my magic in such a way, but it worked. The chain rattled as it freed itself over my shoulder, lashing out with the wind toward the boys. I quickly pivoted to the side to avoid hitting them with force. The drive of my magic felt like a hammer crashing into my chest, and it nearly knocked me from my footholds on the rock.

"Grab on!" I cried. The boys, seeing my abstract idea, struggled to grab onto both the chain and me. One of them released my hand, so I got a grip on the chain and urged it out with as much length as I could use. The weight of the wind forced Ragnarokkr into my shoulder. All three boys had a hold on the chain, but they were struggling to get the girl to grip on it. She was probably scared out of her wits from being completely out in open air. If she couldn't grab on, dropping from this distance would surely kill her.

Before they could rope her in, another blast of winds struck us. The girl let out a strangled cry as the boys lost their grips on her, and she flew into the winds. Cursing everything I knew, I rammed Ragnarokkr's blade between the rocks and kicked off with a frantic leap.

I flew past the three boys with unpredented velocity toward the girl, hand outstretched. My hand flailed through the air, grasped – and caught onto hers. I grinned triumphantly as I clasped her hand firmly. She held on, and brought her other hand around to grab my wrist.

The gravity of the situation hit me. I quickly grabbed onto her and pivoted around, aiming to take the impact of a landing fully upon myself. If I mustered up some quick magic, I could cushion my landing.

The sound of steel on rock ruined my plan. Ragnarokkr jarred loose from the rocks, throwing a drawn steel weapon and three children into open sky. The concerned noise I let out in surprise probably didn't make me look like much of a hero.

Thinking fast, I pivoted again to throw out one of my arms. Three frantic pairs of hands latched onto me tightly enough to bruise. Combined with the gale, it threw all of us in a dizzying spiral. Four sets of screams rang in my ears as I struggled to regain control and somehow work this out. All I could see was the four kids, scared out of their minds, and a rapidly spinning earth-to-sky ratio as a blur.

A dark shape shot out from the rocks. It came at us with unprecented speed, and a strong hand grabbed onto my ankle. I saw a hand grab onto Ragnarokkr as it came through the air along with them. Before I could comprehend it, the force yanked the lot of us down with the ease of plucking a ripe apple from a tree.

My heart was in my chest as we hit the ground. Ragnarokkr landed first, and me with it. The four kids landed on top of me, each knocking the wind from my lungs.

I only recognized Rex as our savior when the world stopped harshly spinning. He had a grip on each of us, keeping us pinned to the ground as wind still screamed overhead. Ragnarokkr pierced the ground a few feet away.

Moments later, the wind died off, leaving the disheveled, gasping lot of us on the ground to catch our breath. The energy given to me by Eckhardt's tonic dwindled fast. My chest burned as I struggled to breathe.

"Thank you!" the four children chorused, catching their breaths much faster than I did. They addressed me.

"It was nothing," I replied, trying to catch my breath. "Rex is the one we should be thanking..."

"I couldn't have done it without you," Rex insisted, rising to his feet and dusting off his coat.

The children regarded Rex warily. I realized the poor guy didn't exactly fit in.

"He's not as scary as he looks," I told them, managing to regain my composure enough to smile convincingly. "Bad people don't just go saving people for fun, right? And he saved us. All of us."

I wasn't sure my words would sink in, but they seemed good enough for the kids. The little girl smiled at him boldly. "Thank you, sir!" she said.

"It was my honor," Rex replied in a gravelly voice, but he was beaming. The little girl actually blushed. Obviously, the three boys couldn't let the girl look like the bravest out of them, so they all rushed into thanking Rex. He looked uneasy under their gratitude, but I flashed him a grin. He deserved the attention. He wasn't a bad guy at all.

After a moment of that, though, Rex's eyes locked onto something behind us, and his eyes turned dark. "You kids should hurry home. Your parents will be looking for you." To me, he added, "I don't think the storm is quite over."

They didn't need convincing, and took off running to their homes past Eckhardt's in the woods. The little girl waved frantically back at us, but nearly fell and one of the boys grabbed her hand. Two worried men rushed them into a nearby house, watching us anxiously. I watched them go, but Rex hurried past me and over to where the others rushed out of Eckhardt's house. A man stood in the clearing, arms crossed. I didn't pay them mind until the kids disappeared inside, then grabbed Ragnarokkr and hurried after Rex.

The lone man watched us with an ugly smirk. Nothing about the man was attractive. His hair was silvery-grey from age and plastered to his angular face. A wretched scar marred most of the left side, from his inflated temple, down the bridge of his stony nose, and ending at a pointed chin. His skin was pale and coarse, like he'd already died once and somebody just stuck his skin onto a new entity. He dressed in impressively cut armor with a long blue cape, but it fit him ill and covered every inch of him from the chin down – even his bulging neck stuck out of his armor. A thick sword sat at his belt, but he made no act to reach for it.

Eckhardt arrived as I did to face the man, clad in one of his huge suits of white armor. Behind him, I saw the flushed faces of Loki, Sira, Katiel, and Kaia arrive from the forest path, giving me a mix of impressed and furious looks.

"What are you doing here, Roland?" Eckhardt demanded. He cut an impressive figure in the oversized armor. "That wind was all you, wasn't it? Why?"

The ugly man grinned, and it was far from a pretty sight. He looked like such a boyish expression should never cross his face.

"Eckhardt Bright," he declared, and stepped toward us with a flourish of his cloak. Nobody moved. "Eckhardt. The great paladin of Southpost, renowned warrior of Laia. Why do you resign yourself to such a post, out in the woods of Bonnin?" He turned to Artos, who appeared to flank the white knight with dual blades drawn, and his smirk only grew. "Ah. Artos Ninjeste. A great and lethal ninja as well. A master of his own unique art. And of course, Kaia," he went on, seeing the girl who hurried in at Katiel's side. "Kaia Oceyen, renowned water mage. The girl who dances with the waves."

He glanced around for another moment. "Ah, no Mayfield. What a shame. Still," he spread his arms out wide, "you all could accomplish so much more at my side! Imagine the holiest of blades, the mightiest of armors. I could augment your body, ninja, to lunge without making a sound, and to do so at such a velocity that your punch could rend flesh. And Kaia, how I could modify your relationship with water! Perhaps allow you such governance over the other elements!"

Katiel only sneered. "You can hardly breathe in your current state, Roland Demizen. What makes you think you'll live long enough to hold up those foolish promises?"

The old man glared back. "And what of you, old friend? What can you bring? The promise of their eventual demise, once again?"

I wasn't sure what he meant, but the words seemed to affect Katiel. He stepped back a little, perturbed. Kaia touched his arm tenderly. Roland crossed his narrow arms as if he'd won a fight. I wanted to throw my sword at him.

"Brings us back to Eckhardt's question," Katiel said. "What are you doing here? Did you come to try to find some happiness in your miserable life, or to try buying my friends? I'm sure you could buy a slave or hooker somewhere else, but they'd probably charge you double."

Roland only scowled, pacing, observing the rest of us in scrutinizing silence. I thought I saw a spark of familiarity in his eye when he saw me, but he kept looking over everyone else as we closed in around Katiel. Then, with a loud gasp, he wheeled back to me, pointing an accusing finger.

"Aha! The boy from the posters! I knew he looked familiar!"

Katiel stepped over to stand beside me. He had his sword out, to my surprise. It was a long blade with a dark green handle that looked something like scales. I hadn't seen him draw it before. "Drop the stupid antics, Roland. What do you want with him?"

Roland's crazed grin only grew. He still made no motion to draw his weapon. "Oh, would you not love to know?" he asked demurely. "As a matter of fact, that was a ruse. I am quite familiar with him. Surely you must realize why, my intelligent friend."

Katiel remained silent, his expression calculative. Did he really know? Did this have to do with my apparent previous time in the spirit realm? The thought occurred to me – my sister.

"What do you know?" I demanded. I made to move forward, but Katiel stopped me with an outstretched hand.

"I know plenty, my boy," Roland spoke carefully, his words as measured as poison, his black eyes scrutinizing. "Ryoku Dragontalen, the meatloaf-headed hero. Nothing compared to the genius that Katiel and I are capable of. You couldn't solve the last piece of a puzzle."

I glared at him, insulted. "And who are you to make such claims? Somebody who can't figure out how to make friends?"

The old man staggered back, clearly offended. "Wh-What!? How dare you make a mockery of me?"

He started forward, and I drew Ragnarokkr from its cloth in response. The dark ringing noise brought satisfaction to my ears. Katiel turned to me with a warning glance, but I didn't heed it. I stepped around him, wielding Ragnarokkr by the handle, leaving its chains to hang along the ground. Katiel might have noticed how I held it, for he didn't stop me just yet.

Roland drew his weapon. It was a plain steel shaft, but thick, only about the quality of a standard soldier. My hand reared back, Ragnarokkr clutched in my fist. Would it work? Could I swing the sword that everyone claimed was to my name, or would it react the same way as any other sword in my hands?

I swung. My grip felt inexperienced. I wasn't used to the act of actually swinging such a weapon – even though Ragnarokkr felt light in my grasp – and I might never find out how to use it properly.

I stared into Roland's coal-black eyes as he readied himself, boasting a much more experienced stance. There was something off about the way he approached. Was he testing me?

As I swung, he prepared to block. However, while Ragnarokkr sailed through the air, I felt the familiar looseness, and my stomach lurched in my chest. I saw the blade in my hands as though in slow motion. I willed it to stay with all my might, but it was to no avail. I flailed as it released and barely managed to grab onto the chains. At least it could be something.

Surprised, Roland staggered back as Ragnarokkr crashed through his dark armor like a knife through paper. The screech of twisting metal and the splash of blood quickly followed. My stomach lurched; the anger I felt toward the ugly man faded like it was never there. I'd committed a terrible injury upon him, one that would definitely take his life. Did anyone deserve that? Especially a man who claimed to have no friends?

The blade moved oddly, and then fell from Roland's chest to clatter to the ground. I averted my eyes from the grievous wound quickly. However, a grin spread across Roland's pale lips.

"Fool," he muttered, and chuckled in a sinister way. Blood ran down from his torn armor freely, but he didn't appear fazed by it. After a moment, the blood started to slow, and then stop completely.

"Such a foolish little Dragontalen," Roland went on, and laughed maniacally, throwing his gnarled hands in the air. "Fool! Just like you've always been, you little meatloaf! You forget, once more, that I am immor—"

Something cut him off – a very *large* something. Something mud-brown crashed in from his left, tearing him from the ground with a loud *crunch* like crushed metal. A vague sound followed, one that I recognized now as world traveling. The brown entity took as long to pass as a train, and then there was nothing left but a twisted, bitten sword and scraps of dark armor in a pool of blood.

Katiel whistled lowly. "Good timing, Reze," he called out, and laughed. He caught my confused glance, and simply pointed up. I looked – and froze.

A huge monster floated above us, hanging in the sky like a banner in the wind. It had the face of a dragon, but it was taller than a regular human was and longer than a train. It must have been the blur that attacked Roland. I couldn't believe the immense size of it. It stared down at us with dark green eyes oddly reminiscent of a dog. Sharp brown spikes ran all the way down its back, ending in a tail that spun out like a fork. I didn't see any wings on it, or anything to explain why it floated like it was.

Kaia sprang forward, and the monster writhed through the air like a snake until it came face-to-face with her. I nervously picked up Ragnarokkr, but Katiel's hand stopped me. I looked up to see that the creature was nuzzling Kaia's outstretched hand.

"This is Rezemetacharuas," she announced to us without breaking glance from the dragon. The dragon rumbled in response, causing its entire snake-like body to tremble.

"Reze—what?" Loki asked anxiously from some distance behind us. "This great serpent, she... is your friend?"

"You can call her Reze for short," Katiel told me with a smirk. "She won't get offended. In fact, if Kaia likes you, then Reze would do just about anything for you."

"I'm impressed you can identify her gender," Kaia said softly. Her usual boundless energy and tendency to cling to Katiel both evaporated in the presence of the dragon. She seemed serene and completely enthralled by Reze.

"She is my sister. We were born of the same mother, in the same place. We are bonded, just as you may be to your brothers and sisters."

"Y-Your sister is a dragon?" Sira asked, dumbfounded.

"A sea serpent, actually," Eckhardt chimed in. He came forward and offered a hand to Reze, who gently turned and rubbed her great skull against the knight's armor. It looked rough, but Eckhardt hardly flinched away, and laughed. "Cut it out, girl – I just got this armor fixed from your mighty scales!" Laughing, he turned back to us. "She's a sea serpent from Kaia's village. She's quite special, actually – she can levitate outside of the water, and she can cross worlds, too."

Lusari nervously came forward to examine the serpent. It shot out a large, forked tongue from its mouth, and the girl screamed, taking refuge behind Will. He laughed, and then approached with ease in his step. Reze approached him just like she approached Eckhardt, rubbing her spiny scales against Will's armor. He chuckled, patting the dragon's scales amicably.

"She is a type of dragon, I think," Katiel explained. "Sea serpent. Wyrm. Dragon. As far as I've ever seen, many with dragon blood can alter and defy the settings of worlds. It's why they can cross realms so easily."

"They're stubborn creatures," Loki commented with a scowl. "Maybe because dragons are ancient creatures, far greater and wiser than even our oldest structures of the world. Even young dragons naturally defy the order of things." He then turned on me. "Speaking of stubborn…"

"Leave Ryoku alone."

Rex's voice cut through the atmosphere like stone. He was near me as I'd faced off against Roland, and now turned on Loki with a scowl. "Maybe he acted hastily and without proper judgment, but he saved the lives of four children with his actions. None of us could have done the same."

"None of us would have even *thought* of that," Katiel admitted, hiding a smirk behind his hand. "You're getting a fast handle on magic."

"You used magic to do that?" Guildford asked me. "We saw you come down from the window just after the storm started. That was…"

"Incredibly reckless," Loki finished for him, crossing his arms. "What a mad action you took! Sailing across an open valley to a boulder we could hardly see! I'm shocked you knew those kids were here, of all things! It's lunacy!"

"Or bravery," Rex corrected with an icy edge. "Bravery and a keen eye."

Loki faltered. "Well, yes, but…"

He couldn't finish before Sira charged between him and Katiel. Nobody moved to protect me this time. As I braced myself for a strike across the face or impaled with Sinistra, she hugged me. It was a rough hug, and nearly took me off my feet with the sheer force of it, but it was affection. Sort of.

"You idiot," she muttered in my ear. "You stupid, moronic, dumb-ass, selfish, bigoted, *idiot*." Then I heard her chuckle. "That was the most fucked up, but badass, thing I've ever seen you do."

"Well, there we have it," Loki gave in, throwing his arms in the air. "Even Sira can't hate you for it, so I guess I have to worship you. How did you even…?"

"Straight to the worship card?" Rex asked dully.

"We only just covered the elementals yesterday," Guildford said. "I'm impressed. I don't know how you did it, but that was impressive."

Sira let me go, and I absently sheathed Ragnarokkr over my back. I'd been hoping it would work as a regular sword, but even that hope dashed.

"If you're interested," Katiel piped up, "why don't we use Reze to cross worlds together? Give your little mage a break."

Loki perked up. "Travel by dragon? That sounds incredible!"

"Can't you cross worlds yourself, Trickster?" Katiel asked him.

Loki shook his head. "Well, not in a group. I can travel alone, yes. That hardly suits our purpose!"

"Can she head to any world?" Guildford inquired. "Could we use her to, say, head directly to Syaoto?"

Will turned his head in interest, and shuddered as Reze licked him with her forked tongue. Lusari succumbed to a fit of giggles. To us, Katiel only shrugged. "Likely only the closest world. Using world-travel magic protects us from the harmful particles outside the worlds. Reze is safe from it, but we aren't. It would be better to play it safe and travel a shorter distance."

Will's expression fell. Guildford scratched his chin. "The nearest world should suit us just fine," I agreed. "If anything, we'll be closer to our mark. It's only a matter of time."

That pretty much sealed the deal. While Katiel and Kaia saddled up Reze to prepare for world travel, Eckhardt treated the rest of us to our promised lunch. It was light, but I hadn't eaten much lately and found the sandwiches more than sating. We discovered that Eckhardt and Artos wouldn't be accompanying us to the next world. Eckhardt was curious of Roland's intentions in this world. Bonnin was small, and signs would make themselves apparent before long.

When I went to sit down with a sandwich, ready to eat, the four children from earlier came out of their home, accompanied by the two men who ushered them in. They approached us, encouraged by Eckhardt waving them over, though they gave Reze fearful looks. One of the men looked more like a logger, the other almost like a butler or rich young man.

"Hello," the one who looked like a logger greeted us with a short bow. "We're the fathers of this crazy lot of kids. We... we saw what you did from the house."

"It's my fault," the richer-looking one wailed. "I should have been keeping an eye on them. Those windstorms have been happening a lot lately. I should have been watching the kids!"

Loki studied the two of them, connecting the dots. "You two... both fathers?"

"Those storms have been happening a lot?" Sira asked. She, unlike the Trickster, didn't seem to see a problem.

The muscular one nodded. "The man you faced out here is the captain of Niin's militia," he explained, "or was, anyway. He's been exploiting the militia and the markets for extra gold. With the way to the capital blocked off, there was aught any of us could do to stop him. The town's supply was dwindling, but I hear you lot have done away with that, too."

"That we did," Loki said proudly, apparently over his personal confusion. "The mountain pass is safe to travel, more or less. But you say that Roland was around here for a time?"

Katiel was frowning, but I didn't have time to ask him why – the one dressed like a butler approached me, holding something behind his back. "We're but simple villagers," he professed. "Not much to our name, but I'd like to repay you for what you've done. You saved our children, after all." He brought out a long parcel from behind him. "I was enrolled in Bonnin's magic school. A childish, young pursuit of mine that I eventually left behind to start a family. We saw that you can use magic, so I thought I might finally part from this little memento of my days as a hapless kid."

He held out a staff. It was a little longer than my oak staff, well polished and made of a fine birch. The same pale blue runes etched along the side, and the head embedded with a green gem.

"We saw that feat of yours – sailing down from the village like a bird," the man said, shaking his head in his own disbelief. "My grandfather made this for me. It specializes in wind magic, and carries two more charge runes than your typical staff. You won't find anything like it in stores!"

He pressed it into my hands, but I protested. "N-No, I couldn't possibly—"

"Of course you can," Rex said for me, raising a brow. "You flew down to save these kids. You risked your life. On top of that, this staff would be great for the magic you just displayed, right?"

"Are you sure you are willing to give this up?" Will asked, stepping in to examine the staff. "The marksmanship is wonderful, even as one inexperienced in magic as I."

"Yes, of course," the man said without pause.

Will nodded, and turned to me. "There you have it – you simply must take it. To refuse such a beautiful gift would be rude. You do not wish to be rude, do you, Ryoku Dragontalen?"

"I—Well, I..." I faltered, flustered by the words of my friends. I looked helplessly at the man, who only smiled further and pressed it into my hands.

"It's the least I can do," he told me firmly. "After all you've done for this village. For my family. My grandfather's memory will live on through his children. You've assured it here, today."

I couldn't protest any further without looking the fool, so I hesitantly accepted the staff. "Thank you so much," I told them both earnestly, bowing graciously. When I bowed, I felt a small tug at my belt. The little girl was pulling on the oak staff at my back.

"Mister, can I have your old staff?" she pleaded. "It looks prettier than the knobby old thing my great-grandpa made!"

I couldn't hide a surprised laugh. The muscular man of the two chuckled, but the butler-like one frowned. "Now, now. You can't just go asking people for their things. What was ever wrong with my grandfather's staff?"

She stuck up her nose. "It's old."

I smiled at the little girl. "It wouldn't be that great to you, would it? It's just a cheap staff I got from Harohto..."

"Sure it will," Will piped up – he plucked the oak staff from its holster on my belt, turning it over in his hands. "Aha!" He pointed at some deep scratches down the side that I hadn't noticed. "These are from the Keeper of the Old Forest that you drove off with this very staff. And more – these are from the thugs you held off, protecting the life of our own young mage."

"Fire is a much better element for a young mage to start with," Loki added proudly. "After all, that's what got our own Defender started up. Lately, he seems to show quite an affinity for wind. This staff would serve him quite well in that light."

The girl's eyes shone already at Will's words, staring at the staff as if it belonged to God. "A hero's staff," she whispered in awe. "May I *please* have it? Pretty please?"

I couldn't say no to that face, especially if I was partially repaying them for their kindness. "Sure," I told her with a soft smile. "Just take care of it, okay? It's seen a lot of trouble! Try not to get in the same dangers I did with that."

Will knelt and handed her the staff in the manner of bestowing a magnificent sword upon her. She took it in kind. "I got it!" she cried excitedly, thrusting the staff in the air. "I got the hero's staff!"

The other kids crowded around her while she waved it around joyously. To my surprise, she flourished it in the air and a myriad of little fiery butterflies lit through the air, fluttering just out of their reach. I was about to ask somebody why I could never conjure up such a trick, but then I caught Loki's mischievous wink. Maybe the Trickster wasn't quite so vain.

After bidding us farewell and a safe journey, the family eventually returned indoors. It was all as well when we crowded around Reze, who now bore a long saddle Eckhardt pulled from somewhere capable of fitting everyone. Katiel still bore a grave expression. I stopped him before we embarked, finally questioning him.

"I'm just curious of Roland's motives," he said quietly, throwing one leg over Reze as he took a seat behind Kaia, still enthralled by her serpent. "He showed up here, in such an innocent world, trying to take control of Niin somehow. Roland doesn't do something for nothing, ever. He's a very selfish old scientist."

I glanced at him curiously. "Why does he take such an interest in you and your friends? And how does he know me?"

Katiel only smirked, gesturing for me to sit upon Reze's back as well. "I'll have to explain that one later. Now come on – Reze gets pretty impatient when she knows she's getting to travel."

Reze let out a shrill cry in response to that. I smiled, and accepted Katiel's hand up to position myself on Reze's back. I sat between Katiel and Lusari on the long serpent's spine, eagerly awaiting departure myself. I couldn't imagine what awaited us after all the wonders we'd seen in Bonnin, Lysvid, and Harohto. The people

I'd helped, the smiles I'd seen, the things I learned. How could it get better?

Of course, I thought as Reze began to hover off the ground, it could always get worse.

...End of Act Five.

ACT SIX: ALTERATION...

*In the eyes of Lamont Declovin, we are in Gahad, in the world of Vortiger.
It is late afternoon
On November 11th, 2017.*

SCENE ONE: HE WHO FEARED

"Well, look who goes there..."

I ignored the voices of the usual men skulking in the slums of Gahad. It was the everyday drivel of those with no hope. I grew accustomed to it long ago. I kept my hands in my pockets; head down, as I sought to pass through the markets without a fuss.

"The bloody coward," a burly man in a turban jeered, jabbing his friend in the ribs. "Lamont Declovin. The last rider in all the lands. He who practically handed over his dragon."

"Legend spreads in all directions of the coward," his friend replied with a nasally voice. "He stands out, no? Walks like the world still hangs on his back."

A young child, part of a group of street rats, spat in my path from atop some dusty crates. I sidled around the saliva in the dirt path and kept walking, head down. I knew the chances of crossing here without conflict were slim to none, but it wasn't worth not trying. I bumped into a massive figure not ten paces from them. A brawly man stood in my path, huge arms crossed against his chest. His neck was probably the size of my waist, if not bigger. Certainly a sellsword from the Gahad Blood, an unsavory group of rebels. Nobody liked our hierarchy. They performed heartless deeds in the name of rebellion. They weren't the only folk like them. I was almost certain Brozogoth personally permitted this one, among others.

"Where does the traitor seek to go now?" the man drawled. He spoke as if it was hard to get the words out past all his muscle.

"Men like you call for a toll in blood," a slighter man piped up beside him. "What home do you plan to go to? Does anyone look at you with aught but disdain?"

I shook my head slowly, keeping my gaze down. "It is no longer our fight," I muttered. "That dragon is a tyrant. He—"

The man shoved me. I wasn't unaccustomed to defending myself, and I held my ground with relative ease. "Not our fight?" the man demanded, and shoved me again. "It was our fight before you handed in our only advantage!"

I was about to retort, but then I glanced around. More were starting to come up and surround me. There were at least six of them, all wearing the typical hoods of the Gahad Blood – interference in their affairs usually meant death. Some were bulky and tough like the first man, and some more like wiry street rats. They knew nobody would stop them.

"There is one thing left in our hands," the big guy growled. "We will die at Brozogoth's behest now. You have granted us that kindness. In turn, we will ensure you don't live to see it!"

With the last word, the man swung. I cringed, but didn't run. A shadow appeared in front of my vision.

"Just who the hell do you think you are? All of you against *one* man? What kind of odds are these?"

The voice was unfamiliar, quick, with a light accent. I glanced down a little to see a blond-haired man standing before me – holding the man's fist in his single hand. He was dressed like a local, with sand-colored pants that puffed around the ankles, leather sandals, and an open brown vest – yet something about him screamed *foreigner*. A diamond band sparkled on his ring finger, and a rich-looking blade on his hip.

"Move aside," the man growled, but his voice strained as he tried to free his fist. "One last chance. Place this rich fist in a fight you stand a chance in."

The blond man turned sidelong toward me, fixating me in his bright emerald eyes. "What do you think?" he asked mildly. "Can we two men beat the shit outta these guys?"

I shook my head. "This is not your fight," I replied dully.

His eyebrows rose delicately. "I've seen slanted odds and come to your aid, so that makes it my brawl. Now come on, old boy. Will you fight with me?"

My glance lowered. "I am not deserving of such."

The man smirked. "Saying that only proves me right," he announced.

With his free hand, he shoved two fingers in his mouth and issued a piercing whistle. The man struggled to break free, and the blond man punched him soundly in the nose. With a snide grin, he said, "Game over."

The other men rushed at the blond. Before any of them could reach him, however, one of the men screamed and toppled over. A tall man rose from where he'd fallen, with chestnut hair and sapphire eyes, also dressed like a local. A soldier's-issue lance hung over one shoulder on a thick rope.

Now the Gahad Blood hesitated. Which one to go after? The blond darted around, striking the closest with quick punches, while the brown-haired man fought efficiently and in a well-taught fashion, using his body like a lethal weapon. He didn't seem to strike until one swung his way, and then his attacker came to regret it.

It couldn't last, though. More men flooded in from all directions. I stayed where I was. Either one would surely weed the other out. When it would end, what was I to do?

Another man went down hard behind me, and an attractive girl stepped out in his place, fists up in an aggressive stance. Her hair and eyes were like fire, and her expression wild to match. She was dressed in a closed vest and wide-legged silk pants – odd attire for a woman, but I supposed there was a reason she dressed like that. A large blade sheathed over her back supported my opinion. Of the three of them, she might be the only one I could believe was a local. She lunged into the fray viciously, but with well-taught precision. Not one of her strikes missed its target, and each caused some serious damage.

"*Bonzai*, you smelly sewer rats!"

The foreign shout came as a fourth figure appeared, striking a man in the small of his back with a taut fist. This boy had shoulder-length red hair with golden eyes, dressed in an open red-and-gold robe and white pants. Inked across his chest were strange black runes, the signs of a powerful *nuvier* –a mage, as was known in Vortigeran.

He came in like a monster. He acted as if *he* was the weapon, wielding strong punches and kicks. He darted through their midst like the edge of a sword himself.

It took mere moments for the growing group to win. Most of the Gahad Blood spread out along the ground, unconscious. Others bolted, tripping over boxes or slipping on sprays of dust in their frenzy. The group of strangers looked unharmed and barely fatigued. The blond, grinning cheerfully, spat at the tails of the men as they ran off. He raised his ringed hand and waved as though he were saying goodbye to an old friend.

"Well, that's that," he said amicably, chuckling as he dusted off his hands. He coughed, aggravated at the dust that rose up in wake of the fight. He only glanced at me after, as though recalling I was there. "Oh hey. Don't sweat what we just did or anything. Don't know why you didn't lift a finger, though. We risked our necks for you."

I only scowled. "Those men were of the Gahad Blood. You knock them down, more will surely follow."

The man grimaced. "Thought as much. Well then, we'd better turn tail and get outta here." He stuck out his ringed hand in greeting. "Might as well introduce myself. The name's… Ymir."

I met his glance evenly, watching the look in his eyes like actual facets of an emerald. He couldn't sit still, fiddling with his emerald earrings, snapping his fingers, or dusting off his trousers any time I blinked. "Lamont Declovin. One… might call me Vortiger's greatest coward."

"A coward doesn't stand up against that many men by himself," the crimson-haired girl said. She stuck out her hand next like a dagger. "Many would have turned tail and run. You stayed and looked them in the eye. The name's Roxy Cleon. Warrior from Id."

I accepted her hand. Her grip came calloused and rough. There was something off about her though, I thought. Vortiger saw many people from Id in its summers. Roxy was tanned, but not quite like that of Id's harsh summers. A princess, maybe? One who lived much of her life indoors, or else very little of her life there at all.

The red-haired *nuvier* approached next, almost as though he was eager for it. "Yo. The name's Crowe Slade. A pleasure."

I searched this one's glance. His golden eyes were alight with adrenaline, and there was humor at the tip of his smile. Seeing his expression, I made an abrupt realisation.

"*Nuvier*," I said, looking him in the eye. "You're a Defender."

He looked taken aback, glancing to the tricky-eyed Ymir for help. "W-What?" he asked, surprised. "What makes you say that? And what's *nuvier* mean?"

I shook my head. "Apologies. Means magic-user in the old tongue. It makes sense a Defender wouldn't know it."

Crowe raised a brow in surprise. "Aye. Well, you have that right then, I guess." A small smile spread across his face. "You're a smart cookie. I like you."

I nodded to him. I turned to the tall man next, who was standing idly between Roxy and Ymir with a spaced look on his face. "And who are you?"

He looked at me like he only just realized I was there. Odd. For such a big fella, he didn't strike me as an airhead. "M-Me?" he asked, surprised. His eyes darted to Ymir, who abruptly turned away from me and mimed at striking his earring like a cat. Then to Roxy, who planted her hand on her head with a depraved sigh. Crowe hid his face in his hands, concealing laughter. "Right. Me. Yeah. Well, it is a pleasure to meet you, Lamont Declovin."

I stared at him expectantly. "That's your name? ''Right me yeah'?"

A fervent blush drove across his face. "N-No, not at all," he said urgently, his eyes darting helplessly between his three friends. "My apologies. My name is... Sir... Sir Todd. Sir Todd Fallenman. Of the world of Orden."

I regarded him with severe scrutiny, noting how Roxy sighed heavily and Crowe laughed outright into his fist. Ymir was the only one who met my glance, and his brows were furrowed.

"Your name is Sir Todd Fallenman?" I asked dully. "From Orden?"

Todd nodded graciously. "Right you are."

"He's shy," Ymir said immediately, sidling out in front of the sheepish man. "An excellent fighter in any right, but his time in the army has scarred him pretty well. Especially against such big and warrior-like men as yourself."

I contemplated his look for a long moment, but finally shrugged. Might as well humor the lad, even though I was more confident that my left foot was an ostrich than this man was who he said he was. They did step in to save me, and that had to mean something. "Right. So what are you lot doing here?"

Ymir looked incredibly relieved. "Glad you asked, my boy," he said cheerfully. "We're looking for a place to stay, you see. Our initial arrival in your lands has proven difficult. You see, we misplaced our gold back in the city of Morghan..."

"A string of terrible luck, really," Crowe added modestly. "You wouldn't happen to know a place, would you? We're part of a group. Another Defender, too, like me."

Ymir shot him a telltale glance that he pretended was nothing when I looked his way.

"How many of you are there?" I asked.

He looked ready to answer, but was interrupted by a surprised cry as a boy stumbled out from the alleyway behind Todd, nearly colliding with the tall soldier. He had golden hair that tumbled all around his head, and I didn't miss the curved tip to his ears beneath them – an elf, or partially. The tall soldier caught him by the shoulder with ease, as though unsurprised by his bumbling nature. He was quite a bit shorter than the others were, and dressed in the same local style as the others. The whole lot of them clearly tried to look like locals, but it was hopeless. Vortiger didn't have elves. Even if that tidbit passed a set of unwary eyes, his shade of blond hair was highly unlikely here. Blond hair in itself was common, but often darker and more sun-kissed than anything. His skin was far too fair, even for those who lived in the Capital their entire lives.

"So this is where you went!" he puffed, clearly drained of breath. He put his hands on his knees for a long moment, doubled over in exhaustion.

"Do you forget what I told you about minding your lungs?" Todd said softly to him. "Running the way you do like a chicken flying from its coop will only leave you breathless all the time."

Ymir turned on the boy with a vengeance. "Are you *mad*?" he cried, throwing an arm around the boy's shoulder before he could catch his breath, dragging him closer, glancing around warily as though a rhinoceros might break free from a building any moment.

"Those *brigands* could still be around! If they laid an eye on your pretty face, surely they would kidnap you and commit naughty things upon your body!"

Roxy strode to him and cuffed Ymir on the head. "Shove it," she said irritably, stealing the boy from him. "What the hell kind of crap are you spewing?" She looked down at the boy, who still struggled to catch his breath. "If you're here, then where are the others?"

As if on cue, a girl approached from the alleyway behind him. She was a pretty woman with reddish-brown hair and an ancient quality to her eyes. She glanced at me mildly, but remained silent and drifted between the blond boy and Crowe, who gave her a wary look. Another *nuvier*, I assumed.

"Right here!" a more mature voice came from the alley after her. Three more figures piled out of the alleyway. One was a tall, dark-haired man dressed in dark leathers of Vortiger, a sword tucked askew at his belt. With him came a dark-looking man with crimson eyes, most of himself hidden away in a dark coat with all the buttons done up. One arm hung removed from the sleeve and against his chest. Lastly, another girl followed, this one with snowy hair and dressed in light silks. Her white eyes carried the same quality as many of this group – another *nuvier*. I still hadn't decided if the tall, mature man or the blond boy were also *nuviers*. The blond boy had a white staff bobbing at his back, but he also had a sword concealed over his shoulder, hidden with care by bags. Only a trained soldier's eye like mine could discern it among his other belongings.

"You lot were supposed to keep an eye on him," Ymir jeered at the older man, who only laughed heartily in response.

"He was fine until word spread of your little brawl," the reddish-haired girl replied sourly. "You're lucky I followed him, or this lot would still be back at the markets watching all the pretty girls pass by in silks."

Only now did the blond boy's head tilt up, and I caught his glance with surprise, for his left eye was an odd shade of violet. The other was a deep, earnest color of green. How strange. This must be the important one Crowe mentioned.

"H-He did protect me, back in Harohto," the silver-haired girl spoke up timidly, aware of my presence as I watched this odd exchange. "I-I think he's capable of looking after himself."

The blond boy beamed at her, and she practically hid her face away, blushing madly.

"This is different!" Ymir snapped, making the girl jump. "This is one of the places that posted—"

Now everyone rushed to shut the wiry-eyed man up. Roxy elbowed him so hard that I thought he'd surely cough up his liver in a moment. All of their eyes turned to me. If this group wasn't suspicious, then I was a frog.

The blond boy approached me, somehow the least distrusting of them all. His openness came as easily as approaching a brother. "Hi there," he said kindly, and extended his hand in greeting. "I'm Ronyx Curtis."

He didn't try to claim a world he was from, or introduce himself as a Defender. Even though I harbored some doubts about this group, there was an earnest quality to his eyes that I couldn't help trusting. I introduced myself in kind, accepting his hand. His grip was starting to newly form calluses, masking a few burns and scars that dotted his light fingers.

The dark-haired man stepped forward next. "A pleasure to meet you. My name is Darrold Fitton, Curtis' instructor." I didn't miss that Ronyx gave him an odd look, but the teacher was blind to it.

The dark-haired man in the coat nodded once to me. "Tristan Bareult." He offered no more, no less. What an enigmatic fellow, even among this group.

The silver-haired girl followed suit to the others. "My name is Belle Collier, a fledgling mage from the country of Fayzr." She spoke much more smoothly than she did when speaking up for Curtis.

"A pleasure," I told her, accepting her hand. Her snowy eyes gave nothing away. If it were her alone, I might believe this weird group's tall tales.

Ymir rounded up his little group. "Alright, guys," he said urgently. "This gracious man has offered us his hospitality, so perhaps we could retire to his home where we can explain everything."

Darrold was the first to look to me. "Pardon me, I didn't realize. That's quite gracious of you to offer. We would be eternally in your debt."

"Are you alright?" Belle asked me, looking me over. "I'm sure I could muster up some healing magic if you took any injuries…"

I smiled. If nothing else, this group was kind. Well, maybe all but Ymir, considering I hadn't actually offered anything. Since this odd group had done me a considerable kindness, I neglected to bring that up. It happened that my home was suitable for a large amount of company, anyways.

"I'm fine," I told her in kind. "Your friends came at the perfect time." I looked to Ymir. "My lodgings are suitable for... a group of your size, as it so happens. Consider it as thanks for saving me."

The young man beamed as if I'd just signed him up for everything I owned. The relief that flowed through the rest of the group was tangible. I observed them all as they gave each other gratified looks. As a past soldier, I was familiar with world structure and knew none of them was from this world at all. At the very least, Crowe and Ronyx were both Defenders. They were being dishonest about something, but maybe they meant to explain in the safety of my home. Normally I wouldn't trust a group, but... perhaps my prayers had reached them.

I observed the blond boy carefully as Ymir and the younger, reddish-haired girl who hadn't introduced herself fussed over him. He looked oddly familiar, somehow. His golden hair, the one forest-green eye, his boyish expression... He caught my glance and gave me a warm smile.

My home was a stop between the city of Gahad and the Capital, a common place for travelers to visit during the extremities of Vortiger's weather. This group had saved me, after all.

While the group gathered their things and prepared to follow me – with due haste, since I warned them of the Gahad Blood possibly returning – my mind wandered, trying to squander the hopes flaring up in my weakened, brutalized heart. That maybe this strange boy, and his strange group, may be the ones who could finally save us.

SCENE TWO: A SHADOWED ABODE

...Of Act Six: Alteration

In the eyes of Sira Jessura, we are in Lamont's home, in the world of Vortiger (warm season). It is early evening On November 11th, 2017.

The trip to the home of Lamont Declovin – the tall, dark-haired stranger we'd saved in the city – was a long and arduous one. Nobody mentioned how his home came after a long trip across the vast expanse of desert. I guessed that, with little option left, it was our best choice.

At the very least, he rented out horses at the stables just outside the city. His own steed, a bold black stallion, had been waiting at the ranch. He saw to the lot of us, though, which was an act far too kind for a group that lied to his face about their identities. His kindness saw Loki seated like a king on a tall white mare, and Ryoku bumbling along astride a spotted pony that he could hardly control. Luckily, Lamont's stallion led us all; else, Ryoku's wild pony would have surely taken him to the depths of the desert.

Lamont rode like a reaper at the head of our group, broad shoulders hunched upon his steed. He was a huge man, perhaps close to Will's height, with dark hair that fell across his muscular shoulders, parted from his eyes with a white scarf tied across his brow. He dressed in a sleeveless shirt and loose pants, and bore no weapon that I could see. His hawk-like green eyes were usually studying our group when he presumed we weren't watching. He had the build and intellect of a trained solider, but the hunch in his shoulders and the pain in his eyes suggested those days were behind him. Something had taken his determination and his soul. Was that why he'd been under attack when we found him?

Ryoku remained silent behind Lamont. Usually the kid was full of questions, but he was quiet today. He'd been oddly quiet since the encounter with the Diamond Dragon. I still felt like crap thinking about how *no one*, save Rex and Artos, saw him coming and attacked him. Sinistra had come upon him with violent intent. The thought made me sick. It wasn't often I couldn't look at my own sword.

On top of that, I could tell he was bitter about staying behind while the rest of us got into a fight. He could hold his own now, a little bit. I had to admit he'd improved since he first tried to pick a fight with those thugs in Harohto. He'd tried to fight them head-on while Will and I had our hands full, and he honestly fought like a dog. It was one of the things I liked about him the most, even if he didn't really have the skills to back it up.

Things changed in Lysvid. He tangled in fights well above his skill level. Against the werewolves, he nearly got killed and almost turned into one. The scenario with Geri still haunted me. I couldn't erase the initial look Ryoku gave me when his one eye turned violet. No matter how much I didn't want to, I could only see the emperor of Orden when I looked at him.

What he did in Bonnin astounded me, and I started to hate myself for how I was treating him. When he deflected all of our attacks on his own, then used magic to save the lives of those kids, I started to realize he was actually growing *rapidly*. Our little Defender was starting to use magic – and he was actually good at it. Creator forbid he should ever wield that sword properly.

We found Lamont's home after hours of trekking through the scorching desert. Most of the men had torn off their shirts and wrapped it around their heads in an attempt to stay cool. Unfortunately for Lusari, Kaia, and I, that wasn't really an option. Not without the lecherous Loki ogling over us, anyway. I thought poor Ryoku might swerve his horse into quicksand.

Lamont's home looked more like a mansion. The width of it was only about that of a regular home, but it was at least four stories high. The sandstone walls gleamed with an unfamiliar sheen to them, heightened to peaks that reminded me of old Arabic pillars. Everything had a solid gold trim to it, and the sandstone was polished white. I saw Ryoku staring up at it as if he'd never seen anything like it. Keeping to his right side, I could remember how innocent he actually was. It was only when I saw that eye that I had to look away.

Lamont directed us around back to his own private stables buried behind a chained-up gate. I thought they looked much larger than any regular stables I'd ever seen. The walls were higher than those of a normal home, and the soil was tossed and churned. Part of it looked like it was from recent activity, but the bigger, swathing marks looked older.

"What sort of animals do you keep?" Will asked lightly. Privately, nobody could let him live down his second name blunder. Todd Fallenman. How could he space out at such an important time? Even Guildford, Rex, and Katiel could come up with better names, though we all discussed it prior. Will must have spaced out on even that conversation.

Lamont's reply was simple. "Horses. What else?"

"These are awfully high walls for steeds," Will commented innocently. He stroked part of the midway barrier, and dark marks came off on his hands. He looked at Lamont curiously, but said nothing. Perhaps it was because we weren't entirely honest with him ourselves.

The inside of Lamont's home was more welcoming. We entered into a large entryway adjacent to a closet stuffed with both heavy coats and light silks. Boots and sandals sat all over the place, along with scarves, gloves, heavy fur hats, and other accessories for both extremes of weather.

"You're well equipped," Loki admitted, letting out a low, impressed whistle.

Lamont nodded. "My home is a defense to the most extremes of weather. A certain stone protects my home, but working in the city means I must travel frequently. Neither season is easy."

I could only imagine. I'd never been to Vortiger personally, but I'd heard of it. A world that fluctuated between scorching summers and icy winters daily. Since today had been hot out, tomorrow would be freezing. Vortiger was always either a scorching desert or unforgiving tundra.

The main room was more welcoming. An assortment of mismatched chairs and couches circled around a warm hearth at the head of the room, where a small window opened into what looked like a well-stocked kitchen. Despite the odd choices of seating, the interior wasn't badly decorated at all. Three huge watercolor paintings hung on the walls. One was of a forest spring, one of an enormous waterfall, and one of a boreal forest. In other spots hung a few portraits. One was of Lamont with a dark-haired girl, both quite young in the visual. Another of the two of them, older now, holding a boy with dark hair. He also had pictures of just him, the boy, and another boy with blond hair, and there were spots where it looked like other portraits used to hang.

I didn't dare ask about the three other people in the pictures. In light of them, the house felt horribly silent. I recalled hearing the things they called Lamont before we stepped in.

He gestured for us to find seats in the main room. He made to enter the kitchen to prepare something cold for us, but Lusari and Kaia offered to do so instead. Surprised, he nodded, and settled against the wall while the girls ran into the kitchen. I saw his glance flit toward me as though I might offer as well, but he didn't say a word. Surely he knew I wouldn't cook for a soul. They'd wind up poisoned if I tried.

Loki settled in the grandest armchair, spinning around to face Lamont against the wall. Shrugging, Will followed Lusari into the kitchen while the rest of us found chairs. Rather than dive into anything huge, the conversation remained light while the others prepared food. Loki tried to discuss Vortigeran women with Lamont, who was uninterested. I studied the portraits of the children in the pictures with Lamont. One of them, the light-haired one, resembled Ryoku a little.

Ryoku didn't remain seated for long. He shifted oddly, as though waiting and listening to the small talk was unbearable. Finally, he asked if he could go assist the others in the kitchen. Hadn't Cleria said something about Ryoku being a cook? He'd never brought it up.

Since Ryoku left me behind, I sulked in the corner while the conversation largely remained dull. Katiel asked about the word Lamont called him – a *nuvier*, which was apparently the Vortigeran word for mage. Apparently, people didn't use the language itself very often these days, but key words still seemed the frequent identifiers for things in their world. The words meant nothing in the common language, so, even with Ryoku and Katiel in our midst, it couldn't translate to anything. *Nuvier* was a common one, and he voiced others that I couldn't pronounce. He assigned the word to Kaia and Lusari as well, and asked about Ryoku and Guildford – of course, by their aliases, which took a moment to recall.

Our friends actually produced some decent food. Ryoku brought out a large bowl of cold pasta mixed with vegetables and a citrus-based sauce. They also brought cut vegetables and fruits, large pitchers of lemonade, and a platter of various sandwiches. Will juggled a heavy amount of cutlery and plates.

"Ah, perfect," Lamont exclaimed in delight. "You all are quite thoughtful. Such food is perfect for the heat."

Everyone indulged. Loki attacked Ryoku's vegetarian tendencies once more, which he was able to shrug off with relative ease. Almost everything save some of the sandwiches was meat-free, so he indulged a little more bravely than he had in Lysvid. He looked exhausted, too. I thought that the tonic Eckhardt gave him in Niin might be wearing off.

Once our light dinner was complete, the same crew that cooked the meal quickly took to the kitchen to clean up. Lamont almost went to help, but Loki stopped him with a hand on his shoulder.

"Lamont, what is going on in the world of Vortiger?" he asked. "Whispers spoke of a tyrant ruling the Capital. Upon my last visit, it was led by a council, was it not?"

Lamont's disposition immediately darkened, and he leaned against the wall heavily. "Much transpires in the Capital. Some may argue the source, but it is largely upon the emperor himself for having shown up here."

Loki pressed the question. "We overheard you in Gahad against those sellswords. You spoke of a dragon? Surely that is a mere nickname..."

His expression was almost pleading. Lamont studied him for a long moment. "I could explain. For that, I would require honesty on the behalf of my current refugees. For that is what you are, yes? Refugees."

The others started to return from the kitchen warily, noting the tension between Loki and Lamont. "You could call us refugees, I suppose."

Lamont's arms tightened around his chest. "That is the only price I ask of you. I am no supporter of the emperor. Should he have any reason to seek you out, he would not hear so from my lips, that I can assure you." He fixated Loki in his raptor-like gaze. "I offer you refuge, food, supplies. All in the name of having saved my life – an unarmed man against bloody sellswords. My only price is honesty."

Loki frowned. "What would you like to know?"

"Start with your names," he said, jabbing his thumb at Will as he entered the room, who flinched at the gesture. "Todd Fallenman. While that is an interesting alias, I would pray it is not your real title. Honor me with your names, and I shall tell you the story of Vortiger."

Loki didn't quite give up yet, but Ryoku returned behind Will. "Let's trust him," he said. It wasn't a question, but a light push in the right direction. I liked Ryoku when he stood up for someone. "He's right. He's helped us out where we'd be freezing to death in a few hours. The least we can do is trust him a little." He turned to Lamont, and bowed in the Ordenite style he'd apparently learned. "I am Ryoku Dragontalen."

Tension clouded the room. Surely he recognized the name and realized the hefty bounty on our Defender's head, but Lamont only smiled at him. "So I thought. You have a unique appearance that dressing up in otherworldly attire cannot quite mask."

Rex leaned forward on the chair. "You recognize him, then."

Lamont nodded. "Fear not, however. As I have said, I don't support our emperor. I once had a sizeable bounty on my own head, but it..." He trailed off, and faintly gestured with his fingers. "Your young friend may be so brave, and he is one with much at risk. I would have all of your names."

After a few looks of hesitation around the room, we all gave in and told him our names. Lamont met us all in kind as a proper introduction, but faltered when Loki gave his real name. I thought Lamont might call him a liar, but he laughed outright. "The name Ymir," he said. "That stems from the tales of your brother Odin, no? A clever little trick. But your mischief speaks for itself, Trickster. I believe you."

Everyone visibly relaxed once Lamont knew all of our true names. Only Loki leaned forward in his chair, resting his chin on his thumbs. "Alright, Lamont. We gave you our names. Now tell me: what has transpired in Vortiger?"

However, Lamont was shaking his head. "Were I you, I would arrange for your travels tomorrow morning. Surely after your incident with the Gahad Blood, he has already heard of you."

"Who?" Guildford asked, speaking with much more hospitality than Loki. "Who controls the Capital? Is it…?"

The thought was on the tip of everyone's tongues. The reach of Orden. It made sense. If Vortiger suddenly succumbed to a dark ruler, what else could it be? Lamont looked us all in the face, shaking his head.

"I spoke the truth to those men," he said. "The dragon. The emperor, Brozogoth, is a dragon."

A moment of shocked silence spun through our group. "A dragon rules Vortiger?" Katiel asked, dumbfounded. "How?"

"That should be impossible," Loki tried to reason. "As much as we know dragons don't like the natural order of things, surely they cannot thrive in such an environment."

"They do," Lamont said. "They have for over a hundred years. My father and his father before him, both became dragon riders. They were once commonplace in Vortiger."

Loki looked visibly distraught. "Dragons weren't here when last I visited," he said. "That's impossible. Such a thing… that rewrites the laws of the realms! Why, it doesn't make any sense at all!"

"What are you talking about?" Ryoku asked. "Why can't that make sense?"

"Worlds follow a natural structure assigned to them," Guildford explained when Loki appeared far too frazzled to respond. "Lysvid is the vampiric world. Bonnin was the world of happiness. Vortiger, of course, is the ever-changing world. Worlds have a designated quality to them."

"Do not worry about discussing the realms here," Will said to Ryoku, who was getting a little bug-eyed at the topic of the spirit realm. "Soldiers are often familiar with the world structure. And Lamont, you were a soldier in the past, were you not?"

Lamont nodded, though he looked a little surprised at Will's observation. "Go on."

"Vortiger is a strange world," Loki said, having regained his composure a little. "Vortiger changes seasons every day. As such, it's impervious to many spiritual norms. The season is autumn, just as it is in your world, but Vortiger does not see it. Many worlds experience a… somewhat altered flow of time. Worlds that experience an alternative flow of seasons can also experience a different passage of time. Orden, for example, and Vortiger. Both worlds suffer extreme weather that alters the flow of seasons. Wintry worlds such as Fayzr and Jerule also apply, as does Id."

He hesitated now, as though pondering the truth of his own words in his mind. "See, as I have said, each world largely has its own quality, and they must never overlap, lest you encounter 'glitches' in the worlds. For example, imagine the vampiric qualities of Lysvid passed over to Bonnin." A few of us laughed – Loki silenced us with glares. "Imagine Harohto began to follow a strict schedule of changing season each day. Imagine Syaoto may fall into the eternal summer of the desert. Such would be utter chaos! The worlds would follow no rules at all, and we would surely all give way to Chaos!

"So," Loki concluded, sitting practically at the edge of his seat, his eyes gleaming like true emeralds, "why is Vortiger doing *exactly* that? How could it change?"

Nobody offered him a response. "Is it that enormous of a change?" Will asked. "I mean… a few worlds have dragons, correct?"

"But not interfering with its structure," Loki insisted. He turned like a whip to Lamont. "Explain how the dragons have lived here for the last century. You said your father and grandfather were dragon riders?"

Lamont nodded. "They were. As far back as I recall, there were families known as dragon riders. We struck bonds with the dragons for life. Their life spans are long, but they bonded with us to form middle ground. Mankind would live longer, and dragonkind sacrificed years to find strength in our bonds. We were stronger together than we ever were apart, even though dragons gave us their life force. Because, when we rode into combat together, nothing could stand in our way."

There was a fire in his eyes all the sudden. Poor, broken Lamont who had been about to let several men beat him to death, had a fire in his eyes.

"You were once one of them, weren't you?" Ryoku asked softly. "A dragon rider."

The fire blinked out like it had never been there. I was sure Ryoku hadn't intended it, but it happened. "I was," he said in hardly more than a whisper. "I was, yes. A dragon rider, as my father and his father before me. As my sons."

He fell silent like a candle extinguished by the breeze. The silence filled the room. I could only imagine where the story went.

"How did that change?" Guildford asked. If anyone were to press the question, it must be him. Only Guildford, or perhaps Will, could breach such a ginger topic.

"Brozogoth used to rule alongside the head of our council," Lamont said. "His rider, a man named Rassaq Elias. Many of the council rode dragons, but many did not. I, and my father and grandfather before me, had a seat on the council once. My dragon was Leiogrey. A strong and noble dragon of twin elements: ice and kinetic energy. Atop that, he breathes fire."

"A strong, unique dragon," Loki commented. That sounded crazy powerful to me, too. Couldn't dragons just breathe fire normally?

"He is," Lamont said softly. "He found the eggs of my two sons' dragons – Malak and Rhovh. Respectively, dragons of fire and ice. Peter rode Malak, the dragon of fire, for he was the more rambunctious of my boys. Malak was a wild spirit, difficult to tame. Rhovh was gentler, more suitable for Jordan, my youngest.

"Unfortunately for the world of Vortiger, Rassaq departed from the world at quite a young age. Younger than I am now. Plague spreading through Loghain took many lives. Rassaq went to personally see to the matter, but fell to the plague. In his wake, his dragon, Brozogoth, succumbed to madness. As a lone dragon parted forcibly from his rider, they also drove him from the council. He soon returned, however, in a fit of rage, and fought against all the other riders himself. Brozogoth is a dragon who controls mind and earth elements, and that gave him certain power over the other dragons. He single-handedly weeded out the council and did away with most of the dragons."

"Most of?" Loki noted. "So others live still?"

Lamont nodded sadly. Before he could elaborate, Katiel closed him off. "What happened then? Why do the folk blame you for Brozogoth's rule?"

"Because my sons and I were the last riders left," he said. "I've always been an outside member of the council. My place is here, as a stop for travelers between Gahad, Morghan, and the capital. The news of what happened hit me later than most. My father also fought against Brozogoth, and he lost his life. I'm unsure what exactly transpired between them, but Brozogoth chose to keep my father's dragon – Deltorah, an entity of pure fire – as his own.

"Brozogoth already had full control of the city, but he sent word to me. He ordered me to surrender my dragon. If I did so, then he would allow the rest of my family to live."

"And you listened to him," Loki said sadly. It wasn't an accusation or anything of the sort, but a sad realisation. "When offered the safety of your family, you chose as any sane father would. But once Brozogoth had your dragon in his clutches…"

"He arrived and slew my children," Lamont finished, "bringing an end to the dragon riders of Vortiger forever."

His words hung heavy on us all. Lamont had lost his family because of the very things that seemed to make up much of his purpose. On top of that, the people of Vortiger actually held it against him.

"What of your wife?" Loki asked gently. The emotion in his eyes was apparent. "The woman in the pictures. Where is she?"

Lamont didn't speak for a long moment. By the look in his eyes, his mind was living in the past. "She died," he said, "giving birth to my second son. I raised them largely on my own."

I knew the reason Loki's eyes turned so soft. He'd told us of his wife in Lysvid, a story that shook us all to the core. If there was anything he could understand, it was the pains of a father and a widowed husband.

"Well then," Loki said, rising from his seat with some difficulty. "I suppose that makes our path evident. Does it not, Ryoku?"

I looked to Ryoku, who had much the same expression on his face as Loki. The slight Defender didn't take a seat, but leaned against the arm of the couch next to me. From here, I only saw that apathetic violet eye. "It does. Given the situation, we'll have to wrest control of the capital from the dragon emperor, Brozogoth." He looked around at all of us, ignoring Lamont's dumbfounded expression. "What do you think, guys? Any protests?"

"I see nothing wrong with this," Guildford said easily. "We have the chance to do some great good in Vortiger. We can only get stronger from this. After all…"

"Vortiger is one of the worlds which posted a bounty," Will picked up the idea. "Perhaps Brozogoth has some sort of connection to the empire. It would not be unwarranted to go after Brozogoth in search of this information."

"I'm with you, as promised," Rex assured Ryoku readily. His crimson eyes gleamed bright. For such a dark-looking character, Rex always seemed to bear a strong devotion to Ryoku that only continually grew. "Until we get to Syaoto and I do what I have to do, I'm at your command."

"And we're your Guardians," I added, crossing my arms irritably. "Whatever you decide to do, you have your flock of bodyguards to try and stop you from doing something stupid again. And protect you or whatever."

Ryoku beamed at me, and I couldn't help a little smile of my own at his happiness.

"Even if you don't succeed," Lamont said, standing at his full height to bow to Ryoku, "your plight is fiercely noble, and highly appreciated. I will lend my assistance to you however I can."

"You got us, too," Katiel volunteered, jabbing his thumb at Kaia, who nursed a glass of water in her lap. "No way am I sitting back while you have all the fun. Maybe I'll get to show you my power, too."

"Your power?" Loki asked, but Katiel nodded him off with only a wink. Meanwhile, Lamont turned to Ryoku.

"Your own plight draws my curiosity," he said. "Why do you travel the realms with such a large and diverse group? What is your goal?"

Ryoku didn't respond immediately, but glanced around for help. With everyone chiming in, Ryoku explained his reasoning for entering the spirit realm and his eventual plight in Orden. Lamont listened thoughtfully. I saw some interested reactions when Ryoku explained how he was hoping to reconnect with his sister, a fact I knew he had initially been very sensitive about bringing up. In turn for the trust Lamont gave us, it seemed Ryoku was ready to be fully honest in response.

"So you believe Orden holds your charge prisoner," Lamont said. "Why?"

Everyone exchanged odd glances. "It seems the most likely place," Ryoku said guardedly. "Of all the places that posted my bounty."

"The bounty is literally signed *by Orden*," I added. "Who else would have this kid as their prisoner?"

Lamont shrugged. "It could be a ruse," he said. "A smaller world surely could not provide such a large bounty. It would take a rich kingdom like Syaoto or Orden, and I could see many smaller worlds beseeching the dark empire for assistance. You could be looking at any world in the spirit realm."

Ryoku looked thoroughly disturbed by this information. "Any world in the spirit realm?" he echoed desolately.

"The fact still stands that they are a high suspect," Loki said, a little defensive. "The dark kingdom. They're infamous in the spirit realm for causing trouble, warring with other nations, and meddling in otherworldly affairs."

"That is true," Lamont agreed. He turned back to Ryoku. "What about your charge? The boy Chris Olestine. Do you know why they imprison him? Perhaps he has committed a crime against their people. Perhaps they are in the right, even as it is a smaller chance given the nature of the kingdom. What then? Would you have the resolve to break Chris Olestine free if it could be wrong?"

Ryoku visibly hesitated. "We have a connection," he said, and this was with more affirmation. "There is something between us. Like we're related somehow, or else of like minds or souls. That's why I'm sure he can connect me to Roxanne somehow."

"Why are you pressing the matter so much?" Loki asked suspiciously.

Lamont looked at him for a moment, and then shrugged, leaning back in his chair. "Call it curiosity. I'm merely playing Dante's advocate for those who might actually seek to break his resolve." He turned back to Ryoku, who had gone somewhat steely-eyed. "Your determination is fairly sound. Just remember your friends if need be."

"Dante's advocate?" Ryoku asked blankly. "What does that mean?"

A moment of stunned silence washed across the room. We'd been with him since the start, and he still didn't know something so simple. If I ever needed reminding that the pretty Ryoku Dragontalen was still new to the spirit realm, it always came quickly.

"Dante is considered the devil in the spirit realm," Katiel answered. "There are a lot of different gods of Chaos, dark gods, deities, demons, and anything else you can think of. Dante governs them all. He's an Ancient, which means he has governance over most gods."

"Opposite him is the Creator," Loki added. "The Creator is the entity responsible for all of Creation. It is mightier than Ancients and Gods. The Creator is not much of a combatant in that sense. It governs over all."

"And then there's the Destroyer," Lamont said. "What the Creator will create, the Destroyer will destroy. Rumor states that the Destroyer is a wildcard. It doesn't sit on golden thrones like the other gods, but actively seeks to undo everything that the Creator has done. In that sense, it isn't much of a governing god."

Lusari only just returned from the kitchen, and I thought she gave Lamont an undeservingly dark look. It was gone so quickly that I thought I imagined it. A few heads turned to her as she entered.

"You didn't call them by genders," Ryoku noted. "Why?"

Only Loki seemed able to answer this. "Because they aren't simply defined as such. The Creator and the Destroyer can freely change form. I could converse with the Creator while it turns from a young, attractive woman, to an elderly man, to a mere infant. That said, they do settle on certain forms once in a while."

Ryoku looked stunned by this. "Loki, have you actually talked to the Creator?"

Loki responded with only a small smile.

"So we shall travel to the Capital tomorrow?" Will asked with a strangely heavy sigh. He seemed to avert his eyes from Loki a little at the Creator topic, though I couldn't imagine why.

"It's settled," Loki declared, sprawling back in his armchair like a king. "We shall liberate Vortiger of the dastardly dragon emperor tomorrow. Or at least, we will depart there tomorrow."

"Dastardly, Loki? Really?" I muttered dryly.

Ryoku looked Loki in the eye. "How are we going to fight a huge dragon on our own?"

"Well!" Loki began, his expression one ready to elaborate on grand tactics – but then he hesitated, and turned to Katiel. "How?"

"How large is this Brozogoth?" Rex asked.

Lamont stared at Rex for a second. "Enormous," he eventually replied. "Impossible to explain. If you're going to defeat him, I hope you can grow to several times your current size. Otherwise, your only bet may be to somehow outsmart him."

"We might not be out of luck just yet," Katiel assured us when a few of us looked at each other anxiously. "We'll see. We never accomplished anything by doubting ourselves, did we, Ryoku?"

I thought Katiel's encouragement was meager, but Ryoku nodded. "Yes. You're right. I guess we'll face that problem when we get to it."

Lamont grinned half-heartedly, but I could see kindling burning in his eyes. No matter how small, this broken man found hope in us.

"You had best be ready for the trip to the Capital tomorrow, then." He rose, standing as though the dragon emperor's claws bore down on his shoulders. "You'll need to rest. I have suitable lodgings for you all, but tomorrow is the cold season. You'll need to pack your beds with everything I have available in the spare rooms."

Loki gave him an incredulous look. "You don't have heating?"

Lamont shrugged. "I do, Trickster – it just isn't enough for the cold season."

SCENE THREE: VIOLET

...Of Act Six: Alteration

In the eyes of Lamont Declovin, we are in The Western Vortiger Sands, in the world of Vortiger (cold season).
It is early morning
On November 12th, 2017.

"You weren't kidding about the cold!"

The Defender, Ryoku Dragontalen, shuddered violently as if in agreement. Wrapped up in multiple layers of clothes, fur-lined boots with snowshoes and mitts, and even my son's old parka, the boy still looked like he might freeze to the spot. Part of me couldn't believe I trusted this poor boy to save my world.

I was long since used to the biting winters of Vortiger. I could make out the assembly line of his group behind me whenever I glanced back. Little else stood tall in the winter. Trees only grew near certain oases that could survive when everything froze over. The ground beneath the snow was the same dunes that the horses stomped through yesterday, likely with our very tracks frozen into the sand.

We were still in the early hours of the winter. In a state of constant blizzard, the snow churned already several feet high. Convincing the Trickster to depart any earlier was in vain, and so this company stamped through the snow in snowshoes, wrapped up like bundles of kindling for the fire. It had taken all of my winter supplies to cloak this group, plus the little they carried with them.

I was beginning to understand this group. The fiery Sira, the violent Swordstress from Orden, clung to Ryoku's right side like the plague. Nobody spoke to Ryoku about that violet left eye, and Sira seemed terrified of it. She'd shared a room with him the night before, too. I thought the meek Defender and the angry warrior was an odd pair, but I didn't remark on it. She seemed fiercely devoted to him, anyway.

Another couple seemed to be the tall, broad-shouldered Will and the quiet, introverted Lusari. Will was a constant guide, a shoulder for the rest of the group, and even a bit of the comic relief at times. He could answer a million questions about armor, weapons, combat techniques, and anything about nature he was familiar with. If one were to ask him something complex – such as coming up with a fake name on the spot – he turned as clueless as the Defender. Next to him, Lusari was quiet. She kept to herself, usually somewhere between Will and Ryoku, and was oddly helpful. She cooked, cleaned, set up and cleaned up all the rooms for everyone, and helped usher everyone out of the door like a mother hen. Yet, when I tried to speak to her, she didn't have much to say.

Loki was the opposite. He could banter about anything, even making a new subject sound like something he'd studied for millennia. He spent a lot of time strolling alongside either Ryoku or the polite Guildford, who was easily one of the most respectable denizens I'd ever taken in. I felt like both of them were too polite to hush the Trickster at any point. Given that point, he still seemed to care for Ryoku a great deal. All of them did to a degree, I thought, but what I knew of their history seemed to clash with that bond they shared.

I got along with Guildford quite well, possibly the best out of the company. We spoke late into the night, and found we had much in common in strange ways. He left his wife behind when he died in the land of the living. Mine passed giving birth to my second child. Guildford confessed to wanting children, though he sympathized with me for raising them alone. Somehow, I felt that the kindly man could relate to me even if we lived entirely different lives, which wasn't all too far from the truth. Guildford grew up in a normal world and became a teacher. I was raised a dragon rider.

Katiel and the girl always clinging to his shoulders provided mostly for themselves. They were polite, of course, but insisted on setting up on the couches rather than occupy a room. When I went to the kitchen late at night for a pitcher of water, the Defender had pitched up two tents in the center of my living room. A faint flickering from within suggested they even had fires going, but I couldn't remember approaching it or reacting in any way. There was no sign of it in the morning, and I became certain I dreamt it.

I thought Rex might be the troublesome one at first. I hadn't seen someone of his ilk before – a hybrid of vampire and werewolf. Such races didn't exist in Vortiger, only in dusty old texts hidden away in ancient libraries. However, Rex was an excellent role model. He acted polite to everyone, didn't make a mess, and seemed to maintain strong relationships with his comrades. He could hold a conversation with Loki, Sira, Lusari, Kaia, or especially Ryoku with ease.

It had been a long time since I connected with a group of travelers. Most distanced me after the deaths of my sons, or else soon after they learned the story behind it. Vortiger was an old and rigid world. Especially in the Capital, people held to their customs. In the eyes of many, it was my responsibility to keep Leiogrey and fight, even if that had been an ensured route to the deaths of my sons. I should have seen through the dragon emperor's deceit. I didn't disagree.

To find a group of travelers that readily accepted my story – even offering to *help* – was profound. Travelers didn't usually stay in Vortiger for long, once they realized dragons were virtually extinct and that they couldn't become Riders, or else remained in the Capital for their entire visit to avoid the deadly weather.

Defenders, though, weren't highly uncommon. Minerals from the frozen desert were invaluable in constructing strong weapons and armor that they sought out. Bounties in the cities offered high rewards for slaying the ilk that roamed the desert during the summer or winter. They brought economy to our rich world, and Vortiger loved it. It wouldn't be mistaken for caring about our world, though.

It was almost noon when the sheen of the Capital's reflective walls started to gleam through the snow.

"We're nearly there!" I shouted, and quickened my pace a little. I didn't hear any replies from behind me, only their rushed footfalls in the snow at the promise of warmth.

When the city itself started to come into view, I saw Ryoku stop in his tracks, stunned. I couldn't hide a grin. A large glass dome encased the entire city to sustain a permanent warm season within – something between the extremes of Vortiger. The dome soared well above our heads, looming out from the blizzard like a shining mountain. The beating sun of Vortiger even reflected from somewhere above the snow.

"It's incredible!" Ryoku exclaimed. "Is this why you said we don't…"

I couldn't make out all his words through the blizzard, but I could assume his intent. "Inside the dome is always warm," I called back. "Keep pace, Ryoku – we've got a ways to walk yet!"

It took almost an hour from there to reach the huge doors to the city. They stood ridiculously large for things such as incoming caravans and other entities that may need to get through the city – dragons, of course, included – but there was also a smaller door in the center of one of the larger frames. I yanked it open against the blizzard, ushering everyone inside before slamming it shut behind us.

We entered into a packed lobby. Lockers and storage rooms lined all the walls. People didn't readily leave during the wintry seasons, but people still rushed around here no matter the weather. Storage rooms were expensive, and required heavy sums of gold to keep over the turn of season. Merchants packed their caravans in wait of the summer season, setting up shop in the meantime for those who did prepare to set out. At the other end of the lobby was another set of huge gates, sealed just as tightly as the entrance. People were unhappy if even a breeze of the wintry cold entered the actual city.

"Thank the Creator!" Loki proclaimed, yanking his hood off his head and shaking free pounds of snow. "I'd begun to think we traveled into the heart of winter itself! I was waiting for Hod himself to approach us and ask what I was doing in his home…"

"Hod?" Ryoku asked curiously.

"A relative of mine," Loki replied, struggling to undo his top jacket with trembling fingers. "Self-proclaimed god of all things cold and dark. Namely, he's one of the stronger gods of winter. Him and Skadi, or Ullr. In my mythos, we don't seem to give just one person *one* job."

"How many Norse gods does it take to change a light bulb?" Katiel asked. He looked around, waiting for a laugh or response of some sort, but only Ryoku vaguely chuckled, still half-icicle.

"Are we renting out lockers?" Guildford asked lightly, having already undone most of his wintry clothes and stood in a pile of shaken snow. "I like the idea. It reminds me of my old teaching days."

"No need," I replied. It took a moment for me to explain as I unfastened my layers, but I eventually pulled out a jet-black satchel from my belt. Once we stepped away from the entry gates and to a more secluded spot, I dropped it onto the ground in front of us. "Throw all your things in there. Don't worry about them being dry or not."

"Ooh, a gravity bag!" Loki exclaimed happily. He and Katiel both zoomed in on the satchel, but most of the others hovered back, confused.

"It's almost a necessity for travelers like myself," I said, a little glad that the Trickster was impressed for once. "I have warmer clothes packed away in there for the return trip."

"What is it?" Ryoku asked.

"They're very handy objects," Katiel replied, still studying the bag. He picked it up and dropped it, as though hoping its contents might spill out. "Defenders love them, too, but I've had difficulty lately finding a world that sells them for anything less than half the organs in my body. They're practically pocket dimensions meant for storing a vast amount of supplies. Traveling merchants will use them to hold their wares at the weight of a penny. Armies will hide most of their stores in them. Only the owner of the bag – marked by a little trick with buying it – is able to open it, and can designate others with the same magic to open it as well."

"That is truly magnificent," Will whispered. He poked the bag with the head of his lance, then recoiled like it might turn into a cobra. "Ryoku, imagine if we could carry all of our supplies in one of these! And perhaps one for our gold, keyed so that Loki could not get his grubby claws on it."

"Perhaps we can buy one in your markets," Loki said to me, completely ignoring Will's shrewd remark.

I finished unpacking my things into the gravity bag while everyone else did. The wait was worth the reactions of those like

Will and Ryoku, who regarded it like it might swallow their arm. Once they packed up their winter gear, I fastened it shut and wrapped it around my belt once more. No matter the weight of objects in it, the bag remained as light as an empty satchel. We crossed the large lobby and, with Will's help, I turned the heavy steel bar to open the gates to the inner city. The Capital of Vortiger – and the lair of Brozogoth, my sworn enemy.

Compared to the sand-swept villages of Gahad and Morghan, the Capital was highly prosperous. It did have its slums, hidden away in the back end of the city and far from view. Immediately upon leaving the lobby, we entered into Vortiger's upper markets. The smells of tanned leather, burnt metal, and various foods filled the air. Men and women here dressed richly. Vortiger soldiers patrolled the area in flocks, dressed in full suits of dark golden armor. I ensured to steer the group clear of them. I tweaked their outfits the best I could, but I still feared the group would stick out like tomatoes among cucumbers.

I instructed some of the group to wear hoods or wraps over their heads. Lusari, Ryoku, and Rex especially. Loki could almost pass as a Vortigeran noble. Sira and Katiel might pass if nobody got a very good look at them. Other than that, I was more worried about being recognized. I kept my hood pulled over my face as much as possible.

"Where are we headed, my faithful champion?" Loki asked loudly, coming up to throw an unnecessarily comradely arm over my shoulder. The abrupt movement threw back my hood. Almost immediately, I caught the stares of several passerby folk. Great. Evidently, Loki wasn't as skilled in the art of stealth. I knew it was only a matter of time before the word got out. Either sellswords like the Gahad Blood would return, or Brozogoth would hear of my entry alongside a squad of foreigners.

"The markets," I replied shortly, annoyed by the Trickster. "If we can survive the next ten minutes without the emperor himself swooping down upon us, then I'd like to gain some intel. To find out if the dragons are all here, for starters. My father's dragon included."

"So there are three." Loki didn't sound mad, astonishingly. Only grave. "Well, alright. What about splitting up? Some of us head to a different part of the markets. We can find out what we need to know much faster, and gather less attention."

I contemplated his company. None truly blended into the world of Vortiger. However, he had a point about the smaller groups. If he couldn't master simple stealth, at least he could think.

"That would work. I will head to the lower markets and try to shake off the unwarranted attention *you* just garnered us. Another smaller group can check the upper markets – back that way."

Guildford politely raised a hand. "Allow me," he said. "Rex, would you mind coming as well?"

He didn't explain why he chose Rex. It could have been because Rex stood out, so removing him from my group might draw less attention. I'd also heard Rex was a proficient fighter. Rex agreed, and they took Lusari with them. We decided to meet outside the slums after.

As a smaller group, we delved deeper into the lower marketplace. Loki stopped to gander at a stall selling gravity bags, but found the price far too steep for his hollowed pockets. Sira and Will took great interest in a weapons stall boasting locally made glaives, scimitars, morningstars, and a variety of other weapons.

From the lower city, I subtly pointed out the dwelling of Brozogoth – the previous abode of the Vortigeran council – in the city center. The grand palace stood atop a plateau that rose far above the lower markets and the slums, peaked with great spiraling towers and built of the same sandstone as my home. I couldn't see him from here, but I could practically feel his presence. With Brozogoth's psychic energy, it was highly likely he could sense us. I only hoped we blended in somehow.

Near the lowest level of the markets, Ryoku suddenly stopped, bringing our company to a halt. He was fixated on a man standing at a stall set up near the fountain. "D-Dagger? Is that you?"

The man turned around, a Vortiger-made scimitar in his hands. "The hell?" he asked, surprised. He had a loud, almost obnoxious voice, but there was friendliness to his coal-black eyes. When he saw Ryoku, he set down the sword at the stall and grinned. "Ryoku, no freakin' way. What are you doing here?"

Ryoku looked too stunned for words. Katiel stood with him, arms crossed and trying to hide a happy smirk. The stranger stood proudly, hands on his hips. He had dark skin and a shaved head, almost a match for the general appearance of Vortiger if not a little too dark.

He dressed somewhat like a pirate, with triply pierced ears and ink tattooed on his chest in unfamiliar spirals. A pair of daggers rest at his belt.

"You're not dead, right?" Ryoku asked tentatively.

The man stared at him incredulously, jaw dropped – then started laughing boisterously. "Dead? Me? Hell, no way! I'm just like you, clearly – unless you're dead, in which case I've got some ass to murder!"

Ryoku raised his hands. "No, no, I'm not dead, either!" He smiled a little now, none too perturbed by the loud and boisterous nature of this man. Ryoku called him Dagger, I thought, but that could be just some sort of nickname. "So what are you doing here?"

Dagger picked up the blade he'd been looking at and raised it toward us. "New toys for the ol' guild," he said easily. "Brooklyn's got shite in terms of metals in the grand scheme of things. Vortiger, boy, that's where the rich stuff's at! And... you have no freakin' clue what I'm talking about, do you?"

Ryoku's gaze had gone blank. "Guild? What are you talking about?"

Dagger chuckled. "Right, I guess you wouldn't have a clue, would you? I run a guild in Brooklyn. It's a fancy term for a team of guys who take up bounties, protect the city, and all sorts of other fun things – all in the name of the people. Since I run the place, it's international! We base ourselves in Brooklyn and operate across tons of worlds, keeping the peace and a low profile about the whole grand scheme of worlds. Syaoto, Orden, Fayzr, even damned Bonnin – you name it, we've probably done something for it." He paused, studying Ryoku with scrutiny. "Now let's chop to the point. What are you doing here? And what the hell happened to your eye?"

Dead silence fell across our group. Everyone looked between Ryoku and Dagger. Ryoku blankly returned Dagger's look for a long moment – then, finally, intelligence flickered in his glance. He turned to Loki.

"What did happen to my eye?"

There was no holding back the imminent explanation. I sat back by the fountain while they explained everything. Loki had explained some of it to me the night before. Dagger listened, too, intent on every last detail of Ryoku's story. Will sat with me, watching the topic unfold uneasily. I made small talk with him while we waited.

The encounter put us a little behind on meeting with the others, but Ryoku didn't seem to mind. He had an alien quality to his expression now that worried me. I knew that, for all the trust he placed in his allies, they lied to him. It may have been for good reason, but I wasn't sure Ryoku saw it that way.

"That's seriously messed up." Dagger heaved a sad sigh, as though he went through everything Loki just explained. "Well, makes sense now that it's just the one eye. I mean, your other eye's—"

Ryoku cut him off with a look. Just as I wondered what he might be covering up this time, Loki stood, rising from the fountain as smoothly as the wind. To my surprise, he walked straight up to Ryoku and embraced him around the shoulders. It was a gentle act for the Trickster. By Ryoku's expression, he'd probably never done anything like it before.

"It's alright, Ryoku," he said. "We know. Guildford... he already explained it to us. Your glass eye, that is. I respect that you hid it from us." He chuckled, pulling back from Ryoku. "By the Creator, we might never have known if not for that violet eye. You are an excellent feint, you know. But, perhaps we should reconsider how we've distanced one another."

He stepped back, crossing his arms over his chest. Will and Sira came to stand with him. Kaia watched from afar while the three Defenders stood together. The Trickster fixated Ryoku in his gaze. "No more secrets. Keeping from you that... eye problem, was a judgement call. It was something I cannot explain, so I didn't know how to tell you. Deciding this was wrong, I'll admit. Other than that, I believe we've told you everything we know. I would be so bold as to ask the same of you."

"He has been as open with us as he is entitled, Loki," Will said, "however, I do agree. From this point on, there should be no more complexities between us. Standing a chance in Orden will be easier if we do not keep such important things from each other."

Ryoku seemed at a loss for words. He looked to Dagger, who shrugged. "Sorry, kid. Didn't mean to spill the shit."

"Okay," was all Ryoku said. With almost immediate purpose, he turned to Sira, who flinched. "If we aren't keeping secrets, can you tell me why you're afraid of this eye?"

I thought that Sira would surely cleave him in half for his forwardness, but she kept silent, arms crossed. As a bystander, I felt I was witnessing something quite personal.

Finally, Sira sighed. "You know where I'm from, right?"

"Of course," Ryoku replied. "Orden. What… what does that have to do with it?"

She seemed at a temporary loss. Perhaps Ryoku was asking too strongly, or else she was highly uncomfortable with the topic. In the end, Loki answered for her.

"Orden is ruled by a royal family. The Ordenstraums." Sira deliberately turned away, as Ryoku's expression began to change. "Hence Vincent Ordenstraum, the current reigning emperor of Orden. Their infamous trait is their violet eyes."

I saw Will's glance flit to the back of Sira's neck. At the nape of her neck, just above the collar, looked to be part of a scar that disappeared under her shirt. Were they connected somehow?

Ryoku reacted hesitantly. He seemed to have some connection with the girl, and I wondered how this information made him feel. Bearing a resemblance to something that reminded her of an evident trauma was unbelievable.

"There you all are," a voice popped up from my other side – Guildford arrived through the crowd, Rex and Lusari in tow. "I was getting worried. We were at the market for some – oh."

He stopped, meeting Dagger's glance as the boisterous man bounced on his heels. Dagger shared a similar reaction. Rex and Lusari came up to stand with everyone else. It looked like Will leaned over to fill them in.

"G-Guildford. No way."

Ryoku immediately beheld an expression of guilt. "Sorry. I didn't know how to say…"

The teacher smiled. "Well, now I've begun to understand. Your entire circle of friends is involved somehow in the spirit realm, aren't they?" To Dagger, he held out a hand. "Dagger. I'm quite proud of you for how far you've come. Ryoku tells me you graduated."

Dagger looked to Ryoku first, who nodded subtly. The big man was at a loss for words for a moment, staring at his teacher's outstretched hand. Then he laughed – a great, booming laugh that Brozogoth himself probably heard from the palace. He ignored Guildford's hand and gripped the older man in a crushing embrace.

"Holy crap! I never, not once, thought I'd lay eyes on you as long as I freakin' lived! They always told me at the guilds 'Dagger, people don't often reunite with spirits who they lost in their lives.' Well, screw them! Screw the stats! Cause Ryoku actually freakin' found you! Of course he fucking did! Don't tell me otherwise!"

Guildford laughed uneasily, not speaking until Dagger released him, still clutching his arm. "Well, sort of," he said, chuckling. "I was taken in by the Timeless One. Ryoku found him. So I suppose it was something of a middle ground."

Dagger frowned. "The Timeless One? The fuck kinda name is that?" He glanced around, examining the full group that formed around Ryoku. "You know, you've gathered up a pretty solid group here. Why don't you actually introduce us?"

Ryoku blushed. Maybe it was because he'd let us sit here for almost an hour while he caught up with his old friend, but I thought it was needless. He introduced us one by one. When I offered Dagger a hand to shake, he returned it in critical condition. How had Ryoku befriended such a beefy, strong man? Was I to assume Ryoku and Katiel were the same age as him?

At Loki, Dagger gave him a skeptical look. "You're the Trickster god? Really?" He looked him up and down. "A bit shrimpy, eh? Fuck, I heard you're supposed to be a giant."

Loki was miffed. "I've grown awfully weary of that misunderstanding," he muttered cynically. "Blame the translators of mythology in your world, if you must. I assure you I am Loki in all rights."

Once introductions finished, I couldn't take it anymore. "Guildford," I began, drawing the teacher's attention from Dagger and the others for a moment. "Did you find anything out in the upper markets?"

He looked unprepared for a moment, then his brow rose again in kind. "That's right. My apologies – matters took quite a distracting turn. As a matter of fact…"

A loud crash sounded off somewhere in the markets. Everyone whipped around to face the source of the noise. Dust and smoke billowed up from something only a few narrow streets away. A moment later, the ground beneath our feet quaked. Lusari stumbled, but Will boldly caught her and held on. Ryoku didn't flinch, but mildly turned toward the source of the noise. Something had come over him ever since he found out about his eye.

"What was that?" Sira demanded, whirling around to me as though I, solely, would have the answers.

"I believe we have our answer," Loki said. "Correct me if I'm wrong, Lamont, but I believe we're about to have company."

Guildford nodded shortly. "That is what I was to tell you. The dragons – all three of them – are in the Capital at present."

SCENE FOUR: BATTLE IN THE CAPITAL

...Of Act Six: Alteration

In the eyes of Lamont Declovin, we are in Vortiger Capital, in the world of Vortiger (cold season). It is early afternoon On November 12th, 2017.

The sight around the next corner was not welcoming.

The great dragon Leiogrey charged down the street toward us. My old partner was silver in color, with a broad skull, heavy wings, thick arms, and a tail that broke out in spikes. Long horns ringed his snout and skull, as well as his wide shoulders and the crest of his wings. His intelligent black eyes latched onto us as soon as we rounded the corner, all weapons drawn. My heart plummeted at the sight of my old partner, even though I saw no betrayal of similar emotions in his eyes. My dragon, my lifelong friend, was under Brozogoth's control.

This was not good. The streets of the lower markets were narrow. Fighting such a beast in the open would devastate the buildings. The source of the uprising dust was the mayhem his wide wingspan left as he charged. I knew that this was no longer my dragon.

Perhaps he didn't even remember me. Leiogrey would never endanger people like this when we were together.

"H-Holy fuck," Dagger breathed, urging Ryoku back a step. "You're not serious, right? You wanna take on *this* brute?"

"We must," Ryoku replied solidly. He'd drawn out the shortbow from his back, notching an arrow carefully. "If we don't, Vortiger is—"

An interfering gale cut him off. The sun above blotted out for a moment. My heart sank further in my chest, if that was possible, as an even larger dragon swooped down from the sky, landing atop the buildings and crushing them with his mighty claws. This was Deltorah – my father's dragon. One look at the beast told me that he was not himself. He looked more reptilian and wild than I had ever seen, his dark scales shades of dark orange and red. Sharp spines lined most of his body.

As he landed, Deltorah dropped his jaw and unleashed a primal roar that made the entire city shudder.

"There's no getting out of this now," Loki shouted, flipping his sword experimentally in his hands. "You in or not, baldy?"

Dagger shot Loki a brief glare for the nickname, but drew his shortswords in response. "Hell yeah I am! You'd better be able to keep up, Trickster!"

Everyone launched into action. Will and Sira rushed to the front lines. Sira's mighty scarlet sword was unleashed with a vibrant ring as Leiogrey closed in.

"The civilians!" Guildford cried. He looked torn, hesitating between rushing to his friends' aid and to the people who still flocked the streets, frozen in place for fear of the dragons.

The world wasn't waiting for me. Deltorah emitted an enraged shriek, then leaned forth and blasted flames down upon the street. Since one of Deltorah's main elements was fire, the flames bore an intensity most dragons couldn't muster. Market stalls didn't stand a chance. The blaze ensnared many citizens, screaming horrendously in a futile attempt to extinguish the fire. People I knew succumbed to the inferno. Flames rushed through the wide street as though trapped.

Kaia broke past Guildford and dragged her hands into the air as though she tried to lift the flames themselves. To my incredulity, water lifted from seemingly every artifice, every crack in the streets – and bore down upon Deltorah's blaze.

The other *nuviers* rushed forward. Guildford raised his hands to bring soil and dust from the cracks in the street into the effort of choking out the fire. Lusari used her staff to target smaller bursts of fire and turn them into frozen entities. After escaping Loki's attempt to stop him, Ryoku joined Kaia at the head of the fray, looking the roaring flames in the face as no attempts could stifle the inferno. He raised his hands with much less force than Kaia did, and it took a moment for anything to happen.

I took a step back in surprise as a full wave of water soared from nowhere before the flames, as though Ryoku stole a snippet of a summer storm in the middle of the ocean. Even Kaia gave him a startled look, but then she was back in focus, manipulating the wave Ryoku summoned to encompass the width of the roaring flames.

As soon as there was room to pass, Sira and Will squeezed through an opening and dashed toward Leiogrey. The approaching dragon unhinged his jaw and unleashed a violent jet of flames. Without the mages to protect them, Sira sprang forward with her mighty sword and took the brunt of the attack on the flat of her blade. Flames licked at her arms.

In a hasty maneuver, Ryoku dove to the side and shot an arrow down the street at Leiogrey. Wind tunneled through the street in an odd way with the arrow. It didn't land anywhere near Leiogrey, but had a surprising effect – the wind thinned out the flames against Sira and extinguished many of the flames from Deltorah's first attack. I couldn't help but be impressed. He was a *nuvier* after all, and an intuitive one.

Guildford shepherded any citizens who survived the blaze out of harm's way. Lusari accompanied him, and the two spared any quick work they could muster on healing those burnt by the flames. Some, I could tell, wouldn't survive the day. Still, Guildford treated them the same way.

While Sira and Will rushed after Leiogrey, Loki and the others went for the bigger dragon as he charged down the street. These streets were too narrow for the dragons, and each movement crushed stone under their feet, their tails decimating buildings in their wake. Deltorah snatched up a shopkeeper in his mighty jaws just before Guildford could reach him, ripping him in half. I saw Guildford, disgusted, shield the eyes of a few children he'd saved. I looked on with disgust and horror. These were not the dragons I knew.

Deltorah rumbled in the way and made to smite through the entire group Guildford led with his huge, spiny tail. However, some force slowed Deltorah enough that Guildford could usher everyone out of harm's way. In their wake, Rex struck Deltorah's tail with his one fist as hard as he could muster. Before Rex fell out of view, I could only hear the sound of stone on dragon skin.

As violent as they were, I knew Leiogrey's abilities anywhere. He was slowing Deltorah where he could. The thought made me wonder – did he have some control after all?

In the other brawl, Leiogrey drew back and unleashed another blast of fire upon Sira. She stepped into it, cleaving through the flames with her violent red sword. Somehow, the flames abated before her, shrouding their company in smoke. Will dove into the fray after her. Ryoku loosed another windy arrow to brush away the smoke, but he was closing into the battle itself.

Annoyed, Deltorah turned on Rex and unleashed a mighty ball of flames, but the fire had a dark edge to it. Kaia called upon water once more to save Rex, but the flames spread out into a dark flare that spilled out to cover Deltorah himself.

"What the—?" Loki cried before darkness swallowed him. Katiel and Dagger stepped just out of the range of the darkness, the latter nearly stumbling into Ryoku as he chased Leiogrey. When Katiel glanced back, one of Deltorah's mighty claws lunged out of the flames.

Katiel whipped around and took the full strike against his arm. I cringed back, expecting his arm to wind up a bloody stump, but he stepped back virtually unharmed. I thought something about his arm seemed to flicker, but I could have been seeing things from the darkness. Swallowing a deep breath, he lunged into the darkness.

Leiogrey's smoke abated, revealing Will and Sira pressing Leiogrey back with a violent onslaught of attacks. Leiogrey drew back where Sira swung her mighty blade, only for Will to lunge in and strike with his lance, slicing a bold cut across Leiogrey's claw. I cringed in spite of myself – he was still my dragon. He uttered an enraged snarl, lowering his head to strike at Will with his full spiny jaw. Will drew back, but he couldn't outpace the dragon and took a full strike. The soldier hurtled back, blood already spilling from several wounds.

Sira shouted, lunging in at full strength to repel Leiogrey. The dragon withdrew and started to rear his iron tail back, dragging it through buildings in a rush of strength. Another second and Sira would surely be struck by it.

Ryoku rushed out in front of Sira, his dark sword raised, just as Rex stumbled out from Deltorah's dark flare near him. With hardly a split second to react, Leiogrey's tail slammed into them both with enough force to topple buildings. The combined strength of the one-armed hybrid and Ryoku's dark weapon stopped the tail short.

In the brief respite, Sira spun around and rushed to Will's side. Just as quickly, Leiogrey reared around and made to snap her up in his mighty jaws. A shimmering barrier shot up between them at the last second. Leiogrey repented with a pained wince. The dragon withdrew, snarling in rage. It looked like Guildford and Lusari were the conjurers, who quickly returned their focus to emptying the street.

While Sira dragged Will to safety, the dark flare in the other battle against Deltorah finally abated, revealing the mighty dragon snapping at Loki and Katiel. The Trickster repelled every mighty blow, sparks raining from his sword like a storm. Katiel had his side in full strength. Dagger made to close in from behind, but Deltorah spotted him and struck him with a mighty whip of his tail. It hurled him into one of the few remaining walls standing, crashing straight through the stone and spraying dust everywhere. Flying stone hit Kaia, who stumbled back as a ball of water she'd collected exploded around her. She aimed a glare Dagger's way, but the Defender struggled to rise among the ruin.

While Sira dragged Will away from Leiogrey, the mighty dragon reared and snapped at Rex and Ryoku. Ryoku lashed out with his sword held by the chains, but Leiogrey's tail didn't relent and knocked the two fighters off their feet. Leiogrey nearly trampled them in an attempt to take down Sira and Will. Behind him, Rex caught his footing and lunged, grabbing Leiogrey by the tail. Rex's sheer strength jolted the dragon and dragged him back – only a foot or two, but it worked. The dragon reeled, roaring in fury. His claw nearly swept Ryoku aside, but Rex backed into the strike instead, taking the brunt of it. One leg crumpled beneath him, and he struggled to rise. Ryoku rushed to his side to support him, eyeing the hybrid worriedly.

After leaving Will in Lusari's care, Sira returned and rushed at Leiogrey. The dragon was ready, and he lunged at her with a heavy-handed claw. She made to defend, but the claw glanced off her sword, knocking it from her grip and clear through the air to land near me. Sira's glance shot back. She had a reserved glare for me, still frozen in place, but I couldn't move my legs.

Seeing her disarmed, Leiogrey closed in. Rex swung openly at his claw, but he appeared to have taxed a lot of his energy and his strike didn't do much. Seeing this, Ryoku ducked under Leiogrey's chest and swung up mightily with Ragnarokkr. The blade glanced off Leiogrey's chin, but the force jolted the dragon's head back. Where Leiogrey temporarily lost interest in Sira, he turned down to face the vulnerable pair right within his grasp.

As Sira rushed to regain her sword, a sharp *crack* shot through the air. A blinding flash briefly illuminated the entire street, and then lifted the dust and sand from the stones with a resonating boom. Deltorah crashed backwards, his claws, wings, and tail dragging through everything as some mighty force pushed him back. Loki stood before him with his hand raised, breathing heavily.

Deltorah's path sent more rubble upon Dagger, who'd been struggling to recover from his fall. Kaia attempted to birth a barrier of water, but came up dry. Katiel appeared before them suddenly, as though he'd simply stepped from Loki's side to Kaia's. He flung his arm before him. Some sort of dark flash emanated from his skin, and the spray of rubble fell short inches from them.

Meanwhile, Ryoku seemed to be barely holding off Leiogrey with Ragnarokkr clutched above his head. Rex winded up for a mighty strike, but Leiogrey struck him aside with a mighty claw, sending the hybrid crashing into another stone wall. Leiogrey plucked Ryoku from the ground by ensnaring Ragnarokkr in his mighty fangs.

Sira slid the rest of the distance near me and snatched her sword from the stones. She caught me in her fiery glare for an instant. "What are you waiting for?" she shouted. "Can't you do something!?"

She was gone before I could try to defend myself, sprinting across the ground toward Leiogrey as he plucked Ryoku from the ground. With a mighty heave, Leiogrey tossed Ryoku and his sword across the street, where he landed roughly near Lusari and Will. The young mage girl had her staff held up against Will's injuries – they would take time to heal. Will struggled to push away Lusari and find his footing, but his injuries were severe. A broken spike jutted out from his ribcage. One shoulder hung back loosely. Leiogrey reared his head toward them again, looming overhead like a giant grey reaper.

Ryoku Dragontalen fought his way to his feet to bring himself before Lusari and Will, his dark sword held before him like a lifeline.

Sira rushed toward him like her life depended on it, but Leiogrey was fast. I tried to force my legs to move. I could only envision Leiogrey's last glance casted at me before I surrendered him to Brozogoth, and then the horror in my sons' eyes as the emperor himself slew them.

When Leiogrey lunged, Sira's sprint intensified. She threw force into her run that she didn't even have. It was Ryoku before the mighty dragon, and it couldn't end well.

However, it was too late.

(Meanwhile, in the eyes of Sira Jessura...)

No.
Crap.
Creator curse it!

I couldn't make it in time. I knew that. A fight like this wasn't one where we could just rely on luck and speed to win. Dragons were mighty creatures. They weren't limited as much by lungs and a heart as us humans were. One snap, and Ryoku was gone.

There was no way he could survive. Once I saw the strike land, I cringed away, unable to look and see my Defender like this. I was so damned stupid. How could I let him think I hated him for so long? He'd only just learned why I shrank away from his gaze, and it wasn't even his fault.

I was too stubborn. I knew this. Even my younger brother was more levelheaded than I was, the black sheep of the Jessura clan. I knew that, and yet I still insisted on being so *angry*. What else did I have? All I had in this world was Sinistra. All I knew was how to fight my way out.

What about when that didn't work? How could one fight their way *in*?

An odd sound forced me to finally raise my head and look.

There he was. Standing there, with the dragons' fangs sunken into his shoulder all the way to his hip. His sword hung at his side. I could only see Ryoku's violet eye from where I stood. Blood stained his blond hair, dripping freely from his hair, his face, his skin.

Something hit the ground. Katiel dashed toward Ryoku, ignoring a deep gash on his own shoulder. Loki was right on his tail despite how heavily sweat dripped from his brow. Dagger pulled himself from the rubble with torn hands. Kaia swayed, but followed Katiel devotedly. Even Will struggled to rise, only kept down by Lusari's firm and impatient hand on his shoulder. She didn't dare look up at Ryoku. I heard a sharp gasp of pain behind me as Rex fought to rise.

Then I saw it. Black streaks snuck through Ryoku's hair like snakes crawling from Leiogrey's great maw. That violet eye seemed to spiral, collapsing in on itself until it turned scarlet.

Before his comrades could break past him, Ryoku shot his arm out, clutching Ragnarokkr by the handle. The blade flashed like a living thing, and everyone stopped in their tracks.

"*Valiant. How truly valiant.*"

The voice sounded older and slow. It took me a moment to realize, with no other source, that it belonged to the dragon. Going by what Lamont told us, this had to be Leiogrey – his dragon. It explained why Lamont couldn't will himself to fight.

"*You are quick, little Defender. I felt confident that I could finish the warrior and his healer before you rose to your feet.*"

The dragon didn't draw back from Ryoku. The Defender merely turned his head upward a little, and a small smile spread across his lips. It wasn't Ryoku Dragontalen's normal pretty smile, but something sinister. I knew the demon within was stirring again. Leiogrey was none the wiser.

"*A costly mistake. One movement, and I will cleave you in half. Do you understand?*"

Ryoku offered no response. The dragon's lips curved upward into a sort of grin. Nobody else moved, frozen in place in fear of what could transpire. Half our group froze to the spot several feet away. The other dragon was down for the time being, and it didn't close back in on us yet.

Ryoku grip on Ragnarokkr tightened. He straightened up, causing a stream of blood to spurt from his injuries. His shoulders squared, and then he raised his other hand – and grabbed Leiogrey's jaw.

A cold, cruel laugh emanated from Ryoku. "He's pathetic."

Leiogrey's dark eyes narrowed. "What?"

Ryoku chuckled still. There was the sinister quality to his voice once more, just as it had appeared against Geri. More darkness leaked into his hair like the blood from his wounds.

"I said he's pathetic. So pathetic."

He raised his other hand, still clutching Ragnarokkr, to grasp Leiogrey's jaw. As his arms moved, something started to shimmer on his wrists. I saw Leiogrey clench his mighty jaw in what should have severed Ryoku in two. Somehow, the demon put enough strength into his grip to it from ripping him asunder.

As I stared, bewildered, the monster in Ryoku started to pull himself free of Leiogrey. Whatever light came from his wrists intensified, turning into something with a glaring sort of power. An instant later, Ryoku retreated from Leiogrey's jaws. The dragon snapped at him, but he stepped out of the way. The demon in him stepped away, studying those glowing things on his wrists.

"Huh. Interesting. So the Remnant has some value."

He spread his arms out on either side of him. I thought I saw some markings within the light on his wrists, but the light increased, blinding me. Bolts of bluish lightning escaped from his skin, dancing across the stone ground. Dust and rocks skittered around him in wild arcs. The monster stared around him, chuckling all the while in the manner of some kind of killer.

Leiogrey lunged again. This time, the monster barely stepped aside, and he cast Leiogrey a look of annoyance like he was interfering with something. "Right. I suppose I must deal with you."

The lightning died away around Ryoku's body. An instant later, Ryoku vanished in a burst of light, burning images into my eyes. I found him a moment later – he stood in the air as lightly as though walking on an unseen path, hovering well above Leiogrey's head. I saw the dragon's astounded blink, and then realization as he located the demon above his head.

Emitting a sinister chuckle, the demon above leveled Ragnarokkr out to one side. A dark gleam seemed to run the edge of the blade, interrupted by the light glaring from Ryoku's wrists. I realized that, as much of him was currently manifested by the demon, the light coming from him belonged solely to Ryoku himself.

"Wait!" Lamont cried from behind me. Ryoku stopped for a moment, and I thought the dark highlights in his hair flickered like the crests of waves. "Don't do it! Ryoku – he is still my dragon! Please!"

There was a moment of hesitation, but then the demon shot down like heavenly lightning, emitting sparks of dark and light energy around him in wild waves. Lamont advanced for the first time, his hand outstretched in fear. I saw the look in his eyes. Not again. He couldn't lose somebody else.

However, when the monster landed full-tilt against the skull of Leiogrey, it wasn't with the blade of Ragnarokkr. He flipped in the air and landed full-tilt with the heel of his boot. A loud *crack* shot through the sky with all the intensity of lightning itself. I was sure that it was the sound of Ryoku's foot shattering, but that opinion changed when Leiogrey's skull slammed into the street.

Dust and stone shrapnel sprayed everywhere. Leiogrey's mighty tail lashed into the street, ripping out chunks of stone the size of large animals and sending them down the street. Luckily, none was left in harm's way.

Ryoku flipped away with the ease of a seasoned gymnast, the lights on his wrists still gleaming. I caught a glimpse of the same lights at his ankles. They burned trails of light in the air as he moved, coming to land on the balls of his feet where he'd started. Will stared up in shock, having given up fighting off Lusari's care.

When he landed, the darkness dripped out of his hair almost like a liquid, but did not leave any pools of shadows in their wake. Ryoku stood there, his wrists still shimmering oddly. He held the stance that his demonic form had landed in – his legs apart, his hands held open and loose before his face. It looked almost like a functioning stance.

Puncture wounds riddled his shoulders, ribs, and arms, but he still stood strong – they must not be as bad as they looked, messily stained with blood as they were.

"The hell was that?" Dagger demanded, rushing to take his place at Ryoku's side. He glanced over at Ryoku's arms, then away sharply as the light burned into his eyes. "Argh, can't you tone those things down or something?"

Ryoku gave him a helpless look. Loki ran up on his other side, beaming. He looked as proud as though he'd written the marks on Ryoku's wrists himself.

"Here, try evening out your footing. If you relax your stance a little…"

Ryoku obeyed, and the gleaming settled down to a faint light emitting from his wrists, and then to nothing. I could see the symbols now on the inside of his wrists. Three intersecting waves and something like a narrow bolt of lightning running through them. He looked at them as though they didn't belong to him anymore.

I wanted to find out what the hell just happened, but there was no time. Leiogrey lifted his head from the rubble. Startlingly, a row of scales upon his brow was marred from the attack of Ryoku's monster. Deltorah wrestled his way out of the rubble, snarling madly all the while. Black streaks marred some of the scales along one leg, but he still clambered back toward us.

Guildford rushed to Ryoku's side, steel sword in hand. It seemed the road was fully clear of the populace, but it landed Guildford as the only one of us left fighting-fit. Lusari shrank back with Will as though she could make them both sink away into the sand. Loki actually uttered a frustrated sigh. Half of us could barely stand. Even Rex had taken a beating from Leiogrey, clearly favoring one leg even as he hobbled toward Ryoku.

"We can't last like this," Dagger realized aloud, taking a step closer to Ryoku. "We're damned near beat, my old friend, unless your weird trick can apply to us all."

Ryoku shook his head. "N-No, I don't think it works that way. I think it's limited too. I…"

He winced, and a red flash snaked across the golden light on his arms. At a gesture from Loki, he evened out his stance, and the light abated for the moment. It seemed he might actually be able to control it, whatever it was.

Everyone fell back into a circle. I was one of the last to circle back to Ryoku, keeping my back against Rex's. We'd fought the dragons separately until now, and that had pressed us to the bone. Now, beat as we were, I couldn't imagine fighting them both off at once.

That was when I caught a glimpse of Lamont. He stood at the end of the street still, rummaging in his small gravity bag. As I watched, he pulled out two small objects. A sapphire and a ruby. With his eyes locked on Leiogrey, he brought them to his lips.

Only then did I realize what they were – whistles.

They didn't utter a sound. At least, nothing we could hear. Leiogrey and Deltorah both halted their advances, turning their attentions to Lamont. Neither dragon moved, nor did Lamont.

I heard the urgent beating of wings coming from two separate sources. A wild breeze rolled through the street, lifting up boughs of tumbleweed to toss across the empty road. The sound grew closer until it was almost right behind Lamont.

Two shapes burst out from behind the buildings, taking flight high into the air above his head. One dragon looked smooth and blue, the other red and spiny. Each was the color of one of the whistles Lamont had produced. He held up one hand in silent command, and the red dragon released a parcel from its clutches. Lamont caught it – it looked like a sword.

The dragons spiraled down with impressive speed. Leiogrey and Deltorah surged forward, but the dragons zoomed in between them with ease. They looked much smaller than the other dragons, I realized. That must be why Lamont waited to show them. The red one snatched up Will, and the blue one caught Lusari. Like bees, they shot up to the rooftops behind Lamont.

I thought they retreated for a moment, but the dragons returned almost instantly to land like a pair of dogs before Lamont. It suddenly made sense; they followed orders, evacuating our healer and injured soldier. Everyone was in rough shape, of course, but Will was the worst off. For the other injured, the sight of the dragons filled them with vigor.

Standing before Leiogrey, I saw the pair were only about the size of the Diamond Dragon, if not a little smaller. They stood like a pair of large wolves, covered in scales, winged and horned. One was blue as the ocean, the other scarlet like flames. While the blue one held itself tall, its slender neck craned upward, the other bent forward like a savage beast, its face, neck, and back framed with spines. Both emitted low growls that made the air hum with power.

"Rhovh. Malak." Leiogrey's old voice sounded slow and tired. He almost seemed to anticipate their arrivals. "It has been a long time."

"Shut up, you old bastard!" the red one howled, practically slashing the earth in its impatience to attack. It was quite clearly male and violent. "You abandoned us! You killed my rider! You would have been better to roll over and die than face me now! I'll tear you limb from limb!"

"Patience, Malak," the blue one spoke with a clairvoyant, clear tone. This one was definitely female. "Leiogrey may not know what it is he has done. If he is innocent…"

Malak cut her off with a vicious snarl. "I don't care! Peter and Jordan – they're dead, sis! He might as well have murdered them himself!"

He lunged. With a responsive roar in challenge, Leiogrey lurched forward to meet his offense. Everyone jumped to action in defense of the young dragons. With a piercing, savage howl, Deltorah sprang right at us.

In response to Malak's attack, Rhovh wheeled back to Lamont. The rider wasted no time in hopping upon her back, yanking free a silver blade from the parcel Malak dropped.

"Ride Malak!" Lamont shouted to us frantically. "They're stronger with a partner! If you do not, we'll just lose again!"

Desperation rang clear in his voice. By the sound of it, Lamont made a huge risk in bringing the young dragons to battle. Bringing them in meant that he trusted us to finally end this for him. If not, then the only remaining dragons he had would perish. The dragons that, obviously, once belonged to his two sons.

When I looked to see who went to Malak, something rammed into me, knocking me clear off my feet. I tried to regain my footing, but that was impossible.

Sorry, girl, the male voice of Malak growled, but it sounded different than his normal speech – it was like he spoke into my mind, his loud voice projecting off everything I experienced. *I'm not messing around this time – you're the one that makes the most sense. You and me will do just fine.*

"You're fucking kidding me," I protested, but the dragon already flipped me over his head and onto his shoulders. I flailed to grab onto his rough scales and spines. I pressed myself against his back as the dragon lurched to the side, narrowly avoiding Leiogrey's incoming claw. "Fine! Fine, whatever! But this is only temporary, I need to protect—"

The Dragontalen, Malak replied shortly. *The blond one. He looks like my rider's brother. I see. We share a common goal, girl. Tell me your name.*

A smirk played across my lips, but quickly slipped as Malak leapt, easily flying over Leiogrey's shoulder. Deltorah was momentarily close enough to touch, but I was too worried about losing my grip to swing at him.

"Sira Jessura," I replied. "Have it your way. As long as he's protected, then I'm yours."

Malak roared in response. Rhovh let out a responsive howl, her cry like a swan over the water.

Leiogrey wheeled around to face Malak and I, but Rhovh and Lamont appeared at our side like they'd been there the whole time. I nervously glanced back, and saw Will returning to the fight. Lusari was trying to drag Ryoku off for healing, and Guildford appeared to be seeing to Loki.

"How amusing," Leiogrey droned. His head became level with ours. He was so close that I could make out every detail in his dark irises. "Dragons with riders. How foolish. Dragons do not require such a partnership to exist. You could have revealed yourselves two years ago and saved yourselves the trouble of dying here."

"Only impertinent dragons believe such a thing," Rhovh replied loud and clear. "You have changed, old friend. We used to train together. With Lamont, you were stronger than ever. You sound like you would sooner pass of old age now."

Leiogrey snarled, exhaling a burst of ashy smoke upon us. Malak and Rhovh circled around it with ease. "I have never needed a rider," he cursed. He swung again with a heavy silver claw. At the same time, Deltorah flew overhead and unleashed a wicked burst of dark flames down upon us. The pair of dragons skirted around it with synonymous ease. Watching their movements, I realized the dragons might be as much twins as Peter and Jordan Declovin were.

"Bastard!" Malak screamed. He spun around Leiogrey's unfurled wing, arching into the air. I gripped on for dear life as he circled over Leiogrey and zeroed in on Deltorah. "Brozogoth addles your mind! You probably don't even remember the days with the old man!"

Deltorah whirled around with a vicious snarl, beating his wings to stay afloat, and lashed out at us with his tail. Malak was far too quick for the savage dragon, and he easily spun out of the way. Below us, the others ganged up on Leiogrey. I saw Loki and Dagger lashing out wildly, backing the dragon down the street as Rhovh circled around, Lamont's sword striking at any opening. In the sky, it was only us and Deltorah.

"You dare insult the master?" Deltorah hissed. It was the first time I heard the savage dragon speak, and his voice sent a chill running down my spine. He sounded diseased, addled, and possibly insane. Was he always like this, or was Malak right and the emperor to blame?

Deltorah lunged again, this time snapping out with his sharp array of fangs. Malak circled around close to the head of the beast. Finding my grip on Malak's scales, I spared my other hand and lashed out with Sinistra at Deltorah's scaly brow. The dragon howled, writhing through the air and slashing out at us wildly. It forced Malak into frenzied flips through the air to avoid the attacks. I clutched onto his spines for dear life.

After a moment, Deltorah froze entirely, hanging in the air with only a heavy wing beat keeping him afloat. Malak, too, halted; uttering a low growl that sprayed sparks across his muzzle. I wondered what the two were experiencing until a shadow passed over me.

The wingspan of the arrival was near silent, but the entity was huge. It dwarfed Leiogrey and Deltorah easily, making us like ants in comparison to the beast that silently flew overhead. It circled above us, blotting out the sun for a good while. I saw huge, forked wings, a long tail, and claws that caught the sunlight like molten lava.

Deltorah lowered himself to the ground, and Malak followed. Even Leiogrey came to a pause, leaving my friends scattered around the dragon, glancing around in confusion. Lamont simply stared up, his weapon dropped absently at his side.

Malak was squirming oddly, as I stayed upon his back, retreating next to Rhovh as we contemplated the new arrival. I noticed Rhovh shuddering, too, and Lamont's eyes turned skyward. I realized, to my horror, that the dragons shook with fear.

The mighty monster landed before us with a crash. Buildings crumpled to practically dust before his great wingspan. Screams signified that some citizens apparently hid within those buildings. The ground shook like an outside force rattled the great city dome.

This dragon was a shining gold color. He was even more magnificent than Leiogrey, but wasn't laden with nearly as many spikes. The only set he bore fanned around his giant skull, giving him an eerie look as though constantly grinning. A pair of dark topaz eyes were already taking us in with fervor, eyes the size of Malak or Rhovh easily.

"Brozogoth," Lamont said, his voice small in the destroyed street. "The emperor of dragons."

SCENE FIVE: TRICKSTER GOD'S LYRIC

...Of Act Six: Alteration

In the eyes of Ryoku Dragontalen, we are in Vortiger Capital, in the world of Vortiger (cold season) It is early afternoon On November 12th, 2017.

"Here, let me deal with this."

Loki stepped out at the head of our group. He stood before Sira and Lamont, both upon their chosen dragons, and the rest of us as we contemplated our new foe. The Trickster flashed me a confident grin.

"What is he planning?" Lamont whispered hesitantly. Loki heard him, and he winked at the rider while he strolled up to the huge dragon. Brozogoth seemed to humor him, staring down at the puny human before him like food strolling up to its prey. As Loki strolled up, I noticed green sparks coursing over the back of his hand like an electric current. Brozogoth couldn't see the sparks, but I thought Leiogrey might be able to from where the silver dragon perched. However, he said nothing.

"Brozogoth, the emperor of dragons, keeper of Vortiger." Loki spoke loudly and gallantly, clear enough for all to hear.

"And you are Loki, the Trickster god," a deep, strong voice came from the dragon, resounding clearly through the street. I thought most of the huge city must hear it, as it surely stood still at the emperor's arrival in their midst. Personally, I found my feet frozen to the ground. I'd agreed to face the dragon emperor, but I hadn't even considered his size. He was close to the size of Deltorah, but that was still enough to crush our two dragons underfoot.

Loki scowled. "Dragons are always messing with the natural order, but this is beyond me. How did you possibly come to this world? How does this make any sense?"

Brozogoth chuckled, a noise that made the very streets shudder. "You refer to the natural order of a mess of broken realms, Trickster. Anything is possible here, just as it has ever been before. I grew up in this world of ever-changing weather. I faced summer after winter of the harshest weathers alongside my master, Rassaq. I do not recall having a family. It was only the two of us against this cruel world.

"When the plague took Rassaq from this world, I was shoved aside." Brozogoth's voice turned harsher than the worst summer. "It seemed that, by the natural order of things, I had no standing. Once Rassaq was gone, that became quite clear. I was but his tool, an accomplice to the great things he accomplished at the head of the council. Others had dragons, but they still held reign. The natural order you claim to be so great merely shoved me aside, Trickster, once my master was gone."

"I apologize for the council's actions, Brozogoth," Lamont spoke, incurring Rhovh to step a little closer to Loki. The Trickster tried to silence him with a look, but Lamont stayed. "The council has always been harsh and unruly. They consider themselves higher than all else. My father was no different."

Brozogoth glanced down at Lamont, and exhaled a burst of dark smoke from his snout. "Ah. Lamont Declovin, son of the great Raimundo Declovin. He took the seat Rassaq once held with seemingly little remorse." He bared his fangs, but it took me a moment to realize it was more of a grin than a dangerous gesture. Given the size of this dragon, though, even a hiccup could kill us. "You were kinder. That is why I gave you the choice of handing over your dragon. I meant to allow your sons to continue, but they resisted. I apologize for that."

His grin faded. "But you looked a gift horse in the mouth. You spat in the name of my kindness. I kept Leiogrey and Deltorah alive to serve me as the last remaining dragons of Vortiger, and you hid these two young dragons from me. For two full years, you have avoided me. That changes now."

"Why did you capture the city?" Loki demanded. "Surely Rassaq was not a terrible ruler. Why would you become a tyrant in his stead?"

Brozogoth chuckled once more, the noise quaking the very streets of the Capital. "A tyrant, Trickster? You would call me a tyrant?" His glance slid over the dragons before focusing on Lamont again. "I have done this miserable world a favor. By eliminating the council and destroying all other dragons, I have brought life into this world again. I have stamped out the minds of those who would think otherwise. I have rewritten the laws of trade and commerce. Risen taxes, the return of the death sentence, and slavery are all but means to an end. This world needs structure to prevent an insidious council from wakening again. Under the longevity of my rule, such a thing will never happen.

"You have a choice, Lamont Declovin," he rumbled. The volume of his voice rose so that the entire street seemed to shudder. "Surrender to me once more. I will keep your dragons alive. With Rhovh, I could birth an heir and keep dragons on Vortiger for the rest of her days. This minor confrontation will end with good things, despite the nature of your assault against my fellow dragons."

Then, inevitably, his glance slid over to me. Despite the enormity of this dragon, I could easily feel the weight of his topaz eyes upon me. I was little more than an ant to him. "Of course, you must surrender the wanted fugitive as well. You were a well-tamed sheep until now. Has he sparked the idea of revolution in your head, Lamont? Has he given you false hope where there is none?"

I faced Lamont with a bit of trepidation. Would he actually sell me out? Those were almost workable terms. Brozogoth would let him live on without fear.

"Lamont, don't listen to him," Loki said urgently. "You've only known us for a few days, I know, but you must listen to reason. You have the means to end this battle here and now. You can free your world into a golden age. Brozogoth would only lie to you, deceive you, ruin you. He would stamp out or use anything in his way. Surely you know this."

"Of course I do," Lamont snapped. As a smile lit Loki's lips in response, Lamont turned Rhovh to face Brozogoth. "You murdered the entire council, including my father. You killed dozens of dragons. You demanded my surrender, took Leiogrey for yourself, and then killed my sons."

"All necessary losses," Brozogoth responded. "At the time. You could join me now, and end this foolish fight. You currently harbor a team of fugitives. Orden has issued a weighty bounty on his head. For that price, we could expand the domes surrounding the capital. We could even build tunnels leading from city to city. I see nothing but prosperity in our future."

I watched Lamont nervously. To a world that suffered as much as Vortiger, that was hugely promising. Were it not for my own personal goals, my sister's sake, and for those of my comrades that placed hope in me, I would almost surrender to such terms. Knowing Vortiger could prosper in my stead would almost be worthwhile, but when I thought of my sister's face, stuck alone in an orphanage, I had to stare Brozogoth in the face. His topaz eyes studied me curiously. In front of me, the sparks around Loki's hands behind his back were expanding widely. Surely Brozogoth was about to notice them.

"The world can't grow like that under your rule," Lamont told him. "We might build pathways and expand the city, but that won't eliminate the fear. If you would kill my children, murder the entire council, and press dragons almost to extinction, what else would you do?"

Brozogoth was ready to reply, but Loki interrupted. He flung his hands in the air before him. A brilliant *clap* shot through the air, hammering against my eardrums as though somebody shot a gun right beside me. Bright light overtook the entire street, even seeming to reflect from the outside dome, as Loki launched a massive bolt of lightning from his hands.

I couldn't have seen what unfolded next, shielding my eyes from the blinding light. I only heard the sound of lightning slamming into something. The whole street shook with enkindled ferocity. Buildings that remained standing in the street collapsed. The stone beneath my feet shuddered so violently that I was sure some of it broke. Above us, something shattered and caused a cold draft to break through – the outer shield. Not for the first time, I wondered what Loki was truly capable of.

When I could finally uncover my eyes, my breath caught in my chest.

Leiogrey and Deltorah both crumpled before Brozogoth, their sides blackened terribly from the lightning strike. Brozogoth remained behind them, unharmed and looking quite pleased with himself.

Loki crumpled to his knees. The power he mustered seemed to take a vast amount of energy from him. Chuckling darkly, Brozogoth pushed both dragons aside with a mighty claw.

"Leiogrey," Lamont whispered. He vaulted from Rhovh's back and ran to the older pair of dragons. Both were clearly unconscious, and I wasn't sure they could survive such a mortal blow.

Malak threw back his head and unleashed a horrible howl. "You *bastard!*" he screamed, and kicked off from the ground with such strength that the stone crumpled beneath his claws. I saw Sira struggling to remain on his back. "I'll murder you myself! I'll avenge the race of dragons by erasing you from this world!"

Rhovh kicked off the ground with just as much ferocity as Malak. Guildford rushed forward and grabbed Loki around the shoulders, dragging the Trickster out of harm's way. Everyone else was ready to back the dragons if they needed it, but none was quite so sure how to fight Brozogoth.

Each dragon shot over a shoulder of the emperor and unleashed wicked bursts of flame. Brozogoth didn't even try to dodge them. The flames licked angrily at his scales, and he seemed impervious. Once both passed overhead, he started to flap his enormous wings, creating a gale that set both dragons off kilter. I saw Sira clinging to Malak for dear life while the dragon careened close to the next street's buildings, narrowly avoiding colliding with them. Rhovh wasn't so lucky, and she crashed into the roof of a building.

"*Sis!*" Malak screamed, narrowly avoiding collision again in his anger. He veered sharply off course and rushed straight at Brozogoth again. The emperor glanced over, his topaz eyes alight. When Malak got in range, Brozogoth unhinged his jaw. A massive column of flames shot from the dragon's open mouth, and Malak only narrowly dodged it, swearing and screaming all the while.

Seeming to dismiss the threat, Brozogoth took a huge step toward us. That was all it took for the dragon to tower overhead. He fixated me in his gaze. Everyone closed in around me, but it didn't prevent his piercing gaze.

"Ryoku Dragontalen," the dragon rumbled. He was so close that I could almost feel the heat from his recent blast of fire. His sheer voice shook the entire street. Would there be anything left of this area by the time we finished? "You have a choice to make. Surrender now, and see the world of Vortiger prosper. Put an end to this ridiculous chase with the empire of Orden and let your judgement catch up to you. Or you can die. Either way, I will be cashing in your bounty to make my own world prosper."

I stared the dragon emperor in the face. He could easily snap me up in his jaws before I could do so much as smile. Malak had landed atop a nearby building, ready to strike. Rhovh returned to us with a light glide.

I saw Dagger's glance – he flashed me a grin. I recalled his words from the Day of Black. *Never surrender. Never take prisoners. It's all do or die in this fucked-up world, and if we don't do this now... it'll just happen to somebody else.*

Even if I hadn't been myself those days, I still vividly recalled them. The rage struck as I saw Guildford collapse against the chalkboard, eyes wide in disbelief. The rage remained through the following days: the nights at home where my foster parents consoled me, the nights with my friends where we consoled one another, standing with my hands folded before me at Guildford's funeral. It was stronger than ever when Joey, Katiel, Dagger, and I assembled near Varis' hideout the same day, dressed in our funeral clothes, ready to combat the darkness.

After everything – the skirmish, the screams, the blows exchanged, the flash of a hot knife – it never left. Still Dagger assured me that we stopped the same thing from happening again, even though it was at a high personal cost.

Now, I stood before a similar enemy. A dragon that would have me shipped to Orden in exchange for riches. From what Lamont told us, I wasn't even sure Vortiger would receive the special treatment he promised. His promises were clear poison, meant to appear harmless until we dropped dead.

I knew what I had to do. Determined, I stepped forward. My limbs stung from the wounds peppered across me from Leiogrey's fangs, but they didn't hinder me. I was far too close to Brozogoth, I knew, but I still strode forward. The dragon emperor stared down at me like I was a new species of bug – curious, but a pest nonetheless.

"Do your worst," I told him, loud and clear. "You'll never take me alive."

Nothing happened for a moment. An almost shrill silence hung in the air. I could faintly hear footsteps that hardly had more impact than the footfalls of a cat, but Brozogoth still stared down at me, dumbstruck. Then, very slowly, he grinned, baring all rows of fangs.

"Very well," he rumbled. His voice, even quiet, shook the ground at my feet. I felt like I was standing before a tank. "I rather hoped it might end this way, if we are being truthful. Why the empire wanted such a dangerous criminal taken in alive is beyond me – this will serve much better."

His claw lifted from the ground like the executioner's axe. The sun from the barrier above caught the steely ivory of his claws, making them gleam like a true weapon. One talon would be enough to sever me in half, but he would decimate me with the entire claw.

I readied Ragnarokkr, only hoping that the blade entrusted to my name could save my life. I could run, but I would only make it nary a foot before his huge jaws snapped me up. After all I'd said and done, there was no running now.

Something slammed into me. It swept me off my feet like I'd never walked the earth. I felt cold scales beneath me –Rhovh. Then my mind started to catch up, and I saw diamonds under my grip.

I will repay my debt to you.

The familiar, clairvoyant tone sounded like water drops upon crystals. She sounded older, but there was no mistaking the voice that transfixed me in Bonnin. The dragon that I stood against my friends to protect – the diamond dragon, Sapphense.

Brozogoth's claws tore through the stone, spraying an enormous cloud of dust across the street. My friends stepped clear of the fight. I saw Loki, weakly leaning against Guildford, flash me a brilliant grin. Malak howled and ripped into the sky like a flame.

As Lamont remained by the sides of Leiogrey and Deltorah, I saw somebody else run to Rhovh's side and take to the air. By the glint of steel, I knew it was Will.

You face a perilous foe in this strange new world. By saving my life, you may have forged an unintentional bond, for I sensed your danger from far away. It was all I could do to rush to your aid. With you astride me, we will defeat this terrible foe.

I was so grateful I almost collapsed on her back, but I had a job to do, so I adjusted my position on her back in open air. The closest I'd ever done to *this* was getting Rex's help to sail the wind and help those kids in need. This was a different matter altogether. The ground was dizzyingly far below us – Sapphense was fast.

With some effort, I maneuvered around to keep my legs by her wings and my arms around her neck. Maybe it was because I'd never ridden her before, but I thought she was bigger now than she had been.

"Interesting," Brozogoth's powerful voice rumbled. It couldn't possibly quake the ground at my feet now, but the volume of his voice seemed to make the very air shudder. "Another dragon. A female, too. With you, I could repopulate this world of dragons all under my command. They would be strong."

"I would sooner perish," Sapphense responded like a cut diamond. She leveled out, keeping afloat with a steady flap of her wings as we faced the emperor. Even Sapphense was only about as large as this monster's head. "What sort of devilry have you done? Dragons and humans are not meant to clash – we are to coexist, as my rider's clan has known many centuries."

That sounded odd to me. Was she talking about my family?

Brozogoth chuckled. "Coexist? Truly?" His laughter only grew, and his tail crashed into the street, sending stone spraying up for yards in all directions. "You did not live here, diamond one. You did not see how I was treated at the death of my rider. To think we can coexist is foolish naivety. As young dragons, you do not know any better. Abandon your passenger, and I will show you the future."

Sapphense snorted, and a rich blue flame shot from her snout. "Never."

Brozogoth's laughter only ceased now, and his narrowed topaz eyes turned to Sapphense. "Then you will perish with the lot of them."

That was all the warning he gave – he reared up and swung with one of his heavy-handed claws. The speed with which he swung was frightening. I realized he'd been merely toying with me when he struck at me before. Sapphense circled around it with ease, and pivoted past him, circling around to Malak and Rhovh.

"Take up arms with me!" she cried, the song of her voice rising up in a way Brozogoth's never could. "Dragons of Vortiger, heed my cry! This day, we will free you from tyranny!"

Malak and Rhovh howled into the sky like wolves, joining Sapphense in the brave cry. Brozogoth didn't utter a sound, his eyes following Sapphense like a pesky fly. On the ground, I saw Katiel and Kaia step forward. Katiel removed his robe, handing it to Kaia, who kept a grey flute in her hands.

A moment later, I heard the sound of world travel resonate through the air. It opened up next to Kaia, and out came the giant sea serpent I met in Bonnin – Reze, although he had a full, longer name I couldn't hope to recall. Although he was a skinny sort of dragon, his length was easily more impressive than the three dragons we had.

Next to him, Katiel started walking toward Brozogoth. As he did, he began to change. My jaw dropped, stunned. Was this the power he talked about before? His *Omega*?

He grew much taller and wider. His skin turned to red, and I saw the scales grow from his flesh. Before my eyes, my six-foot friend Katiel Fereyen changed into an enormous dragon.

He stood closer to the size of Leiogrey than anything else, and unfurled a set of great red wings with gold webbing from within himself. He used these wings to take off into the air and avoid crushing our friends. Everyone else backed away a great deal, whether out of surprise or respect. Maybe even fear. As he reared up, I saw a golden emblem on his chest, while the rest of his scales were scarlet and his webbing gold. His golden eyes caught mine, and a dragon's smirk spread across his lips.

"What do you think, Ryoku?" Katiel called out in his normal voice, but it now carried gravity that reverberated through the air. "This is just a taste, but I thought it'd be fitting to help you out now. My Omega."

Kaia was shining like it was her own power he demonstrated, but I was completely awestruck. Lamont herded everyone else back to a safe distance while Kaia hopped onto Reze's back. If the assembled five dragons couldn't handle Brozogoth, then all was surely lost.

"What a show!" Brozogoth declared, snorting flames all over the stones. "Two more dragons to destroy. I must commend the pair of you, dragon and rider, for bringing me such a trial!"

Katiel snorted derisively, conjuring a blast of flames twice the size of Brozogoth's. "Now that I'm riled up, I could take you on myself. Me and Reze, maybe. The rest of you should sit back. I don't want you getting hurt. It wouldn't do if you lost your rider, Diamond Dragon."

Sapphense looked over at him. "You seem to think I *could* lose my rider. And my name is Sapphense." Then she turned to Malak and Rhovh. "You two are young. The Omega, the serpent, and I will take the lead. Steer clear of his claws. For a big oaf, he is fast. A dead dragon can protect no one."

"Don't underestimate us!" Malak warned, but Rhovh seemed to demand his attention with a stern glare. They knew how dangerous their foe was.

The dragons all locked eyes with one another. It seemed a silent call to action, as all conscious dragons reared their heads back and roared. The significance of the sound jarred the air and made everything feel heavy. I didn't even cover my ears – I was transfixed, staring at the beauty of the Diamond Dragon before me. Without her, I wouldn't be able to stand in this battle. Now I could keep my promise.

SCENE SIX: THE DECIDING BATTLE

...Of Act Six: Alteration

*In the eyes of Ryoku Dragontalen, we are in
Vortiger Capital, in the world of Vortiger (cold season)
It is early afternoon
On November 12th, 2017.*

The battle began like the ignition of a flame. Rearing back from his roar, Brozogoth lunged straight at Sapphense and I with a heavy claw. Sapphense was faster, and spun aside in the air to avoid it. A blast of fire from Katiel's maw struck the emperor in the back of the head. Brozogoth howled in defiance, striking back with his horned skull in the hopes of inflicting some damage, but Katiel swerved aside.

Malak and Rhovh took the opportunity to sweep through under Brozogoth's unfurled wings. I saw Will and Sira each brandishing their weapons before disappearing from view, then Brozogoth snarled in rage, attempting to beat them off by bashing them with his wings. Katiel flew in and swept them up with his own wings just in time.

When the emperor turned on Katiel, Reze sprang in like an uncoiled serpent, latching huge fangs onto Brozogoth's neck. The emperor swung madly, but Reze was far too slippery to take a hit. In the attempt, a claw struck Katiel's back. He snarled in pain, but threw himself and the smaller dragons out of harm's way. The toss gave the smaller dragons more velocity, and they ripped through the sky like freed banners.

Sapphense took flight upward, trying to lure Brozogoth above the city. It didn't seem to be doing much. Katiel and the two smaller dragons followed suit, but Reze still grappled with Brozogoth. Sapphense reared back her head and unleashed a blast of bluish-white flames down upon Brozogoth's back. The dragon screeched, and Reze broke free, slithering its way up into the sky after us.

When Brozogoth saw us all above him, the plan was far too obvious. With a wide grin, Brozogoth brought his mace-like tail down into the nearest building, spraying dust and stone everywhere. The cries of human pain were enough for Sapphense, with an aggravated growl, to lunge back down.

The other dragons followed suit. Brozogoth waited, unhinged his jaw, and I saw the embers birthing within his open maw. Sapphense didn't cut away until a livid batch of flames birthed into the air, and she unleashed what looked like a burst of diamonds into Brozogoth's neck. Before Brozogoth could react, she spread her wings and rode the hot wind from the flames higher into the sky. Katiel rushed right past us, and into the flames.

I leaned forward on Sapphense and screamed in shock. Hadn't he seen the flames coming up like we did?

The flames curled away to reveal Katiel, unharmed, flinging himself down at Brozogoth. He landed upon the dragon's back and clamped down with his huge fangs. Brozogoth roared, enraged, rolling around in an attempt to shake the big dragon. When Katiel withdrew, Reze snaked down and unleashed a mighty blast of water into the emperor's neck, aided by Kaia's own magic. Brozogoth flailed, nearly ramming Katiel with his giant wings, but Katiel flung himself out of harm's way.

Malak and Rhovh shot out from behind him and blasted Brozogoth with parallel jets of fire. When Brozogoth reared on them, Katiel caught them with his hind legs to drag them all out of the way of Brozogoth's flame. Reze dodged on his own, and the flames sputtered out only yards from Sapphense and I.

In the wake of the flames, Sapphense unleashed another blast of her diamond breath. Brozogoth saw them coming and swatted them aside, but one buried itself in the center of his claw. He swung his head back and roared in pure rage. He aimed another blast of flames at us, but Sapphense didn't move – we were safely out of range, and the flames died out long before hitting us.

While Brozogoth struggled to remove the diamond in his claw, the dragons launched an all-out attack. Sapphense sprayed an array of diamonds downward, while Katiel and Reze closed in from either side to try and grapple the dragon. He stepped out of Katiel's way, but Reze latched onto his other claw. Brozogoth flailed until he freed himself, then batted Reze aside with a powerful claw. The dragon spiraled in the air, but seemed unhurt. Malak and Rhovh swooped in before Brozogoth could refocus on his claw, both blasting him with parallel jets of flame. He snarled in annoyance, but appeared overall unfazed and yanked the diamond from his hand with his fangs.

Brozogoth's head shot up towards us. A spurt of pain shot through my head. I cried out, unconsciously tightening my grip on Sapphense. The surprised dragon reared, glancing back at me to see what the problem was. I clutched my head, checking for blood, but there was nothing. Then my hand blurred before me as another jolt of pain shot through me.

I heard the roar of flames as the loudest noise I could recall, jarring against my splitting head as though a train just hurtled past my ear. Brozogoth was attacking. Sapphense, caught off guard, took wing to avoid the attack. I suddenly had no grip beneath my hands.

I lunged through the splitting pain in my head, trying to latch onto Sapphense, but she'd already flown free of my grasp. I tumbled off the dragon and into a terrifyingly open sky.

(Meanwhile, in the eyes of Sira Jessura...)

As Malak peaked in the sky, I saw Sapphense spiraling up through the air, uttering a frantic hum – Ryoku was gone. A cold clutch gripped my chest, and I glanced down just in time to see Brozogoth snatch Ryoku out of the open sky.

I almost felt the tension spike between Malak and Rhovh, sharing the anxiety that probably gripped Will, too. The pair of young dragons shot downward through the sky, but we couldn't keep up with the Diamond Dragon. She zoomed past us, wings tucked against her sides to accelerate her descent.

All movement ceased when Brozogoth clamped his jaws down against Ryoku's body. It didn't impale him, but Brozogoth kept him secured. It looked like he was unconscious.

"Enough is enough!" the emperor snarled past Ryoku in his jaws. "I have humored your plight – now I demand your surrender. An ounce more of strength, and I will crush your hero between my fangs."

The dragons hovered anxiously in the air for a moment. Malak and Rhovh exchanged glances, then huffed in anger. Sapphense came to land before Brozogoth, her crystalline eyes boring into his. Katiel and Reze landed on either side of her, and Reze's rider dismounted. After a moment, Malak and Rhovh descended, too. Once Malak hit the ground, though, I vaulted off his back. I saw Will follow suit as I yanked Sinistra from my back.

"*Drop him!*" I screamed, running at the dragon emperor with my blazing blade. Brozogoth's topaz eyes stared back at me, and I saw pain within them. The last strike had hurt, and so he turned the tides. Now he was done playing fair.

Brozogoth only chuckled darkly. "And why would I do that? I should have done this from the start. Now I demand your unconditional surrender."

I halted next to Will, our chests heaving like a single unit. I couldn't keep my eyes off Ryoku. I heard the others run up to the dragons, just as helpless and angry as I was. Loki was up, which was good news.

"Your surrender?" Brozogoth asked lethally. He closed his jaws a little tighter, and Ryoku's body convulsed. Katiel, still in his Omega-dragon form, hotly blasted the walkway with fire out of frustration. Reze and Sapphense hovered, growling deep within their throats. Rhovh held Malak back with her jaws clamped around the snarling dragon's tail.

"Allow us a moment," Guildford requested politely, but his tone was tense. He beckoned Will and I over. Hesitating angrily, we obeyed. The dragons circled around us. I wasn't sure whether it was to protect us or listen in.

"This looks fuckin' bad," Dagger muttered. His fists clenched like vices around his dagger hilts. "The hell are we gonna do? He'll chomp our boy in half if we don't throw in the towel."

"You think?" I retorted angrily, but regretted my outburst when Guildford scowled. His eyes didn't defer from Ryoku once.

"We must act quickly," Rex murmured. "What are we supposed to do, though?"

"Maybe I could use my magic?" Lusari suggested.

Katiel shook his dragonhead gravely. "Even I couldn't snatch him up before Brozogoth takes a chunk out of him. Look at that grip. We have to persuade him somehow. Surprise him."

"What if we surrender?" Kaia asked gently. When all eyes turned to her, she smiled sadly. "Maybe we could work something out after."

"Even if we surrender," Loki said heavily – he still leaned on Guildford, and his brow was thick with sweat, "Brozogoth would kill him anyway. You heard him. He supports the bounty of Orden."

Silence shortly fell over us. I punched the ground, frustrated. There was no way we could get this far just to be thwarted now, was there? We were so damned close to Orden! Without Ryoku, there was no common goal holding us together. Loki would never lend us his strength without his favorite Defender. Even Will wasn't likely to follow me to Orden. None of this group would actually follow me without him. Then what would I do?

Something stirred out of the corner of my eye, drawing my attention. I turned around just as Leiogrey and Deltorah rose to their feet just out of sight of Brozogoth. My heart sank deeper than it had ever before. We stood absolutely no chance now, I knew. Five dragons could take Brozogoth if we had to, but against three fully-grown dragons?

Leiogrey lunged, quick as a crocodile, and latched onto Brozogoth's injured hand.

The emperor let out a mighty bellow of anguish. "What the—"

Deltorah threw himself on Brozogoth's back, cutting the emperor short. Those two were close in size, and Deltorah pushed Brozogoth down with startling ease even as Brozogoth's spikes pressed into Deltorah and drew blood.

Sapphense took the opening. Without a word, she took to the sky, cutting through the wind like a hot blade to paper. If I had blinked, surely I would have missed Sapphense latching straight onto

Brozogoth's lower jaw. Blood sprayed in all directions, the weight of it crushing stone beneath the dragon.

The realization made me cringe back, but immediately lean forward as I saw Ryoku fall from Brozogoth's clutches. He had huge splatters of blood across his chest. Leave it to our Defender to not be chewed on by only one dragon in a day, but two. Still, the sight made my blood run cold.

I didn't have time to react. Malak and Rhovh kicked off the ground, flying in sync below Brozogoth's open jaw, and Rhovh managed to catch him on her back. Malak flashed me a cocky grin of victory, and the twin dragons reeled toward us.

Will caught my glance as the dragons returned, and we ran forward to meet them. Everyone was a mere heartbeat behind us. Rhovh landed softly before Guildford, who, with Lusari's help, unloaded Ryoku from the back of the dragon. The teacher nodded gratefully, but Rhovh shook off his thanks with a gentle smile.

With a scornful cough, Malak returned our attention to the brawl. Leiogrey and Deltorah were actively grappling with the emperor. Now Katiel and Reze joined in, coming from either side to take as much force off Sapphense as they could. Brozogoth held strong, Sapphense clutched in his massive jaw. Blood poured thickly from the pair. It was impossible to tell whose was whose.

I returned my stare to Will, who nodded shortly. With not a word to the others, we vaulted onto the backs of our dragons and drew our weapons once more. I thought the telltale ring of Sinistra would alert the emperor dragon, but he was helpless either way. The odds were finally ours.

When the dragons peaked above Brozogoth's head, Will and I dove off in unison. Our screams filled the air as we plummeted. I briefly wondered if this was how Ryoku felt when he fell from Sapphense, but I forced the thought from my mind as I maneuvered Sinistra downward.

Our weapons crashed into the emperor's skull with matchless force. Will's lance sank in next to the bloody face of Sinistra. Dark blood sprayed out in rivulets, splashing across our pants and drenching our weapons.

I felt the dragon's life force fade beneath us. I stumbled, and Will fell into me. It occurred to me that becoming a dragon rider was much more fatiguing than I could have ever imagined. The bond between Malak and I pulled at me constantly during our battle. We took each other's strength and fought with it in accordance to our own. Even though Will had risen to the occasion of riding Rhovh after Lamont went to his dragons, did it affect him too?

I didn't realize we were falling until we landed on Reze's back, who caught us on its lengthy body mid-air. The dragon-serpent flashed us an oddly human grin before snaking back down to the ground.

Everyone gathered around, smothering us with congratulations. Lamont was grinning from ear to ear, his sword carelessly discarded behind him. Guildford patted me on the shoulder like I'd just returned from war. Rex appeared to support me – only then did I realize how much trouble it was to walk. Ryoku was awake, and I caught the glance of his true green eye. A selfish part of me wanted him to run to me, to embrace me and congratulate me for defeating the great emperor dragon.

Then his smile was gone, and everything came crashing down.

I watched him run past me in slow motion. He went fast, possibly aided by those strange glowing marks of his. I felt a drop of water hit my elbow – a tear.

I turned to face the gruesome sight. The fallen body of Brozogoth lay amid the wreckage in the street. His giant topaz eyes were lifeless, blood still gushing from the sockets, his horns, and seemingly every interval of his golden scales. Leiogrey, Deltorah, and Katiel clambered away from him. Katiel reverted to his human form in the blink of an eye, stumbling straight into Kaia's waiting arms.

There lay Sapphense, discarded like a ragdoll next to Brozogoth's body. Blood soaked her normally pristine scales, her flawless exterior, pouring from her agape jaw that hung in a twisted angle.

Ryoku ran to the dragon's side and flung himself against her. "No," he whispered – the singular sound seemed to hang like a grave over the dusty street. When I knew what he found there, my heart felt like it sank to the center of the world of Vortiger. Sapphense, the same Diamond Dragon he'd narrowly saved in Bonnin, was dead.

Nobody approached him for a long moment, hanging back, shameful of the pride and happiness we felt for the moment. I knew it was still there – we'd won, by the Creator's name! – but we'd lost this beautiful dragon in the effort. The dragon that Ryoku stood against all of us to protect. He was the last voice of this beautiful creature. It was the only thing that saved her in Bonnin, and they both knew it. Our combined attacks would have killed her. Now she had survived all that, for this? To die in an alien world?

Loki was the first to approach. I made to follow, but stumbled – Rex steadied me, and then we carefully approached. Ryoku laid his head against the dragon's shoulder. Sobs gently shook him, and his eyes hid from us.

"She lived since you last saw her," Loki told him gently, putting his arm around the Defender. "Time has passed. Perhaps Sapphense went to another world like this one, and she grew older. We will mourn for a time, my friend. Remember your journey, the purpose for it. We cannot tarry for long."

"If this is what my journey beholds," Ryoku mumbled against his fallen dragon, "then I don't want to continue it."

SCENE SEVEN: GOODBYES

...Of Act Six: Alteration

*In the eyes of Ryoku Dragontalen, we are in
Vortiger Capital, in the world of Vortiger (warm season)
It is late afternoon
On November 12th, 2017.*

In the strange world of Vortiger, where the seasons changed every day, a week passed since the dire battle of Brozogoth. It remained the same day in my world, but that didn't seem to affect the laws of Vortiger. So, while only an hour passed by in my world, I lived a week in Vortiger.

A week after I lost a friend. At the same time, a mere hour.

Three of those days had been spent in the infirmary along with most of my friends – Will, Katiel, Dagger, Loki, Lusari, Rex, and even the dragons all sustained injuries that needed urgent attention. I was no exception. The others were always at our side while we recovered. Sira irritably insisted she only joined because of everyone else, but she held my hand the whole time. I couldn't meet her glance, not since I learned the truth about my eye. I tried to avoid looking at her with my violet eye. She ignored all those attempts, and bravely stared me in the face.

Will and the dragon twins recovered before me. The others took most of the week to heal. I hung around for most of that time.

Alongside the others, I got to know the dragons Leiogrey and Deltorah since Brozogoth released them from his mental control – the same mental power he'd used to attack me atop Sapphense in the battle.

Leiogrey was old and wise, while oddly similar to Lamont. He knew a great deal about Vortiger's history and loved to talk. Deltorah was more moody and harder to speak with. Lamont assured me it was only due to the absence of his own master, Raimundo – Lamont's late father. Where I couldn't get much out of Deltorah, though, Guildford seemed to be spending a lot of time with the older dragon. I often saw them sitting together, well away from the others and conversing quietly.

As Lamont explained earlier, dragons usually controlled two elements. Leiogrey was of ice and kinetic energy, while Deltorah was darkness and fire. Brozogoth himself was made of fire and mental energy. Malak and Rhovh were quite young, still, and only applied to the singular elements of fire and water. Reze was not technically a dragon, and didn't count – nor did Katiel's Omega form, obviously. All we had about Sapphense's own elements was mere speculation.

We apologised profusely to Leiogrey and Deltorah for their injuries at our hands, but the dragons shrugged it off. They were just happy to be out of Brozogoth's control. It seemed that using his mental energy to dethrone me had lessened his grip on the other dragons, which ended up being our saving grace.

Vortiger itself underwent serious changes during the week, ones which Lamont himself had to oversee. Now that they were free of Brozogoth's reign of terror, much of the city was under construction; partially for the damage done in battle, and partially for damage Brozogoth wreaked during his reign. An election would take place to decide a new council. Forty men and women were participating, but Lamont was the head of operations. Only twelve would become the members of the new council, and it seemed Lamont had earned a place back upon it. We met with all the contenders personally. The world valued our opinions. The candidates all seemed quite honored to meet three Defenders at once. Each of us voted on the contenders, but we would likely be gone before the final votes came into play. Loki particularly voted against a man by the name of Aidrid, while Lamont urged us to vote for his friend, Valerian Vidal; a previous spymaster for the Capital.

We spent all our time in the Capital. The people fixed the outer dome, so the city was safe to walk in and revel in the heat. I explored it to a degree with Sira and the others, but began to grow restless near the end.

They granted us a tidy sum for our services. Delighted, Loki took us shopping. The first thing he bought was a gravity bag for our team, which we stowed away most of our supplies in so we could travel light. Lusari, Guildford, and Kaia browsed spellbooks, while Sira and Dagger practically drooled over the Vortigeran blades. Will traded in our old Harohto cloaks for Vortigeran ones of higher quality, suited to the most extreme of weathers. Only Katiel didn't partake, for he said that his familiar red cloak was more than enough.

On our last day, Loki and I discussed theories of the next world we might land in. I wondered about Orden, but Sira claimed it was still too far from Vortiger to consider. According to Loki, Vortiger was much closer to worlds like Bonnin, Lysvid, and Harohto. Will still sang hopeful tunes about landing in Syaoto next. Nobody else thought it'd be close enough. That, and we knew landing in Syaoto meant we'd be parting ways with Rex. The likeable hybrid had grown on me since we met him, and I secretly hoped he might just tag along with us the whole way. That opinion was selfish, however, so I didn't voice it.

Lamont coaxed us into spending our last night at the palace. It was an incredible honor, but he assured us that we'd earned it. Loki and Will readily agreed, reminding me that we had no way of knowing what sort of roof we might land under next – or, even, if we would have a roof. That, and Loki seemed accustomed to no less if he could get his hands on it.

We each had our own room. I found myself sharing one with Sira again. We had a giant bed that was of finer material than I thought even Vortiger might have. Everything was of the highest quality, including a wide bay window offering a scenic view of the city. In such glory, I should have slept like a baby.

Long after Sira fell asleep, though, I found my way through the palace as silently as a shadow, ensuring I might not wake any of my lightly sleeping allies. Alone, I attracted little to no attention, which worked fine for me. I left all but my knife in my room. It felt banal to leave Ragnarokkr behind, but the huge black blade bobbing over my shoulder had become an emblem of sorts. People recognized it wherever I went, and I despised the attention.

I walked alone to the far east end of the capital. It was a sand-strewn, largely unoccupied square in the lower markets. I had to duck under some blockades to enter. Scaffolding hung everywhere, but none worked on the repairs at this late hour. Cracks webbed across much of the road.

Past the wreckage was hidden a small garden, tucked away in the sheer corner of the markets. Rare palm trees slung across the torchlit view, and the babble of man-made aqueducts that dipped into a golden stream made the only sound. A few of the homeless had strewn up tents, and one brave soul lit a careful fire in a cleared grotto. I made my way through slowly, offering small numbers of coins to the homeless without attracting attention to myself, and approached a crystal statue in the center of the garden.

It stood in the likeness of Sapphense. The height and details were carefully plotted, each diamond faceted in the same way. They had studied the likeness of her damaged body to build the statue. It stood on its hind legs, roaring to the dark dome above our heads where winter began to cry. Protected by its front claws was a simple wooden cross. Even the poverty-stricken would not touch the materials – the memorial of a dragon and her rider.

I approached like it was my first time stepping before the Diamond Dragon. I tentatively ran my hands over the smooth wood of the cross. Flowers from native lands bloomed all over the length of where her body lay beneath the soil. A tear trickled down my cheek. I could recall the overwhelming joy I felt when Sapphense returned, saving me from what would have been certain death. The rising adrenaline, the boundless feeling as we took to the sky.

A grim thought struck me. Maybe Sapphense's time was in Bonnin, where I saved her a mere few days ago. Now I led her to a later, worse fate, and was unable to save her as death snatched her away.

Maybe she was never meant to die. Maybe it was only because she had crossed my path that this fate had taken her. Otherwise, she would never have had a reason to enter Vortiger, to face the monstrosity of Emperor Brozogoth. I stared up at her statue, and shadows from the trees seemed to reach across her likeness as dark claws. Claws that snatched her from this world, and might soon take me as well. I watched for a moment, staring at the darkness, until I realized there were no trees to cast a shadow on it.

A hand appeared on my shoulder. I found myself on my knees, tears streaming down my cheeks as I knelt before Sapphense's tomb. I turned around to an unlikely face.

"...You?" I half-asked, forgetting to wipe the tears from my face in surprise. "What are you...?"

The face of Chris Olestine smiled down at me. He looked thinner than before, his dark hair longer, his green eyes gaunt. There seemed to be a shadowy frame to his appearance, like he could only stand in the darkness.

"I'm not actually here," he whispered, as though afraid the homeless might hear him and report him to somebody. "My energy grows fainter by the day. The time draws near that you must save me by. November 21st. The day they plan to kill me."

It felt like a stone dropped in my stomach. Since the death of Sapphense, the part of me that had been pressing on for Chris' sake fluttered like a dying flame. I knew he promised to help me find my sister, but it suddenly seemed like a road to further death and loss. Who knew what would happen next? Would I lose Will? Sira?

"Who plans to kill you?" I asked faintly. I knew his time must be limited, so I needed to ask the right questions. I stumbled over my words, but asked, "Do you know where my sister is?"

"Orden," Chris replied simply. There seemed a strange quality to his eyes. An inner mystery I had yet to unwrap. He spoke the name of the place, once and for all. Orden. That in itself didn't come as a surprise by this point, but like seeing my name written on a tombstone. The end of my journey.

Chris reached out a hand to me. Instinctively, I backed away half a step, and found the wooden cross at my back. "Ryoku, you must listen to me. I'm running out of power, but in Orden, you must..."

His image faltered, like a shadow with light briefly cast across it. A second later, and Chris was gone, as though he had never been there at all. While I stood, contemplating whether it was possible to see spirits in the spirit realm, a figure appeared at the other end of the garden. Shadows coated the figure, and I couldn't see who it was until they got closer. Loki.

When he found me standing at the head of Sapphense's grave, his usually chipper expression fell, and he looked older than I had ever considered him to be. His hand found my shoulder in the darkness, and squeezed.

"There was nothing you could have done, my boy," he said somberly "Or any of us, for that matter. Sapphense – she repaid you in full for having saved her. She lived since we last saw her, perhaps in another world. She grew older, wiser, and stronger. She chose to find you and repay her debt."

"I killed her."

The words tumbled from my mouth like floodgates releasing their grip on a river. I averted my gaze, unable to meet Loki's gaze. He delicately lifted my chin to face him, and I realized my vision was awfully blurry. His dark emerald eyes looked like grass in the night.

"Listen to me, Ryoku," he said softly. "She lived. She had an egg, remember? I bet that one grew up and hatched into just as beautiful a dragon. She lived for a while before she found us – since you saved her. Had we not come along, maybe other hunters wouldn't have taken pity upon her. But you did. You, the rarest Defender I have ever met, noticed something that this old Trickster couldn't have seen if it was written on my eyelids. You gave her something that none of us could have, not like you – friendship, and love."

I didn't reply. His words were kind, but I wasn't sure of the truth behind them. After all, I had only met Sapphense a mere few days before her death.

"Has Lamont explained the bond between dragon and rider to you?" Loki asked. "About how they choose their rider? Not just anyone can hop onto any dragon's back – they must share a bond. Lamont and Leiogrey. Malak and Sira. In the latter part of that fight, even Will and Rhovh. Lamont's father, Raimundo, and Deltorah. Brozogoth and Rassaq. They all shared certain similarities and a common goal. That means the same for you and Sapphense. You shared an outlook that I'm unsure you realize you have – a desire to see the good in all. To find the kindness in the darkness, so to speak."

His expression turned somber, and his emerald eyes turned to the dragon statue behind me. From the way he stared, I was unsure he was even looking directly at it. He was looking beyond, to some truth behind his own eyes.

"Ryoku. Since you first started your journey, you've never had to walk alone. You've found solid friends in the spirit realm. It's not coincidental, but you've always had a shoulder to walk in stride with. First Kioru, then Will, then all of us in tandem. A time may come when you find yourself walking alone where none of us can reach you. Then, by the Creator, you *must* keep walking. You must keep a hold on your inner resolve and press forward where none of us can guide you. You must not falter a single step. If you do..."

He paused, seeming to lose himself in his words, the statue before him, and the starry reflections in the glass dome. Finally, he turned to me.

"All will be lost. Without you, others will surely fall as well. Many lives hang in the balance. If you cease to press forward doggedly, then surely all we've fought for will be in vain.

"And the day may come," he went on, gazing away again, "where I may not be here to guide you. If that should happen, then you cannot tarry. You must soldier on. For the sake of everyone."

I stared at him, surprised, trying to blink away tears still. This was the most serious conversation I ever had with Loki. Even in Lysvid, he almost felt like an actor taking the stage. Now he looked like a mortal man lost in his own fear, struggling to teach me how to contain that very fear that stole breath from his lungs.

"I will never be alone," I replied, in hardly more than a strained whisper. Now I preached words back to him. Words that had been told to me once before. "Wherever I go, everyone who has helped me, and everyone I've lost, will be by my side. I may have lost my dragon, but I will always be a rider wherever I go. I will always be her rider. She is not the only one with me, either. My mom. My stepdad. My family..."

I straightened, stretching my tired limbs from where I knelt before Sapphense's memorial. Loki was looking at me, shocked. Slowly, it evaporated into a warm smile.

"You're absolutely right, Ryoku Dragontalen," he said. "We never walk without them."

We made to leave the garden. As we walked amid the desert flowers, I looked over at the Trickster. A thought was tugging at the back of my mind, and I couldn't imagine a better time to ask.

"Why did you become my Guardian?"

The question seemed to take him by shock, and he stared at me for a moment, brows raised. Then he absently averted his gaze toward the monument of Sapphense. I followed his gaze, allowing the dragon to infiltrate my mind again. For the citizens to have constructed it in such a short time was phenomenal.

"I... know your father, Ryoku."

I turned my gaze sharply. Loki was still staring at the statue, an odd look in his eyes now. When he saw me staring at him, a lopsided grin spread his lips. "I'm kidding. Thing is, you're a very important person in these realms. All the gods and all the stars have their eye on you, kiddo. And as the Trickster, I could always use a little more fame, right?"

He laughed boisterously, fists on his hips and a twinkle in his eye. I was speechless. Was he being serious? He threw an arm over my shoulder. "Let's head back, Ryoku. Somebody might notice you're gone soon."

I nodded slowly, but watched the Trickster as we left the garden. He resumed his regular Trickster antics. As odd as it was, I had the feeling I might have just helped him as much as he helped me. But... the whole bit about fame and glory. From all I'd come to know of the Trickster, was that really his truest concern?

-~-~-

A company gathered at the lobby to the capital the following morning at a private entry near where we came through. A room set aside for the sole purpose of world travel spells – away from the public eye, but also out of the hazardous weather. We waited outside of it with the dragons and Lamont.

Everyone was already suited up in their regular clothes, stowing away what we had from Vortiger in Loki's new gravity bag. I felt a little like myself again in the red-and-white sweater Loki found for me in Niin. Seeing everyone back in their normal outfits filled me with a sense of nostalgia. We were back on our journey after spending a whole week in the ever-changing world of dragons – even as it turned out to be less in my world – and we left with new lessons learned.

All four dragons in his care – Leiogrey, Deltorah, Malak, and Rhovh – accompanied Lamont. Malak and Rhovh both had homes with Lamont, and the man himself was once more a dragon rider. He dressed richer, his long, brown hair tied back in a loose tail and his sword replaced at his belt. Gone were the shadows under his eyes – for the most part, at least. A youthful smile suited him much better.

"I cannot begin to truly thank you," Lamont told us, and bowed before the entire company of us. "If you hadn't come, this would just be another day of servitude, of dwelling in the shadows out of fear."

"It wasn't any trouble," Loki assured him with his silvery tongue. "Another day in the life of a Defender and his team of elite Guardians." He flashed me a wry smile. "Vortiger has helped us grow."

I self-consciously felt the marks at my wrists. They felt like tattoos that I didn't notice until somebody mentioned them or asked about them. It seemed that, when I blacked out facing Leiogrey, the darkness entered me once more. This time, it left something behind. As odd as it was, though, I didn't feel like those marks came from the darkness. They seemed more like they were something that belonged to me. The markings tugged at my memory somehow, like I happened upon them in a textbook when I was young.

The powers that came with them were something I had yet to master. Drawing upon them was similar to how I used magic. I only had to envision those markings, and the tattoos on my wrists and ankles would begin to tingle. As soon as that happened, it felt like I weighed nothing no matter what I carried. I could jump higher, sprint great distances in single leaps, and move my limbs with little to no resistance. Taxing them too much, though, increased that tingling feeling in the tattoos. Drawing too much from them made them begin to burn. I didn't know what happened past that just yet, and they didn't last awfully long, either. It was a mystery I was eager to explore.

Combined with what I learned about my eye in Vortiger, it seemed to all lead in the same direction. Mysteries, unanswered question, and the eventual darkness.

"We are stronger than ever before," Guildford agreed, clasping my shoulder. "Each world we come to seems to prepare us even more than the last."

"And I finally got to meet your ass here," Dagger nearly shouted, clapping me on the back opposite Guildford. "It's about freakin' time! You know how mad I'd have been if you beat the crap out of a dragon emperor without me!?"

I smiled, wincing from the slap of his hand against my shoulder. Dagger would return to his own world after spending the week with us in Vortiger. He shopped a ton, bought damned near an armory's worth of Vortigeran weapons – at a heroic discount – and now prepared to return to his guild in Brooklyn. In addition, thanks to his own gravity bag, Dagger traveled just as light as any of us. I kept quiet about how odd it was that he chose a world called Brooklyn as his base of operations. The name of our hometown, of course, was Brooks.

"It was good to have you with us," Katiel told him, making a point of gripping our friend's shoulder just as tightly. Dagger gripped back, and both their faces strained in a pointless contest of strength. "You *definitely* made things easier for us!"

"*You guys were a whole lot of fun!*" Dagger replied, putting a great deal of force into it with one hand, his teeth gritted. "*Don't know what the fuck I'd have done without you lot!*"

"*Likewise!*" Katiel half-shouted back.

"What is wrong with them?" Rex asked me quietly. "Is this common in your world?"

I laughed uneasily. "Maybe between them," I admitted.

"*Definitely* between them," Guildford agreed, chuckling.

Kaia sighed loudly, crossing her arms. Reze left again shortly after the battle, so the girl stayed by Katiel's side or mine for the majority of the week. Everyone had questions for her still about the sea serpent, but she didn't offer much of an explanation. It made me happy to know that Katiel and Kaia were still coming with me to the next world.

"You and your friends always have a place at my home," Lamont told me, ignoring the contest of strength between the two Defenders. "Wherever your travels may bring you, you always have a home here. My home is always prepared for travelers. Who knows? You might make more friends here one day."

I smiled warmly. "I sure hope so," I agreed, though I was hesitant. After Orden, who knew what awaited me? I hadn't told anyone about seeing Chris, either. "Your assistance was important to us, Lamont. Without your help and guidance, and without Malak and Rhovh…"

Rhovh smiled bashfully down at me, while Malak butted his head against Deltorah's scales, who reacted like a fly was bumping into him. "It was our honor," Rhovh told me kindly. "To be honest, I never thought we might find potential riders again in our lifetime. The reign of Brozogoth seemed so bleak; neither of us could fly the skies of Vortiger without fear. But now…"

They exchanged grins with Will and Sira. The pairs matched up startlingly well. For their sakes, I hoped we might come back one day but, to everyone's surprise, another dragon seemed to be bonding with a rider. Guildford had engaged with long talks with Deltorah. This morning, I learned that the two had even gone riding outside the city a few days ago. I couldn't recall the last time I saw Guildford so delighted.

Will was laughing at Rhovh's words. He came up next to me, patting my sore shoulder. "I agree, my friend. When we arrived, the world seemed pretty dark and foreboding. Now…" he gestured out to the glass dome above, where snow poured down and gave the illusion of a reversed snow globe.

"It's so pretty," Lusari murmured, hugging herself as she stared up at the sky. "It makes me think of my world before the raiders came along."

"You're lucky to have such fond memories of snow," Sira muttered, and shuddered. "Orden is famous for its storms. In northern parts, they arrive as a blizzard matched by little. Vortiger's weather is intense. Orden is outright deadly."

Rex was staring up at the snow, too. "Lysvid never got snow. At least, anywhere the Timeless One stationed me. I suppose all it can remind me of is life before. A time when I didn't believe anything came after death."

Dagger and Katiel's contest of strength ceased, and they both watched the sky, too. "We don't have snow like that," Dagger remarked. "Maybe looks a little similar, but don't you dare try to catch a snowflake on your tongue. Friend of mine did that when we were kids – hospitalized for three months. Radiation poisoning."

His words made a stunned silence wash over our group. Katiel glanced down at the curious eyes of the spirits looking at us. Lamont looked at me, a brow raised. "You've certainly collected an interesting group."

I smiled sadly, to focus on anything but the state of my home world. "I sure have," I replied. "A day doesn't go by that I'm not grateful for them."

Will and Sira both clutched me a little closer from either side. Dagger decided that would be a good moment to slap me encouragingly on the back, and that sent all three of us bowling over. To topple Will and Sira as well was a little scary coming from my friend.

"You'll get on fine without me," Dagger told me, helping me to my feet – he didn't even offer Will or Sira a hand, but they helped themselves. Dagger was looking me over, scratching his chin, and ignoring the deathly glare Sira gave him.

"You've grown, kid. From the first day I'd seen your face in Gilly's class, what, two years ago? Three? Fuck if I can remember, but you've come a long way. Hell, I think you've grown since I saw you in the damned markets. And that means, since the Day of Black…"

"Will I run into you again?" I asked to cut him short.

He laughed outright now, slamming his fists into his hips. "Hell yeah!" he declared. "You're a Defender now, kid! You know where Defenders love to go for information? The Registry! Guess whose ass controls those!"

"Actually?" Guildford asked, surprised. "That's impressive! Is there not a Registry in every world?"

"Mostly," Loki confirmed with a raised finger. "I suppose that does make sense. The Registries are funded by a 'Neseru Guild,' if I recall, and are a relatively new concept." He turned to Dagger and flashed him a smile. "So we can get a hold of you through a Registry?"

"You bet," Dagger said, laughing like Loki told a good joke. "Any Registry has connections straight to Brooklyn. Damn, if you think you've seen a hot receptionist already, you need to get your ass to Brooklyn! Danielle, now there's a girl…"

Sira gave him a look of disgust, but Will was laughing.

"Don't all the receptionists look the same?" Lusari asked curiously.

I didn't catch the answer. Lamont peppered Dagger with questions about the Registry and the Neseru Guild. Aside from them, Guildford approached me.

"I feel I've not been able to teach you as much as I'd like," he admitted apologetically. "Our foes haven't exactly been something to sneeze at, but yet..."

I smiled. "That's not your fault at all. Like you said, going from some sort of mad scientist to an emperor dragon doesn't leave much room for casual combat."

Guildford smiled uneasily. "Yes, but if I were stronger, I would be able to lend a better hand." His glance wavered, and I followed where his attention went. Deltorah and Malak had started to play, though Deltorah was much bigger and able to pin Malak down easily. He let the smaller dragon break free, then pinned him again just as easily.

"Guildford," I started hesitantly. He turned back to me as though surprised, though we'd only been talking a second ago. I tripped over my words. Was I seeing what I thought I saw? "Did you... Guildford, did you want to stay?"

Guildford's brows rose. There was a telltale spark within them, but he tried to diffuse it. "What do you mean?"

I struggled. I didn't want him to leave, but... I could see the wistfulness in his eyes. Who was I to ask for the afterlife of my old teacher? The Timeless One took care of him since he arrived and until we crossed paths. He'd come along with us, little to no debate offered on the matter. However, this was his afterlife.

"There's no way I could stay," Guildford murmured. The hesitation appeared in his voice. I knew I wasn't imagining things. "You're still learning. I can still teach you. I can grow stronger, strong enough to help you in your plight."

"That's not your responsibility," I told him. "You didn't come here to train me, Guildford. This isn't the reason you're here. Why you came all this way with me."

He was still young, I thought. He died at such a young age. "There's an entire world out here. Thousands of worlds like this, I guess. I have a mission I need to do, but I'm still alive, Guildford. In the way the spirit world works, so are you. There's so much you could do. You're not obligated to stick around with me."

"I would be letting you down," Guildford countered. "You have a higher purpose. I read about it in the Timeless One's study. You have so much you need to do, and I have been given the opportunity to assist you."

"You still can," I told him, "by living your life. Guildford, you... you died young. Maybe I don't know what I'm talking about – I'm still young myself. I think you still have a lot of self-discovery to do. Chances you didn't have in our dying world."

"Our world isn't—" Guildford started, almost angrily, but stopped himself. Some of the others had turned their attention to our conversation with interest, and he appeared almost bashful.

"Ryoku, what are you...?" Loki asked, his eyes wide. He looked oddly transfixed, like I was committing the worst-case scenario.

Lamont came up beside Guildford, putting a hand on his shoulder. "Personally, I think your presence here would be entirely welcome. I suddenly have more dragons on my hands than I know how to care for, if that sort of thing interests you. Deltorah's taken a shining to you as well. After my father, and my sons, I never thought..."

Deltorah had stopped playing with Malak, and he incited Guildford's attention with a low rumble in his throat. The huge dragon, almost the size of Brozogoth himself, stared into Guildford's eyes.

"It is pointless to argue," Deltorah told the teacher. "Your student knows you as well as I do."

They were silent for a long moment, looking into each other's eyes. I wondered if Deltorah was speaking to Guildford with his mind, like Sapphense had to me.

Finally, Guildford turned to me, rubbing the back of his head nervously. "If you're so adamant about it," he said softly, "I suppose I could oblige. *On hiatus as ordered by a Defender.* It does have a certain ring to it."

I laughed. "If you want to call it a hiatus. I mean, if you stay in Vortiger, I'll always know where to find you if I need your help."

Guildford chuckled, but he put a cautious hand on my shoulder. His eyes were earnest and kind. "Be careful out there. Don't you dare die on me, or I'll have to fly these dragons straight to Orden and—"

"I won't let that happen," Katiel piped up, swinging in to throw an arm over my shoulder. "Not in a thousand years. You can count on me, Teach."

"And you can bet your old, saggy ass that I'll keep an eye on him, too!" Dagger cried, popping up at my other side to clap both

Guildford and I's shoulders – the force made us smack heads, and we rubbed them ruefully, smirking in spite of it all. "I can keep tabs on this kid through the Registry. Anyone tries poking their noses into his business, and I'll have their rumps in clumps! Or..."

"Saggy? He's hardly in his thirties, and he can literally stay that way forever," Rex murmured.

"Spoken like a true child," Kaia added, but she was smiling. "Why's everyone being so sad? Come on! This is victory! We kicked Brozogoth's scaly butt and everyone should be happy!"

Katiel smiled at her, making the poor girl light up like a Christmas tree. "She's right, Ryoku," he told me in a playfully stern voice. "Things can only get better from here, right?"

The smile that stole across my face felt alien; like it belonged to a boy I used to be. One that still had his Diamond Dragon, accompanied by his high-school teacher and all of his friends on a world-class adventure. The boy behind it was only a day older. Only a day wiser.

"You bet."

...End of Act Six.

ACT SEVEN: DISOWNED

In the eyes of Ryoku Dragontalen, we are
In-between worlds.
It is early evening
On November 12th, 2017.

SCENE ONE: THE SOLDIER'S FATHER

My eyes flickered open, hesitantly, as though something heavy stirred upon my eyelids.

Everything looked alien. Violet lights swam through the otherwise darkness of my vision in the fashion of a funnel or tube. It felt like I was descending at a slow pace. Looking around, I saw Sira nearby, her eyes delicately closed. Everyone else was around in a similar state. It felt as though we were floating. In the center of us was Lusari, her staff emitting a steady greenish light. It was only then that I noticed the usual glyphs surrounding us, the ones she conjured when we crossed worlds.

Everything around us was dark. It was like how I pictured outer space, but possibly even darker. There was a dim light ahead of us, and I could make out the edges of huge spheres outside of the funnel we seemed to be in, almost like planets. The prospect of staring out into the darkness was utterly terrifying. What could possibly be out there, hiding in the darkness between worlds?

Several minutes passed, and I found I couldn't move beyond tilting my head. The light I'd seen further ahead was getting close. I assumed it might be how we entered the next world, but then I saw some large, ominous shape beyond it. Whatever the source of the light was, it was between us and the next world.

As we neared it, I tried to reach for my sword, but my hands couldn't move. A feeling of warm light flooded over me.

Ryoku Dragontalen.

I hesitated. The idea of something approaching that knew my name wasn't a good thing. The last one I met like that had been Jesanht Olace. The voice was female, though.

In coming to the next world, you will require my assistance to pass a great trial. Merely speak my name, and you shall have all the aid of the goddess of light at your disposal.

I hesitated. It didn't exactly sound like a bad thing. A goddess of light? Her voice sounded awfully familiar, I thought. There was something symphonic and sweet about it, like some innocent tune from my childhood.

"Who are you?" I managed to ask, finding the power to make my lips move.

There was a moment of silence. *You know of me already. I am within you, just as many of the answers you seek are. I am Eos, goddess of light.*

The light grew closer and closer. I tried to muster the strength to ask more questions, but my eyelids suddenly felt heavier as the light grew closer. Before I knew it, I awoke again upon a field of grass.

I found myself staring up at a mostly dark sky scattered with stars. Only a telltale red glow upon some mountains to the west indicated that evening was just arriving, meaning this world was on track with the time I knew. It had been early morning in Vortiger when we left that disorienting world.

Looking around, I found the others scattered around me, unconscious. Our arrivals in new worlds seemed to vary. In Lysvid, we'd all arrived standing in the same way we'd left Harohto, while Bonnin and Vortiger left us on the ground. Unlike Bonnin, though, Vortiger our arrival at this place left us unconscious when we arrived. I seemed to be the only exception.

I propped myself on my elbows to get a better look in the twilight. Rolling hills and plains filled the area around us, eventually fading into mountains that reached into the sky like jagged fingers. To the west, what looked like a grand city surrounded by stone walls took up most of the view. I could see the bouncing torchlight of guards patrolling the walls from here. East of us seemed to be another huge source of light, but I couldn't see the full entity over the rolling hills.

I lay there for a time, relishing the feeling of cool, slightly dewy grass in my clutches, a scarcity in my own world. Everything about this place felt beautiful, cool, and almost devilishly calm.

The others started waking while light still clung to the mountains. Loki was the first to rise, and was similarly enraptured by the beauty of this world.

"What a world," Loki murmured, enraptured. "Where do you suppose we are? It's hard to tell from outside a city."

Will got to his feet eagerly, relying on his lance to support jelly legs. "My friends, it looks like we have finally arrived. Welcome to Syaoto, and her capital city."

He looked out over the stonewalled city like a king. Everyone else rose, looking down at the enormous city below the hills. It was a cloudless twilight, some early stars peering down at us from the sky, and so the silhouette of the great castle stood out like the sun. Torchlight in different sizes dotted the city, some of which slowly moved across the city. I could make out some stone and wooden buildings within.

"So this is Syaoto," Lusari breathed, elated. "It's so pretty out here!"

Katiel turned to Rex. "Have you been here before, Rex?"

The hybrid frowned. "No, this is my first visit, but I have something I must do here." With a look at me, he quickly added, "I'll accompany you to the city. Perhaps we could share an inn once more, but then I must depart on my own journey. Traveling with you has been a pleasure."

"Likewise," I agreed, flashing Rex an earnest smile. "If you ever need our help again or even just want to travel with us, I'd be happy to have you along."

I spoke without being sure my journey would continue, but the words elicited a smile from Rex. "Thank you. Should the opportunity arise again, I'd be honored."

"I thought this world would be too far away to reach," Loki said, scratching his chin in wonder. "It seems I was wrong."

"Guess so," Sira muttered. She kept close to me, but on my right side. Seeing how she gravitated toward my green eye was now unmistakable.

Katiel looked around, squinting in the darkness. "Wasn't there something about Syaoto at night? Some weird quality to it or something?"

Everyone looked at Katiel, then at Will, who was still staring down at the city below. Then his eyebrows popped up. "Oh, right. Perhaps we should get to the city before hordes of demons prowl the plains."

"Seriously?" Sira asked, frowning at Will. "And I thought my world was the evil one."

Will smiled sheepishly. "Life in the capital is hardly perturbed by it. Ancient stones buried within our city walls generally keep the demons at bay at night. It gives work for the soldiers to escort people through the plains, and we are generally safe otherwise."

Loki already drew his sword, though there was nothing suspicious I could see yet. "Then we should get to that city. What do you think, Will? Do we have time before throes of demons fall upon us?"

Will nodded. "It is not immediately as of sunset. In fact, since the sun sets quite early this time of year, then we could still have hours before the demons start to flock."

"*Could* being the key word," Sira muttered. "Let's get everyone to safety before we test that. Afterward, I wouldn't mind coming out here for some intensive training. Are the demons pretty tough?"

Will shrugged. "Somewhat," he said. "Mostly their numbers are formidable. Still, I would advise against going out alone."

Katiel raised a hand. "I got you," he agreed easily. "I've been holding back for a while now. Really need to go out and tear something to shreds."

More than one face turned to him in shock, but Kaia was unperturbed, still clinging to his arm.

"You serious?" Sira asked him. "I thought you were cheerful."

"I am," Katiel replied cheerfully.

"What *is* the nature of your power, exactly?" Loki asked.

"It's called the Omega," Katiel explained. He lifted his right arm as if he were stretching it. Before our eyes, his limb shifted – it turned longer, layered with dark green scales. Thick black claws escaped from his fingertips. He flexed the hand and then, as we watched, he reverted it in the blink of an eye. "Thanks to the creepy old bastard we had the pleasure of meeting in Bonnin, I became the first of this race: Omega. It means I can shift my body into any form I've seen in the past, excluding that of other humans unless they carry subhuman traits. I can either turn into an entire form, like that dragon, or just shift parts of my body: a leg, an arm, a lung, my eyes. As long as I've seen the entity in the past and can recall it to a tee, then I can turn into it."

Everyone struggled to process this. "You mean, you have to know every detail of something to turn into it?" Will asked curiously.

"It has to be clear in my mind's eye," Katiel replied. "So, yes. If I cannot recall the intricacies of the form, it just won't work. If I turn into a dragon but don't know its innards, then obviously I can't breathe fire, or perhaps even breathe at all. I have to know every muscle of the wings, how to work different eyelids, how to breathe with different lungs. And yeah, it was a process to get it down, I assure you."

"You must have an incredible memory," Loki commended, impressed. "That's an interesting power. Come to think of it, I might have heard of it before. It sounds oddly familiar."

"Katiel's been working at it for a very long time," Kaia added, almost gloating. "He keeps getting stronger and stronger. The more he fights, the more he can do."

For a moment, Katiel's expression darkened. It lasted long enough that I knew I wasn't seeing things when he brightened up again. "So you see, I'm the perfect training partner, Sira. What do you say?"

Before Sira could reply, Will directed their attention to him. "You will want to head out there now," he urged. "Find a defendable spot where the two of you can protect one another. The demons will inevitably strike within... perhaps the next hour. Perhaps less."

Lusari was looking between the two of them, panicked. "A-Are you sure that's wise?" she asked weakly. "You two could get seriously hurt! Just how many demons are there?"

Will waved her off. "Two of them will do just fine. The demons themselves are nothing to worry about. Finding a defendable spot will ensure their survival. After all, they are both strong."

"I'm so ready for this," Sira agreed, a fiery look of determination evident on her face. "How long's it been since we could kick something's ass our own size?"

"Too long," Katiel agreed, and again, darkness temporarily clouded his face. He flashed Sira a grin so quickly that I had to think I was imagining it. "Let's do this. See you guys in the city?"

Will nodded. "We should find respite at the castle. Just speak my name at the gates."

That was it – Katiel and Sira took off into the plains, while the rest of us followed the rolling hills to the city. I could see them scouring the plains for a ways off until we neared the city gates, where we could see very little of the surrounding hills due to the small valley that closed in around the city.

Up close, the city looked even more visually impressive. The gates towered well over our heads like a set of great monoliths. Guards crawled the walls above like ants, while a set of four guards manned the entrance to the great iron gates themselves. From here, the stone walls spread out far beyond our view, eventually swallowed by darkness even with torches held by every second guard.

The four guards dressed similarly to Will, except these ones wore black tunics with steel pieces of armor. Will explained that they were simply classified as the city guard, given a ranking of their own. Apparently, the shade of their tunic symbolized their skill level, but all four tunics of the guard looked the same in this darkness.

As we approached, they barred our path by crossing their halberds and spears, scrutinizing us warily while we approached. Will waved a hand in greeting. I saw one of them murmur something to the others, but they kept vigilant.

"State your business," one of them called out in a booming voice when we approached. "The demon hours approach. You lot had better be important, coming into our fine city at this hour."

Will stepped forward, extending a hand out to the one who spoke. "I am William Jesse Ramun, son of Jason Ramun. Traveling with me are Ryoku Dragontalen, Defender; Loki, the Trickster god; Rex Dougo of Lysvid; Kaia Oceyen, water mage; and Lusari Atella of Harohto."

The guards exchanged glances. "Will Ramun? Truly?" One of them, I thought, looked a little skeptical under his helm. "And you travel with one of the dark folk?"

"You tread awfully lightly over the name of the Trickster," Loki uttered. "And of our Defender."

"What do you have against Rex?" I demanded.

Will was frowning. "How long has it been since I left?" he asked.

"Some five years or so," the soldier replied. "Lancet and his group already returned a time ago."

Everyone exchanged equally grave looks. I turned to Loki for answers, but a shadow appeared over his face.

"Very well," the soldier continued before anyone could ask questions, and they parted their halberds. "You may enter on Sir William Jesse Ramun's leave – that is, if you still carry a seat in the King's Own. The king may carry certain qualms about the matter."

Will started. "But King Lionel would never—"

"Open the gates!" one shouted up to the wall, cutting Will short. Anything else we could have asked would've been drowned out by the sound of heavy chains rattling while the huge iron gate lifted. It opened only twice our height, allowing us entry into the capital city. Will hesitated, looking to the guards.

"Does King Lionel still rule?" Will asked in a small voice.

The guard met him with a dark expression. "Best suited you see it yourself, Sir Will. Best of luck in the city. I hear the Iron Bear has reduced rates for travelers at this time of year."

That seemed all we could do, so we entered the city. I stared up at the pointed barbs on the iron gate facing down at us as though they might change their minds, to drop and kill us all instantly.

As we walked through, past the great stone walls, a strange feeling clutched my chest. I found myself frozen in place. It felt like a grappling hook caught in my chest, threatening to tear me asunder if I took another step.

"Ryoku?" Lusari asked timidly, the first to notice that I halted. "What's wrong?"

"The walls," Loki murmured softly, a realization. Will shot the guards a frantic look. I couldn't turn to see their expressions. Whatever feeling gripped me kept me paralyzed. The marks on my wrists began to glow, brightening until they were almost red. I couldn't move, and my wrists and ankles started to burn from the output of energy.

Suddenly, without warning, it broke away. It felt like the abrupt feeling of a weight lifting from my back. I gazed around, startled, to realize I'd taken an automatic step into the city. Whatever it was, it let me go.

"Are you okay?" Loki asked me, grabbing me by the shoulder.

I nodded. "Yeah, I think so. What was that?"

Nobody spoke. I recalled what Loki and the others had told me in Vortiger – the reason my eye had turned violet. The darkness that took over in Lysvid, and not for the first time. The same entity that I knew controlled me on the Day of Black. Was that the reason I struggled to enter the city?

"I wish to make a stop before we retire for the night," Will said, almost apologetically. "If five years has passed, then... I must see my father."

Nobody offered any refusal to the subject. Since the way the guards greeted him, nobody assuaged Will about his home. We simply fell in line behind him as we worked our way through the huge city.

It was easy to tell Syaoto was a medieval world. Buildings of varying sizes stood in stone, brick, or wood depending on the neighborhood. For the most part, they clung close together and left wide streets for mixed usage of caravan, horse, or on-foot travelers. Guards patrolled almost every block. If Will found that concerning, he said nothing. He tried to strike up conversations, but almost every guard ignored us save to glare at Rex. Considering I'd been the one frozen at the gates, nobody seemed to care. In the same light, nobody regarded the Trickster or Defender any differently. If this was a hostile place, I imagined they would be hunting us already.

The city was still pretty active for the hour. Children ran around at play in parks and on the streets under watchful supervision. Villagers on horseback or on foot still went about their business. Beggars crowded together for warmth on benches, below stone bridges that crossed the city's many branches of creeks, or around flaming barrels out of regular eyesight.

We didn't reach the markets for almost an hour. Much of the inner city was rural or farmland. I saw many different sorts of livestock kept on the farms, but the most prominent were easily horses or cattle. The markets themselves were bustling. Different stalls boasted any sort of item I could imagine – all sorts of food, produce, weaponry, armor, materials, clothing, and anything else they could produce or have shipped in.

After traversing the main road a ways, Will directed us down a ruddy dirt road that departed between two stone buildings. The way was sparsely torchlit, and we stumbled over upturned stones, discarded boxes, and other things strewn along the path. We followed it until we reached a distant neighborhood of shoddy wooden shacks, all clumped together in a tight circle.

"You must pass the slums to reach your home?" Loki asked spitefully.

Will replied only with a dark look of his own.

"You said your dad's name was Jason?" Kaia asked.

"Like the engraving on your lance," Lusari added, touching the lance over his shoulder. To my surprise, Will flinched away.

"Yes," Will replied. "Jason Ramun – formerly known as a hero, if you must know. But do not speak a word of it, only treat him with respect."

Loki did a full turn on Will. "Jason, as in Jason and the Argonauts? *That* Jason is your father?"

Will nodded in the darkness, having come to a stop at the entrance to the small, dark cul-de-sac. "One and the same. But it has been a long time since his heroic days."

"Does he live here?" Rex asked. He was the first to voice the idea, and it made an unnerving silence waver over our group.

After a long, gruelling moment, he nodded slowly. "Yes. Jason, hero of Greece, the one who fetched the Golden Fleece, lives here. In the slums of Syaoto."

Nobody said a word. I kept close to my friend, ready to be there for him in what seemed like an increasingly nerve-wracking task.

"We don't have to visit if you don't want to," Lusari offered timidly. "We could just go to the castle."

"The guard said that Lancet's group is back," I said. "Will, we could go check on Alex and the others. Maybe they know something that can help us."

Will shook his head slowly. "No, I must stop in to visit him," he said softly. He contemplated his own darkness for a moment, but finally turned to me. "Perhaps I did not need to bring you here. If you wish, you could go back to the city. Wait for me at the Iron Bear."

Seeing the look on Will's face, I shook my head. "Not at all," I replied, and stepped up ahead of him. "If you have to face your demons, then we will do so at your side. After all, we vowed to stomp through the mud together."

My attempt at a heartfelt joke only caused the smallest of smiles on my friend's face, but he stepped forward with me. Still, as we walked into the circle of homes, a feeling of certain dread filled my chest. What was Will so afraid of?

He stopped before a plain-looking shack at the head of the dirt path. Dim light shone through a shattered window, spilling out onto the fallow grass like it might catch it aflame. A sign hung from the railing beside the stairs – it hung loosely off one chain, dangling in a fell wind. It simply proclaimed 'Ramun.'

Will stood for a moment at the end of the path, staring at the home like it was a ghost. Finally, he muttered, "And so the feline pursues the mastiff." He motioned for us to follow him to the sullen red door. Each of the five steps up to it creaked like frogs. I caught Will glancing back at me, his eyes seeming to scream in whole desolation, but he couldn't meet my gaze. Finally, he stopped at the door, took a deep breath – and knocked. Four quick raps, and then he stepped back.

The home was silent for a long moment. Loki went to stand with Will and put a hand on his shoulder, but then the door shot open abruptly, spilling torchlight down on us. A tall, pudgy man in his forties or fifties stood there. He was the picture of a careless parent. His belly protruded, but his cheekbones were sunken and fallow, his dark green eyes nestled among the wrinkles like a dim light in a chasm. His blotchy beard hung, badly cut, to the middle of his chest, and his greasy hair was about the same length.

"You came back," the man uttered gruffly after a long pause. "Whaddya want?"

He didn't have a trace of Will's proper accent. He came across as more of a drunkard from Harohto than the likeable accent of Will or his friends. Even still, I could see the way his arms bulged with massive muscles under his oversized tunic.

Worse than my impression of him was Will's. He sounded like he hoped for something different, but yet, wasn't surprised. "I-I came back. I just wanted to make a stop. To say I've returned."

Will's voice made me turn toward him in surprise. His normally chipper accent even faltered. Was that fear in his voice?

Jason grunted with disinterest, and he cast his gaze over the motley crew on the steps. "Who're you with? Lancet and his group? They already came in to say you jumped ship on their mission. Lancet Cooper isn't impressed. Given his new position, he might have a few choice words for you at the castle."

None of what he said sounded appealing. Loki cast me a furtive glance, jabbing his thumb at the man and mouthing obscenities. Lusari, Kaia, and Rex stood close to me. Kaia's hand found mine, and clutched it tightly. Everybody seemed nervous to get too close to Will.

"These are my friends," Will started, and began to list off our names.

He couldn't even spit out Rex's name before a loud smack shot through the air. Will tumbled backward. Loki lunged to break his fall and stopped Will short at the foot of the stairs. Jason's hand gripped the doorframe, and it splintered the wood under his fist.

"*Friends?*" Jason growled. His demeanor seemed to change drastically. His dark eyes narrowed to almost slits. He swayed where he stood, his one arm swinging back and forth like a pendulum. "You're tellin' me you left a battalion of soldiers for *friends?* Spit it out, damn it!"

Loki made a step to speak, but Will clutched his hand behind his back, silencing him. Clearing his throat, he quietly continued to introduce us. His shoulders hunched, his head hanging low. Seeing my best friend like this was starting to make my blood boil. Only a tight grip on my hand from Kaia held me back.

"Huh," Jason muttered when Will was done. "A Defender, huh?" He spat ruefully on the ground before us. "Beats me what you're doing in these parts. We don't need your lot around here."

I reflexively spaced my legs apart, feeling an aggravating itch at my new marks. Before I could say anything, Loki finally pushed himself past Will, stepping into the doorway before Jason. In front of the old hero, even Loki seemed to look small.

"*Take that back*," he uttered, and it was as venomous a threat as I'd ever heard. "Your world looks like a stain of manure compared to the grandeur I've heard about it. You're supposed to be a hero – what in Dante's name has happened to you? Speak!"

Jason regarded the Trickster coldly, crossing his arms over his chest. "I ain't afraid of gods, Trickster."

Loki growled, not tearing his glance from Jason. "Maybe you should be, fallen hero." He spat on the ground, all the while keeping eye contact. "You're him, aren't you? The hero Jason, Pathetic. You look like a rueful old man."

Will was starting to edge away from the conflict, foreseeing the outcome. Lusari grabbed onto his arm. I saw Jason's glance shift – then, without further warning, his wrath turned. He shoved Loki aside with a mighty push, throwing the Trickster off balance as he lunged for Lusari.

There was no time to act. Loki was off balance. Will flinched away from his father. With all the strength and speed I could muster, I threw myself in front of Lusari, arms raised to catch his incoming fist.

The force struck my open palms like a train. I gasped in shock and lost all the breath in my lungs. My heels barely caught the off-kilter steps to hold my balance. The marks on my wrists flashed a violent red. I heard a distinctive *crack*! Where I thought it was my wrists giving into the pressure, Jason skidded back, stumbling away. Parts of his shaggy hair stood on end.

Rex and Loki stepped up on either side of me. Will was still behind me. Whatever his father had done to him, he was still petrified.

"Outta the damned way," Jason snarled with a definite slur to his words. "Boy doesn't deserve a girl – she don't know who he is."

"*No*," I protested, holding my ground. Kaia's hand returned to my side, but she held my arm this time, keeping my movement open. "Whoever you think he is, you're wrong. He's my best friend, and far better a man than you could imagine."

Jason chuckled mirthlessly. "That what he tells you? That he's a good man?"

"Step back, Jason," Loki warned, and green sparks started to play around his balled fists.

Before Loki or Rex could step in, Jason swung again, aimed at me once more. I reacted just in time to spring up a barrier of shimmering light. The act itself startled me, and it jolted Jason's fist back like I struck it with a weapon. I had managed to summon a similar barrier when I protected Sapphense, and it took a great deal of energy and concentration then. This time, it was like the energy supplied itself. My marks shone deep red for an instant – then black. Pain lanced up my wrists all the way to my elbows, and the barrier broke away. Only then did the pain abate.

Jason stumbled back, keeping his gaze on me. He didn't go to nurse the evident pain stinging his hand, but he didn't swing back, either. Rex and Loki closed in, ensuring Jason couldn't take another swing at me.

"Quit hidin' behind your goons!" Jason howled, and stumbled outright on the spot. "Let me at her, or I'll gouge out that other eye o' yours!"

I flinched at that remark. How could he tell about my glass eye?

That seemed to be too much for the others. In striking unison, Rex and Loki both lunged at Jason. The combined force of their punches knocked Jason flat on his back in the doorway. Rex stayed back, his chest heaving, but Loki didn't repent. He strode forward and grabbed Jason by the throat, dragging him to his feet.

"*Never,*" Loki uttered, and his voice seemed to carry all the boom of thunder, "*threaten Ryoku Dragontalen again! If I hear you utter one more threat, I will feed your eyes to my sons.*"

Jason didn't speak, only glaring into the Trickster's eyes. Nobody moved. I felt everyone was equally ready to floor Jason or restrain Loki. Then Jason tilted his head toward his son, and spat.

"Get off my lot, mimic. And don't come back."

Another loud crack. Jason fell back into his own home, splintering wood and a table beneath his weight. Loki stood in the doorway like a literal bolt of lightning, his chest heaving, his fist raised.

"Don't talk that way to your kid," Loki snarled. "Actually, to any of us. It wouldn't take much to send your home up in flames. Another word, and I'll burn your manhood to a crisp. Can't be much of an old cock without the equipment, can you?"

He then slammed the door in the old hero's face, and turned on his heel. The rest of us hesitated, almost as afraid of Loki as we were of Jason. "Apologies," Loki told me, his voice still an angry hiss. "Katiel told us about your eye. What happened to it, I mean. And the way he said that…"

"Let's get out of here before he gets up," Rex suggested.

That was a sound enough idea, so we quickly left the torn-up ghetto of Jason's home to return to the city. It was long since time to retire to the inn, and I needed to try and worm out a story from Will. I felt we might have a lot more to talk about than I ever thought. I supposed my sister and I weren't the only ones without a real father.

SCENE TWO: BRAWL IN THE CITY

...Of Act Seven: Disowned

In the eyes of Ryoku Dragontalen, we are in Syaoto Capital, in the world of Syaoto. It is mid morning On November 13th, 2017.

After the events with Jason Ramun, Loki had been irritable the whole night, and Will was as silent as a ghost. We checked into the Iron Boar, a mediocre inn located near the entry to town. Will wanted to connect with soldiers he knew from the castle, but we decided against it for now. If things weren't going so well, we wanted to be rested and ready. It would help to have Sira and Katiel with us.

The night was quiet. We stayed up for most of it, crowded around the hearth in the lobby of the Iron Bear. Nobody could weed out details about Will and his father. Either way, we were all pretty shaken up by the encounter.

Morning seemed to take days to come. At the crest of dawn, we stood outside the Iron Bear to see our fast friend, Rex Dougo, off on his new journey.

"It was good to travel with the lot of you," Rex told us, bowing unnecessarily. "I've been dead a long time, but I learned things from you that I never learned under the wing of the Timeless One."

"Likewise," I told him, and accepted a one-armed hug from the hybrid. He had a faint scent that reminded me of sunlight breaking through the dust of old library books, but in a pleasing sort of way. He'd grown on me quickly since our meeting after the slaughter at Gaevrel, and he turned into a fast friend. It was sad to part ways with him, and I couldn't quite find the words to properly do so.

"I'll remain in Syaoto for a time yet," he told me as he pulled away. "If things go sour, I'm sure I'll find you, and I'd be happy to help again."

Everyone bade him farewells. We exchanged equal hugs and tears. After it all, we watched him walk alone down the street toward the exit to the city. I wondered if we might see him again soon, if ever again. In a world full of spirits, how unlikely was it?

Sira and Katiel had returned just before, and they boasted few injuries for the hours they'd spent battling demons. Neither claimed to need rest after, and so we went into the town of Syaoto.

Our first destination was the castle itself. An enormous stone building that towered in the rear of the city, nestled with its back to a royal forest, while the keep itself stood atop an elevated structure. It looked like anything I'd seen in old European history, but somehow grander. Even on a cloudy, cold day like today, it rose above the city like a king in itself.

Unfortunately, we found our entry barred when we approached the gate.

"Apologies, Sir Will," one of the soldiers apologized, bowing deeply before him. "My liege has gone to Balgena on some urgent business, and he will return later today. Your presence has been noted, and he does wish to make your acquaintance."

Will hesitated. "Are there none present who would see to us? Sir Koteran, perhaps, or Lord Brom?"

The soldier shook his head. "None but the king may grant your entry at this time. My apologies. In the meantime, I recommend the markets if you've a penchant for some new gear. A new blacksmith calling himself Red has the armourers by their hammers, if you know what I mean." He gestured with his head toward Will's shoddy old spear, then to his own brilliant steel halberd. "If you've got gold to spend, an upgraded repertoire couldn't hurt."

but it sounded more for Sira's sake than his own. "Alex. Describe this man to us, if you would."

Alex opened his mouth. Before he could speak, a sharp scream cut through the noise in the city. Without hesitation, Will drew his lance from over his back and beckoned us to follow him.

People flocked away from the noise as we approached what was apparently the city square. Mixed indiscernible shouts beat at our ears. I struggled to listen, but I could pick up little.

"Aye, the gangs are at it again! Someone call the city guard!"

"...the Syaoto Bladerunners are really out for blood this time."

"...The Balgena Flaming Arrows? What a cesspool to get mixed up in..."

Will started shouldering his way through the crowd, aided by the tall and bulky Alex. Growing more nervous, I kept my knife in hand. It sounded like gang activity, and I'd had more than enough of that from my home.

"...Stupid wench got in the middle of it all! Can you believe it?"

"Who does she think she is? A peacekeeper?"

Crowds still clustered around the city square itself, a place I quickly identified from an enormous fountain planted in the center of it, spraying water high above the heads of the people. Now, market stalls stamped down in favor of a huge brawl taking place.

Two huge groups engaged in an all-out brawl, right there in the city. I could pick out the opposing teams by their outfits. No doubt, the ones outfitted mostly in red were the acclaimed Balgena Flaming Arrows, making the ones in silver the Syaoto Bladerunners. Weapons flew through the air in a craze, everything from flails to knives to arrows.

Amidst it all was a girl. She looked about Lusari's age, or a little older, wildly scanning the crowd for an opening to escape from the madness. Her dark blue hair stood out among the crowd. How had she gotten tangled up in such a brawl? If anyone took heed of her, they didn't care enough to stop the brawl and let her escape. Her yellow dress was in tatters, dirt smeared all up the side. A wild scimitar-slinging man rushed past her, and the girl fell roughly to the cobblestone ground.

"We have to help her!" Will cried, and started to push his way through the crowd.

"You know who they are, Will?" Alex called after him, but I was already ducking through the crowd as well. "The Balgena Flaming Arrows? The Syaoto Bladerunners? Death would be certain in mixing up with them! Leif—"

Will shouted back, "What would you have me do? Leave her?"

I caught a glance of the girl again through the crowd of flailing arms and weapons. Her hazel eyes were wide and scared.

Unwittingly, I pictured a different face in the crowd: blond hair, pinned up in just the same ponytail, her blue eyes wide with fright, screaming as Varis' gang tore away at her.

Then, I lost control.

The first red coat of a Syaoto Bladerunner that came between us didn't see me coming. My knife wasn't in my hands anymore, but my reach tore through his arm all the same, sending him sprawling back with a cry of fright. I slashed out at the next one, cutting into the skin above his knee and forcing him to the ground. Two more men staggered back, pointing at me with frantic gazes. I glanced up, but my vision wavered. All I could see was red.

One rushed at me from the side, knife drawn. I swung directly into his elbow, causing a resounding impact that drove the man wholly to the ground, screaming in pain. My elbow struck another attacker in the throat, sending him crashing into the ground.

"Demon! It's a demon!"

Five men appeared before me, all dressed in the reds of the Bladerunners. Or was it silver? Everything looked red as they rushed me, weapons raised.

I dodged around the first incoming sword and lanced into the man's chest with a powerful kick. My other hand flung itself up, channeling power from my staff – a mighty tornado, wreaking havoc through a country plain – and a sharp gust cut through the air before me, severing the head of a steel axe in one fluid motion. Another well-placed kick struck the head of a mace astray.

I was midway into another slash when sudden pain shot through my body. I cried out in shock. The same pain that hit me when I entered the city. It felt like a hook caught in my chest, struggling to tear half of me away. Was it because of the darkness?

It made me recall where I was. I regained control as the sound of steel on flesh above me forced me to focus. Panicked and disoriented, I rolled out of the way. Will was above me, just dragging his lance from the chest of a red-coated warrior. The redness to my vision was abating, but the pain hadn't left yet. Next to him, Katiel shot forward, his arm morphed into a long, jagged red blade that cleaved through another gang member easily. Ahead of them, a wave birthed from the very cobblestones to bear down on a row of Bladerunners.

The next thing I knew, Sira was helping me to my feet, dragging me up beside her. "The hell are you doing?" she muttered. "How many times do I have to scoop you off the ground in a fight?"

I smiled sheepishly, but the pain in my chest hadn't quite abated. I stumbled, narrowly missing a jet of chilly air that Lusari shot into the fray, followed by her frantic apologies in my direction. I caught the look in Katiel's eyes as he flung himself into enemy lines. He had thought of the same thing I did, I was sure.

"Ryoku, what's wrong?" Loki demanded, stealing me from Sira's grip.

"I-I'm not sure," I admitted. I managed to free myself from him, and I drew my knife, starting to feel a bit more grounded. "Whatever happened when I entered the city..."

"The anti-demon walls," Sira said, which surprised me – she hadn't been there when I couldn't make it in. "Whatever that darkness is within you, it doesn't like it. It's strong. Such things can't keep it out."

"How do you—?"

I broke off when more red-coated gangsters stumbled into our midst. Sira didn't hesitate, and she swung Sinistra at them in its full might, bearing down on them like a storm. Before her blade could connect, Loki sprang forward and snapped his fingers. A brilliant bolt of green lightning shot out in a sheet from his fingertips, hurtling the men back and out of harm's way.

When Sira turned on him, he gave her a pointed look. "There have been enough casualties. We don't want to mix ourselves up in a gang war any more than we already have."

A hand dragged me back by the shoulder. Just in time, Loki turned and struck my attacker square in the jaw, sending him to the ground and easily breaking his grip. The Trickster nodded to me. "Now focus – we need to get to that girl."

He was right. I turned around, and I found more opponents approaching. The Bladerunners and Flaming Arrows grouped together to face our threat. Will fell in line next to me, his gladius drawn, and we dove into the fray. I blocked an incoming axe with the handle of my knife, and drove a mark-propelled fist into my attacker's gut. Will caught an incoming strike with a one-handed save, overpowered his foe, and sent them to the ground with a well-placed kick.

I turned to my next foe, but a blast of chilly energy struck him, freezing the man solid. I cringed back in alarm. The magic was a considerable jump from what I knew Lusari could do. I saw her behind Loki, flashing me an innocent smile. Among the rest of us, she was growing, too.

It didn't take long to work my way through the next fleet of men where the girl lay, unconscious. Will picked her up like a pillow and carried her over his shoulder. Her blue hair had come loose from its tail to spill across her shoulders.

"Is she okay?" Kaia fell in beside us. Even now, water clung to her in droplets like some kind of shield.

"She breathes yet," Will told us. "We need to get her to somewhere safe."

"No need," a loud voice came over the crowd. They shouted out an order, and all fell silent to the drop of a pin. Somebody snapped their fingers, and all men in the square fell to one knee, weapons crossed over their upturned knee.

"What the...?" Loki asked, dumbfounded. I quickly found the source. A pair of men approached through the crowd of kneeling men. One was tall and muscular, with dark skin, chopped blond hair and a long red coat. The other was shorter, with dark green hair and excitable eyes, and he wore a silver jacket.

"My sincerest apologies," the bigger man told us as he came closer, not stopping until he stood in the midst of our circle. "I'm Spike Domeran, leader of the Balgena Flaming Arrows."

The younger one raised his hand nonchalantly. "Motley. Leader of the Bladerunners." He shook Loki's hand, the closest one to him. "Apologies for the mix-up. My men had no idea this girl got caught up in the thick of things. If the Bladerunners got one rule..."

"That'd be to wrap up no bystanders as best as we could," Spike agreed. "Our resources are yours if you need."

A figure approached from behind Motley. We only regarded him when Will made a small sound of surprise. It was Leif Cartos, garbed in the cloth of the Syaoto Bladerunners. His brown hair had grown out considerably and hung in a loose tail over his shoulder. Nothing but guilt shone on his face when he caught Will's eye.

"Leif, you..."

The ex-soldier smirked sheepishly. "Yup. Long time no see, Will."

Will and Leif stared at one another for a long moment. "Why did you leave the army?"

Leif shrugged. "If you have to ask, you have not seen it yet. Bladerunners are always looking for new blood, Will."

Will looked like he was about to say something, but the girl stirred on his shoulder. Surprised, he gently lowered her to the ground. Blood trickled down her cheek from several scrapes along her head and chin. Despite that, I realized, she was quite pretty. Her eyelids fluttered open, and she gazed around her in shock.

"Hello," Will greeted her, looming overhead like a tower. "Are you alright?"

"You'd best be ready to pay up if she's lost her mind!" Loki declared, pointing his ruby-lined blade at Spike.

Motley chuckled. "I believe she's fine," he said softly, and gestured to her. She gently lifted her hand to cup Will's face. The poor soldier turned scarlet.

"Are you an angel?" she asked in little more than a whisper.

"N-N-No, I'm not," Will stuttered in alarm. Next to him, Lusari looked miffed, her arms crossed. "You are... alive."

Sira and Leif both snorted in laughter. Will shot Sira a glare as the girl struggled to clear her vision. "She's clearly deluded," Loki proclaimed, and Sira had to pinch herself to stop from laughing.

"We should get her to a healer," Kaia suggested.

"If she's alright, then I believe we're at an impasse," Motley said, and we turned our attention back to him. "The lot of you killed a bunch of our men. Girl or no, that's a crime if I've ever seen one."

"And blood pays for blood," Spike agreed, a hand on the crimson-pommeled sword at his belt. "What say you? Can you go up against the best guys of the Bladerunners and the Flaming Arrows?"

Will stepped in front of the girl to shield her as the rest of us reared our weapons again. Leif stepped behind Motley as though trying to disappear.

"Don't be ridiculous," Loki growled. "You have any idea who you're dealing with? Just stand down like good clockwork soldiers. After all, you had this coming."

"They'll only listen to more bloodshed," Sira snapped. "Whatever. We killed enough of you while holding back. You really wanna test us?"

Katiel was silent, his arm still morphed into a strange blade that gleamed with an ethereal light. Lusari and Kaia stood at the ready. Water droplets hung in the air around Kaia, which clearly unnerved some of the men.

"That won't be necessary, either."

A new voice appeared from the crowd. Rather than bow like before, the men scattered. They jumped away into the alleys, shepherding each other away as quickly as they could. A sharp whistle carried out over the hustle. Guards of the Syaoto army infiltrated their ranks, nabbing any gang members they could. Motley, Spike, and Leif all disappeared.

A giant of a man stepped into the square, broadsword kept clear at his belt. At the sight of him, Will quickly dropped to one knee, letting go of his lance. Alex, a heartbeat behind, quickly followed suit. This man was dressed in more armor than I'd seen most soldiers in Syaoto wearing, and all of it looked to be a dark shade of brown, almost black. As he approached, he removed his helm, revealing an older man with a clean-shaven face and hardened brown eyes. For his age, he still had a full head of trimmed brown hair.

A figure stepped into tandem at his side, clothed in a violet tunic with a silver winged helm. For a moment, I feared it was Lancet, but the figure also removed his helm to reveal Oliver Rouge, Will's senior soldier. The young man smiled at us, but didn't speak. He also looked older, and crows' feet crinkled at the corners of his eyes.

The giant man didn't stop until he stood in our midst, and then drew his broadsword from his belt. The sound was like a gong over the crowds of people, and many of his men who rounded up the gang members stopped to regard him. I thought Brom might swing that mighty sword at Will, but he lowered the blade, choosing to bury the point in the stones and lean on the handles heavily. Standing there, his black cloak thrown over his shoulders, he looked like an executioner.

Oliver cut an intimidating figure next to him, but Brom had all the power in the square.

"My Lord General Brom," Will greeted the giant man. "And... Field Commander Oliver Rouge, if I am not mistaken."

Oliver nodded shortly. "Will. It has been some time."

"Will Ramun," Brom said in an old, heavy voice that still carried certain vigor. "I almost thought I would never see you again. And of all places…"

He cast a steely-eyed gaze at the captured members of the gang, who stood like statues. They didn't pipe up, so Brom returned his gaze to us. I instinctively flinched under his gaze.

"Word travels fast in the Capital, as I am sure you recall," Brom rumbled. "A brawl between gangs. A young girl caught up in it all. My men and I traveled fast, but apparently, this group traveled faster. My work has been carried out for me." He impatiently beckoned at Will and Alex. "Come now. Rise. I am no king. Whether or not I am still your general matters little."

Will popped to his feet bolt straight. Loki was the opposite, leaning heavily on one leg, arms crossed. "What's goin' on here?" Loki demanded wryly. "This city is turned on its head. Surely an old dog like you knows what, in Dante's name, has taken this city."

I expected Brom to strike at Loki, but a crooked smile crept across his face. "Old dog. Hmm. And I hear you are called a fox yourself, Trickster." He cleared his throat in such a way that Alex flinched. "I cannot speak with you for long. As luck might have it, the king has requested your presence in the castle. I am to find you and take you in."

Will looked dubious. "I thought the king was out," he murmured. He met Oliver's glance for a long moment. I couldn't tell what information possibly passed between them.

Brom shook his head. "Not for long, unfortunately." He lowered his voice so suddenly that Will and I leaned in to hear him better. "I can say little. I am Lord General only in title, I fear, and my hands remain quite shackled. I keep to my post for the people. For those people, I beg you to come quietly. Enough blood has been let today."

Loki reared back, hand on his sword. "Are you kidding me?" he demanded. "The king's taking us in by force?"

Will silenced the Trickster with a look. "Enough, Loki." His words carried as much weight to them as a sword, and even the Trickster regarded him with respect. "We are in no position to argue. With a wounded girl and this brawl on our hands, I am afraid we have no choice."

He turned to Brom, and there was ferocity in his sapphire eyes that I couldn't recall ever seeing so bold. "Lead the way."

Alex hesitated, still knelt next to Will. "A-Are you serious? Will..."

Will cast a subtle smile down to his friend. "What would you rather walk as, Alex? A prisoner with shackled hands, or a free man with his head held high?"

Oliver gave Will a curt nod of respect, but Sira was gritting her teeth. "Come on, Will... we can take this guy. This whole army, if we have to. We fought dragons and—"

"No," Will replied shortly. "I very much doubt that we could. To be honest, I would not risk the lives of the people in this city."

At the last second, he spared me a glance. Before the man he called his Lord General, every fiber of the original Will Ramun stood before me – the tall, friendly outdoorsman in steel who escorted me safely in Harohto. I sensed power in his stance, and faith. "Are you with me, Ryoku?"

I cast a quick look around. Most of the gang members stood surrounded by Brom's men. Everyone but Will had their weapons drawn still, ready to fight our way out if we had to. Loki, Alex, and Sira all looked to me. Oliver's lips pursed. Katiel stood ready, but offered no counsel for the decision I was making here.

"You're right, Will," I agreed, sheathing my knife. "We go quietly. At least we can finally get some answers here."

Will's smile was grateful. "Thank you, Ryoku," he said earnestly. To Brom he said, "Lead the way, sire."

Brom didn't return a smile. He only looked grave, and he nodded once. "Very well," he agreed. He nodded to Oliver. "Round up the Bladerunners and Flaming Arrows alike. Milord will deal with them. Ensure no bystanders were hurt."

"What about the girl?" Will asked quietly. "Can you see to her?"

Brom cleared his throat, lifted his sword, and sheathed it at his belt. "Bring her. She is in your care now, and she will be treated as such."

Will hesitated, but scooped up the girl in his arms. She was fully awake now, giving Will a mystified look as she let herself lay in his arms. He whispered something to her, but said no more as we all rounded up next to Will.

"Ryoku, are you sure this is wise?" Loki asked in a whisper.

I nodded. "Will believes so, and I trust him. Let's just see where this takes us."

"If the king is who we think he is…" Loki whispered. Sira said nothing, but a dark look cast over her face.

I nodded again. "Then we will be ready."

SCENE THREE: GRASP OF ORDEN

...Of Act Seven: Disowned

In the eyes of Ryoku Dragontalen, we are in Syaoto Capital, in the world of Syaoto. It is early afternoon On November 13th, 2017.

The march to the castle felt longer than departing from it earlier. As much as Will spoke highly of Brom, I felt like a prisoner in line. They spoke quietly while we walked. Watchful eyes from the soldiers kept me from approaching them. I hoped Will knew what he was doing.

Loki, however, wouldn't let up. He actively pestered soldiers in the line and tried to talk to Alex, demanding information about the king. It eventually took Will's glare to silence him.

"Shouldn't we know what we're going up against?" Sira muttered lowly to us.

I couldn't help but agree. Why they withheld it from us was beyond me, but my guess was concrete. With this sort of treatment, it had to be the same man Sira knew from Orden. Vincent Ordenstraum.

"Don't worry," I managed to assure her, gently putting a hand on her arm – with her temper, even that was nerve-wracking to do. "Even if it is him, he wouldn't try anything against us in this setting, would he?"

"In his own keep, you mean?" Loki asked bitterly. "Who knows. That's why I'd like to be prepared. Maybe we are wrong, and this is simply some horrid coincidence. But if not..."

We reached the bridge to the castle. The guards gave way for us this time, and we marched across the bridge to the great red doors of the keep. The bridge felt like miles, and the slaps of our feet on stone seemed to echo through the moat like drums. Even in daylight, they kept every torch lining the way lit and tended to.

The doors themselves, when we stood before them, were almost as large as the city gates. I felt like I walked into one of my old history books. I only wished I could close the book right now.

The great doors were opening when Brom set foot on the end of the bridge, giving way to the enormity of Syaoto Castle within. Red carpet rolled through the length of the hallway like the tongue of a monster.

Stepping foot into the castle itself, I gasped openly. The room we entered into was higher than the door, extending almost to a point where I couldn't discern the corners of the room from the shadows granted by the flickering torchlight. Folk bustled around here, almost all of whom were either nobility or soldiers. The nobility dressed in fineries richer than anything I'd seen even in the illustrious city of Vortiger. Most soldiers dressed in either black or violet. Others of higher ranking wore full suits like Brom's.

The main room led to another great set of doors a good ways ahead, this one manned by a whole team of guards. Stairs rose up around either side of the entry and far above our heads, leading to what I could only imagine.

"Holy crap," I whispered in spite of myself. Sira shot me a look, as though I shouldn't be impressed when endangered. Will entered behind Brom, and even he stopped to take in the castle. It must have changed a lot for him. Only Loki and Katiel seemed unperturbed, both likely having seen more glorious. I thought Katiel was acting funny since the ordeal with the girl we saved, but it could have just been me.

Only when we reached the last door did Will finally let go of the girl in his arms. A soldier came forward to take her, but she flinched away. She looked better than earlier, well enough to stand.

"Let me come with you." Her voice was clear and sharp in the wide room, and soldiers turned at the sound. "You saved my life. If you surrender me to the army, then who knows if I'll see you again? I must repay the favor!"

Will hesitated. Neither Brom nor any of the other soldiers interfered. "It could be dangerous," he said softly. "I know not what awaits me in there. You would be better off to leave. Accept their medical gratuity, then return home to your family. Surely they are worried sick about you."

The girl shook her head. "My name is Rena Stillwater."

Will's expression changed. I turned to Alex, confused. "What does that mean?"

Alex nodded toward her. "It means she is an orphan, I imagine. Stillwater is the name of the orphanage in Balgena."

That surprised me. If she came from an orphanage, we had a lot more in common than I thought. Now, rather than associating her with the darkness involving Varis, there forged a whole new likeness: to my sister.

"You can come with us," I replied for Will, taking a step forward. Some of the guards reacted to my advance. Only a raised hand from Brom stilled them. The general regarded me with his hawk-like gaze as I approached. "She's with us, then. Simple as that."

Brom looked to Will for confirmation. Will didn't meet either of our glances – he was looking at Rena's pleading hazel eyes. Finally, he managed a small smile. "Right, then. Just stay close to me."

With that, Brom had the great set of doors opened into another hallway. All but Brom now separated from us. Alex loathed staying behind, but Will gave his friend a curt nod. We entered the next hallway, and the doors shut behind us.

No windows reached this hallway. Only several torches lit the way, echoing hauntingly off the stone walls and giving the red carpet an eerie glow. Everyone started walking, but Sira caught me by the wrist and yanked me aside.

"Listen," she whispered urgently. Her crimson eyes looked like a pair of suns in the torchlight. "Please. If this is really him... you can't just rush in like you always do. He'll kill you."

I looked back into her eyes. I was used to looking at this girl and seeing apathy, hatred, or her dry sort of humor. Now, I saw fear. Fear for what waited at the end of this hall. I thought of the long scar snaking down Sira's back. The thought of what this Vincent had done to her was making my blood run cold. Not out of fear for what could happen to me, but out of anger.

It was times like this that I saw through Sira again. For all her fire and bravado, she was just a girl – a regular person like everyone else. She had her scars and her fears. At times like this, I forgot how horribly she sometimes acted and, instead, attributed it to her humanity. She was full of life, and I could never hate her for it.

"Hey," I said, and reached out to touch her. She flinched away, but I kept my hand still. Slowly, I reached out and took her hand, clasping it in my own. For all the fire she declared, her skin felt soft and warm. "I don't know what he did to you. I don't know if I... want to know. But if this is him, the same man..." I looked her in the eyes. "I won't let him near you."

She glared. "You're not nearly strong enough to fight him. You're getting stronger, I'll admit that. But... no, you've heard about him! Come on Ryoku, you have to—"

I cut her off by kissing her. She flinched, but she didn't pull away. Her hands latched onto the collar of my shirt, pulling me against her. My cheeks flushed. We'd spent the night together in Vortiger, but done nothing. This was the first time we kissed since Lysvid.

"Believe in me," I whispered. "I have to do this eventually, you know this. One way or another. If it comes down to this in Syaoto, then he's about to discover who I really am."

"You're retarded," she muttered, and pulled me in for another kiss. When she pulled away, her scarlet eyes still looked sharp. "Come on, you might be able to intimidate your way out of a paper bag – a soaking wet one – but this is different."

I scowled at her. "You're just upset because we haven't kissed in a long time."

My own audacity startled me, but the thought of finally coming face-to-face with my enemy made me feel like the flame of Sira's heart was in my own. To my surprise, she looked guilty.

"That's kind of my fault," she murmured, averting her eyes. "I guess I shouldn't have been so pissed about your eye. Not like that's your doing."

"I understand," I replied softly. My forehead touched hers, and I could almost feel the warmth I associated with her soul. The fire.

Nothing could extinguish that, or surely, I'd grow cold as ice. "But you could have told me sooner."

To my surprise, she chuckled, and pulled me into another kiss. This time her hands started to wander, and I had to stop her out of sheer embarrassment. "The others—"

She shushed me with a kiss, but she trailed her hands down my wrists to clasp my hands. "Why can't you be so cute *outside* of the enemy keep?" I glared at her, and she laughed. "Whatever. Let's catch up to them before Loki blows a gasket."

She took me by the hand and led me away from the wall. None of the others seemed to have noticed our absence. Loki caught me around the shoulders and led Sira and I forward. Will and Brom stood at the final set of doors, where another pair of guards in white armor waited.

"Stay behind me, Ryoku," Loki whispered urgently. "If he is who we think he is..."

I didn't reply, but squeezed Sira's hand. Since Vortiger, when the strange power of my weightless marks appeared, I felt like the times of shying from conflict were over. I could fight now. I stood up against my friends to save Sapphense. I fought Roland with them, and then the dragons in Vortiger. After losing Sapphense, I couldn't bear the thought of my friends getting hurt. I lost enough.

Will turned away from the doors to face me. Rena was behind him, unconsciously clinging to the tall soldier. The look in Will's sapphire eyes was more than enough to push me forward. This wasn't just my battle anymore.

"Let's go," I urged, and started forward. "I need to meet the man responsible for this."

The pair of guards in white opened the door before Will looked ready for it. With a deep breath, we stepped into the throne room.

The room's torchlight threw shadows to even the most innocent things. Cobwebs strung along the ceiling like prepared nets of darkness. The red carpet we'd followed the whole way birthed from here like the end of a dragon's tongue. It started at the head of the room between two windows drawn with velvet curtains. Between the two darkened windows sat the throne.

The toad-like man on the throne was older than I imagined, likely in his fifties or so, and quite a bit overweight. The sides of his armored body pressed against the rigid arms of the throne, where his gnarled hands tapped silent rhythms. Upon his head was what looked like a Victorian era wig, a white piece that looped and curled wildly around his large head. True to the suspicions Sira rose in me, in the center of his hollow, sunken face glinted sharp violet eyes that seemed to offer their own ethereal light, watching us as we entered like a beast served fresh dinner. The red, kingly mantle around his shoulders looked the color of blood in the torchlight.

To the left of him, standing as rigid as a stone, was the pervasive Roland Demizen. Though both equally ugly, Roland managed to look a little younger than the toad-like king. He didn't seem fazed by our last encounter in Bonnin, though every inch of his skin from the high point of his neck to the bones of his wrists was concealed. In Syaoto, he wore armor a little more befitting of a regal general. It still seemed to fit the unhealthy man loosely.

On his other side was a new face. He was much younger than the other two, and a little older than me. Golden hair stuck out on all sides of his head like a barely contained mane. The torchlight seemed to give his blue eyes a dreamy glow, like watching the moon over the ocean. He was dressed in a long-sleeved white shirt with a lace-up collar, and only his left hand bore a black gauntlet on it. He wore no armor or cloak like the other two men, but I spotted what looked like a piece of metal at the left side of his neck and a slight bulge around the shoulder. His ungloved hand tapped the square hilt of a sword at his belt. Compared to the other two, he didn't look nearly as sinister, but there was still something ultimately unsettling about him.

"Welcome," Vincent declared, a satisfied grin spreading across his face. He had a loud and piercing voice, the kind I could easily associate with my timely enemy. He didn't pay much mind to the fact that everyone put their hands on their weapons, nor did he seem to have eyes for anyone but me. "It is high time we finally met. Brom, if you could give us the room."

The old general bowed before Vincent, though the movement was more like a puppet drawn by strings. "By your leave," he said, and quickly left the room. I saw his eyes meet Will's as he departed, closing the door behind him.

"*Vincent*," Sira growled. She was trembling despite all the lethality clinging to her voice. The king's violet eyes slid to her, and he smirked.

"Ah, Sira Jessura," he mused, tapping his fat fingers on the arms of the throne. "Time has been kind to you for the past thirty years."

"Has it only been that long?" Sira muttered. "You look like you could pass away. What are *you* doing here?"

The emperor smiled like a toad hovering over a flock of flies. "I could ask you the same thing," he said, and lifted himself from the throne with great difficulty. Somehow, his weight only served to give this massive man that much more atmosphere. Only two stone steps above us, his visage towered over us like an impassable wall. A sword lay at his belt with a black hilt, embedded with a large, faceted amethyst that glinted in the dark.

"This kingdom is lost to your people. Syaoto will be the property of Orden once my plans are complete. When I learned that the likes of you were meddling with affairs in my new property, I had to see it for myself. To think, the great, chosen hero would waltz right into my throne room and stare at me with such familiarity. You were expecting me, weren't you, boy? Yet, you still came."

He was looking at me now. I knew it. He expected me.

At his words, I finally moved to stand in front of Sira. One of Vincent's thick brows raised – I noticed that they were more of a stormy grey than the white wig he wore – and an eerie smile spread across his face. Roland barked out a laugh, ensuring to bat his cloak aside so the handle of his plain sword was visible for a moment. The blond boy didn't move at all. He didn't even seem to blink. It was like he already studied how I moved, to predict how best to fight me.

"The great hero protects a whore," Vincent mused, crossing his huge arms. Ahead of me, he looked like some kind of Victorian giant, his violet eyes eerily glowing in the dim light. "You are smaller than I imagined. The legends depict you as a young lad, but not quite so small. Tell me, does your waist have has much width as my arm? Are you able to lift that large blade at your back?"

I let out a low growl. I could feel the darkness rising in my chest. It suddenly felt more like an old friend than some alien force within me. We could tear this man apart, here and now. My hand twitched toward the chains of Ragnarokkr.

Loki stepped up next to me. He was the first to move since the great doors closed behind us. We were now mere feet from the emperor and his allies.

"Loki, the Trickster," Vincent seemed to recognize him, nodding once. "Interesting. Now the gods decide to step into the affairs of mortals. My father told me of a time where your refusal to interfere may have cost us our freedom."

Loki growled lowly under his breath. "For a man who spits in the wake of gods, you speak with much higher regard for them than I imagined. Yes, your father would know of such a time, surely."

Vincent didn't reply. He held Loki's gaze for a long time, but he went on.

"Ryoku, I'm sure you have met my chancellor and vassal, Roland Demizen. Perhaps you are familiar with my other vassal, Kimo Goldenhart?"

The blond boy stepped forward for the first time. In the torchlight, his blue eyes looked oceanic and stoic. Something caught my eye about his sword as he stepped forward. Barely noticeable, only enough to catch the torchlight, was an upraised calligraphic letter 'G' in the center of his blade's hilt. It had an archaic loop to it that suggested the weapon dated back hundreds of years. Rather than speak to us, the boy only gave a surprisingly respectful nod in my direction.

"Young Kimo Goldenhart has been at my side for a very long time, you see," Vincent explained. "He is a spirit, not unlike many of you, but hails from the same era as our resident hero. In fact, Kimo tells me you two were once great friends."

My brow narrowed. "What are you talking about?" I asked him. "I've never met him."

I wasn't sure, but I thought I saw the slight tinge of pain in Kimo's eyes. If it was there, it evaporated quickly, giving way to the calm flow of the ocean.

"Don't worry about it, Ryoku," Katiel instructed from behind me. "He's trying to goad you. Remember where we are."

"What do you mean?" I asked, confused.

"So you don't remember," Vincent drawled, expressionless. "Amusing. I suppose you may be even younger than you seem. Forgive me. Perhaps I have overestimated you." He turned away to face the throne and gestured at us over his shoulder. "You are free to go, Defender and friends. I highly suggest you take my offer and leave, now. If this is what your new hero is, then you will lose should we cross blades."

Loki faltered next to me. Kimo's eyes wavered over me without emotion, and then he, too, turned away. I felt my fist clench around the chain of Ragnarokkr, but I did not control the next moment. I only heard the cutting of air as Ragnarokkr swung off my shoulder in a smooth motion.

Kimo turned back around at the last moment and stared, bewildered, as Ragnarokkr flew through the air, striking the wall behind the throne just above Vincent's shoulder and burying deep enough to rest in the stone. Not a soul in the room moved. I stood behind Vincent, shoulders heaving, and now mortally disarmed.

Vincent chuckled. His laugh was somehow both dry and booming. "I see," he mused, and half-turned to face us. A crooked grin had stretched across his face. "There is some fight in you after all, Dragontalen. It is unmeasured and weak, but it is there. Interesting."

Without warning, the massive emperor spun around to face me, clearing his dark blade from his sheath in a lightning movement. Panicked, I yanked my knife free, but the Trickster leapt in front of me. Their blades jarred against each other, igniting a twisted spark like tropical lightning. Vincent's sheer size dwarfed Loki in his shadow, but the Trickster held strong with his silver blade, keeping Vincent back.

"You're slower than I recall, Trickster," Vincent drawled, no strain detectable in his tone. "A shame. I'm intrigued as to why this has become your fight now, rebel god. Did you realize you cannot leave such matters to your own race?"

Loki swung his other hand up, and Vincent maneuvered around a tendril of emerald-colored fire that shot from Loki's open palm. "Enough of your useless banter," Loki snapped, trying to take a step back from Vincent. "Surely you summoned us here for a reason other than to waste our time?"

"He hasn't told Ryoku any of this," Roland spoke, sneering. "None of it. Who he is. Who we are. He doesn't speak for a reason, my liege. He hides something."

When Vincent looked his way, I thought I saw Roland tap his wrist. While they faced away, Loki tried to ease me back. Sira remained by the door with Lusari, Kaia, and Rena, keeping a protective arm across them even while her grip on her sword trembled. Will and Katiel stood between us, both spaced apart with plenty of room around them.

When I glanced back, Vincent's eyes were on me again. Loki was at my side, his sword gripped tightly in his hand. "You have managed to pique my interest, Dragontalen," Vincent said complacently. His eyes twinkled like the amethyst embedded in the hilt of his sword. "You are not the hero spoken of in legends, but perhaps a different sort of intrigue altogether. Kimo, would you?"

My body stiffened, almost sure he was about to sic his vassal on me, but Kimo only glanced at me mildly before turning around. With his ungloved hand, he reached up and yanked Ragnarokkr free of the wall behind him. Both Loki and I halted, surprised as Kimo lifted the sword with only a slight grimace. He flipped the sword in his one hand to catch it gently at the flat of the blade, and took a step forward to offer it to me. Nervously, I reached out and took it from his grasp. The skin on his hand where he'd held it looked burnt, I noticed.

Vincent looked on with a wry smile. "Surprised, Dragontalen?" he asked snidely. "I suppose you have not met many who could hold your weapon. Are you curious to the nature of such a thing?"

Loki's eyes flashed. "Did you say he was a Goldenhart?" he asked, gritting his teeth. "How did you...? They're supposed to serve Dragontalens, not your miserable—"

The next moment happened very sharply. The only telltale noise was the quick scuff of boot on stone, then Kimo appeared directly in front of Loki, his golden blade pointed straight at the Trickster's throat. The alarmed god swallowed hard, looking Kimo in the eyes.

"Do not label me as a servant," Kimo uttered. His voice held the faint note of a refined accent. "Your old ways of labeling people are extinct. I am Kimo Goldenhart; no more, no less."

"Stay your blade, Kimo," Vincent ordered, his voice cutting like a sword. "I did not order you to act. Stay your blade, and mind your tongue!"

From the expression Kimo briefly shot the older man, I almost thought he might turn on him right in front of us. It was a solid, tangible moment before Kimo withdrew his blade and sheathed it in the same moment. As he moved, I noted he'd used his left hand to wield his blade, the one marked at his neck by a piece of metal. Perhaps it was the lighting, but Kimo's left arm looked somewhat bulkier than his other. What was the deal with this guy?

"This is your last chance, Dragontalen," Vincent rumbled, turning back toward me. When our eyes met, I felt like I was unable to hide from his piercing gaze. "Leave now. If you decide to stay, you will never save your charge. You will die in this room. None here – not the Trickster, the Omega, the soldier's boy, the whore…"

His glance slid over us. He paused over Rena, but did not comment on her. "None may save you. Dragontalen, you have drawn my intrigue and my ire equally. I long to discover if the angst that caused you to surprise me is mere coincidence, or if there is someone worth your mettle in your blood. Go. If you return, I will kill you."

I couldn't move. It was Loki's firm hand on my shoulder that shook me back to earth. "We must go," he said quietly, keeping his eyes on Vincent. "Come."

I didn't feel like my legs were my own when I turned away to follow Loki out of the room. I only faintly noticed my friends watching me with a mix of concern and trepidation in their eyes. Will kept his shoulders stoic, his heroic sapphire eyes bold. Sira trembled, hiding her fear with a white-knuckled grip on her sword. Katiel and Kaia were right with me, each putting a hand on me as I approached. Katiel raised a brow at me; Kaia gave me a warm smile. Somehow, Lusari looked almost fearsome in the dark, her snowy eyes glinting like a quiet boreal forest where dark creatures awaited. Rena looked thoroughly confused and worried, but she did not leave and abandon us. She fell in beside Will as we silently exited the throne room, trying to escape a bottomless feeling of dread.

As the doors slowly shut behind us, I stole a last glance back at Vincent, lowering himself back onto his throne wearily. He was watching me until the moment the doors shut. Long after they closed, I could still feel those violet eyes on me. No wonder Sira was terrified.

SCENE FOUR: INDECISION

...Of Act Seven: Disowned
---
*In the eyes of Ryoku Dragontalen, we are in
Syaoto Capital, in the world of Syaoto.
It is mid afternoon
On November 13th, 2017.*

Nobody was in a good mood after our shaky encounter with the emperor of Orden. Brom didn't follow us. I saw Alex rushing after us as we left, but Brom stopped him with a hand. Oliver stood gravely at his side, arms crossed.

After storming out of Syaoto's castle, we all stopped. It seemed like everyone drew breath for the first time since we entered that room.

"We have to fight him." Loki was the first to speak, and all heads turned to him. "That monster has taken this world. If we can expose him somehow..."

Sira threw her arms up in exasperation. "No way," she said scathingly. "I thought you had a real head on your shoulders for a minute. You heard him – we stay, we die."

"What other choice do we have?" Loki asked. "Run away? Hope we can get stronger before Vincent becomes even stronger? No. We have to muster our strength in a decisive burst. Sira, I thought you would be with me on this."

"No, we have to run!" Sira argued. "Get it through your thick skull, Trickster! He said you got slower, and you're supposed to be the strongest of us! How can any of us stand against him now? How can Ryoku?"

"Well, he has to," Loki replied, but he sounded softer than before. He looked at me with a half smile. "That's his goal. Vincent as well as admitted that he has your charge. I'd bet well more than a dime that his home's sitting unprotected while he gallivants around here. He planted himself here knowing that we'd land here eventually. We can't run away from this."

Will was oddly silent while we argued. He looked like he had a thousand different things on his mind. Lusari and Rena both stayed near him. Katiel dragged behind us while we paced the streets, his hands shoved in the pockets of his robes, Kaia clinging to his arm. Sira and Loki argued as we walked, progressively getting louder and less reasonable with the passing blocks.

As the bickering saw the edge of town, the city walls looming into view as the sun became a hot glow over the mountains, Katiel spun on his heel to face Sira and Loki.

"You know it really doesn't matter *what* choice we make," he said flatly, looking between them. "We're gonna have to face him. We try to fight him? He's gonna put up a hell of a fight. We try to leave? Well, you think that fat old spider is just gonna let us out of here without a brawl?"

Sira and Loki stopped, looking at Katiel with slack jaws. "What?" they asked in annoyed unison.

"We can't just leave Syaoto, either," Kaia agreed passionately. "This city's a wreck! You've all seen it!"

"I agree, if that should make a difference," Will added quietly. "This is my world he has settled into. Who knows what happened to my old king?" He shrugged uselessly, and plopped down to sit on the steps of a bakery. "My home. I do not recognize much of it now."

Lusari and Rena sat down on either side of him. Rena seemed awfully taken with him, I thought with a bit of amusement. He was blind to it, absorbed by the strife in his home. The same perfect home he sang about endlessly since I met him, now corrupted by darkness.

"You're absolutely right, Will," Loki said, and plopped down to balance on his heels in front of Will. "This is your home. It lives in the hearts of kids like Alex, still willing to fight the good fight. We can't just let it go."

Sira shut her eyes in frustration. "He's gonna get himself killed," she snapped, tipping her head in my direction. "Vincent Ordenstraum is a *dark knight*. Maybe you lot haven't been to Orden, so you don't get it. Their family trains to swing a sword before they learn table etiquette. He knows how to use a sword better than a spoon. The Imperia Dark Knighthood academy accepts them from the age of *six* to begin teaching them dark magic and swordplay. When I knew Vincent..."

She suddenly trailed off, apparently overcome by her own memories.

"He mentioned it has been some time since you left," Loki said gently. "Thirty years, no?"

Sira muttered something unintelligible. "He looked about your age, or Guildford's, when I was there last," she said. "Even then... *that* was the prowess I was scared of. Thirty years and old age means nothing. A dark knight only gets stronger until they die. Orden sees to that. The things they teach them, he used to talk about it. My page-girl served him closely. He used to wake in the night screaming, still trapped in nightmares of their teachings. That sort of stuff, it doesn't go away. He's stronger now than he ever was."

Katiel made an unimpressed noise. "That gives us two options," he said, starting to pace. "Either we wait out his old age and watch the old toad plop dead on the throne, or we do something about it. Way I see it; he isn't going to get weaker. It sounds to me like he's doing things to the city and the laws, too. He's not just sitting there being a good king. General Brom has no power here. He probably promoted somebody loyal to him, or maybe just gave it to Roland. A bad call, that one."

Will started. "Lancet Cooper," he breathed, and it came out almost a growl. "The guards and my father hinted at that. If he is the Lord General..."

I swallowed. Our last run-in with Lancet Cooper left much to be desired about his character. Vincent would have something to gain by promoting him.

"He's spinning his own web in this city," Katiel said. "Promoting his people. Demoting ours. He's setting himself up for something worse. Said he's got plans, too. With that kind of power, who knows what he's gonna do?"

Sira sighed. "Who cares?" she asked. She plopped down on the other side of Will and the girls. Lusari glanced over at her, but said nothing. "We can't fight him, I told you that. None of us has that kind of experience. The harder people fight him, the quicker they fall. That's what's happening here. Damn it, Will, you've seen your people. They're done."

Will put his head in his hands. Lusari glared at Sira, who sighed wearily and turned away from them. "How can you say such things, Sira?"

She grunted back. "Just telling the truth, 'Sari. Everyone sees it. If we want to press Orden, we need this place. He knows that. If he's got Chris Olestine holed up in his castle, then he has his army protecting them. You think we can take on an army? No? We'd need an army of our own to fight an army, no matter how badass we think we are. Then, what's the first place we'd go to find one?"

Now Loki sat down with the others, burying his head in his hands. "Syaoto," he muttered. "He's two steps ahead of us. He's got this place *and* Orden holed up and on the defensive. If we had any influence in any world, it'd be this one. Vortiger, Harohto, Lysvid... they don't have the numbers we'd need to amass an all-out assault on Orden. This is the only world where we could drum up that kind of support. And so he took it."

"Seems like he's planning more, too," Sira replied. "See? We're fucked. We lose." She threw her arms up, slouching against the bakery wall. "What the hell do we do?"

Nobody else offered anything. Katiel scratched his chin, paced, and clenched his hands into tight fists. Kaia went and sat down on the steps, too. Nobody was coming up with any ideas. Will didn't lift his head. Lusari still gave Sira a bitter look. Sira closed in on herself, arms wrapped around her knees. Even Loki stared at the ground, biting his lip.

"I can't lose to Vincent."

Loki glanced up at me weakly. "Well, kid. We tried."

I shook my head. "No. We didn't try at all. We walked into that room ready to give in. Will, you saw how your home looks and you don't feel like you can save it. Sira, you were ready to let the ghosts of your past walk right back into your life. Loki, I don't know. It's like you were hoping things might go differently. We've landed in one of our worst-case scenarios, but what *hasn't* been the worst case for us? We just fought a dragon emperor, mind you."

"We only just saved you from his clutches," Katiel joked – from anyone else, I might've taken offense. "But you're right. We knew we were going up against some monstrous dragon, and we did it."

"Yeah, and we had other dragons with us," Sira remarked.

"But we didn't know that going in," I replied. "We agreed to do it because Lamont was broken, just like Syaoto is now. Only difference is, they were bent and broken already. According to Alex, things have probably only been this way for six months, not years. One spark, and we have the rebellion we want. We don't have much time – we have to do this!"

"What do you mean?" Sira asked suspiciously. "You never mentioned a time limit before."

I smiled at her uneasily but, with a heavy sigh, explained how I saw Chris Olestine in Vortiger at Sapphense's memorial.

"Hmm," Loki muttered. He got to his feet and leaned against the bakery wall, arms crossed. I noticed a baker from inside the store giving him a dark look. "They intend to execute him. That does imply the possibility of a serious crime."

Katiel snorted. "You met Vincent. He'd sentence us to execution himself if he didn't have the prospect of some kind of game to look forward to."

Loki still pondered the idea in his head. "November 21st, you say? And it's what day in your world?"

Katiel and I replied in unison. "November 13th."

Loki smirked. "We have eight days, then." Then his eyes shot open. "Wait a second. November 21st. That's one of the Demon Days."

I was happy to not be the only one looking confused. Will's head popped up a little and looked at Loki. "Demon Days?" Will asked.

Loki held up five fingers. "October 31st – Halloween." He put one finger down. "November 21st – the middle day. Salem's Hour, as some call it." He wiggled the last three fingers. "These ones change. The Winter Solstice, and the two days counting up to it."

"December 19th, 20th, and 21st this year," Lusari said automatically. Everyone turned to her, surprised, and she blushed madly. "I-I-It was pretty common knowledge at home. I mean, i-in a farming town..."

Loki shrugged. "Well, there you have it. The Demon Days."

"Why would Vincent schedule an execution on one of them?" Sira demanded. "Wouldn't that just make Ryoku's demon thing stronger?"

"That could be part of it," Katiel suggested. "An uncontrollable demon might not be such a boon for us."

"It doesn't seem to work well in this city, either," Kaia noted, raising a finger to collect droplets of water from the street.

"It isn't just demons that get stronger on those days," Loki added. "Evil grows stronger at these times. The Creator demands balance. These days exist as a natural part of their world. Even in your world, Ryoku, the turn of the season is associated with darkness. A time of the year when things end."

"Is there an opposite?" Will asked bleakly. "A time where good gets stronger?"

"Maybe then we'd stand a chance," Sira muttered.

Loki grinned, disregarding Sira. "You bet. There's Hero's Day – summer solstice. That's when the old hero of Laia was born, too."

I noticed Katiel and Will both look up at me. I returned their looks expressionlessly. I was born in January.

"Heroes only get one day?" Rena asked quietly.

"Yup," Loki confirmed bitterly. "I guess heroes always have the upper hand, anyway. Or so the Creator claims."

Sira scoffed. "Okay. Well, what the hell does this do for us now? We know they're gonna be stronger then. Big whoop."

"We're going to fight anyway," I said. Something about the tone of my voice made everyone glance up at me. Will stared through the spaces between his fingers. "You guys have made it with me this far. We've crossed worlds to get here. Syaoto was just supposed to be a stop, but if we have to make our stand here, so be it!"

I knelt down to stare Will in the eyes. "Will. You swore to guide me once. To stamp through the mud alongside me no matter how I chose to travel. We've fought thugs, werewolves, vampires, dragons... all in the name of the here and now. You're finally home again. Just because it's changed does not mean it isn't your home anymore. I'm willing to stand and fight with it if you are."

I turned to Sira. "You came with me this far. You said you'd go all the way to Orden with me if you had to, and we aren't even there yet. Your ghosts have shown up again, but that doesn't mean we have to breathe life into them. You have all of us. We're not as strong as we could be, maybe, but we've grown. You have, too. We won't be defeated as long as we stand together.

"Loki, you too. You followed me from Immortalia to save my life. You swore your vows and promised you'd be enough to see us through every battle. Alongside you, I've gotten stronger than I ever thought I'd become. I still don't know why you did that. I'm not going to lie down and accept defeat until I know exactly why you did. Your *real* reasons."

I turned to Lusari, but she smiled at me. "I don't need a speech, Ryoku, though I'm curious what you might say. Things look a little bleak, but, like you said, they have before. I'm with you. I think we can do this."

Loki pushed himself off the wall, spreading his arms wide with a bright grin. "Well, I know what to do. If Ryoku intends to fight, then so do I. To the last breath, if so must it be. No matter what happens, Ryoku is the hero we all chose. Not only will he find his charge and save him – he'll save Syaoto and Orden in one fell swoop!"

"Ryoku doesn't make the wrong call," Katiel agreed, to my surprise. "If I didn't believe in him, well, trust me – I've got other stuff that needs doing. Uh, not that Dawn would ever let me."

I thought the flicker of a smile passed over Will's face, but it was quickly gone. Instead, he nodded shortly to me. "You have a point. I did swear to stamp through the mud alongside you, and it seems we have landed ourselves in quite the swamp."

Rena and Lusari both smiled now. Sira reached around and clapped Will on the shoulder. Loki beamed down at the soldier. In a way, Will was very much the heart of our group. Seeing him with even a spark of hope made the tasks ahead seem a little less daunting.

"So what's our next step?" Lusari asked.

Loki mashed his fists together. "We must train," he said gallantly. "Luckily, we exist in a world where demons run rampant. If we venture out into the fields at night, I'm sure we can get some practice in."

"And Ryoku has a new ability to break in, if I'm not mistaken," Katiel added. "That thing you used against Leiogrey back in Vortiger?"

I stared down at the marks on my wrists. Even without using them, I thought the black ink of the markings seemed to softly shimmer. "Yeah," I said. "It was sort of abrupt. Thankfully Loki showed me how to control them a little better."

Katiel and Kaia glanced at Loki, who averted his gaze. "It looks like a runic ability. Such things are mostly an inherited ability through bloodlines. Something must have forced it into dormancy for some time, but you would have always had such markings."

"That's really uncommon," Kaia said, frowning. "People aren't just born with markings like that. Magic, sure, but those?"

"She's right," Katiel agreed. "All of my runes are tattooed on." He stared at Loki for a moment, who didn't meet his gaze. "Do they work the same way as tattooed runes?"

Somehow, Loki looked like he found relief in that question. "Sure. Yeah, except they're linked to your bloodline. You'd no sooner be rid of them than you would your own blood. They give you that ability to turn weightless. I'd imagine the boons in that are as boundless as your imagination. Through practice, you could jump vast stretches or heights, carry intense amounts of weight, and perhaps – in theory, of course – fly."

Now everyone gave Loki dumbfounded looks. "No way," Sira muttered. "Ryoku could seriously fly with those?"

"I could see it," Kaia agreed, who beamed. "Weightlessness could translate to a bunch of stuff. Imagine what you could do!"

The intrigue in everyone's faces was clear – except in Katiel, who frowned, arms crossed. "It is interesting," he murmured, and looked deep in thought. "Bloodline ability, you say…"

"Perhaps Vincent does not know of it," Will suggested. "Anything he and his vassals could have missed could be our saving grace."

His words made me recall the banter in the throne room. "What Vincent said back there," I murmured. "Something about the Goldenharts. What was that about? Saying Kimo knows me?"

Loki shot me a look. "Maybe this isn't the best time for that?"

I shook my head. "No, that isn't all. They said his sword is supposed to oppose mine. And… Everything people have said to me. Jesanht wanted to kill me. The Timeless One told me this sword belonged to me. Everything about... this darkness, and the weightless marks. What does it all mean? Wouldn't figuring this out actually help?"

The more I thought on it, the more my head started to throb. Even beginning with Sira and Will back in Harohto, they claimed we were fated to meet. The world hadn't been the same two months ago. The more friends I made, and the more I learned from them, the clearer it seemed that I was involved with that past.

"That Jesanht must've mistaken you for someone else," Sira muttered. "Who knows? Guy was crazy."

"Not quite," Katiel said, to my surprise. I turned to him. My best friend's golden eyes shrouded in mystery, focused on something we couldn't see. "I couldn't say for certain. I didn't meet the guy, never have. However, I could see where he's coming from. Same as Roland. Same as Kimo Goldenhart." He looked me in the eye now, and I couldn't discern anything from his gaze. "There is a truth here, but now's not the time for it. Everything you're asking about – your sword, Kimo, your demon, and all this stuff about the spirit realm... it's a long story, and I don't have every single answer you need. Honestly, I don't know if you're ready for it. Not in this place, with Vincent looming over us and Roxanne's future on the line. This is a truth for another day."

I averted my eyes while he spoke, and he waited for me to look back at him before he continued. "Let's make it through this. I'll help you liberate Syaoto and save this world. We do that, and I'll tell you everything I have an answer to."

He offered me his hand to shake on it. I stared at it. There was so much I couldn't understand. Ragnarokkr belonged to my family name – a sword able to slay *gods*. There was the darkness, and the things it could do, the things it knew about me. Relus once warned me about it. Others weren't surprised by it, including Guildford, Will, and Sira. My eye had turned violet after the first time it took control.

What if Katiel was wrong? What if this had to do with my sister? My family? What if I needed to learn this in order to succeed?

It was with a deep breath that I took Katiel's hand. He smiled like a kid in a candy store. "Thank you, Ryoku," he told me. "We're in this together, you know. All of us."

"Our motley crew from across the worlds," Will agreed, smiling. He rose to his feet with all the valiance of the soldier I knew. "What do you say we get a move on? Check out our things into the Iron Bear, then go out into the fields to train."

Sira's nonchalant smirk turned, quite suddenly, into a grin. "Now that sounds like a plan," she agreed, and snatched me by the arm. "Let's check into that damned inn! Let the king himself rain down on our parade! We're gonna go kill demons!"

She started to lead the way through town, but it quickly became apparent that Will needed to do the leading. Either way, it seemed our resolve put everyone in slightly better spirits. Only Loki looked a little haunted now, I thought. Did he not want me to learn the truth? Did he have to do with it, somehow?

We checked back into our rooms at the Iron Bear. After suiting up, we all rounded up in the lounge, keeping warm in front of the hearth. Sira looked like her own excitement could fuel the fire for days.

"Alright," she announced, one leg up on a stool in the lounge. "We'll go out there and split into groups."

Loki sighed dramatically. I had the feeling he knew as well as I what the pairings would be. Katiel eased himself back onto a couch, arms crossed behind his head.

"There's an uneven number of us," Kaia pointed out. "Rena can't fight, can she?" The blue-haired girl shook her head, and that was all the input Kaia took. "Right. So me, Ryu, Kat, Will, Sira, Lusari, and the other guy. That makes seven."

Loki sputtered. "T-The other guy?"

I blinked. "Ryu?"

"She makes a good point," Katiel agreed, though he bit back a smile. "What'll your groups be then?"

Sira only grinned. "Pretty well the same. I mean, we won't split up far. Three groups – two of two, one of three. Katiel, Loki, you two don't need the practice as much, so you can go with Kaia."

Katiel shrugged. "Sure. The Trickster and me."

Kaia scowled at him. "Me too!"

Katiel shrugged submissively. "Loki, how are you doing? You want me to spot you?"

Loki sputtered angrily. "W-What about Ryoku? Shouldn't he have a large group with him? The demons are dangerous out there!"

Sira smirked knowingly. "No. The pairs are important so we get our training in. We all go out there together, and then somebody can slack off. More specifically, if we *all* went out there with him, we'd all protect him like usual and he wouldn't touch a single monster. You three need less training, plus you're powerhouses. You'd carry anyone else with you."

Loki nodded sadly. "That makes sense, I suppose, but don't you think the monsters outside might be too much for him?"

Sira shrugged. "I was just out there, remember? They're nadda. Plus you saw that kick this kid just about planted on Leiogrey back in Vortiger, right? Or maybe when he fought off *all of us* back in Bonnin? Maybe when he kicked Geri's—"

Will cleared his throat. "Does all of that really count?" he asked. "Demons and dragons are pretty different. Dragons are a big target. There are thousands of demons out there, Ryoku."

"Thousands of targets," Sira brushed him off. "He'll be fine. He'll be with me."

Loki sighed. "Of course you two would be together," he muttered. "Are you sure you won't have one of your episodes and let him get killed?"

Sira's glare could have put holes through him. "Let it go, Loki. I'll look after him better than any of you could. Will, your weird-ass armor leaves all sorts of openings for you to take a hit. You're tough as nails, but you'd falter where Ryoku's life might be on the line. Loki, you need to be with the others. Like I said, you'd just carry him through this."

"So I'm with Will," Lusari breathed, as though that was the only point Sira made.

"You think I have openings?" Will demanded. "I would have you know Syaoto armor is developed for optimal protection! And… I wear chainmail as well!"

"My magic is too wild?" Loki asked in a small voice. "My lightning?"

"Didn't Ryoku use—?"

Sira cut Lusari off. "Seems a *little* erratic. Didn't take out Brozogoth, did it?"

"What about Rena?" Will asked, turning to the blue-haired girl at his side and ignoring how Loki sputtered. "Vincent knows you are with us. Bringing you outside with us would not be safe, but..."

Rena looked up at him. "I would be okay here," she assured him. "If Vincent thinks you left, he should not go looking for me, either. Why would he?"

Will glanced at me, and I saw the unspoken answer in his eyes. To get to him.

"What if she holes up with your soldier friend?" Katiel suggested. "Alex?"

He had a good point. I thought about Leif and Oliver, too, but each seemed to have new responsibilities. With Leif in a gang and Oliver rising in the chain of command, I wasn't fully sure we could trust either one. Alex, on the other hand, supported us even as he stayed in the army.

Will nodded slowly. "I suppose," he murmured. "I wish there was another option. You... truly have nowhere to stay in town?"

Rena shook her head, smiling gently at Will. "Not quite. I only just arrived from Balgena today. I..." she hesitated, and only continued when she noticed all eyes on her. "I... well, it sounds silly, but I was hoping to find my father here. A friend, a pastor at the orphanage, suggested I start looking here. I came with the hopes of meeting him for the first time, but..."

A strange look appeared in Will's eyes for a moment. "You said you were from Stillwater Orphanage, correct?"

Rena blinked. "Yes. I believe it is the only orphanage in Balgena still standing." She giggled, hiding her face behind her sleeve. "I have to say, I never expected to land in such an interesting scenario. Like a story – the tainted monarchy, the reckless band of heroes... If I did not know better, I might presume to be stuck in a novel."

Her words caught Will by surprise, and he laughed, looking around at us. "I guess we rounded up the best reckless fighters."

That was the first time Will actually laughed in Syaoto. I could easily recall his contagious laughter from as far back as Bytold, and the look he got in his eyes when he talked about home. It made me want to save Syaoto more than ever. If nothing else, I could relate to the idea of a tainted home.

While we waited to warm up around the fire and discussed the last details, Loki caught Katiel's attention. "Those runes on your body," he said. "Are those the reason you can use magic without a staff?"

Katiel smirked. "You only take a few days to catch on, Trickster." He lifted his sleeve to show tattoos spanning the length of his arm. "They're multipurpose runes. Strengthen my magic, and they help with my Omega too. Kaia has them, too."

Everyone looked at Kaia expectantly, but the girl blushed. "I'm not showing you mine," she insisted. At the implication, we all glanced deliberately away.

"What about Guildford?" Will asked. "I saw him use magic without a staff, too."

"He has a rune on the back of his neck," Lusari told us. When everyone regarded her with surprise, she actually blushed a little. "I-I saw it from that silly outfit Bonnin gave him."

Loki laughed. "Right, that outfit! That was a good one! The Cheshire Cat – I couldn't believe my eyes! Imagine we ran into his likeness in Bonnin..."

We all shared a laugh. I was glad to see Will brightening up a little. Now, all that was left was to wait while he sent word to Alex to keep an eye on Rena while we were out. The young, tall soldier showed up as the hearth started to die out, and a shrill cold began to settle into the room. It would be even colder outside the city, away from the large amount of bodies.

"Hello," Alex greeted us, standing awkwardly in the room. I'd noticed he grew taller when we ran into him earlier, but it was apparent when he had to duck into the room. "You lot lived through your meeting with the king, so..."

Will gave him a grim smile. "It means little. Alex, he..."

"I know," Alex stopped him. "A lot of our people can guess what kind of man Vincent is. They say he's a Pendragon, too, but he's got none of the features. Until the people have some real proof, there's not a thing we can do."

Sira scoffed. "Like his damned violet eyes? The insignia of the Ordenstraum family."

Alex paled a shade. "Suppose that's true. How would we begin to overthrow such a man?" He clenched his fists on the table. "Leif couldn't take it – he joined his cousin in the Bladerunners not a month after we got back. Oliver got promoted right away. Soon as Vincent came to power, he regretted it. Only Brom's kept him there, and he's just a figurehead now. Lancet controls the city, and it's all Vincent's wishes. The city's in a state, Will. We cannot fight for ourselves. Not against a man like this. You returned at an ample time."

Will gave him a gentle smile, and took his hand on the table. I thought he would pressure Alex about his tardy speech again, but he let it go. "If there is aught to be done, we will do it. Mark my words – Syaoto will be free again soon if I have a say in it."

"Come on then," Sira finally burst with impatience, reaching across the table and grabbing my hand. "Let's go train now. It's not gonna get any warmer."

I smiled shakily, and she led me out the room. After bidding farewell to Alex and Rena for the time being, everyone else followed. All we had to do then was depart the city into the dark fields of Syaoto to fight monsters until the sun rose again.

I didn't dare voice it now, but I was terrified. It was time to test my mettle and find out if I could actually hold my own. At least, if I couldn't handle these demons, I wouldn't have to worry about failing against Vincent.

I couldn't erase his piercing violet eyes from my mind's eye. Even now, it felt as though he was laughing at us, watching us struggle in vain to stop him. At his side was the silent Kimo Goldenhart with his sharp instincts and his even deadlier sword arm. In my mind's eye, he would only scoff in annoyance as we charged out into the fields, struggling to grow stronger. Roland would laugh maniacally, convinced we'd never be able to touch a hair on his ugly head.

All in all, though, the loudest voice convinced of our failure was my own. Was it the darkness in me, or just the back of my mind that knew I was weak?

SCENE FIVE: ASSISTANCE

...Of Act Seven: Disowned

In the eyes of Ryoku Dragontalen, we are in the Outskirts of Syaoto, in the world of Syaoto. It is early evening On November 13th, 2017.

"You don't look so good."

I smiled lightly at Sira, her eyes deceitfully concerned behind the curtain of rain between us. A storm had begun to roll in while we left town, and now it hammered down with the fury of the gods. I was drenched, and I didn't like it. How could we train properly like this?

"What do you mean?" I asked mock-curiously while I scanned the foggy horizon. We wandered a mile or two away from the city until the capital was just out of view – not that we could say that with confidence, given our limited visibility. Mostly squishy grass and mud puddles made up our surroundings, and some shrouded mountains peering out from the distance. Will and Lusari trained just over the hills from us, and Loki and the others opposite them. If we shouted, I wondered, would they hear us?

Sira's eyes narrowed. "Are you having second thoughts about this? Our suicide mission?"

I shook my head, spraying everywhere with water while I slipped on my old black gloves. Watching me, Sira drew Sinistra with an air of practiced mastery, glaring into its fiery face before focusing back on me.

"Why don't I believe that?" she pressed. "You look paler than usual, and you're trembling. If those aren't signs of hesitation, then I'm a courtesan."

I held back a cynical grin, strapping on my other glove – both soaked through already. "What if I'm just freezing?" I teased. Swallowing back some hesitation, I added, "Maybe I'm longing for your touch again."

That brought an unusually soft grin to her face. She dropped her sword-bearing hand to her side, and she pulled me closer with her other. She was no dryer than I. "You're not getting away from it that easily," she muttered in my ear. "If longing for a touch makes you shudder so, then why aren't I trembling?"

I smirked at her, pulling her a little closer. Whether it was because of her affiliation with fire or just her sheer audacity, she made me feel a little warmer. Getting closer to Sira reminded me of the Timeless Castle, and of our first encounter of that nature. Those thoughts could be my only warmth in this battle.

"We'd better train," I said, and had to repeat myself as a boom of thunder shook the plains. The flash followed an instant later, and I blinked it away. "Aren't there supposed to be demons here?"

She scowled down at me. "You ruined the moment," she muttered. "Don't you know anything about romance?"

I scowled back. "Do you?"

Sira looked stricken. "Well, I, uhh..." she stammered, unwinding her arm from my waist to scratch her head. "Oh, look, the demons are coming! About damned time."

"Nice try," I muttered, turning around. "You're just trying to—"

I was wrong. The horizon darkened in all directions, lit only with the glow of red eyes like a sea of fire. It was more monsters than I could have ever predicted. Why were the plains outside such a wonderful city home to a terrifying horde?

It was difficult to pick out in the rain, but I could start to see their diversity. Some were small, others tall and spindly. Some had girth, others bared their exposed ribs. Demons of all colors speckled across the horizon like an evil rainbow. Many crawled or charged across the muddy ground, while others flew with bat-like or feathered wings. Some had scales, others with leathery and deathly skin. Some didn't have visible arms like regular humans, but twisted and savage claws paired with wings. Many of them had horns, tails, snouts, talons, or other unfamiliar appendages that made them even more haunting. Some looked like beasts, while others almost looked human, like the one I'd briefly encountered in Lysvid. The only thing they all had in common was the eerie glow of their red eyes, lighting up the fog in a way most unwelcome.

Most importantly, I knew the city was completely out of our grasp. If this suicide mission went awry, we would surely die out here. Nobody was getting through this horde.

"Not bad," Sira remarked, hoisting her sword up to rest the hilt on her shoulder. "I was hoping for a better turnout."

I gawked at her. "There must be millions here!" I cried urgently, drawing my belt-knife. "How could you want more?"

She only grinned. "I fought more than this with Katiel the other night," she replied. "You'll see. They're nothing special. Like fighting a wave of toddlers."

I looked at her incredulously. "Toddlers? Really? Like that's supposed to help my focus," I muttered, but slipped into a fighting stance. My style was horribly untrained, but it had been effective enough in the past.

Sira fell in behind me; her back brushed against mine, and she took up her sword readily. We stood back-to-back, ready for fighting infinite hordes of demons. I had more romantic dates in middle school.

We lashed out as one. Even as I lurched forward with my weightless marks at the incoming horde, and Sira unleashed a wild battle cry, I seriously doubted I knew what I was doing. I tried to think of my past victories to give me confidence, but it was pointless. Brozogoth could have lay down and hid among this horde.

My foot struck a tall, lanky blue demon with spiky arms. The impact jolted its neck and sent it hurtling back. Four or five demons fell with it, trampled by the incoming horde. I winced. Could this be as easy as Sira claimed? A demon popped up at my side with a raspy growl, and I struck it with the back of my heel. The demon burst at the neck, and its fallen body knocked down another set of demons with it. More rose up to swallow its body into their dead sea.

After striking a few more down, I was starting to see what Sira meant. With growing ease, I could try out different things to improve on my own style. I doubted I could kick Vincent Ordenstraum aside with a kick like these domino demons. My first step was to try and land a proper punch.

Dagger once taught me a few things about fighting. Even back in the days of rolling with him, my kicks always went better than my punches. He liked to work best on my kicks – why not improve a strength I already had? At the same time, he repeatedly tried to teach me how to punch. I always found it difficult. My strikes often ended up with my knuckles bloodied or worse, and the opponent only mildly inconvenienced.

Another demon lunged out from beside me. I acted instinctually, thrusting out with my elbow and a raised forearm. Shifting my weight, I tossed the demon over my head. Surprised at myself, I struck at next demon right away. What kind of instinct was that? It seemed a reflex, something embedded in my muscle memory.

The more I focused on the battle, the more a fractured memory seemed to play in my mind. I recalled talking to a young, black-haired boy with energetic red eyes. Who else had red eyes? It wasn't Sira or Rex, obviously. Maybe somebody from Orden, where unusual eye colors seemed more common. As I kept up my pace, I began to recall some scenario. I wasn't sure if I was recalling it, or inventing it.

"You're hopeless trying to throw a punch like this," the boy insisted flatly. He swatted my arms until I corrected my posture. The memory was fragmented and unclear, but I found my body adjusting as it seemed to in my memory. "Fight like this! It's called the... elbows and knees instead of tryin' to... You're more defensive, less open! ... style of the eight limbs."

The memory ran through my head like a choppy old record, bits and pieces scattered. The boy's face slipped in and out of my mind until I started to see more features. He had a sharp, angular face, an attractive jaw line, and a chaotic tug behind his scarlet eyes. A lady-killer and he knew it. I still wasn't sure if the memory was real, or some kind of figment of my imagination. Still, it seemed to work, and my poise evened itself out just like the boy instructed. Instead of balling my hands into taut fists, my palms opened and loosened, my arms and legs bent. I felt fluid and mobile.

I didn't have time to wonder. A demon stumbled into my midst. I retaliated with a heavy knee, striking the monster in the chest and sending it flying back. Another flew at me; instead of punching, I shot my hand out and struck with my palm, my fingers curled in. The demon hurled back into the crowd beyond my visibility. I whistled lowly, impressed with what I was able to do.

Combining the new, recalled style with my weightless marks, I dove forward and struck out with a leg sweep. Even the way I kicked seemed different than before. I took out a row of the flimsy demons before returning to the ground with a roll. I spun around and narrowly ducked underneath a swipe of claws. I dropped down to my elbows and struck out with a high retaliating kick, knocking the demon into the air.

Oddly, I realized something about the way I was fighting connected to the black-haired boy I thought I'd seen, whether it was a memory or not. I attacked with my palms, elbows, knees, and heels – altogether, the style of the eight limbs. Was it a real memory, or a false image I conjured to remember something else?

I fell into a routine of strikes while I tried to catch a glimpse of Sira behind me, but demons had overtaken me on all sides. I took my first hit. On my left side, my only blind spot, I let my airborne kick extend a little too far. Pain bit through my calf, forcing me back to the ground. I lashed out with my other leg, but the bite remained to put a damper in my step.

I decided to stay grounded more after that. Using the weightless marks allowed me to jump higher and extended the reach of my strikes, but it drained my reserves. I could feel the marks beginning to burn. I could use them on the ground with less strain. I had to adjust my stance to accommodate for my injured right leg.

I became lost in the battle. It was hard to think about anything but my next target, trying to keep all directions in mind, as I became a flurry of attacks. Sira's statement seemed truer every minute: my strikes were rarely blocked or anticipated. I only had to take aim, to keep my eyes and ears open. Wherever it came from, my style of the eight limbs seemed brutally effective.

The brawl seemed to last for an eternity. Each of my new strikes was becoming second nature. Each strike with my closed palms landed true, and my usually brittle elbows could maneuver a demon out of the way or land crushing blows themselves. My legs were capable as ever, and maybe even a little better.

I heard a scream. It ascended over the demonic chatter that infiltrated the sky, the atmosphere, for as long as I could recall.

My heart sank in my chest: Sira.

Everything I'd built up over the hours crashed down. The shrieks and wails of demons faded to a dull din. One thought stole my mind, my focus, erasing all else.

She revealed herself to me now, as though I was only meant to find her when I forgot the hordes. Her soaked red hair fell across her face. She was on the ground, her eyes hidden from me. Her sword was sunken into the marshy ground nearby.

For a moment, I couldn't move. Then I saw the blood.

I sprinted across the mud as though it was pavement, forgetting the demons that surrounded us. Like a familiar cloak, darkness swelled up in my heart, protecting me with its icy grip and surrounding me. The only light in the world was the color of Sira's hair.

I reached her in what felt like an instant. I turned her over into my lap. She was unconscious. Blood from her head smeared my blackened hands. The front of her shirt was torn, and blood leaked from a wound that I couldn't fully see.

Something threatened to burst within me. A primal rage, something both as hot as flame and as cold as winter. Anger. Anger at myself, at everything. Sira hadn't initially wanted to go out training. When she learned Vincent was here, she wanted to run. Why hadn't I listened to her?

I rose like a puppet on strings, bringing Sira with me. She was limp and cold as ice, which already made my stomach churn. I managed to throw her over my shoulder, and I yanked my knife free. I knew I would have to fight my way out. Me – the new Defender, the supposed hero everyone was suddenly looking up to.

The earth fell horribly silent. The demons halted when I turned to face them. The only sounds came from the beating of wings, the rattle of their breathy lungs, and the relentless downpour. A sea of thousands of demons stared at me.

One of them moved. A little black demon with bright gold eyes stepped forward, looking as startled as I felt.

"Prince of Demons?" it croaked.

As I tried to figure out what to do, it took a hesitant step forward. Before that clawed foot touched the ground, the sound of metal striking flesh cut through the air. As I watched, mortified, the demon split in half. The severed halves crumpled to the ground, and those golden eyes remained on me, confused, as they slid apart. A golden blade appeared through it, then yanked free with a bloody *squish*.

"What are you *doing?*" a male voice cried over the thunder and rain. "Fight them! You will die!"

In my moment of confusion, the darkness coating me fell away until color reappeared in the world. Color returned to the sky; the grass remembered it was soaked and muddy. The familiar coat of darkness evaporated, and the horde of demons rumbled, awakening from their own confusion to refocus on me.

"They're coming!" the voice shouted. "Do something! Stop standing around! Put the girl down, or you'll die!"

I shook my head doggedly, shrugging away the demonic calmness with a shower of water from my soaked head. I tried to steal a glance back at the man who took up arms behind me. Could I trust him?

"Put her down!" the boy ordered. "I won't let this demonic scum touch her any more than you would! Just do it, or none of us will make it out of here!"

I finally obeyed. I tossed my cloak off and wrapped it around her before I hurriedly put her down. I thought I saw a glimpse of gold and white from the stranger behind me. Who was he?

I had to force the thought aside, and rose to my full height. I thought the style I recalled had faded away, but it rose up like a toy merely put aside. Now, my precision was pivotal. I had to protect Sira. I measured each strike, contemplated every movement. I only had to make sure no demons got behind me. Easy enough.

Each strike was important. I could almost see the dark-haired boy I imagined barking at me, ordering me to keep my focus. Sira's life hung in the balance. How could I face my friends now?

When the hordes finally thinned out, a reddish glow started up around the mountains, and the rain dissipated to a light trickle. I began to realize how bitterly cold I was, but I couldn't focus on that. I forced myself to keep moving.

When my palm landed the blow against the last demon, it felt like years passed in the fields outside Syaoto. It took all my strength to keep standing. My legs felt like lead, my hands like beaten stones. My vision blurred, but I forced myself to stand tall. I took a moment to steel myself. When I was sure I wouldn't collapse, I turned around to check on Sira.

She remained where I left her, wrapped up in my cloak that had begun to bleed through. Her red hair plastered on the grass around her like coral. Her chest was rising and falling, though, which made my heart sink with relief.

"She lives yet. The wounds look to be shallow enough – she'll make the return trip."

Finally, it was time to look up and face my mysterious accomplice, ready to thank him for his help. He was looking down at me, his ocean-blue eyes twinkling in apparent deep amusement. His golden hair matted to his head, but an easy grin still lit his youthful face. As I recognized him, my heart sank deeper in my chest than ever before. I knew I wouldn't make it out of here in one piece. Not now.

Standing before me was none other than Kimo Goldenhart.

SCENE SIX: FATAL

...Of Act Seven: Disownment

*In the eyes of Ryoku Dragontalen, we are in
The Outskirts of Syaoto, in the world of Syaoto.
It is dawn
On November 14th, 2017.*

"What's the matter? You look like you've seen a ghost."
Kimo Goldenhart stood nonchalantly over us. His hand wasn't near his sword. His eyes were unreadable, standing in a casual posture with his weight planted on both legs. Still, I clutched Sira closer, one hand still on my knife. I'd never seen this boy fight, but he moved quickly against Loki earlier. Could I outrun him?

He knelt down before me and reached his hand toward Sira. I flinched away, and he looked at me. His hand turned palm-up, as though he were approaching a cat or dog and meant to convey no harm. I didn't breathe. His hand continued, slowly, to trace over her wound. His touch was light and gentle, more like a doctor's than a vassal of Vincent Ordenstraum.

After appraising her for a moment, he stood up again.

"She'll live," he told me with a smile. "It isn't deep at all. What you should be concerned of is the blow she has taken to the head, the source of her slumber."

I checked that suggestion with disbelief, parting her soaked hair. Sure enough, a shallow gash spread along her forehead.

"Like I said," Kimo went on, "she'll be fine. You, on the other hand..."

I sensed a threat on his tongue and got to my feet, holding Sira away from him.

"Relax," Kimo said quickly, raising his hands in defense. To my surprise, I noticed he wasn't wearing the glove on his left hand. It looked strangely mechanical. It was identical to a regular hand, but crafted of smooth steel that imitated the shape. He saw my glance, and closed the fingers on his hand as though self-conscious. "We are outside of the king's grounds for the moment. I'd like to speak to you."

Now *that* took me by surprise. While I didn't expect it, staring into his deep blue eyes offered no other explanation.

"Really?" I asked quietly. I tried to keep an edge to my voice, and added, "Vincent claims I'm supposed to know you. Is that true?"

He nodded, and a weak smile flashed across his face. "It is," he murmured. "It seems you don't know much of your old life. Or lives, I should say. You see, we met a thousand years ago."

I almost laughed, but the expression on his face wasn't one I should take lightly. "A thousand years ago?" I asked blithely.

Kimo shrugged. "Is it the most crazy thing you've been told?" he asked, extending his hand out to encompass the fields where we just fought hordes of demons. "You, who had a thousand demons stopped and staring at you when I arrived. I thought they might be trying to trick you, but no. You had them confused. Can you try and explain that while telling me I'm the crazy one?"

So Kimo had seen that, too. I wondered if he'd been watching for a moment before he decided to help this soaked fighter in the dark, surrounded by demons.

"The same energy that drew the attention of Vincent yesterday," Kimo went on, watching me with amusement. "If I were you, I would keep your darkness under wraps. It may be an untold advantage against him if you play your cards correctly. What is its name?"

I hesitated. "Its name?" I echoed disbelievingly. "What do you mean? I, uh..."

I stopped short when Kimo lifted a finger to his face. A light blue flame circled around the length of his finger, then burst out wide enough to surround him. I wanted to retreat, but something kept me grounded. When the flame subsided, Kimo looked... different. His eyes had taken on a fluorescent shade of orange, and his pupils turned to slits. Dark blue stripes painted across his cheeks and neck, where his ears turned catlike and blue.

"His name, Ryoku," Kimo spoke, but his voice sounded different as well. His tone resonated with some kind of ancient power that made my hair stand on end. "This is Romis. A servant of the royal line of demons. A known killer in his own name. Looked down upon by some, but feared by many." He blinked hard, and the changes reversed. Kimo smiled at me with his regular blue eyes twinkling. "So, what's his name? I'm sure you know it."

As perplexed and terrified as I was, memories resurfaced in my mind. The darkness within me which had risen against Geri and hurled my sword at Vincent, and who demanded the attention of a sea of demons, was not appearing for the first time.

The Day of Black. We called it a day, but it consisted of the week where I lost control to that inner darkness. Everything that happened that day was committed through another entity in control of me. We all knew it, but nobody roused the question since that day. It took hold of me the second that Guildford's life faded. The fierce, cold anger in my chest that rose up that day had never left. It may have already been there.

I was only conscious for flashes of that week. I remembered holding him by his throat, six pairs of arms trying to pull me back. I recalled bits of the skirmish at Varis' hideout. The hot knife searing through my eye. My own screaming.

That was not the first time, either. I'd tangled with Varis before, and the memories were murky. I only began to recall it after we met Rena in the midst of a gang war. I could remember following him into an alley where all his friends waited. They held me back as they tore at her clothes. Later, I only recalled their fearful looks when I passed them in the city. Why was my past so foggy? Was there truth in what everyone said about my life? Was the darkness to blame?

An image slowly burnt into my mind. Dark hair. Red eyes. A dark-skinned body wrapped in bandages. Black claws. It whispered, baring its fangs as it spoke to me, chanting a name. It was a whisper, and, just as easily, a primal roar.

"*Advocatos.*"

The name came forth from my lips. I was surprised at the sound. Once I spoke it, it was as familiar as though I'd known it from the moment I was born. I pictured a mark we shared. A star drawn in blood and hidden by our hair. Such had been on us for ages, I felt, though I had no proof of it. Not unless I wanted to shave my own head and find out.

Kimo smiled knowingly. "Advocatos," he said, tasting the name on his tongue. "Yes. The prince of demons. The most wicked of demons, but the one most affected by the trials of sharing a mind with you, a Dragontalen. Purity, they call it."

I tilted my head to the side, my mind slipping in and out of awareness. The images I saw associated with Advocatos still burned into my mind. "The... Prince of Demons." My voice came out pallid and hollow.

Kimo peered into my eyes strangely, searching, as though he might find an answer of his own in there. "Lars wasn't kidding," he murmured, and his voice was distant. "You don't really look like him. You don't really act like him. But...in the end, you're also *just* like him."

My mind was haunted, it felt, but I needed to focus. I stared back into his blue eyes, still paying close mind to Sira. "What are you talking about?" I asked.

He didn't lessen his stare. "Your eyes are just like his," he murmured. "You have the prince of demons, too. The others may not see it, but I do." He pointed at the sword over my back. "I know what that is. That sword belonged to him. To you, I suppose. It is the same weapon, marred by the darkness that it stopped from consuming us before. For a legendary sword of light, it is quite beaten. I wonder if it will ever become the same again."

He kept staring into my eyes. I stared back silently, unsure of what to say. He was making no sense. I knew the sword was supposedly a birthright of mine, though twisted by some form of darkness. Kimo was also able to hold it. What did that mean?

"If you are him..." he whispered, but then fell silent for a long moment. "Never mind. It is not possible."

We both fell silent for a moment. Kimo stared at the horizon, though the glazed look over his eyes kept me from worrying if somebody was approaching. As the dawning sun rose, the steel on his shoulder glinted.

"Your arm," I said, nodding towards the metal peeking out at his neck. "What is wrong with it?"

Kimo, surprised out of his trance, followed my gaze. "Ah, yeah. I guess you wouldn't know, huh."

He pulled up the sleeve on his left arm, and my breath caught in my chest. Machinery made up his whole arm. It all linked together with taut wires that stretched from his shoulders to the metal of his wrist. He showed me the part at his shoulder, too, and the red wires that sank into wide scars deep into his shoulder – almost at his heart, it looked like.

My eyes widened. "*What?*" I whispered. "What on earth happened? That... that is your arm."

His brow raised a little. "Bold statement," he murmured, "and irrevocably true. Yeah, this is my arm, Ryoku. I guess you don't know... that the spirit realm you are in right now was very different three months ago. You don't know the story."

There it was again. The mention of the spirit realm being different.

"Tell me, then," I challenged. "What Vincent said in the throne room about us knowing each other. Your arm. Our demons. All the crap you just spouted. Tell me!"

He peered at me warily, and I realized he was analyzing me as easily as I was him. The posture he held, his sheathed sword, showed he had no plans to attack. However, I hadn't seen him move yesterday before putting a blade to Loki's throat.

"Are you sure you can handle the truth?" he asked. "You look ill. Recalling Advocatos and his meaning in your life strained your mind, I can see. You wonder about the complexities of what I have to tell you. How much of your life has been a lie?"

"Try me," I dared him. I was starting to grow impatient. "I'm tired of people hiding this. I want to know."

Kimo sighed. "For starters," he murmured, "you should know that you aren't really Ryoku Dragontalen."

My eyes widened. I stepped back. "W-What?" I demanded. "You're wrong. I know who I am! I remember everything you said, right? It's all me!"

Kimo shook his head. "You are what has come to be called a Remnant," he explained. "The true version of you sacrificed himself in September. Doing so saved your world, and irrevocably damaged ours. The sheer effort of what he did shattered his soul into thousands of little pieces, of which you seem to be the biggest and, arguably, most important piece. The thing is, a Remnant is not just created. A Remnant appears in an existing being. Whatever, whoever you were before this seems to be gone, and nobody knows who you were before. Your face, your body... none of it is Ryoku Dragontalen. Only your soul partially belongs to that name. Your full consciousness believes you're actually Ryoku Dragontalen."

What was he trying to say? My mind tried to wrap around it, but it was failing. He said I wasn't who I thought I was. How was that possible? I remembered everything!

Although, a voice in the back of my head reminded me hauntingly, I didn't. The feelings about Dawn that resurfaced at the end of summer. The blanks in my past about the Day of Black, and recalling when Varis attacked Dawn in the alley, forcing me to watch. The clippings I experienced of somebody training me how to fight. Adding that on top of my claim to Ragnarokkr, the arrival of Loki, and other odd coincidences, his words rang eerily with the truth.

Kimo was smiling. "Both you and the spirit realm existed before this, but in different ways. Like I said, nobody knows who you used to be. The fact that you drew Vincent's attention is something to be curious about. The fact that you can hold the sword and everything points to the idea that you're closer to him than we imagined.

"Essentially, you may as well accept that you're now Ryoku Dragontalen," he went on, "even if it's not entirely true. Who you could have been before, is dead. Everything that was Ryoku Dragontalen is now you. Before September, you were already a Defender, a spirit reincarnated from a life a thousand years ago. You carried the powers of a boy who once liberated an entire country with his sheer bravery. You carried that into the future, and harnessed that power again in your youth. Enough to become one of the strongest Defenders ever known. You saved this world, and sacrificed your soul in doing so."

He paused, watching my silent expression. "Do you remember meeting your friends? Dawn? Katiel?"

"Yes," I replied, not missing a beat. "Katiel, Dawn, Anna, and Virgo all helped me out back in middle school. There was a group of kids, and..."

Kimo shook his head slowly, and I trailed off. "Not as I have heard. Perhaps Katiel and Dawn were with you from an early age, but prophecy speaks of others. You began as Defenders together. You know some of them, but others seem to be fuzzy in your memory. I suppose there are side-effects to acquiring a memory not your own."

"You're wrong," I protested weakly. I was starting to go frantic. "I remember it so well." That was a lie, and I knew Kimo could instantly tell. I decided to rephrase. "They're my memories! They're fuzzy, like something messed with them a bit, but I know they are mine! They belong to me!"

Kimo's smile faded. "Interesting," he mused. "Perhaps you have a point. Maybe, in some degree, they do belong to you. You could be of the same blood. Family, in some otherwise unpredictable way."

My heart dropped when he reached for the sword at his belt. "Well, enough is enough. I thought I would do you the service of explaining some things to you. I hoped, possibly, that you would come to understand who you were from my words. My mistake. All in all, it is too late for you. We need you to return to who you were."

I swallowed back anger and sadness both. Helplessness flooded me. I finally had answers, even if they made no sense, and I was going to die? I couldn't fight him!

"I almost feel sorry for you," he muttered. He flexed his mechanical hand, and the next thing I knew, he had those cold-steel fingers around my throat. Sira tumbled out of my grasp, landing softly on the ground. Kimo clutched me above the mud, easily holding up my weight with his crushing grip.

"You..." I struggled to breathe, frantically trying to utter something to save myself. "You *don't have to do this.*"

"I do," he replied softly. He was a soldier again. A soldier of Orden. "I truly am sorry it must end like this. It is not the way I would prefer to do so."

He drew his golden blade with his right hand. It was the clearest detail I'd seen the blade in. The rich sound of steel parting from its encasement rang through the silent field of demon carnage. The golden-steel blade caught the timely sunrise like an executioner's axe. The end of the blade curved into a wide hook.

I nearly choked trying to get my next words out. "Please…" I murmured, trying desperately to pull his steel fingers away from my throat. "Don't… hurt Sira."

A transparent smile whickered across his face, but he decimated even that before he could appear soft once more. "I won't touch her," he promised. "A timely last request for a Dragontalen. I do wish I could find out who you really are, but I will honor your last words. Vincent wishes her alive, anyway."

He arched his golden sword over his shoulder in the way a snake would prepare to strike. I stared at the blade in odd transparency, the weapon that would part my breath from my lungs and my soul from my body.

What would happen if I died here?

I wasn't sure how a spirit died while their body was still in my realm. Would I enter a coma? Would my body die as well, or simply blink out of existence? Would one of my Guardians pretend to be me for the rest of my life? Would Kimo take it over himself? Then, his last words kicked in.

Vincent wishes her alive.

I thought of the scar snaking across her back. The terrible fear in her eyes when she confronted Vincent at my side. Her aversion of my violet eye. The way she shuddered when Vincent stared at her.

No. Not like this.

"Goodbye, Ryoku Dragontalen."

The pain felt like nothing I'd ever imagined. It was like being rammed by a dragon mid-flight, or standing between a wrecking ball and a decrepit building. It was like nothing a human should ever experience. My jaw dropped. Words struggled to come out, but all that left my mouth was blood. Blood seemed to fill my vision, blurring the warrior before me.

The realization hit me in my last thoughts. I never stood a chance. Not from the beginning, and certainly not now. Kimo was an opponent far beyond my current ability. Everything that I had worked for led me to this: to die in an empty field, slain by an opponent who didn't know who I was. There was so much I had to do. I needed to save

Chris. I needed to find my sister. My friends all had their own diverse goals that I wanted to help them see through. Who would see to it that Will's kingdom shone again? Who would see that Sira lived a full life, coming to ignore her scars to live happily? How would Lusari find a home? Would Guildford enjoy his afterlife?

A rattling realization hit me while my vision began to blur. A memory resurfaced, foggy and so blurry that I couldn't realize if it was real or not.

I pursued Varis into his hideout. Dawn was in his clutches. Seeing her there, at his control, drove the darkness within to awaken – maybe for the first time. When the darkness left, Dawn was safe. He saved her. Advocatos, the prince of demons.

That presented two things to me. One: Advocatos was on my side. Whether or not it was directly, he needed me alive for some reason or another. Anything that might harm me would harm him, and so he protected me. It made sense. He awoke against Geri, and again to face Leiogrey when my life was in danger. Seeing Sira on the ground, he rose up once more.

Two: Dawn meant something to me, and it linked to my past. Foggy memories brushed past me like long forgotten strangers in a crowd. A prophetic dream. A coffee shop. Dawn's smiling face. It happened probably four or five years ago. I knew we began to date then, but trying to recall how it went was like trying to remember a puzzle from childhood.

Kimo claimed that we were Defenders together from a younger age. Was that the reason my memory was so foggy?

That idea shook me. The possibility that Kimo was actually right about everything. How could he have spun up such a lie for me? It was unheard of to lie in wait and assault somebody with lies about their life, especially in such detail.

No, I already knew Kimo was right. As much as I didn't want to believe it, his words made a frightening amount of sense. It was as though somebody planted me here with the intent for me to never encounter the spirit realm again. They tampered with my memories so that I couldn't remember the spirit realm, and somehow made it so that I didn't try to plunge into my own fragmented memories. All the same, I *knew* that some of it was mine. The feelings that welled up inside me about my friends, my sister, and everyone I met were real. They had to be!

It was too late. I was dying before I could discover who I truly was. I had come close to death before, but there was no assuaging the fact now. My chest grew numb around the cold steel embedded in my chest, dragging out my last few seconds like tangible minutes. I watched Kimo blink as though each frame of the moment lasted seconds. He adjusted his grip on the sword in his hand and made to pull it out. The slow movement tore my chest like unleashed flames within me, and black spots streaked across my vision.

No.

I knew this was it. I couldn't die here, but it was happening. Darkness coated my vision like a curtain drawn on my final moments. The last thing I would see was Kimo freeing his sword from my chest, the gore of slain demons all around us as the rising sun glanced off the metal at his shoulder. It felt like the ending to a story or a movie, looking onto the oddly picturesque world around us in slow motion.

Even the shining light seemed dim, and then black altogether as everything washed away. The last thing I saw were Kimo's apathetic blue eyes, like the calm of a sea after a raging storm that sank many ships.

Then I was gone.

Then, after everything, my eyes shot open.

A new consciousness rose to control, letting the dying host rest in the recesses of my mind. The darkness surrounded me, emanating from me in place of the blood I lost. I became wholly unaware of what was going on – but the new presence took over.

I was not going to lose now.

Kimo's eyes shot wide when I latched onto the golden sword in my chest. My claws clenched, and the blade crumpled under my grip. I fell to the ground with half of it still in me. Kimo staggered back, staring between his wrecked blade and the boy with the other half still embedded in him. My bloody lips spread into a vengeful smirk.

"You..." he murmured, searching the fire in my eyes for words. "You are still here. Advocatos, prince of demons. I doubted you, but you are yet in your full strength."

I growled. "Were I at my full strength, you would not live to see this moment."

I reached for Ragnarokkr over my back, fully intending to dispatch this nuisance and walk myself back to the capital city. Something pinned the sword over my back, and I couldn't move it with all my might. I growled, confused, to find that the other half of the golden sword in my chest had stuck into the sword itself.

"My family heirloom proves true, despite it all," Kimo whispered. "The blades are counters. Our families were never meant to hurt one another."

I snarled, ripping at the remaining blade in my chest. No matter what I did, it wouldn't budge. "Yet your blade remains in me. What do you say to that, bastard?"

Kimo's wondrous expression steeled over again. "If you knew why I did what I have done, then you would heed my words. If we can get rid of this Remnant and bring back the original..."

"That will not happen."

I cut him off, advancing a step toward him. I only made it a step before my legs crumpled beneath me, and I barely stopped my own fall. Growing ever more furious, I fixated Kimo in my glare. "The original version of him is damaged. There is a *reason* he is not here. A *reason* he placed us in control. Interfering is not your place. If you stand in my way again..."

I managed to yank Ragnarokkr free and, from the ground, pointed it level to Kimo's throat. He did not move, staring down the length of blade into my eyes. Along his gaze, I saw a shard of his own sword embedded into Ragnarokkr.

"It is pointless to fight, prince of demons," Kimo told me in a low voice. "He is dead. You know it as well as I. Why waste your words?"

"Because you know I speak the truth. I will live on. Ignore me, and suffer for it. Heed my words. You served us once. Do so once more. Put our lives before your own. He was once your closest friend. Save him, and you will live."

"My closest friend is gone," Kimo replied coldly. "You speak of ghosts."

"He is not gone," I replied lowly. "He lives in the boy you just stabbed. Honor that old claim."

I saw the hesitation in his eyes. If I couldn't convince him, then using the last of Ryoku's strength was meaningless.

"I will heed your words," he said slowly. "If you are right, and he cannot return..." He trailed off, gazing astray for a moment. Something heavy hung on his shoulders. He returned his gaze sharply to me. "When he is well, we must not cross paths again. Not yet. There is much I have to do. I will not allow anyone to stand in the way."

I snarled, annoyed at his arrogance. "You remain at the end of my sword. Speak humbly, Goldenhart, lest my hand slip. I am always here beneath this skin. If you interfere with what I must do, then your days are numbered. Forget about your alliance with the fat emperor. His involvement in our ordeals is less significant than his size."

Kimo smirked. "You could be wrong there, Advocatos," he said softly. "Only there. Nevertheless, for now, I suppose we are at an impasse. I will do as you ask, and may we stay out of each others' way."

I nodded, and Ragnarokkr slipped from my grasp. Supporting the body was becoming too much. I glared up at Kimo, my vision blurring. "Do your part," I ordered, and fell.

...End of Act Seven.

PART TWO
DESCENT

ACT EIGHT: CONQUER...

In the eyes of Ryoku Dragontalen, we are in
Syaoto Castle, in the world of Syaoto.
It is late afternoon
On November 14th, 2017.

SCENE ONE: ROSES

When my eye finally opened, I wasn't sure where I was. What came to be after death in the spirit realm? Was it the mythical heaven and hell that we were always told? Was it just whiteness, like this bright room I found myself in?

I moaned in pain, trying to shake the light out of my eyes so that I could see, and someone stepped in the way of it. I tried to adjust my vision to see them, but it was a slow process. When I made out a set of kind blue eyes and that dopey, worried smile, I groaned.

"What're you looking so worried about, Will?" I mumbled.

He grinned at the sound of my voice. "Ryoku, my friend. You are alive. I thought... We all thought..."

"What?" I asked– but shortly after I spoke, it began rushing in.

I remembered the night of fighting demons with Sira, and then with Kimo. I remembered everything he told me, and my head already throbbed at the thought. Then I remembered being stabbed.

"Am I going to feel it if I move?" I asked simply. Will glanced down in the direction of where the wound must be, then nodded gravely. I groaned again.

Sira's head popped up next to Will's. In the bright light, her scarlet hair shone like fire, and her matching eyes looked soft. "Good to see you're alive," she said. "How do you feel?"

Wow. Sira saw me waking up and didn't make some snarky comment. Oddly, that made me feel worse than anything else. Probably because if she couldn't muster up some sarcasm for me, then she was actually worried. "I don't really feel anything," I replied. "I'm assuming I should."

Sira glanced down, nodding. "Lusari, Kaia, and Katiel put themselves out trying to heal you. Some of the castle mages, too. You were… really on the verge this time."

I nodded painfully. I had adjusted myself to the idea. In fact, I was surprised to see and feel things again. I was certain my last moment was spent.

"How did I get here?" I asked. "Did you find us? Did you bring me here, Sira?"

Will shook his head. "The two of you were the last to return. Everyone got to the Iron Bear. We waited for an hour before we decided to go get you. And…"

He trailed off, glancing away. I saw guilt in his eyes.

"They found us at the city gates," Sira picked up for him. "For almost a day, the medics wouldn't move you. You…"

Now Sira was at a loss. Will looked between her and I, and I almost thought he looked ready to cry. The thought moved me horrendously. For all I'd done, I'd never seen him like this before.

"They had to close you up."

The voice came from the doorway. Loki appeared in my view, his expression taut as an arrow. He completed the picture of my three closest Guardians, all tearing at my heartstrings with their own despair.

"The mages drained their magical stores entirely just to get you into the castle," Will told me. "There, everyone had to *really* fix you."

I couldn't bear the looks on all their faces, and turned away. "Sounds like fun. A Ryoku puzzle to put back together." Nobody laughed, and I looked up at Sira accusingly. "What about you? You were hurt badly. I was worried I might lose you."

She frowned. "You outlasted me out there? Seriously?" She scoffed, crossing her arms. "Sure. Color me impressed, but you took a hell of a beating out there. What happened to you? You looked… well, you looked like you were run through. And your hand. You lost a lot of blood. I should have never taken you out there."

"No, we pressured you into staying in the first place. I felt like hell after you got hurt, but... if you're okay, then it was worth it. I learned a lot."

It was the truth, however bittersweet. I had learned a lot more than I would have if I spent my time brooding over Vincent. I wasn't sure whether to tell them the truth, though. If they knew what Kimo did, I'd never get to him first.

"If you learned something, then we should be proud," Loki said. "One cannot truly learn without investing their well-being. I would have rather it went any other way, but... Ryoku is alive, and we must be forever grateful of that. He has a new look in his eyes. He has learnt a great deal."

"It doesn't mean he had to," Sira snapped. She glanced at me, and she added, more softly, "Not yet. I was supposed to watch him out there."

Loki turned to her with a wink. "Our Ryoku can't be under our protection forever. He will get hurt sometimes, and we can't always help him out." I felt a sharp stab as I remembered our talk in Vortiger. It wasn't the first time Loki brought up such ideas.

Sira looked flustered. "Well, I should have done something," she growled. "I failed you out there, Ryoku. I went down first when I should have been protecting you until the last breath."

I blinked in surprise. "You didn't fail," I replied honestly. "It was training. Loki's right. You guys can't watch over me forever."

"That's not enough," she snapped. "You're too *fragile*. I'm afraid you'll just *break* someday."

I tried to push myself up, but I encountered a sharp pain in my right hand that nearly brought me back down. Loki caught me around the shoulders, steadying me, and he and Will helped me adjust to a better sitting position.

The three of them and an arena of unattended chairs surrounded me in an infirmary bed. Blood stained the sheets even though they still smelled freshly changed. I could tell that healing me had been quite a mess, and this may have been the healers' first break. The curtains were drawn, letting sunlight fill the room.

"Hang on," I remarked. "Where did you say we were?"

Will gave me a tight-lipped smile. "The castle."

I tried to sit upright, but Will quickly stopped me with an outstretched arm. "T-The castle?" I asked warily. "But our enemies are here!"

"As are my closest friends," Will assured me. Despite his tone, a grin was tugging at his lips. "You may be surprised how powerless Vincent Ordenstraum could be in his own castle. Brom arranged your safe passage into the castle where the best healers work. Of course, your friend Katiel is a smidge better than what our Capital medics are capable of. I tried to pull strings and get Balgena mages here, but such was not possible. Nor, it would seem, was it entirely necessary."

I looked up at him as he warily appraised my condition.

"Well, all things considered," I said, "how's it looking, doc?"

He gave me a dry, unimpressed smirk. "Much of the healing focus has been in your chest wound," he admitted. "We put in a lot of work just to bring you into this room. I am unsure how long has passed in your world, but you have been unconscious for several days. I have lost track of how many."

Loki's expression turned dark. "And we have yet to figure out why that is," he remarked. "Once you have fully healed, I will be headed to Immortalia to inform them of these worldly changes. Vortiger was bad enough, but Syaoto... why, it exhibits the time pattern of a fallen world!"

I swallowed hard. In my own world, I quickly ensured to check the date. It was only the afternoon following the demon-night excursion. I couldn't help but be silently grateful for the difference, even unexplained. I was only scandalously late for school in my world, but sleeping further could have resulted in missing Chris' deadline. My world might even take me for dead. If I was spiritually unconscious, could it be taken as a coma?

Will carried on. "Ryoku, you sustained many injuries. Your hand was a prime concern as well. It looks as though you grabbed a blade or something akin to it, as your hand was... near severed at the middle. Other than that, you were largely deathly fatigued and bruised like an apple. As for your overall condition, I think you would not have survived without magical aid."

I could tell Will wanted to know what really happened out there. Before I could ask anything else, there was a small sound at the door.

"Can I come in yet?" a female voice asked timidly. My dazed mind struggled to recognize it for a moment.

"With caution," Will advised uneasily. "He is awake and claims not to feel his injuries, but that could change at the flip of a coin."

She came into view, and my face reflexively lit up. This was our first meeting in the spirit realm, but I'd known the girl for years – Dawn Elethel, my fellow Defender.

Her strawberry-blond hair tumbled over her shoulders and framed her soft, elfin face, lit with a pair of curiously green eyes that always portrayed warmth and loving. She dressed in a somewhat tightly fitting dress layered with pockets and folds of various designs. Only two things differed between the girl of my world and this one: thin vines that entangled through her hair, and a definitive, sharp curve to her ears. Both were undoubtedly signs of her heritage.

No sooner did she meet my glance than did she launch herself at me, much to the fright of Will and Loki. Given the force she used to lunge, she landed on me only as lightly as a discarded coat, wrapping her arms around me as tightly as she dared. Her scent filled my atmosphere; a mix of the beautiful lilac smell she carried in my world, and a nostalgic, earthy scent she beheld as a druid and elf.

"Ryoku!" she cried, burying her face into my shoulder for a long moment. I wondered if she was sobbing, but she'd never let me see that. Being so close to her forced a memory back into my head: how she filled my mind with a strange feeling just as life seemed to be trickling from my grasp at the hands of Kimo. Feeling her against me now, I wondered if it was real. That, and her presence here must mean she had a part in healing me. That was one of her natural talents, I knew.

I noticed Katiel appearing in the doorway behind her, grinning. He looked tired as well. He must have put a lot of energy into healing me.

"Ryoku!" Dawn exclaimed again. She brought her head up until it was inches before mine, and she looked stern. She didn't appear to have been crying, but she was also insanely good at appearing unfazed at a moment's notice. If I recalled, she'd done it plenty when I was getting to know her, and it took me a long time to learn about her home situation. "It's just like you to land in some deadly trouble barely a week after your arrival! You had us all worried! Kat says you could have died! I got here as fast as I could, but a lot of the work was already done."

I smiled sheepishly. It definitely reminded me of last time she visited me in a hospital: right after the Day of Black. "Sorry," I said, resisting a strong urge to play with the vines in her hair. "It's good to see you, too."

She smiled, retreating to sit comfortably on my lap. I caught Sira's glance behind her – she wasn't impressed, clearly. Will was hiding a grin with his hand. Loki watched her with a great deal of intrigue.

"Lots of people came to visit you, just like last time!" Dawn said, still smiling. "Beats me how everyone in your life doesn't have grey hairs because of you! Richard and Breanna must have their hands full with you all the time! You're late for school, too, silly. Can you do anything without almost getting killed?"

"That remains to be seen," I replied mysteriously. I noticed Loki begin to pay a lot more attention to what she was saying. I was trying to think of what to say to the pretty girl sitting on me, but my mind only worked up the strange feelings I'd come to recall about her. Did she remember everything that I couldn't? Would she be able to explain it to me if I asked?

Her expression grew perplexed and she leaned a little closer, looking into my eyes. With her lightly splattered freckles, the cute curve to her nose, and the slight curve of her cheekbones, I started to wonder why I had ever left her. On the other hand, had she left me?

Just when I was sure one of us was going to say something, the door shot open.

It was Rex who burst in, who appeared to have been running. His coat and jacket hung disheveled, his thieves' arm halfway out of the sleeve. We'd only parted ways the other day, but here he was. In Syaoto time, I supposed it had been even longer than I thought.

"Ryoku," he gasped, struggling for breath. "You're alive."

A thought occurred to me. If he was a hybrid, just how fast had he been going to be out of breath?

"Yeah," I replied dully, shocked. "You, too. You're, uh, still in Syaoto?"

"Uh, yeah," he replied, casting his dark hair from his face while he tried to breathe. "The thing is, well…"

If I was already surprised then, the next ones who tumbled through the door behind him left me flabbergasted. There was the Timeless One, dressed in his usual black tunic and cloak that would fit a child comfortably. What he lacked in height, his ridiculous top hat compensated for.

Next to him was his bespectacled assistant, Relus Ashbane, who wore a white coat over his tunic and was easily twice the height of the Timeless One. On their other side, wrapped halfway around Relus, was Cleria Nightfang, dressed in hardly anything considering the weather in Syaoto, her pigtails partially undone and askew. She smiled at me, pigtails bobbing, but it ebbed away a little when she looked at Dawn. Did vampires not like elves?

"Well, well, well," the Timeless One said loudly, strolling into the room like a king. He briefly noted Dawn on top of me. "The hero lives on, I see, despite all that strives to stop him. How are you, my boy? You look more wizened than last we met. Oh, and you've found yourself a strumpet! A true hero, surely."

Dawn looked at him quizzically. "A strumpet?"

I exchanged glances with her. "A hero? What kind of hero has a...?"

Relus adjusted his glasses. "Perhaps it is best we don't elaborate on that," he muttered. "No matter how many decades pass, my master has yet to develop manners." He smiled at me. "But now, look at you! You have grown considerably! A young hero in the making, surely. Have you perfected your magic yet? How has Ragnarokkr fared for you? Oh, and the darkness..."

I tried to sit up a bit. Katiel lurked by the door, clutching his stomach in a silent fit of laughter, and Dawn glared at him. Sira exhaustedly took a seat near the bed, and Will buried his head in his hand. Loki took a seat near the wall and stretched back lazily.

"That's a lot of questions," I murmured, trying to keep up. "I'm working on my magic and everything. Guildford was helping me, but... I can't wield the sword, but... Hey, what do you mean? The darkness! You knew already!"

"Anyone could see it," Cleria replied lightly. "The darkness was always there – your inner demon, slumbering until it was the right time to wake up. Unfortunately, Rex didn't seem to help you much with it."

Rex glowered at her. "You never asked me to."

"The demon is a part of you," the Timeless One explained, butting in on Relus when he was about to speak. "Like two sides of the same coin, Ryoku Dragontalen and Advocatos are one, even if your form is a little... off. The bond you two share relies largely on your strength and potential. He is trained to step in when you're in need, comparable to how once you remove the head of a chicken—"

I did my best to ignore the Timeless One's explanation and demonstration of a chicken with its head cut off. Luckily, the door opened again behind them. I looked up, surprised. More visitors? Or guards coming to remove my current guests?

However, my face lit with glee when Guildford and Lamont entered the room. Both men wore Syaoto attire. It was likely too warm for their winter gear and too cold for their summer. Guildford's dark hair had grown out more, and his face somewhat tanned and well matured. It surprised me to see that he grew even in spiritual form. Lamont also looked older, though he'd trimmed his long, dark hair since last time I saw him. There was a certain level of pride to his posture that didn't exist before. Seeing that made me happy.

Guildford waved at me as casually as though seeing me in the halls at school after a weekend. He noted the Timeless One currently dancing in the center of the room like a headless chicken, and shook his head.

"Some things never change," he sighed, and he smiled at me. "Are you alright? Word spreads fast of a Defender's plight in the spirit realm, and we had all ears to the ground. We came as swiftly as we could."

I listened to his voice with surprise. Was he starting to adopt a Vortigeran accent?

Lamont bowed cordially to me. "I'm glad to meet you again," he said. "Time has passed in Vortiger differently to your world. It has been some time for us. The dragons speak amicably of you to any who can listen."

Introductions carried out around the room. The Timeless One's group, Lamont, and Guildford all appeared to have just arrived. Characteristically, Dawn didn't refrain from sitting on my lap, and smiled at me.

"Interesting friends you've made," she commented. She suddenly fixated the Timeless One in her glare, who froze in his tracks mid-chicken. "You. Do you have any idea who landed Ryoku in this hospital bed?"

Dawn's motherly tendencies kicked in, turning her from the cute girl perched on my lap into a ruthless interrogator. The Timeless One's smile twitched nervously. "I would think some soldiers and medics had to do with it, no? I have no clue," he added earnestly and quickly when her glare worsened. "I figured we'd burn that bridge when we got to it! I mean, it is somewhat of a hammer to the face, us getting to meet altogether like this, no?"

Dawn blinked. "Burn... that bridge... when we get to it?" She scowled. "A hammer to the face? Whatever do you mean?"

Relus adjusted his glasses, appearing between us in a timely fashion. "*Cross* that bridge when he gets to it, I believe he means," he corrected his master again. "Something about a gift horse in the mouth, perhaps, but I cannot say for certain this time. However, I do not disagree – oddly enough. Ryoku's injuries brought us together in a group to culminate our knowledge. As we noted, the demon has clearly surfaced. The most fascinating thing about our hero is his abilities of both light and darkness. A unique blend for a unique battle we must fight."

The door opened again, which drew a furtive sigh from Will, and three more figures piled in. First came Alex and my friend, Joey, chatting and laughing together like old wartime buddies. The two looked a little similar, side-by-side. Both had wild, wavy hair, although Joey's was a little darker than Alex's, and his skin a little more tanned. As was characteristic of him, Joey still wore his red hoodie pulled over Syaoto armor.

Behind them came an alluring figure that I certainly recognized, though I had no clue why she was here. It was none other than the demon girl who assuaged me in Lysvid. She didn't look a day older than before, and sultry in her silky top and hemmed dress. Her bright orange hair looked electrifying, her accentuated black eyes lewdly eyeing me from beneath her lashes. Her orange tail flitted behind her like a happy cat.

Even that wasn't all, apparently. A last guest slid into the room behind her, looking highly uncomfortable as though she tried to slip in unnoticed behind the crowd. Curly black hair tumbled across her bare shoulders, framing a heart-shaped face beset with lazy jade eyes. She wore a simple black outfit that looked like something a ninja might don, a one-piece garb that fitted loosely and left freedom for movement. A green-handled longbow hung behind her back, and a katana slung at her hip. This, to my alarm, was Annalia Rikalla – or Anna, as we called her.

"You weren't kidding about guests," I murmured to Dawn, who nodded once. She was looking at Anna, too. She knew all about our recent history.

"She'll be cool," Dawn assured me softly. "Just don't single her out. You know how shy she is. Honestly, she makes you look like a social butterfly."

I couldn't disagree. It was always difficult to draw Anna into a point of comfort. The fact that she was even here spoke volumes. I tried to focus on the rest of my guests, surprised at so many familiar faces crammed into a white room. I felt a little claustrophobic, and started to notice a faint stinging in my chest. Whatever painkillers they induced into me must be starting to wear thin.

"Was I really this close to death?" I asked as something of a bad joke.

I was met with a bunch of sarcastic looks and raised brows. Lusari, Kaia, and Rena quietly slipped in past the recent arrivals. Lusari gave me a brave smile. Kaia didn't appear happy at Dawn's presence at all, and Rena only had eyes for Will. I decided to single out the demon girl, who continually drew closer to the bed. The Timeless One gave her an intrigued look, but said nothing.

"Uh, what's up?" I asked her faintly.

She smiled, baring fangs in the effort. "Word spreads quickly of an injured Defender, especially one so esteemed as yourself, Ryu." I didn't miss at least half a dozen annoyed expressions in the room at the nickname. Even Loki muttered something under his breath. Probably wished he'd been the first to come up with it. "I thought I should stop by. News spreads quickly, and I heard the one I've been seeking has started to awaken. Advocatos."

"Advocatos," I repeated the name. The demon in my head. Not just a demon, but the prince of all demons. It would only make sense the two were associated. Referring back to our first meeting, it became even clearer. "This is a long way to come for a demon, isn't it? I don't understand…"

She smiled coyly. "Is it, though?" she asked. "Maybe I missed that cute face of yours. Behind it all, I know he's in there."

She winked, and I felt an almost audible chill from Sira. Even Dawn pinched me under the blanket, and I winced.

"Ah," the Timeless One said coolly, looking at Sorha. "Then you are Sorha, princess of demons."

Many heads turned at this. "You're engaged to…" Sira murmured, but she couldn't seem to conjure up the words.

"Relax, girl," Sorha cooed, coming awfully close to the bed. "It was while Advocatos walked the world alone, away from Ryoku Dragontalen. An arranged marriage at the hands of his mother. Still, it would be nice to know when we'll be coming upon our true heritage." She gave me a fanged smile that bore something behind it. "As King and Queen of demons."

A shudder ran down my spine. The heir to such a title was in my head all this time? It was worrying, yet somehow unsurprising. Why wouldn't I just have this last stroke of bad luck?

Was it all bad luck, though? I thought about all the times Advocatos stepped in to save my life or boost me when I could have died. I recalled feeling his presence after Kimo impaled me last night. Maybe he managed to save me then, too. Still, there was no response in my head when I saw this girl. If he was still there, something weakened him. Maybe because I was so damned weak myself.

Loki cleared his throat, rising to his feet. He looked around the room, scratching his chin, murmuring under his breath. He looked awfully pale, too, I thought. I started to wonder if he finally snapped, but he smirked at me.

"What an interesting turnout," he commented. "Most of the Defenders, I think. Who would be missing? Virgo? Dagger? Other than that, I summoned just about all our friends in the big, wide world."

"Virgo would never answer the summons of a god," Katiel said spitefully. "Not even as a personal favor. You know how he is."

"Same goes for Alan," Joey agreed, arms crossed. "Just steps in if he's needed, and I don't plan to need him."

"Virgo just sees Ryoku's injury as a sort of trial," Dawn agreed unhappily. "If he could overcome this, then he can probably take care of himself. It's sort of true, but I think the time for sitting back is over." She smiled at me. "You're getting stronger, Ryoku. Considering how things went up until now, I'm really proud of you. You're getting back to where you need to be."

At my quizzical expression, Katiel approached, grinning. "We made a deal, of sorts," he said, "to not interfere with your mission just yet. You needed to get stronger. The rest of us have... been at this for a while. Mind you, ya did great. You found plenty of friends on your own. You tracked me down by yourself, pretty well. I tried not to interfere." He shrugged at a sharp look from Dawn. "What? Brozogoth was a big deal, alright?"

"His point is," Dawn went on, cutting him off sharply, "that we're here to help now. You've done all we could have hoped for and more. Now, things are getting serious. Loki sent out a call to arms. Vincent Ordenstraum, the emperor who plans to conquer many worlds, has made his move. We don't know what happened out there, but we know one thing."

"It's time to fight," Katiel said, cracking his knuckles. "Now we're all here to help. Dagger's got business to deal with, but we got this. We don't need him or Virgo to knock some heads."

"I'm here, too," Joey piped up. "I've always been down to jump into a fight for you guys. Turns out I have some experience that might prove helpful."

The room fell momentarily silent. The way a few heads turned, I realized they were waiting on Anna, the last Defender present. She never introduced herself to the others. She had moved a bit away from the door, but still lingered near the edge of conversation. Looking at her, I couldn't help but recall our past. The day she moved away. Our last day together, where she told me she didn't want to keep dating from across the country. Since then, we had hardly spoken. She called me twice: the day of Guildford's death, and the day I awoke in the hospital following the Day of Black. Back then, I watched the phone ring.

She blinked, looking around the room – anywhere but at me. "I'm sorry we haven't talked," she said, very quietly. Her voice was always calm and purposeful. She was shy, but she didn't stutter or hesitate like Lusari. She thought out her words carefully before stringing them together. "It's been a while. I know what you're going through, and I'm here now."

Loki leaned toward me, grinning. "She's so precious," he said gleefully. "Your old flame, right? It's so good to finally meet people from your past!"

When he looked up, Anna was staring at him. He froze in place, as though worried movement might alert her further. "Loki," she said calmly. "You're the father of my Guardian, Teoe."

This was news to me, but his face softened. "Yes," he said, sounding relieved. "She did tell me she found a worthwhile Defender, brave and true—"

She cut him off. "She warned me you were a creep."

Thus, Loki retreated to the corner, hiding his face in shame. Katiel and Will approached the point of hysterical laughter. Anna stared at him, expressionless. "She did say you were a good person, though," she added quietly. He didn't seem to hear her.

I looked around the room, still coming to terms with everyone's presence. As if in response, everyone was looking at me. Only Loki still whined about Teoe.

"Are you all here to fight as well?" I asked, as a general question to the room.

Lamont nodded to me firmly. "I apologize I couldn't bring the dragons," he told me. "I've left them to look after my home while I'm gone."

"It could be a long time in your world," I pointed out worriedly. "Is that fine with your council?"

"They understand the need for our absence," Guildford told me. "After all, it is for the boy who saved Vortiger. They couldn't love you more."

I smiled. "If you really want to help... it means a lot to me," I said bravely. I swallowed, and managed to look out to everyone again with a straight face. It was difficult while Loki whined in the corner. "This could be very dangerous; I hope you all know that. Vincent, Roland, and Kimo are all extremely powerful, and they have somehow manipulated this kingdom to their own means."

"We know all of the risks," Sorha purred, taking a silky step forward. "I'm doing this for *you*. Besides, as long as we're all together, the empire will never know what hit them."

Dawn reacted to Sorha's advance, pulling me to her by the collar of my shirt. "We're all you need to protect you," she said pointedly.

Near the foot of the bed, Katiel looked guilty. "Ryoku," he started, "there's some stuff we have to talk about. Stuff I promised I'd tell you."

I didn't miss how Loki glanced up. However, I shook my head. "No, I think I already know," I said. "I think... I think I understand. This world was reset from the old one. Me... I'm not really Ryoku Dragontalen, am I? I'm his replacement, or something."

Silence fell across the room. I felt all eyes on me. Why did they care? Nobody had rushed to tell me this until now. My own enemy beat them to it.

"How did you figure it out?" Sira asked. "How... Who told you?"

I returned her suspicious look. "What about you?" I asked. "You and Will said you didn't know what was going on. You said you'd help me find out about this world. About my role in it."

Both of them turned away guiltily. "We figured it out along the way," Sira remarked, voice lowered. "Once we did, we decided that it might be better not to tell you yet. We didn't have all the answers. Not until this last week. Dawn and Katiel filled us in on everything."

I silently wondered if that version of *everything* was what Kimo told me, or if it differed. I didn't want to press it too much, or they'd remember to ask me who told me. I needed to talk to Kimo again myself.

Still, I noticed there weren't any other surprised looks in the room, Dawn and Katiel least of all. Even Guildford, Lamont, and Rex only looked on. The Timeless One gave me a knowing wink. Relus adjusted his spectacles nervously.

"I see it isn't a secret," I remarked softly. "Okay, that's fine. I guess it just makes it easier."

Will looked at me quizzically. "Makes what easier, my friend?"

I turned my gaze to him. "To keep our promise we made in Vortiger: no more secrets."

I quickly regretted the iron in my voice for the guilty look Will bore. They'd nearly lost me, and I was more wounded of the fact that they hid such dire secrets from me. If I could trust Will as much as I always thought, then they solely considered my well-being as the reason to keep such things to themselves.

"No more secrets," I went on when nobody spoke, "and especially not to protect me. I need the truth from you guys. Honestly, what worse can you hide from me at this point? Everything I learn can only help me now, one way or another."

"That is true," Relus agreed, adjusting his spectacles nervously. "I do apologize. Upon our first meeting, I'm unsure you would have believed me if I explained Advocatos to you."

"I think the same," Katiel told me. "Still, I'll hold us to that. No more secrets."

Some of them came forward. Will, Sira, Relus, the Timeless One, and Katiel all approached, holding out a hand. I raised my uninjured hand, and we crossed our hands over one another's. Dawn included her hand, then glanced pointedly at Loki. Rising to his feet with the weight of the world on his shoulders, Loki added his hand to the ring. Everyone else stayed back. I wasn't sure if it was unnecessarily, or whether some of them may still hide things from us. Sorha looked at me from beneath her lashes. Anna glared at a spot in the corner. Rex sorely rubbed the hand in his coat.

"No more secrets," we spoke in haunting unity before removing our hands.

Once they retreated, Dawn hugged me. "We should let Ryoku get some rest," she said sternly toward the room. She returned a soft smile to me. "You still need a lot of work done on you, mister. Sleep. I'll be back with the others to work on your healing. It will take some time, but we can't do this without you."

"Agreed," Loki declared dramatically, returning to the spotlight as though he had never sulked in his life. "Let us take our leave, good friends. We shall prepare for the moment when Ryoku is ready to fight. The monarchy of Syaoto will fall before us!"

"Who are you calling *good friends,* old man?" Cleria half-muttered, half-sang, but Loki pretended not to hear her. Retreating twice in a single conversation might be too much for the proud god to handle.

Either way, his speech riled everyone up. Guildford and Lamont both shook my hand, assuring me that we could win against our enemies, before taking their leave. Rex softly clapped my shoulder. He looked like he wanted to say something, but he ended up leaving anyway. Cleria hugged me tightly for a long moment, and snaked a long claw along my cheek as she turned to leave, following the Timeless One as he rambled about how this battle closely related to eggs somehow.

Alex gave me a brave smile and saluted me. Grinning, I returned the salute as well as I could, favoring the hand that wasn't injured. Joey went on for a moment about how he was excited to fight alongside me, then he left as well. Sorha drifted out of the door like a sail, her tail bobbing behind her as she went. Anna left silently and unnoticed. Relus was one of the last ones out. His glance lingered over my violet eye. His glasses flashed, and then he was gone.

Katiel left with a simple wave. He never bothered with heartfelt goodbyes like everyone else, especially knowing that I'd already lived through the worst of my injuries and I'd be fighting fit before I knew it. Dawn kissed me on the brow and softly whispered something to me that made little sense. "Think of the cats," she said, and winked. Then was the first time she hopped off me, and she left. I watched her go, trying to ignore how enthralled I felt.

"It is time for you to relax," Will told me as he and Sira helped lower me back into bed, which I protested. I wanted to move on my own, but they must fear reopening my wounds. "Rest, Ryoku. The kingdom will be ours again soon, I promise. I will owe you for the rest of my days."

"You're going to tell me about that *woman* later," Sira muttered coldly at my neck. "I don't like her. How the hell did you meet her?"

I smiled. "Sorha? I barely know her," I whispered. Sira hugged me, which was an odd notion for her altogether, and lightly kissed me on the opposite brow from where Dawn had. She drew the curtains and left quickly, too, but not without looking back at me.

Loki was the last out. He stopped by the door, looking out for a moment.

"Loki, that's what you wanted to tell me, right?" I asked him. "You must have come here because I'm the Remnant of that old hero. That would warrant a god stepping in, so I finally have my answer."

He remained in the doorway, and I couldn't see his expression. "Yes, of course," he replied in an odd way. "I knew you might recall your past eventually, however you might dodge the question of how you came to recall it."

He finally turned to look at me. "I just wanted to say," he murmured, "you've grown so much, my friend. Since the day I met you and you were unable to fend for yourself, you're growing into a fine young fighter. Time and time again, we face perils that I fear will be the undoing of you, and yet you prevail. My point is..." He sighed heavily. "I keep worrying over you when I doubt I need to do so anymore. Maybe all the griping is just for me to feel better."

I looked at him expectantly, vividly recalling the conversation we'd had in Vortiger. What, exactly, was he leaving unsaid? He was silent for a moment, his eyes glinting like true emeralds.

"Soon everything will come together, my friend."

I opened my mouth to voice words I didn't have yet, but he slid out of the door as quickly as he'd ever come into my life, leaving me to stare at torchlight flickering underneath the door in an otherwise dark room.

I tried to relax, but my mind remained plagued. I couldn't forget all that Kimo told me before. He told me that I wasn't really Ryoku Dragontalen, and nobody knew who I actually was. I remembered strange things that didn't seem to add up, like the boy who taught me to fight and details about my relationship with Dawn. I knew the name of the darkness within me. Against all odds, I survived the enigmatic Kimo Goldenhart after fighting hordes of demons and saving Sira. I had to believe there was a reason for it. I couldn't live through all of this only to die today or tomorrow. Everything was starting to come together. Despite what Kimo said, I had friends and people who cared about me – a whole *room* of them.

I learned about Sorha, the mysterious demon who saved me in Lysvid. I even reunited with Anna after months – not that she seemed too happy about it. The other Defenders pledged their support. Everyone vowed to stay honest with me from now on. My friends gathered from across the worlds to support me.

However, there was the matter of Loki. He was acting a little off, and I still wasn't sure why. I knew he'd gone out of his way to rally my friends together in my time of need. However preoccupied and luxurious Loki could be, he proved himself a true friend.

I caught a glimpse of something on the side table. I focused my eyes. It was dark in the room with the curtains drawn, only diluted sunlight and a torch on the other side of the door to light my view. I could make out my weapons scattered on the table. A small glitter caught the torchlight from under the door on Ragnarokkr's black face. What was that?

I carefully reached over to grab my knife and, with patience, used it to deflect pale light from the sun onto the sword. Part of the sword by the hilt shimmered like gold. With a tinge of pain, I remembered the sword that impaled me in the field. Kimo mentioned that our swords were parallels of one another. Was that shimmer of gold tarnish from the sword that ran me through?

Just when I put the knife down and glanced away, resolving to check it out again in proper daylight, my eye caught something by the window I hadn't noticed earlier. Sira had been standing in front of it. A vase full of bright red roses sat on the bedside table. It looked fresh, considering I'd apparently been out for several days. There was a tag on it which showed a large heart, hand-written with *'Get better soon'* in the center.

Though I couldn't be sure who left that for me, I fell asleep with a smile on my face. Maybe, just maybe, Kimo was wrong about one thing. Maybe I did belong here.

SCENE TWO: DISARM

...Of Act Eight: Conquer

In the eyes of Will Ramun, we are in Syaoto Capital, in the world of Syaoto. It is late evening On November 14th, 2017.

"Hey, where're you going?"

"For a stroll," I replied soundly. I felt Sira's suspicion on my back as I hurried down the hall and rounded the next corner. She may have noticed the lance bobbing against my back rather than sitting in my room. If she did, she didn't comment on it.

Try as I might, I could not erase the image of when we found Ryoku. My charge. The boy I promised to bring to safety. Not that long ago, I told him I'd take him through the Old Forest. I promised to take him to my home. I promised to help save his charge. I even promised to help find his lost sister. The fact that he'd gotten so badly hurt in *my* home tore savagely at my heart.

I could only stand back, horror-stricken, as healers and medics surrounded him by the city gates, trying with all their might to fix the gaping hole in his chest. Sira was in better shape, but they still rushed her into the castle. She returned later that day with only a bloody bandage around her head to pace around Ryoku, snapping at anyone who approached her. She hated herself for letting him get hurt as much as I did. I could see it in her eyes.

I couldn't forget Loki's expression. He was more silent than I had ever witnessed. He watched the healers and medics work, hands wrung at his sides like he didn't know what to do with them. Whenever Lusari, Kaia, or Katiel stepped away, Loki ran to them and peppered them with questions. He instructed the other medics on how to do their jobs. He paced, running his hand through his hair and looking like he struggled not to cry. I couldn't pick on him, though, because I was no better.

Dawn arrived before they got Ryoku inside, terrifying much of the city when she did. She strolled through the city gates like she might bring down the whole Capital around her. The trees around her tossed violently in a windless day, leaves raining around her, the soil churning like roots from the earth rushed to greet her. Vines ripped from the earth, crawling through toward the girl as though crawling to her aid.

Many medics abandoned ship, and nobody stopped them. Katiel ran forward to meet her, but she broke past, crying out when she saw the extent of Ryoku's injuries even then. Then she knelt down next to him, and I saw the power Dawn used to heal Ryoku. I understood. She was a druid, and a powerful one at that. The earth itself bent to her will without being asked, like it wanted to please her.

When the time came that Ryoku was stable enough, Loki and I carried him inside. Everyone crowded so closely around us that we almost didn't make it. His wounds were still open, and I had a tunic thrown in my room that I couldn't wash the blood from. Brom and Oliver met us at the gates, and they already arranged for a room for Ryoku.

There – the room he was still in now – we managed to save him. Some of the medics began to tell us he might not live. Loki screamed and raged, and Sira begged until she lost her voice, but it didn't change a thing. In the end, our own perseverance saved him. My limited medical knowledge only let me step in at the end; supplying meager balms to ease his pain and absolve infection. I felt horribly useless the entire time.

"Hey soldier."

A sharp voice sliced through my thoughts. I recognized it right away. Lancet Cooper leaned against the wall in a white tunic. His silver hair hung in his gaunt face, splashing his dark, handsome features with shadow. He smirked, pushing against the wall to stand before me, arms crossed.

"How long it has been, my friend. How fares the Defender?"

I offered a false smile. This was the last man in all of Syaoto that I wanted to see. I would have sooner asked Vincent Ordenstraum to dinner.

"He was awake for a spell, but has gone back to rest now."

Lancet nodded once, his expression unreadable. "That is good to hear. Alex tells me you've been with the boy since you left my patrol in Harohto. I must commend you for sticking with such an inconsolable cause, as opposed to your own kingdom."

He pushed himself from the wall, arms still crossed. "You know, whatever it was in that forest killed most of my men. Only a handful of you survived. A true pity. I managed to recruit some men from the Capital who grew restless in the wake of those bandits you snuffed out. Good work on that one, by the way. It was after that when I wondered if you were actually a loss to my army."

My fists clenched. Vincent ruled this place. Striking at Lancet would do nothing, so I stayed my hand. "Ryoku is a good man. It was by his lead we took out those bandits, Master General Cooper. He stands for something greater than this kingdom."

Lancet raised his brow, and barked in laughter. "So your ears are to the walls, Will," he commended, and he clapped his hands together in bravado. Once. Twice. "It is true. I've become Master General since my return. Poor Brom is too old and dogged for his position, especially at the behest of our new king. King Vincent has graciously let him retain his title, but it is little more than a name these days. He has left all the power of the kingdom to me. You... have met King Vincent, haven't you?"

I narrowed my eyes, and quickly averted them. Alex was right. Egging Lancet on would be detrimental right now.

When I didn't respond, Lancet's eyes narrowed a little. "I apologize. Is that a sore spot for you?" He smirked a little, arms still crossed. "Where are you even off to at this time of night? Fetching new bedsheets for your Defender? Perhaps looking for a strumpet for the night?"

There wasn't an ounce of attempted respect in his tone. I couldn't reply in kind. "A short walk," I replied, "merely to enjoy the night."

I made eye contact with him, and held. Images flashed in my mind about this man, how insufferable he was. The foolishly high prices he demanded in Harohto as a price for escorting them was only the most fallow of his sins. If they couldn't pay up, then the citizens usually landed in some sort of horrid accident, or turned up beaten outside the bar presuming to have been drunk. He deployed similar tactics in other worlds we went to. As long as we were out from beneath King Lionel's watchful gaze, Lancet's deceitful nature always rose to the surface.

Of course, Lancet was a deceitfully skilled combatant. Even being the son of Jason and a trained soldier myself, I could only rise to possibly the best match for him, out of many other high-ranking officers. Even then, I couldn't bring this man down alone. Everyone feared him for both his strength and tendency to fight unfairly. Soldiers disappeared from the army with little to no explanation. Sometimes their wives were defiled, and all they could do was flee. Nobody could really stand against him. I'd wondered if I could finally report his crimes alongside Ryoku to King Lionel, but the current monarchy would never care. In fact, that was probably why Lancet landed Master General. What a conceited title it was.

Lancet didn't seem to care about my response. "So you heard of my new position," he mused. "Did you hear the King's Own disbanded? Sir Koteran turned traitor to the crown when King Lionel stepped down. Even old Brom tried to step up some time ago, but our new liege is impressively strong. Of course, upon my return, he could see my natural talent. He knew I would serve as a loyal servant to the crown, and here I am."

An icy feeling welled up in my chest. So that was where Koteran went. He was the commander of the King's Own, King Lionel's private team of elite soldiers. I was a member of it, too, though unofficially due to my ranking within the army. Being Jason's son landed me in high places among the castle crew, even if my father wasn't so high-ranking himself anymore. Of course, it wasn't something anybody could join without certain skill, no matter their birth. Knowing that Koteran disbanded was both worrisome and a boon. It meant one excellent swordsman I couldn't call on for help, but also one that wasn't on Vincent's side.

"It is interesting," Lancet went on. "King Vincent has his own team of elite soldiers. Rather than the pitiful name of the King's Own – I never liked it, it implied we *belonged* to him, like pets – we are simply his Dark Ring. His vassals from other worlds are included, and there are others who are as strong, or stronger than, myself.

"However," he went on, gauging my reaction with serpentine eyes as he spoke, "there are some who doubt my liege and his longevity. Those of us sworn to protect him must protect him from any and all attempts on his life. I'm sure you're well aware that your Defender is one of them."

He startled a chuckle out of me, which made his eyes narrow. "Your king lacks confidence, Master General," I admitted. "Are you so sure about a king who needs such a squad of protection against a young boy?"

He didn't respond for a moment, fixating me in his icy eyes. "Lest you forget, Will," he hissed, "he is your king as well. You may traipse along with your Defender now, but you will eventually have to decide where your loyalties lie. Your kingdom, or an outlandish Defender. It would be best to decide before your lance must speak for you."

He turned and left. I watched him go, my hands balled into tight fists. I'd have given half the kingdom to settle things with Lancet once and for all, but I had more important things to do. Once Lancet was out of sight, I resumed my pace down the hall.

Even with my long absence from the castle, I could still find my way around in the dark, drawing as little attention to myself as I could manage. It didn't take long to find the central courtyard in the castle.

The sun began to set through the open garden, and servants already lit torches to keep it light. I doubted Vincent cared for this place as much as the old king Lionel, but servants had their habits. They kept flowers of vibrant reds and blues in full bloom all year round. Servants buried stones that drew heat below the garden to keep the earth fresh in the autumn. In winter, they erected a roof over the garden designed to let in the sunlight.

Entering the garden again felt like stepping back in time. The old cobblestone path remained dusted clean of prints, the soil combed, the weeds pulled and the plants trimmed to a healthy length. Servants kept torches clean and frequently emptied of ashes so none spilt on the walkway. I could almost see myself walking through here with King Lionel as he spoke to me about his own matters, anything from the army expenses to the affairs of his love life.

A long time ago, he sat with me on one of these benches to explain the affair he had with a sorceress from Balgena, known as the 'magic capital of Syaoto.' He had been married once – about ten years ago now, I thought – but his wife passed away of an illness in the time Jason was still an active hero. Three years after her death, he confessed to me that he'd had an affair ten years prior. He felt it made him a terrible man and meant he couldn't truly lament his wife's loss, but I set him straight. No matter how a man might sin, they could always redeem themselves. As far as I was concerned, the king was a fair and just man. Humans made mistakes.

The bench was somewhat weathered now, the paint and finishing chipped, scratches dug into the arm of it. Kimo Goldenhart waited there, his golden hair glinting in the light of his own torch resting in the sconce of the chair. The light cast ghosts across his face.

He rose with the gravity of a man who knew he'd sinned. "Will," he greeted me with a curt nod. "I figured you would find me sooner or later."

I swung at him with force. He had plenty of time to read my posture to defend himself, but he didn't. He took the brunt of the hit to his cheek. The sound snapped through the courtyard like a bolt of lightning. His head lolled with the effect, but he didn't move, his blue eyes remaining on me.

"I don't care for your excuses," I snarled, still riled from my encounter with Lancet. "You nearly killed him! Do you have the slightest idea what we had to go through to save him?"

I took a breath. My calmness was slipping, but I didn't care. "I saw the gold on his blade. Your sword is never meant to cross his, but it did, did it not? You attacked him. You are the one who left him for dead out there."

He regarded me calmly. "On the contrary. I left him in a place the guards could find him. He did live, did he not? He who walks among us in the skin of our hero. If he were to die, then surely the old hero would return."

I struck him again. This time he didn't see it coming, and he stumbled backward. "That is not your call!" I screamed. "We all decided without you! You... You were not even involved in this time. The old Ryoku left him in charge for a reason. We have to respect that. He is strong enough, I know it."

"Against *them*?" Kimo asked. He steadied himself, wiping blood from his chin. His cheeks darkened with forming bruises, making him look horrendously tired and gaunt. "Much of the spirit realm has forgotten. I see it in your eyes; you did not. Those who planted the bomb in our realms aren't going to just sit back and watch us regain our footing. Ryoku may have weakened them once, but they'll return."

I squared my jaw. "I did forget. It has only been recently, traveling with Ryoku again, that my memories have begun to resurface about the old spirit realm. I do not remember everything, I can tell. What he did has created several blanks."

Kimo nodded sadly. "It would. The widespread effects of the blast haven't been fully analyzed. Many memories suffer, mostly because of Ryoku and his own loss in the blast. My mentor believes memories were tampered with to create new, less painful lives for the people involved. Maybe he thought it was over."

I smiled grimly. "It could not be further from over," I murmured. "Either way, I believe Ryoku will soon be ready to face Vincent Ordenstraum."

Kimo scowled. He reached for his sword. Whether he noticed my hand twitch toward my lance or not, he didn't remark. He only pulled his golden blade a little from his sheath, enough to show a black scar across the blade. "I am aware of his strength," he assured me. "It is better than I initially guessed, but it isn't enough. Not yet. Still, he does carry Advocatos as well."

I nodded. "We figured that out quickly," I replied. "Advocatos would not join a false host."

Kimo's brow flicked up. "Are you so sure? Nobody knows where this form of Ryoku came from. As powerful as he was, I doubt he could conceive an entire from nothing. No, this Ryoku comes from somewhere, and he must be connected to the old hero somehow.

"Will, I watched him fight a horde of demons at my back. The way he fights is... alien. Those marks on his wrists. His style of fighting. Those do not come from him. They are from some new source, whoever this Remnant is."

He had a point. "His style is interesting, but we know that his old self cannot return to this body. Stopping the blast destroyed him. Who we have is who we must accept. You would do well to acknowledge that."

Kimo gazed at me darkly. "We'll see," he replied softly. "You are not a man without reason, Will. You have traveled with him up to this point, so perhaps you have seen measures of his character that I haven't. Still, I must decide on my own."

"Ensure that does not end with Ryoku at the tip of your sword, and we will get along fine," I replied scathingly.

Kimo's expression didn't lighten. "I cannot promise that," he replied. "However, I could tell you something in good faith. Some information I've recently come upon during my stay in Orden."

"Like what?" I asked.

He kept his gaze level. Even with bruises forming on his cheekbones, he held himself with the utmost self-respect. "Have you, by chance, heard of the Rim of Balgena?"

He had my attention. "Yes. The jewel in the crown of Syaoto. It was last seen with King Lionel's uncle, King Menophres."

"There is more to it than that," Kimo said. "I spoke with a merchant who traveled here from Thralle. The history of the Scepter of Blight, and the first Pendragons in Syaoto. Given that this world is a construct of the old Ryoku, I was surprised at the depths of the mythos. However, it would seem everything here stems from some aspect of the old world."

"I know some of it," I told him, "but the Scepter of Blight? That is almost world origin myth. Does it even truly exist?"

"According to this old historian, it would," Kimo told me. "He suggested that it could be buried in the Enthralmen Jungle south of here. An item like that, a relic possibly of the old world, would have untold power. It could be a useful tool against the likes of Vincent."

I raised an eyebrow. "You would sell me this information? For what, trust?"

He smirked in reply. "Not quite such a simple thing. If my benefactor is right, then Vincent Ordenstraum could be linked to the entity that planted the bomb. Getting to the bottom of it just might give us a lead on them."

I frowned. "You would send me off to the Enthralmen Jungle while my Defender recovers here. That sounds like a means to get rid of me."

Kimo chuckled, shaking his head. As the torchlight flickered off his face, I thought it looked like his bruises were fading away. His expression looked youthful and bright once more. "Not quite. I wouldn't simply send you on a possible fool's errand in some pitiful attempt for trust. I would go with you, as a means of both good faith and a semblance of trust. I wouldn't worry about your Defender, either. He will recover quickly."

He refocused his gaze on me with a small smile. "What do you say? A fool's errand for two? Like old times."

I hesitated. "But Vincent..."

"He cannot hear us here," Kimo said. "You know as well as I do – this garden is enchanted by your old king. It was a place I presume you two, and any other of his close advisors, could discuss matters in confidence. So long as we return within the week, Vincent will not question me."

He contemplated my expression for a long moment. I was sure I wasn't imagining it. His bruises were fading. He smiled, as cheerfully as though we just professed our newfound friendship, and offered me his hand.

"So, are you game?"

(Later that night, in the eyes of Ryoku Dragontalen...)

I shot awake with a start. My dreams threatened me even in waking, and I swore I could still see the haunting violet eyes of Vincent in a dark throne room. Shadows clung to the walls like webs. The curtains were drawn, and pale moonlight streamed through the creases, slowly dispelling the lingering taint of a nightmare. I realized I was sitting upright, the sheets drawn up over my chest. I clenched them hard enough to nearly tear through the fabric.

Forcing myself to take a breath, I settled back into bed, preparing for the sting of pain from my wounds, but it felt easier than before to move. I examined the bandages at my chest, pressing softly against my skin in pretense of a reaction. Nothing. I couldn't find the edges of a wound. Some of the blood on my bandages was still damp, but I couldn't trace the wound.

I tested my limits by working my way out of bed. I put weight on my feet, surprised that I could hold myself up. My hand looked fine as well. Curious, I unraveled the bandages spanning around my fist. All that remained was a pale scar in the form of a neat slice across my palm. The scar spread most of the way around my hand. I was stunned. Was this Dawn's powerful healing at work? How long had I slept?

The floorboards creaked beneath my feet. I fixed the bed behind me, careful not to make much noise. Judging by outside, it seemed well into the night, but I didn't feel as though I needed any more rest.

I dressed and brought my assortment of weapons with me. My knife felt natural at my belt, bobbing back against my staff in its holster. Ragnarokkr and my bow slung over my back. I paused to look in the mirror before I left. Dark circles ringed my bloodshot eyes. My hair looked as though somebody washed it while I slept. I wasn't sure if that had been before or after I was last conscious. My unexpected visitors earlier distracted me from all else.

I expected to find one of my friends waiting outside my room, perhaps Will or Sira, but it was vacant. A single chair sat next to the door, recently occupied. The torch on the opposite side of me was freshly changed. I took it from its holster, lifting it to throw light down the shadowy halls. There wasn't a soul in sight.

A ways down the hall, I encountered a soldier standing at a corner, his chest puffed out even as he guarded a seemingly unoccupied hall. When he saw me, he pulled off his cap to stare at me, perplexed. I didn't realize until I got closer that it was Alex.

"Ryoku?" he asked, puzzled. "What are you doing awake? Your injuries could open!"

I smiled at him, raising my previously bandaged hand. "Looks like they finished up," I told him, just as surprised as he seemed. "I feel great. Everything seems to work, so I'm going for a walk. Tell me, have you seen Will or the others?"

Alex nodded slowly, looking thoroughly stunned. "I-I believe they were to dine with the king in the great hall. But... Ryoku, as far as I know, your healing was not complete! I saw you only earlier today when your injuries were a mess! A healthier man with your extent of injuries would not rise for a fortnight, yet..." He looked me up and down, his mouth agape. "You are truly a remarkable person. Are you sure you can stand?"

I nodded, unable to hide a curious brow from rising at Alex. "I'm fine," I replied, and continued to wave my hand at him. "See?"

He only stared at me, dumbfounded.

"Anyway," I murmured, "did you say they dined with the king? Why would they do such a thing?"

Alex frowned. "I could not say. However..." He scratched his head uneasily, glancing anywhere now but at me. "I think I saw Will headed toward the central gardens earlier. It was a place he and the old king used to speak in confidence. I could take you there if you like."

I hesitated. "I'm sure I could find my way if you point me in the direction. Besides, I could use the walk to clear my head."

"Uh, yes, of course," Alex stammered, and haphazardly pointed where I needed to go. I gave him a quick salute – a pale imitation of what I'd seen other soldiers do so far – and left. If he got over the shock of seeing me awake, he just might stop me from wandering about alone, and I felt like I needed the breather. When I rounded the next corner and stealthily glanced back, he was gone. Maybe he'd gone to warn the others that I was awake. Either way, I felt I needed the time to think.

No matter how much I dwelled on it as I walked the dizzying halls of Syaoto Castle, I couldn't make any more sense of the things Kimo told me than I had earlier. I tried to focus instead on the beautiful paintings and tapestries hung on the walls, emblazoned with bright and brave colors. Vincent must not have affected the décor yet, or else the people of Syaoto were too strong to impose on. Full suits of elaborate armor stood on some corners. Oddly, the statues wore armor better than the soldiers themselves.

Some windows looked outside, over the beautiful royal forest behind the castle, ready to burst with countless trees that glimmered in late moonlit dew. I thought I saw two travelers trekking up a hill in those woods, but they seemed to disappear into the shadows before I could peer more closely. One hallway had no ceiling, and instead opened out to a sky window that boasted a star-spilt sky above me. An interesting trait about Syaoto was that the moon seemed abnormally large, taking up a bigger amount of the sky than I'd ever seen in my world. It hadn't been visible in our demon-fighting night.

    I came across a painting that stole my attention for a long moment. The painting was of a beautiful woman with blue hair and a silver crown, beset with a midnight blue gem that oddly caught the light. I observed it, trying to understand why it seemed so familiar to me.

    I forgot the painting when I saw a wide window at the end of the hall. The view through it offered colorful flowers that caught the heavy moonlight above, glistening like pieces of the moon itself hid among their petals. I approached, forgetting the painting behind me, and circled until I could find a way into the courtyard. Among the darkness of the night, it seemed to glow like anything of magic I'd ever learnt. When I stepped out into it, I found that the grass was dewy beneath my feet, and the air hung with a lingering nostalgic scent.

    I stepped out into the grass as though I was the only resident of the castle, gazing around in wonder at the flowers. Some of them were almost as tall as me. A tree grew in the hidden corner of the courtyard, reaching up to give the area a secluded feeling. I approached the center of the yard and found a white bench. I contemplated it, but ended up putting my torch in the holster beside it and walking past, where a large white mushroom basked in the comfort of the huge tree. I tested it, and then gently sat upon the mushroom. It held my weight, so I sat, fully appreciating the calm quiet of nature. An owl hooted nearby, perhaps perched atop one of the castle walls, and cicada sang into the night as if this world was theirs.

    I lived in a world where the grass was mostly dead and crunched beneath footfalls. Taking deep breaths would eventually hurt my throat, depending on the proximity of power plants. Water was highly toxic and needed treatment prior to consumption. Mushrooms were one of the few plants still alive in my world, but they were usually withered and highly toxic. A boy in my class had once poked a particularly squishy one, only for it to spurt harmful spores into his face. He'd been hospitalized for a week.

There was nothing like this in my own world, and I savored the moment. I'd never seen a mushroom sturdy or large enough to sit on, and it added to a peaceful and magical aura of the courtyard.

At some point, I glanced back at the bench in the middle of the courtyard, and noticed a small letter folded up on its seat. I ignored it for a time, trying to enjoy the glistening courtyard around me, but it ate at the edge of my sight. Somehow, the little letter filled me with a sort of trepidation, like only bad news could come from it.

Eventually, I got to my feet and picked up the little letter. I instantly recognized the handwriting as one that appeared on my Defender Registry forms, which signed the guestbook at inns without fail every single time.

It was Will's.

(Later that night...)

I navigated the halls for a while before I came across a small squad of soldiers, who hurriedly escorted me to the dining room where my friends supposedly waited. I rushed several paces ahead. The feeling in my chest was threatening to burst. When we finally reached the great set of doors, I bolted ahead of the guards and burst into the room.

What awaited me was certainly unexpected. My friends were here – almost all of them, it seemed – and they dined with Vincent and Roland, as well as several other commanding officers and high-ranking officials of Syaoto. I recognized Brom among them, of course, along with Oliver. The room smelt of a surprisingly delicious variety of foods, but my anxiety only made my stomach churn. Dawn dropped her fork when she saw me, and Roland shot to his feet, alarmed.

"What the devil?" Roland demanded. "The—you shouldn't be out of bed! The extent of your injuries should still be quite dire, if I've been told correctly! Those ruddy, good-for-nothing scouts!"

I didn't miss his brief glance to some of the commanding officers as he thought out his words. Clearly, he wasn't keen on making us look like enemies. Vincent patiently watched me from the head of the table, his dark armor surrounding him like the night. His white wig was puffed out nicely, and it looked like he attempted civility. It must have been some sort of ruse, though I couldn't begin to imagine why.

"For once, I agree with Roland," Loki remarked, rising to his feet to approach me. "Ryoku, how—why are you awake? We have yet to work on your healing—"

I strode to him, and he cut himself off when I shoved the letter toward him. He pored over it quickly, his emerald eyes scanning the words with ease. When he finished, Sira snatched it from his hands and read it. I waited, frustrated, while the letter went around the table until it landed in Vincent's hands. He fixated me in his puzzled gaze, dropping the letter to his lap. Roland looked to him, but Vincent didn't regard him at all.

"Where did you find this?" Vincent demanded coolly. He didn't sound either civil or angry. He was interrogating me.

"Where is Kimo?" I asked in turn. I was trying to catch my breath without keeling over, but it was difficult. A soldier stepped up beside me to offer me an arm. Surprised, I obliged, and let him help support my weight. Another soldier went to fetch me water from a pitcher. Vincent fixated him with a glare that froze the soldier in his tracks. A curt stare from Brom returned him to his trek, and soon I had a glass of water held before me. I downed it instantly, and he went to fetch me another. Despite my apparent healing, I felt a dragging fatigue from my injuries, especially after bolting in here.

After a moment, Vincent inclined his head toward Roland. He scurried off into a room behind the grand hall at Vincent's leave. In the time that he was gone, Loki approached me, appraising my condition. A few of my other friends gravitated between their food and me. Dawn stared at me, open-mouthed with disbelief. Katiel looked unsure.

"How are you standing?" Loki demanded, looking me over. He snatched the hand that handed him the letter. The Timeless One strategically slid a bowl of mashed potatoes out of the way as Loki put my hand on the table, unravelling the bandages to inspect the sealed wound.

"This... what sort of sorcery is this?"

"What the hell are you doing?" I asked him vehemently, gesturing widely to the table. "Trying to parlay with Vincent or something?"

"Parlay?" Sira echoed dryly, leaning back in her chair. "Aye aye, cap'n."

"*Parley*," I corrected myself angrily. The room felt like it was slowly spinning. I drained another glass of offered water, trying to drown my quelling anxiety. I fixated Loki back in my glare. "Well?"

"This isn't the place to explain," Loki said urgently, ignoring Sira and I's banter. "We're trying to gather information, which was working just fine until you burst in here waving that letter..."

Roland re-entered the room and strode straight to Vincent's side. He muttered something in his ear, and the king nodded. Vincent got to his feet. In unison, every soldier in the room dropped to one knee, crossing their swords or weapons over their thigh.

"My knights, scour the capital," Vincent ordered. His voice cracked like a whip through the room. "Bring me Kimo Goldenhart."

Every guard in the room saluted Vincent, and then they left. The two soldiers looking after me hesitated, but Loki took over the honor of keeping me on my feet with a respectful nod and a whisper to the soldier that it wasn't worth his head. I agreed; I didn't want to see what Vincent might do to a soldier who hesitated a direct order on my behalf. Oliver hesitated, but Brom rose to his feet with all the gravity of a mountain. Oliver gave me a lasting look as he followed his general out of the room, leaving us alone with our worst enemies.

"How unfortunate that you survived," Vincent drawled, remaining standing while he looked me over with disgrace. "Now you wash back up on my shores like a half-drowned mutt. A true pity."

"These won't be your shores soon enough," I retorted. "Count your last days, Vincent Ordenstraum."

The edge to my voice seemed to have an unnerving effect on the emperor, and he scowled. Perhaps it was the use of his full name.

"It was a mistake to entrust your defeat to the hands of my vassal," Vincent said, and drew the black sword from his belt. The sound of its ringing steel carried throughout the room like a deafened burst of thunder rattling the night sky. The amethyst on the hilt of his sword glinted oddly. "It matters not what my servant attempts to do. I will end you here, Dragontalen."

Katiel had his arms crossed and a wry grin plastered across his face. "You have something in his arm to track him, don't ya?" Katiel asked Roland from his seat.

Roland scowled. "Unfortunately, Kimo has learned how to tamper with the instrument. He learned how to disable it for short bursts of time where I cannot track him."

Katiel only smirked in response. "Huh. Scares you to lose track of your peons, huh?"

"Be silent, Creation!" Roland screamed at Katiel, growing red in the face while Vincent didn't react at all to his statement. "Stand and fight! I don't need you running around wrecking my plans any further!"

Katiel smirked, and made to rise from his chair. Roland flinched back. That was all Katiel needed, and he sat back in his chair, crossing one leg over the other.

"A picture's worth a thousand words," he replied cheerfully. "The look on your face is worth a billion."

Loki slid in front of me, focused on Vincent. "Then what happened out there was your fault," he said. His voice filled with a sort of malice I'd barely seen Loki muster. "You will pay dearly for what you've done. I'm ready for you, emperor. Show me what a dark knight of Orden can do!"

Vincent flourished his blade threateningly. "You look weaker than you did twenty years ago, Trickster. Presume I don't wish to have your body stuffed next to my trophies of war. Would you still deign to challenge me?"

Loki growled lowly under his breath. "It's dangerous to underestimate a god, Vincent."

A thunderous noise burst through the room, bringing everyone to silence. It took me a moment to realize the noise came from the Timeless One, standing upon the table with his hands cupped around his lips. He lowered his hands when everyone looked his way. Even Vincent turned to the diminutive vampire expectantly. The Timeless One clutched a chicken drumstick in his hand, half-eaten.

"This is not the time to squall," he said evenly, but his voice still carried throughout the room. "Ryoku, you are in no shape to perform this fight at present. None of us is! More importantly, we should find Will and Kimo straightaway."

Most of my friends glanced down sheepishly. Loki glared at Vincent from beneath his lashes.

"Loki," I started. "What's going on? You fought Vincent before? Above all else, why is everyone meeting like this and acting like friends?"

"I challenged him earlier," Loki growled, "when your bounty was first posted. I tried to end the threat myself. At the time, Vincent bested me."

"Today, we decided to meet and discuss the looming Shadowheart threat in Syaoto," Vincent drawled, as though discussing something that didn't concern me at all. "As knowingly esteemed guests in my castle, my captains insisted I summon your lot to my council."

"Shadowheart?" I asked. "What sort of unoriginal name is—?"

Loki silenced me with a look. "Shadowhearts are creatures of darkness," he told me seriously. "Nobody really knows their origins. Some say they are spirits who didn't make it to the designated afterlife, cursed to walk in this realm as shadowy monsters. They originated sometime around a thousand years ago…"

"Most importantly," the Timeless One squeaked, abruptly back to his regular voice, "Shadowhearts in this age are commonly associated with fallen worlds. That is, their ancient and chaotic genetic make-up is too much for the new complexity of these worlds. Their presence almost certainly spells bad news."

"But they're in Syaoto?" I asked gingerly. I felt like I loomed over a great chasm of some kind, and the next words would certainly spell out my peril.

Loki nodded solemnly. "Yes. By all accounts, it would seem Syaoto is falling."

SCENE THREE: WHIRLING SKIES

...Of Act Eight: Conquer

In the eyes of Ryoku Dragontalen, we are in Syaoto Castle, in the world of Syaoto. It is well past midnight On November 15th, 2017.

"And what makes you think you can track them down, Dragontalen?"

"Do you want to find them or not?" Loki snapped. I sighed, leading the pair of them around the corner. I traversed the castle with the unlikely pair of Vincent Ordenstraum, the dark emperor of Orden, and Loki, the legendary Trickster God. If I told a past version of myself that I'd be here, even a few days ago, I'd never believe it.

"Hell, you're lucky to have Ryoku and me with you. There's no better duo to locate a pair of lost pups."

"Are we counting the infancy, then?" Vincent asked dryly. "I would have been better off with Roland or a set of my own guards."

Loki glanced sidelong at the emperor. "And trust you on your own?" he asked shrewdly. "As if. You sent all your guards off anyway, remember? We're probably better protection than your anxious scientist."

Vincent didn't readily argue that point. "You believe we need protection against Shadowhearts in the castle?" Vincent asked. "Or perhaps from my own vassal, Kimo? What is your theory, Trickster?"

Loki glanced away. "To be honest, I haven't the faintest," he said softly. "I don't care for Kimo Goldenhart, but I do hope Will is alright. For all that his home affects him, he's a good man."

Vincent made a disgruntled noise. "Kimo is strong," he replied. "Without his arm, however, he would be at a strong disadvantage in combat. The fool relies heavily on the strength that brittle thing gives him."

I frowned. "What do you mean, without his arm?"

Vincent smirked. "When the boy disables his tracking mechanism, Roland rigged it to weaken the strength of his mechanical arm. For how foolish the boy acts, it was a smart move on Roland's part."

Loki winked at the emperor. "Thanks for the tip!" he said lightly. "I'll be sure to remember that when it comes to our battle after this."

Vincent only grinned. "If you take that as an advantage, you will certainly lose."

Loki sounded like he was about to retort, which might just start the fight here, but I cut them off when I spotted movement down the hall. They turned just in time to see a man in white Syaoto armor round the corner a few halls down. A red cape billowed in his wake.

"One of your commanders?" Loki asked, half to himself. "An odd place to find them."

"I did order them to scout the keep," Vincent replied with a scowl. "Altogether, it is not highly unusual. I suggest we keep going."

Loki turned to the king of Syaoto. "Anyone missing from your troupe at dinner?"

"You would still dare suggest—" Vincent paused, seeming to only realize his words after a moment. "Well, perhaps. One absence of worth. Lancet Cooper, my Master General. I was surprised that he didn't join us, especially for his obsession with your soldier, Will."

I recognized the name immediately. Lancet Cooper, the previous leader of Will's squad in Harohto, was no good. Will told me of his corruption and how he leeched from the people of Bytold and the Capital. From the expression on Loki's face, he knew the name, too.

"We should follow him," Loki said urgently, and we both began walking at a faster pace.

"Wait," Vincent cut us off. We both turned to glare, but he directed us to the hall on his left. "By the look of it, he either makes for the central courtyard or somewhere near it. Taking this route, we will likely intercept him."

Loki gave the emperor of Orden an odd look while we skirted around him. "Trusts his commanders, eh?" he asked me with a smirk. "Think we got this one in the bag."

If Vincent heard Loki, he said nothing. We hurried down the hall with more purpose now. This time, Vincent led the way. I had to admit, out of any foe I'd fought, the emperor terrified me the most. Possibly more than the dark-skinned Jesanht, and definitely worse than the egomaniacal Roland. Even Brozogoth was beginning to seem preferable. The way Vincent walked showed he held himself with a terrifying confidence. I'd seen how quickly he could move, too, for someone his size. Loki regarded the man with an air of trepidation. If the Trickster was wary of him, and lost against him once, how could I possibly fight him?

It wasn't long before the wide windows of the courtyard came into view. It was well into the night now, and the garden darker than ever before. I thought there was something strange to its lighting in the center of our view, but I couldn't place it. Something about the sight sent a shiver running down my spine.

"There's nobody here."

Loki sounded annoyed at the fact, glaring over at Vincent. The emperor didn't acknowledge him. He stared over Loki's head into the courtyard.

"There is something off here," Vincent murmured. His shoulders were squared, one hand on the sword at his hip. "Do you see it, Trickster?"

Loki turned around to stare at the glass. "No idea," he said. He wheeled back to Vincent, a hand on his own sword and a dangerous look in his eyes. "This wouldn't be some kind of trick, would it?"

"I need no trickery to defeat you," Vincent spoke plainly. "Use your eyes, Trickster. Or perhaps you are not as used to Syaoto."

A loud noise nearby alerted all three of us. A figure crashed into view at the other end of the hall. They slammed into one of the windows, shattering it in a spray of glass. The figure appeared unharmed, and immediately wheeled toward us. In the darkness, I couldn't quite make it out. Vincent and Loki stepped in the way of the attacker with defensive stances. Next to the emperor, Loki looked like a stick.

The unseen figure slammed into Vincent like a raging bull. Vincent spread his arms and grappled with it, wrestling its hands at bay. Loki's torchlight caught a flash of the man's face, and I stepped back in surprise. It was Jason Ramun, Will's father. He looked to be in a drunken bout of rage. His sapphire eyes glinted dangerously in the light behind a curtain of shaggy brown hair. They locked onto me.

"*Defender*," Jason spat, struggling to break free of Vincent's grasp. It made me think twice about Vincent that he could hold back Jason so easily. "Curse you, false king. Let me at him!"

"Mind your tongue!" Vincent ordered. In a burst of strength, he threw Jason back, slamming him into the wall hard enough to knock the wind from him. As he did, another figure appeared from the next corner: Lancet Cooper. His appearance would have almost gone unnoticed if no one were already looking that way. Vincent straightened, looking at Lancet in surprise.

"Lancet Cooper. What brings you here?"

Lancet looked briefly at Jason as the drunkard struggled to his feet, but returned his glance to the king and bowed. "My liege," he said rigidly, "there is trouble about. I was on my way to warn you when this drunkard burst into the castle. I've been since attempting to capture him."

Vincent raised his brow. "Does it have to do with the Shadowhearts or the missing boys? If not, and you've been wasting your time skipping around the castle to follow some drunken lout, I do hope you have some better excuse. I've not promoted you for nothing, have I?"

Lancet hesitated. It did me good to see the snarky soldier quail before his lord. "Well, not quite," he murmured. "You see, outside—"

Jason clambered to his feet and lunged again, roaring like a savage beast. Before Vincent could react, Loki lunged, spry as lightning, and struck the man in the jaw, hurtling him back several feet. Loki winced, shaking off the pain in his hand.

"Was waiting for the chance to do that again," he said with a grin. To Jason, he added, "You'd best stay down if you know what's good for you. I don't condone this king, but maybe a fortnight in the dungeons would straighten you out."

"I'm not what ye should be worried about!" Jason shouted, his words heavily slurred. He lifted a hand, and pointed one fat finger at me. "He's the reason for what's going on outside! He ruined my boy, he did, and now we're all on the path to ruin!"

Vincent and Loki exchanged glances. "The hell?" Loki demanded, narrowing his brow. "What are you talking about, old man?"

I stepped up between them, keeping a hand on Ragnarokkr. "Where is Will?" I demanded. "You sound like you've seen him."

Lancet cleared his throat. "If I may," he started, "that is why I have come. Milord, by my experience with other realms, I can soundly assure you that Syaoto is falling."

"What?" Loki demanded. He started on Lancet, a hand stretched out like he meant to take him by the throat. Vincent stopped him with a hand on his shoulder. "Kid, we know about the Shadowhearts. Still, such a process takes months or years! Syaoto cannot simply fall!"

"It has been thrown off," Jason growled, pushing himself up onto his elbows. "Whatever that boy of mine's gone and done, that's started it. Take a look for yourselves. Look at the sky. Shadowhearts are popping up everywhere in the Capital. Not only that, the whole damned city's tearing itself asunder."

Loki went stark pale. Vincent still looked disbelieving. "That's impossible," the king muttered, shaking his head. "Word of Shadowhearts only arrived recently. Syaoto surely cannot hearken such destruction so quickly after..."

"We need to go out there!" I insisted. I looked between everyone. Vincent still muttered under his breath, trying to make sense of the whole situation. Loki wouldn't speak. Jason gave up trying to fight us and sat cross-legged on the floor. Lancet rested his hands on his hips, biting his lip in anger.

"What are you waiting for?" I demanded. "If the world is falling, people are in trouble!"

Loki snapped out of his trance. "You're right, Ryoku," he admitted, shaking himself out of a stupor, his face still drained of color. "Let's go outside and see what we have to face."

"I'll go with you," Vincent added, to my surprise. "My vassal is still missing. It would be wise to regroup in this situation."

"I will fight as well," Jason announced, a note which made all three of us stop. He rose to his feet and cracked his neck. He did look awfully sober all the sudden. "Your men know nothing on how to deal with Shadowhearts. If they fight in a panic, they'll only die. That," he added, nodding at my sword, "and you've no idea how to use the only thing that can truly stop them."

Vincent rounded on him. "I should have you tossed in the dungeons," he snarled. "You attacked your mighty king! You have impeded our progress!"

I stepped in. "What do you mean, Jason?" I demanded. "What about my sword?"

Jason scoffed at Vincent, crossing his huge arms. "You'll be the king of a pile of rubble soon enough," he said, "and there'll be no dungeons to rot in. Should we be able to do something, you may decide whether or not to imprison me. But for now, we fight." He finally turned his gaze to me, glaring. "If you don't know about your sword, beats me why you carry it. You're as useful as a lot of manure."

Vincent growled, turning on his heel with impatience. "Lancet, you're to keep an eye on him," he ordered. "I don't trust some fallen hero any more than a regular one."

I tried to get Jason's attention to press him for information, but everyone was already on their feet, taking off toward the entrance to Syaoto Castle. Lancet grabbed Jason by the arm and led him on. With a furious glare at me, Jason kept up with us.

On our way, several soldiers bolted past us in a panic, retreating into the keep. Vincent barked out orders to them, but some ignored him altogether. A few of the more steadfast men listened to his words and made their way back outside with us.

Vincent and Loki led the way. I struggled to keep up. When we finally approached the gates of the castle, both king and Trickster simultaneously shot their hands forward. The set of heavy gates burst open with their combined magic. The effort was so great that I was alarmed to see the doors still standing. Loki and Vincent didn't flinch at that unique moment and strode out in front of the castle. I stayed close behind them, and nearly bowled into them when they came to a full stop.

The scene looked like something out of a nightmare. Darkness plagued much of the city now that the supersized moon had completed its track of the world, but torchlight and alarmingly large fires dotted the city. The fires in the city gave the sky a reddish, eerie glow, and the sounds of panicked screaming rose above all else.

The point that brought us to a dead stop was what looked like a whirlpool forming in the sky. It sucked in the very night and stars at a deadly rate. In the city, ceilings and stones ripped from buildings, dragged upwards into that swirling death in the sky, into something beyond the whirlpool itself. I shuddered, recalling the ominous darkness outside the worlds.

Soldiers ran back and forth, trying to secure as many people as they could. Brom was there, shouting orders while he clutched a small child in his arms. I saw Alex, too, directing a panicking wife, husband, and set of children into the castle. He shot Vincent a look like he expected the king to contest bringing civilians into the castle. It surprised me that he didn't. He only had eyes for the mayhem before us.

"Mother Creator save us," Loki whispered, sounding both awed and frightened. "How could this have happened?" He turned to me, his face ashen. "Ryoku, I have never seen an atrocity like this."

Jason growled beneath his breath. "I told you it was a disaster. Shadowhearts prowl the city freely." He added another unnecessary glare at me. "If his sword was fixed, we might stand a chance."

Lancet struck him in the arm, about as effective as punching a stone. "Keep quiet," he ordered, "unless you plan to fight alongside us. You said that, didn't you?"

Jason grumbled. "Not that there's much point to it." He drew a short sword from beneath his cloak. It resembled the one Will carried, but had a gilded edge and seemed to radiate a strange power.

Loki drew my attention back to him. "Ryoku, I cannot safely say we can stop this, or that we should stick around. We should find our friends and leave."

"You mean us?" came Katiel's voice from behind me. I turned. He and Dawn were just pushing their way through the doors behind us. Dawn smiled at me, but it faded like colors running from a painting when she saw the occurrence behind us.

Katiel stopped short, staring at the sky, and crossed his arms. "What in Chaos is going on?"

"The world is falling," Loki said darkly. "We must find the others and leave. There is nothing we can do here."

Jason spat on the ground, but Loki ignored him. Katiel only stared, jaw agape. "Falling? But it's never looked like this before…"

Sira emerged behind them with Lusari, and both stopped short when they saw the destruction. Katiel turned to them, his brow set and locked. "Help us gather everyone we can," he ordered. "Bring them here. We're to leave here as soon as possible."

Both looked too surprised to do much more than nod and return into the keep. After looking to us, Katiel and Dawn followed them.

Vincent remained where he was, staring up at the sky. Loki gave him an odd look. "Why do you look upset, emperor? Isn't this the kind of thing you wanted?"

"Not like this," Vincent spoke, hardly more than a commanding whisper. "Something is terribly amiss. The fabric of Syaoto has been meddled with."

Loki scoffed, crossing his arms. "Tell me about it," he muttered. "First dragons in a world of ever-changing weather, and now a world decides to change its date of demise? It is not typical. I planned to visit Immortalia already, but that must come with due haste. Something is horribly amiss with the realms."

"You'd let this world fall, Trickster?" Jason growled. He stumbled, and I remembered he seemed quite drunk when he first attacked us. "I recall you threatening me with vigor before. Does that all drain from your toes when faced with unworldly odds?"

"He's not wrong," Lancet murmured uneasily. "I've never seen anything like this. What could we even do but ease our peoples' suffering?"

"We have to stop it," I said, loud enough for all to turn to me in surprise.

Jason spat on the ground, muttering something vulgar about me, but I held my ground before their beguiled looks. I felt dizzy and weak. It was only thinking back that I wondered if I'd eaten anything here in days. It wasn't necessary to consume food here, but I ate little in the physical realm as well, and I felt terribly fatigued. The world spun vicariously around me and it was all I could do to stand straight, but I did so, looking between the king and the Trickster.

"You both agree that it's unnatural, right? Something out there is causing this. Something has disrupted the natural order of this world. If that's the case, can't we stop it? If there is a cause, and we eliminate it..."

"None have ever reversed the falling of a world," Loki advised me with a warning tone. "If a world has reached this point, there is no returning from the brink. Even if it was caused by something, getting rid of that something might not actually reverse it."

"We have to try," I argued. "Will and Kimo are out there somewhere, and all our friends. Would you be pleased with yourself to walk away from this world in such a time? Leaving every soldier that helped us out? Every medic that helped save my life?"

"I would not hesitate to leave this world," Vincent said coldly. "However, someone I know would not appreciate if I left Kimo behind. So, why not. I will attempt to help your folly quest, if only until we find Kimo."

The emperor smirked, studying me with an odd expression. "This will be a good chance to see if you're worth the trouble."

His words took me by total surprise. He was actually going to help us? I was sure he'd leave by the time he found Roland, and didn't care for what happened to Kimo. He said somebody wouldn't appreciate leaving Kimo behind. Was that somebody that Vincent himself cared about? Was that why he was so doggedly searching for Kimo with us?

"I'll come along," Jason agreed, almost as surprising. "You lot have no idea what you're doing. If there's a way to fix this, I'll—"

Vincent cut him off with a cold stare. "You're drunk," he snarled. "You'll only get in the way for us. That said, we could use a meat shield."

"I'll keep him in check," Lancet assured Vincent, saluting his king boldly. "We could use all the help we can get, if I'm to be frank. If Will's involved somehow..."

Loki made an extremely frustrated sound, throwing his hands up in the air. "Well, if Vincent Ordenstraum's going to help you, I guess

I have to agree, too," he said bitterly. "I stand by the same point. If we find Will first, then we must abandon ship. Same goes for if conditions become uninhabitable. If our lives are threatened by this mayhem, we must go. You agree?"

I shrugged. "Sure, whatever," I agreed. "We just have to figure out where they went, once we meet up with the others." I looked to Vincent. "Is Roland going to cooperate?"

Vincent smirked, looking more like an evil toad than ever with the disaster behind him throwing red light across his face. "He is my vassal and servant. He must." I didn't miss Lancet's snide smirk, either.

"Well, sounds like we have a plan," Loki said. "Now we just need to find our friends and figure out where to go."

When I turned back towards the castle, I caught a glimpse of something in the sky behind the castle. It towered so high into my view that I walked to circle widely around the gates in order to see what it was. Vincent and Loki followed me, exchanging weird glances.

Still, I had to back up several feet from the castle to see beyond it, but sure enough, a jet of light connected the sky to somewhere in the royal forest. The bluish hue of the light seemed oddly familiar, and not in a good way.

"What on Gaia is that?" Loki demanded. "Could that be the cause of this?"

"No, just the light catching a pretty stone," Vincent muttered. "Of course it has to be the problem! But what could be the source...?"

Then he stopped altogether. He turned to me, his piercing violet eyes accusing. "That letter. Do you still have it?"

"What?" I asked, taken aback.

"The letter they left you," Vincent said impatiently. "Do you have it?"

Shaking my head, I pulled the letter out from my pocket. As a last thought, I'd snatched it up before we left the room. "Why do you need it?"

Vincent snatched it from my hands and read it over again. After a moment, he cursed, starting to pace between Loki and I. The Trickster looked at me, just as confused as I was. "What are you...?" Loki started.

"They're taking the Royal Forest," Vincent snarled, half to himself. "The boy's accursed magic... Damned Roland was supposed to seal it. Likely he used the tracking chip to do so. Damned, accursed, bloody fool! If you want something done right, best to do it yourself!"

"What the hell are you talking about?" Loki asked quietly. He looked mortally unnerved. "Did Kimo do this?"

Jason seemed to catch on before Loki or I did. "The legend of the hidden lake," he murmured. "Is that what you're talking about? The Dragonstones used in the making of the wall and of the crown?"

Vincent turned toward him with rage in his eyes. To my surprise, he averted his eyes and didn't speak until he calmed himself. "There are points in the royal forest which are said to connect to some underground cave," Vincent explained, teeth gritted. "It is part of the reason I'm here, not that you needed to know that. If Roland put the mechanism to control Kimo's magic in his arm, and the bastard tore it off, then his turbulent magic could react unwisely with those stones. We have spent months trying to safely probe them."

"That means they're in the Royal Forest!" I exclaimed. "That settles it! Loki, we can stop this! We just need to meet up with the others, save anyone we can along the way, and get to that light!"

"Would it be that easy?" Loki asked. He directed his question at Vincent, who was starting to pace uneasily.

"There's no way to tell," he replied, not sounding confident at all. "Kimo beholds a mysterious sort of magic. The strange power has been troubling since we first met, when I was young. Hell if I know where it came from, but it seems to react with the magic stones in Syaoto. Dragonstone."

"Dragonstone?" I asked. As I spoke, a jarring thought hit me. The stones in the walls said to repel demons. Kimo had shown me his own demon. Was that it? Were the stones reacting the same way to Romis as they were to Advocatos? Would it do the same to me?

"However," Vincent kept muttering, "when I was younger, there was an incident with his wild magic that caused him to request assistance in sealing it away. It is not something he can control on his own. We must double back to the courtyard. Check to see if he tossed his tracking device there. Perhaps reconnecting it could cause his magic to fizzle out. Then, and only then, might that beam of light cease to destroy this world. It could possibly react very harshly, however. We should be prepared for either circumstance."

I was surprised to hear Vincent speak of Kimo amicably. Was it possible that he saved him not only for somebody he knew, but... for himself?

"Sounds encouraging," Loki muttered. "Let's go get that device. I imagine that'll be the easiest part of the rest of our night."

SCENE FOUR: ASCENSION TO THE SKY

...Of Act Eight: Conquer

In the eyes of Will Ramun, we are in Syaoto Capital, in the world of Syaoto. It is well past midnight On November 15th, 2017.

"What on Gaia...?"

"I-I don't know," Kimo murmured. I was surprised he could speak in his current state. Atop the plateau we now stood on, a great tremor had shaken the earth. Almost immediately after, a bright light shot through a spot in the earth below and overtook Kimo's entire body, pinning him in place. I could only see his outline within, and his bright blue eyes turned almost dark orange.

Right after that was when everything started. The light channeled through him and into the sky above, where it entered what looked like a deathly whirlpool in the sky. The tremor that shuddered the earth became constant. Across from Kimo, it was difficult to keep my footing. Stones and trees around us tore from the ground, slowly sucked away into the void above.

"Is Syaoto...?" I asked, and found myself unable to voice the sheer thought.

"It is starting to fall," Kimo replied. Even through the light swallowing him, I could hear his fear. The strange energy manipulated his voice to an almost unrecognizable crescendo. "Syaoto is falling. I… I don't fully know what's going on, but I think my magic is reacting with something in the earth."

"Your magic?" I demanded. I tried to lunge through the light and grab Kimo, but it immediately singed my hands to touch. I drew back, growling under my breath. My hand couldn't stay in there even if I forced it. Something kept me out. "You're responsible for this…"

"Will, there's no time to argue the specifics," Kimo insisted. "There might still be time. You have to go find the scepter. If anything can put a stop to this, it would be that relic."

I hesitated. "You mean… To put an end to you?"

"If it must be that way," Kimo replied. A sharp blur of white light overtook him, and he cried out in pain. I reflexively tried to reach out to him, but drew back before my hands touched the light.

"If anything, the scepter is made of an ancient stone native to Syaoto. It can probably put a stop to this. If not… then I am truly sorry."

I couldn't bring myself to move. I stared at Kimo's image surrounded by light. "Am I to leave you like this?" I asked faintly. I had to shove aside the thought that Kimo had done this on purpose. The light was an inconvenience. He'd been just as adamant to get the scepter as I was.

"I don't think you have a choice," Kimo whispered. "The Shadowhearts will come soon. They cannot touch me here, but they will swarm. Staying would be the end of you. If you leave now toward the Enthralmen Jungle, you would be racing against the speed of this event, but away from its epicentre. You might stand a chance."

"But this world will fall?" I asked bleakly. "My home…? It will fall to this accursed power?"

"I cannot say," Kimo replied. "I haven't seen this through. This type of reaction with my magic is unheard of for me. Perhaps it will bring Syaoto to the brink. Perhaps it'll kill us all. If you can find the scepter before that happens, you stand a chance at defeating the tyrant who took your home. He would have escaped already, I'm certain. He'll wait in Orden for you and your friends to find him. Ryoku… if he has any sense, he'll escape. Everyone will make it out of this. You have a job."

"Or he follows this damned beacon and finds you," I muttered. "I should wait. Perhaps we can stop this, and then we go together."

"Don't be a fool, Will," Kimo snapped. "You know as well as I that there isn't much time. If you fail to find the scepter, you would lose your best chance at saving this world. Besides that, it can give your Defender the upper hand. He will need the advantage, no matter how strong he gets. Vincent is a powerful man."

He had a point, and I loathed to admit it. We needed this scepter. It was the reason I'd come along with Kimo, the reason we ditched the device that would lead to Vincent and Roland tracking him. It seemed that might have had adverse effects in causing Kimo to lose control, but Vincent would never have let Kimo go this far with me. We needed that scepter.

"Go into my bag," Kimo ordered. "I have a map of Syaoto on me with what I've deduced to be the area where the scepter is hidden. It could be difficult to find even then, but I have confidence you can do it. You are the son of Jason, aren't you?"

I didn't reply to that. I went into his bag and fished out a battered old map. I took it, unfurled it, and skimmed over its entirety. It covered much of the area around the capital just shy of Balgena to the north. Enthralmen Jungle was a stretch from where I was. I needed to go.

I lifted my hand to place before Kimo's, without touching the light. His orange-looking eyes flashed. "You will make it through this," I told him with confidence. "We have a role to play in the coming battle. Dying here is not that role."

"I hope you're right, Will."

With that, I tucked the map into my own bag and started down the plateau. Darkness was already accumulating around us. The Shadowhearts were coming, and I prayed Kimo was right about being safe.

(Meanwhile, in the eyes of Ryoku Dragontalen...)

It took almost an hour to round up everyone we traveled with, and we found no sign of Kimo's device.

Many of the others were alarmed to see what was going on outside, having been crawling through Syaoto Castle since it began.

The Timeless One hardly reacted, staring up at the sky with a bleak expression. Many had never seen anything like this before. Guildford, Alex, and Lamont stared up at the sky like the ocean had turned upside-down. Even Roland looked a little unnerved. He spoke with Vincent in hushed words, and the king seemed impatient with what he had to say. I couldn't understand any more than that.

"Will and Kimo must both be there," Sira agreed, and didn't sound impressed. "We scoured that castle. If they were in the city, even their thick-ass skulls would've come back by now. They're out there, trapped or worse."

"Are we all to simply charge out into the woods?" Alex asked. "The people here are in trouble! Will is my best friend, but I find it hard to believe we should all run out there and leave them behind. Even if we can stop this, people will suffer."

"Agreed," Katiel said firmly. "Ryoku, we got a lot to focus on. I'll help ya clear a path to your friends, and then I'll double back here to help out."

"Clear a path?" Lusari asked. She kept close to Rena, who looked surprisingly calm for the situation. "What do you mean?"

"Shadowhearts," Anna spoke. I was surprised to hear her pipe up at all. I did know her biggest passion laid in battle, so maybe she was just at home here. She looked brave next to Katiel, Dawn, and Joey. "I don't see them about yet, but they will be here. They feed off the energy a dying world gives off."

Guildford looked unnerved. "Uh, what is a Shadowheart, exactly?"

Before Loki could chime in, the Timeless One took the point. "Shadowhearts are creatures prominent from a lost age. They were noted in history as appearing in our realms a thousand years ago. According to legend, they are souls from the River Styx that leak out through breaches in the river and become these varying beasts that seek havoc and destruction. As Anna claims, in our new age, they populate dead and dying worlds. Something about the breach that sends a world to ruin invites these creatures like the plague. Nobody knows why."

"How do you know more than I do?" Loki asked suspiciously. The Timeless One only winked, and took a bite of a chicken leg he apparently carried over from dinner. After he scarfed it down, I saw Relus dutifully offer him another from a napkin.

"We've dealt with them before," Katiel addressed the entire group. "Someone who doesn't know what they're doing could wind up seriously hurt. Honestly, it ain't that tough. You gotta know how to take 'em down. Each breed has a different weak spot. If we're talking just their base form, called Silhouettes, then we're in luck. A sharp breeze could kill a sea of them. But somehow, going by the size of Syaoto, I doubt it's gonna be that simple."

"They will arrive in waves soon enough," Relus advised, adjusting his glasses. "I suggest we divide our focus. Some of the less experienced fighters should stay in the city and help the people. If there is a way to cease this disaster, then I doubt it requires more than a few capable hands. Others can fan out and stop the Shadowhearts before they reach this city."

Vincent scowled at everyone. "You are mad if you think I'll do anything but head straight for Kimo. Count your blessings that I'm with you at all. I'm tired of standing and talking. We must go, before the ground at our very feet is sucked away."

I felt certainly mixed about the king's help, but he had a point that everyone took. We only took a moment to strategize. Alex would round up some of the officials, including Rena, to keep them safe in close quarters. Lusari, Dawn, and Guildford divided among the task force for their healing magic.

Loki, Sira, Vincent, Roland, and I were making the full trip to the light. Everyone else split up into smaller forces. Katiel and Kaia took a group into the forest to provide nearby support if we needed it. Other strong fighters, like Relus, Rex, and Cleria, split up into different units with soldiers of the army to combat Shadowhearts and save anyone they could. I was surprised to see the Timeless One go out, too. I was also relieved when Lancet and Jason didn't join us in the forest. Vincent ordered them to keep to the forest border.

We took off quickly. I caught Dawn's glance as she hurried off with the others toward the forest. She looked brave. She loved helping people, which probably made her the best of us since she was strong enough to do it. However, I could see a worried look in her eyes. If things went awry, she could probably get everyone out safely, but I still wondered if I might not see her soon.

Our group fanned out and started around the side of the castle. Loki led the way, and I stayed close to Sira and Katiel. Vincent and Roland walked by themselves in hushed conversation. A day ago, seeing Vincent like this would be cause to attack.

Passing the city could be no less than horrific. Emerging from the giant castle revealed the state of the city between the castle's front gates and the forest entrance. Buildings crumbled away before our eyes. I saw everything from bricks to tables dragged into the sky. I spotted a blacksmith's hammer ascending far above a distraught blacksmith. A soldier appeared, dragging the red-haired smith out of the building just as a large portion of the castle tower crumpled. Half of it crashed down, and his shop was no more.

By the gates to the royal forest, a familiar face rushed up to us: Brom, the previous Lord General. Since we saw him earlier, he'd clearly partaken in some battle. Dark matter stained his huge sword, also splashed over his armor. Dirt and grime streaked his weathered face. If I were to face him in combat, I thought, I might back out from sheer fear. Oliver winged him as usual, and the younger soldier appeared distraught. Dark matter clung to his armor and weapon, and some even strung from his hair. His eyes were wild and frightened.

"Milords," the general greeted us hurriedly, bowing before us. I knew the gesture was largely to Vincent, but he didn't seem to be addressing him. "It is good to see capable faces once more! Dark creatures have been appearing in the woods. My men are being picked off like flies! If we do nothing, they will surely reach the city!"

Loki cursed. "So they are already here. Say, who are you again?"

The general's shock at being addressed by the Trickster was evident. "Uh, Brom Gerenadh, sir. I am – was – In full command of the capital army," he added, looking at Vincent pointedly. "I remain a respected voice in the army."

"Alright, Brom Gerenadh," Loki instructed, and the general's attention was rapt. "I want you to come with us. Summon any of your men you can. Many of us are familiar with these monsters. Bring your men to rally around us, and we can clear a path."

Brom's eyes were confused, but he saluted with the utmost devotion nonetheless. "Will do. May I ask where we are headed?"

Loki jabbed a finger toward the light. From here, it was plain as day: a column of blue light streaking through the sky. I stared at it for a moment, just as perplexed as Brom seemed. He set his jaw, and then went about shouting for some of his soldiers. He briefly argued with Oliver, but the soldier wound up at his side when we returned, just as we approached the gate.

There, it was evident that things were not right in the woods. Stone columns reinforced the gate on both sides, but only one hinge remained, leaving the gate dangling above us as the force from the sky tried to drag it off. Claw marks mangled the gate itself. As we drew closer, I saw that the edges of the slash marks seemed to be disintegrating.

I advanced alongside Loki and Sira. As we ducked through, the gate snapped free from its last hinge and disappeared into the sky. Even Sira started at this.

We drew weapons as we started into the rich woods. I might have thought they were beautiful once, but the alien dark matter that seemed to cling to everything gave it an ultimately eerie aura. I felt like I was walking through a nightmare among the shadow-strung trees. The path beneath our feet was heavily trafficked. If I understood correctly, the Royal Forest was normally the hunting grounds of Syaoto's royalty and noble families. Guards who watched for trespassers frequently patrolled the area.

Little of the royal atmosphere remained of this place. Gashes in the earth lay in the wide shapes of once fully rooted trees. Over the entire forest, I could sense something somehow more foreboding than the shining light ahead. A road from the southern exit was supposed to skirt alongside the woods and make for Southern Syaoto, but we knew better than to try that. Will and Kimo were definitely here.

We started in at a hurried pace. Katiel, Kaia, and their group split off into the woods. Everyone else spread out around Loki, Sira, Vincent, Roland, and I. Brom remained close to our inner circle, keeping a stern eye on me. I'd seen Loki mutter something to him earlier, and I had a feeling Brom was enlisted to protect me. The others fanned out until I couldn't see much of them. Shortly into the forest, I began to hear the sounds of combat. A soldier cried out, but it cut short with the whoosh of flames. I dearly hoped that flame was Katiel's work and not some entity of darkness.

In a thick part of the woods, a creature burst out into our midst. How it passed our protective circle was beyond me. The creature was almost my height and dark purple in color, made mostly of four large tentacles, all layered with spikes, and had an orb-shaped head. A single red eye bulged out like a sore. It unleashed a horrific shriek through a mouth ridden with fangs.

Brom stepped in the monster's path, bracing his thick claymore before himself. Before the creature could fall upon him, Loki cut in his way and buried his regal sword straight into the demon's head. It emitted a pained shriek and burst into a spray of black dust.

"Let us deal with those," Loki said to Brom, flicking black matter off his sword. "That was a high-leveled Shadowheart. One of those could wipe out your army if you let it strike first. If those are prevalent out here..."

When he thought I wasn't looking, Loki dabbed sweat from his brow. Taking on these creatures might be a little harder than he was letting on.

Another one burst into our path. This time, Vincent buried his dark sword into the creature's skull. He stormed through it as it burst into dust. "Keep moving," he ordered to me. "They must not overwhelm us. I pray your friends are stronger than you are."

Sira took my arm and made me quicken my pace. "Don't you dare try hitting one of those," she muttered. "Loki's right. Those are powerful Shadowhearts."

I wanted to ask how she knew about them, but I held my tongue. We rushed through the forest trail with the sounds of battle rising around us. I caught flashes of their fights. A blast of fire from Katiel's Omega arms lit the trees around our west side. Relus pounced upon another tentacle-ridden Shadowheart that ran into our midst, burying his short blade into its skull and dragging it away. He flashed me a fanged grin before disappearing again.

More than anything, I longed to rush out and help them. The harrowing thought of losing another friend stuck in my mind. After Sapphense, I promised myself I'd protect my friends no matter what. I hoped that my time spent fighting demons would help that vow become true, but was it worth it? I couldn't fight these monsters like this! I didn't need to cross blades with one of the unnerving creatures to know they were deadlier than the demons we fought outside Syaoto.

The blue light breached from a sharp ascent above us. We reached the plateau, but the edge of land rose probably twenty feet up from where we stood. Likely a path nearby scaled the cliff to the plateau. Judging by the sharpness of the cliff, it wasn't close enough.

We turned around just as another Shadowheart crawled into view. This one was bigger and looked like some kind of horrific centipede on its hind legs. Crimson eyes flashed as it snarled at us. Loki gently nudged Brom behind him, pushing us back against the wall. As he and Vincent started toward it, a pair of tentacle Shadowhearts lunged out from the shadows beside it. Sira dashed forward and ran one through, probably saving Loki's hide in the effort. The Shadowheart's body seemed to flash red as Sira cleaved through it, but it could have been the reflective color of her sword.

Oliver stumbled into the clearing, tripping backwards over a large stone, but righting himself. "We are surrounded, my liege!" he cried out. Just then, a dark shape lunged out from the woods and fell upon him.

"Oliver!" Brom cried, and tried to break out from behind Loki. I was the closest, and I took advantage of Sira's distraction to run to the soldier's aid. I yanked my knife from my belt and lunged.

The thing raised its head as I closed in, and I nearly froze in terror. The creature was about the size of a dog and quadruped, beset with gleaming red eyes and a wagging, forked tongue. Its lip curled up, baring a set of vicious fangs. Shoving away my fear, I rushed at it with my knife. It bounded off the soldier's body with a savage snarl and hurtled straight into me, crushing me to the ground. A sharp pain seared through my chest. I thought it was the thing's claws, but I didn't spot any blood. It was the scars of my recent injury. I cursed – of course; I hadn't tried fighting since my miraculous healing. I couldn't let it hold me back!

I reacted sluggishly and slung my free fist into the monster's chest. It backed off with a pained yip, circling back and pacing around me. I dared a brief glance to see if anyone could help me. Katiel, Anna, and Cleria backed into us in the clearing. Katiel's arms morphed into red, hoof-like appendages that smoked with flames. On his way to help Oliver, Brom wound up engaged in battle with another centipede-like Shadowheart.

The dog-like Shadowheart lunged again. This time, I braced myself and caught the monster in the chest with my knife. It let out another pained yip before bursting into dark smoke. My shoulders sagged in momentary relief. My first Shadowheart slain, and I had a feeling it wasn't nearly as tough as the ones Loki fought.

"Go on ahead!" Loki shouted at me. He held a centipede-like Shadowheart at bay with his sword, his grip shaking. "If you can do anything, stop it! Maybe these hordes will cease!"

If not for his last point, I certainly wouldn't have listened. Could stopping that light spell the end of these Shadowhearts? It was the only way I could save my friends. Fighting these Shadowheart was nothing like scrapping with demons out in the plains, no matter how much I learned out there.

I sighed, sheathing my knife. Oliver got to his feet, flashing me a gratified grin before Brom called him over. If anything, that gave me some pride. One life saved to go along with my first Shadowheart. Maybe I could be a real Defender after all.

I turned my head to the plateau cliff above me and, with a last look around, leapt up.

My weightless marks stung already as I surged into the air. There was a disconcerting energy around me as I went. If I wasn't careful, the sky could suck me up at any given point. What if the pull was stronger atop the plateau? I wasn't exactly a heavyweight champion. It would certainly be a way to go, drifting off to my demise mere feet from the cause of this mayhem.

I landed atop the plateau within a few short seconds, but my marks had a reddish glint to them. I couldn't tax them much more – not that I should, given my proximity to the sky. Up here, the blue light filled most of the plateau. I almost didn't see the boy standing alone in the clearing. I shielded my eyes in an attempt to see him better.

It was definitely Kimo Goldenhart. My heart skipped a beat. Was Will already gone? Sucked into the sky, or fallen victim to the sea of Shadowhearts?

I tried to hide my trepidation and took a step toward Kimo. He was standing with his head turned to the sky. The surging blue light looked to be emerging from beneath him, but it was hard to tell. I had to shield my eyes to see him well enough, and an audible current of energy buzzed at my ears. His eyes snapped open – they were bright orange. Romis, his demon, was awake.

"Will was right about you," Kimo said, just loud enough for me to hear. "You were foolish enough to come here. You must leave. There is naught you can do."

I couldn't work up a response. The electric sound of pulsating energy was the only other sound I could hear. Even the clamor of battle below became inaudible up here. Perhaps I was higher up than I thought. My friends couldn't have lost by now, could they?

Urgency drove me forward. I took one step, and another, working my way toward Kimo. The energy radiating from him made my hair stand on end.

"Ryoku Dragontalen," Kimo warned, "you must leave. You are useless here! Leave me. Take your friends and run to safety. Roxanne will understand."

His words brought me to a halt. For a moment, nothing else existed. The stinging of my marks. My faded injuries at my chest. I felt like a ghost.

"Roxanne?" I demanded. My tone turned to ice. "No, you're not talking about the same Roxanne. Not my sister."

He didn't respond. A chilling anger rose up in me, climbing from my toes to my eyes. I stormed toward Kimo. I wanted to scream at him, to attack, to force him to explain why he'd just uttered that name – but then something hit me.

I heard Kimo cry out, but everything drowned before the current of energy. A tremendous power overtook me quicker than my own anger could, pinning me in place. My hands balled into tight fists. A surging agony channeled through me. It felt like my blood turned to fire. I screamed, but I couldn't hear my own voice over the energy. All I could see was the light.

The pain became irrelevant shortly, replaced by a feeling of calming peace. My fists unclenched, and my hands hung at my sides. The surging blue sea seemed to change a little. I could see Kimo's orange eyes through all the energy before me. In turn, mine were red. Then, even he seemed to fade.

I realized I could see someone in the distance. It didn't appear to be Kimo or any of my friends. In fact, I couldn't say with confidence that I was still on that same plateau.

The figure appeared to be female, and she approached with a gliding movement. She appeared to have shoulder-length hair, but I couldn't decide what color it was. It looked black, but other colors ran through it like a painter spilling their ink. She had a soft and youthful face. I couldn't determine her age from looking. I tried to avert my eyes when I realized her curved body was unclothed, but I couldn't move an inch. Abruptly, she was in front of me, close enough that I could make out details in her oak-brown eyes.

"You have done well," she spoke in a whisper that echoed through my ears and vibrated through my consciousness. Her voice was decidedly feminine, but there was sagely wisdom in her tongue. "Your presence here has saved the world of Syaoto. You have done as I willed it, and you have brought me to the focal point. I'm afraid there is yet one trial you must endure."

"Who are you?" I demanded, but my voice came out soft.

A youthful smile lit her face, but somehow adult and controlled at the same time. The resounding sensation of nostalgia struck me, as though I once knew this girl and had parted with her against my will. Kimo's words rang through my ears, the ones that told me I wasn't truly Ryoku Dragontalen. I thought of the black-haired boy who once taught me how to fight. Were he and this girl from my real past?

"My name is Eos," she whispered, and I felt I couldn't get enough of her voice. It filled my ears like sweet music and made me forget my home. "I have healed you of the impurities that strike you. The taint of the Prince of Darkness corrupted your foreign soul, and I have healed that. The injury you took during the day of his darkness is gone. That is all I can offer to you, of both worlds. It is a gift I give you with love, that nothing you sustain in this world may affect you in the world you call home. If you have further need, please call me. May you survive with faith and valor until you return to me. To home."

In the last moment, she called me by a name, but I couldn't understand her. The name came to fall upon suddenly deaf ears. I tried to speak, to ask her to repeat that last word, but the world around me was quickly trickling away. Before I could speak, I returned in a dark world, kneeling before a duly alarmed Kimo Goldenhart.

SCENE FIVE: REQUIEM OF THE TRICKSTER GOD

...Of Act Eight: Conquer

In the eyes of Ryoku Dragontalen, we are in Syaoto Royal Forest, in the world of Syaoto. It is well past midnight On November 15th, 2017.

Everything rushed back to me. The darkness of Syaoto without that bright blue light was difficult to see in. Even the huge moon hid somewhere in the darkened sky. Most importantly, I realized with an upward glance, that sky returned to normal. A triumphant feeling welled up in my chest. It was over.

Was it actually, though? Who was the girl I saw in the light? She said her name was Eos. How did seeing her end the blight? Oddly enough, she was right about one thing. In both worlds, I glanced down into my lap. In the real world, sitting upright in my bed, my glass eye sat in my open palm. Here, in Syaoto, it had vanished altogether. It was a miracle all in itself. Somehow, saving Syaoto saved a part of me I never assumed I could experience again.

"How did you...?" Kimo asked, astounded. I wanted to question him, to ask if he saw the girl or had any idea what happened there. As I was about to speak, a shadow clambered up onto the plateau alongside us. My heart sank right back in my chest and I reached for my knife. Did the Shadowhearts remain?

It wasn't a Shadowheart, however, that towered into view. Kimo turned around and grabbed his sword as Vincent Ordenstraum appeared. His violet eyes glinted like fallen stars in the darkness. His dark armor blended with the night, and he looked more malevolent and powerful than I could imagine. A sharp realization overtook me: he had no reason to work with us anymore.

"There you are," he spoke. "We've finally found you, Kimo Goldenhart. A pity that your other friend isn't here. Congratulations on saving the world of Syaoto."

"I had nothing to do with it," Kimo said softly. Despite his measured tone, he kept low to the ground with a hand on his sword hilt. "Ryoku saved this world, and me. I... don't quite know how he did it."

Vincent's violet-eyed glare turned to me. "How interesting," he murmured. "It would seem you have some talents after all, Remnant. Your origins may be a mystery to us, but you are still far from the hero I anticipated. A pity that this is where it must come to an end."

When he reached to draw his sword, another shadow lunged from behind him, latching onto his back like a crab. It was hard to see in the dark, but the resounding yelp could only belong to Loki. I rose to my feet, choosing to grab Ragnarokkr instead of my knife. Kimo rose at my side, cracking his human knuckles with the ones of his mechanical arm.

"Get off me, you insolent godling!" Vincent shouted, and hurled Loki off him. The Trickster skidded across the ground, coming perilously close to the ledge before he stopped. Vincent turned and pursued, his sword drawn now. Loki got to his feet with his own weapon just in time for their blades to cross. A resounding spark flashed light across their faces. Vincent's shone with rage and vigor; Loki's with a brave scowl.

"Leave here at once!" Loki shouted, relenting for a second only to strike again like a vicious python. "Your vassal has been recovered! Go back home and cut your losses, Vincent Ordenstraum!"

"This is my kingdom now!" Vincent screamed. He blocked Loki's strikes easily and batted him back, taking ground on the plateau. "Did you not witness the power Kimo activated? It came from that hidden place! I will find it, bend it to my will, and use it to become the mightiest king that this world has seen!"

Something ensnared his foot as he lunged, and Vincent almost keeled over onto his face. I didn't realize what it was until another silhouette appeared on the plateau: Dawn.

The vines Dawn controlled wrapped around Vincent's foot, nearly bringing the weighty man down altogether. In the dark, her golden hair seemed to catch tomorrow's light.

"Druid whore!" Vincent screamed. He kicked hard, ripping the vine free from the ground and charged at Dawn.

Images flashed past my eyes. The times I knew Dawn was mistreated right in front of me, and times I'd seen Vincent easily overwhelm foes that could defeat me. I saw both as I leapt off the ground and slung my arms around Vincent's throat, Ragnarokkr still clutched in my grasp. His body straightened momentarily, but he reacted fast. One huge hand shot up and crushed my wrist. I cried out, and Ragnarokkr fell from my grasp. The next thing I knew, I was mid-air.

I struck the ground like a rock, the wind slammed from my chest in one whoosh. Dawn threw herself over me. The scent of her hair falling across my shoulder filled my lungs, but I couldn't breathe enough to relish the aroma. My vision swam for a moment. Despite the invigorating rush of seeing that spirit Eos and saving Syaoto, I still had not eaten in days and felt the ghosts of my last injury. How could I win this fight?

Vincent's dark blade screamed through the air toward us. Dawn threw her hand up, and a shimmering golden barrier flashed before us like a strike of lightning. Vincent's sword bounced off it, but he kept his grip on it. In the moment Dawn provided, I was able to take a breath and force air into my lungs. I pushed myself up, and Dawn rose with me, her head on my shoulder.

"The Shadowhearts are not gone," Dawn whispered to me urgently. "Saving the world did not remove them. The others are still fighting. I don't know if we can get any help from them. I just saw Vincent coming up here after the light went away and…"

I clenched my fist, and cursed when I found that painful. Vincent disarming me must have messed up my hand. How could we fend him off in this shape?

Loki recovered to strike again. His sword rose like a dragon's tail, striking Vincent's momentarily weakened grip, but not hard enough to disarm him. Snarling, Vincent turned on Loki.

"Stop!" I shouted, taking a step forward. Dawn kept a hand on me as I advanced. I tried to scan for the dark glint of Ragnarokkr somewhere on the ground, but couldn't spot it with Vincent centered on me. "The Shadowhearts are still here!" I cried. "We have to work together and fight them!"

Vincent relented from Loki, who took a second to recollect himself. Each time Vincent attacked him seemed to hack away at his energy even further.

"Work together?" he drawled. "Why should I do such a thing? I can kill the lot of you here and return to the city. With an organized army and my dark power, the Shadowhearts will never be able to penetrate our defenses."

Vincent's smirk widened. "What a shame, I would have to explain, that Ryoku Dragontalen and his allies fell in defense of our great city. I could do you that service, if only because you captured my interest when you seemed most unworthy. You could be a hero in the eyes of the people."

"Not interested," I retorted. "You really think they'll believe you? These people gave us lodgings and hid us from you. Those people dragged me into the city and brought life back into me. This is more my home than it is yours."

The words escaped from me before I registered them. Home. Was that what Syaoto was to me now? I had fought to protect it, slain my first Shadowheart, and even worked alongside Vincent Ordenstraum to get here. I entered that horrifying blue light and somehow saved Syaoto. It seemed meager compared to the things people did for me, but it was a start. I was a Defender, and I saved people almost on my own for once.

Vincent chuckled. "Interesting that you might call something home, Dragontalen. Do you know what a home is? A place that accepts you for who you are, no? Who are you, really? You are not Ryoku Dragontalen, yet everyone will call you such because of the man who gave you his soul. You are taking credit for prophecies you had no part in. You are saving people under a false visage. You seek to save the criminal Chris Olestine, no? The man imprisoned for the murder of my mother?"

I paused. I knew little more than Chris' name and what he looked like. His soul seemed to resonate with mine somehow. Was he actually a murderer, or was Vincent manipulating me?

"You didn't know that, did you?" Vincent asked. He stepped closer, dragging the tip of his sword along the ground as he advanced. I held my place, keeping a grip on the knife at my hip even while I hoped to spot Ragnarokkr.

"You seek him based only on a flimsy feeling. A connection? Some meager hopes? Perhaps he is the same as you: a piece of the hero you once were. Maybe you were hoping he is stronger than you are, and that he can take up this mantle thrown upon your shoulders. Wouldn't that be a relief, to give up the weighty cloak of prophecy and hand it to someone else?"

I hated the look that Loki flashed me. He considered the words of this emperor. I loathed admitting that it made sense, and that I had fully considered it. If Chris was the same as me, then maybe he could take on this life of prophecy people somehow expected to fulfil.

"I thought so once," I said. My voice sounded hauntingly calm in the presence of the approaching emperor of Orden and dark king of Syaoto. I noticed Kimo was still behind Vincent, and he didn't move for or against us. The mention of my sister's name before the light took me gave me the strength to keep talking.

"Once I started realizing what people expected of me, it was terrifying. I got this twisted sword that the Timeless One said belonged to me. People kept saying they know me when I don't even know myself. I became familiar with the darkness, and along with that, my light. Not even that long ago, this was terrifying. I'd have done anything to run away."

I took a deep breath. Vincent paused to listen to me with a wry sneer. Loki seemed enthralled by my words. Dawn was silent, only a hand on my arm as comfort. Just then, I saw something. Just behind Vincent's leg, something caught a brief flicker of light. It was the slash of gold across my blade, the scar left upon it by Kimo Goldenhart.

I glanced at Kimo, who quietly slid his own sword back into his sheath. I saw a black line along the hilt of his weapon that wasn't there before.

It hit me. He purposely directed his blade to reflect off the golden scar on Ragnarokkr. He made it possible to find my sword. He gave me a fighting chance. I couldn't imagine why, seeing as that scar was from him trying to kill me. Right now, he wanted me to win. I needed every chance I could get.

I refocused my attention to Vincent. I needed to buy just a few seconds.

"Then I lost someone. Not a friend I'd had for long, but one that showed me devotion and died for me. At first, that made me want to quit so badly. I wanted to give up even trying. It still hurts like hell. I would resurrect Brozogoth and fight him again just to feel a little better. But over time, it just made me even stronger. It made me realize that this mission is my own. Maybe not for the same reasons. Maybe not how whoever made me this way intended for me to be strong."

I paused. Vincent was hanging onto my every word. Now was my chance. I smiled.

"But I will fight on."

I lunged. It caught Vincent by surprise enough that he hesitated. I dove straight at him, and ducked down as he recovered enough to retaliate. I snatched up my sword by the chain and swung with as much might as I could muster. My weightless marks screamed an angry shade of red as I threw everything I could into one strike.

The clash of steel on steel met me. A strong force slammed into my shoulder that threw me back. I hit the ground hard enough to hurl head-over-heels. My hand screamed with pain; I'd tried to use it, knowing it was injured already, and felt I only strained it further. Whatever struck my shoulder left a burning pain that ignited as I hit the ground. Once more, Ragnarokkr slipped from my grasp

In the split second it had taken to snatch up Ragnarokkr, Vincent's posture differed entirely. He deflected my attack hard enough to deter me, and his open palm emitted smoke from a recent burst of magical energy. From there, he spun around to deflect Loki's incoming strike and knock the Trickster away once more.

The realization hit me like a train. Vincent was going easy on us, and a moment of trying to outsmart him made him prove just how tough he was.

He let out an enraged roar and threw both hands out. Dark waves of energy shot out to both Dawn and Kimo like tsunamis from a black ocean. Their screams were stifled for a moment. When the darkness abated, both fell to the ground, unconscious. A black shroud hovered over Dawn.

"What did you do to her?" I demanded. That darkness rippled through my voice. Before I could move, though, he flexed his hand. Spikes jutted out from the shroud covering Dawn, coming inches from her skin. My heart sank in my chest.

"Enough is enough!" Vincent shouted, and he turned his other hand on me. His violet eyes flashed as dark energy spiraled around his open palm. That darkness must have been what damaged my arm. Even with Advocatos riled up under the surface, I couldn't do anything.

"To think a petty Remnant might try to outsmart me," Vincent snarled furiously. "Well, no more! Here ends the Defender's tale. If luck is with you, perhaps you will rise again as the real hero to face me once more. That might be an opponent worthy of my true strength. If not… then I suppose this is the end of your charade."

Violet energy expanded in his palm and grew to the size of a dog. It cast ghostly light across his old face, making his dark armor shine and the lines in his face appear like grooves.

My mind raced, searching for some bit of information that could save me. Something to distract him long enough for me to force myself to move. My friends below were too busy fighting Shadowhearts to help us. That showed no signs of ending yet.

I only just escaped the clutches of death. It felt like death meant to take me, for the idea never stopped pursuing me. I was only sixteen, and yet faced death more times than I was able to process. There were so many questions I needed to find answers to. Maybe death was the only way to find them. Maybe I could find out who I really was, somewhere in the great beyond.

Even Advocatos didn't respond. I wasn't sure if it could help at all here. Seeing Dawn in a state riled it up, but it couldn't move any more than I could. I remembered feeling it rise as I faced death against Kimo. It might have been the reason I lived. Perhaps it drained all its strength to get me this far, and now I was on my own. Maybe it didn't care. Maybe it knew from Vincent's words that this was what it came down to.

I was helpless as Vincent released his spell. The orb grew to the full height and width of the emperor, and blasted across the ground with a foreboding power that seemed to stretch at the world itself. The dark aura surrounding it could very well be the outside world, the space-like void I'd seen between worlds.

The incoming magic mesmerized me so that a sudden movement before it made me freeze up. A flash of green shot between the blast and I.

My heart seemed to stop, and an instant became an eternity until the next time it would beat.

I saw the face of Loki before me, a bead of sweat trickling down the hook of his nose, his emerald eyes more alight than I had ever seen them, and an easy grin on his face. His arms stretched out, and he looked as though he were holding the entire world at his back.

The violet orb of energy tore at him, flaying his skin, tearing his green tunic asunder as it raged like a living flame. Even as it throttled him, it expanded until it could almost reach around him.

"Loki!" I screamed. I hadn't realized I was able to draw enough breath to speak until I did.

He smiled at me like it was any other day but for the sweat dripping down his face. "I used to hold doubts about you. Now I believe in you more than I ever believed in myself. I need to give you… a fighting chance."

I tried to swallow, but my lungs felt useless. I tried to reach out to him, and my arms couldn't muster up the force. The power radiating from Vincent's orb pinned me to the spot, dragging my heels into the ground. If I could just push forward, I could take the blast and Loki could get away. He was stronger than me. If anyone could defeat Vincent, it was him.

Even then, I knew I was lying to myself. I knew what it meant to see him blocking this attack.

"Loki, stand down," I whispered. My voice came ragged. My face soaked with tears I never saw falling. "Let me take the attack. You… you can still survive! Just stand down! I… I order you, as your Defender!"

He winked, so cheerful-looking for a moment that I pictured him just as easily in Lysvid, or Bonnin, or Vortiger, or even Syaoto before we realized how dangerous it became here.

"Don't fret," he said, voice strained. "You don't have to pretend to be happy for everyone. Don't be afraid to... let that smile relax."

He screamed with force. He threw everything he had into tossing the attack off his shoulders. I didn't realize I was screaming with him, only for the note of my own agony in the air. I tried to reach him, to give him all my strength, but I couldn't.

Loki reared back with all his might, and a rim of golden energy surrounded his body. Only then did the giant orb of violet energy desist. The entire world turned into violet light. When I could see the edge of it, it took on a green rim like a dragon circling the earth.

It struck, and exploded with such ferocity that the entire plateau shuddered violently. I found my numb fingers digging into the earth to hold my ground.

It felt like an eternity before the world fell to darkness once more. It was like when I left the company of Eos, but the air filled with anything but that triumph

Loki teetered before me, his legs slackened, arms hanging limp at his sides. I wasn't sure how I managed to catch him before he fell, or how I lowered him slowly to the ground. A visible outline of his body was charred black from the effects of the blast. I could see his torn skin across his shoulders, neck, and arms. One of his ears was gone, the other charred black. A sob racked my chest from just looking upon him.

I fumbled for my staff, and his own weakened grip stopped me. "I don't recommend doing that," he whispered hoarsely. "The draw on your power would kill you."

"No," I whispered. "You promised to come with me all the way. You... You can't..."

"Ryoku, listen," he whispered. A dry cough struck him, and he almost doubled over. I heard rushed footsteps. Possibly the sound of others climbing up the cliff. I only glanced up briefly enough to notice that Vincent was gone.

"Ryoku, you have to listen. I don't have much time. Remember... what we've spoken about."

I shuddered uncontrollably. I only fought the urge to go for my staff because I had to hold him up. "What do you mean?" I asked. "No, wait, stop. You can't do this! Dawn's here! She can heal you! Dawn!"

Loki's fingers rose enough to stop her as Dawn's hand approached. "To restore energy to a god requires more than just a talented healer," he murmured. "Do not do it. Promise me."

"He's right, Dawn," Katiel's voice said from somewhere nearby, and he appeared to kneel on Loki's other side. "Loki, there's no more honorable way to go. You've done us all proud."

Dawn let out a small cry. Loki only closed his eyes in acknowledgement, but he weakly peered at me. "Ryoku. Stop and listen, please. If I do not speak… you may never come to know the truth."

"Loki, I…" I struggled to speak, but couldn't find words.

A hand appeared on my shoulder. "Let him speak," Katiel told me. "He would not rest otherwise, my friend."

Feeling utterly broken and helpless, I leaned closer to Loki as his words fell to a pained whisper.

"I'm sorry I cannot explain everything," Loki said. "Your father – your true father, is my brother. Odin, the chief of all gods. Seek out my son, Fenrir. He can help you soldier on. That attack may have weakened our foe, but…"

He coughed hard, and I saw the mortal pain in his eyes as they shot wide. I felt all the nerve I had slink away at the sight of him in this state. I knew, in that moment, that I would give anything to save him. It took a long moment for his hazy emerald eyes to return to me. They were as dry as mine were drenched.

"I'm sorry for lying to you for so long. I didn't want you to discover the new part of your soul… because… you are my nephew… first and foremost. But I changed my mind. Maybe… just maybe… you can be both. Fight on, my boy. Until the… last breath…"

I couldn't speak as his emerald eyes shimmered with emotion. I saw his bravery and redemption, his solitude, the love he bore for his late wife, for his daughter and son, and for me. Everything I knew of him, and more, conveyed through his suddenly transparent eyes. I saw the Trickster who defended me from the very moment he met me, and I saw a man built on envy who turned toward the path of light. He brought us laughter, safety, and kindness.

Then, in one shallow breath, he took it all away, and I felt my heart break.

Brom appeared, and knelt next to Loki. He brushed his calloused hand across the Trickster's face. When he removed it, Loki's eyes delicately shut.

"A brave soul," he said gravely. He remained kneeling and looked at me, his eyes like clay. "You would do well to heed his words. The emperor may be gone, but darkness reigns. We are not safe."

A sharp movement occurred behind him. Heads turned. I glanced, but it was hard to feign interest until I saw what was happening. Lancet and Roland stood at the far end of the plateau, blades crossed over Rena's exposed throat. The poor girl was rigid with terror, a single tear rolling down her cheek.

"Surrender now, Dragontalen!" Lancet ordered. He looked somewhat battered since earlier, but his eyes were sharp and clear. "We'll kill her if you move! You don't have the Trickster to save you anymore!"

I couldn't have stood if I wanted to. My arms were hardly in usable condition. Luckily, I didn't have to. I heard what sounded like a pair of heavy footfalls. A figure stumbled into view and struck Lancet soundly across the face with enough power to floor him. The figure towered over him, clothes smeared with dark matter, his greasy hair tousled with sweat – Jason Ramun.

Roland made to retreat, but Kimo appeared, his golden blade laid across Roland's throat. The scientist froze, perturbed.

"It is time for you to leave," Kimo said coldly. His eyes flashed orange once more. Kimo's demon, Romis. "Return to Orden. Tell them what has transpired. If either of you move against the girl, I will kill you both. Do not think I won't."

Roland stared Kimo coldly in the eye for a long moment. "Do not think she will be safe, Goldenhart. If you cross us—"

"You will not. Now leave."

Even Roland, who didn't seem to fear Kimo, quailed before the tone he spoke with. With a lasting glare, Roland snatched Lancet's arm, and the pair vanished with the sound of travel. Kimo's sword dropped, and Rena, stunned, collapsed to her knees. Jason didn't move, his shoulders heaving.

I saw Lusari and Dawn flock to Rena like motherly hens. I saw Katiel hesitating, looking between them and me. Brom stood with his hands clasped over his sword in silent prayer. I saw Sira's haunted expression nearby, but she didn't approach. Kimo stood above his sword, hands trembling.

"Maybe I haven't paid enough attention lately," I heard Jason growl. "Letting these villains do what they would with my home. And now it has come to this."

Nobody replied. Now, our company was more broken than ever before.

(The next day...)

Time moved on no matter how much I wanted it to stop. Everyone stayed on the plateau for a short time – Shadowhearts were still rampant. We had to return to the city.

Brom left to regain command of his army and rout the Shadowhearts remaining in the royal forest. Katiel and Kimo carried Loki's body to the castle. The rest of our company spread out and protected us along the journey back.

In town, our company split. Sira vanished immediately, not to return until the funeral just after sunrise. Many went out into the city to help with the restoration effort. I found myself wandering the city in a convoluted daze. I helped any I came across, but I felt hollow inside. No matter who I helped, I couldn't fill that void. Not from the blacksmith's amicable handshake after helping clear rubble from his store. Not from the innocent smile of a child I reunited with his mother.

How could I keep going like this?

I crossed paths with many of my friends and some from the castle who offered condolences. Many didn't seem to know Loki that well. I wondered why, until I wondered if I even knew him that well.

I found myself sitting at a torn-up fountain in town square. I stared into the markets where we met Rena for the first time. I could almost see Loki where he'd stood up to Brom without understanding the situation, or where he haplessly strutted out of the clothing store in his new Syaoto attire.

"A sorrowful day for all those present. A lament hangs on the winds like a requiem."

The voice came from nearby. I almost didn't heed it, but something told me to look up.

The marketplace wasn't empty, by any means. Peasants, soldiers, and carpenters alike worked together on the restoration effort. A man and woman sobbed openly over a small urn that contained the ashes of their child. Two soldiers escorted a man with a severe limp toward a medic, already bustling between injured patients. One man who I'd helped reunite with his child fought to spread his joy with anyone around him.

I noticed the man sitting next to me on the fountain. He had blond hair spiked up in some precarious wave, clearly of a foreign style. Sky-blue eyes stared up at the sky – hours before, any one of us could have been consumed by it. He dressed foreign, too. I thought he looked like some kind of mercenary. His arms looked well muscled, but they hung listlessly at his sides. He wasn't interested in fighting now.

He turned to me, and I almost jumped when his eyes zeroed in on mine. There was something strange about them. "You were a part of this great loss, weren't you? A tumbler in the lock, a stone in the river. A boy standing alone on a plateau of wizened shadows."

I didn't know what to say. I wasn't sure if he didn't make any sense because of my grief, or just because he didn't seek to make sense. "Yeah, I guess."

He turned away. "Huh. You're no stranger to it, that I'm certain of. Yet it haunts you like none other. Why?"

Now I looked away when he turned to me for answers. "How can you tell that from a look?" I asked him.

He shook his head. "Not a look. A story, written on your skin in blood and ink. I've seen many stories, kid." He sighed, staring up into the listless clouds. "Stories. A thousand words that, in the end, just talk about a simple thing. A fallen hero. A deluded messiah. A misled child. An abandoned warrior. A poorly raised emperor. And when they all come together, they create stories of their own."

He looked at me once more, catching me off guard. "What's your story, kid? What did your loss write in blood for your future?"

As strange and alien as his words were, I felt an odd distillation of comfort. I averted my eyes from him, staring into the heart of the hurt populace of Syaoto. "I don't know," I told him. "A leader, but a follower. He guided me, but followed my guidance. I think he meant a lot more to me than I would address, because he liked acting aloof about the whole thing."

The man chuckled. "Funny how love does that, doesn't it? Hides in plain sight until the object of your love is gone."

I stared at him incredulously. "Uh, not like that. I mean, I didn't—"

"You're not listening, kid," he said, and chuckled. "People call love the star-struck sort between a man and woman – guy and guy, girl and girl, or whatever you want to call it. Sure, that's a big, huge thing in everyone's lives. I think there's an even more important one, though. Comradery. The people you meet who each write a word on the scripture of your heart. Who you'd more than miss if they were gone, and who you might not even appreciate in the minute.

"Its love, it is, and it's more important than anything in this world. It's gotta be what you fight for. It'll always have a hand on the hilt of your sword. If you ever find that something else leads your hand, then you should put down your weapon."

I stared at him as he spoke. "It'll... always have a hand on the hilt of my sword...?"

He smiled grimly. "Yup. You know that, don't you? You just needed somebody to remind you."

I looked away again, and tears threatened the corners of my eyes again. The stranger unwittingly drew on things I could picture Loki trying to tell me. "I..."

Where I looked away, I saw Guildford approaching. My teacher looked lonely and hurt. I'd never seen such a look on him before. I turned to the stranger to excuse myself from him, but the figure was gone without a trace.

Guildford came and sat with me for a time. He didn't speak, only offered his company. I couldn't meet his gaze, and he didn't expect me to. Later, others hung in the shadows with no idea how to approach me. I wasn't sure if I wanted them to.

I was no stranger to funerals. The deaths of both my parents happened for me at a young age. Guildford's own funeral was only earlier this year. I had even been to one in the spirit realm already for Sapphense. This was a funeral for one I hadn't known long, but possibly one of the biggest impacts on me. Loki broke into my life in the loudest way, and his flame didn't die until he sacrificed himself for me to go on fighting. Maybe not even then.

Everyone gathered at the funeral, some for the last time. I knew some would be returning home. We must be continuing from Syaoto soon, but I didn't want to think about it.

What could I do now? Charging on to Orden felt useless and stupid. What could I accomplish? Startle Vincent once more with my own stupidity? I already knew I wasn't strong enough to fight him. We needed an army if we wanted to wage war on the dark empire. I couldn't possibly muster the nerve to rile up a whole world to go fight another. I could lose others in that battle. Will. Sira. Guildford.

On the day of the funeral, we found ourselves deep in the Royal Forest amid the trees. Loki's grave was the sole tombstone in the woods. The ground was been smoothed over by soldiers after the turmoil, and the beginnings of new grass crept up amid the tossed earth. The trees cleared at the end of this path, where daylight shone through the dusty air and made the pollen sparkle like ashes. I found myself sitting at a vantage point, alone atop a small hill above the scene.

Soldiers and commanders of the army stopped me to give me their condolences. By the sound of it, they regarded Loki as something of a martyr, and they respected me in the same light. It was undeserved on my end. All I'd done was become the reason this happened.

I sat by myself while Guildford was speaking for Loki in the center of the clearing. All eyes were on the teacher. Nobody noticed when the tree behind me shuddered. I glanced back, sure that I was just imagining it, when a strong grip latched onto my ankle. Before I could make a sound, it dragged me into the earth, swallowing me into deep, utter darkness.

...End of Act Eight.

ACT NINE: SEPARATION

*In the eyes of Sira Jessura, we are in
Syaoto's Royal Forest, in the world of Syaoto.
It is high morning
On November 15th, 2017.*

SCENE ONE: PLAN OF ACTION

"Any sign of him on your end?"

I shook my head futilely. "Nothing. What about you?"

Kimo stared away deliberately. "We scoured the forest. If he were still in Syaoto, he can't have gone far. At the least, we should search the Capital."

"He'd never have made it that far," Katiel said. He leaned against a tree with his arms crossed, glancing away. "He's not replyin' in my world, either. This whole city knows his face now if they didn't already. Somebody would see him. Same goes for Will."

"The latest hero of Syaoto isn't cutting through town without word spreading," Anna agreed. The mysterious black-haired Defender seemed perturbed enough by the situation to help, the most emotion I'd seen her display yet.

Kimo stared at his feet. I watched him with trepidation. It seemed, during the events of fighting Vincent, Kimo tried to help Ryoku. There was no chance our Defender could have really succeeded, but now Kimo was here helping us track him down. The whole situation was weird. Ryoku somehow slipped out of view in the middle of Loki's funeral and vanished. We had no idea how long he was gone for, but it had to be less than an hour. Someone with his weightless ability could have made it to the capital by then.

"No way he just left," Kimo muttered. "He can't cross worlds alone yet. No one who could even help him was anywhere near. He must still be nearby somehow."

"Ryoku isn't the only one who has disappeared as of late," Guildford said in a somewhat intense tone. "For what reason did you and Will embark from the castle? It was dangerous, and it sparked events I don't believe you intended to happen."

I didn't think he'd spare Guildford a response, but he looked him in the eye. "I heard rumor of something which could help against the emperor," he said. "When that... phenomenon, occurred, Will continued on toward the Enthralmen Jungle."

I wasn't the only one who gave Kimo a mistrusting glance. "You really wanted to help against Vincent?" Katiel asked. "Why? We heard what you did to Ryoku, y'know. You don't seriously think we'd blindly place our trust in you now?"

"Will chose to go with him," Guildford inferred, "assuming that was, in fact, a choice."

"Will was angry with me, too," Kimo admitted. "Quite so. I offered the information as a means to partially redeem myself. We were to go to the Enthralmen Jungle, procure the Scepter of Blight, and return before anyone noticed our absence."

"The Scepter of Blight?" I asked dryly. "The hell's that? Can't anyone think up decent names for things anymore?"

Kimo scowled, clearly not appreciating my humor. "According to legend, the scepter belonged to the first Syaoto king, King Ramenas Pendragon. It likely has a history predating that of this new world. The important thing is that the scepter can apparently negate any magic used against it. If anything could make Ryoku Dragontalen survive against Vincent..."

"This new world?" Guildford asked. "What do you mean by that?"

Kimo exchanged a dry look with me. "What a favor the old hero has done us, making all forget what once was," he said morosely. "The old version of him, Ryoku, destroyed the old spirit realm we once had in an attempt to stop a grave enemy. The attempt was largely futile and has done more harm than good, according to my mentor."

Guildford had an intriguing look in his eyes, as though Kimo's words tugged at something in his memory. He didn't elaborate, though.

"Who's this mentor?" I asked. "You workin' for some kind of third party or something?"

"A favorable party," Kimo said. "An interestingly changed man who is a placeholder in this war. However, that discussion is not for this moment. I wouldn't disclose his name for now."

"We're supposed to trust that?" Katiel asked suspiciously. "You're not doing a great job of this. Didn't I overhear that you can be tracked through your arm?"

Kimo regarded Katiel with his own mistrust for a moment, but it evaporated. He raised his mechanical arm. The appendage was an oddity I hadn't initially noticed about Kimo Goldenhart in the throne room, but something about it rang with familiarity. "Correct," he replied, "but I have some time, I believe. Vincent Ordenstraum must have taken damage during his fight against Loki. On top of that, I dismissed Roland, who has probably fled to the capital. As flighty and minor as Roland is, he won't strike against me yet."

Katiel smirked. "Sounds about right," he muttered. "Needs to update his revenge journal first."

Kimo smiled at that. "It only leaves one question," he went on, turning to me with a serious expression. "We have multiple things that require our attention. You'll want to arrange something in an attempt to track Ryoku, I imagine, but I would ask to borrow your strength. I wish to follow Will and resume the hunt for the scepter."

I gave him an odd look. "Will went after it last night, didn't he?" I asked. "You think we can catch up with him?"

Kimo nodded. "Now that the world is safe, I want to follow him. Lending some of your strength to me would help me catch up to him. After all, your current numbers are pretty impressive."

"This world is not entirely safe."

A familiar booming voice cut through the forest. I was getting too used to that voice to be alarmed, and sighed instead. The Timeless One approached us, winged by his regular assistant, Relus, and his returned one, Rex.

"The dark creatures remain on this tainted world. Any who walk outside the city walls without due protection are in certain danger. I admit that their severity has been weakened, but they are more than a match for any wandering citizen. It's a highly curious scenario that I am unable to calculate entirely on my own. Perhaps this idea of yours will give us a toe on the monkey!"

The Timeless One's words brought stunned silence to our small circle. "Toe on the monkey?" Katiel asked wondrously. "Has anyone ever taught you how to talk?"

Relus cleared his throat. "I believe my master may have meant 'a leg up on the situation.' Currently unclear, however." He adjusted his glasses, sunlight flashing across his eyes along with a beguiled smile. "Point being, we overheard your conversation. The Timeless One suggests that we followers of Ryoku hold a council over our next move, for there are several things that require our attention. Yours is but one of our responsibilities."

"As he says," the Timeless One agreed, and bowed deeply before us – his hat fell from his head, and Relus swooped down to catch it by the brim and replace it on his master's head before it could touch the ground. Loyal, much. "You are all aware of the prophecies, no? The time of reckoning is nearly upon us. Ryoku requires us, and yet, the boy is nowhere to be found. We must seek each others' counsel."

"Syaoto is broken after the events that shook it to the core," Relus added. "If we can spare the manpower for a short time, I would very much like to help them with their reparations. Of course, the land is also without a reigning king or queen since the departure of Vincent. We owe this land certain respects in helping them solve their affairs."

"Couldn't agree more," Katiel said. "It wouldn't hurt to still send word out around neighboring towns, on the off chance that Ryoku is still around."

"We should go to the castle," Kimo said. He started walking, tapping his sword with his metal hand. "Summon all of your allies. We can figure out our next move there."

"Let us hurry," Guildford agreed. "This is not something to leave to rest."

(Later, in Syaoto Keep...)

"Say what?" Guildford asked the general disbelievingly. "Are you sure about this?"

The reinstated Lord General of Syaoto's army and good ally to us, Brom Gerenadh, nodded affirmatively. "Miss Atella was last seen in the castle courtyard early this morning prior to the funeral of Master

Loki. She refused any close guard detail despite the lurking danger. Regardless, some of my men stationed themselves near the door. No guards saw her depart, or, for that matter, anyone else arriving. She seems to have vanished."

"This sorta makes sense," Katiel said with a shrug. "If she disappeared like this, maybe Ryoku left the same way? We were all there at the funeral. The odds that none of us saw him go are a little backless. Maybe they somehow left together, wherever they are."

"That would be a preferable scenario," Guildford agreed. "At least Ryoku wouldn't be alone. Lusari is a capable young woman."

"Lusari wasn't seen at the funeral, either," I argued. "You seriously think something could have snatched them up at the same time?"

"Another matter we must consider for this meeting," the Timeless One noted. "Let us take council now. Everyone appears to be here."

With the arrival of Brom and his news, the Timeless One was right. What a group we had. I spotted the tall, sandy hair of Alex among a group of fellow soldiers, winged by Joey – the two seemed to have become fast friends – and Oliver, sporting his field commander armor. Cleria drifted up to join the Timeless One's little group. Lamont clasped hands with Guildford in kind. Even Sorha, the strange demon girl that Ryoku never properly explained, hung in the shadows in the room.

Dawn and Anna discussed something urgent with Katiel apart from everyone else. As strong as they were, the pair of female Defenders were unnerving. Dawn nearly tore the city apart with her nature magic the day she arrived. In contrast, Anna was like a shadow, drifting in and out of the group with as much ease as though she weren't there at all.

Among all the warriors, mages, and vampires, Rena was a little out of her comfort zone. Still, she made a point of sticking to Will's side since we saved her from the brawl in the city. She didn't look like herself without him here.

With the appearance of Dawn Elethel, Kaia became a fly on the wall. The girl kept to the sidelines since her arrival. Dawn kept close to Katiel or Ryoku at all times – Kaia's two favorite people, I thought – and the fact made the water mage anxious. Now, though,

Katiel's friends from Bonnin returned to hang in the shadows with her. Artos, the dark-clad ninja, and Eckhardt, the friendly knight in white armor, kept Kaia company as she glared at Dawn in total envy.

After looking around, Kimo scowled. "What of that man who stepped in on the plateau?"

"Jason Ramun?" I asked, and shrugged. "Beats me. Haven't seen him since we left the forest. After what I heard about him, it's probably for the best."

Everyone fell silent as the Timeless One took the center of the room with Guildford and Brom.

"Welcome, friends old and new," the Timeless One greeted us. "We have quite a predicament on our hands. Three of our own are missing. Ryoku Dragontalen, Will Ramun, and Lusari Atella are all gone. Our priority remains to find Ryoku, but tracking down the others are likely connected."

"Will has departed to the Enthralmen Jungle in search of a relic," Guildford spoke, loud and clear. That must be his teacher voice. "A relic exists that may assist in our battle against Vincent. Kimo Goldenhart wishes to lead a few of us in pursuit of him."

A few people gave Kimo distrusting looks. The blond warrior leaned against the wall, arms crossed, the picture of an angtsy, ambiguous character. His blue eyes stuck on the center of the room, and he didn't appear to notice any discontent aimed his way.

Guildford turned to Brom next, who cleared his throat. "With the betrayal of our last king, Syaoto seeks a new ruler," Brom spoke. "It is hardly the concern of you who have done us such a great service already, but we would humbly request your presence to help select a new ruler. We highly value what opinions you might have to offer toward our choice. On another note, we could use the manpower to battle the Shadowhearts that have appeared around the city. If any are able to assist in instructing my men how to fight them, the kingdom would owe you eternal gratitude."

"Then, we must find Ryoku," Guildford finished. "I will be heading to some neighboring towns to ask about him. In the effort, I'll battle any Shadowhearts we cross paths with. I'll keep an eye out for Lusari, too, although we don't have much in the way of clues on her behalf."

I looked at Guildford in surprise. For a schoolteacher, he cut an astonishing figure standing next to Syaoto's own Iron Bear, Brom Gerenadh. The general shifted, looking around at the table.

"One thing before we begin," Brom spoke with the clipped voice of a general. "Many of you have mentioned these... prophecies that Ryoku is in. I have heard nothing about these. What are they about? Not that I wholly have any doubts, but why is Ryoku Dragontalen so... special?"

There were a few knowing looks around the table. "You're correct," the Timeless One said. "Those prophecies are not exactly commonplace. Perhaps Balgena's magic school would have them, but not the kingdom of Syaoto."

"They derive from Ryoku's past," Katiel added. "Our past. His. Mine. Dawn's. A past that brings everyone together as a stem of the legend."

"A thousand years ago, Ryoku Dragontalen was a normal villager," Dawn said. She smiled wistfully at the thought, as though she personally recalled it. "He managed to rise up and save an entire continent stemming from his actions. His family name comes from a long line of warriors. His sword has been cast down through their family for centuries."

Relus adjusted his glasses. "Even though Laia eventually fell to ruin, the spirit of Ryoku Dragontalen went on to be reborn almost exactly a thousand years ago. He rose up as a Defender in the spirit realm that existed up until a few months ago – where we all stem from, one way or another."

Katiel nodded amicably. "And then he saved us again."

"With our help." Anna added quietly. Dawn and Katiel looked at her, but she didn't appear bitter about it, nor did she elaborate.

"He wasn't the only Defender who fought, yes," Katiel agreed. "We all played a pivotal role. We do have our opinions, though, that we might not have come together without him. Or stayed together, for that matter. Some of us are particularly diverse."

Dawn and Anna both nodded vigorously. I thought I saw the Timeless One's glance flicker in amusement.

"There is a lot to the legend, naturally," Relus said. "Right now, that's all we need to know. It's all most of the spirit realm remembers, if they do recall his name." He directed his attention to Brom. "Know that Vincent Ordenstraum acts against not only Ryoku Dragontalen – no doubt he knows just who he is – but against the entirety of the spirit realm. Given the chance, he would not stop at conquering Syaoto. He would sweep up as many of the realms as he could. Isn't that right, Sira?"

I jumped, surprised at being called upon, but my expression quickly melted into steel. "About sums it up," I replied. "I don't need Ryoku as a reason to fight Vincent – I have my own. We all do, now."

"He is a smart man." Kimo spoke from the edge of the room, drawing everyone's attention to him. "Given he's with Roland Demizen, a genius in his own name, Vincent has no shortage of plans to conquer. Having been thwarted by Loki's attack – which I have no doubt he survived – he'll go on to the next plan. He'll infiltrate Jerule, or Vortiger, or Harohto, or Bonnsyara. He has the plans. He needs only to act."

Lamont's expression turned sharp. "He has plans to conquer Vortiger?"

Katiel shrugged. "Roland's annoying, but he's damned smart. With his backing, Vincent has all the brainpower he needs."

Brom cleared his throat. The simple action turned everyone to look at him. He stood at the head of the table still, his rough face chiseled into a steely expression. Looking upon him, I had no doubts that the man was as much bite as he was bark.

"I have no doubts," Brom told us. "None. Vincent Ordenstraum seized my kingdom, likely killing my liege King Lionel to do so. Out of the entire kingdom, your company was the only one to attempt raising a hand in revolt. Prophecies or no, I do believe Ryoku Dragontalen, and your entire company as a whole, is capable of change."

As he spoke, he strolled over to stare out the window of the council room. The wide bay window opened out over the east wall of the castle, out into the plains where Ryoku and I fought demons a few days ago. From the heights of Syaoto Keep, the hills that closed in the castle were like mounds of sand, and we could see for miles to the east. A small village nestled in the crook of a mountain, and a river jutted across the land not far from where Ryoku and I had been. In the black of night, we could have never seen it. Sharp mountains jutted up in the distance, and forest grew on them like beards. Under the view of an autumn, cloudless sky, Syaoto was pretty – even I had to admit that.

I probably shared those thoughts with Brom, but this was his homeland. To him, this was a place worth dying for. In lieu of death, he'd stand and fight for it like nobody else ever could.

"You will have our armies," he said gravely, with all the weight of the world he stared down on. "Syaoto will be as it if it were yours. In Ryoku Dragontalen's name, and in the name of my close friend Will Ramun, knight of the King's Own."

A few heads turned. "The King's Own?" Guildford asked.

"Will was that high-ranking of a guy?" Cleria asked teasingly. She looked like she relished the idea.

"The King's Own disbanded, didn't it?" I asked. "We heard it disbanded because nobody wanted to serve Vincent."

A smile spread Brom's wizened face. "Disbanded, perhaps. It does yet exist, waiting for a king to fit into the throne once more. Will was at the heart of it, and losing him for a long time dampened the hearts of our knights. If he should return…"

He didn't elaborate, but I saw the hopeful smile return on Alex and Oliver's faces. In the lull of the moment, Brom approached Guildford and held out a hand.

"You speak for Ryoku Dragontalen, yes?" he asked. "In his absence, I would put a great responsibility upon you. I have already asked you to help us find a king and to help save our people. What you have done – what *all* of you have done for us – outweighs that. As Lord General of Syaoto's Royal Army, I would pledge our armies to serve you. You, Guildford… is that a title of yours?"

Guildford smiled, a little uneasy. "John Guildford, if you must know. I do prefer just my last name, however."

"Sir John Guildford," Brom repeated. "I like you. You are a modest man. Ryoku Dragontalen is the hero of your group. Aside from that, Will is the only link between us. I would place upon you a title that grants you the same privileges. Specifically, I want you to be one of our leading men in the battle against Orden. An ambassador, a commander."

Guildford stared at Brom with an unreadable expression. Surely, the words must have moved him. He began an original school teacher, then moved on to study and train with vampires, to travel alongside a Defender and past student, then to live among and ride dragons. Now he was being offered a serious place in Syaoto?

"Perhaps we could discuss this at more length later?" Guildford asked. "I don't wish to dishonor you, but I hope that our quarrel with Orden can end without total war. If Ryoku winds up in battle with them, then I will charge on with all that I have at my disposal. Otherwise, I would end things peacefully. Our fight leads to Vincent Ordenstraum, not to his people. Ryoku needs me right now."

For a moment, I thought Brom might be mad. His expression looking stony as ever, he stepped toward Guildford and clapped his shoulder. "You do not cease to surprise me, John Guildford. As well, you do not cease in showing me that I have chosen the right battle. I wish you would stay and help us find our next ruler. Surely your judgement would help us."

Guildford smiled, putting a hand on Brom's. "I cannot. Ryoku has helped me in many ways I cannot explain, and I cannot leave him to his own devices now. If I have my way, I'll walk into Orden at his side."

"You would be a fool not to," Brom told him. "Very well. Let us resume the moot point of this council. Friends of Ryoku, speak your piece. What path will you take?"

A buzz of conversation filled the room as everyone discussed the options. Brom, Guildford, and the Timeless One waited it out for a long moment, letting everyone decide. After a few minutes passed, the Timeless One cleared his throat with his booming voice, and all turned to him.

"The Defenders will speak first," he said, and nodded to Katiel.

"I'll do a comb-over of nearby worlds," Katiel announced. "Best if I just take my people. I've got Eckhardt, Kaia, and Artos with me, and I'll send word through Dawn if I find anything out."

"I'll stay to help you allocate a new king," Dawn added with a smile. "You could say I've got past experience with this sort of thing. After that, we'll see. I'd be better with Ryoku if we can find him."

Joey shrugged. "I'll go for the adventure. Heading to the Enthralmen Jungle sounds more my style. From there, I'll see what else I can do to help out."

Expectantly, all heads turned to Anna. When she realized it was her turn, she glanced away, going a little red in the face.

"I'll do my own thing," she said. Even from the side, it looked like her eyes were alight with emotion. She attempted to sound uncaring, but was it a ruse?

Everyone waited a moment for her to elaborate, but she didn't. A few glances exchanged. Dawn shrugged and mouthed words that Guildford seemed to understand. "Alright," he agreed with a nod. "Next, we'll go on with the order in which our allies were met by Ryoku. Sira, if you will?"

I jumped, surprised at being called upon first. Of course, Guildford had to pick some meaningful way to go about this. I froze for a moment. I hadn't thought this through. More than anything, I wanted to ditch everyone and go hunting for Ryoku on my own. Before shacking up with this group, that was how I did things, and I was fine by it.

However, glancing around at all the familiar faces, I knew I couldn't abandon them. Everyone here had some sort of stakes in the coming battles. Besides whatever thing Ryoku and I had going, I needed to face my past and fight against Orden. With Loki gone, it just made this fight a little more personal. Ryoku must feel the same way.

After some thought, I met Guildford's glance. "I'll go with you. If he's here, we'll find him. I guess we'll check anywhere that makes sense, but hopefully we figure something out before we prowl the entire countryside. Until then, we'll knock some Shadowheart heads together."

Guildford smirked. "Glad to have you, Sira," he replied. I had a feeling he knew what I'd choose before I did. He turned to Alex next. "Alex, our group considers you a friend to us after all you've done on our behalf. If you'd like to come along with any of us, you're welcome to."

Alex nodded fervently. The young soldier looked a lot older than when we first worked with him back in Harohto. He was still scrawny and nervous, but there was a glow to him he never had before. "I will go with Kimo to the Enthralmen Jungle," he replied easily. "Don't worry – I already asked Brom about it, seeing as he *is* my Lord General again. Anyway, one of our recent expeditions led us into that jungle after a Mandragora. I could help navigate the area."

"Ah, the Mandragora," Brom recalled with a frown. "I'd forgotten about that. Pray you don't run into one of those foul beasts again."

Alex agreed with a furtive nod. "What about you, Ollie? Are you gonna come with?"

Oliver and Brom exchanged a furtive glance. We hadn't heard much from Oliver Rouge since learning that he was a Field Commander now. He'd been nothing but helpful to us back in Harohto.

Oliver gave Alex a tight smile. "My place is here, with my Lord General. I will help oversee the affairs of finding a new king for Syaoto. In Will's stead, I believe I could help out to some degree."

The room fell momentarily silent. I could tell I wasn't the only one worried about Will and the others. We'd been inseparable for so long. I'd gone off in Bonnin once, but otherwise I was practically glued to Ryoku's side. At his other side, no matter what, was always Will, and Lusari on his other side. That was how it'd been for so long.

"Is it on us next?" the Timeless One asked excitedly, clumping together with Relus, Cleria, and Rex. Rex looked most unhappy with getting drawn in, but he tolerated it. "Oh, I was excited to share this! You see, I have considered Loki's last words carefully." His eyes flashed oddly, but the moment seemed to pass quickly. "I would like to seek out his son, Fenrir, and see if he would not come to Ryoku's aid."

His words carried an enormity to them that many of us hadn't come to terms with. The death of Loki was a sudden and terrible loss. One of the last things he'd told Ryoku was to find his son, Fenrir. The idea of fetching his son to replace all that Loki had done for us carried some gravity to it that I wasn't ready to accept.

"Send him our best," Guildford said softly, "for his father. His loss is one that has wounded us deeply."

Rex inclined his head. "I will pass on the message," he assured us.

The Timeless One turned to his assistant. "Why don't you go with Guildford, Relus?" he asked. "I won't be gone for long. I could use Rex as a witness, and you could prove useful to the others here while I'm away."

Relus looked surprised. I wondered if he was ever apart from the Timeless One. "Very well," he agreed, and smiled at Guildford. "At least it is with an old friend. I only hope I can be useful."

"Absolutely," Guildford agreed cheerfully. "We could catch up on matters since I left the castle."

While they conversed, I noticed Katiel was giving the Timeless One an increasingly confused look. By the time the Timeless One finally looked at him, Katiel's brow rose and his eyes seemed to flicker. He turned away as though he'd seen a ghost. Perplexed, I turned my attention to Lamont as Guildford turned to the Rider for his opinion.

"I could attend the coronation," he said. "I have experience with judging council members. However, I can also help you reach the Enthralmen Jungle with more haste. I will summon Leiogrey to aid you."

"You can summon your dragon from here?" Relus asked, intrigued.

"It only makes sense," the Timeless One said with a wry smile. "Dragons defy the newfound structure of our worlds. A dragon in Lysvid could overhear our conversation and decide to drop in. They only have to know we're here."

"Are there dragons in Lysvid, then?" Alex asked curiously, but the Timeless One only gave him a funny look.

"That being said," Lamont went on, looking at Kimo. "I am unclear of your allegiance. I trust Leiogrey only for the presence of other friends of Ryoku. If I find him to be mistreated, or your methods are discovered less than savory, I will see to it that you don't return to your kingdom."

Kimo nodded gravely. "I would never mistreat a dragon, no matter its keeper," he promised. Although it didn't sound the most enthusiastic, Lamont seemed to take it for its value and didn't protest. He still had the young man locked in a wary glare when they called upon Rena. Many curious faces turned toward her. Was she going to stay with us?

"I could attend the coronation," she said, "provided I am welcome there. After seeing the corruption that nearly seized this kingdom, I would like to play a part in securing it. Friends of Ryoku, you all seem like excellent and wise people. I would love to be another voice in finding the best leader for my kingdom."

Guildford smiled at her. "You are welcome with us, Rena, but do you have nowhere to go? No family waiting at home for you?"

Rena shook her head. "My pastor told me that I would find family here," she replied. "I may have found something even more valuable. I will wait and see. Until my birth family should make itself apparent, I will join you. Perhaps I can learn how to wield a sword and be of some use. Shadowhearts will not cease on their own after all, it seems."

I didn't miss Brom exchanging words with another soldier waiting on the room who'd approached him, looking at Rena. Oliver listened, arms folded over his chest. The girl was blind to it. Will had also shown a great deal of interest in her. Maybe her home was here.

Guildford called on Sorha next. The demon glided into the center of the room like one of the evil creatures swarming outside. "About time, teacher," she mused, looking around at us all from beneath her lashes. "Order-wise, you're a little late getting to me, I'd say. Ryu and I are old acquaintances."

"Just who are you?" I demanded. She glanced at me, a smirk tugging at the corner of her lip.

"Ryu introduced me, didn't he?" she asked demurely. "The real story is not important right now. I could go out and track him down all on my own, but the Prince of Demons is still asleep. I'll stay with you for now. In fact, girl, you're going with the teacher to check out the neighboring villages? I'll tag along. Dante knows I can fight Shadowhearts with much more efficiency. You'll be glad to have me."

The way she spoke suggested Dante actually knew she could fight, rather than a figure of speech. Either way, I didn't like her involvement with Ryoku in the slightest. Even if it was with the Prince of Demons in his mind, that almost made it worse. The only part of her words I didn't doubt was her effectiveness against Shadowhearts. I'd seen her fight last night.

"Alright then," Guildford spoke with an inward sigh and looked around at us all. "I trust everyone is pleased with their decisions. Let us move swiftly. Sira, Relus, Sorha. We'll leave as soon as we're prepared. I hope the rest of you will act with as much urgency. As well, do recall that we are but humble guests at the castle of Syaoto. Act with respect and help wherever we can. On your way out, if anyone needs help, I hope you'll stop to help them. Don't do it for me. Do it for yourself, or for Ryoku."

He cut off the short council with that. Guildford, Relus, Sorha and I grouped together at the corner of the room while everyone split off. Kimo, Joey, and Alex spoke with Lamont only for a moment before all of them left the room. Katiel and his friends departed directly from the room after Katiel bade Dawn farewell. Kaia hung closely to him, seemingly eager to have him to herself again. When they left the room, the faint sound of world travel seemed to echo behind them, and the pale afterimage of Kaia sticking her tongue out at Dawn.

Dawn was alone, wringing her hands as she stared into an upper corner of the room. Rena approached her with a tentative smile. The Timeless One, after a brief word with Brom, left the room as well, winged by Rex and Cleria. Anna watched them go before she, too, world-traveled from the room.

Brom and Oliver spoke quietly for a moment. Brom looked at Guildford with admiration, and Oliver looked hopeful. After their piece before the council began, I wondered how things would play out between us and the kingdom.

"Are we ready to go?" Guildford asked. He looked confident in his leadership, which I supposed a teacher should be. "I need only grab my supplies. A quarter of an hour, and I'll be set."

"Be swift," Sorha said cuttingly, crossing her arms. "If Ryu is still in Syaoto, he could have crossed half this world by now. If we walk by night, Shadowhearts thrive alongside the demon ilk of this world. Neither is a problem on their own, but together... I might have to let one of you die."

Guildford and I exchanged furtive glances. Relus adjusted his glasses meekly. Nobody seemed entirely happy to have this demon with us. I didn't like her affectionate nickname for Ryoku, either.

"I'll grab my supplies," I said.

"Do it," Guildford replied softly. "Relus, could you consider renting horses from the stables for us? I believe I have something quick I must tend to before we depart."

"Of course," Relus agreed quickly. Maybe he saw the odd look in his eyes, too. We all glanced at each other once before leaving the room.

SCENE TWO: THE KEEPER OF DEATH

...Of Act Nine: Separation

In the eyes of Ryoku Dragontalen, we are in Crater Field, in the world of Vxxyura. It is late morning On November 15th, 2017.

The next thing I knew, I was laying face-up on some sort of craggy ground, a strange, twisted sky above me, murky-colored and filled with oddly parted clouds. It looked almost like the sky in Syaoto if it completed its falling process. This place carried an eerie atmosphere that gave me the chills. A golden orb shimmered in the sky behind a miasmic cloud. It didn't quite look like a moon, but it was too dull to be a sun. It offered dull light to the eerie world I found myself in.

My body felt enflamed and sore, and I rose with great difficulty. It felt as though I'd been carried here and tossed to the ground. That, and I hadn't eaten in either world for quite some time. It wasn't a necessity to consume food in my spirit form, but I felt weak as a result.

As I looked around, I wondered if finding food was even possible here. The ground near me was rocky and uneven with a purplish-grey hue to it, filled with craters and erratic slopes. It made me think of pictures I'd seen of the moon. I couldn't see anything around me but uneven ground and lurking fog of a pale toxic color. No buildings, no trees or grass, and definitely no people.

I felt like shambles from the battle yesterday, let alone from everything else that transpired in Syaoto. My wrist, injured by Vincent, died down to a dull ache. I wondered if it was broken or merely twisted. My shoulder suffered some kind of severe burn from his energy blast – the skin reddened all the way from my mid-arm to my bicep, and a darker hue around my shoulder blade where it struck. My chest still ached from the field of demons. Getting anywhere was going to be tough.

It was difficult to will myself to move. I had so many questions I couldn't ask anyone about since Loki's death. The events surrounding Syaoto brought me to a greatened height of understanding my role in this world. Facing off against Vincent was now personal, as much as part of me wanted to run away with my friends and never see the powerful, toad-like emperor again. He was ready and waiting for me. Maybe Loki's rebounded spell injured him, but I couldn't hope for an advantage. I needed to increase my skills in order to face this evil.

He wasn't alone, either. Lancet was on his side too, a fact that didn't surprise me about the corrupted officer. Twisted as he was, Lancet was a seriously tough knight. I recalled his brief duel with Will just after our first meeting. Getting past him could be almost as difficult as the inevitable fight with Vincent.

Katiel downplayed Roland and assured me that the man was no problem, but Katiel was stronger than me. Roland was wickedly smart, even if he didn't seem physically strong by any means. An intelligent enemy could be just as bad. He seemed unkillable. A smart, persistent enemy might be worse. I had to be prepared for all of this opposition when I recollected myself to go after Vincent again.

While I contemplated, movement caught my eye that made me clutch my knife, and I winced from the pain in my wrist. The movement occurred again, coming from one of the craters in the craggy ground nearby. As I stared, trying to figure out how I could defend myself while in such pain, a head appeared over the edge of the rocks. It looked like some kind of shadowy orb beset with a pair of luminous golden eyes. Bent black appendages stuck out from both sides of its circular head, possibly horns or ears.

The creature stared at me from afar for a moment, and blinked. I froze to the spot, one hand loosely gripping my knife, staring back. Was it faster than me? Could it reach me before I freed my knife? More importantly, could I fight like this?

"Hello."

A small, rotund voice came from the creature. It sounded distinctly childlike, but with a haunting note to it that kept my hand on my knife. While I stared at it, perplexed, it lifted one claw. The hand looked as twisted as its bent ears, hooked with four sharp talons made of the same dark substance. Still watching me like a boy attentively approaching a stray dog, it lifted its other hand, and started to rise from the pit. I watched as the creature climbed out, examining me warily. It was about the size of a small dog and walked like a primate, using a pair of spindly back legs and supporting itself mostly with those huge claws. Darkness made up its entire body, and a spiraled tail poked from its rear.

It hit me. "You're a Shadowheart," I murmured. The creature froze, almost as though surprised I could speak. It tilted its large head to the side, its large golden eyes unblinking. Then, it shook its head.

"No Shadowheart," it responded almost irritably. Speaking opened up a small mouth below its eyes that I couldn't discern from its face until it opened. "Name Bohko. Just Bohko."

"Bohko?" I asked. "But you're clearly a Shadowheart. What else is made of shadows like you?" I stopped myself. I was arguing with a shadow.

Bohko shook its head again. "No Shadowheart. Just Bohko." It pointed between itself and me with one of its clawed hands, using a single claw as emphasis. "Bohko was like you. Shadowheart not like you. Bohko was like you, so Bohko is Bohko."

I didn't understand a lick of what it was trying to say. "But you're made of shadows."

The creature giggled, a high-pitched, squeaky laugh. "Shadows made of Bohko," it responded. If I didn't know better, I thought it sounded smug. "Bohko came first. First light, then dark. Sun, then moon. Bohko, then Shadowheart. Bohko, then boy."

"You came before... me?" I asked, trying to discern what this little creature could possibly mean. "Well, where are we? Is this your home?"

Bohko shook its head fiercely. "No home. Home gone. This place not home. This Vxxyura, fallen place. Nothing home here."

I glanced around as long as I dared with this creature staring me down from a few feet away. It could attack at any moment. Although, I thought, it surely realized I was hurt and couldn't fight. If it meant harm, wouldn't it have attacked by now? Those big claws would make short work of me.

When I registered what it said, I realized I heard of this place. "Vxxyura. The fallen world. So this is near Syaoto." Bohko looked at me, but didn't reply. "This is a fallen world?" I asked. "This world… ended?"

Bohko nodded. "This world once great jungle. Once grass beneath feet, not stone. Time takes away. All worlds fall to this soon. Then Bohko go home."

"Where is your home?" I asked quickly, and was unsure I should have.

"Same as you," it said, pointing one long claw at me. "World below. A past place. Half-worlder like you goes there, but home gone for now."

I had to think hard to discern its possible meaning. "Half-worlder. Defender?" It nodded, and I thought deeper. "The old spirit realm Kimo talked about?" I asked, half to myself. "You know about that?"

Bohko tapped its dome impatiently. "All know, only forget."

"Right," I said. That sounded a lot like something Kimo would have said, only not like a caveman Shadowheart creature. "Well, how do I get out of here? I have places I need to be, but I was dragged here somehow."

Bohko shook its head. "No easy leave," it said sadly. "Vxxyura hard to leave for Ryu. No settlements. No people. Only tower."

I struggled not to strangle the frustrating creature. "A tower?" I asked. "You said hard to leave, not impossible. So is this tower the way?"

Bohko tapped its chest proudly. "Bohko know where tower is. Bohko help Ryu get there."

It took me a long moment to realize what he'd just said. "Do you know my name?" I asked. "How could you know my name?"

Bohko looked confused. "We share home," it said softly. "Bohko home is Ryu home. Ryu knows, only forget."

"Right," I agreed half-heartedly. "Share home. Sure. So where is this tower?"

If Bohko sensed the sarcasm in my voice, it didn't seem to care. Excitedly, it waved its arm behind it. "Tower that way," it said, and added, "Must go fast! Danger out here."

My brow furrowed. My grip, having relaxed on the handle of my knife, tightened once more, lancing pain down my arm. "What do you mean?"

Bohko's spiky ears shot up as a familiar sound sang in the distance. The noise made me freeze.

"Like screeching," Bohko complained, pinning down its own ears with its claws as though pained. "Ryu must come with Bohko! Ryu cannot fight the Cloak!"

Only when Bohko mentioned a cloak did I recognize where I knew the noise from. Back in the Old Forest, long before my life became this complex, the same noise had rang through the air as Will and I crossed the rickety bridge over the river. The sound of an approaching Keeper. I couldn't forget the sheer terror I'd once felt when that noise echoed over the water and the ashen expression on Will's face when he realized. What was one of those monsters doing here?

My mind raced. If I had to fight another one of those, I was woefully unprepared. I couldn't fully use either arm. Last time we got rid of one, I'd called upon fire to dispel it. Would that work again? Rather, could I summon fire properly now? I'd practiced magic enough in Bonnin, but it had been a while since I actually needed it. If weapons worked on it, that didn't give me an advantage, either. I could barely move.

"Follow Bohko!" the small creature urged me, beckoning me with one of its big claws before ducking into the crater it came from. I looked after it, then wildly around, scanning for a sign of the impending creature. When I couldn't catch sight of its deathly cloak, I struggled to rise and follow Bohko. I wasn't sure I could trust this little Shadowheart, but it seemed a better option than waiting for the Keeper.

Akin Minds

"Hey, wait up!" I cried after the Shadowheart after managing to clamber to my feet. My body felt as though my bones swapped out with fire, whittling away at my skin.

Then, abruptly, I felt a wave of intense cold pass over me. A shadow cast overhead. I didn't need to look. I didn't *want* to look. I already knew what it was.

I whipped around with all the force I could muster, lashing out at it with my knife. I could vividly recall what happened when Will and Sira attacked a similar creature not long ago, but I couldn't let that hinder me. My knife met a solid force that ground it to a fast halt.

The first thing I saw were folds of a greyish cloak that made up the tall creature. It didn't seem to touch the ground, but it certainly towered over me. A pair of crimson eyes leered like a pair of floating candles behind its furled hood. It didn't move, keeping my knife at bay with a set of ivory claws double the length of my knife.

"You stand in the terrain of Death," the keeper spoke in a deep, profound voice, taking me aback. I was sure the last one had never spoken to us. It withdrew to hover before me like an ominous reaper. "You are in a place devoid of life. I am Death's Keeper. Leave, or join that which I must protect."

I was too stunned to reply for a moment. The Keeper didn't seem intent on trying to outmaneuver me yet, though. "You're the Keeper of Death?" I asked, surprised. "What's there to protect here? Isn't this a fallen world?"

The Keeper growled deep within its throat. There was something distinctly familiar about the sound, but I couldn't place it. I decided that this beast was far different than the one we last faced. Maybe it wasn't as strong.

"Death is as much a virtue as life," the Keeper responded. "The abstinence of breath and life. Things do not grow here, and entities come only to die. Death belongs only with death. It is no place for the living. So begone, human."

"I can't," I replied with gritted teeth. The arm clutching my knife felt enflamed. If the Keeper attacked again, I'd easily be disarmed with my current lack of strength. "I don't have the power to cross worlds. Something brought me here, and I'm afraid I have to find a way out."

The monster snarled, making me jump. "That is not a possibility I can grant you. Should you stay in this realm, you will die. Your optimal fate would be to die at the behest of my claws."

I wanted to glance over my shoulder and see if Bohko was still here, but taking my eyes off the opponent would surely spell my demise. I didn't stand a chance against the Keeper alone, especially in my current state. I wished I knew more about magic. Fire might not have the same effect on this particular Keeper as it did in the Old Forest, but it was worth a shot if I could reach my staff. If the creatures had elements like I theorized, I'd have to guess my advantage lay in light magic – not that I could control it if I wanted to. If Bohko really was to be trusted, then maybe it could help me out of this somehow, but I didn't dare check if it stayed to face this monster with me.

I was in bad shape. It was possible I still had some juice in my weightless marks, but it wouldn't last long if that was all I could muster. Still, if I could attempt a spell from my staff, at least I was putting up a fight. Maybe I could even put Ragnarokkr to use somehow, although wielding it by the chains took a lot out of me.

I was out of time. The beast lunged without any sort of warning. I sapped my marks in order to step out of its elongated reach in time. My boots dragged against the craggy ground when I dashed and nearly made me trip. This would be difficult ground to fight on.

The creature didn't slow down when its first attack didn't land, and flung at me again with its claws lashing like scissors. I didn't dare try to block again, and used my marks to pull myself out of the way. My energy was already trickling away like a hole in a boat, but I would surely fail in a test of strength against the Keeper. As I stepped aside, I thrust my knife back into its sheath and drew my staff. As soon as I had the rod in my hands, I could picture images behind my eyes as though painted on my eyelids. The visualisation mustered its strength. So far, I'd only managed to wield it a few times.

The images flashed past my eyes. A hot campfire. A flame under the element of a stove. A wildfire coursing through a forest.

The next thing I knew, a flash blinded me. Hot air exploded before my staff, the sheer force of it almost enough to tan my skin. The whoosh of rushing flames slammed against my eardrums as though I thought to listen to a thunderclap closely. After the initial flash, I could see the velocity of flames I'd summoned taking up my entire vision.

The Keeper held them off with its claws crossed before it, flames licking at its cloak and claws like a living thing. Behind it all, its red eyes glowed like lanterns.

For all the glory of the flames, they dissipated in less than a minute – hardly long enough for me to catch my breath and try to regain feeling in my arms. The black cloth that the Keeper wore was hardly singed, its claws painted with ash. In the moment the heat dispelled, the Keeper's eyes flashed like living flames.

It was on me again in a flash. With only the staff in hand, I panicked and lashed out, hoping to get lucky and save my own life. A heavy force struck the staff just above where my hands were, shooting pain down both my arms. Rather than press, the Keeper spun and retaliated. With phenomenal force, it struck the staff in an uppercut and ripped it from my hands. I used my marks to throw myself backwards, but caught my heel on a stone and flipped mid-air. My marks flashed white-hot from overcasting them.

The Keeper appeared above me mid-air, scaring the wits out of me. I narrowly dodged a fatal sweep of its long claws and forced myself back down. When I landed, I used my momentum to launch myself into a heavy axe-like kick upward, presuming it followed me. It did, but my boot struck the solid bone of its claws. It held for a moment, but the Keeper lashed, throwing me back with full force. I only managed to land on my feet with a quick sap of my weightless marks.

When the Keeper dove again, I yanked free my knife and raised it to the assault. The force of its clawed strike nearly forced my knife from my grip. I backed my heels into the ledge of a well-placed crater and held my ground. It unleashed a savage roar and rained blows down upon my knife, each singularly tougher than the last. Keeping myself pinned quickly became more of a downfall than a good plan. In a moment that the Keeper reared back for an even tougher slash, I dropped down, jammed my knife in its sheath and pulled Ragnarokkr free by the chains. My whole body screamed in pain, but I swung upward with all I could muster.

The Keeper slid out of the way, letting Ragnarokkr sail uselessly past it. The thick blade flew its course and crashed into the craggy earth, and it took another burst of effort to drag it free to swing again. The Keeper floated aside, watching me with mocking fiery eyes.

It was no use. Trying to fight with Ragnarokkr like this was far too slow, and would certainly cost me if I tried again.

Thinking fast, I dropped Ragnarokkr altogether and drew my bow and arrows. It was a weapon I had made little use of since Lysvid, but maybe it could be my advantage here. The arrow I freed was hasty and misaimed with the monster lurking so closely, and the arrow broke against the ground. I stepped around the Keeper's retaliating slash and used my marks to launch myself back a good distance while I notched another arrow, trying to keep the beast in my sights.

Time seemed to slow while my mind raced. Running around and trying to shoot this beast with a wood arrow was foolish on its own. Maybe I could land a lucky shot, but the monster would certainly rip me apart in the aftermath. My whole body seared with pain that was becoming increasingly difficult to ignore. My staff was down, Ragnarokkr abandoned, and none of my weapons seemed effective against this foe. I couldn't hold out for much longer.

I successfully manifested fire, but that had little effect on the beast. Was there naught else I could do? Guildford explained little about the element that might actually turn the tides in this battle: light. I managed to summon some water and wind in the past, but had little experience with the others aside from the shield I conjured before. Darkness and light were ones I couldn't wrap my head around. Guildford had explained how their energies worked in the world with little detail. Darkness and light: the two sovereign elements that could vanquish all else.

Different images flashed by my eyes. In the entire ruckus since, the memories of my fateful encounter with Kimo and my brief meeting of the spirit Eos sat in the back of my mind. I remembered Kimo's orange eyes turning to me. The bright light entering my entire being. I met Eos, who appeared in the midst of that blinding light. In the rush of the battle after, and the grave cost of it, I had almost entirely forgotten her words.

If you have further need, please call.

Maybe that was it. The ace that I needed in order to walk away from this fight, otherwise I would surely die here. If nothing else, Eos said she was a spirit of light. She requested I call her if I needed. Whoever she was, she seemed to vie for my safety. If there was ever a moment I needed some sort of divine intervention, it was now.

Time seemed to grind down as I strung an arrow to my bow. As though in anticipation, a stray ray of pale light seemed to catch the tip of my arrow. Given that Vxxyura had little in the way of light, I couldn't imagine where else it came from. The light grew in mass until it was difficult to focus on the arrow itself. The Keeper drew ever closer, advancing so quickly that my time was running out. I had only one chance. I only had a few arrows left, and I might not get the chance to notch them if I missed this shot. Even if it hit, was this actually going to work? My doubts were the loudest noise on this empty planet, louder than the screeching whistle the Keeper emitted as it closed in on me.

"*Eos!*"

Her name burst from my lips with every ounce of strength I had. Surely if this idea failed, it was the last thing I would ever do. I tried to channel all my waning strength into my cry as my fingers unleashed the string on my bow, releasing an arrow that took on a blinding light as though it were a ray of the sun itself. The effort of loosing an arrow jolted my wrist in a near-excruciating way.

For a moment, I thought I could see her somewhere in the light. Her distinct hair, smooth features, and unclothed body seemed to appear for but a moment. She smiled softly, but with a bit of chastise, as though impressed I managed to land myself in deadly trouble after just one day. Just before the blinding arrow struck, Eos raised two fingers to her lips, kissed them gently, and held the fingers out toward me. I blinked, and she vanished as the arrow of light struck its target.

A shrill, whistling shriek shook the air with the sound of impact. For a moment, the light was blinding. I almost thought I could see Eos smiling from within, but the image blurred from sunspots in my eyes. All too quickly, the light abated, and the world succumbed to darkness again. The Keeper was gone.

My shoulders sagged in relief. My plan actually worked?

It took all the self-restraint I had not to lie on the ground and fall asleep. I couldn't forget how Bohko had warned me about the dangers of this place.

Speaking of Bohko, it seemed that he was the one thing I should be focusing on right now. I forced myself to limp over to my discarded weapons, retrieve them, and then turn in the direction Bohko had disappeared. I tried to think that the worst of this forsaken world was over, but a little voice in the back of my mind begged to differ.

SCENE THREE: SEEKING THE SCEPTER

...Of Act Nine: Separation

In the eyes of Alex Retton, we are in Enthralmen Jungle, in the world of Syaoto. It is late afternoon On November 15th, 2017.

"So this is the presumed location of the mythical scepter?"

"Supposedly," Kimo replied, grunting with effort as he slashed thick knots of jungle overgrowth with his hooked sword. "It seems we are headed in the right direction."

"I hope you are correct," I grumbled. "This heat is sweltering."

"It would be easier without all your armor," Joey poked at me with a smirk.

"Without my armor?" I asked incredulously. "Are you mad? This armor symbolizes my homeland. It is everything I fight to protect. Shedding the armor is as well as shedding my own dignity. That, and it is protecting me from the hazardous overgrowth quite well. What of that thick sweater you wear?"

Joey's expression was immediately defensive. "What *about* my sweater?" he demanded, adjusting the collar of the red sweater as though to reinforce its comfort. I smirked in reply. Point made.

The Enthralmen Jungle, located to the distant south of the capital, seemed hotter than our capital city up north ever got at this time of year. The sun seemed to blaze twice as bright in the beaming sky above us, the same sky recently consumed by a dark magic which made it toss and turn like the sea. Looking up now, one could never tell what had befallen this grand world only yesterday. Despite that, we still gazed up at the sky with trepidation as we rode here on Leiogrey's back.

It would have significantly sped up our process if Leiogrey had been able to land deeper into the enormous jungle. Unfortunately, we'd circled overhead for quite a time and been unable to find any landing spot close to the circle drawn on Kimo's map. We were forced to land only a stone's throw into the jungle. Leiogrey circled over us, prepared to overtake the woodlands if a sign of trouble arose. I admired Lamont's silvery beast, a truly massive dragon with a fiery resolve to match any of us. Of course Will, in Ryoku's company, would come across such a man who befriended dragons.

On the other hand, the Enthralmen Jungle was strikingly beautiful despite the stifling heat. The ground was largely even and flat, like much of Syaoto, and only trees that grew in patterns of the wind made it difficult to walk. Moss and fungi swarmed all over the trees and nestled in vines. We passed strange mushrooms that were half the size of us. We tread carefully as we cut a path through the overgrowth. Striking any of the abnormal mushrooms doused the area in harmful spores that made our skin burn. We'd nearly done it once, and that was enough. Nobody wanted to know their adverse effects.

Speaking of blades, my regular steel shaft felt a little underwhelming against these two. Kimo, the striking vassal of Orden who temporarily sided with us, wielded a fancy sword with a golden blade. It was only a few inches longer than the regular issue, but the sharp hook at the end combined with its brilliant sheen made it look like the weapon of kings. No amount of thick vines threatened to dull its fine edge.

Joey, too, used a magnificent sword that he didn't seem inclined to speak of. It had an off-white blade with almost a foot on the length of Kimo's hooked sword. Its crossguard and handle were forged of an entwined black steel cord, spiraling to form a sun-shaped pommel that hooked out like two talons. The blade itself ridged with hooks and groves, ending smooth-ridged for the last foot of the blade. Symbols etched along the flat of the weapon. Those gave me an odd feeling the longer I looked at them, and I couldn't bring myself to ask about it. I'd already spent a long time studying the fanciful blade. What I wouldn't give to have such a thing to my name.

One thing I forgot about him often was that he, too, was a Defender. He knew Ryoku from their home world, supposedly, but they bore themselves quite differently. Joey knew the ways of the spirit realm and could blend in with ease. Only among us, he always donned the foreign red sweater. In unfamiliar lands, he could blend in just as easily as anyone else. One could take him for a resident of Syaoto, even.

Among these two legends, I wished I were with my squad again. Leif and I worked side-by-side for a long time despite our differing ranks. After learning Vincent Ordenstraum took over our kingdom, Leif couldn't stand by and left, choosing to join the Syaoto Bladerunners with his cousin. We hadn't spoken since Vincent fled, but I doubted his resolve changed much. My dear friend had changed quite a bit since he joined the Bladerunners. Oliver, too, wasn't much for adventure these days. He was older, and life at the precipe of the army suited him best. He grew to be Brom's right-hand man over time, and he served the role well. One day, he might even join the King's Own – if they reformed.

The trail we forged opened out ahead of us abruptly, landing us in a mild clearing beset with a couple mossy stones and a ton of hacked-away overgrowth. Stumps of trees littered the ground. Without much thought, the three of us each took a stone and sat down to catch our breath. After a short moment, a great wind fell upon us. I went for my sword, but glanced up to see that it was only Leiogrey's massive wings as he descended, landing his large, serpentine body in the clearing with us. I was surprised he managed to fit. The beast was so large, his tail wrapped around three different stones, one of his massive claws clenched around a fourth. He brought his head down until his amphibian eyes were level with Kimo.

"I have located the temple you seek," the dragon rumbled. The sheer volume of his spoken voice seemed to rustle the grass around us and create a breeze through the trees. "It is in the crest of a hill ahead. The entrance descends into the earth. Walking blindly, one might simply pass it. It has a wide door. I may be able to enter it if you clear a path."

I smiled to myself. The thought of traversing some wicked underground temple alongside a dragon was much more comforting than without.

"What does the area look like?" Kimo asked.

Leiogrey growled. "Press on southwest and you shall find it. If not, I shall direct you. It also seems to be rich in the way of monstrous activity. Tracks and scents litter the jungle in the area."

I grumbled under my breath. Couldn't a remote temple be free of monsters for once?

"Any sign of Will?" Kimo asked. Leiogrey shook his head, and Kimo's jaw set. "I shouldn't be surprised. He may well already be inside."

"You would be able to tell better than I," Leiogrey admitted. He didn't wait around for further talk, and he took flight once more. The unwarranted beating of his wings nearly floored some nearby trees.

"Was it just me, or did he not tell us how far we have to go?" Joey asked, defeated.

Kimo smirked, pushing himself to his feet. "He did not. I don't know about you, but I don't require much of a rest. Should we press on?"

It was the last thing I wanted to do, but I nodded. Maybe the hidden temple would be cooler.

We rose together and pressed on in the direction Leiogrey gave us. The journey seemed even more overgrown and dangerous than before. Kimo managed to deflect our way out of a basilisk encounter that we were seriously unprepared for. Demons prowled any opening big enough to stand comfortably in.

It took a long time, but we found ourselves at the place Leiogrey hovered atop. Were it not for the dragon, we might not have stopped here. The setting looked no different than anything we'd encountered yet. The only telltale sign was of an overgrown mural buried halfway into one of the trees. After Kimo slashed away the vines covering it, we could make out the design: an ancient carving in worn gold, of a man with blue hair, wielding a golden sword and a matching scepter.

"I take it that's our scepter," Joey said, "unless every king in Syaoto has their own scepter."

Kimo smirked. "It lies here then."

His eyes warily scanned the area. It took a moment, but he picked out something in the opening of the trees. A few tree-hacking minutes later, and we found ourselves literally on the doorway of a temple. The door appeared seemingly out of nowhere, blending into the gaps between the trees like it was the earth itself. Vines covered the door from top to bottom, and it was with some hard work of our swords that we managed to open it. I couldn't help but be impressed that Leiogrey spotted this. Maybe it was easier from above.

The dragon himself came to land among us once we cleared the doorway. We had to clear even more room for him to land, and he still crushed great trees under his mighty claws when he came to rest.

We stared down into the temple uneasily. The gate opened out to a flight of stairs descending into utter darkness. Kimo dug into his bag. He gathered three sizeable branches from the slashed-aside vines and wrapped them in torn rags. He pulled a flask from his bag and poured oil onto the rags. He turned away, touched his ear in an odd way, and returned to hand us each a lit torch.

"How did you do that?" I asked him.

Kimo shrugged. "I carry supplies like this everywhere," he replied. "You never know when you'll need something like a torch, or equipment for first aid, excavating, or what have you."

He said no more than that and started out into the dungeon below. Joey and I exchanged glances.

"He totally didn't understand you," Joey told me dryly.

I shook my head. "No. He avoided the question like a dragon avoids lakes."

Leiogrey grumbled next to me. "I am rather partial to lakes myself, thank you."

I frowned up at him sheepishly. "Does that not put out your fire or something?" Leiogrey only stared, so I shook my head. "Oh well. Let us go on, then."

Joey nodded vigorously. Exchanging a last set of nervous glances, we delved in with Leiogrey right behind us.

(Meanwhile, in the eyes of Sira Jessura)

"Not even a single sighting of him?"

The officer shook his head. "The closest we have come to Ryoku Dragontalen is by ear. A Defender has not passed through Reulio in ages, let alone one so famous."

Guildford nodded, dejected. "Very well. Thank you for readily greeting us strangers."

The officer saluted us. "Not at all. Word spreads fast of a Defender. Any friends of his are friends to the common people."

He returned to his post with that. Guildford turned to the rest of us, shaking his head.

"This doesn't seem like such a great idea now. Thanks to those bounty posters from Orden, everyone here knows what he looks like. They would have reported anything already."

Relus put a friendly hand on his shoulder. "Your actions had good intentions, Guildford. We deal with a complex matter."

Guildford frowned. "It troubles me. We can't figure out how or why he left Syaoto in the first place. He just... vanished."

Relus crossed his arms, matching Guildford's scowl in full. "He was likely distraught with Loki's death as well."

"I doubt he'd do this on purpose," I argued against their implications. "All his friends are here! Katiel, Dawn, whoever else. Me. He wouldn't just take off on purpose."

"Then how else?" Guildford asked. He didn't sound accusing, only frustrated. "What possessed him to leave?"

Sorha scoffed at us. "I don't see why he would stay."

I turned to her in aggression, but a sharp glance from Relus stayed my hand. "What do you mean?"

"I mean the part of him that is my fiancée," she said dryly. "Advocatos, the prince of demons. I know he has a strong presence in Ryoku right now as he gains strength. As was with their bond before, that can influence his personality. Perhaps he sought something else after losing Loki. After all, according to you lot, he's already experienced recent loss."

Now both Relus and Guildford kept me at bay. I felt a bit glad for their silent intervention. Part of me knew I didn't want to piss this girl off.

"Okay, but what about Lusari?" Guildford asked calmly. "Why might she have left around the same time?"

Sorha studied him. "You suspect foul play of some kind?"

Guildford shrugged. "We have powerful enemies," he replied. "Ones that know just how many friends Ryoku has. Part of our strength lies in our numbers. With the power Vincent and Roland have displayed, perhaps this is possible for them? Or Kimo Goldenhart."

Sorha was intent on him like a cat upon a mouse, and it made me want to step in. "You have a point, teacher," she mused. "There may be another possibility, however. Remember the fact that Syaoto is now considered a fallen world."

"It didn't actually fall," I argued. "Whatever weird magic Kimo has was at fault."

Sorha shrugged. "It came close. Close enough that Shadowhearts still reign here. Don't tell me none of you noticed the time unraveling before this even happened, too. Syaoto took on a different time flow long before this happened."

Guildford and Relus exchanged glances. "Loki did mention that," Guildford said softly. "What does that mean?"

"The Creator works in strange ways." Relus tapped his sword idly, studying Sorha. "The Creator, or the force that made these realms the way they are. Either way suggests that this was going to happen either way."

Guildford contemplated Sorha. "Those rifts that we create to cross worlds in world-traveling magic. Is there a way that they could be... caused by other methods?"

Sorha smiled in a way that was far too attractive. Her familiarity with Ryoku made me nervous. "Those rifts are a passage between worlds. A glimpse of what lies between. An unstable world might find these to be ultimately common. After all, that's what Shadowhearts come from."

Everyone was silent while Guildford mulled over this idea. "So a rift could have passed through those very woods," he murmured. "Just because Shadowhearts didn't clamber out doesn't mean it didn't pass through our very midst. And... That could cart somebody to a new world." He looked up at Sorha. "That would account for Lusari, too. I should have noticed the circumstances. Ryoku can't cross worlds on his own, and nobody for miles around has seen him. He's gone."

Sorha shrugged, glancing away. "No point in blaming yourself. The point is, now we have to figure out where he went. There are many worlds near Syaoto."

Guildford looked to Relus, who was already numbering them off. "Syaoto is near Vortiger, Brooklyn, Vxxyura, Bonnsyara, Rune, Emsahl…"

He numbered a few more off before his eyes widened.

"What?" Guildford asked him. "What's wrong?"

Relus hesitated, scratching his chin. "It's not an ultimate possibility," he reasoned, "and there are a number of worlds considered closer in alignment to Syaoto than this one, but…"

He didn't need to finish. I noticed where he was leading. I wasn't the only one. Guildford looked at me. For the first time I could think of, I saw panic in his eyes.

"Orden."

(Meanwhile, in the eyes of Alex Retton)

"Not much further now, I imagine."

Kimo nodded in agreement to my mild complaint. Even the youthful Goldenhart looked fatigued. "Hopefully. I'd like to find it before I must return home."

Joey grunted in agreement, wiping blood from his sword onto a battered tapestry. It was one of many dirty pieces that lined the walls of this rustic old temple, and one of the better standing. They all depicted the same things. A king with blue hair, a golden crown with a blue gem on his head, wielding both a mighty sword and the very scepter we sought.

This place had clearly been unoccupied for a long time. We exchanged guesses, but Kimo was the smartest of us. He gestured to the sand-swept tiles, cracked and misshapen in spots, and reasoned that this place must have once had open windows to the jungle outside. All that remained of that was the huge, thick vines that broke through, the surface too far above to grant us even the dustiest sunlight. Time and neglect essentially buried the huge temple under the jungle itself. Where it must have once been widely accessible, now only one entry remained. With that and the moth-eaten murals on the walls, Kimo guessed that the temple was above land at least six hundred years ago.

The hallways strung out in a maze around us like the endless trees of the jungle, spiralling out into a myriad of paths that winded throughout the underground. We had only our instincts and Leiogrey's keen senses to guide us. He didn't explain why, but Syaoto harbored an old myth that dragons could smell gold from miles away. I wondered if that was the case now.

Of course, given the mazelike interior of the temple and the moth-eaten, dusty odor, the worst part had to be the monsters. Shadowhearts hadn't made it to these halls yet, but other beasts that lurked in the shadows made me long for the creatures of Syaoto's end times.

Golems as tall as Leiogrey ambled through the halls. We stumbled upon one of them once, even though its heavy footfalls alerted us from afar. A couple, however, hid among rubble in crumbling hallways to reassemble at full height when we drew too close. Were I alone, I would have been squashed like a bug. Joey and Kimo both wielded mighty blades capable of damaging the shambling monsters. Where they fell short, Leiogrey's flames did the trick. They still held us up for a good while to defeat them.

Where there weren't giant golems, dark demons lurked in the shadows with hands like swords. Like the shambled golems, they only lashed out when we drew close, making them almost impossible to protect ourselves from. The only monster that didn't hide in the shadows was large, ugly turtle monsters with spiked shells. They were slow, but they hit hard. Leiogrey could break through their tough shells with his mighty fangs that even Kimo and Joey had a hard time cutting through.

A ways down the hall, Leiogrey lifted his head until it almost hit the roof. Blood stained his fangs and claws so badly that they appeared black.

"There is a doorway ahead," he informed us. "A room of golden doors, lined with sapphires and precious gems."

I nearly doubled over in relief. "Thank the Creator," I said, exasperated. "Perhaps the end is finally near!"

Kimo smirked. "We'll still have to fight our way out after," he said, but he couldn't hide his own glee.

Without warning, Joey took off down the hall ahead of us. I stared for a moment, stunned, but he grinned back. "Come on, Alex! Don't they teach you how to have fun in the army?"

I bit back laughter and rushed after him. Kimo was right behind me, to my surprise. Either he was glad to be almost done with this, or he had more youthful enthusiasm than he showed. Leiogrey kept up easily at his own pace. I wheeled around a corner and nearly crashed into a wall, but pivoted around it just in time. Joey wasn't so lucky, but he pushed himself off of it as easily as though he meant it. I sensed the Defender had a few more abilities than he readily let show.

A creature lunged out at us, taller than Joey and as spindly as a skeleton. Joey didn't flinch, drew his sword, and ran through it without a second thought. Kimo and I skipped around the pile of shadowy remains.

Soon, we came to the door that Leiogrey sensed. The doors were fashioned of pure gold and stood high enough for Leiogrey to enter easily. Cryptic runes and symbols etched into the breadth of the door. Staring at it, though, I couldn't see any sort of knob or way to open it.

"What do we do with this?" Joey asked, half to himself. He started at the gems on the door, trying to pry some out or find some switch beneath his fingers.

My stomach sank. Did we really come this far to find a sealed door?

Kimo stepped forward, his hand on his chin. "This is an ancient text indeed. I do recognize some of the letters, but not enough to make sense." He turned to Leiogrey. "Can you understand this at all?"

Leiogrey shook his great head. "It must be a language foreign to this world. An ancient Syaotoan dialect. Perhaps Will could…"

He trailed off, turning his head toward another hall adjacent to the one we came from. A low rumble emitted from his throat.

"What are you…?"

I stopped, too, as I heard a noise from further down the hallway. It sounded like a long, drawn-out whistle. Something about it tugged at the edge of my memory, and I shuddered violently.

"What's that noise?" Joey demanded, drawing his sword.

Kimo's sword flashed into the air, seeming to glimmer with a golden light. "Of course," he murmured, drawing the blade to stare down the face of it, pointed down the hallway. "Each treasure must have its keeper."

The shrill noise grew louder, and I drew back, freeing my own sword from its sheath. Then the noise abruptly stopped – and something charged from the hall, mid-air, to clash against Kimo's sword. Kimo lashed out, but the figure vanished in the blink of an eye. It reappeared to hover in the air nearby.

When I saw the full figure of the entity, my blood ran cold. It looked like the creature that appeared to attack us in Harohto – the Keeper of the Old Forest, Will called it. Only, this one had robes of a different color, a mix of darker greens and sandy brown. I couldn't see beneath the creature's ragged hood. Long claws hung out from the folds of its cloak – or, at least, it looked like a cloak. For all I knew, it *was* the creature.

"Leave this place," the creature hissed, surprising me. I didn't remember the last one speaking. "Only the worthy shall pass."

"Like the Syaotoan royal family?' Kimo asked. He sounded remarkably calm considering what he faced. "Unfortunately this world's a little short on that. Why don't you just let us take the scepter?"

The creature snarled under its breath. I kept alert, unable to remove my eyes from it. "You know a curious amount for an interloper. Explain that to me, agent of Zachariah."

Kimo went rigid. I couldn't begin to understand what the creature meant by that. It snarled once more. "It matters not. I am the Keeper of the Scepter, and I shall only surrender it to the royal family. You are not of royal blood. Give up and return home, or else die here."

"We don't have time for this!" Joey lashed out with his regal blade. I was sure the blow would land true, but the creature vanished, reappearing behind Joey like a reaper. Kimo recovered quickly enough to dive to his rescue. He maneuvered around Joey to block the incoming claws with his hooked sword.

"Joey's right," Kimo growled. "You're charged to protect a sacred relic for Syaoto. Yet, when the world is endangered, you refuse to give it up. What a flawed existence you lead."

"That is not my concern," the Keeper replied boldly. "I am charged only with protecting the scepter. The governance of Syaoto is not mine."

The creature shoved Kimo back, and he staggered, struggling to regain his footing. When the Keeper reappeared, Joey lunged into his midst and slashed at the Keeper, who vanished again. Kimo uttered an irritated growl, and turned his head to me.

"You should run," he said quickly. "I don't know that I can guard you against this kind of foe. Take Leiogrey and get out of here."

Leiogrey, however, let out a derisive burst of flames with a snort. "I shall not run," he proclaimed loudly, and unleashed a full blast of flames from his jaw just as the Keeper reappeared near him. The creature emitted a pained screech and vanished again. Leiogrey reared his head on Kimo. "Dragons do not cower before other entities."

Kimo smirked. "Right."

The Keeper reappeared near Kimo and spun in a whirl of claws. Kimo backed out of range and dashed ahead when the Keeper slowed. His blade met a spray of sparks from colliding with the Keeper's solid claws, and both leapt away. Joey lunged again in the moment, but the Keeper drifted out of the way of his strike. Leiogrey hung near, his eyes never leaving the monster.

I swallowed hard. I didn't want to run, and this fight seemed to be going nowhere fast. If this was the same as the creature in the Old Forest, how could they possibly defeat it? I wasn't even sure Ryoku properly put a stop to the one back in Harohto. How could we get into the scepter's room without fighting this creature?

I heard footsteps down the hall. I turned, tightening my grip on my sword. Who else could be down here? Some other Keeper?

The answer came quicker than I expected as a figure dashed into the hallway. He rushed out of the darkness and leapt into the air, straight past Leiogrey and into the Keeper. He strode with such purpose; it took me a moment to recognize him.

"Will!" I exclaimed, unable to hide my surprise. We'd been hoping he was here, but to find him at the right time seemed too good to be true.

His sapphire eyes flashed to me for a second as he lunged at the Keeper. Whether it was by sheer luck or his unanticipated arrival, his attack seemed to land. I heard the tearing of cloth, a sharp, rasping cry – and the creature vanished, leaving Will to land lightly on his feet.

I stared at him, stunned. I looked up to Will ever since I joined the army. He stayed a median-rank soldier, but he had friends among the King's Own and the most high-ranking officials in the army. Some of it was to do with his father, Jason, but most of it was his own doing. He shared drinks with Brom, sparred with Koteran Ruesto, and many knew him as King Lionel's confidant. Still, he insisted on bearing no titles and walked the lands like a free man. Only two shadows ever clouded across his face: Lancet Cooper and Jason Ramun.

"What the–?" Joey asked, stunned. "Did you...?"

Will sheathed his lance over his back, taking a moment to see who all was here. He gave me a knowing smile, but quickly turned his attention to Kimo.

"I doubt it," he replied. "Merely drove it back. I heard the ruckus and followed the noise." He gestured to the door, smirking at Kimo. "Seems I followed it the right way."

Kimo met him in the middle of the room and they gripped hands. "Impressive, Will," Kimo said coolly. "Still, I doubt it served for much in the end. We still have to get this door opened."

Something about Will's smile twitched. "Yes, and about that..."

He didn't continue, only turned toward the hallway he'd come from. I hadn't noticed in the action, but a man was there, leaning against the walls. His skin was so dark that he may easily melt into the shadows. His eyes and hair, however, were both snow-white, and he had the build of a sailor or a fearsome warrior. Thick vambraces on either arm seemed strained by his muscles.

"You are..." Kimo faltered, still clutching his sword tightly.

The man stepped out lithely, his step oddly reminiscent of some kind of wolf or panther. "Greetings," he declared in a bold, decisive voice. "I am Jesanht Olace. At the moment, you may call me a friend." He paused, looking around for a moment. "A Defender walks with you, I sense, but not the one I seek."

"Guilty as charged," Joey replied, raising a nonchalant hand. He was regarding Jesanht with a cool stare. Were I the recipient of that look, I'd be worried. "You must be talking about Ryoku."

"What do you mean, at the moment?" I asked. His name rang a bell, but I couldn't quite place it. Had Ryoku and the others mentioned it before?

The man's glance turned to me. He didn't seem to have irises and pupils, or else they were as white as the rest of his eyes. It was a symptom I associated with blind men, but somehow I knew he was looking at me.

"At the moment," he repeated, with finality. "I've made a deal with your friend. I can open this door at a price. One that has already been agreed upon."

"What deal did you make, Will?" Kimo demanded.

Jesanht didn't butt in this time, so Will replied. "Once we are done with the scepter, it belongs to Jesanht," he replied. "He would not explain why, but…"

"There is no other way to open this gate," Jesanht said. He turned lazily toward the door and spoke, with a reverent, heavy tone, "*Thou hast reached the ancient resting chamber of the holy scepter, thy tool of magickal undoing. In the hands of the Pendragon line, thusly a weapon of holy blight; in the hands of darkness, thusly a weapon capable of ensured havoc. The wielder of this weapon shall find an assault toward themselves to ensure this item is safe. To find entry into this holiest of gates, thou must present an item of absolute balance.*"

Kimo looked between Jesanht and the scripture on the doors with disbelief. "And you have an item of absolute balance?"

Jesanht shrugged mildly. "If you so doubt me, you are welcome to try on your own. There is no penalty for failed attempts." His eyes narrowed for a moment, and he tilted his head the other way. "Except, of course, the inevitable return of its keeper."

As he spoke, I remembered hearing of his name from Ryoku. Jesanht Olace – the unexplained man who'd attacked Ryoku and the others in Lysvid. Will surely knew who he was, didn't he? Why did he entertain his company?

Joey nodded toward Kimo. "Try your sword," he suggested. "That dark sliver in your blade could be just what we need."

Kimo smirked broadly, shooting Jesanht a victorious look. I noticed a dark piece attached to Kimo's blade. Against the golden face of the rest of the sword, would that work?

Kimo strolled past Jesanht and pressed his blade against the door. Nothing.

Jesanht smirked knowingly as Kimo turned back to him. "You've had your fun," Kimo said coolly, stepping back. "Open the door. When matters in Orden are finished, you will have your scepter."

Jesanht studied him, crossing his arms coolly. "Now what does Kimo Goldenhart have to do with the downfall of Orden? Why are you so invested in this? I understand you work for Vincent Ordenstraum."

Kimo returned his stare. "I am his vassal, yes. My reasons for securing his downfall are my own."

They locked eyes for a long, tense moment, but eventually Jesanht nodded and stepped past Kimo toward the doors. He stood in front of them and inhaled a long, deep breath, rolling his shoulders back and straightening his spine. Then he brought both arms before him, and pushed them together as forcefully as though pulling closed a heavy door.

Light reflected from his thick white bracers. A reaction of some kind sparked in the door. A returning light shone from the door, then split apart into two. Just when the lights became nearly blinding, they blinked away altogether, revealing two holes big enough for Jesanht to put his arms into. Rather than do that, he only lowered his chin to his chest and the doors began to open.

Joey and I stepped in behind Kimo to watch the unveiling of the great room. Both trepidation and glory filled my chest. This was something no soldier in the army had ever seen. An ancient room within a hidden temple, boasting a relic said to have been lost to the ages. I was already imagining how I would explain this scenario to Brom, to Oliver, to all my friends in the army. Leif occurred to me, but I wondered if he was not lost to us after joining the Bladerunners.

The room unfolded into a set of descending stairs, and was, to my surprise, well lit. The whole chamber was solid gold as the doors, and every few bricks in the wall shone like the doorway when Jesanht opened it. The stairs descended into a chamber, the focus of all the white lights, where the scepter rested upon a small pedestal.

It was smaller than a regular sword, the handle gilded and laden with small, precious stones. It looked like the focal point of a thousand years of crafting. The head of it spiraled out into a pair of twin dragons ensnaring a cluster of precious gems – emerald, sapphire, silver, rubies, and even a bite-sized black opal in the center.

Joey and I both let out a low, impressed whistle. The value of such an item must be astronomical!

"This is our only chance to reconsider," Leiogrey warned us, his heavy voice echoing through the chamber. "This man could be an enemy to us in the future. Simply wishing for the downfall of the Ordenstraum Empire does not make us kin."

Will sighed, skirting past Jesanht into the room. "We have no choice," he said softly, though the words echoed like a storm in the room. "I assure you, he is stronger than us. We could not leave here with two enemies at our backs."

Kimo turned to Jesanht. "You will allow us to leave with this scepter? At only the assurance that it would see its way back to you?"

Jesanht shrugged cordially. "It is all I can do. For now, we do share a common goal. Use the might of the scepter in your decisive battle against Orden, but then it belongs to me."

Joey scowled at him. "Why don't you just use it against Orden yourself, if you're so powerful?"

"Because I dare not," Jesanht replied. He shrugged once more, spreading his hands out like as innocent as any a man. "A fool's errand is for naught but the foolish. And when the aftershock begins... I shall be long gone."

With only that, the man slunk away into the shadows. Standing before the golden room, his image seemed to shimmer for a moment with world-travelling magic of his own.

"Are we making the right choice?" Joey asked.

Will shrugged. "It is the only choice to make. I would prefer to have such a weapon in our hands than to see it in Orden's clutches. If Jesanht seeks it…"

"It could be no better in their hands," Kimo agreed. "According to that script he told us, the Scepter of Blight is the ultimate defense. Their venomous magic can be erased, or maybe even turned against him, without any damper on our own energy reserves."

Will turned toward Kimo and nodded solidly. "This is our best shot."

"Perhaps our only shot," Joey agreed. "However strong we are, he's stronger. Who knows what other kinds of aces he has up his sleeve."

"Including me," Kimo muttered, "though I wish it were not so. I have other obligations of whom I must protect, no matter what."

"Are you going to try and kill Ryoku?" I demanded. Joey and Will both turned to me in alarm, as though the thought hadn't occurred to them. Why wouldn't it? Kimo was one of Vincent's vassals – they knew that.

"Not if I can help it," Kimo replied. "Alex, you are a valued soldier of Syaoto's armies. In my time serving in Syaoto Kingdom, I heard great things about you and the devotion you bring to the royal army."

He waited until I met his glance – his eyes were like pools of the sky, seemingly earnest, clear, and true. "I would not feel right if you opposed this. To use the relic of your old kings in battle against the empire. It is matters not entirely of your world. I would understand if you think it blasphemic."

Surprised, I shook my head. "No way," I replied. "This is entirely personal. Vincent Ordenstraum stepped into our kingdom, trying to turn the entire world on its head. No, Kimo – this is not some alien affair of other worlds. This is the truest possible battle I think Syaoto has faced. If they could, the kings of old would stand with us in battle, each with a hand upon the Scepter of Blight."

Will's smile was proud. It shouldn't be – I was sure, deep down, that Will felt much the same way. He had his obligations to Ryoku, too, but facing Orden had become a very personal matter. I had seen the fat old toad of an emperor demote Brom, to cause the King's Own to disband, and to turn the entire kingdom on its head. He promoted the likes of Lancet Cooper to his fold – a perfect fit, I thought – and nearly killed Ryoku in my own home. I would do whatever I could to stop him.

"Very well," Kimo agreed. "Then the Scepter of Blight is ours."

SCENE FOUR: TOWER OF THE FALLING RAIN

...Of Act Nine: Separation

In the eyes of Ryoku Dragontalen, we are in The Twisted Tower, in the world of Vxxyura.
It is late evening
On November 15th, 2017.

I pushed myself through the doors of the great tower, my skin stinging badly from the hours of acidic downpour. The musty odor of an abandoned place filled the air like a living thing around me. Bohko clambered in after me. I wrested the door shut. Darkness fell like a cloak around us, and all fell to silence.

I quickly tore off my cloak and shirt. The acidic rain here was much the same as in my home. Keeping wet clothes on after would only worsen the stinging. The rain picked up on us over an hour ago, and I was soaked to the bone with the painful acid. I delved into the bottom of my bag for a dry shirt and struggled into it, mindful of my reddened, sore skin. My hair felt like the roots were aflame, and my skin was flushed and painful. It was the icing on the cake. Nothing was going my way.

"Does anything live here, Bohko?" I asked, keeping my voice as low as possible.

The small creature shook its head doggedly. "Not live. Nothing live here."

I gave it a dry look. "But there are creatures here? Shadowhearts, like you?"

Bohko nodded fiercely, then paused – and shook its head aggressively. "Yes, creatures. Shadowhearts, not Bohko. Bohko not Shadowheart."

"Yeah, yeah," I murmured, exhausted of the way this entity talked. I supposed Shadowhearts didn't speak, or else they didn't when they swarmed Syaoto. The thought of Syaoto brought in a stinging pain unlike the burns of the acid rain – Loki. My fast friend, the Trickster, who had given his life to save me from Vincent. I shook my own head angrily, shutting the thoughts out from my mind. Not that this pitch-black tower wasn't a fitting place to let my grief catch up to me, but I had more immediate concerns.

"So in this tower..." I paused, trying to catch my breath. Running through acid rain only made my prior injuries flare up even worse, but I couldn't stop. "Is there a way out there?"

Bohko nodded. "Exit and answers. We must climb."

Bohko started ahead of me like some kind of dinosaur, walking with most of his weight on his front claws. Shaking my head, I followed.

I was still adjusting to having my eye healed by the spirit of Eos, but it didn't make a difference here. I could only see the odd thing in the darkness. Luckily, being blind in one eye for six months increased my other senses, it seemed. I could differentiate parts of the tower from one another by listening to the dripping of acid rain from within.

Walking blindly after Bohko, I closed my eyes and loosened my knife in its sheath. The small sound of steel echoed across the walls, bouncing along the railings of a flight of stairs before me, and echoing off each step in kind. The sound fell to nothingness above me – nothing, as far as the small sound could travel. There had to be one eventually, or the rain would still be pouring down on me still.

Using the sounds around me, I found the stairs and followed the small creature up them. My mind mapped the stairs from each sound upon them, and I was able to walk as though I could see perfectly. Bohko must have noticed, for I heard him come to a stop at the height of the stairs and turn toward me.

Behind Bohko, around the corner, was a narrow window, letting in the faintest ghost of moonlight. I could glimpse the acid rain still falling without relent, turning the ground into craggy pools and even more dangerous than ever. It was part of a hallway that wrapped around, and intermittent windows dotted the way like sad streetlights. I followed it with my eyes until I was sure it wrapped around the second floor, ending in more stairs that rose out above me. I could reach them with my weightless marks if I wanted, but I needed to conserve my energy.

"Ryu interesting human," Bohko commented. The creature watched me with unblinking eyes. "Uses sound to walk, not sight. Senses objects? Senses *me*?"

"Uh, no," I replied. "Just sound. Hard to explain, but I only had one normal eye until recently. I learned how to use my other senses to make up for my lack of vision."

Bohko's eyes seemed to widen, if that was even possible. "Interesting human," he repeated. His ears twitched madly, and he spun away, swirling into the shadows until he practically became them. "Not alone! Not alone!"

Now that primitive speech was clear. I yanked my knife out as something darted past the brief interlude of light ahead. My heart thudded in my chest. If the Shadowhearts here were anything like in Syaoto...

The creature that popped out ahead of me, however, looked more like Bohko than anything else, except its eyes were scarlet. It still had the same huge claws like Bohko, ones I didn't want to catch the wrong side of.

It only took a well-timed uppercut with my knife to the creature's chest to extinguish it in a puff of dark smoke. I stared into the extinguished puff, surprised.

"What was that?" I demanded, but Bohko already slipped away, slithering away through the shadows like he was entirely one of them. Cursing, I made after him. I thought to try and capture the slippery little creature, but I wondered if he might fight back.

For now, there was only Vxxyura, Bohko, and this twisted tower, with no guaranteed method of leaving. The Keeper of Death was likely not dead and gone as I hoped, and I was sure I'd see it again. Of course, the place Bohko led me to might be crawling with Shadowhearts, so I kept my guard up.

Following Bohko down the hall, I tapped the blade of my knife or bumped my staff against the wall to map out my way or search for things hidden in the darkness. I saved myself from tumbles more than once with that trick. Sometimes the twisted tower had steps hidden between the small batches of light.

As we climbed up the stairs to the third floor, an acute sense overtook me. I heard a noise that I couldn't quite assign to a location. It didn't seem to be in the range of my knife's tap, and it didn't make any other moves to indicate what it might be. I frowned in concentration as we came to the next floor, trying to figure out where the entity was.

Before I could conclude, a shadow jumped out at me, knocking me onto my back. I made to swipe at it, but I quickly noticed its golden eyes – Bohko.

Something crashed from the ceiling above where I'd just been, causing a great ruckus to shudder the ground at my feet. Now I could hear its breathing easily as the boulder-shaped entity growled, turning a set of crimson eyes toward me. It was definitely a Shadowheart, but it was almost as tall as me and thrice as wide. It pretty much looked like one of the basic Shadowhearts if it had led a richer life. Its arms were short, but there was a lot of muscle to them. Most of the creature's bulk existed in its sheer size and weight.

When Bohko clambered off me, I had half a mind to finally snatch the little creature and demand some answers, but I knew that had to wait. The monster rumbled toward me like a train. Despite its size, it was quicker than I would have guessed. I managed to skirt around it just in time, but one of the monster's brawny shoulders struck me in the edge of my arm. I cried out, slammed into the wall, and my lungs rattled in my chest.

The creature snorted like a wronged bull, but it kept its charge until it hit the end of the stairs before it slowly started to turn around. When it wasn't charging, it moved like an inchworm. An idea occurred to me. If Shadowhearts were as simple to defeat as Katiel and Loki claimed, maybe I knew how.

I waited it out by stepping into the middle of the hallway, giving myself plenty of room on either side. The creature sorted itself out slowly, angling itself in just the right way to come at me. No wonder it had been undetectable. I theorized that Shadowhearts might be able to blend into the shadows ultimately well, which was about the only way to explain how it got above me. Its angling process was almost as silent as air.

Finally, the beast charged. When it actually moved, I'd almost forgotten how quickly it came at me, and dove aside in a rush. This time, as the creature barreled past, I swung around and drove my knife into the meat of its back. It let out a horrific wail, and burst into a boulder-sized cloud of black smoke. I stepped out of the way, coughing hard. The air outside was bad enough – no need to inhale Shadowheart, too. That couldn't be healthy.

After besting the creature, I found myself sliding down the wall, and took a defeated seat on the ground of the tower with a heavy sigh. I wondered if what everyone said about me was true, and about these things. Did we used to do battle with their ilk once? Did we all actually used to fight together, or was I still the odd one out? Kimo said I didn't have the same soul as everyone thought.

Unwittingly, I started to think of Loki's last words to me. He told me I was his nephew, and the son of Odin. If I made the right sense of his words, then maybe that was who I was before this soul came into me. The son of Odin. I chuckled to myself in the darkness bitterly. If I was supposed to be this hero, this demigod, then why didn't I remember any of it?

Of course, I remembered some things. There was Eos, the spirit of light who looked so familiar, and those strange hallucinations that reminded me of learning how to fight. Did they have to do with the past Loki claimed I had?

The thought of that unsung past brought a tear to my eye. I'd only known Loki for a short time, but somewhere in my memories existed time spent with the god that I couldn't remember. Times we'd laughed and cried together, fought together, and maybe even traveled together like we did before. I wondered if I knew more about him somewhere in my mind. Would I like him more for them? Or less?

The shimmer of Bohko's golden eyes in the darkness brought me back to reality, and I felt my cheeks damp with tears. The small creature looked at me from the shadows. Something about it looked almost pitiful, and I felt a pang of guilt for treating this creature with some animosity. In the rush of things, sometimes I forgot that other creatures went through the same ordeals as me. Well, okay. Maybe not *exactly* the same, but that wasn't the point.

This time, Bohko didn't scamper away. He watched me inquisitively, as though I were the odd creature in the tower.

"Is there actually a way out of this tower?" I asked, half-pleading. "Tell me you aren't leading me up this thing for nothing."

Bohko shook his head doggedly. "Not nothing!" it cried. "Truth, and way to outside place. Bohko will guide! Bohko will show, and Bohko will prove!"

I raised my hands. "Okay, okay," I gave in; unsure I wanted to get the creature so excited. Still, I bit back a smile. "Bohko will guide. Okay. As long as you can help me get out of here."

Bohko emitted a strange purring noise. "Bohko help. But must hurry! Long way to top of tower, and Cloak will surely follow!"

I began to understand his dialect more readily. I wasn't sure whether that was a good thing, or whether I'd pick up on his speech by the time I left. I could imagine introducing myself at the next town. *Ryoku, Defender. Come from bad world.*

I chuckled to myself, but Bohko didn't appear to notice – he was already traipsing down the next hallway. Trying to find the brightest possible side of my situation, I pushed myself to my feet, and followed.

SCENE FIVE: CHOICE OF KINGS

...Of Act Nine: Separation

In the eyes of Dawn Elethel, we are in Syaoto Capital, in the world of Syaoto. It is early evening On November 15th, 2017.

"The candidates for the new reigning king of Syaoto have arrived. Are you ready to meet with them?"

The team of us exchanged glances – Lamont, Rena, and I. The resident judges of to-be kings. It was a humorous thought, but one I didn't comment on. Syaoto needed our help, and Ryoku seemed attached. In addition, I learned that Lamont was from a council of another world. If anyone could help judge the rightful king, it might as well be him.

Of course, we were additional voices to Syaoto's own council. Three esteemed nobles from the higher end of the city sat among us. Lord General Brom was absent, to my surprise, and Oliver Rouge sat in his place.

Lamont nodded for us. "Yes, sire, we will see them. Thank you kindly."

The chancellor seeing to us looked flustered. "S-Such formalities are not required of my position," he stammered. "I am merely the royal chancellor, and you are our esteemed guests."

"Of course," Lamont agreed easily. "By your word, then."

The chancellor bowed to us, then went to open the door behind him. Five men entered the room in single file. Leading the pack was a tall, young, and handsome man with his long blond hair pinned back in a tight braid. He was done up in dark armor with regal grooves cut into the plates, complete with a Christmas-red cape pinned over his shoulders. Immediately from the way he held himself, I could tell he gauged himself as the most important man in the room. Typical men.

I was shocked to see the massive figure of Brom Gerenadh behind him. The man was still a giant even out of his armor, now donned in a light silver doublet of a ceremonial texture. His chopped hair looked freshly washed, his skin reddened from a fresh shave – but it didn't ease the tired, gaunt look in his eyes. There was an earnest crispness to this man that I couldn't help but admire. I heard locals call him many things. Predominantly, he was the Iron Bear, and seen as something of a legend to the people of this world.

Behind him was a younger man, closer to our age than the others. He looked like a discount version of the first man, but his blond hair was closely chopped and of a dirtier shade. He looked nervous, and his dark-green armor looked a little big on him. I did note that the armor was expensive. This man certainly came from a royal family of some sort.

Behind him was an unusual contestant, to say the least. He was so tall that he had to stoop to enter the doorway, and his spiky blue hair brushed against the doorframe regardless. His face was earnest and plain. He must be around Guildford's age, and dressed in simple traveler's clothes – a laced brown shirt and black pants. He and Brom were the only ones who came in with a sword at their belt.

The last one looked familiar somehow. I couldn't recall why, but it made my eyes follow him into the room. He must have been about the same age as the discount contestant. Silver hair fell to his shoulders, framing a sharp and angular face with piercing blue eyes. He dressed in sharp clothing, and I noted the edges of a dark bruise framing his left eye. Adding that to the muscles pressing against his tunic and his large, calloused hands, I gauged him to be a member of the army as well.

The five men lined up before us, each standing with their hands clasped before them. The chancellor stepped out in front of them.

"I present to you the first of five royal candidates," the chancellor began, and cleared his throat. "Sir Arthexus Mandrake the Second, the young lord of Balgena and son of the great Duke Arthexus Mandrake the First, descendant of the cousin to the crown, Lord Menophres Pendragon."

Lamont raised a brow. "He is of royal blood, then?" he asked.

Arthexus cleared his throat. "Yes, mortally speaking," he said. "Royal blood does exist in my veins, though not of any more pure-blooded Pendragon than my estranged great uncle, Lord Menophres Pendragon. Although my family eventually took on the name of my grandmother in part of a winding tale, I assure you that it is there, and that I have inherited much of my great uncle's talent for magic, thirst for knowledge and power. If you are not familiar with my home kingdom..."

"Balgena is known as the magical capital of Syaoto," Rena told us. "He's right. The Mandrakes have ruled Balgena for generations, and do descend from the royal line – according to history, that is."

"Perhaps not entirely to be trusted," the blue-haired man murmured under his breath. When Arthexus shot him a glare, he glanced airily up at the ceiling, as though he paid the conversation no mind. He did catch my eye, though, and winked.

"Secondly," the chancellor said pointedly, as though to force the conversation back on track. "The next representative is Lord General Brom Gerenadh, a man in life service of the royal army and a past knight of the King's Own – a total of forty-six years in servitude to the crown."

Brom bowed deeply before us. He might be the only contestant to do so.

"We owe a great debt to Ryoku and his fellowship for saving the realm of Syaoto. In absence of our true king, Lord Lionel Pendragon, I thought to offer my assistance. No descendants to the royal family appear to remain, and I fought at King Lionel's side for many a battle, for many years."

I thought the silver-haired man shot him a glare, but he kept his head down when I glanced his way.

"Thirdly," the chancellor went on, "Lord Kergo Bassonet, duke of Fort Issomas to the north."

The blond man bowed, a little more shakily and nervously than Brom. It was noticeably less deep than Brom's. "How do you do?" he asked. His voice was very polite and warm, but there was a tremor to it. I couldn't help but see the young man's anxiety.

The chancellor didn't give us a chance to answer. "Fourth of all," he went on, and then paused, turning to the blue-haired man. "I'm sorry – *who*, exactly, are you?"

I expected him to falter, but the man sauntered forward, one hand on his hip and the other at the hilt of his sword. He bowed in a very strange way, probably a style from another world. He twirled his left hand extravagantly as lowered himself, bringing his pointy chin nearly to the floor.

"Ragekku Gero." He spoke in a somewhat deep and elaborate tone. "I come from a manor in Balgena, but I'm no lord; merely a warrior who has traveled across the lands, and I've heard plenty about your team. My blade sings praise to your hero, Ryoku Dragontalen."

A murmur started up behind us with the other council members. "Ragekku Gero?" one asked another. "They say he's party to the King's Own. Koteran trusts him with his life."

"He's married to that beautiful songstress. Melodia Harmony, if I'm not mistaken."

"Their children go to the Balgena academies. The School of Black and the Magickal academy..."

"I-I see," the chancellor muttered, though he didn't appear overly impressed. He turned to the last. "And lastly, from our very own army. Field Commander Lancet Cooper, hailing from the town of Thralle."

When the last man bowed, it hit me. He was none other than the man who attacked us atop the plateau in the Royal Forest. During Vincent's reign, he'd climbed the ranks to assume Brom Gerenadh's role of Lord General. Brom said nothing in his presence, nor did anyone else. Did they not recognize him?

No. For some reason, Brom was keeping quiet about the affair. I wasn't familiar with Syaoto politics, so maybe it was best to stay silent. After all, we'd be pulling a record check on the candidates. Lancet surely wouldn't escape that with his chastity – would he?

"Well met, everyone," Lamont spoke, but he sounded a little nervous. Understandable, I guessed, when we stood before five kingly candidates. Some more likely than others. He bowed in kind before them. "I am Lamont Declovin, son of Raimundo, residing on the council of Vortiger. I am a friend of Ryoku and rider of the dragon Leiogrey."

"I am Dawn Elethel," I introduced myself after a pause, realizing they expected it of us after a look from the chancellor. "I'm a Defender, elf, and druid."

A slight murmur started up behind me, and I saw Arthexus' eyes twinkle with interest. For a Defender to reside over such a matter usually made it quite important, and he knew that. These were all men who would be aware of the outer world structure.

"Um, just Rena," our shy friend added, curtsying before them deeply. "Well, Rena Stillwater. From the Stillwater Orphanage in Balgena."

Kergo cleared his throat. "Forgive me, milady," the boy said kindly, "I do not mean to seem rude, but what brings you to reside over our jurisdiction?"

"She is a friend of Ryoku as well." Lamont's voice was like a cutting edge, and he made it very clear that she was under our wing. "Will Ramun saved her during a skirmish between Syaoto's gangs.

"Why don't you tell us about yourselves?" I asked. I meant for the question to distract the candidates, and it seemed to work. Arthexus turned to us and straightened, standing like an upright lizard with his hands on his hips.

"I am Duke Arthexus Mandrake the Second," he repeated. "My father has been the reigning duke of Balgena for seventeen years. Before him was my grandfather, Thelonious Mandrake, who inherited the throne when my great-uncle Menophres Pendragon... lost his way. The Mandrake title is more of a penname, you see, for my family's penchant in dabbling with alchemy. My great-great grandfather, Amarant Mandrake, was the first to stray from the royal line. That is where the impurities begin."

Lamont crossed his arms. I wasn't sure he absorbed a bit of what Arthexus rattled on about. I sure didn't. "Tell us more about Balgena. I am new to your world."

Arthexus lit up like a lamp. "Balgena is known as the magical capital to Syaoto," he explained. "While the Capital holds the King and the royal army, the King's Own, Jason Ramun, and many other things, Balgena is known for her sorcery. We host the greatest magical academy in all of Syaoto, as well as a prestigious swordsmanship academy and the infamous School of Black. Respectively, the latter trains individuals of... darker, roots. Assassins."

"It's not a darker path," Ragekku commented airily, gazing up at the ceiling. "My daughter attended. Arthexus belittles the fact that many of the King's Own and Syaoto vassals graduated from the school. Our greatest spymasters have that school under their belt."

He rolled his gaze downward and smirked at me. "No good king holds an attendant unschooled in the Black. Consider it the dagger behind the crown, if you would."

Arthexus gave Ragekku a sharp look, but Lamont's interest was piqued. "So a school of espionage? In addition to the magical and sword academies?" He let out a deep breath. "Formidable. Balgena is a place of power, I see. I have a friend from home who would, no doubt, like to see this school one day."

Arthexus looked pleased now, and Ragekku smirked. "They accept international students, if the friend is a traveler. They've put out such people as the leader of the Flaming Arrows gang here."

Rena looked taken aback at this. "The leader of that gang is from Balgena?"

"Our prestige outdoes us." Arthexus glowed like a smug pug.

Rather than continue to prod the man's already bursting self-esteem and pride, Lamont turned to the general next. "Forty-six years," he commended. "That is a long time to devote yourself to the army."

Brom nodded. The movement was like a boulder churning in the earth. "I started from the roots of the army. A fledgling from the village of Balegar. It is so far south that many people think it belongs to the swamp," he added, when even Kergo and Arthexus looked confused. "As good as nothing ever was, and it remains so. I could be a pig farmer and still be the best thing that came from that town. Either way, I worked my way up. Started in the latrines, not even good enough to be a scout or page. I had to empty more latrines than we have in the new sewers beneath the keep."

Lamont raised a brow. While some of the other council members leaned back, bored, Lamont took a chair before the contestants, seated backward with his arms across the back of it. "How did you come so far? Please, sit. A king needs practice for their thrones, no?"

Everyone except Ragekku Gero turned to the chancellor for confirmation, who shrugged, exasperated. When they looked back, Ragekku already sat just like Lamont and looked thoroughly exhausted.

"A low-ranking field commander found me sparring with a friend in the swamp," Brom explained. "Measly little sticks, but apparently I wielded mine with some promise. Since most of the army does *not* hail from Balegar and the swamps, they do not have the same practice in keeping their footing on marshy ground. Galahad noticed this technique of mine, and it served to later win encounters for us that they never knew they might face."

"So Galahad scoped you out," Lamont said, smirking. I thought maybe he noticed how bored the other contenders looked, and how one of the council members yawned hugely. Maybe Lamont just found it terribly interesting. "And you climbed the ranks yourself from there?"

Brom nodded soberly. "Aye. From my closeness to Galahad – who also climbed the ranks – I began to realize what a winning battle looked like, and how to form that from the jaws of defeat. I eventually grew close to the king from there, and became a knight of the King's Own."

"I have heard that name before," Lamont said. "Tell me, what, *exactly*, is the King's Own? The best knights of the realm?"

Brom nodded. For the first time, I was starting to see a light in the tired old man's eyes. "The legend stems from the first king of Syaoto, King Ramenas Pendragon, and the round table he had forged to protect his son, Arthur. He handpicked knights from around the realm to form a fellowship in protection of his son. When that fell through, the knights eventually passed down generations and became known as knights of the King's Own. Some were still hand-picked by each king, though some served for generations before their children tired of the royal duty."

"And this table disbanded recently," Lamont stated, though still with the edge of a question, "due to the latest king."

Brom nodded. "Aye."

Lamont leaned forward further. "What became of them? Do they still adhere to the realm? And... dare I ask. What became of your old friend, Galahad?"

The reception was mixed. Everyone behind us seemed bored and tired. Arthexus yawned loudly and openly, but Kergo and Ragekku looked thoroughly interested. Lancet stared off behind us, eyes narrowed.

Before Brom could respond, the chancellor cleared his throat loudly. "We *do* have other guests to speak with," he said pointedly. "As fascinating as Lord General Brom Gerenadh's history must be, there currently sits no king on the throne."

Lamont leaned back now, clearly losing interest. "Very well." He nodded to the next blond, Kergo Bassonet. "What do you bring to the throne, lad?"

Brom appeared to take his interruption fairly well, clasping his hands neatly before him as he sat back. Even sitting, he had the posture of a mountain. Kergo, however, struggled for words.

"R-Right," Kergo stammered. "I come from a royal line. My father, Maestro Bassonet, was reigning lord of Fort Issomas for thirty years. My brother, Baron, and I are contenders to that particular throne. However, the events that took Syaoto by storm the other day took the life of my father and mother. In light of that loss, and of other losses I experienced, I wondered if my time may be better spent doing something more. And so I came here."

"I see," Lamont said softly. "My condolences for your father and mother. Losing family is a difficult, and often life-changing, affair."

He spoke like he knew what he was talking about, and Kergo nodded solemnly. The boy didn't seem to have much more to say, and the chancellor turned to Ragekku next. "What of you?"

Ragekku cleared his throat, leaning so far forward in his chair that I thought it might tumble. "We hold an estate in Balgena. I was traveling when the world started to fall. Not abroad in other realms, but still far from home. We suffered property damages and my horse was victim to a falling column, but no losses in the family or estate. Thing is, that whole event really hit me where it counts."

He slammed a fist over his heart – an abrupt movement that made Kergo nearly launch from his seat next to him. "My family. I've been away from them for a long time. Taking this job would mean a lot to them. Balgena is only a days' ride, and this place needs a good king."

"What did you do before now?" I asked.

Ragekku shrugged. "Mercenary work. I've been able to wield a sword better than fat nobles wield their salad fork, and from a younger age. I work closely with an old friend from the King's Own, a man who I've entrusted a great deal of my estate, and we've trained together for decades. My combat expertise is next to none."

"And what of lordship?" Lamont asked. "Have you ruled any lands next to your estate? A dukedom, perhaps? Even an army?"

Ragekku thought about it visibly, but shook his head. "Nadda. Never piqued my interest before, y'know. My old man used to always tell me that it's never too late to travel a given path."

Lamont nodded solemnly. "A wise man, your father," he said. When Ragekku leaned back, Lamont slowly turned toward Lancet. "Well, I suppose I must hear of you next. So what do you have for us, Lancet Cooper?"

Lancet got to his feet and bowed before us. It didn't impress anyone. "As spoken prior, I'm Lancet Cooper of Enthrall, a field commander in Syaoto's royal army."

"You were the Master General before, were you not?" Lamont interjected dryly. "Under the reign of Vincent Ordenstraum?"

Tension snapped through the room. A few of our fellow council listened intently. How could the enemy work his way out of this one?

"Aye," Lancet said with a solid nod. He resumed his seat, but sat at the edge of it. "In service of my world, no matter which king sat upon the throne. Many of our people did the same. After all, there was little else we could do but find positions of power in such a dark time. Becoming Master General ensured the safety of many people, both beneath me and simply of the common people."

I very much doubted anyone was safe beneath this snake-faced man, but a few of the council seemed satisfied. Lamont, however, kept Lancet in his sights.

"You weren't one of many," Lamont reasoned. "The King's Own disbanded. Others vacated the capital until the tyrannical emperor was dethroned."

Lamont leaned forward even further, maintaining eye contact with Lancet. "My home was taken by an enemy once as well. Many could say I was at fault. I stepped down from the council and hid myself away unless I needed supplies. That emperor killed many that I loved, and harmed a great deal more. Would it have been different if I served him? Would he not have harmed so many people?"

"Perhaps you should have," Lancet replied guardedly. "I only know that I could help more from a position of power."

Lamont shook his head sadly. "Perhaps I am a man of different honors, but I would never serve the enemy. Not from such an auspicious role where, surely, you had to carry out his dark bidding more than once. Or is there another reason he found you to promote?"

His words seemed to be impacting Brom, too, which I felt guilty for. I hoped he wasn't setting up a double-edged sword. Ragekku listened intently, attention rapt on Lamont.

"I served the army well," Lancet replied. "Vincent saw this when he rose to power. He needed a strong ally in his field, and sodding Brom was far too pertinent to serve him well. Too many would have turned coat if Brom left, though. We needed to abdicate his role and create a better one."

Brom made to speak, but Lamont stopped him. "There is a story I'm quite interested in," he said. "Vincent's rise to power. How, exactly, did an alien emperor come into the kingdom of Syaoto in time to interfere in King Lionel's reign?"

Lancet was rigid as stone. "You would not dare suggest—"

"Now, now," the chancellor interrupted, stepping between them. "These matters are of no relation to the royal election! Lamont Declovin of Vortiger, I pray you find another topic to impeach upon."

It was around then I wagered they paid off the chancellor. My eyes wandered to the council behind us. Just how many of them were the same?

"Very well," Lamont gave in, leaning back once more in repent. "One last question from me. You're familiar with the King's Own. Ragekku is affiliated with a member of the previous legion. Brom, too, professes to be a past member. Were you ever on the chair?"

Lancet shook his head. His eyes had a whole new quality of ice to them now. If Lamont kept pressing him, I wasn't sure what would happen. Lancet had proven to be a formidable combatant. "I was not, no. I am spirit-born and quite young still. It takes many years to join such a prestigious group."

"Koteran is close to your age, lad," Ragekku commented lazily. "The captain of the King's Own became a member when he was a teen."

The chancellor silenced further commentary with a look. Lancet spared the man a look of daggers before returning his attention to Lamont. "These are people who attended prestigious schools. An old captain favored Brom. Koteran and Will were both very close to the king."

The last note took me by surprise. Will was a member of the King's Own? I'd hardly gotten to meet Ryoku's first Guardian, but he spoke highly of him. I wondered if he should not be here himself, seated before us as a proper candidate. We had all that we could muster in the short time. Syaoto needed a ruling king before anarchy surely struck.

Lamont studied Lancet evenly. "Have you attended a school of any kind? You said you were from Enthrall, correct?"

Lancet looked a little flustered. "Uh, yes. There is an academy in Enthrall..."

"But you don't quite look like you're of Syaoto heritage," Lamont ventured. "Silver hair? Blue eyes? You have a wirier build. Nothing quite like I've seen of Syaoto folk."

Lancet made to rise from his chair, but the chancellor stopped him with a look. "I do believe I called an end to this interrogation some time ago."

Everyone turned deadly silent. Lancet sat on the edge of his chair. Oliver appeared near Lamont's elbow, a hand on his sword, eyes locked on Lancet.

Finally, Lamont rose from his chair, stretching like he'd spent days there. "Very well," he said heavily. "Thank you all for your time. I believe we should conduct our personal council now. By your leave."

All five men rose as one. Kergo looked horribly nervous. Brom's poker face was made of stone. While Arthexus looked confident and snide, Ragekku didn't seem to mind either way. For that man, this was just a gamble. Lancet left rigidly, his eyes on Lamont until he left the room.

As soon as they piled out, Lamont turned to us. "Fetch me any files you can on those five men," Lamont ordered the chancellor. "I want criminal records, medical history, anything that can pertain to the case. Rena, if you could act as a second pair of arms for our chancellor. I'm sure he could use the help to carry all those files."

The chancellor went rigid. Lamont clearly suggested Rena's accompaniment to keep him from interfering or leaving anything out. "Yes, of course," Rena replied immediately. She curtsied to Lamont and left with the chancellor, who walked like he'd stuck a broom between his legs on the side.

Lamont looked at me and smirked. "Now it is up to us," he said softly. "You seem of a brave and noble heart. I hope you can help me decide the best possible candidate here."

I nodded, glad to have Lamont on my side. With that, we all exited into the back room to begin our judgment.

(Later that day...)

"The council coronation has reached a verdict."

It was almost half a day after we first convened. The group of us had scarcely left the room save for bathroom breaks. They brought lunch to us, which was a pleasantly filling meal to help clear my mind.

When Rena returned with the chancellor, she brought news that lifted our spirits. The party that left to the Enthralmen Jungle returned, scepter in hand. Kimo returned to Orden as well. I was horribly uncertain about his intentions, but he'd just done us a huge favor. That, and Will was back. Lamont wanted to summon him to the council, but he had already taken off somewhere with Sira. My heart did somersaults at this. Were they pursuing Ryoku? Was I in the wrong place right now?

The five kings had returned to their seats just before we came into the room, their eyes immediately upon us as though we'd never left. The kingly candidates weren't the only ones who looked nervous. The chancellor dabbed at his brow with a handkerchief. Many of the council exchanged uneasy glances. Oliver kept to himself, but his eyes were always on Brom. Even Lamont looked uncertain. He was, of course, an emissary from another world about to present our final decision.

Lamont cleared his throat. "We've tarried long enough," he spoke, his voice like the crack of a whip. "The night will fall soon, and I would have the new king readily upon the throne by morning. This world needs a firm hand to guide it through the chaos of the previous night, to begin the reparations and to unify its people."

Everyone nodded solemnly. Arthexus was practically glowing, like a child who awaited presents he'd already seen. Lancet's expression wasn't too different. Next to him, Kergo was sweating almost as badly as the chancellor. Brom sat like a neutral mountain in his ceremonial armor, a man who would take defeat the same way as victory. Ragekku leaned over the back of his chair, but he was uncharacteristically grim.

Lamont turned toward Arthexus first. He fell silent for a long moment, studying the duke of Balgena with scrutiny.

"Duke Arthexus Mandrake the Second," Lamont began, "will remain the young lord of Balgena."

Arthexus made to rise from his chair, but the chancellor came to our defense. "I would remind you that this is a royal proceeding," he said shrilly. "Any actions against our council are actions against our kingdom."

It took a moment, but Arthexus leaned back into his chair. His eyes looked like balls of ice as he glared at Lamont. "Very well, then. Why have you, a man of Vortiger, come to this verdict?"

Lamont was glad he asked. "You reside as the son of the current duke of Balgena," he said. "Thus, certain ill effects would come into play. The Capital would be tucked under Balgena's wing – which, if I've read about your father correctly, may well be his intention. The Capital cannot be swayed or chosen by another. Its king must be sovereign above all the lands, and no man's father can control the kingdom under their nose. You are also, if I understand correctly, the sole heir to the throne of Balgena. With matters between the two cities already boiling, this would cause further turmoil between them."

Lamont leaned forward in his chair, fixating Arthexus' gaze in his own. When he spoke, it was with such fluid, levelled rage that it sent chills down my spine.

"I am sure you understand that Syaoto, as well, is an even community. Vortiger has women in her armies, which I admit to not seeing here in Syaoto. However, they do hold an auspicious role in this kingdom, one that must not be underestimated. They hold our trades, our commerce, have revolutionized the courtesan trade, and uphold farms and estates. There are many within the kingdom."

He gestured to one of the council members behind us, a middle-aged lady. "Annalise here controls the flow of taxes in the community. Syaoto expects its strong men to protect them, to uphold the army and maintain peace, but we are not the smartest, I can assure you. Without Annalise, we may have already scourged into debt. I watched her scrawling notes throughout our meeting on how to budget with the recent disaster. She has already divided our funds between the different sectors of this city. A great deal has gone to finding homes for those who lost them. Funerals, for those who lost their loved ones, funded by this city and her pockets. Even Vincent Ordenstraum let her work. Yes – even the dark emperor knows a certain respect for women. I wager that they hold a higher place in Orden's armies."

Arthexus was growing red in the face as Lamont leaned even closer. "I suggest you learn to respect them as well. Given some of your criminal history, I should hope to never see you upon a throne in a city I walk."

Arthexus sputtered. "T-This is an outrage!" He turned on the chancellor, red as a rose. "How did these people come to have such records?"

Rena bowed meekly before him, and his head inclined toward her. "My apologies, Lord Arthexus. Given that I was asked to accompany him and retrieve all these files, I also helped carry them back to our room. We had to be certain we didn't miss anything."

The glare Arthexus gave her made me unconsciously lean out next to Rena. When he glared at me, I stuck out my tongue at him subtly. "Na na," I murmured in a singsong voice, and waved to him with one hand. "I'd say we'll see you later, but…"

At this, Arthexus stood upright like an aggravated porcupine, quills all on end. "Very well," he snapped. "I should have known better than to entrust my future to the likes of these outsiders. I'll see myself out."

He stormed out, his face almost as red as his cherry cape. I smothered a giggle as he left, reminding myself that we had to be professional. Lamont caught my gaze, and winked. "Your turn," he told me.

I swallowed. Right. Public speaking… not my favorite.

"Kergo Bassonet, lord of Fort Issomas." I drew a couple surprised looks. Technically speaking, in the order they presented themselves in, I was skipping over Brom. I took a deep breath. "Respectfully, we have decided you are not yet fit for the throne. Don't worry – it's not as bad as Arthexus, I promise!"

Kergo smiled shakily, to my relief, and it gave me the courage to go on. "From our talk with you and our search into your records, you are more than fit in terms of the heart. Syaoto needs a kind king, and we would love to have you on the throne, but it is a stressful and exhausting job. As a lordling from Fort Issomas, a smaller dukedom, we're unsure you have the right experience for the job.

"However," I went on, "we wish to keep that path open for you in the future. You said that you do not wish to reign over Fort Issomas any longer, and so we offer you a position on the royal council. With the promise of our new king, we harbor strong hopes. Reforming the King's Own and a strong supporting council are on the agenda, and we would like to see you in that position. Come the next opportunity, you could honestly be ready for the role."

Kergo nodded. He looked a little upset, but at least we didn't send him packing like Arthexus. "I would be honored," he said softly, with more confidence than he used in our interview. "I'd be happy to serve under our new king. If I can make our world a better place in any way, I'd happily do so."

"We'll gladly have you, Kergo Bassonet," I assured him. My glance turned to Lamont. It was time for our next candidate. I wanted to leave this one to him. By his expression, he was all too happy about it.

"Lancet Cooper." Lamont took a deep breath. Again, we were skipping Brom and Ragekku onto the last of the five candidates. If the tactic confused Ragekku, he didn't show it. "You are unfit to be king of this land."

Lancet's eyes flashed. "What brings you to this delusion, may I ask?" he demanded. The chancellor shot him a warning glance. At least now, since Lamont ensured he didn't leave anything out, the chancellor more readily took our defense.

"Partially, your lack of expertise," Lamont replied, "in any matter. We looked into the swordsmanship school at Enthrall, which... lacks any evidence of your actual attendance. That said, there *is* a letter of graduation from the academy in Syaoto Capital. The letter is dated about seven years ago, which is more than a little steep for somebody of your age.

"The council enlightened us on the promotion process through the army. Ten years in the academy, beginning as a mere page. That last year is an intermittence into the novice rank, which can last anywhere from one year to twelve, depending on the amount of community services carried out, victories you participate in, recommendations, and whatnot under your belt. Our friend, Alex Retton, passed only a year as a novice before accepting the role of a median soldier. From there..."

He looked to Oliver, whose chest puffed out. "A median soldier will hold rank for up to five years, or else branch off into the castle guard. High rank is reserved for only the best among the army. These are men who can oversee their allies in combat, fully medically trained, outdoor survivalists..."

He looked up, and held Lancet's gaze. "From there, promotion to field commander is only on personal recommendation, usually by Lord General Brom, or from another man of similar stance. King Lionel, perhaps, or..."

Oliver turned back to Lamont, who fished out a paper from a stack on his lap. "I have your letter of recommendation here, Lancet Cooper. The signature baffled us, as I'm sure you know. The implications of such a thing worried me. And then we compared them to this..."

Lamont held that up with another document, one of newer print. The chancellor stepped closer to observe, and his eyes widened. We all knew what it was. Lancet's fists curled up under his chair. More than ever, I worried he'd attack us.

The chancellor looked perturbed. "Why, this is the bounty for Ryoku Dragontalen."

Lamont was already fishing out another documentation. "And his graduation papers," he added, shoving them toward the chancellor. "Whose signature would this be?"

The chancellor stared at them, jaw slightly agape. "The dark emperor. Vincent Ordenstraum."

Kergo looked at Lancet incredulously. "Then that means... you're from the Ordenstraum academy?"

"The signatures match," Ragekku added, peeking over the chancellor's shoulder. "Well, hell. Looks like he's had his claws in

Syaoto for longer than we knew." He smirked knowingly at Lancet. "That seems about the cue for you to high-tail outta here, boy."

"I second that," Lamont said sternly. All eyes turned to Lancet, who sat upon his chair like a cornered dog, one hand at his belt. Then, with an outcry of rage, he lunged at Lamont, rearing his lance over his head like a scorpion tail. I screamed in alarm. How had he possibly snuck a weapon like that in here? Magic?

Lamont didn't have his weapon. He stumbled back over his chair, scrambling for something to defend himself with. Before Lancet could reach him, however, Ragekku and Brom sprang upon him. The combined weight of the stranger and the Lord General brought Lancet down like reeds to the wind. The soldier cried out, voice strained, struggling to free himself as a team of guards entered the room. It seemed, to my pleasure, that they were ready for such a thing.

"Wrong move, Lancet," Ragekku quipped, tapping the hilt of his sword proudly. "You're already an enemy of the keep, and you wanted to add assault charges onto that? Tsk tsk..."

Lancet spat at him, but the swordsman deftly maneuvered out of the way, chuckling under his breath. He couldn't get another word out as the soldiers escorted him out, and the door slammed behind them. I caught Lancet glaring back at us before he vanished from view.

"Wretched child," one of the council members muttered angrily. "A spoiled lad since he joined the army. I'm glad we uncovered what we could!"

"No kidding," Ragekku said, leaning back on his chair. "A soldier of Orden actually infiltrated you guys. Well, hell. Whaddya say? Let's get this show back on the road. I'm guessin' I'm next?"

Lamont and I exchanged glances. I really liked Ragekku, especially after he stood up for us like he did. At Lamont's behest, I cleared my throat.

"Ragekku Gero," I began, "you are not fit to be king." I sucked in a deep breath, afraid to look at his expression. However, he just looked bored, still. "You have the heart and courage it takes to guide people. Regrettably, that doesn't translate to ruling an entire world, let alone a kingdom. But we have looked into you – what records exist on Syaoto, anyway."

Ragekku gave me a mock look of terror. "Whatever that handmaiden in Balgena said about me—"

"Hush," Lamont warned him, but he was snickering. "Let her speak."

Ragekku gave me a concerned look. "Of course – how rude of me. Go on, lass."

I cleared my throat again. "However," I went on, "we recommend you apply for a recently opened position in the castle. By our studies, there are few soldiers currently left in the city who might fit the role of Lord General. That may be the best role for a man who fights with his heart rather than his head, someone young and full of initiative. You'll have a few noble warriors at your call who, no doubt, will work well with you. Perhaps an opening for another field commander, too."

Ragekku seemed more pleased by this idea than anything else. "Gotcha. I might have a recommendation for some field commanders. We'll look into it later."

All eyes turned quickly to Brom. As soon as I'd mentioned the open title of Lord General, the man went rigid and attentive – the general waiting for orders. For a moment, there was such shining enthusiasm and youth in his face that I could almost see a quite young Brom behind his years of stress.

"Brom Gerenadh," Lamont started, in a bold and loud voice. "You may have noticed your previous position is now open. This is because, as of today, we wish for you to stand as the new king of Syaoto. You have served the army loyally for over forty years. You dealt with many grievances and sufferings for the kingdom. You lost people you loved, and kept vigil to the crown even during Vincent's reign. You fought among the King's Own and climbed your way through the army from the bottom. Most importantly, you were close with King Lionel. You have witnessed both how a good kingdom and a corrupt one runs. We acknowledge this as we offer you the crown."

Brom's face was poker-straight, a soldier's expression. Whatever his face hid, his shoulders gave way to a bursting sense of pride. He stood like a mountain before us. We couldn't actually put a crown upon his head, unfortunately – apparently, the relic had been lost to the ages. All knew Brom's face, though, and that was enough.

"I am forever grateful to you," Brom told us. "I will rule Syaoto as the great King Lionel did before me. I will never let darkness infiltrate this kingdom again."

Ragekku stood as well, hand on his sword. "I'd be honored to serve as your Lord General," he said bravely, and bowed deeply before Brom now. "You sound faithful and true. I might like you a little more than the last king."

Brom smirked. "And I would have you." He pulled Oliver in with an arm around his shoulders. "This is Oliver Rouge, my second-in-command. I would almost take him as a royal assistant, but I sense the man would be better at your command. He still has many years of good service to offer."

Oliver smiled at them both. "Absolutely. I beckon the other worlds to try us now!"

Excitedly, the chancellor led Brom and Ragekku out of the room, all too eager to announce the news. Lamont was grinning to himself, and turned to Rena and I. "We've made history today, girls," he said proudly. "Declaring a king and a general to this kingdom. I have faith in them, and I think Ryoku would, too."

That made me smile.

SCENE SIX: ESCAPE

...Of Act Nine: Separation

*In the eyes of Ryoku Dragontalen, we are in
The Twisted Tower, in the world of Vxxyura.
It is late evening
On November 15th, 2017.*

"Ryu, terrible storm stopped!"

"Yeah," I yawned, trudging behind the energetic Bohko. "How long until we get to the top?"

"Not long!" Bohko cried. "Not long at all!"

I nodded, too exhausted to feel fully relieved. Since I started following this little creature through the tower, we must have climbed at least ten stories, navigating complex paths of stairwells and corridors. Bohko dubbed this the Twisted Tower, and I soon realized why. Last time we passed a window, I glanced out to see the hallway we'd just been in across from us, even though we'd just ascended a flight of stairs. From there, we could glance up and down the height of the tower, and nothing seemed to match up with what we'd trekked through.

To add to the confusion, Shadowhearts roamed the place. They never flocked in great numbers, but clambered out of the darkness like they'd been sleeping in the shadows for centuries. Bohko tried to describe to me the different breeds. I knew people called the little ones Silhouettes, and the big, dumb ones Brawns. Honestly, I wasn't sure if these were their real titles or just the Bohko dictionary edition anymore.

Some of them did have strange names. When I explained the tentacle beasts that attacked Syaoto, Bohko fell silent for a long time before dubbing them 'Gokri.' He eventually told me that those particular creatures might be as strong as the Keeper of Death. I couldn't be glad enough that I'd been with my stronger friends in Syaoto.

Bohko told me that they were part of a breed called 'Complex Shadow,' a manmade variety of Shadowhearts somehow developed in labs a thousand years ago. To contemplate the complexities of that made my head spin.

We mostly encountered more Brawns and Silhouettes, but later, encountered a particularly pesky one Bohko called the Grabber. This one had me stumped. It was dark orange and a little bigger than a Silhouette, but with claws fashioned like a sloth. Its main method of attacking was to lunge from the shadows and latch onto the enemy's back, where its sloth-like claws gripped tight. It took some maneuvering to stab the creature in its weak spot, the small of its back. I didn't speak to Bohko for some time after he let me figure that out on my own.

I couldn't help but notice more similarities between the anatomy of Bohko and the Grabber. I wondered if they bore relation somehow, despite Bohko adamantly insisting it wasn't a Shadowheart.

"Ryu, look!" Bohko cried, stunning me out of my tired thoughts. I followed its voice to a window looking out over the tower.

"I already know the tower tw…" I trailed off when I reached the window. Right across from us was the very peak of the Twisted Tower, casting a wicked shadow over us. My tired mind didn't even want to understand how it worked. We were finally close.

"One floor left!" Bohko wailed. "One floor, and then Ryu go bye-bye."

It sounded awfully sad about this fact, which tugged at my heartstrings. I didn't imagine Bohko had much company here. Still, I couldn't tarry any longer.

"What are we waiting for?" I asked, as though unperturbed by the idea, and started walking at a faster pace. Bohko trailed along with me, hopping sideways like a strange little frog. I watched it as I hurried along, trying to ignore the residual pain in my limbs.

"Hey, Bohko."

The little creature's ears perked up. "Ryu calls?" it asked meekly.

"You say you're not a Shadowheart. If that's the case, what are you exactly? A demon? A monster?"

Bohko's eyes narrowed. "No demon. No monster. Just Bohko."

"Just Bohko?" I echoed. "Well, what do you mean? Like I'm Ryu—" I immediately chastised myself for using *his* name for me "—but I'm a human. Like that. So what exactly are you?"

Bohko looked at me for a long moment as we kept on walking. "Well, Bohko used to be human. Like Ryu."

I raised a brow. "You used to be human?"

Bohko opened its small mouth, but a sudden noise made us both stop. A certain feeling of dread filled my stomach. No. Not now.

It was, undeniably, the screech of the Keeper of Death.

The monster appeared suddenly between Bohko and I, forcing us each to push ourselves back. Bohko swung up its claws in an apparent defensive maneuver. This time, it stood with me as the Keeper hovered between us like the Reaper itself. Its cloak wavered in a fell wind that I couldn't feel in my hair, its claws glistening like the outside ground, dewy with acid.

"I told you to leave," the Keeper rasped, its voice like rattling chains. "Despite my warning, you remain in the world of death, one where the living must not tread."

"Are you serious?" I demanded. More than anything, I was frustrated by now. "I'm literally minutes from this method of travel that can get me out of here, and you show up *now*?"

The Keeper hovered between us, seeming to judge me silently beneath its hood of shadows. "I see," it rumbled. "The object which keeps this world standing. That would make sense."

I released my grip on my knife. "Wait, what?"

The Keeper emitted a low growl. "This world hovers in a state between life and death. From death, new life will be born. I would be released from my vows."

I hesitated, still keeping my hand close to my weapon. "This world would die if I take that method of travel?"

The creature contemplated my words. I couldn't believe it was listening to me now. These creatures didn't seem to act the same each time I encountered them.

"So I theorize," the creature replied. "It makes sense. As a Keeper of Death, it is not my duty to set foot into this tower unless trespassers walk in it."

"Despite the Shadowhearts," I muttered, unable to help myself from one snarky comment. "So, wait. You're going to let me go?"

The Keeper let out a low, trailing growl that reminded me of some kind of predator. "So it would seem, if it is capable of being used."

To my surprise, the Keeper reached up toward its hood. With its long, ivory claws, it pulled back the hood of its cloak to fall to its shoulders. I looked upon the creature's face for the first time, and wasn't sure exactly what I beheld. It looked almost like a lion, but the creature still hovered in the air. It had gleaming red eyes and appeared as much a Shadowheart as Bohko did.

"W-What are you?" I asked, taking a nervous step back.

The Keeper looked me in the eye. "I am the Keeper of Death," it replied solemnly. Much of the shadowy aspect to its voice seemed to dissipate when its hood was off. "I am sworn to protect this place, the place of death."

"Yeah, but you're... a lion?" I asked tentatively. "Are you another Shadowheart?"

Bohko made a noise, seeming to alert the Keeper to its presence for the first time. "Keeper not Shadowheart, either," Bohko told me irritably. "Keeper is shadow of another thing. Almost same to Bohko. Keeper cursed to protect place. Why I told you, no fight Keeper."

I gave Bohko a dry look. "You were actually serious?" I hesitated, half-turning behind me. I thought I sensed movement. When I looked, though, there was nothing there. Only darkness.

When I turned back, the Keeper stood on two legs. It was an odd sight to behold. Whatever that cloak was made of, it seemed the reason for half its darkened attributes. Its raspy voice, the way it floated off the ground. Maybe even those foot-long claws.

"Bohko is here," the Keeper growled, studying both of us with interest. "Does that mean...?"

Bohko waved its arms frantically. "I tried telling you! This Ryu!"

The Keeper studied me intently. I felt somewhat naked before its crimson gaze. "...Ryu. Ryoku Dragontalen."

I gave Bohko a dry look. "You know me too, I guess?"

The Keeper averted its gaze. "Correct. In a sense." It paused for a long moment. "We are the Keepers. We are of a race that once used to protect people like you, but have been cursed to this darkness. We were once the Gallians. Long ago, we were warriors of human and lion blood. When this world was reformed, there was... darkness within it. Darkness which touched many hearts."

"You're cursed?" I asked. "So... you're not *actually* like this. Like a Shadowheart."

The Keeper growled lowly. "Not a Shadowheart. However... yes. Very similar."

I nodded, unsure I really understood. "So when this world was reformed, this happened to you?"

I remembered what Kimo had told me. About my old self, the one who'd sacrificed themselves to save the spirit realm. Apparently doing so had caused all these new worlds to form. "What are you saying, exactly?"

"Much of these realms were born from that Defender," the Keeper said. "There was more. While his soul reforged much of these realms, there was... something else. Certain darkness seeped into the realms. It cursed my race into these dark monstrosities." Its claws rattled at its side. Under its cloak, I guessed it was clenching its fists. "With no heroes left to these realms, we have taken to protecting ancient locations. Pieces of my ancient homeland."

"Why?" I asked. I felt overbearingly exhausted, and I wasn't even sure I could retain this whole conversation. "Why do you have to sit here and protect death?"

Bohko waved its claws. "Tower linked to places below!" it cried. "To old world. Keepers made to protect places. Stop old world from coming back."

That surprised me. "To stop them from coming back?" I asked. "Like, they still exist? Below these realms?"

The Keeper nodded. "These worlds are like bandages over the old world. While they remain, the old world may recover from the damage in that battle."

"What battle?" I asked. "What did... my old self or whatever, have to sacrifice himself against?"

The creature's head lowered. "The enemy of our entire realm. The –"

A thud cut us off from behind me. All three of us turned. I knew I'd heard something before, but now I was certain. "More Shadowhearts?"

The Keeper let out a low snarl. It turned to Bohko. "You are certain this is the boy?"

Bohko nodded fervently. "No mistake. Ryu is Ryu."

The Keeper straightened to its full height. Its crimson eyes gleamed like flames. "Then you must go on, Ryoku Dragontalen. Something here seeks to impede your journey."

I hesitated as the Keeper turned away. "Wait," I demanded. "What is this enemy? Is it something I'll have to face?"

The Keeper replaced his hood, and the creature's feet lifted once more from the ground. It was, once more, fully a Keeper. It turned to me and uttered, in its raspy voice, "I believe you are already on your way there."

The realization hit me as the Keeper turned. "Orden," I murmured. It made sense. Every friend I'd met spoke of the darkness of that place. I knew Chris Olestine was connected to me somehow – did this make him another part of the person who sacrificed themselves?

I felt a greater sense of purpose than ever. It almost drove all my aches away in its power. I knew exactly what I needed to do. My mission had more reason than ever before. Saving Chris Olestine. Defeating Vincent Ordenstraum. I could avenge Loki and figure out the messy puzzle of my past, all grouped up in one neat bundle.

"One last thing," the Keeper rasped, now facing away from me. Bohko was scrambling behind me somewhere, and I heard him open a door – pale moonlight flooded the room. Ahead of the Keeper, something stirred in the darkness. "My name was once Cobalt Bagaro. If you can find him... seek out Kohmar Issilrin. Speak my name to him. He will know who you are. He will help you."

Bohko scrambled up to me, clutching a source of light in its claws. "I found it!" it cried. "Ryu must take this!"

I hesitated, nearly dropping the item Bohko pressed into my hands. "Wait," I said, "stop! We can leave together! Come with me to Orden!"

Bohko crawled ahead of me next to Cobalt. "Ryu must go. Travel only good for one. Bohko and Keeper hold off enemy."

I stared down at the item in my hands. It was the size of both my hands pooled together, and seemed the truest source of light in this fallen world. This was my ticket out of here.

"No, wait," I protested wearily. "You both helped me! We can—"

Cobalt emitted a frustrated howl. "Go, or else never leave this place! Time runs shorter than you realize."

I still hesitated. Bohko turned on me, its golden eyes wide, and then slapped the pearl in my hand with its claw. I flinched back as a bright light swelled up from within it, expanding to all around me. The last thing I noted was a shadow appearing in the hallway before Cobalt and Bohko before the light overtook me, and I was gone.

...End of Act Nine.

Act Ten: The Serpent's Nest...

*In the eyes of Ryoku Dragontalen, we are in
Orden Capital, in the world of Orden.
It is nearing the end of the night
On November 15th, 2017.*

SCENE ONE: THE SERPENT EMPEROR

Landing in the next world was rough. My legs jolted beneath me and I lost my balance, stumbling into a thick wall with the brunt of my shoulder. My breath slammed from my chest, leaving me struggling to breathe, trying to gain my bearings.

I was outside some kind of city or fort. The wall I rammed into was tall, black and made of some sort of reflective iron or steel. It spread out on either side as far as I could see, interrupted only by a tall black gate further down, the height rimmed with spikes. Crisp frost crunched under my feet across a wide expanse of grass, only interrupted by the odd tree and a path leading to the gate.

Above me was a bleak and grey sky, a sign of recent and coming storms. I could faintly smell the usual scents of a city – burnt metal, tanned leather, fresh baked bread, and other such items. Even then, the smell of rain clung heavy to all else.

There, I noticed two guards wearing black clothing who patrolled the gate. Luckily, neither seemed to notice me.

As I finally caught my breath, I let my back rest against the wall, my mind racing. I could be wrong, but I had a good idea of just where I had landed. My last thoughts upon leaving Vxxyura.

Orden.

I pictured my charge's face clearly in my mind. His hazel hair, olive skin, delicate nose. All too easily, I could recall how he appeared before me in Vortiger once more, and that feeling of closeness remained. Now that I knew about my old self and the bit about a shattered soul, it only made sense. He was a part of me, and probably the key to figuring out everything that was going on.

He was here. If I was in the right place, anyway. My heart filled with resolve, I pushed myself away from the wall. Now I just had to get in. I was right next to the gate. It was only manned by two guards, but I didn't doubt that there were more on the other side, ready to snatch up the boy likely posted all over the kingdom. If I had any chance, it was to disguise myself.

I dropped my bag and unclasped it, rifling through my belongings. To my surprise, the pearl I'd used to travel here was nowhere to be seen. Crossing worlds must have expended it, however that worked. Luckily, I still had parts of my outfit from other worlds. I picked out the coat I wore in Lysvid and shrugged it on. With some work, I was able to cover Ragnarokkr behind my coat and tucked the other weapons in my bag, except my knife that I kept at my belt. I wished I had the gravity bag Loki bought in Vortiger. One of my comrades had that, which carried most of my other clothing and our amassed coins.

With a deep, inward sigh, I holstered my bag on my shoulder, tucked most of my hair in behind my hood, and started toward the gate. A few steps in their direction were all it took for the guard closest to me to turn. He elbowed his accomplice, and they both watched me as I approached.

For a long, terrifying moment, I feared my meager disguise was pointless. Did they recognize me? Could I luck out, walking right through the front doors of my enemy's lair?

"Hail, friends," I called out, hiding the tremble in my voice behind my best attempt at a Syaoto-esque voice, and gestured with my hand.

The two guards returned the gesture. I was a little surprised to notice they weren't dressed like I expected. They both wore dark vests over black button shirts, and breeches puffed out at the shins where they tucked into tall boots. Each had a rapier at their side, and one had a halberd slung over his shoulder. Was I wrong about the world?

The closer one had flame-red hair and a brave grin. The other guard looked a little less friendly, with messy black hair that ended in sharp violet tips. Despite my imagination, they both looked horribly human. My mind turned them all into monsters while I journeyed here. Maybe that was a dangerous mistake.

I was worried I assumed the wrong world. Then again, I knew Sira hailed from Orden and she had unusual hair. It could be an Ordenite characteristic.

When I approached, the red-haired one strolled toward me. I held back a terrified flinch, but was surprised when he came to clasp my arm in a friendly gesture. "Good day," the guard told me in a sophisticated accent. "What brings you to the Capital of Orden today, world-traveler?"

So I was actually here. Orden.

My mind steeled over. Time to lie. Why was it so hard to figure out a reasonable lie? What if they tried to escort me inside for some reason? Disguise or no, Vincent would recognize me instantly. I realized, too, that my location gave away that I was from another world. I never considered the possibility that travel spots weren't entirely random. If world-travelers were directed here, it meant they had to pass the guards to enter the city.

"Hail, friends. I come from the world of Ellithea."

They both scrutinized me. I gulped. Was it really a good idea to bring attention to my elf ears?

"You speak like someone from Syaoto," the black-haired guard said. "You dress... outlandishly, I'll admit. Elves rarely come here either. What's your business here?"

"You do speak Ordenite rather well," the redhead commented with a smirk. "An elf who studies languages?"

I swallowed hard. Right. Defender magic and whatnot. At least they believed I was an elf. Passing off a Syaoto heritage would have been tougher. They all seemed way brawnier than me.

"Uh, yes," I replied. "I came from Syaoto recently. And... well, I learned the Ordenite language quite well there. From their king, Vincent Ordenstraum."

I chose the right guise. "Ah, you met our senior emperor," the red-haired guard said. He visibly relaxed now. "A good man, if a little too driven. Syaoto is our sister country, but the old emperor was never too fond of them. I've nothing against them myself – I have family there. My cousin just had a wedding there."

"You must forgive my friend."

A voice came from behind me. As soon as I heard it, a thousand notes of relief sang through my body. There stood Will, garbed in his usual Syaoto garb. It hadn't been long, but my eyes almost teared up to see him again.

"A terrible tragedy has befallen Orden, hence the reason for my elven friend here. He does not speak much of the Orden tongue, so I fear you may have confused him."

The red-haired guard scratched his chin. "A tragedy? In Syaoto? By the Creator, that explains why our emperor has not returned. Are they alright?"

I couldn't stop myself from exchanging a glance with Will. Vincent hadn't returned? Did that mean Loki's magic was effective?

More importantly, it spelled out something that threatened to flood me with enthusiasm. The throne was empty.

"I pray so," Will replied. "If we wish to make sure, then allow us to pass. We were to speak with his vassals and send reinforcements."

The black-haired one looked confused. "With the vassals? Very well then. I cannot question our senior emperor."

They turned in unison to open the gates. I swallowed hard when the red-haired one moved aside, and I saw my own wanted poster right behind him, pinned on the black wall. Will glanced nervously at me, but said nothing.

The screeching of the opening gates was like screaming cats, but it only lasted seconds before the very jaws of Orden hung opened before us. A short tunnel led to another gate that another set of guards were opening ahead of us, signaled by the first gate. I gazed into the brief darkness ahead ominously, but Will caught my arm and hurried me through, stopping to bow to the guards in turn. I hoped they misplaced his rush for the purpose of his lie.

I could see the city within as we neared the second gate. Cobblestone made up much of the path, parted only for a great sign that directed the populace through the markets. Hawkers of different commodities lurked around the entrance to snipe out newcomers as soon as they entered. For us, that only meant unwanted attention. Not only that, but guards seemed to patrol every few feet in the initial square. As we got closer, I saw rich-looking buildings of fine woods and smoothed stone splitting into two main paths into the city.

Will and I didn't speak until we passed the second pair of guards. "That was nerve-wracking," I muttered anxiously.

"Orden is just another city, hardly expecting their biggest bounty to just stroll into it." He looked me up and down subtly. "You are in rough shape. Why did you come here?"

"I didn't really mean to. I used a method of travel from Vxxyura and it just took me here."

He gave me a sharp look. "From Vxxyura? How on earth did you get there?"

"I'm not sure," I replied. "Then again, that's some timely event – you showing up here like that. Did you know I'd be here somehow?"

He gave me a look like a closed book. "Turn left here," he said.

I obeyed, but studied him curiously. He didn't look so well himself. The guards may not have seen it, but twigs and odd leaves stuck out in parts from his chainmail. Dirt and grime stained parts of his face, but others hastily scrubbed away. He was getting the beginnings of a scratchy beard, and dark shadows clung beneath his eyes.

The right turn went to the main markets, crowded with merchants and shoppers alike in huge crowds. We took to the left, more of a residential area with a few inns and some smaller shops. As soon as we passed the first bend, the quality of homes began to decay. Orden was a city squared on first impressions.

"Have you been here before?" I asked. "You seem to know the streets."

"Not in a very long time. But somebody else does."

I tried to see what he was looking at. Not as many people walked these streets. A few guards converged at the corner ahead. Somebody approached hastily in a brown cloak. I didn't realize until she reached up and adjusted the hood around her head.

"Sira," I breathed. The name came from my lips with a surprising delight.

She closed the distance between us in a lunge, clutching me like a pet that had gotten lost in the outside world. Her atmosphere smelled of strawberries and the faintest familiarity that made me feel like I finally came home. I hadn't realized I missed her. Then again, while pursued by Shadowhearts and the Keeper of Death, I could hardly tell what I was thinking.

She pulled back far enough to kiss me. I melted into it like candle wax. Her lips tasted like a spice, something that kept my lips searching.

"Ryoku," she whispered, pulling back enough that our noses were touching. "I thought I'd never fucking see you again."

"But you did," I replied. "How did you know I was here?"

"Guys!" Will cut in warningly. I almost ignored him, caught up in the spell of Sira's crimson eyes – but Sira's glance cut past mine, and then she stepped back. In a flourish, she threw aside her cloak and drew Sinistra in a mighty arc.

I whipped around. Where I swore there'd been only a few guards around us before, they closed in on us at all sides. Not only guards, but ranking soldiers and higher officers surrounded us. A field of rapiers, halberds, and – to my surprise – guns, all leveled toward us.

"What the..." I murmured, reaching over my back. My hood had fallen when Sira hugged me. Even then, that surely couldn't have summoned such a huge host of soldiers.

"He cannot be trusted." I thought I heard Will curse under his breath.

"It can't be helped," Sira growled. "Willy-boy, I've been waiting to see how you fare against Orden soldiers."

Will glanced sharply at her. "You think we can fight our way out?"

Sira snorted. "Tell me what the hell else we're gonna do."

While they bickered, one of the soldiers stepped forward. Where the guards had vests, he had a sleeveless black coat that came to his knees. A mane of wild blue hair fell in shocks around his face.

"Ryoku Dragontalen," he barked. This was no general like Brom or the others I met – he looked only a little older than Will. "By the imperial command of the crown of Orden, you are under arrest. You and your comrades shall accompany us in silence, or else be brought in bags."

I took a step forward – a quick lunge of Will's hand kept me from approaching further. The sound of dozens of guns cocking filled the area around us, blending with the ripe steel of drawn weapons.

"I don't want to hurt you," I told him loudly. "You don't realize what kind of man you serve. Stand down – let him come to me himself. I'll stand before him and challenge him. When I do, you'll all be freed."

The man snickered. "We won't be falling for your tricks, boy. If you insist on challenging us, then we have no choice!"

"Wait, that's not what I—"

The cracking of a multitude of guns shot through the air like nutcrackers. Smoke lit the air and went alight with the flash of the rifles. Will's big hands forced me down to the ground. A myriad of bullets burst above my head.

On the ground, somebody grabbed me by the shoulder. "Come on!"

I blindly allowed them to lead me. It was only when I hit a run off the ground that I realized it wasn't Will's voice. I caught a glimpse of Will and Sira in the smoke, running alongside me. Someone else led the way.

We broke out of the smoke into a side road. I heard shouting behind us, making me nervously glance over my shoulder, but the figure ahead of us urged my attention forward. I registered only a black cloak and a red sword naked in their other hand.

"Keep running!" he insisted.

The sounds of conflict broke out behind us. I still tried to glance back, surprised. It sounded like the soldiers were fighting another force. Was somebody defending us?

A small group of soldiers broke out in front of us, and looked as surprised as we were. One of them holstered his rifle. The figure leading us didn't break pace and lunged forth with his sword. I yanked out my knife with sore hands. I wasn't in the shape for this, but I didn't seem to have a choice.

The figure buried his crimson blade into the one wielding a gun. He didn't delay at all and drew back to block an incoming halberd. As he did, the hood of his cloak fell. He had stark-white hair.

My heart leapt in my chest. Kioru – the boy who helped me when I first arrived in the spirit realm.

In my lapse, a soldier ran out in front of me. I panicked, lashing out with my knife, but I didn't make it to the enemy. He fell dead right before me, a feathered arrow stuck between his eyes.

"Pay attention, kid," a flamboyant-sounding male voice demanded. I half-turned to see a boy with golden hair, the tips accented an electric blue. He dressed like a traveler in a white shirt and breeches, but belts layered much of his calves and across his chest.

He notched an arrow to his longbow with delicate fingers. "You're in the beast's jaws now."

Another soldier was coming at me. I lurched forward and caught his incoming rapier against my knife. The soldier pressed back, forcing me to retreat half a step. I struggled, trying to adjust my grip so I could hold this enemy off. I was horribly regretting jumping into Orden. I hadn't even properly rested since my fight with Kimo. The guards said Vincent wasn't here, but the kingdom was surely prepared for battle. Was this the work of the vassals? Kimo, even?

Before I could maneuver myself, the enemy's grip slackened, and I fell into him as he toppled lifelessly to the ground. Will yanked his lance free before he got caught up in the fall. He gave me a worried look and shoved something into my open hand.

"Drink," he ordered. "This could be our last fight. If you are still weak from your last battles, you will not survive."

I looked at the object. It was a small blue vial with oddly familiar contents. Trusting Will, I popped the cork and downed the substance. When a blueberry taste touched my lips, I recognized it. It was the same brew Eckhardt made for me in Bonnin.

Relief flooded me with the effects of the tonic rushed through my system. I knew I was still recovering from injuries, but my limbs felt like extensions of my soul, entities that would do as I commanded at a thought.

Kioru ran his blade through the last enemy ahead and glanced back at me. He spared little more than an apologetic smirk before beckoning me to follow. Experimentally, I tapped into the marks on my wrists – replenished. I'd barely been able to use them in Vxxyura without instigating stinging pain. The sounds of battle still raged behind us, and we kept running.

"Thank you for your help," Will said loudly to Kioru. Despite our pace, he sounded as though he were only on a brisk jog. "I do not surmise how the enemy knew of us."

Kioru made an annoyed noise back. "Whoever's intel you trusted, you weren't their only informant. Lars knew you were coming. If Kimo hadn't warned us…"

Sira faltered so strongly that her grip on my arm almost wrenched free. "Lars? Who the hell's that?"

"I doubt it matters," Will told her, surprised. "The guards said Vincent is not here. If we can avoid battle with the emperor, we should be alright."

"Kimo helped you?" I asked.

Kioru turned back like he was going to say something – but all four of us slammed into a wall. All at the same time, with shocked expressions, we stumbled back. I caught a horrified look in Kioru's eyes.

We knelt in the midst of a littered alleyway, the sounds of battle far behind us. I'd lost sight of the blond archer, and it was now just the four of us in the center of this narrow road. One building was the back of a bakery, burnt breads and bags of flour spilling from a waste bin. The cobblestone was thick with grime. Paint smeared the walls, and I caught sight of a snoozing homeless man behind a crate. He didn't as much as stir at our presence.

When I realized there was nothing we could have run into, a thick chill ran down my spine.

There was no wall.

"Well, well, well."

The voice didn't seem to come from anywhere for a moment. It hovered around us like a tangible thing. It spoke with rich power and authority, but there was insidiousness to it like a snake slithering out of the shadows.

"It pains me to believe we have such a tidy sum out for this stupid child. Little more than a boy, foolish enough to stumble *right* into my open arms. What a pity."

A figure appeared out of nowhere before us. He was tall and slender like a skeleton, with pale skin to match and a straight sheet of black hair that fell to his shoulders. His eyes were closed as he stepped out toward us, the heels of his shoes clapping like the only sound in the universe. He dressed in an open black robe of the most intricate quality, where the black shirt and pants beneath looked skin-tight.

I tried to get to my feet, but it felt like everything from the alley was forcing me to the ground. I noticed the man's fingers twitching as he strolled calmly toward us. Magic.

Kioru had better luck than me, struggling to rise to his feet and leaning heavily on his scarlet blade. "B-Bastard," he growled heavily. "Are you too afraid to fight us on fair ground? En garde!"

The man chuckled as he came to a stop mere feet before us. "Now, now, Kioru Rasale. I've entertained your game of lost boys with sticks and stones for quite some time, haven't I? I've not had the honor of meeting the full entourage until now."

He kept chuckling, almost uncontrollably, like a boy trying to withhold his excitement at Christmas. Finally, slowly, his eyes opened.

They were violet.

It felt like a shockwave hit me, my breath trapped in my chest. Was this another Ordenstraum? Somebody akin to Vincent?

The man chuckled giddily. "Oh my. I've been horribly excited for this moment, I promise you. Your eyes are filled with such confusion, Ryoku Dragontalen. I can see the puzzle pieces struggling to fit behind your gaze. You're trying to blend together any possible theory that would make sense, aren't you?"

Sira snarled next to me. She struggled against whatever power kept us down. "Quit playing games," she snapped. "Fight us! We don't have time for this!"

The man's violet eyes fell upon her. "Silly wench. Be quiet. The men are talking."

His tone made me push against the magic holding me down. My marks emitted a pained light. The man only gazed at me, bemused.

"To one of your caliber, fighting back is the most pointless thing you could do. It's a little pathetic, truly. As though I've stepped on the legs of an ant underfoot, and I watch the little creature struggling to get away." A cruel smirk spread his thin lips. "The more you push back, the stronger my magic becomes, and the weaker you will be. You could hardly hope to inflict a scratch upon a dark knight of Orden."

In my mind, the faintest spark went off. This man seemed to see it in my eyes, and he smiled widely.

"Watching you struggle to understand is hopelessly amusing, I hope you know, but it is getting a little dry with time. You truly do not have an inkling of the truth? No little breadcrumbs to follow to a solution?" His smile only spread further, until he looked like a snake ready to strike. "Or did my father not speak of me?"

When he saw the understanding finally appear in my eyes, his smile broke, and he laughed outright, throwing his head back like a wolf baying before the moon.

"There it is! The truth! Oh, how beautifully it should strike when my foe finally realizes just how hopeless his journey has become!"

He leveled his head again, drawing one of his twitching hands up to his face and eyeing me between his fingers with a cruel smirk. As his fingertips curled, the power pressing us back intensified, and I fell back onto my wrists. Even with the tonic Will gave me, my damaged wrist buckled.

"That's absolutely correct, that little realization you just had. My name is Lars Ordenstraum – the son of Vincent Ordenstraum, and reigning emperor of Orden!"

The blood ran from my face. His words had to be true. Nobody could speak with such confidence about a lie. Horribly enough, it rang true with me. Vincent had a son.

Each second threatened to shatter all the resolve I had built up over time. I knew the power Vincent wielded against me, with which he struck down Loki. How did his son compare?

"Enough games!" Will shouted. He pushed up with all his might and managed to rise to his feet, his shoulders hunched with the weight Lars put into holding him down. The emperor blinked, taken aback. "Cease your magic and fight us, as your father did!"

His words startled Lars even further, and the mention of his father made his delicate brows furrow. "Well, if that's all you wanted."

His hands fell to his pockets, and the energy holding us down dissipated. Will swayed oddly on his feet, released from the pressure he'd fought. Sira, Kioru, and I got to our feet. I jammed my knife in its sheath and grabbed Ragnarokkr from my back.

This was it. No soldiers around to interfere. No Roland or Kimo backing him, and it was four against one. My grip tightened on Ragnarokkr, and then I yanked it free, letting the steel sing through the air.

Kioru went at Lars with a wild cry, bringing his sword about in an arc. From the meager distance between them, I was sure the blow would land. Lars hadn't even drawn a weapon yet. When the sword came close, Lars bent doubly backwards, letting the blade sail overhead harmlessly, the steel inches from the tip of his nose. He rose effortlessly once more, unamused.

"You're awfully slow," Lars commented airily. "Haven't my soldiers forced you to fight better? I suppose they're but peons."

Will's lance levelled behind him, aimed for Lars' heart. Lars flashed a mock-shocked look, then pivoted to the side, watching as the lance brushed the fabric of his cloak. He let out a low whistle. "Now there is some raw power, if I've ever seen such a thing! Splendid! Even that brooding toy of my father's isn't quite like this!"

When Will sailed past Lars, the emperor smirked, and, with the hand still in his pocket, drove his elbow straight into the side of Will's ribs. In the same move, he lashed out with his other hand and struck Kioru in the center of the chest with enough force to knock him back. Will dropped to his knees, clutching his chest, and Kioru stumbled away.

Sira ran in, screaming as her crimson blade coursed through the air. Lars opened up his position, stepping away from the boys on the ground. "Hmm," he commented lazily. "You look Ordenite, but that weapon is simply archaic. Color me curious."

"Shut up!" Sira shouted, and swung with her broadsword like a baseball bat. Sinistra screamed through the air like an inferno. Lars watched it coming, brow raised.

"How curious."

At the last second, he ducked underneath the volatile swing and lunged forward. His empty palm rammed into Sira's stomach, bringing her down quickly. Lars straightened, looking around at my three comrades he'd taken out with a single blow. He chuckled softly to himself, facing away from me.

"You didn't even try to attack me. Why? Do you profess to be smarter than your friends? Or is it the opposite – are you a coward?"

"N-No," I hesitated, tightening my grip on Ragnarokkr. "Truth be told, I'm wondering if you know how to attack head-on."

His head lifted, then he turned his head, a look of great amusement on his face. "Oh? A quirky hero? A sense of humor?"

I shook my head. "Not so much. I mean, you haven't even drawn your sword."

He chuckled in response, now pivoting his body toward me. "How do you know I have a sword? Either way, I thought it best to even the playing field. Why would I draw a sword against someone who can't actually use theirs?"

I clenched my teeth, tightening my pose. The air of Lars suggested he could attack without a second's notice, but he was acting more like a creature playing with his food.

"What makes you think that?"

"Oh, come now," Lars said, and scowled. "You don't seriously believe that I haven't done my research? Do you ignore the games going on around you, too? The half-truths, the outright lies, the literal chessboard of a team you have going? It's all just like that now – but everyone's been playing far longer than you, and I've read your whole side of the board."

I gulped. If not before, it was truly setting in how great my disadvantage was. Whether Lars was stronger or weaker than Vincent, he knew a great deal more about me than I did of him. Until moments ago, I hadn't even anticipated the existence of this sadistic boy.

"I've quite anticipated this battle, you know. The broken little toy of a Defender, and the great emperor of Orden. A true battle for the books, no?"

I shrugged. "We know how the books always turn out." I could only think of Vincent's magic aimed at me, and when Loki stepped in.

Lars' brow rose, and he laughed. "Funny. You know, I do appreciate people that can make me laugh." He reached to his belt beneath his robe, and carefully plucked out a long, needle-like rapier. It was a wholly different style of weapon than Vincent had, and wasn't one I'd ever tested my luck against before. The blade of it was jet-black. "Call me amused. If you can pretend to wield a sword, then I shall humor you. En garde, Ryoku Dragontalen!"

He danced toward me in a flawless gait. His strike was so smooth that I didn't anticipate the force he struck with. I shifted, working my balance to better face this foe, but he didn't relent. He lashed out several times with his rapier, and it was all I could do to maneuver Ragnarokkr around to block each attack. I could tell by his coy smile that he was only still playing. He moved perfectly from strike to strike, his footwork levelled and practiced, but he kept his eyes on mine rather than scan my body for telltale motions.

I counted his strikes as well as I could. He struck like heavy hail, hitting multiple spots at once often with his impressive speed. I kept one hand on the chain, one on the handle as I prepared to strike.

As soon as I detected a half-second of slowed movement, I latched my other hand onto the chain, throwing Ragnarokkr forth with all I had.

I couldn't complete the switch. My grip faltered, and Ragnarokkr slipped from my grasp as blood started to soak through my shirt. Lars smirked transparently, sticking his rapier back in under his robe.

"What… how did you…?"

"That was an admirable effort. Raising your sword to an enemy a thousand times stronger than you. Maybe you're just a naive boy who believes he can fight with a stranger's sword, or maybe you actually thought you could win. Maybe you were truly brave, but I doubt it."

My vision swam, and the ground started to close in on me. Soldiers came from all around, grabbing my friends off the ground. One grabbed each of my arms, dragging me off. I saw one try to lift my sword, but scowled. Behind him, Lars still watched me, his violet eyes swirling.

"Perhaps you would have been a worthy foe to me in the future. Given time, maybe you could have amounted to some feasible amount of skill. Maybe you could have actually landed a blow. But your chance is over, would-be hero." He turned away, his robe billowing behind him like a storm cloud. "Take them to the upper dungeons."

SCENE TWO: BOUNTY ROSE

...Of Act Ten: Serpent's Nest

In the eyes of Ryoku Dragontalen, we are in Orden Castle Dungeon, in the world of Orden. It is past the sun's rising On November 15th, 2017.

"Well, isn't this just fucking peachy."

"At ease, Sira," Will said, leaning against the wall of his own cell, head down. Despite the tone of his voice, torchlight danced ferociously in his sapphire eyes. "We must escape. There is much yet to accomplish before we allow ourselves captive."

"A little late for that." Sira clutched the bars so hard that I thought they should just crumble beneath her hands. A growl rose up under her breath until she finally whipped around to us, flames roaring in her eyes. "Damn it! Why the hell did nobody tell us he had a kid?"

"You hail from here, Sira," Will replied tonelessly. "We assumed you might be partial to such knowledge." He lowered himself onto the bench, hands clasped before him, and sighed wearily. "What is done is done. Here we have landed, and now we must figure a way out."

"Orden's dungeons are locked tight, I'm afraid," Kioru said gravely. He leaned into the gate, his hands neatly clasped on the other side of the bars – given something the right size, he might be able to reach the lock, I thought, but there was nothing like that in reach. "I've expended many resources breaking my people out of here in the past, and they only keep fixing the loopholes."

"So it is not impossible," Will commented, facing Kioru. "You are Kioru Rasale, correct?"

Kioru nodded. "Yes. Kioru Rasale, leader of the Orden Rebellion. Or, I suppose, that may be a tentative title at present." He rested his head of white hair against the cell bars as though the cool steel may chill his nerves. "Though you have a point. Not impossible."

"So you don't work for Vincent anymore," Sira said with certain edge.

"I never truly did," he responded. "Not for a very long time. I could once hide within the walls of the castle and play the most direct set of ears. However, as you saw, Lars knows me now. There's no hiding in plain sight anymore."

"What can we do even if we bust out?" I asked hopelessly. "Fight our way out? We don't stand a chance against the emperor. He proved that."

All three looked toward me. Sira crossed her arms. "Don't you dare give up now," she said fiercely. "We're in his nest. We fought damned hard to get here, and we lost people on the way for it."

"This isn't my first time in these cells, Ryoku," Kioru told me. "We'll bust out, and I have many supportive of your cause under my command. One signal from me, and they'll storm the keep."

Will pushed himself to his feet, arms crossed, examining me. "You battled Vincent once. The difference was that Lars picked us off one-by-one. He is not like his father. He has no honor. Given that fact, we only need to adjust how we try our luck against him again."

"Do you have others coming?" Kioru asked him. "I hear you've amassed quite the following in Syaoto."

Will and Sira exchanged glances. "Possibly. Not likely," Will said. "Honestly, we were supposed to fetch Ryoku and return. Our source told us where we might stand a chance at meeting with you, so I thought we would head here and try our luck."

"You didn't make it, clearly," Kioru muttered. "Who was this source of yours?"

"Some bounty hunter," Sira replied. She didn't sound happy about the matter. "He was at the castle when I came back from scouting with Guildford, and asked to see him. Guildford paid him off for the information that you'd be here. Turns out Lars must've paid more."

I frowned. "How would anyone have known I was here?" I looked to Will. "I'd only just gotten here and fixed up my plan when you showed up. Five minutes, maybe."

Kioru planted his head against the bars, looking defeated. "No mistaking it. That's Sover."

"Sover?" I echoed.

"He's a common hunter around here," Kioru said morosely. "He doesn't take up any flag. Syaoto, Orden, and any other world are open to his business. Civil war, rebellion, or total war. Nobody really knows how, but rumor says he can see parts of the future. Bastard uses them for personal gain. Takes on the biggest bounties and dishes out information on them, or hunts the mark himself."

Will sat back down, shaking his head sadly. "There are powerful enemies wherever we turn."

Sira struck the bars with her hand in frustration, making Kioru jolt back. "Damn it! Even if we bust our way outta here, there's just more coming!"

"Yes, but is that not what you prefer?" Will asked dully.

A spark lit in my mind. "Yes," I agreed, and they turned to me when I spoke. "From what everyone says, I'm the Remnant of this guy who sacrificed himself to save the spirit realm. I don't know what that all means, but I know one thing. We made it this far despite all the odds."

Will smiled sadly at me. "You are beginning to learn the truth," he acknowledged. "Good. The more you know, the stronger you will be. You are absolutely right."

"Both of you are," Sira added. She was grinning; her crimson eyes alight like a pair of torches. "Bastard seems impenetrable now, but we'll see how many swings of Sinistra he can dodge in a row!"

"Once we get our weapons back, that is," Kioru agreed. "You'll see. We have a following ready to fight as well."

A small noise came from the cell next to us. None of us would have heard it if we'd been speaking still, but the faint noise alerted all four of us. In the next cell over, almost completely swamped in darkness, a figure pushed themselves up from the flat bed. The small sound was the clink of chains around their ankles. The figure rose with difficulty, their shoulders hunched, head down. I could only tell their hair looked to be of a darker color in the dim lighting.

"Impressive," a boy's voice came from the figure, who inched toward our cell with the weight of the world dragging at his legs. "For all I've heard of you, you are quite brave considering the forces stacked against you."

He slowly approached until he came to the cell walls. The swinging torch in the jail hallway swung away, keeping the figure in total darkness still. I could only see a faint smile on his lips.

"You are the one who will save us all."

"Who are you?" Sira jeered half-heartedly.

The boy's smile spread, and the lamp returned on its cycle to shed light on the boy. Greasy brown hair hung in his face, all but shrouding a pair of dark eyes locked solely on me.

My heart leapt into my throat as I recognized him.

"My name is Chris Olestine."

(Meanwhile, in the eyes of Dawn Elethel...)

"So they have gone to Orden."

Seated with me, at the same table we once dined with Vincent and Roland, were the remaining members of Ryoku's company. At one end sat Brom, garbed in a Christmas-red tunic with ceremonial pieces of armor attached overtop. Guildford sat at the other end, our designated leader in the time of Ryoku's absence, in new clothes not stained with blood or Shadowheart matter.

"I must express my envy!" Alex declared, slamming his hands on the table. "The three of them run off to face the emperor of Orden without us? What are we, chopped Ragul?"

"Recall your place, Alex," Guildford chastised him. "You're still a member of the army with your royal commander and king watching."

Ragekku waved Alex off. He'd changed from his beaten traveling clothes, donning instead a golden tunic with cobalt-blue pieces of armor atop. "He's but a lad. If he doesn't speak his mind in the kingdom, nobody will."

"Often speaking one's mind can lead to revolt," Brom said heavily, eyeing his new Lord General warily. "In this case, however, I agree. Alex has proven to be one of my largest assets as of late. In light of recent events, I may have to start considering him for some higher positions in the army."

Alex lit up like a lighthouse. "Truly, my king? You would think so highly of me?"

"I'll keep that in mind," Ragekku said, tapping his head with his knuckle. Guildford hid a smirk behind his napkin. "Either way, what now? What are we supposed to do?"

"They've been gone for a long time," Joey said darkly.

"Many of us are absent now, too," Lamont pointed out. He gestured to the table. Compared to the dinner with Vincent, there were many absent chairs. "Ryoku, Will, Sira, and Lusari could be together. Katiel has gone. The Timeless One and his assistants have not returned."

"There is the kingdom to think about," Brom said. "Shadowhearts run rampant since the event. The world is in a state of ruin."

"And Ryoku faces the might of Orden with such a small group," I said in a small voice. "They're strong, yes, but... If Vincent captured them..."

"I believe in them," Guildford said without a note of doubt in his voice. "Those four have handled themselves well enough before. If things have gone sour, we may only worsen our situation by trying to step in. A small group could escape on their own."

"If Ryoku knew we thought to leave Syaoto in such a state..." Joey didn't have to finish – his words were met with many sets of furtive nods.

"So what?" Sorha demanded in such a sharp tone that Joey and Alex, both seated near her, nearly leapt from their seats. "This is the mission he is meant to encounter. Orden has grown a ridiculous amount of power since the new world began, and we're allowing him to walk right in there!"

"The bounty hunter said Ryoku would go undetected," Guildford reasoned.

Sorha gave him a reserved glare, causing the teacher to flinch back – more than ever, he looked like our old teacher right then. "You trust a bounty hunter to promise you Ryoku's fate?"

Guildford glanced down in shame. "We paid him much of my gold for those words."

"And gold never loosened any lips," Sorha snapped like a whip.

"Who is this bounty hunter you speak of?" Brom asked. His position combined with his previous one served to give his voice extra boom across the table, turning all heads when he spoke. "Perhaps we could find this hunter. Ascertain the truth from him."

"You mean me?"

The voice came from among those at the table. I took a glance up and down the seats, expecting one of the guys to be hiding a grin and a fake voice – but then I saw the man at the table, who made Rena jump out of her seat in alarm. Blades all around the table sang steel in the air. Only a raised hand and a brief shout from Brom left the interloper alive long enough to get a look at him.

The first thing I was of him was a brimmed hat laden upon shocks of electric-blue hair that fell to his shoulders. Both of his huge black boots rest on the rich council table, some of the plates from our lunch pushed aside for it. He carelessly kept his eyes closed despite the countless blades pointed at him, his arms crossed loosely over his chest. A set of jagged scars ran the length of his left eye from the bridge of his nose to the base of his sharp cheekbone. He looked beaten and unkempt, though his outfit seemed quite new.

"You must be the bounty hunter we spoke of."

"Who else could I be?" the man asked, shrugging. The movement made his shoulder touch Ragekku's drawn blade, but he didn't flinch at the touch. "A lowly urchin from the slums of Vortiger, perhaps having stolen into your chambers? A jester among the royal court of Orden to entertain you? Perhaps a famous actor from Brooklyn?"

"If we wanted to play games, I would hire someone to juggle for us," Brom said levelly. "Do you understand the company you stand in, hunter? I could have my guards escort you to the dungeons in pieces if you wish."

"Aye, I don't doubt it," the man said calmly, and opened his left eye. The eye was such a bright shade of teal that it seemed to glint beneath his hat. "Only, then you wouldn't know what became of your Defender."

"What do you suggest by that?" Guildford asked in a startlingly lethal voice. "Your information sent Will and Sira to protect him."

"Right-o," the man said, "but that ain't the whole story." He held out a gloved hand and beckoned toward Brom. "Whaddya say, your highness? Does my information sound good enough to line my pockets?"

Brom glared at him. If I were the recipient of that look, I thought I'd escort myself to the dungeons to escape his wrath. Brom looked like a great bloodhound sitting at the head of the table suited up as a king, or a mountain in disguise.

"What sort of price do you demand?"

"Seventy thousand should suffice."

The room exploded in anger. Everyone was on their feet and shouting at either Brom or the stranger. Only I remained sitting, and sighed heavily. At this rate, I might as well go to Orden myself. I bet Katiel would happily tag along.

"Why would I obey the demands of a hunter who does not present himself?" Brom asked. "If you are so prestigious, tell me your name."

The man chuckled. "Heh. I like you, Iron Bear."

He pushed his chair back – it spun wildly and nearly toppled, but the hunter came out landing on his two feet. Standing tall, he was dressed in a long black open coat with a red trim to match his rimmed hat. A pair of daggers shaped like lightning hung at his belt. He bowed in a most extravagant and showy way.

"Huzzah. I present to you, my lordship, the mightiest and most renowned of bounty hunters – Sover Brandhall." At the peak of his bow, he opened out his palm like an unfurling leaf. "And I'll take your gold, too."

A tight smirk spread across Brom's old face. "Sover Brandhall. I have heard of you after all. You have dodged the law a great many times in the Capital."

"And done away with many of your peskiest of pests," Sover said, and winked deliberately with his one eye – the other looked scarred shut. "Army only takes care of so much. How about that bounty for the old leader of the Balgena Flaming Arrows a few years back? I tell ya, the look on his face when I caught up to him was worth more than the bounty." He stopped to chuckle, covering his mouth with his fingers. "How about that killer running rampant last summer? The Red Snapper or whatever folk called him. Guess who snapped him up in the end?"

"Counting that upon cases you have taken against the people in the Capital, I would consider your actions impeding of the royal army and our judgment."

"That's what I—" Sover seemed to catch onto Brom's words a second too late, and cut himself off with a sigh. "Oh. Didn't realize you were that hard to convince." He stroked his chin for a moment. "Well, my actions against those particular murderers stopped a great deal more lives from being taken. If that's the sort of thing that sells you. Sells me, in this case."

"One of the most common things I hear from other worlds," Brom said wearily, "is that your loyalty cannot be bought. You take sides as you wish. Who says I would not buy your information, only for you to sell mine to Vincent Ordenstraum?"

"Because I do not wish to sell you mere information," Sover replied. "I asked a steep price, and I know it. Buy me out. Consider me Syaoto's Royal Hunter, if you will. For the time being, at least. Maybe a better name than that. I'm sick of double-crossing. I've double-crossed so much, I forget who I originally crossed to double-cross their cross."

Brom leaned forward, his elbows weighing on the table. "You wish for me to buy a bounty hunter?"

Sover's smirk twitched. "Not just any bounty hunter, milord. The best of the best."

Brom studied Sover's expression for a long moment. Finally, he signaled Ragekku, who let his sword fall to his side. His glare, however, didn't dull. Brom leaned back in his throne and started fumbling with something in his lap. "Very well. There is a role for what you dubbed 'Syaoto's Royal Hunter' – the Spymaster."

Sover smirked. "Spymaster. Cool. Gotcha. Sounds better, anyway. And the money?"

In response, Brom dropped a heavy satchel onto the table and slid it across toward Sover. The hunter stared at it, not quite reaching for it yet.

"No way that's seventy thousand."

Brom shrugged. "You want to be our spymaster. A spymaster earns a salary. There is the payment for your first week."

Sover contemplated the satchel for a long moment. "You know what? Forgive my mistrust. I think we're gonna get on great." He snatched up the gold and shoved it in his pocket immediately, as though Ragekku might steal it first. Then Sover spun his chair and somehow took a seat on it whilst it spun, landing with his feet back up on the table. "Alright, kids. Listen up, cause I've got news for you."

As Sover began to talk, something happened in my world. My cellphone chimed. It was early morning in the real world despite being noon in Syaoto, so the action startled me in both places. Only Joey noticed, and he gave me a curious look. In my own world, I reached over to my bedside table and checked the message. My heart leapt – it was from Ryoku.

"Hey, don't freak out. We got captured. Working on escape route. Don't let anyone come here. Trap."

My brows rose in alarm. It was abrupt for a text message from Ryoku, but it spoke a great deal.

"What? He's captured?"

The outcry from Joey surprised me back into the room. Sover nodded and went to speak, but I cut him off. "He's captured in Orden. He said it's a trap and to not follow him; he's working on an escape."

Sover glanced at me beneath the rim of his hat. "Another Defender. Interesting. Fear not – I've got more information than you have rooms for. Things Ryoku might not know himself."

"We're going to listen to our newbie?" Sorha challenged. She turned to Guildford. "Why don't we just bust in anyway? He wouldn't know what we can handle."

"She has a point," Guildford said toward me. Despite the frenzy slowly starting to clamor in the room, Guildford kept a calm and level gaze on me. "What do you think? Should we try to rescue him?"

I hesitated. "We just paid for the new spymaster of Syaoto," I suggested. "Why don't we hear him out?"

"Smart girl," Sover agreed, relaxing back into his chair. "You'll be glad you did."

The voices of protest started up, but Brom silenced all by raising his hand into a gentle fist.

"Don't keep us waiting," Ragekku told him, keeping his sword at the hunter. "What've you got?"

Sover smiled. "First off, you're all talking on about Vincent Ordenstraum like he's been waiting like a toad in the throne for Ryoku this whole time. Thing is, old Vincy's been gone for a long, long time."

"Well, yes, he was here," Brom said. Then his brow furrowed. "He was. And from your expression, I doubt he was on a temporary leave."

Sover nodded. "Aye. Took ya long enough to surmise that one on your own, didn't it? I guess things work differently in different worlds. Orden and many other worlds have a complex flow of time, so I could see your lot thinking mere days passed over there since he took over Syaoto. Truly, it's been about a decade."

I wasn't the only one surprised by this idea. "A whole decade?" I asked. "How long was Vincent in power *here*?"

"Six months," Brom said, his voice hardened. "Our world began to flow oddly because of the falling event." He turned to Sover with the gravity of a churning mountain. "If Vincent was gone for an entire decade, then someone else sits on the throne."

He nodded. By the gleam in Sover's bright teal eye, this was the bit that would match the worth of his salary, the coin toss on whether or not saving Ryoku was a good idea.

"Aye. Orden has entered a new era of steam engines, guns, and the like. A pseudo British Empire, if some of you travelers may catch my drift. Heading the trip into this new school of thinking is the new emperor, Lars Ordenstraum – the son of Vincent."

SCENE THREE: TRICKSTER'S SIGNATURE

...Of Act Ten: Serpent's Nest

In the eyes of Ryoku Dragontalen, we are in Orden Lion Pits, in the world of Orden. It is early afternoon On November 16th, 2017.

"Go on, felon! And try to keep that pretty face intact this time!" The guards jeered behind me as one of them unceremoniously shoved me into the room before slamming the iron gate. I stumbled. My legs felt as though they'd been broken several times over. At this point, I wasn't sure they hadn't.

Sensations flooded in as I walked into the bright light of day. The sounds of a jeering, cheering audience rammed my ears like a living thing. My head churned and pulsed in pain. I squinted, wanting to shield my eyes with my arms, but it was pointless. My arms remained behind my back, trapped in a wooden block.

"...And today, we have the felon Ryoku Dragontalen once more! Is this the fifth time? Sixth? Has it been weeks or months? We don't know, but eventually it'll be the last!"

Whoever spoke with the loud, magic-enhanced voice over the crowd drew raucous cheers and applause from the people of Orden within the coliseum. It was hard to tell if they were rooting for or against me. I was just a criminal to them. Day after day, forced into this coliseum, I hoped that some of them were in support of me, waiting for the day I'd bust out of here at last.

Only my knowledge of the real passing of time kept my mind from permanently snapping. In my world, I was free, and little time passed while days and weeks churned together in Orden. Sira told me once that Orden flowed differently because of extreme weather patterns. Secretly, I hoped it was because the world was dying.

Once my mind adapted to the brightness and loudness of the audience, I could appreciate the clean, sunny air that filled my lungs. It felt like I drew a breath of pure hope. I was short on that lately, but I still intended to let it shine. Somehow.

Over the sound of the cheering populace came the clanging of steel ahead of me as my opponents released into the pit. The guards used chains from above to raise the gate, so that they didn't have to encounter the wicked beasts themselves. I heard their low growling before I saw them.

The first one prowled into the arena. A lion, though its fur was a dark, fallen grey, and twice the size of what I thought a normal lion should look like. It sauntered in, its dark eyes locked on me and drool dripping from its sharp fangs. The poor creatures were starved. I could see their ribs even through bleary, unadjusted eyes. Welts and scars dotted their backs, suggesting I wasn't the only prisoner in Orden forced against them.

The leading lion came, followed by six more, all of varying sizes and shades of fur. I doubted they came from the same pack, but hunger led them to unify in their hunt – for me.

They prowled closer, some of them circling around, but none leapt yet. They awaited their leader, the largest lion, to act first. I heard some of the other prisoners dub him Proudclaw after a deformity in his dominant paw that made it appear split in two. Proudclaw stalked to the center of the arena at the head of his pride, watching me with those hungry eyes.

A long moment passed. Oddly, it seemed like the lions always waited for the arena to silence before they struck. Maybe the deafening noise unnerved them. It gave me time to prepare myself.

Finally, Proudclaw lowered its head and let loose a loud, ripping roar. I stared back with sorrowful eyes. It was time to fight for my life.

Before any of the lions moved, I kicked up into the air with my weightless marks. I already heard several groans from the audience. I was tempted to rush into the stands and attempt my escape, but three prior attempts dissuaded me from any further. It usually landed me beaten by the guards and with a battle yet to fight.

My usual strategy involved grabbing onto something mid-jump, but my hands were disabled. I could only stall for time as I hovered just out of the range of their first lunge. My marks didn't have much energy these days, and they already seared red from usage.

I landed lightly by the door they'd come from, already shut and locked behind them to prevent escape. It had always been this way. I was to either win by dispatching the lions, or become their food in my loss. Since Lars first ordered me into the pit, I averted killing the lions. I only swung at them the odd time when I couldn't escape quickly enough, and it made me feel just as terrible as Lars for thinking to inflict pain on them. However, if the lions fell unconscious, they usually let me go. Lars was more interested in making me kill them than in a simple matter of victory. He was an enemy of psychological warfare.

The smallest of the lions yowled at me and lunged. I dodged with a pang of guilt. Such a small cub shouldn't have such a vicious look in its eyes. I knocked the wooden block on my arms against the all, and yelped in pain. The skin under them was beyond raw. Backed against a corner, I had to leap up to avoid the starving young lion.

Mid-air, I caught the violet-eyed glance of my constant surveyor. Lars Ordenstraum, seated in one of the nearer chairs at the head of the stands. A malevolent smile painted his oddly perfect face. His expression was one of merely watching his favorite theater performance, only short of popcorn on his lap. The smugness of his victory against me was always clear.

One day, I would wipe that look from his face.

I landed hard across the arena, but botched my landing and rolled my shoulder straight into the wall. I reeled, but I had to catch myself quickly as Proudclaw closed in. The poor lion had blood trickling from his bared fangs, presumably from whatever torture he endured before coming here. I couldn't force myself to hate this creature enough to kill it. He was but another prisoner.

He roared with just as much fury as a free animal, and shot from the ground like a bullet. I leapt away with as much power as I could, but my back struck a wall much sooner than intended. Proudclaw's talons lashed through my chest, inciting a strangled cry from my lips. The pain felt blurred now, after all the suffering since I'd arrived here.

I heard a mixture of reactions from the audience. I struggled to escape, but another of the lions popped up in my blind spot, forcing me back with a wild swing of its claws. I fell to the ground, feeling the constant dragging of claws through my skin. Red filled my vision, splashing across my face, my clothes, my eyes... and everything slowly turned black.

(Later that day...)

My eyes slowly flickered open to another white ceiling. I sighed inwardly. How many times would I wake up somewhere like this?

My hand shot to my chest, but there was nothing there. No injuries, no flayed skin from the savage lion attack. Just the fabric of a cloth tunic.

"...have him losing like that again. Lars would be furious."

"The young emperor is already furious. The rebel boy intervened."

I went still listening to the voices. Two males were speaking, and one of them sounded awfully familiar somehow.

"You really think he'd want him dead? After all this time?" A soft chuckle. "No, I think Kioru's escape was allowed. You know how Lars likes to play with his food."

"Please don't speak of him that way..."

I stiffened. There was a new speaker, a girl. Something about her voice struck me in the oddest way. I lay in bed, torn between remaining to listen more and rushing to find out who it was. I tried to lift my wrist, only to the clanking of chains. Of course. No prisoner was left unattended.

"My apologies. You know I don't mean such things personally."

"I know." The girl sighed. "What are we to do?"

"We have done our part," the other male replied. "Thanks to you, I've done a good job on his injuries. Lars would have a partial healing done, but he has fully recovered. Hopefully we've given him a chance – and I don't speak of the lions, madam."

"He's right, you know," the familiar-sounding boy said, presumably to the girl. "You know we cannot do more, but I wouldn't write him off just yet. He's more resourceful than the emperor would judge."

"I know," she replied sadly. "I just…"

"Come. We must prepare for the ball tonight. If Lars finds us in this wing of the castle…"

I heard retreating footsteps. Before they completely died out, a head popped around the corner. The doctor'd seen to me a few times, a dark-skinned young man with black and red hair. He was always shirtless under a white lab coat, and dreadfully thin. "You're awake," he said, sounding pleasantly surprised. "How do you feel?"

"Fine," I replied, a little wary still. "Who were you just speaking with?"

The doctor's brow furrowed. "Ah, you heard that? It'd be best if you disregard ramblings within the castle."

I looked him in the eye. "Ramblings that can save my life are hardly just ramblings."

He averted his eyes. "One should be very careful of who they speak around," he said nervously. "I'd scarcely risk telling you that it was a vassal of Orden and the emperor's sister."

I raised a brow. "Lars has a sister?" I could feel a pit opening up in my stomach. More Ordenstraums could never sound like good news, but why was her voice so familiar?

"I can say little more," he said, turning away to study his clipboard quite intently. "Though know this: not all in Orden are your enemies."

I nodded, deciding not to press the matter further. His words served to give me some hope where it had been dwindling over the days. "Who saved me? Why did the lions not tear me apart?"

"The rebel leader," he replied, jotting something down on his clipboard before setting it down and turning back to me. "Kioru Rasale. He was waiting for the next brawl and escaped to save you. Were it not for him, I cannot say your injuries would have been something to come back from."

Kioru had saved me once more. I didn't press anything else as the doctor checked my reflexes, my vitals, and everything else. Compared to many worlds I'd been to, his medical supplies were quite advanced.

After he confirmed I was in good health, a few guards arrived to escort me back to my cell. One of them was the red-haired guard from the city gates. He didn't meet my glance, only took me roughly by the arm and led me back to the dungeons. I tried to study the hallway patterns again, hoping I could retain some of the knowledge upon my escape. I thought that, but I didn't know how long it would be. It could be days, or months.

When he shoved me back in my cell, he briefly caught my hand and shoved a piece of paper into it, just out of sight of the other guard. I tried to meet his glance, but he spat on the ground and left the dungeons.

A few candles flickered into being within the dark cell, and Will and Sira came forth, scooping me up off the ground. "Are you alright?" Will demanded, steadying me.

I nodded. "Fully recovered," I whispered. I lifted my hand with the crumpled piece of paper in it. "Bring the light over. Quietly."

Sira glanced between me and the small, illegible note in my hand, then fetched one of the makeshift candles Will made, bringing the flame over gently. I unfurled the small piece of parchment and we crowded together to read it. When I saw the single word scrawled on it, my heart sank in my chest.

"What the fuck?" Sira growled, snatching the note from me

"Is this some kind of cruel joke?" Will demanded. "Who gave this to you?"

I took a moment to reply. "The guard who just dropped me off. He was from the city gates when we entered."

Sira struck the wall with her fist in rage. I wasn't sure whether it was her anger or sheer strength that didn't make her flinch back from it. She paced the room angrily a few times.

"Why would they write that?" Will asked. The anger in his voice was starting to ebb away already. "Perhaps there are many among the kingdom who wish us ill."

"They know about his death, that's for fucking sure," Sira snapped. "What the hell was the point of that? Rubbing it in?"

"They only scrawled his name," Will murmured, bringing his hand thoughtfully to his chin. "Why? Perhaps the guard is a follower of the Trickster."

"Perhaps it was from one of my men," Kioru suggested. His voice surprised me. I thought he was sleeping, but he lay on one of the stony cots in the corner, his back to us. "I didn't see which one it was, or I could just tell you. I don't know what it could mean. Think on it."

"Or they just fucking hate us," Sira muttered angrily, squatting down in her corner of the cell again. She snuffed out the candle with her fingertips. "Whatever. A whole lot of good Loki could do us now."

Her words hit Will and I hard. Will sat down in his corner bed. I remained standing for a long moment in the darkness as my friends extinguished the other candles.

"Hey, Kioru."

The rebel leader made a sound. "What is it?"

"Thank you for saving me."

He didn't reply for a moment. "I'm only lucky I got the chance. Lars will not be that careless again." He breathed softly. "You could be the only hope the rebellion has in seeing a free Orden in its lifetime. Considering that, I'd gladly face any amount of lions in open combat again."

I didn't know what to say to that. "Did you kill them? The lions?"

Kioru didn't reply for so long that I thought he fell asleep. Finally, he said, "No. It was tough, but I routed them and made them go after one of the guards. Even for starving animals, they'd take a meaty Orden guard over a scrawny Defender."

I smiled. I wasn't keen over one of the guards getting mauled by lions, but I was glad the animals were still alive.

Judging by the silence, Kioru eventually fell asleep. I remained awake for a long time in my cot, my hands tracing over my scars. I could count the injuries I'd sustained on my hands and recognize them. Many of the scars came from my practice fighting demons. Others, more recently, came in the patterns of lion claws.

The fact that somebody had the gall to give me a note stating only Loki's name stirred a great deal of stifled emotions. Since the death of my comrade and Guardian, I'd forced myself to deal with the matters at hand. First had been landing in Vxxyura at the behest of the Keeper of Death, an event that only landed me with even more questions. Here, it felt like every day was another attempt on my life that Lars proudly oversaw, his violet eyes gleaming in entertainment.

As glad as I was to be with Will and Sira, I found myself terribly missing Loki. My mentor. My Guardian. My friend. It felt like ages since I'd seen his mischievous green eyes or his tricky smile, or endured his unnecessary, but witty, commentary. I tried to visualize that easy smile of his, but all I could see was that demure grin he gave me while he held off Vincent Ordenstraum's attack.

I struck the stony ground with my fist, digging my knuckles into the ground. How could this have happened? Why was this mission so important that Loki would give his life to protect it? To protect *me*?

What would he have done in this situation, locked away with us in the dungeons of Ordenstraum Keep? Debating that Lars could even pin him down like he did to us, I imagined him sitting down here with us. Maybe he would comment on the drab tunics we donned as prisoners, and demand his own, more illustrious, version. He'd somehow be the only prisoner in a woven silk tunic, proudly displaying it as he outsmarted Lars' lions in brawl after brawl. Even as a prisoner, Orden would love him like we did.

The tears started down my cheeks, hotter than blood. The singularly demure grin I couldn't erase of Loki's last moments drifted away, and I remembered fonder moments. The way he stepped out in front of Lusari and I when Jason threatened us. His painfully mortal expression as he told us about his wife and daughter. When he handed me the sweater he bought me, something that was probably gathering mildew in a locked chest nearby with all our other belongings.

I remembered our conversation in Vortiger. How he warned me to prepare for life without him, and without the others. How could I have known it'd end up like this? The days where we traveled together were painfully short, yet they seemed like they should never have ended. I didn't appreciate it enough. I always drove forward so painstakingly that I forgot to look alongside me.

An urge overtook me. I couldn't explain where it came from. I pictured the note, simply scrawled with the word "Loki" in quotations. Who could have given that to me? What was its purpose?

I needed to say it. I needed to speak his name. He'd come up in passing conversation in our cells over the last few days, but had we ever properly acknowledged him? The man who gave his life to further our own?

My gaze locked onto the cell door, still swimming with hot tears. A fell breeze came from the hallway. Orden was apparently so stormy that often the weather affected the castle. Stray currents of wind would flow through the keep itself, rattling doors and opening others, knocking objects over in the night where the storms were most livid.

My cell door rattled, a strong wind for a place so deep in Orden's dungeons.

I wasn't sure when it started, but I felt it. The cool, gripping darkness from within me that rose when I needed it the most. It wrapped itself around my heart, my mind, my eyes. I hadn't decided whether it was comforting or invasive, but it sidled into control as easily as the tears streaming down my cheeks. Everything stilled until there was only us. The note, the darkness, and I.

The door rattled loudly enough that I heard Will stir near me in the cell. Still, I couldn't remove my gaze from it. I didn't know why I had such a mission, but I knew what had to be done.

My hand lifted. Blood dripped along the back of my knuckle from striking the ground. It oddly glinted like fire, wrapping around and encircling my hand. With it, the word rose up in my chest like a hurricane, begging to be spoken. It was a matter of life and death. To speak it would serve several purposes, I knew, though I couldn't claim exactly what they were. To reaffirm myself after Loki's death? To serve homage to the fallen god? Maybe the words would crawl through the insidious darkness of Ordenstraum Keep, finding and stilling the heart of Lars Ordenstraum.

When the words parted from my lips, I could almost see Loki with me. His glinting emerald eyes, twinkling mischievously as though telling a joke he failed to properly explain before he left us.

"Loki."

Click!

The sound snapped me out of my trance. The darkness fell away like a coat I merely shed after its purpose. Will, Sira, and Kioru shot up, their eyes on the cell door. The quiet guest in the next cell over stirred, rising up from his bed painstakingly.

"What was that?" Will asked softly, his words slurred by exhaustion. Had they all been asleep? How long had I been awake?

"It sounded as though..." Kioru started, but trailed off. I felt his eyes on me in the darkness. His eyes were so like Lars', but so different.

The four of us rose like spirits from the grave. On our feet, we hesitated, as though wondering whether we'd all just had the same strange dream. Will chided us under his breath, strolled forward, and put his hands on the gate.

The sound of that cell door opening would stick with me for a very long time. The sound of our freedom, of the flames of hope rekindling, soaring back up into a great and wild flame.

"No fucking way," Sira breathed. "How... How did...?"

A smile started to find its way onto my face, carving a forgotten path across tear-stained cheeks. I wasn't sure how it happened, exactly, or whether it had even be real. Maybe I dreamt the painful need to speak his name, but I knew a sign as well as anyone.

Loki had left us his last signature.

SCENE FOUR: ESCAPE

...Of Act Ten: Serpent's Nest

In the eyes of Ryoku Dragontalen, we are in Orden Dungeons, in the world of Orden It is late night On November 16th, 2017.

In the baleful darkness of Ordenstraum Keep's dungeons, my boot came from the shadows as easily as just another shadow itself, to strike the jailer in the temple.

He went down, but Kioru caught him before he could make a noise, and his quick hands swiped the keys from his belt. He tossed them to Will, who fiddled with them for a moment before unlocking the dungeon's chest, unveiling our belongings.

Sira fished out Sinistra like she was struggling to breathe without it, and only looked like herself once more when she strapped its baldric over her shoulder. Will replaced his armor, lance, and gladius on his person, stuffing away our regular clothes into another backpack.

While we reequipped ourselves, Kioru took back the keys and started opening the other cells. An older man with dark skin, a shaved head, and a rough scar across his brow stepped out like it was his first time outside the cell. Kioru clasped his arm amicably before handing him part of the key ring, and they set to freeing the others.

Seeing Chris Olestine escorted from his cell by the muscular friend of Kioru's made my heart sail. His posture suffered, looking at me from beneath a tangle of greasy auburn hair, scars visible on every inch of his skin – but he was free. He managed a weak smile when he saw me.

Kioru freed at least twelve more prisoners before dumping the keys back onto the unconscious jailer. "Arm yourselves suitably," he told the prisoners. "Guard said Lars was holding a ball tonight. I suspect there will still be guards stationed at regular intervals."

"We know the routes," the big man said, lugging a broadsword from the chest of arms. "Hosting a ball changes little in their routine. Given their prisoners, security will be tight."

We waited while everyone armed up. Kioru introduced me to the big man, Liragon Elto, who turned out to be one of his finest rebels. Apparently, he'd been arrested in some kind of marketplace skirmish a few months ago. Despite his best efforts, Kioru was unable to free him – until now.

He knew at least six of the other prisoners, and introduced me by name to each one. I tried to retain them, but the adrenaline of our pending escape was starting to push all else out. I watched Will supporting Chris down the hall, where he helped him stoop and retrieve a rusted longsword from the chest. For the first time, I saw a light in the prisoner's eyes.

We were just about to leave when the dungeon doors flung open. Four guards piled in, and the enthused, nervous silence broke.

One of them holstered their gun and fired at one of our prisoners. The *crack* of a point-blank gun shot in an enclosed space hammered on my eardrums like a living thing, and the prisoner fell dead in a pool of his own blood. Liragon's eyes fell upon the fallen prisoner, and he let out a howl of rage.

I was right with him. I danced around an incoming rapier, ramming my elbow into the soldier with all the force I used to shove myself forward. I intended to leave him, but Sira ran her broadsword through the man without hesitation. My next strike bent the head of a rifle, dissuading the bullet to ricochet off the walls with a sound like contained thunder. I shot my other hand forward, calling on magic I hadn't fully used since I was in Syaoto, and rammed the gunner with strong winds. They threw him down the hall like a doll, breaking his gun beneath him. One of the prisoners fell upon him like lightning.

Will tore his lance through one soldier's skull, kicking away the body before grabbing Chris to direct him into the hallway. Kioru dispatched the fourth with a mighty swing of his crimson blade.

"Stealth will be out of the question now!" Kioru barked. "They know we've escaped. Follow my lead! We'll stick to the least manned route."

Halfway down the hall, a dazed guard burst out from a side room, his leather armor only half done up and his rapier halfway from its sheath. Will ran him through before I could see the whites of his eyes. My stomach churned. Seeing my friends dispatch enemies so easily scared me, sometimes. I preferred to incapacitate them and move on.

Kioru and Sira hesitated between a fork in the path. "This way goes to the servant halls," Sira protested.

"And passes the barracks," Kioru argued. "We'll be swarmed before we can say—"

Neither could claim their stake as groups of soldiers started around each corner.

"Curse it! Straight, then! Up the stairs! Keep some heavy force in the back!"

Another snap of a bullet came from our left side. To my surprise, Chris stumbled forward in time to deflect the bullet with his blade, narrowly avoiding Kioru's shoulder. Kioru regarded him with surprise, but Chris stumbled, and Will caught him around the shoulders, helping him onward.

Combat waged all around us. I kept to the back left, running alongside Will and Liragon Elto. Our enemies suited up in full armor, so trying to take them out unarmed wasn't going to work. I drew my knife and kept shoulder-to-shoulder with the two warriors at my sides. I heard shouting rise up from behind me, and Kioru's resounding curse. More soldiers appeared from atop the stairs.

"Knot together!" Will shouted. "Do not let them through!"

We fell back, converging into the hallway at the foot of the stairs. Enemies surrounded us on all sides. I gritted my teeth, tightening my grip on my knife. I knew what was happening, deep within the pit of my stomach. Lars knew we were escaping.

He was directing us. Leading us. Forcing us to clash with him once more.

This time, I would be ready.

The battles only grew in ferocity. From the cornered battle in the stairway, a constantly thriving army battled us back, forcing us up the stairs and in a continued plight down the hallway. I fought at Will's side, then at Sira's back, and alongside Kioru and Liragon at different intervals. I saw three of our people fall in combat. Chris wasn't among them.

Injuries dotted my body in mixed severity. My ankle bled freely enough that it left a trail where I ran along with the others, but adrenaline kept the throbbing injury from impeding me. A cut bled slowly into my eye, and other scrapes and cuts crossed my arms.

It was evident that the armies were forcing us a certain way. We were far from the path Liragon suggested. There would be no respite from the soldiers now, and I knew exactly where the conflict would land us.

At the least, no sign of the Ordenite vassals showed up. I knew one appearance from Kimo might spell the end of our resistance. Even Roland Demizen could ruin us. I dreaded the thought of running into Lars or his father, especially. I knew my friends were strong, but they were stronger by far. Even Loki couldn't defeat Vincent in the end.

We kept in a tight formation, pushed along by the conflict, and we kept dealing out blows against the army. Each soldier felled by a burst of my magic, or thrown back with dire injuries, or finished by the others, was a strike against their main force. Yet, I couldn't bring myself to land any mortal blows. These were men with families and loved ones. The darkness of Lars and Vincent might not belong to their entire army.

As we rose to a higher level of the castle, I could see and hear the savage storm outside. Winds not belonging to my magic throttled the hallways, sometimes strong enough to push the soldiers back. Thunder shuddered the great stone keep, accompanied by flashes a thousand times mightier than the bursts from Ordenite guns. At times, I could even hear the torrential rains hammering against the stone walls outside.

At some point, the sounds of classical music echoing within the chambers reached our ears above the sounds of the storm. I caught a desperate glance from Kioru. The ball. The armies pushed us this far, and we were certain who we might encounter near here.

It was impossible to push back against the army. They had their orders, and we couldn't hope to push our way back. Three immediately replaced any soldier we knocked aside. I flung myself at them recklessly, lashing out with my knife, striking out with weak bursts of magic so as not to wreck my inner stores. If I used my weightless marks, the guns they kept from using in these close quarters appeared at their shoulders. I could only dodge so many of those bullets, especially if I took to the air.

It was no use. The music grew louder even over the rage of battle. Sira and Liragon fought side-by-side with their huge swords, but the enemy lines wouldn't cut. Soon, even they were stumbling back.

When we neared the ballroom, a great and terrible noise rose out above all else. Even the armies halted as a bright flash overtook the hallway. A horrid roar shook the ground at our feet. I felt the energy of the lightning from where I stood, making my hair stand on end.

It was only when I saw charred stone hurtling through the doorway ahead, accompanied by harsh winds, that I understood. Lightning had struck the castle, tearing part of the ballroom ahead asunder in a violent rage. Every lamp and torch in the vicinity blew out in the wind, and a shrill silence washed over the army, parted only by the fierce licking of flames.

After a long, harrowing moment, the classical music picked up again. It sounded somewhat stressed now. The violinist panicked, playing eerie and harsh notes, and the pianist hammered on the keys.

Ahead of us, the army parted, paving the way into the room torn apart by lightning. Out of the corner of my eye, I saw two figures retreating. A blond boy rushed a girl in a beautiful white dress out of harm's way. I swore I caught the glint of Kimo's blue eyes as he dragged the girl.

There it was. For just an instant, I thought I saw her face. A feeling greater than anything the storm could conjure birthed in my chest, like my heart swallowed up bolts of the ferocious lightning within it, and my breath fell from my chest.

It couldn't be. I knew that, but my eyes disrupted the fact with the truth.

My sister.

Movement in the center of the ballroom ahead tore my glance away. Smoke and fire filled most of the ballroom, but a figure strode forward from that smog, smoothly drawing out a long sword from his belt, a different blade than the flimsy little thing he used before. He dressed in an elegant coat with white ruffles emblazoning his chest and sleeves. His shoulder-length black hair was slick with rain and tarnished with ash, but his violet eyes gave none of that away now, for they were as cool as ice.

Everything else seemed to vanish. I could only see his unsettling violet gaze from afar in the clearest detail. I recalled that, until the spirit of Eos repaired it, my eye was previously that very same shade, and it caused a shudder to wrack my body that wasn't from the cold.

"This is the end, Ryoku Dragontalen!" he cried, flourishing his sword in a practiced arc before raising it, pointing it across the room toward me.

"This is where Orden will reign supreme! Fight well, child – this will be your last battle!"

SCENE FIVE: A GODSEND STORM

...Of Act Ten: Serpent's Nest

*In the eyes of Ryoku Dragontalen, we are in Ordenstraum Keep, in the world of Orden.
It is late night
On November 16th, 2017.*

The monster spawn of the Ordenstraum family lurched toward me like nothing but air was between us, and a terror unlike anything I ever realized flared to life inside me.

His chalky-perfect face twisted with a malevolent smile that flickered like the flames engulfing the ceiling behind him. Even from afar, I could see my terror reflected in his eyes.

Was that really Roxanne who left with Kimo? How could she be here, after all this time?

I swallowed my resolve back into my chest. Questions and anxiety filled my lungs, but I had to bite them back. I raised my knife, and Lars bore down on me with all the fury of the storm.

My treacherous mind already calculated odds I didn't want to think about. Lars was supposed to be a dark knight like his father, which suggested prowess beyond my wildest dreams. I suspected he wielded elemental magic from the way the flames of the storm licked around him, and how the savage rainfall from above glinted around him.

For such a slender man, he struck with ferocity and deadly intent. Each strike was like the lash of a snake, hammering down against my knife with each blow. I staggered back, stumbling to block each blow unless I fancied losing a limb each time Lars rained down on me. When his blade came too close, I panicked, and shot out my hand. I unleashed a wicked blast of wind magic.

It did little more than land, heaving Lars back as effectively as though I shoved him. Before I could fall back on my head, a hand grabbed me around the shoulder, dragging me upright just in time to gain my footing before Lars came rushing at me again. Now Will planted himself before me, lance raised in a practiced form.

Lars rushed us like he *was* the army. He lashed out at Will relentlessly, pushing the soldier back until he was level with me. Given the moment of respite, I lunged next to him and aimed for Lars' ribcage. My knife fell astray from a bullet from the army around us – which largely dwindled, to my surprise. Lars granted us more than enough room to fight, and only a steady squad's worth did battle against the few rebels we had left. I saw Chris among the fray, battling a single soldier on his own. Given his condition, I prayed he could last by himself.

Lars recovered from a brief opening by lashing out at me with his sword, but Will stepped in and blocked the blow with his lance, then struck Lars with the blunt end. The young emperor stumbled back, brow furrowed in a delicate line of rage.

The thought occurred to me. Compared to out in the alleyways where he apprehended us, Lars was going easy on us.

I'd never fought side-by-side with Will like this. He dove with his lance, pushing Lars back, and I stepped into the opening close-range with my knife, aiming for blood. My knife glanced off his sword – once, twice, three times before the grip on my knife jolted. Will rammed Lars with the butt of his spear before I could lose the knife entirely, but Lars was upon me again in an instant. I thrust out with a burst of wind magic supported by a quick hand on my staff, shoving Lars back a good foot or two.

Lars recovered quickly and pranced forward in a thrust. I stepped aside, the blade raking the skin as it narrowly passed by me. A wave of heat from behind me made me stumble, and then lurch forward – part of the flaming ceiling crumbled behind me, spraying us with hot debris. Will's arm pushed me away, and Lars looked unperturbed.

A red spectre appeared from the smog. Lars spun around just in time; Sinistra broke through the smoke, slamming into Lars' blade with a mighty force. Anyone else would have fell to such a mortal blow, but Lars only skipped back, quick to lash back. As Sira stepped into the brawl, I saw that her other hand hung uselessly at her side. She wielded Sinistra with one hand against Lars. Even given how good she was, there was no way I could let that happen.

Quick as a flash, I lunged just as Will came in beside me. Lars' blade repelled Sira's strike and spun to meet Will's lance mid-air. I managed to swing in below his blind spot.

The sound of ripping flesh tore out above all else. The roaring flames, the anxious orchestra forced to perform for the battle, and all the sounds of skirmish around us. Everything muted as my knife bit into flesh.

An intense feeling of glory washed over me. I landed a blow! I actually pierced him!

It was hardly anything to be proud of in any other battle. The blade only sank in an inch before Lars dragged himself back. A second later, a violent energy slammed into me, knocking the wind from my chest and forcing me down. Pain flashed across my whole body. Lars' dark magic?

"Bastard! You inconceivable fool!"

Will lunged in beside me, but Lars' sword screamed through the air like a bolt of dark lightning. It broke through Will's lance like air, spraying wood splinters and bits of steel everywhere. At the last second, Will hooked his arm around me, dragging me out of harm's way as Lars' blade throttled the ground where I stood. Dark energy radiating from his weapon cut a scar into the stone.

Sira stepped in before Will or I could take the next blow, blocking a wild strike with Sinistra. The first strike jolted her grip, nearly forcing her own blade against her. I lunged when the second strike landed, forcing her onto the ground with a shriek.

The strangest noise filled the air, then. Of all the strange, alien noises of Orden, what came next managed to surprise me. A bluish-white streak shot through the air past me and onto Lars with a frenzied howl. Lightning snaked in the air like living entities.

"Go!" a familiar voice shouted. "Run! We can hold him off!"

I caught glimpses of what was going on, but my mind wasn't quite willing to register them. I saw the Timeless One like a small child amidst the battle, but he wielded a large black sword, exchanging blows with a figure of which I only saw red hair. I heard familiar giggling, and the curtain of black hair and claws that was clearly Cleria skipped through a line of soldiers. She caught my stunned gaze, and winked.

"Rex! Go with them!"

The speaker was unfamiliar, but the arm that latched onto mine wasn't. There was no mistaking that doggish scent – Rex Dougo. He couldn't spare me a look as he put all my weight behind him and dragged me off. Will and Sira appeared on either side of me now, both shooting frantic gazes back as they fought to keep alongside me. Sira plowed through enemy soldiers like her sword was a shovel. I thought I caught a glimpse of Kioru nearby, too.

I couldn't make sense of the scene behind us. Lars got to his feet, thrusting aside what seemed to be *a huge wolf*. It had bluish-white fur and was even bigger than the lions I fought in the arena.

I caught the emperor's glance from miles away, and I knew I would never forget that look. Those intense violet eyes locked onto me, instilling themselves into mine to never forget one another and what transpired here today.

I had to focus forward. Rex had me in his arm, lashing out at soldiers where he could with wild kicks, his coat billowing around him like a shadow. Will, Sira, and Kioru were the front lines, cutting a way blindly through enemy forces. I broke free of Rex and lashed out myself, using what I had left of my magic to blast brief respites into the relentless force ahead of us.

My mind wasn't there, fighting hordes of soldiers alongside Rex, Will, Sira, and Kioru as our life depended on it. Secrets and mysteries flooded my consciousness, tugging at me, demanding the light of day. Had I really seen my sister here?

Something shot at me from the darkness. I flinched back, lashing out with my dagger, but something else hit the soldier that came out at me. I saw the whites of his eyes flash, and then extinguish.

What looked like a dark blade shot through the man's chest, stopping only an inch from my own heart. I stared into the man's quickly lifeless eyes, trying to catch up to the moment and understand what was going on. The dark blade disappeared, and the fallen soldier tumbled into the stampede of continuing battle. I searched for my savior, expecting maybe Cleria or Relus – he was always with the Timeless One, after all – but only saw what looked like the wide rim of a hat vanish into the shadows.

I couldn't tarry behind the others, or I would surely die here. The amount of soldiers lessened as we worked our way in the opposite direction from where we came. Will was fighting with his gladius only, something I'd seen little of in my close friend. Even one-handed, Sira was a mighty force at his side.

It felt like only moments passed before a great set of doors became visible in the hallway ahead. Our vigor spiked, and Rex pushed me onward, each strike he landed fatal against the soldiers of Orden.

It was only within feet of the great doors that I realized, and I halted in my tracks. Sira saw, and she flashed me an annoyed glance.

"Chris."

It was only the five of us. None of the other prisoners we'd escaped with was among us. Even Liragon, Kioru's trusted ally, was gone.

"Oh shit," Sira growled. Her fiery eyes glanced back the way we came, and she cursed under her breath. "No way. We can't fucking go back."

"I abandoned him! We helped him escape, and he..."

Will stepped forward and put a heavy hand on my shoulders. There was a prevalent light in his eyes.

"Lars would not kill that particular prisoner, I am certain. There is a reason he kept him alive. For now, my friend, we have to escape. We will not get a second chance at that battle today."

"But..."

"Look at us!" Kioru told me urgently, gesturing to Sira's arm. "I'm the leading force against Lars, and I would do anything to cease this reign of terror. We cannot win this fight today. Your friends did us a great service in letting us get away, or I do not think we'd have survived."

Footsteps echoed behind us. I turned, about to heave a huge sigh of relief, but it wasn't Chris who approached. Liragon was bolting down the hallway at a full run, hindered by a slice across his thigh.

"Go!" he barked. "Lars comes this way! You will die!"

Kioru shot me a sharp look. "We have to go! Now!"

I couldn't protest if I wanted to. Sira and Rex charged and heaved the great doors open. A great blast of wind slammed into us right away, but Will grabbed my arm and dragged me forward into the storm.

What little drying we'd done since leaving the main battle was quickly useless. The force of Orden's unhindered rain broke through us to the bone. I felt like my very heart was soaked. Lightning snaked and flashed across the sky like wild dragons locked in battle. Behind us, Rex and Liragon managed to force the doors shut – our only hope at evading pursuit.

The soldiers didn't persist outside the keep, which was hardly a boon for us at this point. We forged on with everything we had, torn at by the savage winds and drenched by the relentless rain. Will slipped in the mud and went down. Kioru dragged him to his feet and supported him. Sira kept at my side, her fiery spirit offering me a faint source of warmth as we trudged along the courtyard through the vicious storm.

The worst lay ahead. A great moat encircled the outer keep. A small footbridge led the way across, but it churned and tossed horribly in the wind, and water from the moat tossed in waves across it. Helpless fish flailed on the bridge before gravity eventually tossed them back home.

I swallowed hard. This made the bridge back in the Old Forest seem like a cakewalk.

"This looks bad!" Will shouted over the storm. "If the wind picks up at all, it will toss us!"

"Orden is used to the storms, my friend," Kioru shouted back. "The bridge will hold."

"Let's run it!" Sira yelled. "If it goes down, it'll slow down our pursuers!"

"And if we are on it?" Will demanded.

"Pair up!" Liragon ordered. "The storm will not take us!"

I hesitated as Rex approached me, silently the best choice for the lightest of us. I couldn't imagine falling into the waves of the moat. Orden felt unnaturally furious, though it was just a force of nature at work in this world. No mage could conjure a nightmare this terrible.

"Hold on tight!" Kioru shouted. Then we started running.

Kioru and Liragon charged first, latched onto one another. I tried to ignore how the bridge tossed below them as Will and Sira ran after them together. Rex and I exchanged glances – then we charged.

A wave hit us as soon as we set foot on the bridge. It lasted seconds, but I swallowed a mouthful of salty water and choked, clutching my chest. Rex kept me going, not slowing his pace no matter how the bridge churned beneath us. It felt like I was walking on the rain itself, hoping I might not slide off into the sky.

Thunder howled in the night. A nearby bolt of lightning threatened to throttle the very world of Orden. Seconds later, another huge wave slammed into Rex and I. This one brought Will and Sira to a grinding halt, their knees buckling ahead of us. Liragon and Kioru reached the other side, and each grabbed onto one of the posts supporting the bridge.

"Come on!" Kioru screamed, but it was like a whisper in the ferocity of the night.

Another wave throttled us, filling my lungs with salty water. When it passed, Rex lost his grip on me. I lost touch of what was going on for a moment. Something heavy struck my head.

"*Ryoku!*"

A hand wrapped around my arm. It was Will's. I saw Sira stumble behind him, and Rex caught her, spitting out enough water to drown a normal man. My head swam like it had gone off the edge itself.

Craaaaaaaaack!

The second I heard that noise, I knew we were done for. The bridge gave way to the relentless waves. A huge crack split down the breadth of the bridge. Splinters caught the wind, spraying into the air.

"*Run!*"

Will didn't need the motivation. We charged, even as I spat out seawater and my head throbbed. The wood slid beneath my feet, and I swayed heavily, fighting for balance. It was only a lunge to dry land.

Another wave struck us. I lost contact with Will, and open sky churned beneath my feet. Images rushed past my face between waves. I saw the bridge flail through the air, ripped from the earth. Will's body spun with the force of the wave. I saw Sira, a horrified look on her face.

The next thing I knew, my lungs filled with water. The tide ripped at me like hundreds of strong fingers, fighting to drag me away. I saw Sira lurch past me, and I managed to catch hold of her arm. The force of the water yanked on us – but something stopped me from going downstream.

The next thing I knew, we were back in open air – and then we landed hard on the marshy ground, Relief and air filled my lungs in equality. Rex had a firm grip on my ankle, panting heavily, drenched to the bone with his dark hair matted to his stony flesh. His other hand was on Will's ankle, who was coughing out a river full of water from his own lungs.

Nobody spoke, but a pair of hands urged me to my feet. Liragon's grip was like a gentle giant, and he supported Sira and I as we found our footing in the horrible storm. Kioru helped Rex and Will to their feet, and then we were trudging again.

Once air found our lungs, our march turned into a run. Only the slapping of stone beneath our feet told us we reached the city.

Kioru led the way. For a few minutes, the streets were empty – sensibly, none dared venture out into this wicked storm like we did, but then we were whispering in a panic, and Kioru led us into the shadows. A squad of Ordenite soldiers appeared in the streets, clutching glass lanterns to light their way in the storm. They swung the lamp on a long, thick bamboo rod, scanning the shadows for any sign of us.

We only had to dodge them for a few minutes before we found our destination, and Kioru wrenched a rickety wooden door open. He ushered all of us into the building before he entered himself, slamming the door behind us.

Warmth flooded into me. It was something I'd never thought I might feel again. I shuddered terribly, and the shock numbed me to the bone.

"By the gods! Look at you kids!" A deep male voice greeted us. Only Kioru seemed unsurprised, striding forward to clasp hands with a pudgy innkeeper who clutched a tankard of ale.

"Alphonse," Kioru greeted him with a shaky grin. "Can you shelter us for a spell?"

The man chuckled. "Of course! Anything for the rebellion forces, and—"

He faltered, noticing me for the first time. I thought I might look like a small lap dog, drenched to the bone.

"Ryoku Dragontalen," Kioru spoke, and there was unmistakable pride in his voice. "This is Ryoku Dragontalen. Ryoku, this is Alphonse Loras – innkeeper of the Prancing Bolt."

"Welcome!" the innkeeper greeted me, grabbing my hands and shaking them enthusiastically. "It's my honor and privilege! Ya see, I've been..."

Kioru silenced him with a look. "Keep quiet, Al. Soldiers were prowling the streets when we got in."

Alphonse's humorous eyes solidified. "Aye. They'd brave this storm, they would. Very well."

He beckoned Kioru to help him, and the two retreated to the back room. In their absence, Liragon led us to the back room where a fire pit sat mostly abandoned, though a small flame still licked at a pot that smelled like vegetable stew. A few faces sat around the fire, including a boy with golden hair who looked a little familiar. He shot to his feet when we entered, staring at Liragon in mute shock.

Liragon smiled wistfully. "It has not changed." To me he added, "The Prancing Bolt is the rebellion headquarters. Old Alphonse has been accommodating us since Kioru started out."

"L-Liragon? Liragon Elto?" the blond boy stuttered. "No freaking way. Kioru *actually* did it."

They gripped one another in a comradely hug. I thought I saw a tear in the corner of Liragon's eye. "Never thought I might see you before my execution date, kiddo."

The boy laughed shakily. When he did, I realized where I recognized him from. He was the archer that helped us out just before Lars caught up with us in the city.

He stuck out a hand to me next, which I accepted. "Belto Rasale," he introduced himself. "Cousin of Kioru. Big-time fan of yours." He observed us, a brow raised. "Now come on. I'll stoke the fire."

Belto and one of the other men started picking up the fire. Kioru and Alphonse returned with heaps of towels and fresh clothes. While I huddled with Sira for warmth, Belto and Alphonse dished out heaping bowls of stew, cheese, mashed potatoes, and vegetables for us. I didn't realize how hungry I was until I took in the first sip of stew. I wound up hopelessly lucky that it had no meat – somehow, Kioru knew I was vegetarian.

We sat by the fire for hours, and I still didn't feel dry. Liragon, Kioru, Belto, and Alphonse all exchanged vivid stories, with Will chiming in at certain intervals. They loved hearing about my adventures up until now, but I was too cold and exhausted to properly relay them myself.

Sira held me close, quiet as a dormouse, staring into the open flames. Seeing them reflected in her eyes made me think of the flames in the ballroom, and I shuddered.

After some time, Will got my attention. He'd been the most active of us, and had eventually changed into some dryer clothes. Compared to how we'd all looked when we got here, it was like watching a slave turn into a king.

"We have rooms for the night," he told me. "You look dead on your feet. Rest. I must discuss some things with Kioru."

I was too tired to do anything but nod. Sira came with me, and we took a room near the fire pit. We stripped out of our wet clothes and huddled together under the covers. Sira felt like the entity of fire, the heat of her skin like a warm hearth against mine.

I had no grasp of the time of day when we awoke. Sira and I remained in bed, awake, for a short time. We kissed passionately, but neither of us seemed to have the energy for anything more, even though being together made a different sort of flame awaken in our chests. I remembered how it felt to see her again when she strolled up to me in Orden. It was something that took me by storm.

Eventually, we found the ambition to dress ourselves and return to the fire pit. Will was there, speaking about something with Kioru in hushed tones. Alphonse served them breakfast, and Belto was jeering about how he would surely turn into an egg himself if Alphonse didn't cook them another way for once. Rex greeted us as we entered, and then all heads turned to us.

"Good morning," Kioru told me warmly. He rose from his discussion with Will and embraced me. I returned the gesture, and he stepped back, holding me by the shoulders and smiling at me. "Well, to be honest, good afternoon. It is well into the day, though I cannot hold any misgivings to you."

"Don't go riling up the boy first thing, Key," Belto insisted, easing Kioru away from me. "Let them get some real food in them and wake up for the day before we assuage them."

Kioru obeyed, though an unspoken tension remained as Alphonse piled up my plate with food. Unlike when Kioru gave me food, I stealthily slid the meat off onto Rex's plate, who accepted it without question. Will noticed, and hid his laughter behind his hand.

Although Kioru looked eager to speak, conversation didn't spark up until almost an hour after we'd eaten, and Sira and I curled up by the fire once more. I felt like I might never work the chill of the unforgiving storm from my bones.

"Ryoku," Kioru finally started.

It was only a word, but all eyes and ears turned to him. Belto glanced over from carving a figure of a dragon next to the fire. Liragon looked up from polishing his sword. Alphonse was wiping out glasses from suspiciously nearby while he watched from the corner of his eye. Will sat next to Kioru, and Rex near Sira and I.

"We cannot stay in Orden," Will said. "More specifically – you, my friend, cannot remain here. It would be impossible. With the bounties against you, every soldier and every peasant in Orden knows your face. You could not hope to see the light of day for a long time.

"But I will stay," he went on. He kept going as he saw my mouth open to protest. "I would stay for you – to arrange this rebellion force and align with the effort in Syaoto. You are smart, Ryoku. Surely you see there is little to no hope that a small force can infiltrate this world again. For our next efforts, we require a full army."

"We spoke with our friends in Syaoto," Rex added, to my surprise. "That's how I got here with Fenrir and the others."

"Fenrir?" I asked. I recalled the bluish-white wolf that leapt upon Lars.

"Loki's son," he said quietly. "We went to speak with him after your disappearance in Syaoto. He may be sympathetic to your cause, but that remains to be seen. Either way, King Brom has pledged his armies to your cause."

"King Brom?" I asked, surprised. Will's face light up in pride. So he was the new king?

"We knew that last night was not our night for total victory," Kioru reasoned. "It was our escape. You arrived far too prematurely to consider revolutionizing Orden. Even if you managed to save your charge or defeat Lars, the kingdom would capsize. Powerful vassals lie in support of the throne."

"Fenrir and the Timeless One acted to give us an opening to escape," Rex told me. "They planned to hold him off until you could get away, and they've likely returned to Syaoto. I'll be doing so as well, as instructed. I'll be conveying messages to connect the rebellion with Syaoto's army."

"And Sira," Will said, "will go with you. Out of all of us gathered, I believe you have already professed to be the most protective of our Defender."

He couldn't help a smile at that. Sira shut her mouth and nodded, so Will turned back to me. "You have to get stronger. We know you can. Everything we have come to know of you and seen you display *proves* that you can defeat Lars one day. You may be the only one who can."

"Why can't you come with us?" Sira insisted.

Will shook his head. "I am the representative for Ryoku in Orden. I know him best, and so I can stay here to grow the rebellion further in his name. I hail from Syaoto, so I can work between the two armies and ensure we meet our goal at the same time. Besides, I am a soldier. It is my sworn duty to my world, and to you. This is the best way I can do just that."

I raised my hands. "There's still a lot I don't know here," I argued. "Why couldn't I just rush back in and save Chris? They wouldn't expect me to come running in. His execution is supposed to be—"

"The twenty-first of November," Kioru finished for me, cutting me off. "Going by the universal date, of course, which is a little muddled in Orden. Clearly, Lars intends to call you out by using that date. Vincent has bred him to be the strongest of dark knights, and he has forged a brutal weapon out of his son against you. According to their legends, you are the enemy."

"That means little," Will assured me when he saw the look in my eyes. "Ryoku, I presume I can speak openly with you now. The theory is that Orden comes from the enemy that you – your old self – sacrificed himself to foil. Naturally, such an entity would see you as the ultimate enemy. Do not let that inhibit you. Lars and Vincent are both powerful dark knights, both of whom will stop at nothing to destroy you, but you are strong, and you need to embrace that. You need to return and strike the decisive blow upon them."

I didn't question Will now. I couldn't. The truth of everything I'd learned was a dizzying one, and difficult to make any sense of, but I knew that Lars was linked to that force that threatened the spirit realm two months ago, causing my 'old self' to sacrifice himself and landed me here. Chris Olestine was another link to the puzzle, and so I had to save him to figure out that next piece.

I had a greater goal than that. Saving the world was all good by me – as long as I could actually do something – but there was a very personal stake in it. When I first met Chris Olestine, I was convinced he could help me find my sister by that odd connection between us. Now I knew that connection was between our souls, and I knew – though I didn't dare speak it – that Roxanne was here. She was in Orden, just as Kimo had let slip back in Syaoto. Above all else, she was the one I needed to save. She was my family. She was all I had left in my own world.

"Are we in agreement?" Will asked.

I looked from face to face. I finally reached my destination only for my mission to turn on its head. I felt much clearer purpose than before, but one thing rang true in my mind: so far, I had failed. Lars was far too strong for me, forcing me to leave behind not only Chris Olestine, but my sister.

Even if I didn't yet voice the true reason I would return, I knew this group was faithful to me. Will – my Guardian, my guide, and my best friend – would see to it that this place readied for my success later on. I would speak with him before I left and explain Roxanne to him. Surely he, if anyone, could somehow see to her safety. He protected me all this time.

Most of those who helped me get this far weren't here, and I was leaving my closest friend behind directly in the line of danger while I ventured further away, biding my time until the last minute.

Rex, too, showed up to save me, and I knew I couldn't have made it out of the castle without the impressive hybrid at my side. He had done a great deal for me since we met in Lysvid, and I knew I could count on him. He would head to Syaoto to see to my other friends – Guildford, surely, and Dawn, among others – and link up our two causes into one great army. I hoped I wasn't done with him while I ran off to get stronger. Rex was a huge asset to that particular road.

I exchanged glances with Sira. Despite it all, she looked a little excited. She relished the time we might finally spend alone, and here I was delaying it. She was one of my first and fastest friends in this world, one of my first Guardians, and my first cross-world girlfriend – if I understood how we were correctly, which could be a grave mistake. Still, I had her with me. Just like Will said, she was fiercely devoted to me.

Kioru worked at the head of the rebellion. He was in full support of me since before I even knew who he was. He gave me the knife that saved my life more than once, especially against Lars, and continued to work with me toward the same ends. What work existed so far to raise the rebellion was largely his doing, and I knew he'd be glad to keep going. He might even do so without me. With strong allies like Liragon and Belto, and with Will at his side, he would succeed. I almost believed in him more than I did in myself.

There was only a week until the date of the execution. However, given how time flowed in some worlds, it could wind up being a very long or short time away from me at the present. It was an amount of time where I anticipated to grow strong enough to return, to face Lars and Vincent Ordenstraum in combat, to prevail in my quest, to save my sister and Chris Olestine, all to the boon of the people of Orden – or not. I was already stronger than I ever thought I could be, but it still wasn't enough.

Then there was Loki. Speaking his name unlocked the doors to my cell, otherwise escape could never have been feasible. I could have been stuck here long enough to watch Chris Olestine's execution. I lost a great and valuable friend, but somehow, his loss ended up saving me.

A hand grasped my shoulder; Will roused me from my thoughts with a warm smile. A means of encouragement, and the gentle reminder that worlds counted on me.

"I know you can do this."

He had *zero* doubt in his voice, which either spoke volumes about my skill or Will's unsound mind. Still, his words straightened my back and loosened my grim, stubborn chin.

"We will be waiting for your return. You will lead us into battle, and we will prevail over the forces of darkness once more." He smiled at me like back in Bytold, long ago, after he had just dispatched eight or more drunkards on his own. "Nothing new, am I right?"

I couldn't help but grin. Indeed, in the last few weeks, we'd overcome ridiculous odds. Lars Ordenstraum was still on a whole new level. I watched his father defeat a god, and I crossed blades with him myself amid a terrific storm. What manner of human he was, I couldn't ascertain.

Yet, it was there – my drive. My need to continue, to prevail. Sapphense and Loki died to see me come this far, and I couldn't let that go in vain. The memory of each funeral stung behind my eyes, and I knew I had to keep fighting for them, if not for my own personal reasons. If I ran and hid, never to return, more would perish.

Will, Sira, Lusari, Katiel, Kioru, Dawn... Everyone who came to mean something to me was counting on me. If I stopped, they might be next. Although it was a naïve thought, I didn't want to attend another funeral.

No. There was no backing down now.

Finally, all at the same time, the company of rebels nodded.

...End of Akin Minds.

CHARACTER GUIDE

Advocatos – the prince of demons affiliated with Ryoku.

Alex Retton – novice soldier from Balgena. Outspoken and bold.

Annalia Rikalla – Ryoku's ex-girlfriend, fellow Defender. Quiet and rigid.

Arthexus Mandrake – duke's son from Balgena. Shallow and callous.

Artos Ninjeste – assassin from unknown lands. Katiel's friend. Helpful and kind.

Belto Rasale – archer from the Orden Rebellion. Cousin to Kioru, flamboyant.

Bohko – a small creature claiming not to be a Shadowheart, but looks like them.

Brom Gerenadh – lord general of Syaoto Capital, called the 'Iron Bear'. Stalwart man.

Brozogoth – dragon emperor of Vortiger. Savage and resorts easily to trickery.

Caryl Cerone – pretty bartender from Bytold. Dreams of adventure.

Chris Olestine – prisoner of the spirit realm. Believed to be connected to Ryoku.

Cleria Nightfang – vampire of nobility from Lysvid Capital. Promiscuous.

Cobalt Bagaro – a Gallian creature from Vxxyura.

Dagoriph Neseru – Defender and guild leader. Foul-mouthed but loyal and loving.

Dawn Elethel – Ryoku's ex-girlfriend, fellow Defender. Bubbly and cares too much.

Eckhardt Bright – noble paladin, Katiel's friend. Enjoys quiet and helping others.

Gale Destrow – leader of the Ritual cult in Lysvid. Arrogant and snide.

Geri – wolf god of the moon. Likes only two things: his sister and fighting.

Grezen – commander of Harohto Capital army. A bold man.

Jason Ramun – Will's father. A fallen hero from mythology.

Jesanht Olace – mysterious man from Id. Powerful and graceful.

Joey Elder – Defender and friend of Ryoku. Adventurous and reserved.

John Guildford – spirit of a schoolteacher. Friendly and likes to help.

Kaia Oceyen – water mage. Reserved and sweet. Likes only her dragon, Kat, and Ryu.

Katiel Fereyen – Defender and Ryoku's best friend. Omega. Protective and comical.

Keeper of Death – monster from Vxxyura.

Keeper of the Old Forest – monster from the Old Forest.

Keeper of the Temple – monster from Enthralmen Temple.

Kergo Bassonet – lordling from Fort Issomas in Syaoto.

Kimball Cragg – excitable blacksmith from Bytold.

Kimo Goldenhart – vassal of Orden, home unknown. Personal intentions unclear.

Kioru Rasale – rebel leader from Orden Capital. Hides his intentions well.

Lamont Declovin – previous council member from Vortiger. Dragon rider, scarred past.

Lancet Cooper – corrupt field commander from Thralle. Competitive streak.

Lars – an enigmatic figure from Orden.

Leif Cartos – kind-hearted free spirit, soldier from Syaoto Capital. Median rank.

Leiogrey – Lamont's dragon. Wise and slow to trust.

Liragon Elto – rebel from Orden Capital, Kioru's friend. Selfless and commanding.

Loki – Trickster god, a vain man who hides kindness behind humor.

Lusari Atella – orphaned mage from Harohto Capital. Quiet and reserved.

Malak – Peter's dragon. Angry and vehement, but protective. Accepts Sira.

Mosten Clienne – stalwart officer from Harohto Capital. Cares for his men.

Motley – leader of the Syaoto Bladerunners.

Oliver Rouge – high-class soldier from Syaoto Capital. Strong-willed and wise.

Ragekku Gero – wild mercenary from Balgena. Callous and free-spirited.

Relus Ashbane – intelligent vampire from Lysvid. Loyal to a fault.

Rena Stillwater – orphan from Balgena. Will is soft for her. Quiet, cares for friends.

Rex Dougo – hybrid from Lysvid. Kind but reserved.

Rezemetacharuas – water serpent belonging to Kaia. Likes attention.

Rhovh – Jordan's dragon, quiet and serene. Accepts Lamont and Will.

Roland Demizen – mad scientist, creator of the Omega. Capricious and cowardly.

Roxanne Mercy – Ryoku's sister. Her location is currently unknown.

Ryoku Dragontalen – main protagonist, Defender. Brave and a little sarcastic.

Sapphense – beautiful diamond dragon from Bonnin. Accepts Ryoku as her rider.

Sira Jessura – snarky ex-soldier from Orden Capital. Ryoku's Guardian.

Sorha – demon girl connected to Advocatos. Promiscuous and satirical.

Sover Brandhall – infamous bounty hunter across worlds.

Spike Domeran – captain of the Balgena Flaming Arrows.

Thorne – governor of Harohto, a stout man with a lion heart.

Timeless One – mysterious old vampire from Lysvid. Takes in those in need.

Will Ramun – brave soldier from Syaoto Capital. Ryoku's Guardian.

Vincent Ordenstraum – emperor of Orden Capital. Sinister and vile man.

Virgo Rytalen – fellow Defender to Ryoku. Known as standoffish by the others.

Made in United States
Troutdale, OR
05/08/2024